U0136424

2011 不求人文化

2009 懶鬼子英日語

I'm 我識出版集團
I'm Publishing Group
www.17buy.com.tw

2006 意識文化

2005 易富文化

2004 我識地球村

2001 我識出版社

2011 不求人文化

2009 懶鬼子英日語

2006 意識文化

2005 易富文化

2004 我識地球村

2001 我識出版社

2018
TOEIC Reading

50次多益滿分的怪物講師

多益閱讀

攻略＋模擬試題＋解析

只學考試會出的內容就夠！

現在的社會，報考多益已經成為一件不得不做的事情。想要就業或升遷，高分的多益成績單就跟履歷、作品集一樣，是不可或缺的條件，分數愈高，受到公司青睞的機會也會愈高。

你正在為了一張「好像只有我沒有」的高分多益成績單，翻著堆疊如山的相關書籍、在各家補習班間奔波嗎？

很累吧？讓我們來幫你終結這痛苦的生活。這本《全新制50次多益滿分的怪物講師TOEIC多益閱讀攻略＋模擬試題＋解析》可以讓各位的實力有明顯的變化，同時也改變你的人生！

無可取代的特色！

1. 內容包括多益改制前後的考試總整理，以及怪物講師們對於多益出題模式的研究、在補習班教授的考試專用祕訣……等。簡單來說，就是滿分50次的怪物講師們，將分析考題與挑選答案的全部過程公諸於世。為了避免造成學習者的混淆，我們秉持最基本的原則——就是把考試裡不會出現的冷門內容排除掉！

2. 淺顯易懂的說明方式，就算學習者的英文程度是只認得英文字母，也能逐步學習、一讀就理解。從Part 5到Part 7，為什麼這是答案、為什麼那個不是答案，每個選項都一一解釋。這是因為我們相信——基礎實力必須要穩固，才不會遇到難題就逃避。

3. 當學習者差不多看完這本書的時候，會發現我們藏在書中的一個禮物——看完這本書，不只能掌握多益閱讀考試的技巧，連多益寫作（Writing）也都學會了。

在多益改制之後，為了做出符合最新趨勢、最好的多益教材，我們不斷進出考場，蒐集與研究多益改制前後的資料，以求提供學習者最完整的學習內容。為此，透過序言我們要向朋友們表達謝意：謝謝一起經過漫長辛苦作業的同仁們，還有出版以來一如往常支持我們的忠實讀者們。

怪物講師教學團隊（韓國）代表作者 **鄭相虎、金映權** 敬上

2小時內能游刃有餘作答的方法！

多益考試的應試時間僅有2小時，時間其實滿緊繃的。因為我一緊張就會慌亂，所以相當佩服那些能在時間內作答完畢的高手們。而這本書提供「在5秒內解題的祕訣」，甚至還標示常考題型，讓我能針對重要部分學習，也能在2小時內游刃有餘地作答了。

申瑟姬，28歲，首爾牙山病院，護士

這不只是書而已，可說是老師了吧！

努力準備多益考試時，最煩惱的問題就是「拼命背下來的理論，要怎麼活用在題目中？」如果因為看不懂而無法解答，是自己能力不足；但明明知道卻答不出來的話，更是令人感到懊惱！這本書呈現出怪物講師們實際破解多益考題的過程，方便讀者可直接演練。鄭相虎和金映權老師，是連實戰習題的解答都仔細說明的又親切又聰明的怪物講師。

權圭莉，23歲，龍仁大學，食品營養系

怪物講師果然是解答怪物！我太喜歡了！

一個人自己埋頭準備多益又累又毫無動力，讓人容易中途放棄。而這本《全新制50次多益滿分的怪物講師TOEIC多益閱讀攻略 + 模擬試題 + 解析》是自學者的最佳工具書。一般市面上的多益書籍，不是沒有附題目的解析，就是解析過於冗長無重點。但本書開門見山切入重點，詳細說明成為解答的原因，可說是引領著考生往目標分數前進的重要後盾。

李孝真，26歲，又石大學，教育學系

補習班老師都不教的Part 7攻略法！

我最想要學的就是Part 7文章理解題的攻略法。因為考試時，Part 7會需要花最多時間做答，但分數卻是最不理想的。看到這本書時，真是令人眼睛一亮！讓我發現答題時的盲點。在補習班裡從來沒有老師提示過解題順序與重點的祕訣。現在，我心中不禁偷偷期待下次的考試到來。

安治勳，28歲，仁荷大學，建築研究所

明快、確實、基礎穩固，最佳應考攻略！

準備多益考試時，多做題目固然很重要，但累積「正確地分析題目的基礎實力」也很重要，面對題目時才能不慌張並提高分數。現在你手上拿的這本書，就是可以替各位鞏固基礎的優良工具書。明快的解說、不枯燥的架構、怪物講師的解題祕訣，只要擁有這本書就能一手掌握多益考試祕訣。

李祖恩，24歲，總神大學，社福系

英文不好的人，也能考好多益！

本書從基本文法和單字開始教起，循序漸進，任何人都能輕鬆跟上進度。是一本讓初學者也能輕鬆上手多益的文法、閱讀攻略。只要對內容感到疑惑，就會馬上出現怪物講師的提醒；剛學習到的內容也可以在Quiz馬上確認；還有筆記整理讓學習者可以反覆練習；還有各章節的Review Test和Preview，在多益奪高分的精華都在這裡！

李侑智，28歲，上班族

多益閱讀的精華就是文法！

多益閱讀考試中，最重要的似乎就是文法了。只要了解文法，分數就會毫無阻礙地扶搖直上。本書最大的優點就是文法理論比其他書更加地簡潔明瞭，不論翻到哪頁，一眼就可以看到重點精華。很幸運地有這個機會，可以釐清以前混淆不清的文法概念。

閔恩慶，28歲，中央大學，醫科專門研究所

分類清楚，馬上可以找到想要的部分！

和其他的多益書籍比起來，我最滿意這本書的地方是Part 5單句填空和Part 6短文填空的地方，讓我能很快找到解答。練習實戰習題時，遇到不懂的地方或是忘記文法時，可以像查字典般可以快速地翻到要找的資料。

金煥錫，38歲，上班族

多益是什麼？

TOEIC是Test of English for International Communication的縮寫，針對非英語母語者以工作或日常生活裡需要的「溝通」為主測驗實用英語能力的考試。因此裡面大部分出現商務以及日常生活裡所使用的實用主題。

多益考試的出題領域以及特色

公司內研發	研究、產品開發
財務相關	投資、稅務、會計、結帳
餐飲	業務上的聚會、聚餐、晚宴、預約
娛樂、文化	電影、音樂、藝術、博物館、大眾媒體
一般業務	合約、協商、併購與合併、行銷、業務
健康相關	健康保險、診療、牙科診療、醫院
住宅／公司不動產	建設、採購與出租、電氣／瓦斯費用
人事相關	僱用、退休、升遷、申請工作、錄取公告、薪水、年薪
製作	組裝工程、工廠管理、品質管理
辦公室相關	理事會、委員會、參觀、電話、傳真、電子郵件、辦公用品
購買相關	購物、訂單、配送、費用請款單
旅行相關	大眾運輸、船舶、入場券、廣播、飯店、延遲、取消

多益考試會盡量避免只屬於特定文化的內容，各個國家的人名與地名都平均地分布在考試題目裡面。另外，美國、英國、加拿大、澳洲等的發音與語調也平均分配出現。

考試的結構

結構	Part	內容	考題數目	時間	分數
聽力測驗	1	照片描述	6	約45分鐘	495分
	2	應答問題	25		
	3	簡短對話	39		
	4	簡短獨白	30		
閱讀測驗	5	句子填空	30	75分鐘	495分
	6	段落填空	16		
	7	單篇閱讀	29		
		多篇閱讀	25		
Total	7個Parts		200	120分鐘	990分

考試時間介紹

時間	內容
9：30～9：45	分發答案表格，以及說明填寫表格方法
9：45～9：50	休息時間
9：50～10：05	第一次身份證檢查
10：05～10：10	分發考卷，以及檢查考卷上的瑕疵與否
10：10～10：55	進行聽力考試
10：55～12：10	進行閱讀考試（第二次身份證檢查）

＊ 無論如何，在九點五十分以前得入考場。以上時間視考場狀況可變。

多益報名方法

報名期間與報名處：請參考多益委員會網站／考試費用：1,600元

❶ **網路報名**：費用1,600元，加網路處理費40元。

報名網址：http://www.toeic.com.tw/register/index.jsp

❷ **通訊報名**：費用1,600元，須以郵政匯票方式繳費。

報名表可臨櫃或致電索取
（台北市復興南路二段45號2樓，02-2701-8008分機109）。

❸ **臨櫃報名**：費用1,600元，平日早上9:00至下午5:30。

地址：台北市復興南路二段45 號2 樓。

❹ **APP報名**：可使用APP報名，在便利商店繳費。

Android下載　　iOS下載

考試準備事項

❶ **身份證**：限中華民國國民身分證或有效期限內之護照正本。沒有身份證的話，絕對不能參加
考試。一定要記得喔！

❷ **文具**：電腦用鉛筆（先弄成粗一點比較方便；一般鉛筆或自動鉛筆也可以，但不可使用有墨
水的筆），橡皮擦。

確認成績以及成績單寄發

在指定的發表日期，在多益官方的網站或透過電話可以確認成績。成績單是以應考生指定
的方式領取，且僅有第一次成績單是免費的。

Part 1

出題趨勢

此部分已不再能說是最容易得分的題型了,因為近幾年常常出現以東西描述為主的陌生說法。這些說法是以前完全沒有出現過的,所以應考生的錯誤機率也劇增。有人可能會想,在Part 1裡錯兩題左右也不會有礙於考到高分,畢竟數目不大嘛。但千萬別這麼想,如果把失去的分數類推到聽力考試其他部分,就等於在各個部分裡錯六題那麼嚴重。只要錯一個考題,也有可能會造成很大的影響,而不容易得到高分數。

出題比例分析

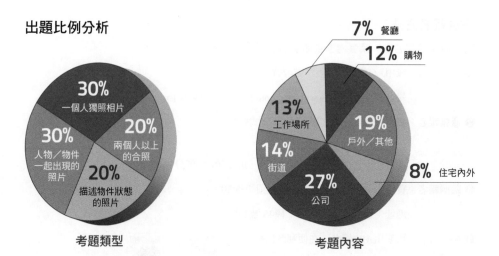

考題類型

考題內容

學習策略 & 應考策略

1 人物照片的出現比例為60～70%,所以得熟知人物的動作以及狀態相關的說法。

2 要達到一看照片就能判斷是什麼狀況的程度。即使聯想不到動作或狀態相關的英語說法,還是要能先正確分析照片,在聽錄音的時候才能容易選出答案。

3 若出現描述在照片裡沒出現的東西或動作的選項,立刻排除在答案之外,然後繼續看別的選項。

4 聽錄音的時候應該同時填寫答案。在Part 2之前的單元立刻填寫答案會節省時間。

5 有時也會發現找不出完美答案的情形。此時得選擇最接近的答案。

Part 2

出題趨勢

即使是同樣類型的考題，前面第7～19題大部分很簡單，但愈到後面題目通常會愈難。尤其在第25題以後，混雜出現了能評鑑出高分數應考生的高難度考題的情形。因此，第25題以後回答考題時得特別注意。最近陳述句的比例正在增加當中，且疑問詞疑問句裡常出現why與how。

出題比例分析

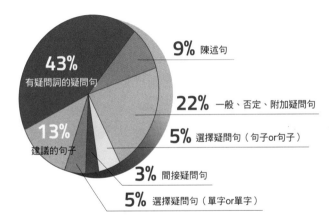

學習策略 & 應考策略

1 需要依照疑問句前面部分出現的疑問詞來決定答案。即使聽到了考題後面的部分，但如果一開頭沒有聽到疑問詞，還是無法找出正確答案。

2 最近常出現看起來很容易，但聽起來很難的說法。Part 2的答題線索沒有在考卷上，必須專心聽這些說法。

3 若將類似的發音、時態、同義詞等先整理下來學習，會有幫助。尤其是如果先將自己很容易弄錯或選錯的選項整理好，可以提高以後選出正確答案的機率。

4 聽選項的時候，偶爾會記不住剛聽過的疑問詞或句子開頭的地方。即使多麼專心，進行25個考題時還是會失去集中力。

出題趨勢

Part 3前面的部分（第32～40題），對話長度很短且考題也是有關地點、說話者、下一個行程等，比較容易回答的問題為主。但在後面部分（第53～70題），對話長度比較長且選項為句子形式的「詢問具體內容的考題」最常出現。「詢問概括性內容的考題」是與主題、地點、說話者、要求與建議事項、以及下一個行程相關的為多。Part 4裡，電話留言以及活動開始公告的類型在增加當中。

出題比例分析

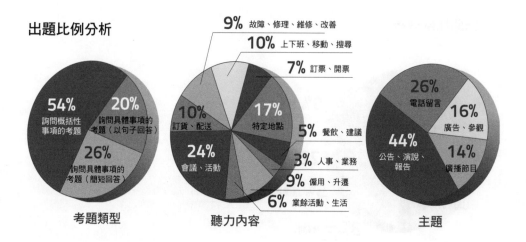

考題類型　　　　　　聽力內容　　　　　　　主題

學習策略 & 應考策略

1 無論如何，在聽錄音之前，需要了解考題裡的核心詞彙。先知道是哪種考題，才能有選擇性地聽錄音，聽到考題重點時也不要猶豫，要立刻選擇答案。

2 需要多做邊聽錄音邊看考題與選項的訓練。雖然先看了考題再聽錄音是好的，但還是需要將所看過的考題做確認的過程，這種練習剛開始的時候很難適應，但經過多次就會熟練的。

3 大部分的情形之下，考題的順序與錄音內容進行的順序一樣，所以需要做依序回答考題的練習。

4 在錄音前段部分出現答案的情形尤其多，得專心聽該部分！

5 有些主題、情況的內容大部分相似：影印機總是故障、想找的人都是出差當中，因此若習慣了這些刻板的內容模式，會更容易回答考題。萬一真的沒有時間或不想讀書，起碼看看錄音內容的翻譯吧。

Part 5, 6

出題趨勢

雖然每個月都有所不同，但文法與詞彙考題佔各一半。大部分的考題與以前的類型和難易度沒有太大的差別，高難度的考題仍然會出現。另外，大部分的考題長度以及詞彙難度正在慢慢調高當中。Part 6裡所使用的詞彙量更大，而且也會出現了解脈絡才能回答的考題。

出題比例分析

Part 5 考題類別

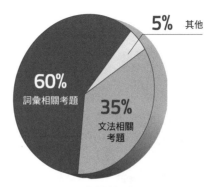

Part 6 考題類別

學習策略 & 應考策略

1 Part 5 & 6是可以最有效率找到答案的部分。回答考題的時候，要先很快看過選項，判斷此題是否為需要經過翻譯才能回答的。

2 若有不知道怎麼回答的考題，先標記之後直接進入別的考題更省時。最多要在二十五分鐘之內結束Part 5 & 6，才有充分的時間完成Part 7。

3 無論如何，文法考題的部分全部都要答對。多益總分數高的人，大多是在詞彙考題方面獲得高分。

4 學詞彙的時候，得將常用的組合一起背下來。有些句子是我們看來沒問題，但在以英語為母語者的眼裡是很奇怪的說法。將詞彙常用的組合熟記，才能在考試時縮短答題時間且提高分數。

Part 7

出題趨勢

Part7是最近難度變得最高的部分。除了考題的難度提高，文章的長度也變長，所以讓應考生感到吃力。除了最容易的詢問主題類的題目，現在考生也需了解文章裡隱藏的含意。詢問具體事項的考題也是如此，在選項裡找出線索變得更不容易。推論相關考題也提高了難度，且持續出現同義詞相關的考題。信函與電子郵件類型仍然最常出現，此外，說明文與報導類型文章的出現機率最近也增加當中。愈後面部分的文章長度會愈來愈長，有時可能會出現考生無法看完文章的情形。

出題比例分析

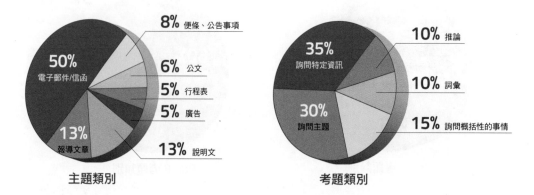

主題類別

8% 便條、公告事項
6% 公文
5% 行程表
5% 廣告
13% 說明文
13% 報導文章
50% 電子郵件/信函

考題類別

35% 詢問特定資訊
30% 詢問主題
10% 推論
10% 詞彙
15% 詢問概括性的事情

學習策略 & 應考策略

1 若沒有自信管理好時間，先完成Part 7再進入Part 5 & 6也是個好辦法。

2 要練習先看考題，之後在文章當中閱讀需要的地方。選擇答案時沒有必要將長篇文章都看完，只要了解考題的核心，然後有選擇性地閱讀。

3 為了得到高分數，選出答案之前還是得再次思考。多益裡不常出現一眼就能看出答案的考題，若再多想一次，常有會找出別的答案的情形。

4 文章最後部分也有答案。有時在文章最後出現的幾個說法會決定考題的答案。

「多益只不過是一種考試。
為了這種考試，學必要該學的東西就好！」

若是很會英語的人，可以隨自己的實力將考試考好，這樣多麼好呢？不過在多益達到高分數的階段不是一件容易的事情，何況我們又不能整天只學英語就好。然而英語夠厲害就會自動得到多益滿分嗎？不是，因為所有的考試裡都設有為了預防得滿分的陷阱，這就是為什麼不太可能隨著實力而得到分數。

那麼，眼前面臨考試的我們要怎麼辦？最重要的就是，即使只學一道題目，都得學有助於解決實際考題的方式。透過徹底符合實戰考試的學習法，並依照最適當的答題法來準備多益才行。前面說過，所有的考試裡都有陷阱吧？如果有陷阱也就會有漏洞。出題者挖陷阱不是什麼卑鄙的事情，所以應考者鑽漏洞同樣不是卑鄙。縱使只學一題，我們也要使用在考場上行得通的方式來學！

NEW 　逐步拆解，讓你更了解句子結構，奠定良好基礎！

很多人會認為要準備好多益閱讀，就要能夠熟練「閱讀英文→翻譯成中文→理解意思→答題」這樣的過程，但光是閱讀英文與翻譯中文，就會耗掉許多寶貴的作答時間。多益只是一種考試，不需要拘泥於每句話、每段文字的翻譯，只要能夠找到關鍵資訊、答對題目就好。

這本書的主旨是帶領考生考好多益閱讀題，而多數考生在閱讀測驗時最常碰到的問題就是「時間不夠」，時間不夠用的主要原因是大家很容易陷入在英文逐字翻譯的情境裡，認為要把每字每句都讀懂了，才能夠正確答題。

怪物講師想要改變多數人的學習方式，希望傳授能夠在實際考場上立即運用的解題法，所以在英文的翻譯部分，特別拆解英文句子的結構，按照英文句的結構逐段翻譯成中文。

!! 　**例如將097頁的句子「The applicants (whom) she waits for have not arrived yet.」刻意翻成「申請者們／她等待的／沒到達／尚未。」透過這樣的方式，培養讀者拆解句子、分段了解句意的能力，如此即使無法馬上將英文句完整翻譯成中文，也能夠透過拆解句子結構來推敲句意，迅速作答，再也不用怕時間不夠用了。**

教你真實考場上可以立刻使用的方法！

這本書是基於「多益只不過是一種考試而已」的想法誕生的。大部分的多益教材是教你把「英語」與「考試」兩隻兔子都要抓住。

但「多益」是在有限時間之內，答對愈多考題的人，就可望得到愈高分數的一種遊戲。即使是英語相當不錯的人，如果不太懂遊戲規則，十之八九會失敗。

這本書是徹底為了實際考試撰寫的。因此將考場上用得到的內容放在裡面，連帶著把回答的方法一起很實戰的教給你。

不僅是單純的理論書，更是實戰手冊

這本書不同於別的多益參考書，不是單純的修改幾個句子或增加幾張頁數，而是脫胎換骨的「全新版」。雖然多益的考試模式沒有變得很多，但我們想要脫離多數多益書會有的盲點。

學了文法之後，實際考閱讀部分時，曾因為不知道到底要如何應用於考題，而為此懊惱過吧？為了解決這樣的問題，我們加入了「依照考題直接聯想適當理論」，做為找出答案的過程與練習活動。

以前準備多益閱讀考試時，得將理論、考題分開學習，市面上也沒有一本書將這些攻略做乾淨俐落的整理。因此這本書提供「看考題→預測→作答」的流程，這樣就能有助於考生學習了。

訓練你最適當的解題方式！

這本書的每個單元以「理論→Quiz→沒有答對會後悔的考題（低難易度）→考題實戰練習（實際難易度）」的四個學習階段而構成。

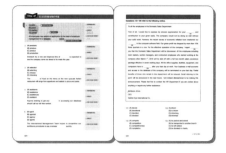

「沒有答對會後悔的考題」裡，學習者可以將前面透過理論學到的解題方法逐一應用。按照例子練習的過程中會發現，即使沒有看過很多考題，但自己正使用怪物講師的解題法。國內沒有任何教材是這種「實戰型」的學習書。

一目瞭然地整理所學過的內容！

無論是上補習班還是自己學習，最重要的就是複習。但這一點可不容易，為了讓讀者有效的整理所學過的內容，每個單元後面的部分都安排了「一目瞭然整理」的專欄。透過易懂的圖示化方式，學習者可以很快在頭腦裡整理內容。考試前總複習所學過的內容時，沒有什麼是比這個專欄更有效的。如果學習者沒有太多時間從頭學習，看這個部分也能提高分數。

比任何參考書還要詳細的解說！

這本書不同於其他書的解說，除了理論說明以外，解題的部分比起任何書還要詳細。怪物講師根據自身長久以來的經驗，不只有解說錯誤的理由，同時也很仔細說明為什麼是正確答案。如果你想找一本仔細解說的書來學習，就算學一個題目也想要明確了解，那你就找對書了。

自我診斷測驗

1 Representative Dickens gave a speech today about _____ corporate taxes and won general applause.

(A) reduces
(B) reducing
(C) reduction
(D) being reduced

2 Industrial Technologies, Inc. has released a new calculator in hopes of attracting students _____ plan to study advanced physics.

(A) whose
(B) who
(C) which
(D) what

3 The prospects of the marketing department for the next year _____ optimistic enough to invest funds amply.

(A) have
(B) is
(C) are
(D) has been

4 CMOS Industries' annual aim is _____ its business in Europe and therefore intends to hire more employees.

(A) expanding
(B) expanded
(C) to expand
(D) expansive

5 The annual team building exercise _____ an opportunity for employees to work together outside of the office.

(A) providing
(B) is provided
(C) provides
(D) provide

6 The most _____ friendly solution is to use alternative energy as much as possible, such as solar or wind power.

(A) environmentally
(B) environment
(C) environmental
(D) environments

7 If Matthew had left for Paris a day early, he _____ able to meet with our European clients before the seminar.

(A) could be
(B) will be
(C) could have been
(D) is

8 The current time schedule should be adjusted for the benefit of our _____.

(A) works
(B) working
(C) worked
(D) workers

9 No sooner had they received numerous complaints _____ the software developers attempted to solve the problems.

(A) because
(B) when
(C) than
(D) such

10 The charity event benefiting the poor will _____ place next week with the help of our ex-president.

(A) be taken
(B) be took
(C) take
(D) is taking

11 For two years, the product warranty guarantees free repairs for _____ may happen to the item.

(A) however
(B) who
(C) if
(D) whatever

12 Some senior executives receive the highest salaries, though _____ may also earn more through bonuses and sales.

(A) others
(B) other
(C) another
(D) the other

13 Alexander Petrokov's new film "Roses, Daisies, You" is expected to be a hit at the box office _____ it receives negative reviews.

(A) even
(B) where
(C) even if
(D) in order that

14 Jonathan's favorite form of acting is theater, _____ he plans to pursue a career in television and movie acting.

(A) so
(B) yet
(C) and
(D) for

15 The staffing committee _____ to recruit more than 100 new employees for an ambitious project this year.

(A) decision
(B) has decided
(C) decided
(D) was decided

16 The supervisor does not like to allow her assistant _____ even at a lunch time.

(A) to rest
(B) resting
(C) rest
(D) rests

17 How a company contributes more to worker health care plans _____ becoming an important factor.

(A) are
(B) being
(C) is
(D) been

18 President Patel promised to increase the export of automobiles _____ domestically.

(A) to manufacture
(B) manufacturing
(C) as manufactured
(D) manufactured

19 Because the market remains _____, many leading economists are predicting a cut in interest rates by the Reserve Bank.

(A) volatile
(B) volatileness
(C) volatility
(D) volatilizes

20 The health and fitness facility, located _____ the corporate headquarters downtown, is open for any employee to use.

(A) inside
(B) throughout
(C) upon
(D) up

▶ 解答在004頁

自我診斷測驗做完了嗎？我們來診斷你的結果是屬於下面A、B、C型中的哪一種。
並且來看看何種學習方法適合你！

自我診斷表

A型
答對數7個以下
初級

你是剛開始學習多益沒幾個月的學習者。擁有的基礎詞彙和文法數量不足，對於多益題型的熟悉度也不夠。簡單來說，是基礎不穩的階段。

此階段
學習者
的特徵

- 找不到主詞和動詞，光聽到5大句型就頭痛。
- 對於多益裡出現的詞彙很生疏，都憑感覺在解題。
- Part 5裡的每一道題目裡，一定會有很多看不懂的單字。但還是會把題目讀完。
- 做Part 7時，時間絕對不夠用。遇到比較難的類型或閱讀測驗時，大部分都做記號跳過。

B型
答對數8～15個
中級

你接觸多益已經有一段時間，或是已經掌握了多益大部分的出題型態了。具備基本的詞彙和文法實力，但一有變化就面臨困難。也可能是你實戰的經驗不足，時間分配不夠完善。在這階段想要拿高分的話，需要多練習詞彙。

此階段
學習者
的特徵

- 覺得新多益詞彙中的商用單字很困難。
- 在分析句子時，一直在前後來回檢視沒有效率。
- 時間分配不完善，在試題上做記號的數目超過10題。
- 無法有效整理艱澀的文法。

C型
答對數16～20個
高級

你相當了解多益的出題類型，時間分配也相當恰當。解題也幾乎能通暢無阻，光靠解析題目就可以正確解題。但是在選項中一一探討為何非正解時，可能就會產生疑慮。

此階段
學習者
的特徵

- 任何題目都能迎刃而解，但在詞彙部分常會出錯。
- 在Part 5解題時，使用消去法摒除2個選項後，卻會在留下的兩個選項間猶豫。
- 閱讀的理解能力出眾，但常會遺漏重點部分的閱讀理解。
- 在考試時，常會花了時間思索正確答案，卻選到錯誤的答案。

此類型的學習者需要60天的學習課程！

整體看來此類型的讀者大部分都接觸多益不久，基礎實力不夠穩固。歸納於這類型的讀者必須要反覆的熟讀整本書，從基本的詞彙開始累積基本實力。

60日學習計畫

第1週	Day 1	Day 2	Day 3	Day 4	Day 5
本書	自我診斷測驗	Warming-up	Chapter 1 理論	Chapter 1 問題	Chapter 2 理論
背單字範圍	／	／	Chapter 1		Chapter 2
第2週	Day 6	Day 7	Day 8	Day 9	Day 10
本書	Chapter 2 問題	Chapter 3 理論	Chapter 3 問題	Part 1 複習	Chapter 4 理論
背單字範圍	Chapter 2	Chapter 3		／	Chapter 4
第3週	Day 11	Day 12	Day 13	Day 14	Day 15
本書	Chapter 4 問題	Chapter 5 理論	Chapter 5 問題	Chapter 6 理論	Chapter 6 問題
背單字範圍	Chapter 4	Chapter 5		Chapter 6	
第4週	Day 16	Day 17	Day 18	Day 19	Day 20
本書	Chapter 7 理論	Chapter 7 問題	Part 2 複習	Chapter 8 理論	Chapter 8 問題
背單字範圍	Chapter 7		／	Chapter 8	
第5週	Day 21	Day 22	Day 23	Day 24	Day 25
本書	Chapter 9 理論	Chapter 9 問題	Chapter 10 理論	Chapter 10 問題	Part 3 複習
背單字範圍	Chapter 9		Chapter 10		／
第6週	Day 26	Day 27	Day 28	Day 29	Day 30
本書	Chapter 11 理論	Chapter 11 問題	Chapter 12 理論	Chapter 12 問題	Chapter 13 理論
背單字範圍	Chapter 11		Chapter 12		Chapter 13

day60

第7週	Day 31	Day 32	Day 33	Day 34	Day 35
本書	Chapter 13 問題	Chapter 14 理論	Chapter 14 問題	Chapter 15 理論	Chapter 15 問題
背單字範圍	Chapter 13	Chapter 14		Chapter 15	
第8週	Day 36	Day 37	Day 38	Day 39	Day 40
本書	Part 4 複習	Chapter 16 理論	Chapter 16 問題	Chapter 17 理論	Chapter 17 問題
背單字範圍	／	Chapter 16		Chapter 17	
第9週	Day 41	Day 42	Day 43	Day 44	Day 45
本書	Part 5 複習	Chapter 18 理論	Chapter 18 問題	Chapter 19 理論	Chapter 19 問題
背單字範圍	／	Chapter 18		Chapter 19	
第10週	Day 46	Day 47	Day 48	Day 49	Day 50
本書	Chapter 20 理論	Chapter 20 問題	Part 6 複習	Chapter 21	
背單字範圍	Chapter 20		／	／	
第11週	Day 51	Day 52	Day 53	Day 54	Day 55
本書	Chapter 22-23 理論	Chapter 22-23 問題	Chapter 24-25 理論	Chapter 24-25 問題	Chapter 26 理論
背單字範圍	Chapter 22-23		Chapter 24-25		Chapter 26
第12週	Day 56	Day 57	Day 58	Day 59	Day 60
本書	Chapter 26 問題	Chapter 27 理論	Chapter 27 問題	實戰測驗	實戰測驗解説
背單字範圍	Chapter 26	Chapter 27		／	／

B型

答對數8～15個

推薦此階段的學習者30天學習課表！

雖然熟悉多益的考題型態，但是想要得高分的話，文法、詞彙、閱讀實力還是稍嫌不足。雖知道大部分的文法，但了解得還不夠透徹，所以作答時遇到活用的變化時，就顯得相當吃力。這階段需要針對細部的理論部分加強。詞彙的庫存量也不夠，所以在Part 7應答時，會不知不覺發現時間不夠用！屬於這階段的讀者，需要針對細部的內容去學習，並設法提升詞彙和閱讀能力。

30日學習計畫

第1週	Day 1 8/19	Day 2	Day 3	Day 4	Day 5
本書	自我診斷測驗	Warming-up	Chapter 1	Chapter 2	Chapter 3
			Chapter 21	Chapter 21	Chapter 21
背單字範圍			Chapter 1	Chapter 2	Chapter 3
第2週	Day 6	Day 7	Day 8	Day 9	Day 10
本書	Part 1 複習	Chapter 4	Chapter 5	Chapter 6	Chapter 7
	Chapter 21	Chapter 22	Chapter 22	Chapter 22	Chapter 22
背單字範圍	Chapter 21	Chapter 4	Chapter 5	Chapter 6	Chapter 7, 22
第3週	Day 11	Day 12	Day 13	Day 14	Day 15
本書	Part 2 複習	Chapter 8	Chapter 9	Chapter 10	Part 3 複習
	Chapter 23	Chapter 23	Chapter 23	Chapter 23	Chapter 24
背單字範圍	Chapter 23	Chapter 8	Chapter 9	Chapter 10	Chapter 24
第4週	Day 16	Day 17	Day 18	Day 19	Day 20
本書	Chapter 11	Chapter 12	Chapter 13	Chapter 14	Chapter 15
	Chapter 24	Chapter 24	Chapter 24	Chapter 25	Chapter 25
背單字範圍	Chapter 11	Chapter 12	Chapter 13	Chapter 14	Chapter 15
第5週	Day 21	Day 22	Day 23	Day 24	Day 25
本書	Part 4 複習	Chapter 16	Chapter 17	Part 5 複習	Chapter 18
	Chapter 25	Chapter 25	Chapter 26	Chapter 26	Chapter 27
背單字範圍	Chapter 25	Chapter 16	Chapter 17	Chapter 26	Chapter 18
第6週	Day 26	Day 27	Day 28	Day 29	Day 30
本書	Chapter 19	Chapter 20	Part 6 複習	複習	實戰測驗
	Chapter 27		Part 7 複習		
背單字範圍	Chapter 19, 27	Chapter 20	／	／	

C型
答對數16～20個

此類型的學習者適合20日課程表！

相較於五花八門全面性學習，有效的重點整理更適合以滿分為目標的學習者。高分族群更要減少失誤的發生，因為熟悉考題的類型，因此可以多練習看題目的重點。作答時，必須要清楚了解非正解的選項為何不是答案的理由，這裡所謂的「了解」指的是到可以對其他人說明的深入了解。

20日學習計畫

第1週	Day 1	Day 2	Day 3	Day 4	Day 5
本書	自我診斷測驗	Warming-up	Chapter 1	Chapter 2	Chapter 3
			Chapter 21	Chapter 22	Chapter 22
背單字範圍			Chapter 1	Chapter 2	Chapter 3
第2週	Day 6	Day 7	Day 8	Day 9	Day 10
本書	Chapter 4	Chapter 5	Chapter 6, 7	Chapter 8	Chapter 9
	Chapter 22	Chapter 23	Chapter 23	Chapter 23	Chapter 24
背單字範圍	Chapter 4, 22	Chapter 5	Chapter 6, 7	Chapter 8, 23	Chapter 9
第3週	Day 11	Day 12	Day 13	Day 14	Day 15
本書	Chapter 10	Chapter 11	Chapter 12	Chapter 13, 14	Chapter 15
	Chapter 24	Chapter 24	Chapter 25	Chapter 25	Chapter 25
背單字範圍	Chapter 10	Chapter 11, 24	Chapter 12	Chapter 13, 14	Chapter 15, 25
第4週	Day 16	Day 17	Day 18	Day 19	Day 20
本書	Chapter 16, 17	Chapter 18	Chapter 19	Chapter 20	實戰測驗
	Chapter 26	Chapter 26	Chapter 27	Chapter 27	
背單字範圍	Chapter 16, 17	Chapter 18, 26	Chapter 19	Chapter 20, 27	

Warming-up

1. 文法用語的理解——名詞、動詞等的涵義和標示

本書和其他多益攻略書籍一樣，充滿文法用語。有許多考生嫌麻煩，不願意深入了解其涵義，但其實文法的用語比想像中簡單。只要清楚了解文法用語，便可以輕鬆理解文法的說明。在記文法用語的同時，也可連字典裡常使用的簡寫一起記下來。字典不只是在查單字時使用，從字典中也可了解單字詞性、涵義的變化、實際使用的例子…等，查一個單字可以得到10倍的效果。

用語	簡寫	內容
sentence （句子）		英文句子的第一個字母通常須為大寫，句子末端要有句號（.）、問號（？）或是驚嘆號（！）。
subject （主詞）	S	某種動作或行動的主體，「何人」或「何事」…等型態出現。
verb （動詞）	V	表示主詞的動作或是狀態，文法標準用語為「謂語」（predicate），但一般常稱之為「動詞」。
object （受詞）	O	敘述句中的動詞動作對象。第4大句型裡的**IO**（indirect object）是間接受詞；**DO**（direct object）是直接受詞。
complement （補語）	C	在第2大句型裡補充主詞，第5大句型裡補充受詞。
noun （名詞）	n.	表示人、事、物的名稱。
pronoun （代名詞）	pron.	代替前面曾經出現過的名詞。
adjective （形容詞）	adj.	描寫人、事、物的狀態，修飾名詞。
adverb （副詞）	adv.	修飾動詞、形容詞和副詞，常以方法、程度、時間、場所等型態出現。
verb transitive （及物動詞）	vt.	需要受詞的第3、4、5大句型的動詞。
verb intransitive （不及物動詞）	vi.	不需要受詞的第1、2大句型的動詞，部分與介系詞結合的動詞。

preposition （介系詞）	prep.	位於名詞之前，用在句子中表示動作、行為對象的時間、場所、方向等之間的關係。
conjunction （連接詞）	conj.	相互串連字和單字、句子和句子、子句和子句間，使其有關係。
interjection / exclamation （感嘆詞）	int.	表達悲傷、高興、驚訝…等情緒的詞。
article（冠詞）	art.	未被明確定義是不定冠詞（indefinite article）a／an，被限制的是定冠詞（definite article）the。
infinitive（不定詞）	inf.	簡單來說就是動詞的原型。to + 原形動詞，我們稱之為to + 不定詞。
participle（分詞）	pple.	基本上分為過去分詞和現在分詞兩大類，扮演著形容詞的角色。
phrase（片語）	phr.	兩個以上的單字組成的短語（其中不含「S + V」）。
clause（子句）	cl.	和片語一樣由兩個單字以上組成的，但是其中包含「S + V」。 （sentence，也可以稱做句子）
-(e)s		1. 接在動詞後：主詞是第三人稱單數時，表動詞現在式。 2. 接在名詞後：表名詞複數。
-ing		1. 動名詞：是由動詞變來的名詞（扮演著主詞、受詞、補語的角色）。 2. 現在分詞：表示主動或進行的狀態（扮演著修飾名詞的形容詞角色）。
-ed		1. 動詞過去式：指過去發生的事。 2. 過去分詞（p.p.）：表示被動或完成的狀態。
be p.p.		表被動狀態（被…）。
be -ing		表主動語態；或正在進行式（正在…）。
have p.p.		表完成式（已經…）。
phrasal verb		稱為片語動詞，由超過一個單字組成，必須要整個當成一個動詞來看。又稱two-word verb。 例：deal with（處理）、turn up（出現、發生）

一眼看出詞性！

在這本書會常看到名詞、形容詞、副詞、動詞…這些用詞。不過，各單字的詞性要怎麼得知呢？最好的方法是翻字典查找背誦的，但這麼多單字怎麼可能一一找出、背完呢？這個時候，下面的圖表就派上用場了！

只要看單字的後面，就可以推測出單字的詞性。大部分的單字字尾都可依下面圖表例示，推測詞性，但也有例外。舉例來說，「-ment」結尾的單字幾乎都是名詞，但是implement（執行）是動詞，類似這樣的情況也不少。但討厭的是，這樣的例外很常出現在考題中。像close既可當動詞，也可以是名詞、形容詞、副詞，這種單字是考試中的常客。因此可以把下面的規則當作基本常識背下來後，規則以外的單字再另外做整理背誦。

可將單字轉換成名詞的字尾

字尾	範例
-tion, -sion, -cion	information 資訊、decision 決定、coercion 強制
-ty, -sy, -cy	responsibility 責任、autopsy 驗屍、accuracy 正確
-ce, -se	diligence 勤奮、defence / defense 防禦
-ture, -sure	creature 生物、exposure 暴露
-ance, -ence	assistance 輔助／幫助、experience 經驗
-ment, -ery	government 政府、recovery 恢復
-ness, -dom, -hood, -ship, -ism, -tude（表思想／主義等抽象的意思）	kindness 和善、freedom 自由、childhood 童年時期、scholarship 獎學金、industrialism 工業主義、attitude 姿勢／態度
-logy, -ics（表學問）	psychology 心理學、economics 經濟學
-er, -ee, -or, -ar, -ist, -ian, -ant / -ent, -ic（人的稱呼）	employer 雇主、employee 職員、editor 編輯、scholar 學者、biologist 生物學家、technician 技師、applicant 申請人、president 總裁／總統、critic 評論家

可將單字轉換成動詞的字尾

-ize, -fy, -en 做…；使…等及物動詞	**memorize** 熟記、**satisfy** 使滿意、**strengthen** 鞏固
-ate （也當作形容詞的字尾）	**concentrate** 集中於…

可將單字轉換成形容詞的字尾

-ous, -ic, -ical, -ive, -ful, -less, -able / -ible, -ish	**dangerous** 危險的、**economic** 經濟的、**economical** 節約的、**competitive** 競爭的、**careful** 小心的、**hopeless** 絕望的、**understandable** 可理解的、**sluggish** 懶惰的
-ing / -ed，**-ate**（也可當動詞），**-al**（也可當名詞）	**interesting** 有趣的、**interested** 感興趣的、**delicate** 纖細的、**normal** 正常的
-y, -ory，名詞 + ly （副詞為形容詞 + ly）	**sunny** 陽光照耀的、**preparatory** 預備的、**friendly** 友善的

可將單字轉換成副詞的字尾

- ly是副詞，你知道嗎？但是你還要知道，副詞是「形容詞 + - ly」。請特別注意，前面也有提到形容詞是「名詞 + - ly」，千萬不要搞混了。

愈常碰字典,對英文學習的幫助愈大。只要好好充分利用字典、查字典的話,也能得到充分的學習。所以請各位一定要好好活用字典,培養不必上補習班也能獨自學習的力量吧!

查詢英英字典

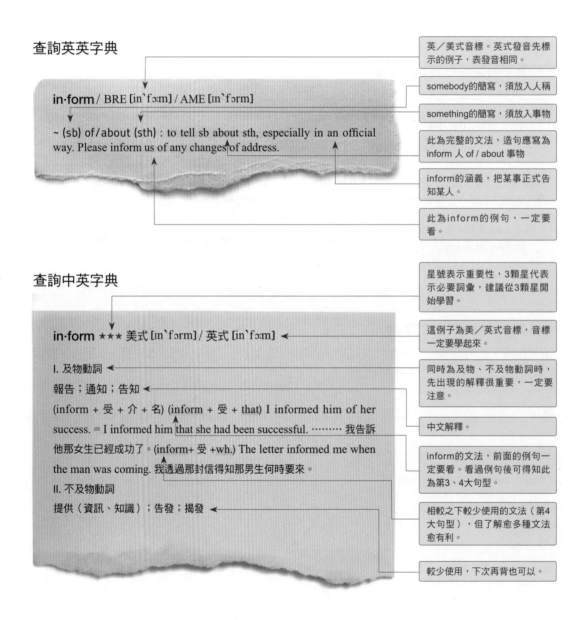

英/美式音標。英式發音先標示的例子,表發音相同。

in·form / BRE [ɪnˈfɔːm] / AME [ɪnˈfɔrm]

somebody的簡寫,須放入人稱

something的簡寫,須放入事物

~ (sb) of/about (sth) : to tell sb about sth, especially in an official way. Please inform us of any changes of address.

此為完整的文法,造句應寫為 inform 人 of / about 事物

inform的涵義,把某事正式告知某人。

此為inform的例句,一定要看。

查詢中英字典

星號表示重要性,3顆星代表示必要詞彙,建議從3顆星開始學習。

in·form ★★★ 美式 [ɪnˈfɔrm] / 英式 [ɪnˈfɔːm]

這例子為美/英式音標,音標一定要學起來。

I. 及物動詞

報告;通知;告知

(inform + 受 + 介 + 名) (inform + 受 + that) I informed him of her success. = I informed him that she had been successful. ……… 我告訴他那女生已經成功了。(inform+ 受 +wh.) The letter informed me when the man was coming. 我透過那封信得知那男生何時要來。

II. 不及物動詞

提供(資訊、知識);告發;揭發

同時為及物、不及物動詞時,先出現的解釋很重要,一定要注意。

中文解釋。

inform的文法,前面的例句一定要看。看過例句後可得知此為第3、4大句型。

相較之下較少使用的文法(第4大句型),但了解愈多種文法愈有利。

較少使用,下次再背也可以。

1. 英文的語順

英文的基本語順是「主詞 + 動詞」（S + V），但也有例外，就是「動詞 + 主詞」（V + S）的倒裝句。在本書的Chapter 07和20有針對倒裝句做詳細的說明，在這裡僅簡單介紹疑問句的倒裝。

❶ be動詞的情況（單純地將SV對調為VS即可）

He is a manager. 他是位經理。→ **Is he** a manager? 他是位經理嗎？

❷ 助動詞的情況（單純地將SV對調為VS即可）

He can arrive soon. 他馬上就會抵達。→ **Can he** arrive soon? 他馬上就會抵達嗎？

❸ be、助動詞以外的其他動詞（加入助動詞do就變成疑問句）

He works hard. 他努力工作。→ **Does he work** hard? 他努力工作嗎？

He worked hard. 他有努力工作。→ **Did he work** hard? 他有努力工作嗎？

You work hard. 你努力工作。→ **Do you work** hard? 你有努力工作嗎？

2. 單數、複數

❶ 動詞是單數加-s，名詞是複數加-s

我們先一起來看名詞吧！名詞加上-s是複數，而動詞相反的是加上-s或-es是單數。這兩種千萬不能搞混了。

> 名詞 + -s = 複數 　 動詞 + -s / -es = 單數

a boy （單數名詞）, **boys** （複數名詞）

makes （單數動詞）, **make** （複數動詞）

另外主詞和動詞的單數、複數的搭配如下：

A boy makes （單數名詞 + 單數動詞）

Boys make （複數名詞 + 複數動詞）

上述兩個例子不是完整的句子，請看單、複數的搭配即可。

❷ 動詞接-(e)s的規則

主詞為「第三人稱單數，現在式」的情況才會加上-s或-es。我們在前面有學到動詞加-(e)s是單數吧！那麼如果是單數主詞的話，該不該加-(e)s呢？事實上規則有點複雜，我們先記住下面三個規則吧。

1 主詞是第三人稱時	
2 主詞是單數時	動詞後接-(e)s
3 動詞為現在式	

同時符合上面三個條件時，動詞後才能接-(e)s。

第一，主詞必須是第三人稱。但是第一人稱、第二人稱的單數主詞，動詞後面不加-(e)s。所謂的第三人稱，就是除了第一人稱的I與we、第二人稱的you以外，其餘通通都是第三人稱。

第二，如同上面提到的，主詞必須是單數。雖然employees是第三人稱，但為複數名詞，為了使前後單、複數一致，這時候就不在動詞後面加-(e)s了。

第三，動詞的時態必須是現在式，後面才可以接-(e)s。像He worked的過去式和He will work的未來式，就算主詞是第三人稱單數，動詞也不能接-(e)s。若不是現在式，能區分單、複數的只剩下be動詞的was和were了。

3. 現在、過去、未來

在本書的Chapter 06會學到動詞的時態，在此先了解現在、過去、未來的基本時態。

現在式：動詞的原形，或是原形動詞後面加-(e)s。

過去式：規則變化是在動詞後面加-ed，但也有動詞像made一樣是不規則變化。
　　　　（不規則變化必須背字典後附錄的不規則變化表）

未來式：形態主要為「will [shall] + 原形動詞」。

我們從動狀詞開始說起吧！動狀詞指的是-ing、p.p.、to不定詞，這三種以外的形態叫做限定動詞，句中有主詞的話，後面一定要有一個限定動詞。如果題目中的句子沒有限定動詞，那空格位置就要填限定動詞，這時候就可以把動狀詞的選項直接刪除。另外，連接詞連接兩個以上的「主詞＋動詞」的子句時，限定動詞也要有兩個。

1. -ing

-ing形態的動詞叫做動名詞（參閱Chapter 08）；也稱為現在分詞（參閱Chapter 10）。動名詞，可當作名詞使用；現在分詞，當作形容詞使用時，表示「正在…中的」。

2. p.p.

過去分詞（參閱Chapter 10）用來修飾名詞，當作形容詞使用，表示被動「過去已完成動作的…」。舉例來說，指的就是fall-fell-fallen中第三個fallen。fall有「掉落」的意思，是動詞的原形；fell是「掉落」的過去式；fallen有「掉下的」的意思，是過去分詞，當作修飾名詞的形容詞使用。很多單字像fallen一樣，可明確區分出限定動詞和動狀詞，但也有很難區分的單字，如：make-made-made、set-set-set、revise-revised-revised。那這種單字要如何分辨呢？如果made、set或revised這些容易混淆的單字放在冠詞、所有格、介系詞、及物動詞等和名詞之間的話，是限定動詞還是動狀詞呢？是形容詞的位置嗎？（參閱Chapter 01）是扮演著形容詞的動狀詞，也就是過去分詞p.p.的位置。另外，我們來看這句子The law revised recently will be in effect starting next month.，在這裡，revised很清楚地就是動狀詞。因為will be是限定動詞，所以不需要再有一個限定動詞了，而且「法令」不會自己主動修改，若想成「法令被修改」就比較說得通了。

3. to不定詞

to不定詞在句子裡扮演著名詞、形容詞，或是副詞的角色（參閱Chapter 09）。很複雜吧？這3種詞性的涵義如下，名詞時表示「所謂的…」；形容詞時表示「將要做的（動作）」；副詞時表示「為了做…」，不管怎麼樣都不會是限定動詞。

4. 限定動詞和動狀詞的結合

在使用上，常常看見have、be這類的限定動詞和p.p.、-ing的動狀詞結合而成的have + p.p.、be -ing、be p.p.形態，這些組合都叫做限定動詞。是限定動詞？還是動狀詞？這得由前面的單字決定。前面是have、be動詞的話，就是限定動詞；如果前面是having p.p.、being p.p.、been p.p.的話，就是動狀詞，因為having、being、been本身就是動狀詞。

你常因為時間分配不均，只作了10題或20題就走出考場了嗎？那我可以明確地告訴你，這不是時間管理的問題，而是實力不足。或許你聽了心情會不好，但這是很殘酷的事實。那麼難道沒實力的人就沒有其他辦法了嗎？當然不是！現在就來公開我自己在考場上使用的方法，只要遵照這方法進行，就能拿到好成績。你千萬不要懷疑！心裡想著「就憑你說的？行嗎？」的人現在就把書闔上吧！不然就是照著我的話去做，絕對不會吃虧。來吧！想提高多益分數，卻又無所適從嗎？英文程度不錯，但又想知道50次滿分的怪物講師的撇步嗎？想知道就一起來傾聽祕訣吧！

Part 1

在答案卡上標示時，用簡單的「＾」就好。這時將手指頭放在考卷上Part 1第一題的位置上，當聽到「Now, Part 1 begins」就將注意力集中在Part 1，手指頭從(A)～(D)依序移動，把不是答案的一一刪除。當你覺得答案是(B)時，手指頭就停在答案上。（也可以在答案卡上做記號）這是為了要避免你聽完題目，卻想不起答案是哪一個的情況發生。這樣做至少可以幫助你發揮最大的注意力。此時，即使你心裡已認定答案是(A)，也不要忙著去看下一題。把選項(A)～(D)一一的仔細聽完是很重要的。

Part 2

在答案卡上標示時，也是用簡單的「＾」就好。Part 2開始作答時，盡快將注意力集中在Part 2後，注意聽問題，再用中文把問題在腦中重複思考兩、三遍，避免發生聽選項聽到一半，突然想不起原本題目的情況發生。仔細把選項聽完後，再將你心中認定的答案選出來。Part 1和Part 2將答案直接畫在答案卡上。注意！不是「＾」標示，是畫出真正的答案。時間很充裕的！如果遇到答案很模稜兩可的題目時，絕對不要執著於該題。當下一題開始進行時，要毫不留戀地放棄，隨便選個答案就跳過，過度執著只會造成更多的分數損失。

Part 3

這裡就需要有快速的解讀能力。每段內容都會有3道題目，如果解讀能力較差的話，就先讀題目別看選項（當然這樣很難得高分）。看題目時，默記重點單字，一邊集中注意力聽內容，一邊用「︿」在答案卡上標示可能的答案。此時也要注意，作答時不要占用到閱讀下一題的時間，再慢也要在第一題播放結束時，就將三個問題的作答完畢。在第二、三題播放時，你就應該在閱讀下一個題組的題目和選項了。在時間內未作答完畢，影響到下一題作答時間，導致錯誤的機率升高。如果錯了就讓它錯了吧！猶豫的話只會讓損失擴大。

Part 4

這部分也跟Part 3一樣，先看過題目後再來聽題目內容，最好連選項都全部看過。Part 4和Part 3一樣，高手們光看題目，就大約可以猜出答案。像我的話，不聽播放內容光看題目和選項，我有70%的自信可以答對。當然，如果有聽內容的話，其餘的30%要答對就很簡單了。這樣的預知力是怎麼來的呢？從平時多閱讀英文文章，多做題目中學來的。到Part 4為止，答案都在答案卡上作記號後，就迅速填好。另外，選用較粗的考試用鉛筆筆芯有利於作答，這也是一個訣竅。

在做Part 5、6的題目時，最好是先完成Part 7以後，留下20分鐘回頭作答Part 5、6

Part 5,6

的題目比較恰當。這時候應該趕快答題，不要回頭看已經做完的題目。20分鐘包含填答案的時間。作答Part 5時，先用簡單的「^」符號在答案卡上標示後，等全部Part 5作完以後再一次畫卡，這是為了避免趕時間，而不小心劃錯答案格的憾事發生。作答Part 6題時，只要注意看空格前的2～3個單字即可；詞彙的部份，只要看有空格存在的句子就好。當然，如果是高手的話，將所有的文章看完也有充裕的時間作答，可是這對一般的考生來說是不太可能的，所以才會叫大家看空格前的2～3個單字就好。

Part 7

做完聽力的題目後，緊接著開始做Part 7。如果時間只剩10～20分鐘，面對Part 7的長篇文章，肯定讀不下去吧！請不要慌張失措，這樣絕對無法拿高分的。Part 5、6的題目是由較短的句子組成，即使只剩下10分鐘心裡也不至於那麼慌張。甚至1分鐘就可以做完2～3題。（Part 7的文章都那麼長，1分鐘根本起不了什麼作用吧？）所以我建議Part 5開始的解題順序是Part 7 → Part 6 → Part 5。Part 6的文章長度比Part 5長，所以先將容易造成心理負擔的Part 6解決後，最後再來做Part 5的問題。所以無論如何，做完聽力的題目後一定要先做Part 7！知道嗎？這時候，不論文章有幾段，一個題目作答時間不可超過1分鐘。也就是說如果一段文章有4個題目，那麼此段文章的作答時間要在4分鐘內結束。

讀解和詞彙漸漸在TOEIC考試中佔有愈來愈大的比重，英英字典將是你再好不過的重要嚮導。建議平時多接觸、閱讀英文文章，也可參考本書的句子結構分段方式，熟悉語句與文章架構。以上是多益各部分的時間管理要領，建議各位在平時寫模擬測驗時就要實踐。最後在下頁也用圖表整理出實際在考場上的時間管理表，讓大家一眼就可以了解。

怪物講師的時間分配

時間分配（各考場的時間有所不同，請留意畫答案卷的時間）

Part 1, 2, 3, 4 聽力	10：00～10：55（55分鐘，第1題～第100題）
Part 7 多篇文章閱讀	10：55～11：20（25分鐘，第176題～第200題，每題組5分）
Part 7 單篇文章閱讀	11：20～11：50（30分鐘，第147題～第175題，每題1分鐘）
Part 6 短文填空	11：50～11：57（7分鐘，第131題～第146題，每題組1分45秒）
Part 5 單句填空	11：57～12：10（13分鐘，第101題～第130題，每題26秒）
總共120分鐘 + 考卷缺損檢查及direction的時間4分鐘要答第101～110題	

剛開始準備多益的人大部分都會習慣先讀完題目再看選項。但是Part 5、6不需要理解完整的題目內容，看過選項就能知道答案，可以節省寶貴的時間。因為即使掌握題目意思後再作答，也可能會遇到在兩個答案間猶豫不決的情況，先看選項至少省去了一些不必要的理解時間。快速地掌握題型後，選出空格的答案。

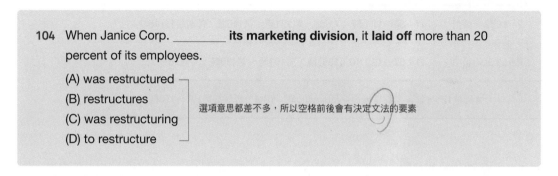

104 When Janice Corp. _____ **its marketing division**, it **laid off** more than 20 percent of its employees.

(A) was restructured
(B) restructures
(C) was restructuring
(D) to restructure

選項意思都差不多，所以空格前後會有決定文法的要素

上面的選項都是以動詞restructure為根本，差別在「be動詞 + p.p.」、「第三人稱單數動詞-s」和「be動詞 + -ing」、「to不定詞」，可得知這是「文法題」。這樣一來，不用花太多時間去知道題目的語意，也可以找出正確答案。

110 We **are** _____ **to announce** that our revenues have increased by more than 30%.

(A) pleased
(B) pleasing
(C) please
(D) pleasure

可看出選項意思都差不多，僅詞性不同。

上面的選項都是以動詞please為根本，差別在詞性和型態上。這種情況可以不用花太多時間翻譯題目的語意，可藉由確認空格前後，找到決定文法的要素。這種問題叫做「詞性題」，也是不用花時間了解題目語意就可解題的代表性例子。

接下來請看下題。

---

115 We are able to avoid pitfalls primarily because the supervisor _____ checks the materials in and out of the factory.

(A) generally
(B) assuredly
(C) rationally
(D) regularly

可看出詞性相同，要根據語意選擇。

上面選項全都是副詞，也就是說無法利用詞性或文法的方式解題。遇到這樣的問題時，一定要了解題目的語意才有辦法知道答案。這種題目類型叫做「詞彙題」。

這些方法並不完全適用於Part 5、6的所有題目，但即使是節省一點點時間，在考試時的幫助很大。請各位善加運用並發揮最大的效用。

Q1 Something should be done in order to improve the _____ of the retail store to attract more customers.

(A) environment 　　　　　　　(B) environmentally

(C) environmental 　　　　　　(D) environmentalist

▸ _____

Q2 The report written by the head manager _____ finally approved by the board of directors.

(A) was 　　　　　　　　　　　(B) were

(C) have 　　　　　　　　　　　(D) has

▸ _____

Q3 A common news topic in many countries today is _____ ways to reduce government spending.

(A) foundation 　　　　　　　　(B) found

(C) finding 　　　　　　　　　　(D) to finding

▸ _____

Q4 Most modern cities have a complex but convenient network of subway rails that run _____ the surface.

(A) beneath 　　　　　　　　　(B) from

(C) above 　　　　　　　　　　(D) outside

▸ _____

| 正確答案 | 1. 詞性題(A)　2. 文法題(A)　3. 詞性題(C)　4. 文法題(A)

Part 01

30% 解題看例句的
結構！

理解基本詞性
5秒內解決20個詞性問題！

請猜猜看下列單字的詞性，如果連意思都知道就更好了。（可能有2個詞性）

1 responsibility

2 accurately ▸ adv. 正確地

3 preparatory ⌐ex¬ preparatory school ▸ adj. 預備的.
　　　　　　　　預備學校 (prep school)

4 friendly

5 widen ▸ v. 使變寬

6 accountant ▸ n. 會計師.

7① critic　n. 評論者. ②criticize v. 批評 ③ critical a. 批評的

8 representative ▸ n. 代表者 ／ a. 代表性的

句子中最重要的基本詞性是**名詞**、**形容詞**和**副詞**，而且各個詞性在句子中所扮演的角色如下所示。

1 基本詞性的功能
　❶ 名詞的角色：主詞、受詞、補語
　❷ 形容詞的角色：名詞敘述
　❸ 副詞的角色：修飾動詞、形容詞、副詞、所有句子

2 基本詞性問題的解法
　　如果你在前面Warming-up部分有認真學習，看到結尾是-tion（名）、-ty（名）、-ly（副／形）、-en（動）等的單字，大概就知道詞性是什麼。但就算實際的型態是這樣，也有不少例外的狀況。如果像機器人一樣不知變通地作答，很難考到好成績。基本的詞性經由Warming-up部分記清楚後，在各種英文考試中常常出現的例外狀況，也要好好地熟記。

| 正確答案 | 1. 名詞／責任 2. 副詞／正確地 3. 形容詞／預備的 4. 形容詞／友好的 5. 動詞／使變寬 6. 名詞／會計師 7. 名詞／批評者 8. 名詞；形容詞／代表者；代表性的

攻略法
01

名詞是答案的5大情況

要讓句子具有意義的話，除了要有動詞、形容詞、副詞等等的詞類，還一定要有指稱某人或是某事物的「名詞」。如果沒有名詞，句子中的「主詞、受詞、補語」就不具有任何意思。

名詞在一個句子裡具有主詞、受詞、補語的作用，但考試時，只知道這些是不夠的。以主詞、受詞、補語來找出名詞的位置，會佔用太多解其他題目的時間，因此，要學會看空格的前後文，快速掌握名詞的方法。

1　**A man** is trying to open **his briefcase**.
　　冠詞後面是名詞！　　　　　所有格後面是名詞！

2　**A supervisor** will ask for **the information**.
　　冠詞後面是名詞！　　　　　定冠詞後面是名詞！

3　**With his right**, he could finish the job.
　　介系詞後面的名詞right！中間就算有所有格也沒關係！

4　The new born baby will **resemble its mother**.
　　　　　　　　　　及物動詞後面的名詞mother！中間果然有所有格！

5　**The employee who was diligent** was promoted.
　　who後面是形容詞子句，employee是先行名詞！

1　一個男人正要打開／他的公事包。

2　一位主管將要求／那個資訊。

3　以他的權利／他可以完成／那項工作。

4　新生兒／會長得像／他的媽媽。

5　那位職員／勤奮的／升職了。

稍微清楚名詞的位置了嗎？只要先理解基本概念，仔細觀察名詞的前後文，很快就能找到答案。**與其他的詞類相比，看前後文會更正確判斷名詞。**在實戰中該以哪一種方式來應對呢？

5秒　解決名詞問題的方法

① 觀察句子空格的前後文。

② 空格前面有冠詞、所有格、介系詞和及物動詞。

③ 確認名詞的位置。
　　（此時，確認空格內是否要填上主詞、受詞、補語，另外，確認語意正確的話，就100%是正確答案了！）

Quiz

Q1 The shop will offer its (customers / customize) discounted rates.

Q2 Without the (helpful / help) which I need urgently, I would fail.

▶ 解答在008頁

形容詞是答案的3大情況

形容詞是用來修飾句子中的名詞。不管名詞放在形容詞前方或是任何地方，形容詞的主要任務就是修飾名詞。由此可知，如果沒有名詞的話，形容詞也就沒有用了。

1. 形容詞修飾名詞

形容詞是修飾名詞的詞類，因此如果是修飾名詞的問題空格，通常正確答案就是形容詞。**如果句子中有形容詞的話，前後方一定會有名詞**。

1 **A diligent supervisor** will ask for **the accurate information**.
冠詞與名詞之間是形容詞。

2 **His main responsibility** does not include this one.
所有格與名詞之間是形容詞。

3 **With his own right**, he could finish the job.
介系詞與名詞間插入形容詞的情況！（也可能在所有格與名詞之間）

4 The new born baby will **resemble its beautiful mother**.
及物動詞與名詞之間插入形容詞的情況！（也可能在所有格與名詞之間）

5 **The diligent employee** was promoted.
左頁原本是The employee who was diligent，也可以用The diligent employee表示！

在這裡，**形容詞是修飾名詞的修飾語**，因此如果不需要的話，**也可以省略不用**。

Quiz

Q3 Due to the ongoing financial difficulty, we require (additional / addition) layoffs.

Q4 (Qualified / Qualification) applicants are to submit their resumes.

▶ 解答在008頁

2. 第2大句型動詞後面常出現的形容詞，be、become、remain是第2大句型（S + V + C）的常見動詞！

在這些動詞後面可以是名詞及形容詞，但在多益的考試中，這些動詞後面幾乎不會是名詞！

《講師的補充說明》

形容詞大部分都是放在名詞前面，但是並不是說名詞之前一定是形容詞。因為也有「名詞 + 名詞」型態的複合名詞會出現。

1 一位勤奮的主管／將要求／正確的資訊。

2 他主要的責任／不包含／這個。

3 根據自己的權利／他可以完成／那項工作。

4 新生兒／好像／自己美麗的媽媽。

5 那位勤奮的職員／升職了。

相信我，be、become、remain後面請選擇形容詞當答案。

1 We **are able** to finish it in no time.
      be動詞後面是形容詞的情況！

2 The supervisor **became interested** in the new project.
    become後面是形容詞的情況，interested是把過去分詞形容詞化，帶有「有興趣」的意思！

3 The company has **remained competitive** since its founding.
        remain後面是形容詞的情況！

Quiz

Q5 Our products are (compatible / compatibility) with your system.

Q6 Because of the newly adapted system, our department became (efficient / efficiency).

▶ 解答在008頁

3. 常常以第5大句型的受詞補語形式出現的形容詞

make、keep、find是常見第5大句型（S＋V＋O＋OC）動詞。在這些動詞後面常會看到當作受詞的名詞，為了修飾當作受詞用的名詞，**形容詞會被當作受詞補語使用**。

1 The revised regulation **made** the staff **confused**.
      第5大句型，動詞make後面是被當成受詞補語使用的形容詞confused（困惑）！

2 I **found** this movie very **exciting**.
    第5大句型，動詞find後面是被當成受詞補語使用的形容詞exciting（刺激的）！

5秒 解決形容詞問題的方法

1 觀察句子空格的前後文。

2 空格後面是名詞，空格前面會有第2、5大句型的動詞。

3 確認形容詞的位置。

（如果有時間的話，可填入形容詞之後，確認看看是不是可以修飾名詞。）

Quiz

Q7 Please always keep your room (cleanly / clean) so that you can concentrate.

Q8 We (became / found) anxious about the proposed plan.

▶ 解答在008頁

1 我們可以完成／那件事／即時。

2 那位主管／有興趣／對於那個新的計畫。

3 那間公司維持／競爭力／自從公司創立之後。

1 這修正過的規定／使職員／困惑。

2 我發現／這部電影／很刺激。

攻略法

副詞是答案的3大情況

副詞是修飾動詞、形容詞、副詞以及整個句子的詞類，但和形容詞一樣，並不一定要在句子裡出現。由此可知，答題之前，要在腦中想一想，隨著需要修飾單字的詞性，來選擇要使用形容詞還是副詞。

1. 修飾動詞的副詞

(1) 句子的最前面或最後面，動詞的正前方就是副詞的位置

副詞有①放在句子逗號前面的情況，②在主詞與動詞間出現的情況，③動詞後面的受詞、補語等詞類位置都確認好後，在句尾出現的情況。

Presumably, you **certainly** have no reason to do it **swiftly**.

逗號前面的位置！　　　主詞與動詞之間！　　　　　　　　句子的最後面！

> 大概／你／無疑地／沒有任何理由／去做那件事／快速地。

(2) 插入動詞群組之間的副詞

副詞大部分的位置是在動詞群組之間，因此一定要好好了解在考試中常出現的動詞群組型態，「**助動詞 + 原形動詞**」、「**have + p.p.**」、「**be 動詞 + -ing**」、「**be 動詞 + p.p.**」等代表性的動詞群組。而且「**動詞 + 介系詞**」、「**動詞 + 副詞**」等動詞群組都被當作片語使用。因此需要特別熟記。那麼我們現在來觀察這些動詞群組之間插入副詞的情況吧。

1 | I **can hardly hear** you.
　　助動詞與原形動詞之間的副詞！

2 We **have recently hired** a few workers.
　　　have p.p.之間的副詞！

3 The woman **is now sobbing**.
　　　　　be 動詞 + -ing之間的副詞！

4 The construction **is not yet finished**.
　　　　　be 動詞 + p.p.之間的副詞！

5 She **depends wholly on** me.
　　　動詞片語（depends on）之間的副詞！

> 1 我幾乎聽不到你。
>
> 2 我們最近雇用了／一些工人。
>
> 3 那女人現在正在啜泣。
>
> 4 那個工程尚未結束。
>
> 5 她完全地依賴我。

(3) 非限定動詞（動狀詞）也是以副詞來修飾

在英文中有一種具有動詞機能，另外還具有名詞、形容詞、副詞等其他詞性作用的詞類，那就是非限定動詞（動狀詞）。

最常見的非限定動詞（動狀詞）就是**to不定詞及-ing型態的動名詞、分詞**。非限定動詞也是動詞的一種，因此**也需要副詞來做修飾**。另外要注意的是，依照to不定詞及-ing型態的動名詞或是動詞的屬性，後面不是副詞而是**受詞**或是**補語**。

1 We expect **to promptly begin our operation** efficiently.

to＋副詞＋原形動詞＋受詞（所有格＋名詞）＋副詞！

2 They considered **showing us the picture** immediately.

-ing＋IO＋DO＋副詞！

《講師的補充說明》

IO是 Indirect Object 的簡寫，代表間接受詞。DO 是 Direct Object 的簡寫，代表直接受詞。

1 我們期待／馬上／開始／我們的操作／有效地。

2 他們考慮／展示給／我們／那幅畫／立即。

Quiz

Q9 After (careful / carefully) considering it, we decided not to go with you.

Q10 If you are not (full / fully) satisfied, we will gladly refund your deposit.

▶ 解答在008頁

2. 修飾形容詞與副詞的副詞

副詞也修飾形容詞與副詞。請一定要記住，在副詞的後面並不一定都是形容詞，這需要觀察詞性來做判斷。

1 The audience thought the presentation was **really good**.

副詞＋形容詞！

2 The show **is exceptionally well prepared**.

be動詞＋副詞＋副詞＋形容詞！

1 觀眾覺得／演出太好了。

2 這次的表演／很好／準備。

5秒 解決副詞問題的方法

1 副詞, 主詞＋副詞＋動詞＋受詞／補語＋副詞

2 助動詞＋副詞＋原形動詞

have＋副詞＋p.p.

be 動詞＋副詞＋-ing / p.p.（進行式／被動式）

動詞＋副詞＋介系詞 例 depend heavily on

3 動詞 to 副詞＋原形動詞＋受詞／補語＋副詞

動詞 -ing＋受詞／補語＋副詞

《講師的補充說明》

對於 Chapter 01 的說明與例句你都了解、熟悉了嗎？如果還是不太清楚的話，不要草率直接做題目。最好再把前面的說明熟讀幾遍。要知道，蓋房子如果地基不穩，房子馬上會倒的！

Quiz

Q11 It is (certain / certainly) true that he will pass the exam.

Q12 The faculty of the university handled the issue very (ease / easily).

▶ 解答在008頁

攻略法01	名詞是答案的5大情況

1 冠詞

2 所有格

3 介系詞

4 動詞（及物動詞、主動型）

+（副詞）+（形容詞）+ 名詞 + **5** 形容詞子句

攻略法02	形容詞是答案的3大情況

1 冠詞

所有格

介系詞

動詞（及物動詞，主動型）

+ 形容詞 + 名詞 + 形容詞子句

2 be

become

remain

+ 形容詞 （第2大句型）

3 make

keep

find

+ 名詞 + 形容詞 （第5大句型）

攻略法03	副詞是答案的3大情況

1 副詞 , 主詞 + 副詞 + 動詞 + 受詞／補語 + 副詞

2 助動詞 + 副詞 + 原形動詞

have + 副詞 + p.p.

be 動詞+ 副詞 + -ing / p.p.（進行式／被動式）

動詞 + 副詞 + 介系詞

3 動詞 to 副詞 + 原形動詞 + 受詞／補語 + 副詞

動詞 -ing + 受詞／ 補語 + 副詞

例子 1 (A) employee ── ❶ 把握問題的類型
　　(B) employ
　　(C) employed
　　　　　　　　　❸ 空格中要填什麼詞類？
　　(D) employment

The experienced _____ who was recently hired must report to me directly.
　　　　　　　　　　　　　　　　　　❷ 把握提示

1 把握問題的類型	
2 把握提示	
3 空格中要填什麼詞類？	

2 (A) necessary
　(B) necessity
　(C) necessarily
　(D) necessaries

It is _____ for candidates to show a high level of eagerness to deal with the task.

1 把握問題的類型	
2 把握提示	
3 空格中要填什麼詞類？	

3 (A) noticeable
　(B) noticeably
　(C) notice
　(D) notify

You have to know that the flight schedules are subject to change without prior _____.

1 把握問題的類型	
2 把握提示	
3 空格中要填什麼詞類？	

4 (A) affords
　(B) afforded
　(C) afford
　(D) affordable

As the shopping mall provided discount coupons to visitors, they found the place _____.

1 把握問題的類型	
2 把握提示	
3 空格中要填什麼詞類？	

5 (A) Although
　(B) However
　(C) Despite
　(D) As

_____ , the accounting director accepted the proposal because it was impressive.

1 把握問題的類型	
2 把握提示	
3 空格中要填什麼詞類？	

6 (A) adequately
   (B) adequate
   (C) adequateness
   (D) adequacy

   You'd better _____ prepare for all the questions in case there are demanding customers.

1 把握問題的類型

2 把握提示

3 空格中要填什麼詞類？

7 (A) attracting
   (B) attraction
   (C) attract
   (D) attractive

   We should make our display _____ to shoppers in order to increase our sales.

1 把握問題的類型

2 把握提示

3 空格中要填什麼詞類？

8 (A) apply
   (B) applying
   (C) appliances
   (D) to apply

   We can deliver all our _____ which we have in stock within three working days.

1 把握問題的類型

2 把握提示

3 空格中要填什麼詞類？

9 (A) interests
   (B) interesting
   (C) interested
   (D) interestingly

   The R&D department showed us really _____ results of the experiment.

1 把握問題的類型

2 把握提示

3 空格中要填什麼詞類？

10 (A) strictly
   (B) strict
   (C) strictness
   (D) stricter

   According to the new policy, employees are _____ prohibited from smoking within this area.

1 把握問題的類型

2 把握提示

3 空格中要填什麼詞類？

▶ 解答在008頁

101 The current time schedule should be adjusted for the benefit of our _____.

(A) works
(B) working
(C) worked
(D) workers

102 Something should be done in order to improve the _____ of the retail store to attract more customers.

(A) environment
(B) environmentally
(C) environmental
(D) environmentalist

103 You should submit the financial report _____ to the personnel department by May 7th.

(A) direct
(B) directed
(C) directly
(D) direction

104 Thank you for offering the position to me and I am _____ to accept your generous suggestion.

(A) more happily
(B) happiness
(C) happily
(D) happy

105 We guarantee that we will replace the defective item with a new one _____ free of charge.

(A) complete
(B) completely
(C) completeness
(D) complement

106 According to the newly _____ newsletter, all employees will get subsidized when using buses.

(A) publish
(B) publication
(C) published
(D) publishes

107 The sales _____ who developed the marketing strategy will be awarded the first prize.

(A) manage
(B) manager
(C) management
(D) managing

108 _____, you should ask for the approval from your immediate supervisor first before doing anything.

(A) Generally
(B) General
(C) Generalize
(D) Generalizing

重要
109 After completing the form, he has _____ agreed to work in another branch.

(A) final
(B) finalize
(C) finally
(D) finalist

110 If you agree _____ with the terms of the contract, please write your name at the bottom of it.

(A) absolute
(B) absolutely
(C) absoluteness
(D) absolutize

收集了多益考試中常出的題目。請當作正式的考試，確認時間並解題。

高難度
111 As the economy remains _____ sound, there will be more job openings.

(A) financing
(B) financial
(C) financed
(D) financially

112 _____, the merger between the two companies did not have much influence on the industry.

(A) Despite
(B) Although
(C) But
(D) However

113 We must adhere to the time schedule so that the construction can be _____ on schedule.

(A) current
(B) currently
(C) more current
(D) most current

114 Most of them have _____ hard to buy and maintain their own vehicles.

(A) work
(B) working
(C) worked
(D) works

115 All the system engineers are to participate in the seminar next Wednesday to raise our _____.

(A) productivity
(B) productive
(C) product
(D) produce

116 _____ the damage to the operating system, Mr. Jones won't be able to use his laptop computer.

(A) Because
(B) Because of
(C) Nevertheless
(D) Into

117 The board of directors is expected to rule _____ on all disagreements between the labor union and the management.

(A) impartial
(B) more impartial
(C) impartiality
(D) impartially

118 It is essential that we try harder to improve customer satisfaction levels and keep our company more _____.

(A) competitive
(B) competitively
(C) compete
(D) competition

高難度
119 It is unanimously agreed that the company's _____ new line of products will dominate foreign markets as well as its domestic one.

(A) impression
(B) impressive
(C) impressively
(D) impressed

重要
120 Easier access to the public transportations is making the factories in the region more _____ to commuters.

(A) attract
(B) attraction
(C) attractively
(D) attractive

▶ 解答在010頁

Questions 121-124 refer to the following article.

"The first moment of truth" is _____ idea where a consumer has made up in their
                                    121
mind if they demand to purchase a product or service upon first encountering any aspect

of the product or service, as many studies of economics have revealed. Undeniably, it

sounds a bit _____ and subjective, yet it truly exists. For one thing, purchasing is not
              122
a purely rational behavior even though plenty of consumers may express their concerns

about the price, quality, or customer service while they are considering if they want to buy

something or not. The truth is they _____ whether they want to buy it or not at the
                                      123
very first moment they see the product or experience it. They merely take advantage of

the expression of those concerns to convince themselves that _____
                                                              124

121 (A) a
    (B) an
    (C) the
    (D) some

122 (A) mystery
    (B) myth
    (C) mysterious
    (D) mysteriously

123 (A) to decide
    (B) decided
    (C) have decided
    (D) had decided

124 (A) this deal is a sensible action rather
        than an impulsive one.
    (B) this deal is a sensible action rather
        than a cautious one.
    (C) this deal is a sensible action rather
        than a wise one.
    (D) this deal is a sensible action rather
        than a clever one.

Review Test

請先回答下面的問題，並複習在Chapter 01中所學習到的基本詞性內容。

1 形容詞存在的理由？　　　　　　　　▶ _____

2 副詞存在的理由？　　　　　　　　　▶ _____

3 be、become、remain後面所接的詞類？ ▶ _____

4 make、keep、find後面所接的詞類？　▶ _____

5 名詞是正確答案的證據？　　　　　　▶ _____

6 形容詞的位置會在哪3個地方？　　　▶ _____

7 副詞的位置會在哪3個地方？　　　　▶ _____

Preview

1 5大句型的特徵

英文句子中有5大代表的句型，你知道哪些是5大句型吧？不要覺得我又要講解落伍的文法了，5大句型真的是所有英文的根本。

- 第1大句型：主詞 + 動詞（S + V）
- 第2大句型：主詞 + 動詞 + 主詞補語（S + V + SC）
- 第3大句型：主詞 + 動詞 + 受詞（S + V + O）
- 第4大句型：主詞 + 動詞 + 間接受詞 + 直接受詞（S + V + IO + DO）
- 第5大句型：主詞 + 動詞 + 受詞 + 受詞補語（S + V + O + OC）

2 句子構成的要素與區分的方法

- 主詞：確認是不是名詞類（名詞、代名詞、動名詞、to不定詞、名詞子句）
- 動詞：限定動詞與非限定動詞（動狀詞）的區分（數 → 態 → 時）
- 受詞：雖然屬於名詞類，但是要注意它會在動詞後面出現
- 補語：名詞類與形容詞類（主要被當作3大形容詞類來使用）
- 修飾語：形容詞類與副詞類（4大形容詞類、4大副詞類）

主詞位置問題的check point！

大部分的句子中最先出現的就是主詞，因此要尋找填入主詞位置的答案，需要去確認什麼東西呢？有好幾個重點需要熟記，希望在多益考試中可以100%活用。

首先，先來了解在主詞的位置要填入什麼，要留意的要點是什麼。好好熟記以下的內容，活用在解題上吧。

1. 要填入主詞位置的名詞類

通常在主詞的位置，我們都會想到名詞，但是只靠一般名詞無法表達多種意思，有幾種可以具有名詞詞性且可以被當作主詞使用的詞類，只要是稱得上名詞的，都可以歸在名詞類。在名詞類中有名詞、代名詞、動名詞、to不定詞、名詞子句。

1 The man
句子最基本的名詞！

2 He
可以代替名詞的代名詞！

3 Speaking English
是動詞且具有名詞作用的動名詞！

4 For him to speak English
具有名詞、形容詞、副詞作用的to不定詞！

5 That he can speak two languages well
句子中具有名詞作用的名詞子句！

1	那個男人
2	他
3	說英文
4	他說英文
5	他精通兩種語言

像這樣在句子中可以**當作主詞使用的代表性名詞類有5種**。另外，這種名詞類在句子裡可以當作受詞、補語使用。

2. 沒有主詞的命令句

通常在句子中一定要有主詞，但是**命令句卻是以沒有主詞的原形動詞開始的**。

Please **contact** us if you have any further questions.
動詞contact前面沒有主詞！

請聯絡／我們／如果您還有其他的問題。

3. 可以取代真正的主詞，使用it的情況

主詞如果很長的話，在主詞的位置可以使用虛主詞it，再把真正的主詞放到後面去，請見以下例句。

1　**It** is not so difficult for you **to master English**.
　= **It** is not so difficult **that you master English**.
　it雖然在主詞的位置，但是to和that後面才是真正的主詞！

2　**It** is useful for our employees **to use the public transportation**.
　= **It** is useful **that our employees use the public transportation**.
　如果to不定詞與that子句是主詞的話，理解上是不是變得困難！

1　並不是這麼難的／你要／精通英文。

2　有用的是／我們的職員們／利用大眾交通工具這件事。

4. 主詞在動詞後面的倒裝句

倒裝句在後面章節會做仔細的講解，在這裡先講解倒裝句中的一種形式——以there開始的句子，意思是「…有什麼」，表示「有什麼存在」的時候使用的。

1 There **is a book**.
is後面的a book是主詞！

2 There **remain attendants**.
remain後面的attendants是主詞！

3 There **exists a border**.
exists後面的a border是主詞！

這種情況下，there就是帶出句子內容的副詞，is、remain、exist是動詞，那後面的名詞們就是句子的主詞。這就是主詞與動詞位置倒過來的倒裝句。

1 那有一本書。

2 參與者還留在這裡。

3 那有警戒線。

怪物講師的祕訣

1 名詞類有名詞、代名詞、動名詞、to不定詞、名詞子句。

2 名詞具有主詞、受詞、補語的功能。

3 命令句沒有主詞。

4 如果主詞太長，可以先寫虛主詞it，把真正的主詞放在後面。

5 「There + 動詞（be 動詞／其他第1大句型動詞）+ 主詞」中，There不是主詞。

Quiz

Q1 (Attractive / Attracting) customers needs a lot of patience.

Q2 It is necessary for them (to place / place) an advertisement.

攻略法

05

動詞位置問題的check point！

在前面的章節有學到幾種找出主詞位置的訣竅，那現在就要來學習找出主詞後面的動詞位置了。我們一起來看看，如果要找出主詞後緊接而來的動詞位置，需要確認哪些東西。

現在要來學習找出主詞後面的動詞位置了，限定動詞與非限定動詞（動狀詞）的概念，另外先了解限定動詞有3個主要的check points－數、態、時！

依據字面上的意思，所謂的限定動詞就是，在句子的主詞後面只會有一個表示主詞動作的動詞。動詞的型態大多都是（to原形動詞／-ing／-ed），不是限定動詞之外的都稱作非限定動詞（動狀詞）。但是，如果有連接詞的話，動詞的數量也會變多，那限定動詞也會變成2個吧？

1. 限定動詞及非限定動詞（動狀詞）的區分

主詞後面一定要有限定動詞，非限定動詞（動狀詞）無法取代限定動詞的位置。也就是說，如果空格中要填入限定動詞的時候，請先把非限定動詞（動狀詞）刪除後答題。那非限定動詞（動狀詞）有哪些呢？

1 **Swimming** is my hobby.
　名詞功能的動名詞！

2 She **is swimming**.
　　　表示進行中的現在分詞！

3 She **was hired**.
　　　表示被動意思的過去分詞！

4 My hobby is **to collect pictures**.
　　　　　句子中，表示名詞功能的to不定詞！

5 I have **an ability to finish it**.
　　　　句子中，表示形容詞功能的to不定詞！

6 We study English **to succeed**.
　　　　　句子中，表示副詞功能的to不定詞！

《講師的補充說明》

動詞之間結合的being p.p.等都是非限定動詞（動狀詞）。但是限定動詞只有be -ing或是have been -ing形式。另外動詞的過去型態是限定動詞，與非限定動詞（動狀詞）的p.p.很像，很容易混淆，請您要特別注意。

例 make-made-made

made是限定動詞（做了）也是非限定動詞（動狀詞）p.p.（被做的）。

1 游泳是我的興趣。

2 她正在游泳。

3 她被錄用了。

4 我的興趣是收集圖片。

5 我有能力／完成那個。

6 我們讀英文／是為了成功。

2. 在限定動詞中找出答案順序的數、態、時！

依據上述的訣竅，如果判斷這個位置是限定動詞的話，非限定動詞就會被刪除。因此在這個問題的答案選項中通常會有兩個以上的限定動詞。這個時候就需要再以其他的判斷基準來解題，這個基準就是數、態、時！

(1) 單、複數的區分－數！

The managers in this plant **have** many complaints about it.

主詞是單數的話，動詞也是單數型。主詞是複數的話，動詞也是複數型（只有現在）

> 管理者們／這個工廠的／帶有許多不滿／關於這個。

主詞是managers，因此絕對是複數型，符合答案的動詞就是複數動詞的have。這句還有常被出題者使用的小陷阱，就是在動詞旁邊的單數名詞plant，會讓你感到混淆，這也是多益典型出題的方式。

(2) 主動、被動的區分－態！

The supervisor **was hired** just last month.

有受詞就是主動型態，沒有就是被動型態！！

> 那位主管被錄用／就在上個月。

句子中was hired是被動型態，just last month的意思是「就在上個月」，是修飾was hired的副詞句。如果句中was hired的位置是空格的話，句意可以看成「錄用了（主動）」以及「被錄用了（被動）」，所以這個時候就要看有沒有受詞。

(3) 時制的區分－時！

They **have discussed** the plan since **last June**.

在句子中一定有讓你知道時制的提示語！

> 他們一直討論／那個計畫／從去年6月以來。

have discussed是現在完成式，提示就是後面出現的since。從6月「持續⋯以來」的意思，因此要寫上現在完成式的答案。

5秒 解決限定動詞的方法（數、態、時！）

1 數：觀察單、複數，如果主詞是第3人稱單數的話，確認動詞後面的-s。

2 態：觀察主動、被動，如果有受詞是主動，沒有就是被動。

3 時：觀察時制、主要依據提示語及句意來決定。

✎ Quiz ....

Q3 The bridge built thirty years ago still (standing / stands) there.

Q4 Companies specializing in manufacturing (take / takes) advantage of this system.

> ▶ 解答在014頁

攻略法 06

受詞位置問題的check point！

受詞在句子中不會時常出現，如果出現大多是在動詞的後面。另外受詞大都是名詞類，但是並不全都是名詞類，這要依據當時的動詞來決定。

與主詞一樣，受詞大多是名詞類，但並不是所有的名詞類都可以當作受詞使用。

1. 受詞是第3、4、5大句型的必須詞

主詞與動詞是不論任何句型中都要存在的必須詞，但受詞或補語則是依據句型而出現，所以這兩個詞也可以叫做句型必須詞。受詞是第3、4、5大句型的必須詞。

1 I read **the book**.
　　只有一個受詞！（第3大句型）

2 I gave **him a chance**.
　　受詞分成間接受詞與直接受詞！（第4大句型）

3 I made **her frustrated**.
　　受詞與修飾用的受詞補語！（第5大句型）

2. 受詞的位置大多都是名詞類

上面的read、give、make等動詞後面，受詞位置填入的是名詞，但並不是所有名詞都可以填入，名詞與代名詞大多可以當作動詞後面的受詞，剩下的名詞類就要依據動詞來決定是否可以填入。

1 I **want to pass** it.
　　動詞want是把to不定詞當作受詞使用的動詞！

2 Would you **mind opening** the door?
　　動詞mind是把動名詞當作受詞使用的動詞！

3 I **know that he was fired**.
　　動詞know是把that子句（that S + V）當作受詞使用的動詞！

《講師的補充說明》

把名詞子句當作受詞用的動詞

想像動詞：think, suppose, agree, guess, know, find, insist

未來型動詞：promise, predict, expect, hope, wish

1 我讀了那本書。

2 我給了他機會。

3 我讓她感到挫折。

1 我想要／通過它。

2 可以幫我開門嗎？

3 我知道／他被解雇的事情。

3. 受詞很長的情況

主詞很長的時候可以寫上虛主詞it，而真主詞寫在後面對吧？相同的，受詞很長的時候可以寫上虛受詞it，真受詞寫在後面。

當然，並不是所有的動詞都可以使用虛構受詞以及真受詞的用法。這個部分請多留意，只有一部分的動詞可以這樣使用。

We find to play soccer interesting. (X)
→ We find **it** interesting **to play soccer**. (O)
受詞to不定詞句太長，移到最後面，另外使用虛構副詞it！

《講師的補充說明》

可以使用虛受詞、真受詞用法的動詞：find, make, believe, consider, think, ...

我們覺得很有趣／踢足球。

5秒 解決受詞問題的方法

1 把握動詞性質。
2 如果是第3、4、5大句型就需要受詞。（主動型態）
3 依照各個動詞選擇適合的名詞類。

Quiz

Q5 I hope (to watch / watching) her growing up.

Q6 I (suppose / am supposed) that we can expand our business in the near future.

▶ 解答在014頁

攻略法 07
補語位置問題的check point！

所謂的補語就是在句子中補充主詞或是受詞的句子或單字。其中補充主詞的就是主詞補語，補充受詞的就是受詞補語。

很多人會對補語感到困惑，其實不用想的太難，只要把補語想成是「補充」或是「修飾」主詞或受詞，就可以了。另外，多益考試中，大部分都是以形容詞補語形式出題，但根據情況也會出現以主詞補語形式出題的題目。

《講師的補充說明》

形容詞補語：修飾主詞或是受詞的補語

受詞補語：與主詞或是受詞有同格關係的補語

1. 補語是第2與第5大句型的必須詞

補語是指在第2與第5大句型出現的必須詞，那我們先來看在第2與第5大句型中常常被使用的動詞吧。

> 第2大句型動詞：be, become, remain, ...
> 第5大句型動詞：make, keep, find, ...

She **became tired.**（第2大句型）　　　　　　　她變得很累。

第2大句型句子主要是以「主詞 + 動詞 + 補語」（S + V + C）組成。在上面例句中的tired的意思是「累」，以形容詞補充主詞狀態，可以叫做主詞補語，是屬於第2大句型的句子。

She **made** me tired.（第5大句型）　　　　　　　她讓我很累。

第5大句型主要是以「主詞 + 動詞 + 受詞 + 受詞補語」（S + V + O + OC）組成。上面例句中的tired是補充受詞me的字，可稱為受詞補語，是屬於第5大句型的句子。

2. 補語的位置填入名詞或是形容詞

不管是第2或是第5大句型，在補語的位置可以填入名詞或是形容詞。名詞補語是主詞或是受詞具有同格關係，而形容詞補語是修飾主詞或是受詞，請好好牢記。

1 **She** became **ill**.

She became **a doctor**.（第2大句型）

主詞補語是形容詞的話，就修飾主詞。如果是名詞的話，就與主詞具有同格的關係！
第二例句中a doctor是主詞，與she具有同格關係的名詞補語！

2 She made **me happy**.

She made **me a manager**.（第5大句型）

受詞補語是形容詞的話，就修飾受詞。如果是名詞的話，就與受詞具有同格的關係！
第二個例句中manager是受詞，與me具有同格關係的名詞補語！

3. 具有形容詞功能的補語

如同前面所說，形容詞常常被當作補語來使用。但是除了一般形容詞之外，也有一些具有形容詞的功能且被當作補語使用的詞類。

1 She is **happy** with the result.

一般形容詞！happy是修飾主詞she的形容詞補語！

2 The book is **of great use**.

of use是以「介系詞＋名詞」型態具有形容詞的功能，而且被當作book（書）的主詞補語使用！

3 The result is **frustrating** in some ways.

非限定動詞。在這裡frustrating是以非限定動詞當作形容詞來使用的主詞補語！

5秒 解決補語問題的方法

1 把握動詞的性質。

2 如果動詞是第2或第5大句型動詞的話，就需要補語。

3 請詳記在補語的位置中可填入形容詞、介系詞片語（介系詞＋名詞）、非限定動詞等。

Quiz

Q7 Furthermore, the board of directors considered (dismiss / dismissing) more directors.

Q8 The recently hired manager became (concern / concerned) about the upcoming merger.

▶ 解答在014頁

----

1 她變得生病了。
她變成醫生了。

2 她讓我很幸福。
她讓我變成經理。

1 她很高興／對於這個結果。

2 這本書真的非常有用。

3 結果是失望的／在某個層面來說。

攻略法
08

修飾語位置問題的check point！

到現在為止看到了主詞、動詞、受詞、補語是答案的情況，現在就要來看不論是主詞、動詞、受詞、補語都無法替代的要素——修飾語。

句子的必須詞——主詞、動詞、受詞、補語之外，還有一些單字，這些單字叫做修飾語。並不是所有句子都需要填入修飾語。

1. 當作修飾語使用的4大形容詞類

當作修飾語且可以省略的形容詞類有以下4種。

1 the **generous donor**

在這裡generous是修飾donor，是可省略的一般形容詞！

2 the **part of this machine**

在這裡of this machine是修飾前面的part，是可省略的介系詞片語（介系詞＋名詞）！

3 the **dancing girl**

在這裡dancing是修飾girl，是可省略的非限定動詞！

4 the **man who works hard**

在這裡關係代名詞who是修飾man，是可省略的一般形容詞子句！

最後所看到的形容詞子句雖然可以跟形容詞一樣修飾名詞，但因為帶有「主詞＋動詞」（S＋V）型態的子句意義，也常常被稱為關係子句。

2. 當作修飾語使用的4大副詞類

當作修飾語且可以省略的副詞詞類有以下4種。

1 He lives **here.**

在這裡here是可省略的一般副詞！

1 慷慨的捐款人

2 這個機器的部分

3 跳舞的女孩

4 認真工作的男人

1 他住在這裡。

2 He lives **in Seoul.**

在這裡，in Seoul是可以省略的介系詞片語（介系詞＋名詞）！

3 He lives **to succeed.**

在這裡，to succeed是可以省略的to不定詞！

4 He lives **because she loves him.**

在這裡，because...him是可以省略的副詞子句！

對於考生來說，覺得最難的部分就是to不定詞與副詞子句。在例句3中的to不定詞部分解釋為「為了」，跟副詞一樣修飾動詞lives。而例句4中的because之後的句子，可以把它當作是可省略的副詞子句。

5秒 解決修飾語問題的方法

1 確認主詞，動詞修飾語。

2 找看看需要修飾動詞的受詞或補語修飾語。

3 如果主詞、動詞、受詞、補語都在的情況下，尋找當作修飾語來使用的形容詞類或是副詞類。

Quiz ....

Q9 The firm (although / which) will be acquired soon has many merits.

Q10 You will be offered a position (due to / because) you're so qualified.

2 他住在／首爾。

3 他活著／為了成功。

4 他活著／因為她愛他。

攻略法04　主詞位置問題的check point！

1️⃣ 主詞的位置只能填入名詞類。

2️⃣ 句子中沒有主詞的例外情況，用命令句。

3️⃣ 虛主詞it及真主詞的用法。

4️⃣ 主詞與動詞倒裝的情況。

攻略法05　動詞位置問題的check point！

如果是限定動詞的情況，確認填入空格的答案是限定動詞還是非限定動詞。

1️⃣ 數：觀察單、複數，如果主詞是第3人稱單數的話，確認現在式動詞後面有沒有加上-s。

2️⃣ 態：觀察句子是主動或被動，如果有受詞是主動，沒有就是被動。

3️⃣ 時：觀察時制，主要依據提示語及解析來決定。

攻略法06　受詞位置問題的check point！

1️⃣ 受詞只存在於第3、4、5大句型中。

2️⃣ 在受詞的位置只能填名詞類（包含to不定詞、動名詞、名詞子句）。

3️⃣ 受詞也可以填it。

攻略法07　補語位置問題的check point！

1️⃣ 補語只存在於第2、5大句型中。

2️⃣ 補語可以是名詞也可以是形容詞（主要是以形容詞問題出題）。

3️⃣ 可以當作補語的有一般形容詞、介系詞片語（介系詞 + 名詞）、非限定動詞，另外形容詞子句不能當作補語。

攻略法08　修飾語位置問題的check point！

1️⃣ 修飾語不是構成句子的核心要素，是可以省略的。

2️⃣ 當作修飾語使用的4大形容詞類：一般形容詞、介系詞片語（介系詞 + 名詞）、非限定動詞、形容詞子句。

3️⃣ 當作修飾語使用的4大副詞類：一般副詞、介系詞片語（介系詞 + 名詞）、to不定詞、副詞子句。

例子

1 (A) popularity　❶ 把握問題的類型
(B) popularly
(C) popular
(D) popularize　❸ 空格中要填什麼詞類？

Please confirm your reservation well in advance as it was so _____ last year.　❷ 把握提示

1 把握問題的類型
　詞性問題

2 把握提示
　was是第2大句型動詞

3 空格中要填什麼詞類？
　形容詞

---

2 (A) assign
(B) assigns
(C) assignment
(D) assigned

The new recruits had a complicated task _____ by their picky manager.

1 把握問題的類型

2 把握提示

3 空格中要填什麼詞類？

---

3 (A) Raising
(B) Raise
(C) Raises
(D) Raised

_____ my employees' morale is the first priority in this time of difficulty.

1 把握問題的類型

2 把握提示

3 空格中要填什麼詞類？

---

4 (A) to
(B) that
(C) if
(D) which

It is likely _____ this kind of business will make considerable profits in the foreseeable future.

1 把握問題的類型

2 把握提示

3 空格中要填什麼詞類？

---

5 (A) looking
(B) to look
(C) looked
(D) looks

The accounting department decided _____ over the plan as recommended by the CEO.

1 把握問題的類型

2 把握提示

3 空格中要填什麼詞類？

6
(A) to
(B) heavy
(C) while
(D) on

On the other hand, we must abide by the existing rule so that the plan can be _____ schedule.

1 把握問題的類型
2 把握提示
3 空格中要填什麼詞類？

7
(A) make
(B) bring
(C) remain
(D) confirm

Before mailing it in, please _____ sure that you enclose your reference letters with your resume.

1 把握問題的類型
2 把握提示
3 空格中要填什麼詞類？

8
(A) sell
(B) sells
(C) is sold
(D) sold

The grocery store which I often go to _____ a lot of daily necessities and produce.

1 把握問題的類型
2 把握提示
3 空格中要填什麼詞類？

9
(A) totally
(B) total
(C) totals
(D) totalling

The shop will refund the full price if you are not _____ satisfied with their goods.

1 把握問題的類型
2 把握提示
3 空格中要填什麼詞類？

10
(A) donation
(B) donating
(C) donate
(D) donates

Each year, every resident in this area _____ their money to help the poor.

1 把握問題的類型
2 把握提示
3 空格中要填什麼詞類？

101 The staffing committee _____ to recruit more than 100 new employees for an ambitious project this year.

(A) decision

(B) has decided

(C) decided

(D) was decided

高難度

102 The recent survey indicates _____ few companies regard the product quality as the most important thing.

(A) although

(B) that

(C) despite

(D) which

103 This up-to-date smart phone is specially aimed _____ those who trade stocks every day.

(A) at

(B) that

(C) if

(D) therefore

104 You will have to accept my _____ since there is no appropriate alternative.

(A) offering

(B) offered

(C) offer

(D) to offer

105 In addition, the program of those seminars _____ its own merits.

(A) have

(B) having

(C) has

(D) to have

106 Be _____ not to offend your supervisor by taking a day off during the peak season.

(A) care

(B) careful

(C) carefully

(D) careless

107 Accidents can be prevented if you are _____ careful while you are in the factory.

(A) very

(B) particular

(C) enough

(D) too

重要

108 We take great _____ in announcing that we are offering special incentives to all of you.

(A) please

(B) pleasing

(C) pleasurable

(D) pleasure

109 It is essential that we try harder to satisfy customers and keep our company more _____.

(A) competition

(B) compete

(C) competitive

(D) competitively

110 It usually remains _____ to make sure that you read the user's manual carefully.

(A) used

(B) of use

(C) use

(D) useless

111 I am enclosing a catalogue in which you may _____ something that would suit for your purpose.
(A) find
(B) finds
(C) finding
(D) are found

重要
112 You are entitled to health benefits if _____ have lived in this country for more than one year.
(A) you
(B) your
(C) yours
(D) yourself

113 This new device for infants _____ with a manual in three different languages.
(A) coming
(B) comes
(C) come
(D) to come

114 _____ the online shopping mall has only been open for two months, it has already been visited by thousands of people.
(A) When
(B) Although
(C) However
(D) In spite of

115 Information on the new product _____ on the company's website this afternoon.
(A) post
(B) will post
(C) are posting
(D) will be posted

116 We will not be able _____ the deadline unless we hire more employees immediately.
(A) meeting
(B) meet
(C) to meet
(D) to be met

117 When submitting an application form, _____ sure to fill in all the blanks with accuracy.
(A) is
(B) be
(C) have
(D) has

118 Simon has been displaced from that position, so _____ ought to do something to find a new job.
(A) his
(B) he
(C) himself
(D) him

119 Last year, the federal government _____ a large amount of money on the reconstruction project.
(A) spend
(B) spent
(C) spending
(D) was spent

高難度
120 It _____ true that the manager arranged the breakfast meeting in order to keep an eye on her employees.
(A) offered
(B) took
(C) provided
(D) became

▶ 解答在016頁

Dear Mr. White,

I hope you are having a good day. I am writing to draw your attention to the order number ORD 06302012 of twenty-five sets of meeting room chairs and tables. There are some manufacturing flaws in eight of them, _____ obviously fail our defective rate of 3% in
121
accordance with the terms of our contract. Please find in the enclosed files the pictures I _____ before. Since this incident of faulty goods has happened twice _____,
122   123
it may lead to uncertainty on future orders. _____ as well as send us new ones as
124
replacement without any additional charge to us within three working days. If you have any questions or concerns, please feel free to contact me.

Regards,

Mike Edward

121 (A) who
    (B) where
    (C) which
    (D) whose

122 (A) take
    (B) took
    (C) was taking
    (D) am taking

123 (A) in a row
    (B) in a way
    (C) in order
    (D) in a queue

124 (A) I would be grateful if your company must refine your production
    (B) I would be grateful if your company had better refine your production
    (C) I would be grateful if your company could refine your production
    (D) I would be grateful if your company shall refine your production

▶ 解答在016頁

Chapter 03 | 5大句型
利用常用動詞來輕鬆解題

Review Test

在這邊回憶一下前面學到的句子構造。

1 可當主詞的是？ ▶ ....

2 動詞的確認重點是？ ▶ ....

3 受詞的確認重點是？ ▶ ....

4 補語的確認重點是？ ▶ ....

5 必須詞和句型必須詞都有的話？ ▶ ....

Preview

1 5大句型的特徵

為什麼要學5大句型呢？所謂的5大句型，就是將所有句子的類型整理成5大公式。如果熟悉了這些內容，不僅可以提升多益成績，也可以成為writing和speaking能力的基礎。首先，我們來看看下面四點。

❶ 所有句型的主詞和動詞都一樣！

❷ 但是動詞後面都不一樣！

❸ 動詞後面的變化取決於各動詞。

❹ 學習英文的核心就是記住各動詞後面的變化，這就是5大句型的重點。

2 5大句型的解題法

我們要怎麼樣才能了解5大句型呢？

• 第一：在背動詞單字時，不要只背含義，要連動詞後面會出現的詞組一起背誦！

• 第二：動詞不只有一個意思，要將所有的含義背起來，才有機會得高分！

[正確答案] 1. 名詞類 2. 限定動詞和非限定動詞（動狀詞）區分 3. 名詞類 4. 主要為形容詞和名詞，第2、5大句型的確認 5. 放入修飾句子的形容詞類和副詞類

攻略法

09

第1大句型解題法

這是最簡單的句型，在考試中並不常出現，大概2個月才會出現一次，所以最好平常看到就記下。

第1大句型動詞的後面沒有主詞或補語，是單純說明主語的行動或狀態的完全動詞。也就是「主詞＋動詞（S＋V）」，無其他句子元素參雜在內。

第1大句型的型態：主詞＋動詞
　　　　　　　　　S　　V

1. 第1大句型的典型結構為「主詞＋動詞＋（副詞類）」

第1大句型只要有「主詞＋動詞」就是個完整句子，但也有附隨的副詞類（副詞、介系詞片語、to不定詞、副詞子句）跟著出現。這些對句子的結構不會造成任何影響，反而像佐料的角色增添句子許多風味。第1大句型的主要關鍵在區分副詞類。

1　It snowed.
　　只有主詞和動詞的第1大句型！

2　It snowed **yesterday.**
　　完整句中多了副詞yesterday！

3　It snowed **in the northern province.**
　　完整句中多了in以後的介系詞片語！

4　It snowed **when he visited us.**
　　完整句中多了when後的副詞子句！

1　下雪了。

2　下雪了／昨天。

3　下雪了／在北方的省。

4　下雪了／他來拜訪我們的時候。

2. 第1大句型的代表性動詞——去、來、待在

來看看第1大句型的代表性動詞！第1大句型的動詞主要分為「去、來、（待）在」這3大含義的動詞。

去：go（1, 2）, run（1, 3）, fly（1, 3）, rise = increase（1, 3, n）, leave（1, 3, 5, n）, disappear

來：come（1, 2）, decline（1, 3, n）= decrease（1, 3, n）, happen = occur, emerge = appear（1, 2）, drop（1, 3, n）

（待）在：exist, live（1, a）, stand, stay（1, 2, n）, work（1, n）= labor（1, n）= serve（1, 3）

※ 1, 3, 5等代表可能出現的句型

　　n, a 表示除了當動詞，還可以當名詞（n）或形容詞（a）。

第1大句型只要有「主詞＋動詞（S＋V）」就是個完整句子，後面不需要再有其他必要元素。主詞去、來，或是待著，只要有這3大其中一個動作就是個句子了，所以只要記得第1大句型的代表性動詞就是「去、來、（待）在」，作答時，「去、來、（待）在」的動詞後面選副詞類的解答就對了。

5秒 解決第1大句型的方法

1 看到「去、來、（待）在」的動詞？後面選副詞的選項。

2 看到後面有副詞類？選「去、來、（待）在」的動詞。

Quiz

Q1 Sales in this quarter increased (sharply / sharpness).

Q2 The owner of that store appeared (sudden / suddenly) at that time.

▶ 解答在020頁

第2大句型解題法

有時候主詞後面需要描寫主詞狀態的形容詞補語，或是需要補充說明主詞是什麼。此時就需要利用第2大句型的動詞，豐富句子內容。

只用主詞和動詞就可以完成第1大句型，但是第2大句型「是…」、「成為…」就無法單純靠主詞和動詞滿足。為了補充不完整的部分，需要補語來填滿，這就叫作主詞補語（補充主詞的意思）。主詞補語不是形容詞就是名詞，多益題目大多都是考形容詞補語。

第2大句型的型態：主詞 + 動詞 + 補語（形容詞或名詞）
S　　　V　　SC

1. 第2大句型的代表性動詞3類型——be, become, remain

雖然不少動詞被分類在第2大句型，但在多益題目中，最具代表性的3個動詞如下。

1　She **is gorgeous**.
　　She **is a minister**.
　　後面以補語型態出現了形容詞或名詞！

2　She **became tired**.
　　She **became the president**.
　　意思有一點不同，但當成be動詞使用。

3　She **remains silent**.
　　She **remains my advisor**.
　　remain後面出現名詞似乎有點奇怪，但這是正確的句子。

這3大動詞常出現在多益考試裡，**因此動詞後面有出現形容詞，動詞的答案請選be, become, remain**。如果主詞補語的位置要填入形容詞或名詞其中一個，與主詞為同格關係的話就選擇名詞。目前多益試題的答案大部分都是形容詞。

1 她很有魅力。
　她是位主管。

2 她愈來愈疲倦。
　她當了社長。

3 她沉默著。
　她當我的顧問。

2. 其他第2大句型的重要動詞

除此以外，第2大句型常用的重要動詞整理如下。

(1) be動詞類

be [remain, stay] + 形容詞或名詞（呈現某種狀態、是⋯）

His father **remained silent**.

他爸爸保持安靜。

(2) 第1和第2大句型皆使用be動詞。

become [go, come, get] + 形容詞或名詞（呈現某種狀態、是⋯）

The company **went bankrupt**.
Our dream will **come true**.

那公司倒閉了。
我們的夢想將會實現。

(3) 慣用類

seem [appear]（to be）形容詞或名詞（看起來呈現某種狀態、看起來是⋯）
prove [turn out]（to be）形容詞或名詞（證實為⋯）
remain to be seen （待瞧瞧）

She **seems (to be) hopeless**.

她看起來很絕望。

(4) 感官動詞類

look [smell, taste, sound] + 形容詞或名詞
（看起來、聞起來、嚐起來、聽起來）

They **looked** busy.

他們看起來很忙碌。

5秒 解決第2大句型的方法

1 看到第2大句型的動詞時 → 填入形容詞或名詞。
2 與主詞同格關係時 → 填入名詞補語。
3 如果是修飾主詞時 → 填入形容詞補語。
4 看到形容詞時 → 填入第2大句型動詞。

Quiz ⋯⋯⋯⋯⋯⋯⋯⋯⋯⋯⋯⋯⋯⋯⋯⋯⋯⋯⋯⋯⋯⋯⋯⋯⋯⋯⋯⋯⋯⋯⋯⋯⋯⋯

Q3 The new marketing strategy will be (of importance / importance) to us.

Q4 The mayor seems to be (hope / hopeless) about the upcoming reelection.

《講師的補充說明》
可以當補語的形容詞

形容詞類有四種，其中「形容詞、介系詞片語、動狀詞」可當補語。形容詞子句無法當補語。

▶ 解答在020頁

攻略法

11

第3大句型解題法

第3大句型是英文中最常見的句型。因為「主詞 + 動詞 + 受詞」型態的句子是最常被使用的句子架構，當然也就會常常出現在多益題目中。

第3大句型需要注意：受詞前若有介系詞，有些介系詞類型是不可以使用的。

第3大句型的型態：主詞 + 動詞 + 受詞
S　　　 V　　　 O

1. 第3大句型的型態1

是「主詞 + 動詞 + 受詞（名詞）」的句型，受詞前面沒有介系詞。

1 We will **discuss the topic.**

　discuss後似乎要有介系詞about，但其實不是！

2 I **decided to go** with you.

　to go是動詞decide的受詞。

3 I **know that you will succeed.**

　看起來似乎有點長，that以後是動詞know的受詞。

> 1 我們會討論／那個主題。
>
> 2 我決定了／和你一起去。
>
> 3 我知道／你一定會成功。

2. 第3大句型的型態2

「主詞 + 動詞 + 介系詞 + 受詞（名詞類）」的句型，受詞前面有介系詞。

1 They **waited for me.**

　wait for是一個字組，me就是受詞

2 They **dealt with the problem.**

　deal with (= handle) 是一個字組，the problem就是受詞。

> 1 他們等待／我。
>
> 2 他們處理了／那個問題。

多益考試常出現的動詞大多屬於第3大句型，所以不需要另外背誦。將詞組「動詞 + 介系詞」同慣用語般，一起記住。第3大句型受詞的前面大部分都不會有介系詞，但是「動詞 + 介系詞」的慣用型態一定要有介系詞，這一點一定要記住。

以下第3大句型的必背慣用詞組整理如下：

• engage in 受詞	埋首於…
• enroll in 受詞	註冊於…
• participate in 受詞	參加…
(= take part in 受詞)	
• result in 受詞	導致…結果
• result from 受詞	起因於…；產生
• succeed in 受詞／-ing	成功於…；做…而成功
• succeed to 受詞	繼承…
• abstain from 受詞／-ing	抑制…
(= refrain from 受詞／-ing)	
• account for 受詞	說明…；佔…
• ask for 受詞	要求…
• wait for 受詞	等待…
(= await)	
• agree [consent] in / to + 受詞	同意…
• agree to 原形動詞／agree with 受詞／	同意…
agree that S + V	
• object to 受詞／-ing	反對…；反對（做）…
(= oppose 受詞)	
• be opposed to 受詞／-ing	反對…；反對做…
• react to 受詞	對…做出反應
• refer to 受詞	參考…
• reply to 受詞	對…作回答
• respond to 受詞	對…作回應
• subscribe to 受詞	訂閱…
• comply with 受詞	遵守…
(= conform / abide by 受詞)	
• cope with 受詞	對付…；克服…
(= overcome 受詞)	
• deal with 受詞	處理…；應付…
(= handle / manage 受詞)	
• interfere with 受詞	妨害（干涉）…

《講師的補充說明》

動詞後面不可有介系詞，但名詞後面一定要有介系詞的狀況！

介系詞 to：access (to), damage (to), visit (to), answer (to)

介系詞 about：question (about), discussion about, disclosure about（不過discuss和disclose是動詞，不用介系詞）

其他：regret (for), influence (on), interview (with)

- count / depend / rely / rest on [upon]　　依靠著…；依賴在…
  (= be dependent [contingent] on [upon] 受詞)
- look at 受詞　　　　　　　　　盯著…看
- look for 受詞　　　　　　　　　找…
- look over 受詞　　　　　　　　檢查…
- look into 受詞　　　　　　　　調查…
- look after 受詞　　　　　　　　照顧…
- go through 受詞　　　　　　　　經歷…
- get through 受詞　　　　　　　辦完…
- come by 受詞　　　　　　　　　短暫經過…
  (= drop / stop by 受詞)

5秒 解決第3大句型的方法

1 大部分的動詞都是第3大句型！介系詞後面請選名詞類的受詞。

2 看到名詞的話，它的前面請選第3大句型的動詞。

3 看到第3大句型中的慣用詞，把它當作一組單字。

Quiz

Q5 You should (comply / obey) the rules set by us.

Q6 We didn't expect any severe damage (to / ×) our existing facilities.

第4大句型解題法

第4大句型需要有兩個受詞，也就是「S + V + IO（間接受詞）+ DO（直接受詞）」。第3大句型的受詞後面不能出現名詞，如果出現名詞的話，必須要有介系詞。但要注意的是，第4大句型不需要有介系詞即可接名詞。

第4大句型中，間接受詞在前、直接受詞在後，一般在「給、對⋯」的間接受詞位置上放人，「把⋯」的直接受詞位置上放入事物。

> 第4大句型的兩種型態：1. 主詞 + 動詞 + IO + DO
>
> 　　　　　　　　　　2. 主詞 + 動詞 + DO（介系詞 + IO）

上面是第4大句型的基本組合，其三大特徵整理如下。

1. 第4大句型有兩個受詞

和只能有一個受詞的第3大句型不同，第4大句型有IO（間接受詞）和DO（直接受詞）兩個受詞。一般不會連續出現兩個名詞，但要特別記得第4大句型會出現兩次名詞。

I gave **her a ring**. → 第4大句型
= I gave **a ring (to her)**. → 第3大句型
her是IO，a ring是DO。「給⋯」是IO，「將⋯」是DO。

我給了／她／戒指。
我將／戒指／給她。

2. IO是名詞與代名詞，DO僅可以是名詞、代名詞或名詞子句。

這時IO，也就是間接受詞的位置，是放入名詞和代名詞；DO，也就是直接受詞的位置，是放入名詞、代名詞或是名詞子句。所以其他名詞類的動名詞，或是to不定詞的句型就不能看作是第4大句型。

1 We offer **customers good services**.

第一個名詞customers是IO，第二個名詞good services是DO！

1 我們提供／給客戶／優良的服務。

2 We sent **him what we had**.

代名詞him是IO，what名詞子句是DO！

2 我們寄／給他／我們所擁有的東西。

3. 第4大句型可轉換成第3大句型

第4大句型的「IO + DO」順序也可以寫成「DO + 介系詞IO」。這時「DO + 介系詞IO」成為介系詞片語，變成不是必要句而是修飾句的第3大句型。由上可知，第4大句型也可轉換成第3大句型。

1 We offer **good services** (to customers).

　　　將to customers的to拿掉，再和前面的good services位置對調就是第4大句型！

2 We sent **what we had** (to him).

　　　將to him的to拿掉，再和前面的名詞子句what we had位置對調就是第4大句型！

重要的第4大句型動詞如下所示，用篇小短文幫大家記憶。

> give, offer, send, bring, fax, show, grant, award, cost, lend, tell
>
> 「如果告知（tell）要用傳真（fax）寄送（send）或是直接帶來（bring），和是否會提供（offer）獎項（award）的話，就允許（grant）以低廉的費用（cost）出借（lend）場地給（give）你們舉辦表演（show）。」

整理一下，可以知道在第4大句型句子與第3大句型句子不同，第4大句型的兩個受詞可以不加上介系詞使用，順序為（IO + DO）。

怪物講師的祕訣

assure		of / about 事物（關於…，第3大句型）
notify	人當受詞（給…）	
inform		that 主詞 + 動詞（第4大句型）
convince		of / about （關於…，第3大句型）
advise	人當受詞（給…）	that 主詞 + 動詞（第4大句型）
remind		to 原形動詞（使…能夠，第5大句型）

取上述六個單字的字首稱ANICAR，這些動詞的特色就是受詞僅能是人。如果受詞不是人的話，就必須變成被動式，這時候主詞就必須是人。ANI是第3、4大句型，CAR是第3、4、5大句型。

例 He informed me of the result.（他通知／我／結果。）

例 I advised him that he (should) be quiet.（我勸告／他／安靜一點。）

Quiz

Q7 ACE (provides / offers) you a rare chance this week only.

Q8 The manager (informed / was informed) that he would be promoted soon.

---

1 我們提供／優質的服務／給客戶。

2 我們寄了／我們所擁有的東西／給他。

《講師的補充說明》

為什麼第4大句型要變成第3大句型？我們一起來看看I gave some money.這個第3大句型。

因為很好奇到底給了誰，而有了I gave some money to the man.的表現。（這時一定要有介系詞，因為前面已經是完整的第3大句型，所以加入介系詞to使the man成為修飾語。）不過「把…給…」的句型很常見，也可以寫成I gave the man some money.這已經是一種固定句型。

動詞buy、make的介系詞用for，ask是用of，其餘的第4大句型大部分使用to。

▶ 解答在020頁

第5大句型解題法

第5大句型和只有一個受詞的第3大句型不同的是，句中的受詞後面會緊接著受詞補語。一般句型表現為「S + V + O + OC」，與第3大句型最大的差異就是後面的受詞補語（OC）。

上面提到由「主詞 + 動詞 + 受詞 + 受詞補語」（S + V + O + OC）所組成的句子稱作第5大句型。此種句型的受詞是名詞類，受詞補語就是形容詞或是形容詞類。

第5大句型的型態：主詞 + 動詞 + 受詞 + 受詞補語
S　　V　　O　　OC

1. 受詞補語是形容詞時修飾受詞，是名詞時與受詞同等

第5大句型的型態一直到受詞為止都與第3大句型相同，不同的是受詞後面會出現受詞補語。受詞補語的位置應該放入形容詞，或是與受詞同格關係的名詞。

1　We kept **our room clean.**

　　clean是修飾our room的形容詞補語

2　I made **her a doctor.**

　　a doctor是與受詞her同格關係的名詞補語（her = a doctor）

> 1 我們維持／我們房間／乾淨的狀態。
>
> 2 我讓／她／成為醫生。

2. 第5大句型動詞和受詞補語同時熟悉

平時就要將第5大句型的動詞和受詞一起記憶，例如：在記動詞allow時，最好可以「allow + 受詞 + to不定詞」整組一起背誦，這樣在考場時就可以不加思索馬上應用。

1　I made **the box.**

　　只有一個受詞的第3大句型

　　I made **the box strong.**

　　平時就要「make + 受詞 + 形容詞」一起記。

> 1 我做了／箱子。
> 我讓／箱子／變堅固。

2 We convinced him.

只有一個受詞的第3大句型

We convinced him to accept the proposal.

平時就要「convince + 受詞 + to不定詞」一起記。

2 我們說服了／他。
我們說服他／接受那個提案。

3. 第5大句型中只有受詞補語的話，是被動型句型

如果第5大句型動詞出現，在後面只有當做受詞補語使用的形容詞，就是受詞跑到主詞的位置去，因此答案就是被動式。

The box was made strong.

只剩下當做受詞補語的形容詞strong，受詞the box跑到句子的前面！

這個箱子被造得／堅固。

4. 其他第5大句型代表性的動詞

除上述的動詞以外，其他屬於第5大句型的動詞如下。與其他5大句型的動詞用法相同，動詞後面為「受詞 + 受詞補語」。請好好記住與各個動詞搭配的受詞補語。

1 make [keep, find] + 受詞 + 形容詞／-ing／p.p.
2 「使、要求、允許」+ 受詞 + to不定詞
　　使：force（強迫）= compel, persuade（說服…）
　　要求：ask（要求）、encourage（激勵使…）
　　　　　require（需求）、expect（期望；第3、5大句型）
　　　　　would like（期望；第3、5大句型）
　　允許：allow（允許）= permit, enable（使…可能）
3 使役動詞（let, make, have）+ 受詞 + 原形動詞／p.p.
4 call [elect, appoint, consider] + 受詞 + 名詞

綜合以上的總整理可得知，第5大句型的核心就是受詞補語！受詞補語常搭配的第5大句型的動詞，請一定要分門別類記住。

《講師的補充說明》

還記得ANICAR嗎？其中適合CAR的動詞也有第5大句型的用法。一起看下面的例句。

例 She advised me to take a day off. （她建議／我／放一天的假。）

例 We remind our customers to keep their receipts. （我們／提醒／我們的客戶／保留收據。）

5秒 解決第5大句型的方法

1 看到第5大句型的動詞時，請先確定受詞和受詞補語！特別是受詞補語！
2 依據適合各個受詞補語的5大句型的動詞作為解答！

Quiz ....

Q9 By doing his best, he made her (happy / happily).
Q10 They encouraged us (to be / being) competitive.

▶ 解答在020頁

攻略法 09-13	5大句型的學習法整理

1. 各大句型都存在著「主詞＋動詞」。

2. 句子的重點在於後面的變化，這都決定於動詞。

3. 不要只記動詞的意思，連動詞後面的變化也一起記憶。

4. 解多益題目時，先看動詞後再決定後面的解答，或先看後面的變化再決定動詞的答案。

5. 不是只有動詞後面的句型變化跟著動詞改變，像動狀詞（to不定詞）或-ing（動名詞）也都適用。

6. 這些所有的訣竅也都適用在writing和speaking上。

攻略法 09-13	5大句型各種型態的重點

1. 第1大句型：主詞＋「去、來、（待）在」＋（副詞類）

2. 第2大句型：主詞＋be [be, become, remain] ＋主詞補語（形容詞／名詞）

3. 第3大句型：主詞＋大部分的動詞＋受詞（名詞類）

　　　　　　　主詞＋動詞＋介系詞／副詞組成的慣用詞組＋受詞

4. 第4大句型：主詞＋give [offer, send, bring] ＋間接受詞＋直接受詞

　　＊ANICAR一定要熟記！

5. 第5大句型：主詞＋make [keep, find] ＋受詞（名詞類）＋受詞補語（形容詞／-ing／p.p.）

　　　　　　　主詞＋「使、要求、允許」＋受詞（名詞類）＋受詞補語（to不定詞）

　　　　　　　主詞＋使役動詞＋受詞＋受詞補語（原形動詞／p.p.）

　　　　　　　主詞＋help＋（受詞）＋（to）原形動詞

　　　　　　　主詞＋call [elect, appoint, consider] ＋受詞＋受詞補語（名詞）

例子
1　(A) said
　　(B) announced
　　(C) informed
　　(D) briefed

① 把握問題的類型

③ 空格中要填什麼詞類？

The director in accounting _____ us of the budget for the next quarter.

② 把握提示

1 把握問題的類型
文法題
2 把握提示
選項要填入動詞
3 空格中要填什麼詞類？
動詞

2　(A) effective
　　(B) effect
　　(C) effectively
　　(D) effects

The machine installed last week was more _____ than I anticipated.

1 把握問題的類型

2 把握提示

3 空格中要填什麼詞類？

3　(A) object
　　(B) accept
　　(C) oppose
　　(D) comply

At first, we planned to _____ to his proposal because of the lack of creativity.

1 把握問題的類型

2 把握提示

3 空格中要填什麼詞類？

4　(A) runs
　　(B) ran
　　(C) running
　　(D) to run

We are trying to keep the assembly line _____ while the inspection is being done.

1 把握問題的類型

2 把握提示

3 空格中要填什麼詞類？

5　(A) tell
　　(B) talk
　　(C) convince
　　(D) mention

Ms. Janice was waiting in line to _____ to the service representative about the problems.

1 把握問題的類型

2 把握提示

3 空格中要填什麼詞類？

6 (A) satisfy
(B) provide
(C) force
(D) send

Mr. Carl will _____ the purchasing department an estimate to negotiate the contract.

7 (A) cooperation
(B) cooperatively
(C) cooperative
(D) cooperate

All workers under my supervision need to work _____ to prevent accidents.

8 (A) hope
(B) hoping
(C) hopeful
(D) hopeless

When she was promoted, she seemed to be _____ due to poor maintenance by her staff.

9 (A) to take
(B) taking
(C) took
(D) taken

The CEO allowed the director _____ a day off as her son was so sick at that time.

10 (A) allow
(B) force
(C) consider
(D) let

I won't _____ you do whatever you want, so listen carefully to my advice.

▶ 解答在020頁

重要

101 The supervisor does not like to allow her assistant _____ even at a lunch time.

(A) to rest
(B) resting
(C) rest
(D) rests

102 I would like to have my proposal _____ by you if you are not too busy right now.

(A) edit
(B) edited
(C) to edit
(D) editing

103 We are pleased to _____ you that you need to attend the final interview on Friday.

(A) express
(B) mention
(C) announce
(D) inform

104 We are trying to convince our customers _____ we only offer the best products.

(A) because
(B) that
(C) of
(D) therefore

高難度

105 It is the manager's responsibility to _____ his staff to be competitive all the time.

(A) bring
(B) assure
(C) persuade
(D) suggest

106 Helping others _____ healthy, the instructor is an outgoing person with a lot of energy.

(A) become
(B) became
(C) becoming
(D) becomes

107 In spite of the harsh weather conditions, they might be able to _____ the meeting place on time.

(A) reach
(B) appear
(C) arrive
(D) come

108 Considering the current situation, _____ is another alternative to this terrible plan.

(A) she
(B) it
(C) I
(D) there

109 The new strategy _____ entirely thanks to his motivating the staffs in marketing.

(A) emerged
(B) informed
(C) required
(D) proved

110 After filling out the survey form, please _____ the secretary the form as soon as possible.

(A) deliver
(B) bring
(C) submit
(D) provide

收集了多益考試中常出的題目。請當作正式的考試，確認時間並解題。

111 If you have difficulty in installing the new software, please _____ to the operational manual.

(A) read
(B) refer
(C) look
(D) decide

112 The department manager will notify his members _____ their assignments through e-mail.

(A) that
(B) to
(C) of
(D) by

113 The unexpected sales volume decrease will _____ our company from opening new branches in China.

(A) conserve
(B) deal
(C) prevent
(D) expedite

114 An increase in costs _____ made the board of directors lay off 20% of local employees in Brazil.

(A) is
(B) are
(C) has
(D) have

115 We would like to _____ you that all questions will be answered by Customer Support Center starting next week.

(A) say
(B) respond
(C) remind
(D) endure

高難度
116 Regarding the delivery, the shipping company must _____ our customers of the arrival date and time.

(A) notify
(B) explain
(C) announce
(D) suggest

重要
117 Although the company _____ the division, most of the employees seemed not to be nervous about their job security.

(A) was restructuring
(B) was restructured
(C) restructuring
(D) to restructure

118 While they were in the middle of a heated discussion, he suddenly jumped into it and tried to _____ company executives to improve working conditions.

(A) recommend
(B) persuade
(C) award
(D) assure

119 Our long-term export plans should have helped us _____ the recent problems with the EU market.

(A) overcame
(B) overcomes
(C) overcoming
(D) overcome

120 They could _____ the place after two hours of wandering about in the streets, because they were not told the name of the hotel.

(A) arrive
(B) reach
(C) get
(D) come

▶ 解答在022頁

It seems inevitable that dwellers of cities to fall victim to dire stress on account of their preoccupation with _____ their career or their households. _____ can be deduced
121   122
to be a productive way to eliminate this massive pressure. During their stay in an exotic environment, they may _____ distracted from their tiring daily patterns. Indirectly, they
                                123
will sense that their accumulated stress is gradually melting away. Furthermore, people get to broaden their horizon by learning about different foreign cultures or experiencing different cuisines. It has been _____ that people who travel periodically are able to
                                124
cope with the various challenges in their career or personal life with relative ease.

121 (A) not only
    (B) neither
    (C) either
    (D) nor yet

122 (A) Thus, taking an escape periodically
    (B) Thus, taking an escape infrequently
    (C) Thus, taking an escape once in a blue
        moon
    (D) Thus, taking an escape once in a
        century

123 (A) is
    (B) being
    (C) have
    (D) be

124 (A) document
    (B) documented
    (C) documentation
    (D) documentary

▶ 解答在022頁

Part 02

60%句型一致就能解題！

單、複數的一致
只要了解就很簡單的問題！

Review Test

只要了解英文的5大句型，任何英文句子都可以輕鬆理解。我們來複習一下在第3章學過的內容。

1 第1大句型的代表性動詞是？ ▶ ....

2 第2大句型的代表性動詞是？ ▶ ....

3 第3大句型的代表性動詞是？ ▶ ....

4 第4大句型的代表性動詞是？ ▶ ....

5 第5大句型的代表性動詞是？ ▶ ....

Preview

單、複數的一致

I work (O) - I works (X)	You work (O) - You works (X)
He works (O) - He work (X)	They work (O) - They works (X)
She worked (O) - She workeds (X)	She will work (O) - She will works (X)

❶ 所謂的單、複數的一致就是主詞和動詞間的單、複數要一致。

❷ 所謂單數的動詞就是原形動詞後接-s、-es。

❸ 使用單數動詞的3大狀況

—— 主詞是第3人稱。第1、2人稱單數的動詞不可加-s、-es。

—— 主詞是單數名詞。如果是複數名詞的動詞後面不可加-s、-es。

—— 動詞必須為現在式。過去式或未來式不可加-s、-es。

＊即使非現在式，能分辨單、複數的be動詞只有was和were。

❹ 主詞和動詞的單、複數一致以外，有部分形容詞可決定名詞的單、複數，請一定要記住。

|正確答案| 1. 來、去、（待）在+（副詞類）2. be, become, remain +（形容詞／名詞）3. 大部分的動詞 4. give [offer, send, bring] + 間接受詞 + 直接受詞 5. make, keep, find + 受詞（名詞類）+ 受詞補語（形容詞、-ing、p.p.）

只要了解主詞、動詞的關係，就能解決單、複數

了解單數和複數的一致很簡單，但也是容易錯的地方。請專注在主詞和動詞，把單數和單數、複數和複數送作堆就行了。

主詞的單、複數決定於動詞，動詞的單、複數決定於主詞。但如果主詞和動詞間有各種修飾句和連接語的話，就很難掌握主詞和動詞之間的關係了。在這邊再次提醒各位，句子裡只有一個限定動詞。只要確實分辨主詞和限定動詞，就能毫無困難地解開單、複數的問題。

搭配主詞和動詞的方式！
單複數的搭配規則是主詞決定於動詞，動詞決定於主詞。

1 **The employees** in the plant **work** hard.

employees是複數，因此接原形動詞即可。

2 **The man** who will apply **has** enough qualifications.

主詞man是單數。

3 **The manager read** the memo just **a few minutes ago**.

為什麼是用過去式的read呢？重點就是a few minutes ago為過去副詞。

1 工廠員工們／認真工作。

2 那男生／將要申請／擁有充分的資格條件。

3 那位經理閱讀了／紙條／就在幾分鐘前。

5秒 解決單複數一致問題的方法

1 如果主詞是空格時，答案請選名詞類。這時候選項中常會出現單數名詞和複數名詞混淆視聽。選答時不要猶豫，也不用了解題目涵意，把握時間看動詞找出與其單、複數一致的答案。

2 動詞是空格時，如果是限定動詞，請依照數 → 態 → 時的規則解題（請參閱Chapter 02）。探討單、複數，只要與主詞搭配就可以輕鬆解題。

Quiz

Q1 The (supervisors / supervision) in the West Plant are due to arrive soon.

Q2 The letter confirming your presence (has / have) not arrived yet.

▶ 解答在026頁

拿掉修飾語就能解題

主詞和動詞之間如果有修飾語的話，不要多想，馬上移除，如此，才能一眼看到主詞和動詞。在多益考試裡，修飾語只是絆腳石而已。

修飾語大致分成形容詞類和副詞類。形容詞類有形容詞、介系詞片語、非限定動詞（動狀詞）和形容詞子句；副詞類有副詞、介系詞片語、to不定詞和副詞子句，這些都是在看題目時可以拿掉的修飾語。一起來練習拿掉修飾語的要領吧！

拿掉修飾語吧！

1 **The number** of our new members **is** greater than expected.

拿掉介系詞片語of our new members以後，主詞the number是單數。

2 **The document** showing new trends **has** been distributed.

拿掉非限定動詞（動狀詞）showing new trends以後，主詞the document是單數。

3 **Students** in my class who didn't register yet **are** to receive my mail.

介系詞片語in my class和形容詞子句who... yet是修飾語。

1 數量／我們新進員工的／比…更多／預想的。

2 那份資料／顯示新趨勢／被分發。

3 學生們／我課堂上尚未註冊的／將會收到我的信。

5秒 解決一致性問題的方法

1 主動詞的一致性是，主詞決定於動詞；動詞決定於主詞。

2 看題目時請當作沒有修飾語。

3 請確認主詞和動詞之間的形容詞、介系詞片語、非限定動詞（動狀詞）、形容詞子句、副詞和副詞子句。

Quiz

Q3 Anyone ready to apply for this position (have / has) to call me first.

Q4 One of the rivals who are competitive (work / works) harder than us.

▶ 解答在026頁

攻略法

16

拿掉形容詞子句（＝關係子句）

形容詞子句都長到很難掌握句子的起始處，要清楚區分，才能順利解題和了解題意。這多少會有點困難，但如果仔細學習的話，看句子的眼力也能跟著一起提升。

1. 形容詞子句（＝關係子句）完整的情況

形容詞子句就是關係詞所引導的子句。首先，我們來看看下面的例句，仔細閱讀說明和解法。

1 **The client who visits us every day needs to know this change**.
   先行名詞 關係詞 動詞1 受詞 副詞   動詞2   受詞
   （主詞）

> 1 那位顧客／每天訪問我們的／需要／了解這個變化。

關係代名詞who後面的動詞visits是單數型態吧？這是要符合先行名詞client，動詞2 needs是與主詞client搭配，所以client是先行名詞，也是主詞。上述兩者都是單數型，但是下面的例子要注意。

2 **One** of our employees **who were absent was** James.
   主詞   先行名詞   關係詞主格 動詞1 補語1 動詞2 補語2

> 2 一位／我們的職員之中／缺席的是詹姆士。

本句型的主詞是單數型的One，所以使用的動詞2也是用單數型的was。可是你有看到關係詞主格who後面卻有were吧？和主詞One不合吧？這個動詞是要配合非主詞的先行名詞，而先行名詞employees是複數，所以動詞也要搭配複數的were。如下整理後也是一樣。

先行名詞（主詞）＋（關係詞主格 ＋ 動詞1 ＋ 受詞／補語）＋ 動詞2 ＋ 受詞／補語

5秒 解決形容詞子句的方法1

1️⃣ 先行名詞後若有出現who / which / that（關係代名詞主格），請用括號畫出來。

2️⃣ 從過了第一個動詞後，截到第二個動詞前。

3️⃣ 此時動詞2是非限定動詞（動狀詞），須判別出動、態、時，根據上面提到的單、複數的要領區分出形容詞子句後拿除，使主詞和動詞一致。

4️⃣ 動詞1也是非限定動詞（動狀詞），須判別出動、態、時，與名詞搭配單、複數即可。

2. 形容詞子句（＝關係子句）不完整的情況

也就是句中使用的關係詞受格。首先我們來看下面舉的例子，先了解基本結構後再看解題法。

1 **The book (which) they borrow is** so popular.
　先行名詞(S)　關係詞受格　主詞　動詞1　動詞2　副詞補語　形容詞

1 那本書／他們借的／非常熱門。

此例句中的關係代名詞受格which扮演著及物動詞borrow的受詞角色，也可以省略。乍看之下句子好像沒有受詞，但實際上which在擔任受詞角色，所以使用主動型的動詞borrow。當然，這時候的borrow的單、複數是配合前面的主詞they。此句子的動詞2是is，搭配前面單數主詞book。

2 **The applicants (whom) she waits for have** not arrived yet.
　先行名詞（S）　關係詞受格 主詞 動詞1 介系詞　動詞2　副詞

2 申請者們／她等待的／沒到達／尚未。

這個例句中的wait for是「主動詞＋介系詞」扮演著第3大句型的慣用詞組的角色。因此waits for的受詞是whom，wait的單、複數需配合she，動詞2 have當然就是搭配最前面的主詞——複數名詞applicants。

先行名詞（主詞）＋（關係詞受格）＋ 主詞 ＋ 及物動詞1 ＋ 動詞2 ＋ 受詞／補語
（或是不及物動詞＋介系詞）

5秒 解決形容詞子句的方法2

1 名詞後面出現whom / which / that（關係詞受格）用括號標示出來。

2 動詞1後到動詞2之前截掉。

3 這時動詞2是動狀詞，要區分出數、態、時的形式，尤其是要分辨單複數時，依據上面的要領拿掉形容詞子句，使主詞和動詞一致即可。

4 動詞1也是動狀詞，要區分出數、態、時的形式，這時單複數是要與它前面的主詞做搭配，非先行名詞。

5 關係詞受格與關係詞主格不一樣的是可以省略。也就是說名詞後面只出現「S＋V」，也要知道是省略關係詞受格。

Quiz ··

Q5 The restaurant which (is / are) popular (has / have) a lot of customers.

Q6 The shoes our company (sell / sells) (is / are) so sturdy.

▶ 解答在026頁

攻略法

17

關係連接詞和單、複數

這邊所學的連接詞是對等連接詞和關係連接詞。對等連接詞就是大家所熟悉的and、but、or。若對等連接詞前面有接both、not、either，就叫做關係連接詞。

1. 對等連接詞和關係連接詞

首先各位要知道，在A和B間有and、but、or這類的連接詞，就叫做對等連接詞。對等連接詞在Chapter 04裡會學到，但首先要注意的是A和B的型態必須要一致。也就是說，A如果是名詞，B也必須是名詞；B是形容詞的話，A也必須是形容詞。

對等連接詞and、but、or前面，如果有both、not、either等連接詞的話，使兩個以上分開的單字有關係，就叫關係連接詞。這類的關係連接詞是慣用語法，最好可以背下來。像是看到both的話就要想到and；看到either就要馬上想到or。

以下是常見的關係連接詞。

---

both **A** and **B**：A和B全都

between A and B：A和B之間

not A but **B**：不是A，而是B

not only (= just) A but (also) **B**：不僅A，B也是

= **B** as well as A

either A or **B**：不是A就是B

neither A nor **B**：兩者都不是

好了！那麼句中如果有關係連接詞的話，單、複數的問題會變成怎麼樣呢？

2. 用解釋法來做單、複數搭配

解釋出句子的意思，大部分都可以知道哪一邊比較重要，在重要的那一邊做單複數搭配就行了。就像上面用粗體字整理出的代表性的關係連接詞，標示出的部份做單、複數搭配就可以了。也就是說A和B兩者都

很重要，所以一定要搭配複數動詞，其餘的看B搭配單、複數就行了。
（between A and B是介系詞片語，不是搭配單、複數的對象。）

1 **Both** he **and** she **are** my friends.
　　he和she兩者都很重要，所以搭配複數動詞！

2 She **as well as** you **knows** it.
　　B as well as A中，B比A重要！

特別要注意的是第2個例句，很多人會把you錯當主詞，不小心會把動詞寫成know。這類的句型要直接翻譯出來，才能知道哪一部分較重要，解決搭配單、複數問題的最好方式就是翻譯法。

3. 用近者一致法搭配單、複數

有加入連接詞or的關係連接詞，像either A or B、neither A nor B這類的相關連接詞，即使是翻譯出來也很難分辨哪一方較重要。這時就取離動詞較近的B來搭配單、複數，這種方式叫做「近者一致法」。

1 **Either** you **or** he **has** to go there.
　　動詞has與較近的主詞he做搭配！

2 **Neither** you **nor** I **was** aware of the fact.
　　動詞was與較近的主詞I做搭配！

5秒 解決連接詞的單、複數問題的方法

1 both A and B是配複數。

2 not A but B、not only (= just) A but (also) B、B as well as A，用翻譯法是要與B做搭配。

3 either A or B、neither A nor B用近者一致法，是與B做搭配。

Quiz

Q7 Neither she nor I (has / have) any idea about the project.

Q8 The president as well as you (was / were) quite impressed about the result.

1 他和她都／是我的朋友。

2 不只是你，她也／知道那件事。

1 不是你的話，就是他／要去那裡。

2 不論是你或是我／都不知道那個事實。

▶ 解答在026頁

攻略法

18 其他重要的單、複數一致

到目前為止，我們學到了主詞和動詞間的單、複數一致，現在我們來看形容詞和名詞的單、複數一致性。

1. 決定單、複數的形容詞

有部分的形容詞會影響它後面接的名詞的單、複數型。接下來的說明中，出現的形容詞會讓你一看到就會恍然大悟「啊！原來這就是單、複數的問題啊！」

1 **Every applicant has** to turn in their resume.

every後絕對是出現單數名詞，這是單數！

2 Our manager was asked to finish an evaluation for **each employee**.

each後絕對是出現單數名詞，這是單數！

3 Only **a few chairs were** available because of the ceremony.

a few後絕對是出現複數名詞，這是複數！

4 **A variety of events are** scheduled at the Hankook Theater.

a variety of後絕對是出現複數名詞，這是複數！

> **1** 每一位申請者／必須要提出／個人的履歷。
>
> **2** 我們經理／被要求／要完成／評估／每個員工。
>
> **3** 只有少數的椅子／可以使用／因為那個典禮的關係。
>
> **4** 多種活動／已經預訂／在韓泰劇場。

對單、複數一致有影響的形容詞

1 a / an, one, another, every / each, this / that, either / neither
  + 單數名詞 + 單數動詞

  • a little / little, much + 不可數名詞 + 單數動詞

  • the, 所有格 + ⎡ 單數名詞 + 單數動詞
                    ⎣ 複數名詞 + 複數動詞

2 two / three / four..., a few / few, many, both, several, these / those,
  various / a variety of + 複數名詞 + 複數動詞

3 other / all / most / lots of
  = a lot of = plenty of + 複數名詞 + 複數動詞

Q9 (All / Every) assembler in this factory should wear protective helmets all the time.

Q10 Other (information / informations) will be necessary to activate the procedure.

▶ 解答在026頁

2. 易混淆的單、複數

做題目時常會遇到已經用刪去法一一刪掉不要的答案，但就是會有兩個讓人猶豫不決的情況。接下來要介紹的，就是在題目中讓人在最後感到混亂的代表性範例。趁這機會好好把它記下來。

1 **A number of** students **were** at the job fair.
a number of是「很多的」的意思，這是複數！

2 **The number of** students who participated in the exhibition **was** more than expected.
the number of是「⋯的數量」的意思，這是單數！

a number of是「很多的」的意思，當作修飾語使用，後面要接複數名詞，複數名詞為主詞，所以使用複數動詞就是理所當然！和a number of長的很像的the number of是「⋯的數字」的意思，後面雖然是接複數名詞，但是主詞是the number of，屬於單數名詞，因此動詞也必須使用單數動詞。

3 **One of the keys** to the lockers **was** missing.
one是主詞，後面的修飾語不論是什麼動詞都是單數！

one of the有「⋯中的其中之一」的意思，所以後面會出現複數名詞，但是如果沒有of the只有one的情況下，後面要接「單數名詞 + 單數動詞」。有沒有of the會影響到後方接的名詞單複數，但只要記著有接of the，就跟著接複數名詞、單數動詞；如果要拿掉of the，就接單數名詞、單數動詞。each、either、neither也是一樣的情況。

4 **More than** half of the students **participate** in the job fair.
部分動詞的單複數會跟著of後面的名詞單複數情況而改變。

有些名詞本身無法分辨單、複數，會依據of後面的名詞而決定是要使

1 許多學生們／在／那個就業博覽會。

2 學生的數量／參加那個展覽的／比預計的還多。

3 其中一支鑰匙／置物櫃的／遺失了。

4 一半以上的學生／參加／就業博覽會。

用單數動詞或是複數動詞，也可說是近者一致法的一種。舉例來說，「most of the...」解釋為「大部分的…」，所以most of the扮演著形容詞的角色，後面所出現的名詞就是主詞。所以千萬不要光看名詞就決定是單數還是複數。

整理前面所學的內容，請參閱下表

1 a number of + 複數名詞 + 複數動詞
the number of + 複數名詞 + 單數動詞

2 one of the 複數名詞 + 單數動詞 → one 單數名詞 + 單數動詞
each of the 複數名詞 + 單數動詞 → each 單數名詞 + 單數動詞
either of the 複數名詞 + 單數動詞 → either 單數名詞 + 單數動詞
neither of the 複數名詞 + 單數動詞 → neither 單數名詞 + 單數動詞

3 部分名詞 of + 複數名詞 + 複數動詞
部分名詞 of + 單數名詞 + 單數動詞
部分名詞 of + 不可數名詞 + 單數動詞

有點複雜吧？不一定要背下來，但一定明白為什麼是這樣。如此一來記憶才會深刻。

怪物講師的祕訣

1 觀察決定數量的形容詞後面，是出現單數名詞還是複數名詞。特別是every、each、a few、both、a variety of等，只要仔細想想各單字的意思，就很容易就了解了。

2 要好好掌握主詞後面的修飾句，最後都是句子的含義決定數量。

Quiz

Q11 The number of the resumes we have received (was /were) greater than anticipated.

Q12 (One / Most) of the employees has a lot of complaints about the change.

▶ 解答在026頁

《講師的補充說明》

何謂部分名詞？

most, the rest, half, part, the majority, XX percent等，非整體的，表示一部分的名詞叫作部分名詞。

攻略法 14	只要了解主詞、動詞的關係，就能解決單、複數

主詞 ◀──────────────────────▶ 動詞

根據動詞的型態決定單、複數　　　　　根據主詞的型態定單、複數

主詞是第3人稱　　　　　　　　　　　現在式動詞後加-(e)s

攻略法 15	拿掉修飾語就能解題

主詞和動詞間的修飾句

1 真正的形容詞、介系詞片語、非限定動詞（to不定詞、副詞）、形容詞子句（形容詞類）

2 真正的副詞、介系詞片語、to不定詞、副詞子句（副詞類）

攻略法 16	拿掉形容詞子句（＝關係子句）

1 先行名詞（主詞）+（關係詞主格 + 動詞1 + 受詞／補語）+ 動詞2 + 受詞／補語

2 先行名詞（主詞）+（關係詞受格）+ 主詞 + 及物動詞1+ 動詞2 + 受詞／補語

（或是不及物動詞 + 介系詞）

攻略法 17	關係連接詞和單、複數

both A and B：A和B全都

between A and B：A和B之間

not A but B：不是A，而是B

not only (= just) A but (also) B：不僅A，B也是＝B as well as A

either A or B：不是A就是B

neither A nor B：兩者都不是

攻略法 18	其他重要的單、複數一致

1 後面出現「單數名詞 + 單數動詞」的形容詞

2 後面出現「複數名詞 + 複數動詞」的形容詞

3 後面出現「不可數名詞 + 單數動詞」的形容詞

例子

1 (A) contain —— ① 把握問題的類型
   (B) containing
   (C) to contain —————————————— ③ 空格中要填入什麼詞類？
   (D) contains
   ——————————— ② 把握提示
   The contents of this popular website _____ informative and
   interesting information.

1 把握問題的類型
  文法題

2 把握提示
  數態時的題型

3 空格中要填什麼詞類？
  動詞

2 (A) have been
   (B) were
   (C) being
   (D) was

   The marketing plan concerning our newly developed products
   _____ unanimously approved.

1 把握問題的類型
....
2 把握提示
....
3 空格中要填什麼詞類？
....

3 (A) plans
   (B) plan
   (C) planned
   (D) planning

   The initial _____ to expand overseas branches has been
   announced at the monthly meeting.

1 把握問題的類型
....
2 把握提示
....
3 空格中要填什麼詞類？
....

4 (A) A number of
   (B) Much
   (C) Every
   (D) That

   _____ customers in rural areas have preference for an old model
   over a new one.

1 把握問題的類型
....
2 把握提示
....
3 空格中要填什麼詞類？
....

5 (A) being
   (B) are
   (C) is
   (D) been

   Attracting customers _____ the main reason for renovating the
   department store experiencing a decrease in sales.

1 把握問題的類型
....
2 把握提示
....
3 空格中要填什麼詞類？
....

6 (A) is
   (B) are
   (C) having been
   (D) have been

That your esteemed company offers the most competitive salary _____ why I applied for this job opening.

1 把握問題的類型

2 把握提示

3 空格中要填什麼詞類？

7 (A) offer
   (B) offering
   (C) offers
   (D) are offered

One of the employees who _____ creative ideas to the R&D center is to be chosen.

1 把握問題的類型

2 把握提示

3 空格中要填什麼詞類？

8 (A) being
   (B) were
   (C) was
   (D) to be

Both the design and the theme _____ especially appealing to those who gathered at the exhibition.

1 把握問題的類型

2 把握提示

3 空格中要填什麼詞類？

9 (A) comply
   (B) complying
   (C) complies
   (D) compliant

When you renovate your property, be sure that the building materials you select _____ with all building regulations.

1 把握問題的類型

2 把握提示

3 空格中要填什麼詞類？

10 (A) having
   (B) has
   (C) have
   (D) to have

There _____ to be no obligations to this event, but your voluntary participation is really appreciated.

1 把握問題的類型

2 把握提示

3 空格中要填什麼詞類？

▶ 解答在027頁

重要
101 The prospects of the marketing department for the next year _____ optimistic enough to invest funds amply.

(A) have
(B) is
(C) are
(D) has been

102 The report written by the head manager _____ finally approved by the board of directors.

(A) was
(B) were
(C) have
(D) has

重要
103 _____ of the machine parts is guaranteed for a full one year from the date of purchase.

(A) Each
(B) Some
(C) All
(D) Both

104 Wearing thick clothes _____ strongly recommended in chilly weather not to catch a cold.

(A) is
(B) are
(C) have
(D) has

105 The economy of our nation as well as most developed nations _____ according to the principles of the free market.

(A) runs
(B) running
(C) to run
(D) run

106 The main reason for the weekly meetings _____ to keep our staff informed of rapidly changing market conditions.

(A) is
(B) are
(C) have
(D) will

107 The web-based consulting agency founded a few years ago _____ some of the best services in the industry.

(A) offer
(B) offering
(C) is offered
(D) offers

108 The campaign the local government _____ had a negative effect on the area.

(A) is sponsoring
(B) sponsoring
(C) is sponsored
(D) are sponsoring

高難度
109 The number of the complaints we are receiving _____ so overwhelming that we have to call an emergency meeting first.

(A) being
(B) is
(C) are
(D) been

110 The rest of the refurbished items _____ been returned to their original owners with no further delay.

(A) have
(B) has
(C) to
(D) will

高難度

111 _____ local branch as well as the headquarters is to be renovated to improve working conditions.

(A) Several
(B) All
(C) Little
(D) Each

112 While the directors you met during the interview _____ say, they are expecting your prompt reply.

(A) to
(B) not
(C) doesn't
(D) don't

113 _____ students are required to fill out this form in order to enroll in the next semester.

(A) What
(B) Every
(C) All
(D) That

114 All of the products produced by Freeride Corporation _____ for one year from the date of purchase.

(A) covering
(B) is covered
(C) are covered
(D) covered

115 Every local branch manager in the region _____ fully in charge of recruiting local sales representatives.

(A) to be
(B) have been
(C) being
(D) has been

116 Overseeing the project's progress _____ his top priority until he was transferred to another branch.

(A) considered
(B) had been considered
(C) have been considered
(D) considering

117 Each of the three independent branches of the conglomerate _____ one another.

(A) monitors
(B) monitoring
(C) monitor
(D) to monitor

118 _____ of the businesses in the competition expresses its intention to give up.

(A) Some
(B) All
(C) Most
(D) Neither

119 Most of the local corporations _____ consistently criticized several proposals on the new sales tax plan.

(A) have
(B) has
(C) have been
(D) has been

120 _____ existing factory as well as new office space is to be renovated to include a new staff lounge.

(A) Both
(B) Few
(C) Much
(D) Each

▶ 解答在028頁

Questions 121-124 refer to the following article.

The climate has become abnormal recently. There has been violent rainfall in places where there is usually mild weather, and there have been blizzards in other places that _____ often fairly warm. This situation has impacted people's lives seriously. At first,
                    121
no one seemed to be capable of understanding this chaos. Many believed that it was just a temporary phenomenon. When we had more and more _____ natural disasters,
                                                                              122
everything started to become uncertain. Scientists hypothesize that this abnormal weather might be caused by gasoline use, deforestation, and overpopulation. They have even warned us that humans _____ extinct if we hesitate to take action on dealing with
                          123
this issue. If there is an inexorable rise in temperature, coastal land will be submerged by ocean water due to melting ice from the icebergs, and more people will have no access to fresh water and food due to the soil salinization in some agricultural regions, and more animals on earth will go extinct. We are running out of time. We must take action on addressing this issue. _____
                        124

121 (A) is
    (B) are
    (C) have been
    (D) are going to

122 (A) predict
    (B) unpredicted
    (C) unpredictable
    (D) unpredictably

123 (A) would be
    (B) will be
    (C) is
    (D) would have been

124 (A) The only planet we live on will be better than it ever was.
    (B) The only planet we live on will no longer be inhabitable.
    (C) The only planet we live on will be sustainable.
    (D) The only planet we live on will be as such without failure.

▶ 解答在028頁

主動、被動的區分

受詞的生命！主動、被動的解題法！

在Chapter 04中學到了單、複數的一致性了吧，請回想一下回答下面的問題。

1 想要確認單、複數的話？ ▸ ....

2 主詞與動詞間需要把什麼抽掉？ ▸ ....

3 把形容詞子句抽掉的法則？ ▸ ....

4 相關連接詞的單、複數兩大解法？ ▸ ....

5 every, each, another, either, neither等？ ▸ ....

6 both, few, several, many, these, those等？ ▸ ....

1 主動、被動的特徵

❶ 到目前為止了解了句子的意思，主動、被動的問題還是沒有解決吧？單單以主動、被動來分析是無法解決問題的。

❷ 解題上還是需要了解句子的意思，如果再看有沒有受詞的話，就能更正確的解決主動、被動的問題。

❸ 如果有受詞，就是主動；如果沒有受詞，就是被動。再加上上述的方法，一定能正確解題。

2 主動、被動問題的解法

❶ 第1、2大句型不使用被動式，因此無條件地選擇主動式當答案就可以。

❷ 第3、4、5大句型有受詞的話，就是選擇主動式當答案，如果沒有的話，就選擇被動式當案。最後分析題目後再答題的話會更正確。

❸ 第4大句型的受詞有兩個，如果是主動的話，一個會在前面出現，剩下的一個會在後面出現的句子結構。

[正確答案] 1. 主詞看動詞，動詞看主詞 2. 修飾語，特別是形容詞子句 3. 從名詞後面的關係詞開始，從動詞1到動詞2前面都要抽掉 4. 使用解釋法與近者一致法來解題。 5. 與單數名詞使用 6. 與複數名詞使用

19

主動、被動問題的基本解題法

碰到主動、被動問題,你都是分析題目解題的吧?在多益考試中,常常出現只用分析也無法解決的主動、被動問題。那這些無法光用分析解決的題目,該怎麼去解題呢?

分析主動、被動問題來解題,能解決固然很好,但是如果光靠分析無法解決的話,該怎麼辦呢?這個時候就要來看句子中有沒有受詞了。

We **build a house**.

> 我們建造房子。

這是非常簡單的第3大句型的句子,主詞的we是以主動式來建造房子。如果要變成被動的話,a house成為主詞,房子就以被動式的被建造,所以就會出現A house is built (by us). (一間房子被〔我們〕建造。)這樣的句子。只要知道在被動式的句子中「受詞移動到主詞的位置」就可以了。所以在被動式句子中雖然有受詞,但因為受詞變成主詞,因此也有「在被動式的句子中沒有受詞」這樣的說法出現。

1 The young people **will be hired** as they are so qualified.

> 1 那群年輕人會被雇用/因為他們非常勝任。

分析這個句子,年輕人可以被看成主動性的受雇,也可以看成被動性的被聘雇,但因為動詞後面沒有受詞,因此這個句子就是被動式。動詞以will be hired這種形式變成被動式。

2 The man **was notified** of the result.

> 2 那個男人被通知/關於那個結果。

若將of後面的介系詞片語(介系詞 + 名詞)移除,此句就沒有受詞了,所以寫成被動型態的was notified。

5秒 解決主動、被動問題的方法

1 主動式句子中的受詞變成主詞的話,就變成被動式的句子了。

2 如果有受詞就是主動,沒有受詞就是被動。

3 自己先解析題目,再加上上述兩個方法做驗證的話,就更確定答案了。

Quiz

Q1 She (hired / was hired) due to her creative writing ability.

Q2 It (expected / was expected) that the new plant would be operational from next month.

▶ 解答在032頁

攻略法

20

拿掉修飾語就能解題

主動與被動的區分，可以使用簡單的解析或是觀察有沒有受詞來判斷，但也有例外的情況，
在只有主動式答案的情況下（＝意思就是不能寫成被動），該怎麼解決呢？

1. 第1、2大句型動詞

1 He **disappeared**.

不能寫成He was disappeared.。

2 I believe that God **exists**.

不能寫成God is existed.。

3 He **looked** satisfied.

不能寫成He was looked satisfied.。

1 他不見了。

2 我相信／神是存在的。

3 他看起來很滿意。

主動、被動的基本原理你還記得吧？要寫被動句的時候，受詞要變成主
詞。因此第1、2大句型的句子該怎麼辦呢？在第1、2大句型的句子中有
受詞嗎？答案是沒有，所以第1、2大句型只能寫成主動式。

怪物講師的祕訣

下面是在各種考試中常被出題的第1、2大句型動詞：

1 常被出題的第1大句型動詞

只以「主詞＋動詞」（S＋V）完成的句子是第1大句型，代表性的第1大句型動詞如下
所示。

go, fly, rise, disappear （消失）, come, happen（發生 = occur）, emerge（出現 =
appear）, exist （存在）, live, stand, stay, work（= labor）…等。

2 常被出題的第2大句型動詞

「以主詞＋動詞＋主詞補語」（S＋V＋SC）完成的句子是第2大句型句子，代表性的
第2大句型動詞如下所示。

be, become, remain, go, come, grow, get, appear, seem （…看起來 = look）, smell（發
出味道）, sound （…聽起來像）, taste （…嚐起來）…等。

> Quiz

Q3 The girl was (standing / stood) near me, smiling cheerfully.

Q4 The manager (appeared / was appeared) suddenly through the rear
entrance.

▶ 解答在032頁

2. 狀態動詞

與上面的第1、2大句型動詞不同,狀態動詞有時會有受詞,但是如果寫
成被動式的話會很奇怪,所以請記得只能寫成主動式。

1 I **have** an opinion. (○)
   → An opinion is had by me. (×)

2 The son **resembled** his father. (○)
   → His father was resembled by the son. (×)

1 我有意見。

2 那兒子長得很像他爸爸。

怪物講師的祕訣

代表性的狀態動詞如下所示。

have(帶有), resemble(像), belong to(屬於⋯), consist of(以⋯構成), want(想),
like(喜歡)⋯等。

> Quiz

Q5 The committee (was consisted / consisted) of twelve members.

Q6 The competent manager wants to (belong / be belonged) to our
group.

▶ 解答在032頁

攻略法
21

第3大句型的兩種被動式

還記得嗎？在Chapter 03中有提到，第3大句型的句子大概以兩種型態出現。因此第3大句型的句子以什麼型態出現，被動式也會隨著改變。

第3大句型句子大都以下列兩種型態出現。

❶ 主詞 + 動詞 + 受詞（大部分第3大句型的句子）
❷ 主詞 + 動詞 + 介系詞 + 受詞（請記得以「動詞 + 介系詞」片語出現的特例）

上面兩個的型態如果要以被動表示的話，就會以「be p.p. +（副詞類）」或是「be p.p. + 介系詞 +（副詞類）」其中一種句型來表示。

1.「不及物動詞 + 受詞」型態的被動式

英文的句子大都是第3大句型的句子，且都是「主詞 + 動詞 + 受詞」（S + V + O）。再次說明，大部分第3大句型的句子中，有受詞就是主動，沒有就是被動。出題會有兩種形式，一種是先看動詞的主動、被動，再看後面是名詞類還是副詞類；另一種是倒過來先看後面是名詞類還是副詞類，再來看動詞是主動、被動。

1 It **was discussed** last week.

　　last week是與時間有關的副詞，拿掉之後，就沒有受詞，所以是被動！

2 It **was expected** that he would stay.

　　that之後是真主詞，無法成為受詞，由上可知這是被動！

3 The situation **was considered** to better serve you.

　　consider不能把to不定詞當作受詞使用，所以在這裡的to不定詞是擔任副詞的角色。這個句子中沒有受詞，因此是被動式！

> **1** 那件事被討論／在上個禮拜。
>
> **2** 被預測了／他會留下來。
>
> **3** 這個狀況被認為／會比較適合你。

怪物講師的祕訣

1 有受詞的情況：主詞 + 第3大句型動詞（主動）+ 受詞（名詞類）。
2 沒有受詞的情況：主詞 + 第3大句型動詞（被動）+ 沒有受詞（副詞類）。

Q7 He (planned / was planned) to help others with his energy and enthusiasm.

Q8 The meeting was well attended (by / our) newly recruited staff.

▶ 解答在032頁

2. 「及物動詞 + 介系詞 + 受詞」型態的被動式

與前面看到的「主詞 + 動詞 + 受詞」型態的第3大句型不同點,是在動詞後面加入了介系詞。就像在Chapter 03中所強調的,不要把「動詞 + 介系詞」當作兩個單字來看,而是要看成一個單字。也就是把它當成片語來學。由上可知要看有沒有受詞的話,不是看動詞的後面,而是要看介系詞的後面,如果介系詞後面有受詞的話就是主動,沒有就是被動。

1 We will **deal with the problem**.

　　deal with後面有受詞(the problem),是主動!

2 The problem will **be dealt with** by us.

　　deal with後面沒有受詞,是被動!by us是介系詞片語(介系詞 + 名詞)因此要拿掉!

1 我們會處理／這個問題。

2 這個問題可以被處理／由我們。

怪物講師的祕訣

1 在第3大句型中,在動詞的位置插「動詞 + 介系詞」情況的主動、被動

　　主詞 + 動詞(主動式)+ 受詞(名詞類)

　　主詞 + 動詞(被動式)+ 沒有受詞(副詞類)

2 在考試中常以「動詞 + 介系詞 + 受詞」出現的片語

refer to 事物	參照…
comply with 規定	按照(遵守)…
deal with 事物	管理(處理)…
interfere with 事物	妨礙(干涉)…

5秒 解決第3大句型主動、被動問題的方法

1 大部分的狀況,在後面有名詞類就是主動,沒有就是被動。

2 但是,在片語的情況,要把它看成一個單字,另外看介系詞的後面有沒有受詞來決定是主動、被動,需要特別留意。

3 雖然動詞的主動、被動都會出現,但是考試時常常會依據主動、被動後面是什麼(是名詞類還是副詞類)來出題,因此要時時地觀察前後詞類。

Q9 The topic will (deal / be dealt) with by the head consultant.

Q10 The data must be referred to (us / by us) for fear of losing them.

▶ 解答在032頁

攻略法
22 第4大句型的被動式

受詞有兩個的第4大句型與只有一個受詞的第3大句型的被動式不一樣。為什麼不一樣，請好好看以下的說明。

第4大句型與第3大句型的句子非常不一樣，先回想在Chapter 03所學，再想第4大句型句子動詞give, offer, send, bring, fax, grant, award, cost, lend, tell等（ANICAR），並看看以下說明。

1. 一般的第4大句型句子

第4大句型句子與第3大句型句子非常不一樣，和前面Chapter 03所學的一樣，第4大句型句子有2個受詞。那麼2個受詞中的一個被當成主詞的話，該怎麼辦？因為有2個受詞，因此如果一個跑到前面變成被動式，那後面還會剩下一個受詞。

1 He gave **me a ring**.
IO和DO都有的典型第4大句型句子！

2 **I** was given **a ring**.
IO被當作主詞變成被動式，但是DO還留著！

3 **A ring** was given (to) **me**.
DO被當成主詞變成被動式，但是IO還留著！

受詞有2個的第4大句型，一個受詞變成主詞，變成被動式後還留著另外一個受詞。

1 他給／我／戒指。

2 我收到了／戒指。

3 一個戒指被交給／我。

怪物講師的祕訣
一般的第4大句型句子的主動式及被動式
1 主詞 + 第4大句型動詞（主動式）+ IO + DO
2 主詞（IO或DO）+ 第4大句型動詞（被動式）+ 受詞（IO或DO）

✎ Quiz

Q11 The customer wants to (offer / be offered) discounts.

Q12 A memo will (send / be sent) to you immediately.

▶ 解答在032頁

2. 第4大句型變成第3大句型的情況

這個變形句子是DO沒有被當作主詞，IO跑到後面並且加上介系詞to。在這個情況，「介系詞 + IO」被當作介系詞片語（介系詞 + 名詞）省略也可以，如此這個句子就不是第4大句型而是第3大句型。由上可知，如果有受詞就是主動，沒有受詞就是被動的第3大句型了。

1 The company offered **an opportunity to me**.

   只剩下DO，「to + IO」被放到後面的第3大句型句子！

2 He showed **a picture of his mother** to her.

   只剩下DO，to + her被放到後面的第3大句型句子！

第4大句型可以變成第3大句型句子的這個特點，請不要忘記。如果一直想著第4大句型句子有兩個受詞的話，反而會妨礙解題。

怪物講師的祕訣

1️⃣ 主詞 + 第4大句型動詞（主動式）+ IO + DO → 第4大句型

2️⃣ 主詞 + 第4大句型動詞（主動式）+ DO +（介系詞IO） → 第3大句型
　　主詞（DO）+ 第4大句型動詞（被動式）+（介系詞IO） → 第3大句型

Quiz

Q13 The company didn't want to (offer / be offered) discounts.

Q14 The shop owner gladly (sent / was sent) a letter to her regular customers.

▶ 解答在032頁

3. ANICAR動詞們的主動、被動

和前面Chapter 03所學的一樣，如果ANICAR動詞們後面有人的話，就是主動，沒有就是被動。請牢記在心上，不用去想其他的單字。有ANICAR動詞的情況，只要重視人就好了。

1 He **notified us** of the result.

2 We **were notified** of the result by him.

右側譯文：
1 公司提供了／機會／給我。
2 他展示／自己母親的照片／給她。

1 他通知／我們／結果。
2 我們收到通知了／關於結果／由他。

像這種ANICAR動詞，後面有沒有接人是很重要的。請您在多益閱讀題中活用主動、被動問題的解法。

在ANICAR動詞的情況，只有人可以當受詞這點非常重要。如果沒有人就會變成被動式，主詞一定要是人。ANI被使用在第3、4大句型，CAR被使用在第3、4、5大句型。

再次的整理ANICAR動詞，如下所示。

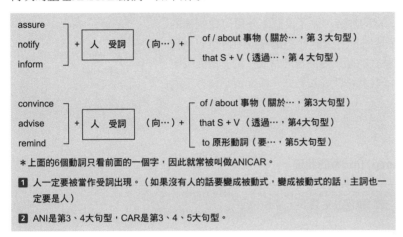

＊上面的6個動詞只看前面的一個字，因此就常被叫做ANICAR。

1 人一定要被當作受詞出現。（如果沒有人的話要變成被動式，變成被動式的話，主詞也一定要是人）

2 ANI是第3、4大句型，CAR是第3、4、5大句型。

Quiz ....

Q15 The information (gave / was given) to the attendees absolutely free of charge.

Q16 The superintendent (offered / was offered) a chance to me once again.

Q17 The customer will (notify / be notified) as soon as the item is in stock.

▶ 解答在032頁

5秒 解決第4大句型主動、被動的方法2

1 後面都有IO和DO的話，答案當然就是主動。

2 後面只有IO（人）的話，答案就是被動式。（因為DO跑到前面去了）

3 後面只有DO（物）的話，先分析看看再來決定是主動、被動。
（因為可以變成第3大句型的句子，也可以是第4大句型被動式的句子）

攻略法

23

第5大句型的被動式

第5大句型的被動式與其他句型句子有哪些不一樣？為什麼會不一樣呢？讓我們來了解第5大句型句子的被動式。

第5大句型與第3大句型不一樣的地方，除了受詞之外還有受詞補語吧？所以具有就算把句子變成被動，受詞補語還存在的特點。也就是第3大句型句子被改成被動式的話，受詞會被當成主詞，後面只剩下副詞類，但第5大句型句子就算被改成被動式，後面還是會有受詞補語。

1. 第5大句型動詞make, keep, find等的狀況

make [keep, find] + 受詞 + 受詞補語（形容詞、-ing、p.p.）

1 He found **her fascinating**.

受詞her後面有形容詞fascinating被當作受詞補語的狀態！

2 **She** was found **fascinating** by him.

後面的例句被寫成被動式，因此後面的受詞補語fascinating就自然地出現了！

> **1** 他發覺／她很有魅力。
>
> **2** 她被覺得／有魅力／由他。

像這樣，第5大句型會具有變成被動式時，對應受詞補語的形容詞類（fascinating）會留下來的特點。但要注意make、keep、find也是會被用在第3大句型的動詞。如果要用在沒有受詞補語的第3大句型，寫成被動式的時候，副詞類會被留下。

Quiz

Q18 He was found (dead / deadly) last week.
Q19 The name of the donor (kept / was kept) secret.

▶ 解答在032頁

2.「使、要求、允許」動詞的情況

「使、要求、允許」動詞 + 受詞 + 受詞補語（to不定詞）

「使、要求、允許」這種第5大句型的動詞，跟前面其它第5大句型動詞make、keep、find不一樣，被改成被動式的時候，to不定詞會被留在後面。

1 He persuaded **me to go** with him.

persuade是「要求」動詞。在受詞補語的位置要填入to go這樣的to不定詞！

2 I was persuaded **to go** with him.

上一句的第5大句型句子要改成被動式的話，動詞的後面自然會留下to不定詞！

怪物講師的祕訣

和下面一樣，使用「使、要求、允許」動詞的第5大句型句子，在主動及被動的情況下，所有動詞後面都會有to不定詞這一點，請牢記在心。

使：force（強迫＝compel）、persuade（說服，讓…做）

要求：ask（要求）、encourage（鼓勵，讓…做）、require（被需要）、
　　　expect（希望，第3、5大句型）、would like（希望，第3、5大句型）

允許：allow（允許＝permit）、enable（讓…變的可能）

* ANICAR中，屬於CAR的動詞都是用第5大句型。

Quiz

Q20 They (encouraged / were encouraged) to actively participate in the project.

Q21 The workers (do not allow / are not allowed) to smoke in the factory.

3. 使役動詞（let, make, have）的情況

使役動詞（let, make, have）+ 受詞 + 受詞補語 +（原形動詞、p.p.）

1 He made **me work** hard.

使役動詞後面出現受詞me，在後面出現沒有加to的原形動詞狀態！

2 I was made **to work** hard.

把上面的例句改成被動式，原形動詞work以to不定詞型態出現！

請絕對不要忘記，有使役動詞的句子要變成被動式的話，當作受詞補語的原形動詞要改成有to的原形不定詞。

1 他說服了／我／和他一起去。

2 我被說服了／和他一起去。

▶ 解答在032頁

1 他逼迫／我／認真工作。

2 我被逼迫／認真工作。

Q22 They (let / were let) to stay.

Q23 The girl (made / was made) to go there against her will.

▶ 解答在032頁

4. 第5大句型動詞call、elect、appoint、consider的情況

使用這4個動詞的第5大句型句子，若要改成被動式，受詞要變成主詞，且在後面留下當作受詞補語的名詞。此時這個名詞具有與主詞同格的關係。動詞consider可以被使用在第3大句型、第5大句型，特別是使用在第5大句型的時候，大都以「consider +（to be）+ 受詞補語（形容詞或是名詞）」的型態出現，因此需要好好牢記。

call [elect, appoint, consider] + 受詞 + 受詞補語（名詞）

1 We elected **him our chairman**.

第5大句型動詞elect後面可以看到受詞及受詞補語（our chairman）！

1 我們選／他／當我們的議長。

2 他被選／當我們的議長。

2 **He** was elected **our chairman**.

在上面的例句中，受詞him被改成主詞he而變成被動式！此時，受詞補語our chairman與主詞的he具有同格（＝）的關係！

Q24 The data must be kept (confidential / confidentially) as they contain very important secrets.

Q25 You (require / are required) to inform your supervisor first in case of any emergency.

Q26 I wasn't let (enter / to enter) the restricted area at that time.

▶ 解答在032頁

5秒 解決第5大句型主動、被動的方法

1 第5大句型也是一樣，有受詞的話就是主動，沒有受詞就是被動。

2 第5大句型句子如果要變成被動式，就一定會有受詞補語。

3 請記得這個時候留下來的受詞補語，會隨著第5大句型的動詞是哪一個而改變。

攻略法

24

被動式相關的片語

被動式的表現中，很常出現在後面會加上什麼樣的介系詞的問題。像這種與被動式相關的表現，是包含介系詞的。

如果要分析被動式片語的話，會有一些主動、被動分不清楚的狀況，但是像這樣的片語很常出現在考題中，因此平時就要好好的熟記。

1 He **was pleased with** the result.

be pleased with（高興…）要看成是一個單字！

2 She **was satisfied with** her promotion.

be satisfied with（對…滿足）要看成是一個單字！

3 I **was disappointed at** the low revenue.

be disappointed at（對…失望）要看成是一個單字！

1 他很開心／對於結果。

2 她很滿足／關於她的升遷。

3 我很失望／對於低收益。

如上所述，被動式的片語，最好都要把它當成一個單字來熟記。在之後的考題中出現時，就可以立即寫出答案，對listening和speaking部分也會有很大的幫助。

怪物講師的祕訣

下面整理了所有在前面加上介系詞，且合併在一起被當成一個單字的被動式表現。

1 使用介系詞 with 的被動式表現

be pleased with	對…高興
be satisfied with	對…滿足
be covered with	被…覆蓋
be crowded with	被…塞滿
be filled with	被…塞滿

2 使用介系詞 at 的被動式表現

be disappointed at	對…失望
be surprised at	對…驚訝
be alarmed at	對…驚訝
be frightened at	被…驚嚇
be astonished at	被…驚嚇
be shocked at	受到…衝擊

3 使用介系詞 in 的被動式表現

be interested in	對…感到興趣
be involved in	介入（牽連）…
be absorbed in	熱衷於…
be dressed in	穿著…的衣服
be disappointed in	對…失望

4 使用介系詞 to 的被動式表現

be known to	讓…知道
be opposed to	對…反對
be inclined to	有做…的意願
be married to	和…結婚

5 使用其他介系詞的被動式表現

be made of	被做成…（物理性的）
be made from	以…而做的（化學性的）
be tired of	對…厭煩
be tired from	因為…而疲憊
be used to	對…習慣

 Quiz

Q27 They (involved / were involved) in the insignificant matter.

Q28 He was interested (with / in) the upcoming project.

▶ 解答在032頁

攻略法 19-24

1 要把第1、2大句型動詞改成被動式是不可能的，所以只能寫成主動式。

2 第3大句型句子如果要改成普通的被動式，受詞要往前移動變成主詞，而且後面剩下副詞類。但是「動詞＋介系詞」形式的片語要看成是一個單字，並且注意後面的受詞。

3 第4大句型的特點是句子中有兩個受詞，如果要改成被動時，一個受詞要移到前面變成主詞，後面則剩下另一個受詞。但是如果要把第4大句型改成第3大句型的時候，不會留下受詞，因此解題時一定要解析題目再答題。

4 第5大句型中有受詞和受詞補語，變成被動式時，受詞要移到前面變成主詞，後面則剩下受詞補語。另外要留意第5大句型隨著使用的動詞不同，受詞補語也會跟著改變這一點。

5 在考試中常常會被出題的被動型片語「be動詞 + p.p.」，後面會出現各種介系詞，請一定要熟記。

例子 1
(A) advise ← **①** 把握問題的類型
(B) advises
(C) be advised ← **③** 空格中要填什麼詞類？
(D) to advise

Interns must _____ that they should always wear lab coats before entering the restricted areas.
← **②** 把握提示

1 把握問題的類型	文法問題
2 把握提示	數、態、時！
3 空格中要填什麼詞類？	動詞

2
(A) please
(B) are pleased
(C) are pleasing
(D) is pleased

Usually, customers _____ with our outstanding services and products as we are doing our best.

1 把握問題的類型
2 把握提示
3 空格中要填什麼詞類？

3
(A) exist
(B) are existed
(C) existent
(D) existence

Problems always _____ only when you are worried about them, so please calm down and relax.

1 把握問題的類型
2 把握提示
3 空格中要填什麼詞類？

4
(A) offering
(B) offer
(C) be offered
(D) offers

Customers will _____ a considerable discount for a limited time since we celebrate our tenth anniversary.

1 把握問題的類型
2 把握提示
3 空格中要填什麼詞類？

5
(A) dealt
(B) interfered
(C) handled
(D) kept

Our population is rapidly decreasing, which must be _____ with instantly for our bright future.

1 把握問題的類型
2 把握提示
3 空格中要填什麼詞類？

6 (A) say
   (B) is said
   (C) saying
   (D) said

It _____ that we can make more money by offering customers what they really want.

1 把握問題的類型

2 把握提示

3 空格中要填什麼詞類？

7 (A) disappear
   (B) be disappear
   (C) be disappeared
   (D) disappears

As mentioned just a minute ago, the evidence may _____ if you don't come on the scene right away.

1 把握問題的類型

2 把握提示

3 空格中要填什麼詞類？

8 (A) convinced
   (B) to convince
   (C) was convincing
   (D) was convinced

The candidate _____ that she will be informed as soon as her resume is reviewed by the committee.

1 把握問題的類型

2 把握提示

3 空格中要填什麼詞類？

9 (A) refuse
   (B) intend
   (C) discontinue
   (D) remind

We must _____ selling those defective products and recall all of the already sold items.

1 把握問題的類型

2 把握提示

3 空格中要填什麼詞類？

10 (A) be notified
   (B) notify
   (C) notification
   (D) notified

Managers should _____ before you take a day off, which is our current company policy.

1 把握問題的類型

2 把握提示

3 空格中要填什麼詞類？

101 The charity event benefiting the poor will
_____ place next week with the
help of our ex-president.

(A) be taken
(B) be took
(C) take
(D) is taking

高難度

102 Frequent customers will _____ a
big discount this week only, so hurry up!

(A) be offered
(B) offer
(C) offering
(D) offers

103 New employees are not allowed _____
the confidential data unless otherwise
noted.

(A) access
(B) accessing
(C) accessible
(D) to access

104 Although the rare book is presently out
of print, it can be _____ from the
largest on-line bookstore.

(A) ordered
(B) remained
(C) considered
(D) found

105 Your idea of expanding business will be
considered _____ as that fully
makes sense.

(A) care
(B) careful
(C) caring
(D) carefully

106 After you completely fill out the application
form, it should _____ to the
personnel department directly.

(A) submit
(B) submitted
(C) have submitted
(D) be submitted

重要

107 Any staff member who voluntarily
contributes to our company considerably
will be _____ a special bonus.

(A) awarded
(B) taken
(C) obtained
(D) kept

108 My counterpart was _____ to sign
the contract even though the terms were
not so favorable for him.

(A) made
(B) decided
(C) appeared
(D) had

重要

109 The oil price _____ sharply owing
to the unstable market nowadays, which
will have a negative effect on us.

(A) has risen
(B) has been risen
(C) was risen
(D) raised

110 The article dealing with the stock
investment _____ published in
today's newspaper.

(A) was
(B) were
(C) have
(D) has

111 To obtain a promotion, the performance evaluation form must be filled out and _____ to the human resources department.

(A) return
(B) returned
(C) returning
(D) were returned

高難度
112 I _____ that the application form for the mortgage loan was received and final decision will be made soon.

(A) assure
(B) have assured
(C) was assured
(D) was assuring

113 The boss instructed his employees to be conscious about office supply waste because resources _____.

(A) limited
(B) have limited
(C) limit
(D) are limited

114 The employees of the promotion team _____ that the model can be a big hit in the highly competitive market.

(A) was expected
(B) has expected
(C) were expected
(D) have expected

115 All of the applicants who are qualified for the position will _____ a chance to take a job interview.

(A) be given
(B) give
(C) have given
(D) be giving

116 Mr. Jones who is motivational and entertaining _____ as a keynote speaker for the upcoming conference.

(A) have chosen
(B) has chosen
(C) were chosen
(D) has been chosen

117 We tried to prevent the order from going out, but only found that the delivery man _____ for the warehouse earlier than expected.

(A) had left
(B) has been left
(C) had been left
(D) left

118 Every spring, steel companies' operations in the area are frequently _____ by regular labor strikes.

(A) disruption
(B) disrupting
(C) disrupt
(D) disrupted

119 There have been a lot of positive changes made to us since Mr. Baker, who had been in charge of Space International, _____ the president.

(A) elected
(B) to elect
(C) electing
(D) was elected

120 Because the periodical is already out of print, it can't be _____ from even the largest on-line bookstore.

(A) ordered
(B) designated
(C) notified
(D) allowed

▶ 解答在035頁

The majority of nine-to-five workers all face the dilemma of maintaining a healthy diet. They are all hesitant to make their own lunches when they _____ ingredient
121
preparation into account. As a matter of fact, making yourself a club sandwich won't disturb you that much if you follow the steps below. Making a tasty and nutritious lunch is a simple chore. First of all, _____ some vegetables and a meat that you like.
122
Afterwards, wash all the ingredients and tear off some handfuls of the vegetables and slice a few pieces of meat. Please bear in mind, if chicken is your selection, you can just have a whole piece without _____. Secondly, heat a pan and put some oil in it. Then,
123
put the sliced meat in the heated pan and turn it over from time to time until the surface of the meat turns light brown. Meanwhile, you can start to toast the bread and scramble two eggs. Finally, put all the ingredients on one piece of bread in the following order: fresh vegetables, cooked meat, and scrambled eggs. Close the sandwich with _____. If you
124
enjoy stronger flavors, you can add some salt and black pepper on the top before you close the sandwich. Finally, you can enjoy your club sandwich during your lunch break at work.

121 (A) get
(B) put
(C) take
(D) have

122 (A) selecting
(B) selected
(C) selection
(D) select

123 (A) chop it off
(B) chopping it off
(C) chopped it off
(D) chop

124 (A) the other piece of bread
(B) some more vegetable
(C) some other meat
(D) another kind of sauce

▶ 解答在035頁

句子的時態
時態問題的解題法！

Review Test

確認在Chapter 05中所學到的主動、被動內容，請在下面的空格中填入適合的答案。

1 主動、被動基本原理 a. 如果句子中有受詞　　▶ _____

　　　　　　　　　　　 b. 如果句子中沒有受詞　▶ _____

2 第1、2大句型及狀態動詞的特徵　　　　　　▶ _____

3 第3大句型的被動式的兩種形式　　　　　　 ▶ a. _____

　　　　　　　　　　　　　　　　　　　　　 b. _____

4 第4大句型的被動式的兩種形式　　　　　　 ▶ a. _____

　　　　　　　　　　　　　　　　　　　　　 b. _____

5 第5大句型的被動式　　　　　　　　　　　 ▶ _____

Preview

1 時態問題的特徵

你知道副詞是用來修飾動詞吧？雖然不是所有副詞都是這樣，但有一部分的副詞可以決定時態。因此先了解與時態相關的副詞、介系詞片語、副詞子句的話，可以更快且更容易地決定時態。另外，可以讓與時間相關的副詞類與動詞的時態變成一致後使用。

2 時態問題的解法

不管你對於時態問題多有把握，還是請你遵守原則，也就是遵守以下的順序。

❶ 把握這個位置是限定動詞還是非限定動詞（動狀詞）。
❷ 如果這個位置是限定動詞，就要以「數、態、時」的順序。
❸ 觀察單、複數及主動、被動後還是沒有答案的話，最後請觀察時態。
❹ 觀察時態的時候，請先看可以讓我們了解時態的副詞類，再來解題。

[正確答案] 1. a.主動 b.被動 2. 不可能是被動式，因為只有使用主動式 3. a.主詞＋be動詞＋p.p.（副詞類）b.主詞＋be動詞＋p.p.＋介系詞（副詞類）4. a.主詞（IO）＋be動詞＋p.p.＋DO b.主詞（DO）＋be動詞＋p.p.＋IO 5. 主詞＋be動詞＋p.p.＋形容詞／-ing, p.p.／to不定詞／名詞

攻略法

25

基本3時態問題的解法

首先，我們先來看看在日常中最常使用，而且在各種英文考試中最常出現的3大時態，也就是過去式、現在式、未來式，在基本3時態主要會出現什麼副詞呢？

講到時態，一定會想到**過去式、現在式、未來式，這三個最基本的時態就叫做「基本3時態」**。那在各個時態中主要常出現的是什麼副詞類呢？

1. 過去式（-ed、was / were、had等）是正確答案的情況

過去時態就是在**過去所做出的某種動作（大部分都是動詞的情況）或是說明過去的某種狀態（be動詞的情況）**會使用。大多在原形動詞加上-ed，be動詞就用was、were，而動詞have就使用had。在句子中如果看到像是yesterday、...ago、last...這種副詞類，就能大概知道這個句子是過去時態了。

1 He **was promoted** to the position of vice president **last year**.

　有看到last year吧？當然是過去時態！

2 **Yesterday**, we **met** the retired minister on the street.

　yesterday就是提示，當然要填入過去動詞met！

3 We **were ailing** like other companies **just two years ago**.

　以just two years ago這樣的副詞類來決定時態！

1 他升職／到副總裁的職位／去年。

2 昨天／我們見到／退休的長官／在街上。

3 我們很辛苦／像其他公司／就在不久的兩年前。

平常如果看到上述提示過去時態的副詞類，就可以馬上解答時態問題了吧。但是再強調一次，**要以限定動詞／非限定動詞（動狀詞）→ 數 → 態 → 時態的順序來解題**。因為如果看到了過去時態的提示後，馬上把過去時態當作答案填入是不行的，因為這有可能是出題老師的陷阱。

怪物講師的祕訣

如果看到下列表現時，在大部分的情況下過去時態是正確答案。

- yesterday、時間 + ago、last + 時間

- in + 年度／世紀

- once（一次、曾經）

- those days（那時、那個時候）

✎ Quiz ··

Q1 The scholar (submitted / had submitted) the report last week.
Q2 We (have / had) an important meeting two weeks ago.

▶ 解答在039頁

2. 現在式（-(e)s，am / are / is，have / has等）是正確答案的情況

表示現在常常反覆的事情或是習慣性所做的事情、不變的真理或事實、現在的狀態等，都要使用現在式。 主要與現在時態一起使用的副詞類有 now、just now（就是現在）、these days（最近）、always、usually。

1　I **always wake** up at 6 in the morning.

　　像always一樣一直反覆的事情，大多要使用現在時態！

2　I **usually have** a TOEIC test once a month.

　　像usually或是once a month這樣反覆性且習慣性的事情，大多要使用現在時態！

看到與現在時態一起使用的副詞類的話，答案大多是現在時態。但有時候卻不是這樣，例如always、usually在過去時態的題目中也會被使用。因此如果想要得到高分，在解時態問題的時候不能只看副詞類，多考慮幾個變數再答題會更好。

1　我總是起床／在早上6點。

2　我通常考多益／每個月一次。

怪物講師的祕訣

如果看到下列詞彙時，在大部分的情況下，現在式是正確答案。

- now, just now, always, often, usually

- every year = each year

- these days

✎ Quiz ··

Q3 We (live / lived) in a dangerous and unpredictable world these days.
Q4 Coffee, tea and soft drinks usually (contain / contained) caffeine.

▶ 解答在039頁

3. 如果看到下列表現時，在大部分的情況下未來時態是正確答案

未來時態是說明還沒發生的未來時使用。**表現未來意思的副詞類有 tomorrow、soon、before long、next...、in the future等，如果沒有特別的情況的話，看成是未來時態就可以了。** 未來式有以下幾種形式：「will / shall + 原形動詞」、「be to + 原形動詞」或是「be going to / be expected to / be used to + 原形動詞」、「plan to + 原形動詞」。

1 **Next year**, we **will expand** our business into a new area.

　　有next year這樣的單字，就可以馬上知道是未來時態！

2 We **are going to meet** our client **tomorrow morning**.

　　有tomorrow這個單字，應該是未來時態，那are不是現在時態嗎？
　　be going to與will一樣是表示未來時態的表現。

如果看到與下面相同的單字，當然就是未來時態。但在考試的時候，因為壓迫感及緊張感，時常會連這種簡單的副詞類都沒看到。如果在平時常做這種題目的練習，應該可以克服這種不必要犯的錯誤。

怪物講師的祕訣

如果看到下列表現時，在大部分的情況下未來時態是正確答案。

- tomorrow

- soon, shortly, before long

- next + 時間（week / month / year / Friday...）

- in the near [foreseeable] future

Quiz

Q5 We (are / will be) holding a press conference tomorrow when he arrives.

Q6 The task (is / will be) assigned to the new manager in the foreseeable future.

5秒 解決基本3時態的方法

1 首先一定要以限定動詞／非限定動詞（動狀詞）→ 數 → 態這樣的順序來分析題目。

2 依照上述順序解析題目之後再來觀察時態的話，這時就要趕快來看副詞類了。

3 看過表示時態的副詞類後，決定動詞的時態，另外也有看動詞的時態，來選擇副詞類的情形。

1 明年／我們會擴張（擴大）／我們的事業／到新的地區。

2 我們要見／我們的客戶／在明天早上。

▶ 解答在039頁

132

攻略法

26 完成3時態問題的解法

完成時態是在哪一種型態或是哪一種情況下使用呢？所謂的完成3時態就是過去完成式、現在完成式、未來完成式。看起來比基本3時態更複雜吧？

1. 過去完成時態（had p.p.）是正確答案的情況

比起過去更之前已經發生的事情，或是從過去以前開始到過去為止持續發生的事。下面兩個例句所使用的就是過去完成時態，以had + p.p.表示。不管是過去完成式還是現在完成式，在完成時態中大部分都會出現 already, just, since, until, by, before, for這樣的單字。

1 He **had waited** for her **until** she finally **arrived**.

「她到達」是過去式，另外因為是在她到達之前就在等待，因此用過去完成式！

2 **Before** you **said** so, I **had not been** aware of it.

「你說話」是過去式，「不知道事情」在過去那個時間點停止，因此用過去完成式！

> 1 他等了她／直到她最後到達為止。
>
> 2 在你說之前／我都不知道／那件事。

怪物講師的祕訣

如果看到下列表現時，在大部分的情況下過去完成時態是正確答案。

- 主詞 + had p.p. + since [until / before / by / by the time] + 主詞 + 過去動詞

✎ Quiz

Q7 The man, living next door, (causes / had caused) many troubles before I moved in.

Q8 By yesterday, he (has / had) been in the bed because of a bad headache.

▶ 解答在039頁

2. 現在完成時態（have / has p.p.）是正確答案的情況

現在完成式以have p.p.或是has p.p.來表示，只要把它想成是比過去完成時態離現在式的距離更近就好了。也就是比起現在，在之前已經發生的事情或是從過去開始到現在所發生的事情。

1 We **have known** each other **for more than a decade**.

for之後的提示，認識10年以上的時間，這是現在完成的持續用法！

2 I **have just finished** my homework.

just是提示，不知道從什麼時候開始做到現在的作業剛剛結束了，這是現在完成的結束用法！

怪物講師的祕訣

如果看到下列表現時，在大部分的情況下現在完成時態是正確答案。

主詞 have / has p.p. ⎡ since + 過去時間名詞／主詞 + 過去動詞
⎣ for [in / over] + 以數字表示的期間

Quiz ....

Q9 I (don't hear / have not heard) from my son for almost five years.

Q10 The client has grumbled about the product (since / for) she bought it.

▶ 解答在039頁

3. 未來完成時態（will / shall have p.p.）是正確答案的情況

未來完成時態是說明在未來的特定時間點，或是到之前為止持續性的或是完成的事情。以「**will [shall] have p.p.**」表示。也很常與when、before這樣的連接詞一起使用。

1 I **will have completed** the work **before you come tonight**.

到今天晚上你到之前會結束，是表示在未來會結束，因此是未來完成！

2 **By next week**, we **will have finished** the construction.

建設會持續到下周結束，因此是未來完成！

Quiz ....

Q11 I expect he (has / will have) finished it by tomorrow evening.

Q12 He (has / will have) visited Jeju Island three times if he visits again.

▶ 解答在039頁

5秒 解決完成3時態的方法

1 看到by、before、until的話，就要好好看看它後面是過去還是未來。

2 如果是未來的話，就是未來完成。如果是過去的話，就是過去完成，當然也是要了解句子的意思。

3 選擇現在完成的時候，不要只看since，也要確認後面有沒有過去的時態。

4 如果答案要寫現在完成的話，請記得答案要寫「since + 時間點」、「for + 期間」。

攻略法 27 其他常出現的時態問題解法

在英文的時態中，除了基本3時態和完成3時態之外，還有其他幾種時態。不管是在哪種時態下，都能讓你找到時態的提示，因此熟記找出時態的方法是很有幫助的。

1. 在時態問題中最常出現的時間，條件的副詞子句

要不要試試看用「如果你認真讀英文的話，我就會幫助你。」來造句？

If you **study** English hard, I'**ll help** you.

< 你如果認真讀英文的話／我會幫助／你。

應該是這樣寫。在這裡我們用中文與英文來做比較，「如果認真讀的話」是現在式吧？所以要寫**study**。「幫助你」是未來式吧？所以要寫上**will help**。但是「如果認真讀的話」感覺上是未來式，所以就會有「**在時間條件的副詞子句中以現在式取代未來式**」這樣的說法出現。時態雖然是寫現在時態，但實際上的意思卻是表達未來。在上面的例句中「如果認真讀的話」，就是表示「…的話」這種條件的副詞子句，所以要寫上現在時態。

1 When it **rains**, we **will stay** home.

when it rains是表示時間的副詞子句，所以要寫上現在時態的rains，當然在we後面的句子是未來時態！

< 1 下雨的時候／我們會待在家。

2 假使發生緊急狀況／你應該要留下／你的電話號碼。

2 In case we **have** an emergency, you **will have to leave** your phone number.

in case也是表示條件的副詞子句，當然在副詞子句這邊寫上現在時態，在主句子這邊寫上未來時態！

怪物講師的祕訣

如果看到下列表現時，請按照時間或是條件的副詞子句規則！

when before / after until as soon as by the time (when) if once unless as long as = as far as in case	+ 現在時態（或是現在完成），未來時態（或是未來完成）

Q13 When he (visits / will visit) us tomorrow, he will bring a lot of samples.

Q14 You will need to report to him (as soon as / what) he comes back.

▶ 解答在039頁

2. 與時態及單、複數無關，無條件使用原形動詞的狀況

表示主張、命令、要求、提案、勸告的動詞，以及表示理性判斷的形容詞，在後面的that子句中，省略助動詞should的情況非常多。所以在that子句後面就算沒有should，無條件寫上原形動詞並解釋為「…應該要」，完全不會受到時態及單、複數影響。但是在寫上相同的動詞或形容詞，卻不是表示主張、命令、要求、提案、勸告意思的情況，就不能無條件的寫上原形動詞，這一點要特別注意。因此，針對題目要做多方的解析之後再寫上答案。

1 He **ordered** that she **speak** only English in this room.

> 在動詞order本意中就有表示「…應該要」的助動詞should的意思，所以不是寫speaks而是寫原形動詞speak！

2 It is **essential** that he **attend** the meeting.

> 形容詞essential是以「必須性的」的意思，也包含了「…應該要」should的意思，所以要寫原形動詞attend！

1 他命令她／只能說英文／在這個房間裡。

2 他必須要參加／這個會議。

怪物講師的祕訣

如果看到下列表現時，無條件都是原形動詞。

1 主張、命令、要求、提案、勸告的動詞（根據狀況做動詞、名詞、形容詞等詞性的更換）

主詞 + insist [order, ask / request, suggest / recommend, advise] + that + 主詞 + （should）+ 原形動詞

2 理性判斷的形容詞

It is essential [necessary, important, advisable, imperative, mandatory, urgent, natural] + that + 主詞 + (should) + 原形動詞

Q15 We insisted that he (accepts / accept) the proposed plan.

Q16 It was important that she (registered / register) the class in advance.

▶ 解答在039頁

5秒 解決基本3時態的方法

1 看到時間、條件副詞子句時，就把它當作是時態問題。

2 看到表示主張、命令、要求、提案、勸告意思的動詞的話，請以原形動詞作答。

3 看到理性判斷的形容詞，是要以原形動詞作答。

攻略法 25　　基本3時態問題的解法

1 如果看到以下的表現時，在大部分的情況，過去時態是正確答案

－ yesterday、時間 + ago、last + 時間、in + 年度／世紀

－ once（一次、曾經）、those days（那當時、那個時候）

2 如果看到以下的表現時，在大部分的情況，現在時態是正確答案

－ now, just now, always, often, usually, every year (= each year / these days)

3 如果看到以下的表現時，在大部分的情況，未來時態是正確答案

－ tomorrow, soon, shortly, before long, next + 時間（week / month / year / Friday…）

－ in the near [foreseeable] future

攻略法 26　　完成3時態問題的解法

1 如果看到以下的表現時，在大部分的情況，過去完成時態是正確答案

－already, just, since, until, by, before, for等

－主詞 + had p.p. + since [until, before, by, by the time] + 主詞 + 過去動詞

2 如果看到以下的表現時，在大部分的情況，現在完成時態是正確答案

－already, just, since, until, by, before, for等

－主詞 have [has] p.p.　┌ since + 過去時間名詞
　　　　　　　　　　　│ since + 主詞 + 過去動詞
　　　　　　　　　　　└ for [in / over] + 以數字表示期間

3 如果看到以下的表現時，在大部分的情況，未來完成時態是正確答案

－主詞 will / shall + have p.p. + by [before, when] + 未來表示

攻略法 27　　其他常出現的時態問題解法

1 表示時間、條件的副詞子句出現時 → 以原形動詞作答

2 主張、命令、要求、提案、勸告的動詞出現時 → 以原形動詞作答

　理性判斷的形容詞出現時 → 以原形動詞作答

例子 1 (A) will interview
　　　(B) interviewing
　　　(C) interviews
　　　(D) interviewed

❶ 把握問題的類型

❸ 空格中要填什麼詞類？

The company _____ several people for the advertised position, but none of them were deemed suitable.

❷ 把握提示

1 把握問題的類型
　文法問題

2 把握提示
　數、態、時！

3 空格中要填什麼詞類？
　動詞

---

2 (A) had worked
　(B) has worked
　(C) worked
　(D) works

Mr. Ramirez _____ for Meditech Inc. for twenty five years, and he's planning to retire next month.

1 把握問題的類型

2 把握提示

3 空格中要填什麼詞類？

---

3 (A) will have upgraded
　(B) has upgraded
　(C) will be upgrading
　(D) was upgraded

All employees should not use the company network tomorrow, as the IT department _____ the company servers.

1 把握問題的類型

2 把握提示

3 空格中要填什麼詞類？

---

4 (A) has had
　(B) will have
　(C) had had
　(D) does have

James _____ several severe cases of the flu before he came back to his routine work.

1 把握問題的類型

2 把握提示

3 空格中要填什麼詞類？

---

5 (A) displayed
　(B) have displayed
　(C) were displayed
　(D) will be displayed

Company security regulations were once so strict that personal security passes _____ while employees were on site.

1 把握問題的類型

2 把握提示

3 空格中要填什麼詞類？

6 (A) will move
(B) moved
(C) have moved
(D) move

I had taken the bus to work for years until I _____ and started to use the subway.

1 把握問題的類型

2 把握提示

3 空格中要填什麼詞類？

7 (A) have closed
(B) are closed
(C) will have closed
(D) closed

By the end of this week's extended European business trip, we _____ the long-awaited contract.

1 把握問題的類型

2 把握提示

3 空格中要填什麼詞類？

8 (A) examine
(B) is examining
(C) examines
(D) has examined

Dr. Smith _____ sick patients every weekday morning, but he often does house calls to very sick patients in the afternoon.

1 把握問題的類型

2 把握提示

3 空格中要填什麼詞類？

9 (A) is
(B) are
(C) to be
(D) be

I advised him that cutbacks _____ made, as our annual budget was unsustainable in all areas of our operations.

1 把握問題的類型

2 把握提示

3 空格中要填什麼詞類？

10 (A) after
(B) until
(C) because
(D) due to

The company had made a profit _____ a bad business decision caused a sudden drop in profits.

1 把握問題的類型

2 把握提示

3 空格中要填什麼詞類？

▶ 解答在040頁

101 The annual team building exercise _____ an opportunity for employees to work together outside of the office.

(A) providing
(B) is provided
(C) provides
(D) provide

102 Parking spaces were limited when the new plant opened, so employees _____ to use public transport to travel.

(A) are forced
(B) were forced
(C) had forced
(D) forced

重要
103 Once we _____ of any dietary restrictions, we will be able to make appropriate arrangements for our planned dinner.

(A) are informed
(B) were informed
(C) are informing
(D) had been informed

104 He had read the terms and conditions of the agreement before he _____ it on behalf of his company.

(A) signing
(B) sign
(C) signed
(D) signs

105 The real estate agent will contact you if they _____ the offer your consortium has made on the property.

(A) will accept
(B) accept
(C) are accepted
(D) has accepted

106 By the end of this week, the payroll department _____ all employees who went on the business trip for their expenses.

(A) will have compensated
(B) has compensated
(C) is compensating
(D) were compensating

107 Ms. Park _____ her flight when the tropical storm was forecast and she e-mailed her co-workers to cancel the meeting.

(A) cancelled
(B) will cancel
(C) cancellation
(D) is cancelling

108 The company's management _____ for A1 catering service to provide a gourmet lunch in the near future.

(A) arranges
(B) will arrange
(C) arranged
(D) has arranged

高難度
109 The medical supplies company made a mistake as its records seemed to show that it _____ our MRI machine already.

(A) had delivered
(B) delivery
(C) were delivering
(D) will deliver

110 Mr. Hernandez _____ the new employee training program for eight years without a single problem the whole time.

(A) has overseen
(B) was overseeing
(C) is overseeing
(D) will oversee

111 The company had operated without making a loss for 40 years until a series of poor financial decisions _____ to bankruptcy.

(A) has led
(B) will have led
(C) led
(D) was led

112 Company operations _____ while the company reorganization was underway; however, everything is thankfully back to normal now.

(A) will be interrupted
(B) were interrupted
(C) interrupting
(D) are interrupted

113 The results of the second survey of the project _____ released finally next week.

(A) was
(B) will be
(C) has
(D) to be

114 When the job application _____ after the due date, it will not be accepted by the personnel department.

(A) arrived
(B) is arrived
(C) arrives
(D) will arrive

115 Over the past five years, the gross salary of our employees _____ an average of 4.5 percent every year.

(A) will have increased
(B) had increased
(C) was increased
(D) has increased

116 The presentation _____ until the keynote speaker Wayne Hill arrived.

(A) has postponed
(B) had been postponed
(C) is postponed
(D) will have been postponed

高難度
117 The firm has increased the amount of funds invested into research and development by 15% _____ the past 4 years to maintain its lead.

(A) since
(B) before
(C) over
(D) yet

118 When many of the product's defects _____, we considered filing for bankruptcy

(A) founded
(B) found
(C) were founded
(D) were found

重要
119 She _____ for the payroll department at our head office since she joined our company 10 years ago.

(A) works
(B) had worked
(C) worked
(D) has worked

120 By the time Mr. Stone _____ as accounting manager next month, he will have served the company for 20 years.

(A) retire
(B) had retired
(C) retired
(D) retires

▶ 解答在042頁

According to current reports, a 21-year-old girl _____ suicide by jumping off from
the top floor of a 6-story apartment. She died at the scene. From all accounts, the
prospective cause of her suicide was that she had hard time _____ for a permanent
job with decent pay and suffered greatly from this due to the fact that she had to provide
for her family. This story should give us a wake-up call that the unemployment situation
is a severe crisis. _____ more and more graduates have trouble finding jobs, a strong
malaise has descended on them. Especially, some of them probably have a heavy burden
from college loans or come from underprivileged families. _____ so that they can
offset their debts or improve the condition of their families. With such an overload of
pressure and insufficient assistance from the government, it's predictable that more and
more of this sort of tragedy will happen.

121 (A) conducted
(B) comprehended
(C) committed
(D) concluded

122 (A) apply
(B) applied
(C) to apply
(D) applying

123 (A) Due to
(B) Now that
(C) Because of
(D) Owing to

124 (A) Either one may cause them to be
desperate for a job
(B) Either one may cause them to be
reluctant for a job
(C) Either one may cause them to be
unwilling for a job
(D) Either one may cause them to be
passive for a job

▶ 解答在042頁

假設法
只要前後搭配呼應，無其它要訣！

來複習一下Chapter 06裡學過的內容。時態要依據什麼解題？沒錯！就是要看副詞類來解題。來確認下面幾題吧！

1 句中有下面副詞屬於何種時態？

a. those days ▶ ....

b. these days ▶ ....

c. in the near future ▶ ....

2 句中有下面單字屬於何種時態？

a. already, just, since, until, by, before, for ▶ ....

b. by / before / when + 未來 ▶ ....

3 「主張、命令、要求、建議、忠告」這類的動詞
後面出現的子句內的動詞屬於何種時態？ ▶ ....

4 「時間、條件」副詞子句中的動詞屬於何種時態？ ▶ ....

1 假設題的特徵

假設法在最近幾年來出題率降低，所以若是急著提高分數，可以略過此單元。但考試不是全部，如果想要有紮實的英語實力，還是得按部就班作準備。在這邊只要記住，**假設法中最重要的是時態，所以關鍵就是if子句和主要子句的時態搭配。**

2 假設題的解題法

因為if子句和主要子句的時態搭配是關鍵，所以稍微背一下就可以輕鬆解決。如果連倒裝句、變型句都一起準備的話應該就更好了啦！

[正確答案] 1. a. 過去 b. 現在 c. 未來 2. a. 過去完成或是現在完成 b. 未來完成 3. 原形動詞 4. 現在式取代未來式，未來完成式取代現在完成式

攻略法

28 假設法的過去式和過去完成式

過去式和過去完成式常被使用在假設法裡,可說是相當重要。因此如果考題出現假設法時,題型是假設過去式或過去完成式的機率非常高。

再次強調,**假設法最大的關鍵在時態**。所以假設法重視的就是if子句的時態和主要子句有何種關聯。**也就是看if子句的時態決定主要子句的時態,看主要子句的時態決定if子句的時態。**

1. 假設法的過去式

假設法的過去就是假設與目前事實相反的事情。有個假設法的句子相當有名,就是「If I were a bird, I could fly to you.」。這是「現在我不是鳥,如果我是鳥的話」的假設句型。像這種假設與現在事實相反,were和would都是動詞的過去型態,所以叫做假設法的過去式。**假設法的過去式句型為if子句用過去式,主要子句使用「would [should, could, might] + 原形動詞」。**再補充說明一點,假設法的過去式中be動詞的過去式與人稱無關,一律使用were。

1 If I **were** healthy, I **could go** there with you
因為身體不好,所以無法去的意思。這裡不使用was,要使用were。

2 If he **lived** here, he **would visit** me more often.
實際上不住這裡,所以無法拜訪的意思。請注意動詞的過去式是lived。

雖然假設法的過去式使用動詞過去式,但是有「(現在)假如…的話,就…」的假設與目前事實相反的意味。所以時態是過去式!含義是現在式!

> **1** 如果我健康的話/就能和你去那裡了。
>
> **2** 如果他住在這邊/他就會來拜訪我/更常。

怪物講師的祕訣

假設法的過去式就是使用於假設與目前事實相反的事情,一般常見句型如下。

If 主詞 + 動詞過去式(或是were), 主詞 + would [should、could、might] + 原形動詞

= 主詞 + would [should、could、might] + 原形動詞 + if 主詞 + 動詞過去式(或是were)

Quiz ···

Q1 If I (am / were) you, I would not say such a thing.

Q2 If I had enough money, I (can / could) buy her a cellular phone.

▶ 解答在046頁

2. 假設法的過去完成式

如果說假設法過去式是假設與目前狀況相反的話，那麼**假設法過去完成式就是假設與過去事實相反**。假設法過去完成式的句型是**if子句中使用過去完成式（had p.p.），主要子句would [should, could, might] have p.p.**。假設與現在事實相反時，使用過去式；假設與過去事實相反時，使用比過去式更早的時態——過去完成式。這點非常重要，請熟記。

1 If they **had not allowed** us to stay, we **could have caught** a cold.
實際上早就得取得許可了，所以才沒有感冒的意思！

2 You **might have been hired** if you **had showed** your potential.
實際上沒有發揮潛在能力，所以沒有被錄取的意思！

假設法過去完成式的型態雖然是過去完成，但句意是表示「萬一…做的話…應該會怎樣」，以過去式的形式來解釋。雖然時態是過去完成，但是解釋起來卻是過去式。

1 如果他們沒有允許／讓我們留下／我們很可能早就感冒了。

2 你可能早就錄取了／如果你的潛能發揮出來的話。

怪物講師的祕訣

要假設與過去事實相反時，使用假設法的過去完成式。一般常見的句型如下。

If 主詞 + had p.p., 主詞 + would [should, could, might] + have p.p.

= 主詞 + would [should, could, might] + have p.p. if 主詞 + had p.p.

Quiz ···

Q3 If he (was not / had not been) sick, he could have done it within the deadline.

Q4 If you had accepted this idea, the situation would (be / have been) much better.

▶ 解答在046頁

攻略法

29

假設法的現在式和未來式

假設法的現在式和未來式的出題比率，跟過去式和過去完成式一樣低，兩者中現在式和未來式的機率會稍微高一點，主要會以「時間、條件」為考題。

假設法的現在式或未來式都是對未來的假設，如果要追根究底的話，**假設法的現在式更接近現實，未來式離現實較為遠一些**。真正要區分是有困難度的。把這兩種假設法看作差不多，會比較方便一些。

1. 假設法現在式

假設法的現在式使用在假設現在或未來時，**句型為if條件子句使用現在式，主要子句使用未來式**。

1 If you **come** now, you **will get** a discount.
  注意！if子句使用現在式，主要子句使用未來式。

2 If it **snows** tomorrow, we **may have to stay** home.
  也是if子句使用現在式，主要子句使用未來式。

> 1 如果你來的話／現在／你可以享有優惠。
>
> 2 如果下雪的話／明天／我們應該待在家裡。

怪物講師的祕訣

假設法的現在式是對現在或未來的事作假設，常見句型如下。

If 主詞 + 現在式動詞, 主詞 + 未來式時態
=主詞 + 未來式時態, if 主詞 + 現在式動詞

Quiz

Q5 We (notify / will notify) you at once if you submit the enclosed form no later than Thursday.

Q6 If she (finishes / will finish) her homework, I will let her rest for a while.

▶ 解答在046頁

2. 假設法的未來式

如果說現在式是單純地假設未來的事時使用，那麼未來式就是使用在假設遙不可及或是未來不可能會實現的事。雖然假設法的未來式有未來兩字，但其特徵是if子句要使用過去式的助動詞should（或是were to）。

在多益考題中常見到should，（但幾乎不會出現were to）。記得，假設法未來式的主要子句要使用未來式，但必需視整體句意判斷。

1 If I **should fail** the exam again, I **will try** again.
   這句有「考不好的可能性很渺茫」的意思，但如果真的考不好，會再試一次！

2 If the sun **were to rise** from the west, I **would marry** you.
   太陽不可能會從西邊出來，所以跟對方結婚是絕對不可能的，因此主要子句必需用過去式。

考題中出現假設法的未來式通常會以「如果…的話，就…吧」的勸誘或是命令句型的方式出題。

1 如果我考試又沒考好的話／我將會再嘗試。

2 如果太陽升起／從西邊／我就會和你結婚。

怪物講師的祕訣

未來式就是使用在假設遙不可及或是不可能會實現的未來的事，常見句型如下。

If 主詞 + should（或是were to）+ 原形動詞, 主詞 + 未來式時態

= 主詞 + 未來式時態, if 主詞 + should（或是were to）+ 原形動詞

Quiz

Q7 If she (had heard / should hear) of his death, she will be shocked.

Q8 If it should rain this afternoon, we (don't / will not) go there.

▶ 解答在046頁

攻略法

30

假設法的倒裝句型

假設法就和數學公式一樣，感到太規矩，很無趣吧？因此也產生了省略if，倒裝「主詞 + 動詞」的「假設法倒裝句」。

假設法的句中常常會省略if，這時if子句的動詞會出現在主詞的前面。這叫做假設法倒裝句。如果有be動詞或助動詞，又或者有一般動詞時，**be動詞、助動詞或一般動詞都以do動詞取代後，放在句子的最前面**，原本的「主詞 + 動詞」就成為「動詞 + 主詞」的倒裝句型了。

1 Were I you, I would not attend the meeting.

原本是If I were you, I would not attend the meeting.，省略了if，be動詞were放到句首形成倒裝句。

2 Had he studied harder, he would have passed the exam.

原本是If he had studied harder, he would have passed the exam.，省略了if。

第1個句子中，現在我不可能是你，所以才會假設「如果我是你」。因為假設與現在事實相反的情況，所以假設法是過去式的句型。第2個句子的if子句是過去完成式，因此是假設法的過去完成式句型。這句的意思是說，如果當時有用功唸書的話，考試早就及格了，代表當時沒這麼做，所以考試是不及格的。

> **1** 如果我是你／我不會去參加／那場會議。
>
> **2** 如果當時他唸書／再努力一些／他可能早就通過考試。

怪物講師的祕訣

常見假設法倒裝句型如下。

1 Were 主詞 + 補語, 主詞 + would [should, could, might] + 原形動詞

Did + 原形動詞, 主詞 + would [should, could, might] + 原形動詞

（如果…，就能…。假設法過去式倒裝句）

2 Had 主詞 + p.p., 主詞 + would [should, could, might] + have p.p.

（如果當時就…，早就…。假設法過去完成式的倒裝句）

3 Should 主詞 + 原形動詞 + 未來式

（如果…，我應該會…。假設法未來式的倒裝句）

Quiz

Q9 (Had / If) you met me earlier, you would have not wasted your precious time.

Q10 Please e-mail me directly (although / should) you have another problem.

▶ 解答在046頁

攻略法

31

省略if的慣用表現題型

前一頁有提到省略if的倒裝句型，接下來我們會介紹英文中省略if表現方式，下次看到這種句子，就不會再感到慌張。

假設法的表現中**省略if時**，**是假設法的慣用表現**，可以解釋為「假如沒有…」、「假如當時沒有…」，were it not for和 had it not been for就是屬於這種表現方式。這是假設法的必讀範圍，一定要好好的記住。在考試或是speaking、writing時，才能靈活運用。

1. were it not for... 假如沒有…

基本型是if it were not for，是假設法的過去式。這邊省略了if，將were移到最前面，成了were it not for的倒裝句型。有同樣意思的**but for**、**without**、**barring也一併背下來**。是假設法的過去式句型，所以主要子句裡要使用would [should, could, might] + 原形動詞。

1 **Were it not for** his wife, he **could not be** a mayor.

原本是If it were not for his wife, he could not be a mayor. 這邊省略了if，將were移到最前面，成了Were it not for的倒裝句型。**Were it not for也可以用以下單字取代But for、Without**。

2 **Were it not for** music, the world **would be** a dull place.

原本 If it were not for music, the world would be a dull place.這個句子，Were it not for 可以使用But for、Without來寫。

1 假如沒有／他的太太／他應該無法當上市長。

2 假如沒有／音樂／這世界會很單調。

怪物講師的祕訣

Were it not for...（假如沒有…）→ 假設法過去式，表示與現在事實相反

= If it were not for

= But for ⎱ + 名詞, 主詞 + would [should, could, might] + 原形動詞

= Without

Quiz

Q11 (Was / Were) it not for your help, I could not succeed.

Q12 Were it not for air and water, we (can / could) not live.

▶ 解答在046頁

2. had it not been for... 萬一沒有⋯

基本型是**if it had not been for**，可用更簡單的**but for**、**without**取代，值得一提的是**but for**、**without**可使用在假設法的過去式和過去完成式。所以也不必執著探討是過去式或過去完成式，只要注意「would [should, could, might] + 原形動詞」或是「would [should, could, might] + have p.p.」就行了。如果真的堅持要分辨假設法的過去式和過去完成式——雖然從未出過此種題型——**如果翻譯出來是現在的情況，那就是過去式；如果翻譯出來是過去式的情況，那就是過去完成式。**

1 **Had it not been for** your help, he **could not have finished** the project.

　省略了if，had放到句首成了倒裝句！

2 **Had it not been for her** devoted love, I **could not have overcome** the difficulties.

　原文為If it had not been for her devoted love, I could not have...

1 如果當時沒有／你的幫助／他無法完成／那個專題。

2 如果當時沒有／她全心全意的愛／我無法克服／那些逆境。

怪物講師的祕訣

Had it not been for... （假如當時沒有⋯）→ 假設法過去完成式，表示與過去事實相反

= If it had not been for

= But for

= Without

　　+ 名詞, 主詞 would [should, could, might] + have p.p.

Quiz

Q13 (Were it not / Had it not been) for your help, he could not have succeeded.

Q14 They could not have attracted more customers (had / has) it not been for the new strategy.

▶ 解答在046頁

攻略法 28　假設法的過去式和過去完成式

1 假設法過去式（假設與現在事實相反）

If 主詞 + 動詞過去式（或是were），主詞 + would [should、could、might] + 原形動詞

= 主詞 + would [should 、could、might] + 原形動詞 + if 主詞 + 動詞過去式（或是were）

2 過去完成式（假設過去事實相反）

If 主詞 + had p.p., 主詞 would [should, could, might] + have p.p.

= 主詞 + would [should, could, might] + have p.p. + if 主詞 + had p.p.

攻略法 29　假設法的現在式和未來式

1 假設法現在式（假設現在或是未來不確實的事）

If 主詞 + 現在式動詞（或現在完成式），主詞 + 未來式時態（或未來完成式）

= 主詞 + 動詞未來式時態（或未來完成式）if 主詞 + 現在式動詞（或現在完成式）

2 假設法未來式（假設現實的可能性很渺茫，或是未來也不可能會發生的事，如果不可能發生的，要視情況改寫時態）

If 主詞 + should（或是were to）+ 原形動詞, 主詞 + 未來式時態

= 主詞 + 未來式時態 + if 主詞 + should（或是were to）+ 原形動詞

攻略法 30　假設法的倒裝句型

Were 主詞 + 補語, 主詞 + would [should, could, might] + 原形動詞

－Did + 原形動詞, 主詞 + would [should, could, might] + 原形動詞

（如果…，就能…。假設法過去式倒裝句）

－Had 主詞 + p.p., 主詞 + would [should, could, might] + have p.p.

（如果當時就…，早就…。假設法過去完成式的倒裝句）

－Should 主詞 + 原形動詞 + 未來式

（如果…，我應該會…。假設法未來式的倒裝句）

攻略法 31　省略if的慣用表現題型

Were it not for + 名詞, 主詞 + would [should, could, might] + 原形動詞

（假如沒有…，應該就會…。假設法過去式，表與現在事實相反）

Had it not been for + 名詞, 主詞 + would [should, could, might] + have p.p.

（假如當時沒有…，應該早就…。假設法過去完成式，表與過去事實相反）

例子 **1** (A) be able
(B) are able
(C) is able
(D) were able

① 把握問題的類型

③ 空格中要填什麼詞類？

② 把握提示

Globalstar Enterprises requires that all employees _____ to take on the roles of other members in emergencies.

1 把握問題的類型

　文法問題

2 把握提示

　動詞require的特徵！

3 空格中要填什麼詞類？

　動詞

---

2 (A) should have
(B) can
(C) would
(D) will

If I were you, I _____ definitely think twice about going ahead with the new advertising campaign.

1 把握問題的類型

2 把握提示

3 空格中要填什麼詞類？

---

3 (A) can
(B) were
(C) are
(D) will

I wish we _____ able to get a clearer picture of what is happening to our Indonesian operation.

1 把握問題的類型

2 把握提示

3 空格中要填什麼詞類？

---

4 (A) to hold
(B) is held
(C) will hold
(D) be held

As the chairman of the shareholder's committee, I demand that someone _____ accountable for the catastrophic loss.

1 把握問題的類型

2 把握提示

3 空格中要填什麼詞類？

---

5 (A) will maintain
(B) maintaining
(C) maintains
(D) maintained

If it is possible, every company employee _____ detailed records of expenses while on business trips.

1 把握問題的類型

2 把握提示

3 空格中要填什麼詞類？

---

6 (A) are
(B) is
(C) was
(D) were

I wish it _____ possible for employees to use the company's holiday house in the mountains during the skiing season.

1 把握問題的類型

2 把握提示

3 空格中要填什麼詞類？

7 (A) were not
(B) had not been
(C) not being
(D) have not been

If it _____ for the heavy traffic in the downtown area, I would have taken my own car for both of us.

1 把握問題的類型

2 把握提示

3 空格中要填什麼詞類？

8 (A) will have
(B) would have
(C) to
(D) would

If I were to make a suggestion, I _____ say that he should hold off on making an offer until we know a little more.

1 把握問題的類型

2 把握提示

3 空格中要填什麼詞類？

9 (A) am
(B) was
(C) were
(D) be

In other words, I would be more aggressive when pursuing potential clients if I _____ in your position.

1 把握問題的類型

2 把握提示

3 空格中要填什麼詞類？

10 (A) If not
(B) But
(C) Beside
(D) Without

_____ American competitors, many Korean companies could have been a lot more successful in the North American market.

1 把握問題的類型

2 把握提示

3 空格中要填什麼詞類？

▶ 解答在047頁

101 If Matthew had left for Paris a day early, he _____ able to meet with our European clients before the seminar.

(A) could be
(B) will be
(C) could have been
(D) is

102 _____ the global financial crisis, our company could have earned a much larger profit last year.

(A) If
(B) Were it not for
(C) Had it not been for
(D) It has not been for

高難度

103 _____ Jonathan not left the company last year, he would have been able to take over my duties.

(A) Were
(B) Had
(C) Did
(D) If

104 If the marketing team _____ able to spend more money on the advertising campaign, we could reach more customers.

(A) was
(B) are
(C) had been
(D) were

重要

105 If it were not for our dedicated domestic management team, we _____ not be able to handle so many local client firms at once.

(A) will
(B) would
(C) were
(D) are

106 While it would be good if Jose were able to be here, I do not think it's absolutely essential that he _____ included in this teleconference.

(A) was
(B) be
(C) is
(D) were

107 If we were to increase the department's operating budget for next year, we _____ see an improvement in staff morale.

(A) would have
(B) will
(C) would
(D) are

108 If we _____ to begin the project immediately, we would be able to provide the client firm with updates on our progress.

(A) are
(B) will
(C) is
(D) were

109 _____ all the government red tape, Innova Technology's new manufacturing plant would be operating by now.

(A) If not for
(B) In spite of
(C) As for
(D) Because of

110 If I _____ managed to complete the in-house training course, I would have received a promotion.

(A) had been
(B) have
(C) had
(D) having

111 If the conference on genetic engineering
_____ held in America, I would be
able to attend it with my colleagues.

(A) was
(B) were
(C) is
(D) are

重要
112 Had you _____ here a few years
ago when the restructuring began, you
would have thought of quitting.

(A) work
(B) working
(C) worked
(D) been worked

113 _____ for the assistance of federal
government, the county which was hit by
the hurricane could not have recovered
from the disaster.

(A) Yet
(B) But
(C) Nor
(D) Without

114 _____ you find any difficulty
operating this facility, our trainer will be
with you shortly or your money back.

(A) Should
(B) Did
(C) Because
(D) Had

115 Under the reinforced safety measures,
it is imperative that each employee
_____ a photo ID to security
guards.

(A) show
(B) shows
(C) showing
(D) is shown

116 More people would have attended the job
fair _____ they had a better idea
of what we are doing.

(A) unless
(B) had
(C) if
(D) having

117 Had _____ not been for the
approval from the upper management, we
would not have succeeded in closing the
contract.

(A) we
(B) there
(C) it
(D) gotten

118 The inspector urgently requested that
the account book _____, so an
emergency team was called last week.

(A) analyze
(B) was analyzed
(C) analyzes
(D) be analyzed

119 If they had not allowed us to reserve the
seats in advance, we _____ in
spending our vacation comfortably and
freely.

(A) would not succeed
(B) would not have succeeded
(C) had not succeeded
(D) could not succeeded

高難度
120 Did a company _____ from losses
due to the lack of investment, it should
prepare enough capital to be prepared for
the next time.

(A) suffer
(B) suffering
(C) suffers
(D) be suffered

▶ 解答在049頁

Questions 121-124 refer to the following article.

Generally, if someone merely mentions passengers and pedestrians, it appears that there's nothing _____. However, if we look closely, some similarities will come out. For one thing, both passengers and pedestrians need to follow certain traffic regulations. If any one of them _____ the traffic regulations, it will be a big problem and may lead to dire accidents. In some cases, government properties may be damaged or precious lives may be claimed. Moreover, there is some etiquette that needs to be followed _____ both passengers and pedestrians. For instance, if you always speak loudly on the cell phone when you're walking or taking public transportation, it may upset others. Ultimately, both passengers and pedestrians are required to cooperate with each other in order to ensure traffic is smooth. _____, it's likely to cause inconvenience to the pedestrians when they want to pass by or cross the street. In brief, passengers and pedestrians seem to be very different, but actually there are a few similarities if we think about it.

121 (A) on common
(B) at common
(C) to common
(D) in common

122 (A) will disobey
(B) disobeyed
(C) disobeys
(D) had disobey

123 (A) for
(B) by
(C) to
(D) from

124 (A) If the passengers of taxis or buses were desperate to get out of these vehicles wherever they want
(B) If the passengers of taxis or buses had been desperate to get out of these vehicles wherever they want
(C) If the passengers of taxis or buses are desperate to get out of these vehicles wherever they want
(D) If the passengers of taxis or buses is desperate to get out of these vehicles wherever they want

Part 03
動詞完全公開！

動名詞
是動詞、也是名詞的動名詞解題法！

Review Test

在稍早我們學過了假設法，只要知道基本規則就很簡單吧！
我們來複習一下學過的內容吧。

1 if子句中「if + 主詞 + had p.p.」時，主要子句是？

▶ _____

2 if子句中「if + 主詞 + 動詞過去式（或were）」時，主要子句是？

▶ _____

3 if子句中「if + 主詞 + 動詞現在式」時，主要子句是？

▶ _____

4 if子句中「if + 主詞 + should」時，主要子句是？

▶ _____

5 Had、Were、Should出現在句子最前面是何種句型？

▶ _____

Preview

1 動名詞的特徵

舉中文中的動詞「吃」為例，想在句子中當主詞使用時，就要變成「吃的東西」或是「吃這件事」。英文中的eat無法直接當作主詞，需要變換成eating。**想把動詞當作名詞使用時，在原形動詞加上-ing就成為動名詞了。**動名詞本身是從動詞轉換而來，保有動詞原有的性格，這也叫作「動詞性質維持現象」，這時就不是動詞，它是個名詞。也叫作「詞性變形現象」。這兩個是本單元的中心主題，請務必要記住。

2 動名詞的解題法

❶ 動詞要寫在主詞、受詞和補語時，要填動名詞。

❷ 動名詞和動詞一樣，後面需另有受詞、補語，這可別忘了。因為它依舊保有動詞的性格。

[正確答案] 1. 主詞 + would [should、could、might] + have p.p.（假設法過去完成式） 2. 主詞 + would [should、could、might] + 原形動詞（假設法過去式）3. 主詞 + 未來式（假設法現在式）4. 主詞 + 未來式 if + 主詞 + should + 原形動詞（假設法未來式） 5. 省略 if 的倒裝句型。

攻略法

32 動名詞的「動詞性質維持現象」

動名詞是原形動詞加上了-ing形成，特徵是在句中名詞相同，卻又保留著動詞本身的性格，
這又叫做「動詞性質維持現象」。

動名詞是動詞單字本身直接轉換為名詞，因此仍然保持動詞的性格。這
是什麼意思呢？一起來看看下面的動名詞5大特徵，更了解什麼是動名
詞。

1. 動名詞有含義上的主詞

英文的句子中，動詞的前面是主詞，**具有動詞性質的動名詞前面也是會
有主詞，這時叫作「含義上的主詞」。如果說動名詞前面要加些什麼的
話，常出現的是「所有格 + 主詞」的型態。**（動名詞前也會放受格，但
這種情況非常稀少。）下面例句中的括弧內應該要填入什麼字呢？請試
著作答。

(He / His) staying there was not expected at all.

> 他留在那裡這件事／完全沒
> 有被預想到。

只要有看出動名詞staying只是需要有個涵意上的主詞，那就可以解題
了。這句話的意思是他從未想過會在那邊留下，留下的主題是「他」，
所以要使用所有格His，答案就是His。

2. 動名詞有受詞和補語

動詞後面大部分都有受詞和補語，**具有動詞性質的動名詞也可能會有受
詞和補語。這時是要接受詞、還是要接補語，會依據轉變成-ing型態的
動詞及形式動詞而有所不同。**想要徹底了解的話，必須要將Chapter 03
的5大句型了解透徹。

I am ashamed of his **being (lazy / laziness)**.

> 我感到羞愧／為了他很懶這
> 件事。

雖然一直在強調，還是要再說一次這不能用翻譯的方式解題。句中的
being是第2大句型動詞be的動名詞型，所以後面的形容詞當作補語。所
以括弧內的答案是形容詞lazy。舉例來說，在說「他很懶」時，是使用

形容詞寫作He is lazy.，不會寫名詞laziness。這例句就是動名詞的「動詞性質維持現象」。

3. 動名詞有主動和被動機能

動詞有在主動型和被動型，具有動詞性格的動名詞也可轉換成主動型和被動型使用。主動型和被動型的區分**原則是-ing後面有受詞的話，就直接使用-ing；如果後面沒有受詞的話，須轉換成being p.p.使用。**第1、2大句型沒有受詞，無法使用被動句型，只要使用-ing即可。請試著作答。

He was on the verge of (**submitting / being submitted**) **the report**.

他幾乎快要交／報告。

這是動名詞的主動、被動的題型，有看到後面有受詞report吧？這題是屬於主動的題型，所以答案是主動型的submitting，順帶一提on the verge of是「接近於…」的意思。

4. 動名詞也有時態

動詞有時態，具有動詞性格的動名詞也有時態。動名詞的時態和句子的主要時態一致的話，使用最簡單的-ing動名詞即可。不過**動名詞的時態若比句子的主要時態更早時，則要使用動名詞完成式having p.p.**。一起來看下面題目。

He **is** proud of (**being / having been**) rich **in the past**.

他驕傲／曾經富有／在過去。

句子的時態是is現在式，不過因為有副詞in the past（在過去），所以動名詞要使用比現在還要早一個階段的過去式。「他驕傲」是現在式，「曾經富有」是過去式。所以括弧內是動名詞完成式having p.p.。

5. 動名詞被副詞修飾

副詞修飾動詞，具有動詞性格的動名詞也會被副詞修飾。一定要牢牢記住，它叫做動名詞，動名詞是被副詞所修飾。這又再度證明了「動詞性質維持現象」這句話。

I am considering **ordering** the mentioned items (**quick / quickly**).

我正在考慮／要下訂／曾經提到的物品／儘快。

副詞quickly修飾前面的動名詞ordering。像這種副詞修飾動名詞的句型一般都是「動詞＋-ing（受詞補語）＋副詞」。本句中的am considering是現在式，「正在考慮中」的現在進行式；動詞consider後面的動名詞是動詞當作受詞使用，所以使用ordering動名詞狀態。

怪物講師的祕訣

1 -ing前面是空格的話，請填適當的所有格當作含義上的主詞。

2 -ing後面是空格的話，分辨動名詞本身的動詞是屬於第幾大句型的動詞，再填入受詞或補語。

3 其他主動、被動、時態等也需要確認。再提醒，修飾動名詞的是副詞！

Quiz

Q1 We look forward to meeting (your / you) sooner or later.

Q2 Do you mind (my / I) opening the door?

▶ 解答在053頁

攻略法 **33**

動名詞的「詞性變化現象」

不知道各位是否了解這一部分，但是大概知道跟透徹了解是不一樣的。希望大家趁這個機會了解動名詞的「詞性變形象」。

動名詞是原形動詞加上了-ing所形成的，詞性改變了，當然就是「詞性變化現象」。**動名詞在句子中扮演著主詞、受詞、補語等角色，且還具備了動詞的特性，所以後面也會出現受詞或補語。**

首先要知道如何區分現在分詞和動名詞。現在分詞和動名詞形態長得一樣，都是原形動詞後面接-ing。那該怎麼區分呢？**動名詞是名詞，所以可以在句子中扮演著主詞、受詞、補語等角色；現在分詞是用來修飾名詞，在句中扮演著形容詞的角色。**我們來看看下面的例句。

1 **Singing** a song is fun.

　　動名詞 → 名詞 → 主詞、受詞、補語（解釋為「做的…」、「做的事…」）

2 A **singing** man is Tommy.

　　現在分詞 → 形容詞 → 修飾名詞（解釋為「正在做…」）

1 唱歌／很有趣。

2 正在唱歌中的男生／是湯米。

1. 動詞當主詞時

想把動詞當作主詞使用時，在原形動詞後接-ing變成動名詞即可。但不要忘了，因為它具有「動詞性質維持現象」，所以後面還要放受詞或補語。被當作主詞使用的動名詞也可以用to不定詞替代。

1 **Knowing** oneself is difficult.（動名詞）

　= **To know** oneself is difficult.（to不定詞）

2 **Taking** pictures is prohibited here.（動名詞）

　= **To take** pictures is prohibited here.（to不定詞）

1 了解自己／很困難。

2 照相／被禁止／在這裡。

✎ Quiz

Q3 (Notifying / Notification) them of the result was to the point.

▶ 解答在053頁

2. 動詞當受詞時

想把動詞當作受詞使用時，在原形動詞後接-ing變成動名詞即可。因為它具有「動詞性質維持現象」，所以後面還要放受詞或補語。但記得，並不是所有的動詞後面接-ing就會成為受詞。

(1) 可當作受詞使用的動詞

需要受詞的及物動詞中，**只有某些動詞可接上-ing當受詞**。這樣的及物**動詞叫作「MEGAPAS ID動詞」**。「MEGAPAS ID動詞」須接-ing的單字當受詞，但不接受to不定詞當受詞。「MEGAPAS ID動詞」如下。**可利用「MEGAPAS的服務要一直持續（-ing）下去」的口訣記憶。**

M mind 在意
E enjoy 享受
G give up 放棄
A avoid 避開、advocate 支持
P put off = postpone 延期、finish 結束
A admit 承認
S stop 停止、suggest = recommend 提議、consider 考慮
I include 包含
D discontinue 中斷

上述的動詞加了-ing就有受詞的意思，是主動詞；如果是上述以外的動詞加-ing，不一定會有受詞，也要思考是否為被動詞。可試著直接翻譯出來會更確實了解句意。

1 I want to **finish editing** this report by the end of this week.
   MEGAPAS ID中的finish後面有出現動名詞editing！

2 He **considered hiring** all of them.
   MEGAPAS ID中的consider後面有出現動名詞hiring！

1 我希望／結束／這份報告的編輯／在這週末之前。

2 他考慮／雇用／他們全部。

✏ Quiz ....

Q4 They intended to discontinue (producing / to produce) the old model.

▶ 解答在053頁

(2) 動名詞被當作介系詞的受詞

動名詞也是名詞的一種，前面可以接介系詞，所以又被稱作介系詞的受詞。接下來講解考題常出的「介系詞＋-ing」，此種用法須牢牢記住。

by -ing 以⋯的手段、on -ing 一⋯就⋯（＝ upon -ing）、without -ing（不做⋯）、besides -ing 不只是⋯；除了⋯之外還⋯（in addition to）。

3. 動詞當補語時

動詞當補語使用時，原形動詞後加-ing。-ing也當作動名詞使用，或當作現在分詞用於現在進行式。**當作動名詞時解釋為「⋯的事」，與主詞同格關係；當作現在分詞使用，表現現在進行式或是形容詞時解釋為「正在⋯中」。**一起來看看動名詞現在分詞的差別在哪邊吧！

1 The purpose is **making** a contract for mutual benefits. 動名詞（補語）

2 They are **making** a contract for mutual benefits. 現在分詞（現在進行式）

3 A **rolling** stone gathers no moss. 現在分詞（形容詞）

> 1 目的是簽約／為了互惠利益。
>
> 2 他們正在／簽約／為了互惠利益。
>
> 3 滾動的石頭／不會聚集／青苔。

有看到例句1和2的原形動詞make後面加上-ing嗎？例句1「目的是簽約」比「目的是正在簽約中」更順暢吧。making是動名詞，當作名詞「做⋯的（這件事）」的意思，當作補語使用。但是例句2是「他們正在簽約中」比「他們是簽約」更像個合理的句子，所以現在進行式須用現在分詞構成。那麼例句3呢？這句的rolling的-ing型態是「滾動的」的意思，用來修飾後面的名詞stone，是現在分詞。若是翻譯成「正在⋯中」就是現在分詞。請一定要記住喔！

怪物講師的祕訣

1 句中若要把動詞當作主詞、受詞、或補語使用，使用動名詞（-ing）。

2 千萬別忘了！根據動詞的形式，後面要接受詞或補語。

3 動名詞有「做⋯的（這件事）」的意思，可當作主詞、受詞、或補語；現在分詞是「正在⋯中的」代表現在進行式，用來修飾名詞。

4 動名詞用來當補語使用時，可與to不定詞交替使用。
Seeing is believing.（百聞不如一見）
= To see is to believe.

5 現在分詞用to不定詞表現會變成另一種意思。
The store is having a sale.（那間店正在特價。）
≠The store is to have a sale.（那間店即將要特價。）

攻略法
34
名詞和動名詞之間選個答案

你應該有碰過名詞和動名詞同樣都是名詞，但很難區分的問題吧。多益考試中，這樣的問題很常出現。

1. 含義不同時，先解讀意思後選出合適的答案

如果名詞和動名詞的含義不一樣時，當然要選出符合句子意思的選項。

1 We are **in the (process / processing) of hiring** employees.

雇用職員的「階段中」的意思，process是正解。在背誦時，要in the process of -ing（正在…的階段中的）整段一起背。

2 The **(process / processing) of your order** needs some time.

解釋為「處理訂單（這件事）」比較通順，processing是正解。processing當作名詞時有「過程；階段」的意思。

1 我們在階段中／雇用職員的。

2 處理／你的訂單／需要／一些時間。

2. 含義都差不多時

如果填入名詞或動名詞後，意思差不多時，**請注意後面有沒有受詞。後面有受詞的話，就搭配動名詞；沒有受詞的話，就搭配名詞。**

1 **(Discussion / Discussing) is** needed to resolve conflicts.

不論是名詞或動名詞，意思好像都差不多呢！不過仔細一看，後面沒有受詞，直接就接動詞is吧？動名詞discussing需要接名詞，所以這題要選擇名詞discussion。

2 We object to **(discussion / discussing) the matter** in front of others.

看到後面的受詞the matter了吧，所以動名詞discussing是正確答案。

1 需要討論／解決矛盾。

2 我們反對／討論／那個問題／在別人面前。

5秒 解決名詞和動名詞區分題的方法

1 如果詞義明確有不同時，就利用平時所知道的詞義解題。

2 如果詞義幾乎差不多時，如果後面有受詞或補語，答案就是動名詞；沒有的話，請選名詞為解答。

Quiz

Q5 We are so glad that we have received many qualified (applicants / applying) for this job.

Q6 The (reporting / report) was well written and will be accepted.

▶ 解答在053頁

攻略法 35 動名詞的慣用片語整理

英語系國家的人已經有固定習慣使用的動名詞句型表現。這些表現我們在平時就要整組記憶，有利提升英文能力。

有動名詞的慣用片語主要分成三大類。比起沒系統地亂背一通，建議還是細部分類後再記憶，比較有效率。

1. 「to + -ing」形的慣用片語

在to後面很常加上原形動詞變成to不定詞，因此如果不記得下面的慣用片語，在考試中，很容易因為選擇動詞原形而答錯。因此，請謹記以下「to + -ing的內容」。

• object to -ing	反對…
• look forward to -ing	引頸期盼…
• be [get, become] accustomed to -ing	習慣（熟悉）做…
• be dedicated [devoted, committed] to -ing	埋首於做…

1 We **object to hiring** any more employees.

2 They **were used to receiving** complaints from customers.

> 1 我們反對／雇用／更多員工。
>
> 2 他們習慣／接收抱怨／從客戶。

2. 「介系詞 + -ing」形的慣用片語

看看下面的慣用片語吧！和介系詞一起出現時，後面不論出現名詞，或是動名詞一點也都不奇怪吧？不過問題來了，**很多時候，片語會把介系詞省略，但即使如此，還是要當作介系詞存在，後面必須接-ing形式的動名詞。**

• keep (on) -ing	繼續做…
• be busy (in) -ing	忙於做…
• have a hard time (in) -ing	因為做…經歷了艱困的時期
(= have difficulty (in) -ing)	
• spend 時間／錢 (on, in) -ing	花時間／錢做…
* succeed in	成功於…（此狀況不省略in）

1 He **was busy preparing** for an important presentation.

be busy -ing要整組背下來！

2 We must **spend** more money **building** homes for the poor.

spend 時間／錢 (in) -ing要整組背下來！

1 他很忙／因為準備／重要的
發表會。

2 我們必須／花更多的錢／蓋
房子／為窮人們。

3. 你不能不知道的慣用片語

如果不背好下面的慣用片語，會很難去判斷要寫動詞原形，還是to不定
詞。

• cannot help -ing	不得不…
• feel like -ing	想要…
• be worth -ing	有…的價值
• come close to -ing	差一點就做某事…
• go -ing	去做…
• there is no -ing	無法…
• it is no use -ing	再…也沒有用
• it goes without saying that ...	不必再多説…

1 I **cannot help cleaning** this room.

2 We are planning to **go fishing** this weekend.

1 我不得不打掃／這房間。

2 我們正在計畫／去釣魚／在
這週末。

怪物講師的祕訣

1 如果出現look forward to -ing這種整組片語時，to後面接名詞或是動名詞。而一般to後面
會接原形動詞。

2 如果遇到像be busy (in) -ing這種省略介系詞的片語，如果平時沒有準備的話，很難會寫
對答案。

3 go -ing這類的片語，得靠平常多看多背，這樣實際在考場上才不會被考倒。

Quiz

Q7 He is now used to (cooking / cook) meat products.
Q8 This knife must only be used to (cutting / cut) meat.

▶ 解答在053頁

攻略法 32	動名詞的「動詞性質維持現象」

1 動名詞有含義上的主詞。（所有格 -ing）

2 動名詞和動詞一樣有受詞和補語。

3 動名詞有和動詞一樣主動和被動機能。

4 動名詞也有時態區分。

5 動名詞和動詞一樣被副詞修飾。

攻略法 33	動名詞的「詞性變化現象」

1 動名詞在句中當主詞。（做…的）

2 動名詞在句中也可當受詞。（MEGAPAS ID！）

3 動名詞在句中也可當介系詞的受詞。（介系詞 -ing）

4 動名詞在句中也可當補語。（be動詞 -ing）

攻略法 34	名詞和動名詞之間選個答案

1 含義不同時，先解讀意思後選出合適的答案。

2 含義都差不多時，試著找出受詞。

攻略法 35	動名詞的慣用片語整裡

1 「**to + -ing**」形的慣用片語

object to -ing 反對…（＝ be opposed to -ing）、look forward to -ing 引頸企盼…、be [get, become] accustomed to -ing 習慣（熟悉）做…（used to -ing）、be dedicated [devote、committed] to -ing 埋首於做…

2 「**介系詞 + -ing**」形的慣用片語

keep (on) -ing 繼續做…、be busy (in) -ing 忙於做…、have a hard time (in) -ing 因為做…經歷了艱困的時期、spend 時間／錢(on, in) -ing 花時間（錢）做…

3 其他你不能不知道的慣用片語

cannot help -ing 不得不…、feel like -ing 想要…、be worth -ing 有…的價值、come close to -ing 差一點就做某事…、go -ing 去做…、there is no -ing 無法…、it is no use -ing 再…也沒有用

例子

1　(A) Recognized
　　(B) Recognizing
　　(C) Recognition
　　(D) Being recognized

① 把握問題的類型

③ 空格中要填什麼詞類？

_____ talented employees has been shown to improve productivity of the entire office.

② 把握提示

1 把握問題的類型
　文法題

2 把握提示
　動詞和數的一致

3 空格中要填什麼詞類？
　動名詞

2　(A) celebrate
　　(B) celebratory
　　(C) celebrations
　　(D) celebrating

Each year, the office staff look forward to _____ the new year with a festive office party.

1 把握問題的類型

2 把握提示

3 空格中要填什麼詞類？

3　(A) looking at
　　(B) taking
　　(C) marking
　　(D) listening to

One of the keys to academic success is _____ careful notes during all the lectures.

1 把握問題的類型

2 把握提示

3 空格中要填什麼詞類？

4　(A) foundation
　　(B) found
　　(C) finding
　　(D) to finding

A common news topic in many countries today is _____ ways to reduce government spending.

1 把握問題的類型

2 把握提示

3 空格中要填什麼詞類？

5　(A) to search
　　(B) search
　　(C) being searched
　　(D) searching

Victims of Hurricane Hugo gave up _____ for a dry place to stay after the storm passed.

1 把握問題的類型

2 把握提示

3 空格中要填什麼詞類？

6　(A) learning
　　(B) learn
　　(C) learns
　　(D) learned

New employees are encouraged to spend enough time ＿＿＿＿＿＿ the company's latest products.

1 把握問題的類型

2 把握提示

3 空格中要填什麼詞類？

7　(A) submitting
　　(B) submission
　　(C) submitted
　　(D) being submitted

Please be advised that ＿＿＿＿＿＿ a payment after the due date will result in a heavy late fee.

1 把握問題的類型

2 把握提示

3 空格中要填什麼詞類？

8　(A) exercisable
　　(B) to exercise
　　(C) exercising
　　(D) exercised

I should make it certain that our people enjoy ＿＿＿＿＿＿ to release stress after a long tiring week.

1 把握問題的類型

2 把握提示

3 空格中要填什麼詞類？

9　(A) I
　　(B) Mine
　　(C) Myself
　　(D) My

＿＿＿＿＿＿ expecting delays during the busy holiday season seemed to be so reasonable at that time.

1 把握問題的類型

2 把握提示

3 空格中要填什麼詞類？

10　(A) refuse
　　(B) object
　　(C) stop
　　(D) mind

In order to ＿＿＿＿＿＿ receiving these notices, please contact our customer service department.

1 把握問題的類型

2 把握提示

3 空格中要填什麼詞類？

▶ 解答在053頁

101 Representative Dickens gave a speech today about _____ corporate taxes and won general applause.

(A) reduces
(B) reducing
(C) reduction
(D) being reduced

102 Frequent airline passengers are used to _____ their flight schedules during periods of extreme weather.

(A) changing
(B) change
(C) being changed
(D) have changed

103 Increased sales of the new smart phone are linked with the decreasing cost of _____ a service subscription.

(A) established
(B) being established
(C) establishing
(D) establishment

104 Philanthropist Miguel Carrera appreciated the mayor's _____ his efforts to harmonize with everyone at all levels.

(A) acknowledgement
(B) acknowledged
(C) being acknowledged
(D) acknowledging

105 _____ responding to the customers' needs is essential until our revenues increase.

(A) Actively
(B) Act
(C) Active
(D) Action

106 The tour guide apologized to the museum visitors for _____ them to wait for the tour to begin.

(A) to cause
(B) causing
(C) being caused
(D) cause

107 The store manager decided that _____ the store open an extra hour on Friday nights would increase sales by ten percent.

(A) kept
(B) having kept
(C) keeping
(D) being kept

108 After he retired from sports, Frank is committed _____ motivational speeches around the country.

(A) delivering
(B) to delivering
(C) to deliver
(D) delivery

109 Most doctors recommend _____ at least eight hours a night to maintain a strong immune system.

(A) slept
(B) sleepy
(C) to sleep
(D) sleeping

重要
110 Our company earns strong customer loyalty by _____ the durability of all our products even after a warranty expires.

(A) to guarantee
(B) guaranteeing
(C) guarantee
(D) being guaranteed

111 Juanita stayed up late with the aim of _____ the international conference to be held in the next morning.

(A) preparing for
(B) preparation
(C) preparatory
(D) prepared

高難度
112 As the manager of a large team, Teresa is quite busy _____ extensive training sessions.

(A) conductivity
(B) conducts
(C) to conduct
(D) conducting

高難度
113 Thank you for _____ the contract with our company for additional 3 years as an exclusive agency in this region.

(A) renew
(B) renewal
(C) renewing
(D) renewed

114 We have the right to approve contracts less than $10,000, but in case of more than $10,000, it is subject to our executive's final _____.

(A) approve
(B) approving
(C) approval
(D) approved

115 The mechanic didn't mention beforehand that _____ the battery for my laptop takes more than half a day.

(A) recharges
(B) recharging
(C) recharged
(D) recharge

116 The newly elected executive is considering making her subordinates _____ by allowing them to have more time for themselves.

(A) satisfied
(B) satisfaction
(C) satisfying
(D) satisfy

117 A tax reduction is being considered _____ small to medium-sized companies.

(A) to benefit
(B) benefitting
(C) beneficial
(D) benefits

118 We need to reorganize our profit structure to make more money by _____ new lucrative business projects.

(A) add
(B) added
(C) to add
(D) adding

119 The software company, which was founded in 1990, enabled users to enjoy _____ the Internet freely and comfortably.

(A) using
(B) used
(C) user
(D) use

重要
120 Most of the employees _____ to working overtime throughout the week to meet the tight deadline.

(A) want
(B) object
(C) refuse
(D) promise

Questions 121-124 refer to the following letter.

Dear Mr. Wyllie,

Sincere greetings from Ares International Co. Ltd. In regard to our appointment, we _____ at World Trade Center at 14:00 PM on June 27th to further discuss
    121
our cooperation in emerging markets. However, I regret to inform you that I have to

_____ our meeting owing to the approaching exhibition. My sincere apologies for any
    122
inconvenience. I wonder if it would be convenient for you to set up the meeting _____
                                                                                    123
anytime on June 30th. I will send you the agenda of the meeting by the end of this week,

so if you have any further concerns, please don't hesitate to contact me at my e-mail

address or my cell number. _____
                              124

Best Regards,

Edward Alison

Project Manager of the Overseas Department

Ares International Co. Ltd.

121 (A) will meet
   (B) are going to meet
   (C) meet
   (D) are meeting

122 (A) postpone
   (B) delay
   (C) cancel
   (D) change

123 (A) in
   (B) on
   (C) at
   (D) of

124 (A) I look forward to having a dinner with you.
   (B) I look forward to receiving your confirmation.
   (C) I look forward to having a conversation.
   (D) I look forward to attending the convention.

▶ 解答在055頁

Chapter 09 | to不定詞
一起來解決常常搞混的to不定詞！

Review Test

在Chapter 08學到了動名詞，動名詞的根本是動詞。在原形動詞加上-ing，在句中被當作很重要的角色，那麼我們要不要來複習一下在Chapter 08所學到的內容？

1 什麼是動名詞？　　　　　　　　　　▶ ....

2 動名詞在句子中具有什麼樣的作用而被使用？ ▶ ....

3 如果動詞要當作主詞使用的話？　　　▶ ....

4 如果動詞當作受詞使用的話？　　　　▶ ....

5 與MEGAPAS ID對應的動詞有？　　　▶ ....

6 如果把動詞放在介系詞後面使用的話？ ▶ ....

7 如果動詞當作補語使用的話？　　　　▶ ....

8 現在分詞在句子中修飾什麼？　　　　▶ ....

Preview

1　to不定詞的特徵

　　沒有辦法讓動詞當作名詞、形容詞、副詞來使用嗎？這個時候就出現了to不定詞，只要熟記to不定詞的話，就可以自由地運用動詞，真的很方便。另外to不定詞有兩個很重要的特徵。

　　❶ 維持動詞性質現象：to不定詞也跟動名詞一樣，起源是來自於動詞，因此與動名詞一樣維持動詞的性質。

　　❷ 詞性變換現象：雖然動名詞在句子中扮演名詞的角色，但是to不定詞在句子中不僅扮演名詞的角色，也扮演形容詞、副詞。

2　to不定詞問題的解法

　　to不定詞與動名詞一樣，具有「維持動詞性質現象」以及「詞性變化現象」，但還是有些微的差異，因此正確了解to不定詞與動名詞的共通點、相異點非常重要。

[正確答案]　1. 在原形動詞加上-ing，被當作名詞使用　2. 主詞、受詞、補語　3. 製作動名詞　4. 前面的動詞一定是「MEGAPAS ID」動詞　5.mind, enjoy, give up, avoid, advocate, put off, postpone, finish, admit, stop, suggest, recommend, consider, include, discontinue　6. 以-ing的形式（要區分現在分詞與動名詞）7. 寫動名詞，此時的動名詞具有與主詞同格的關係　8. 名詞

to不定詞的「維持動詞性質現象」

to不定詞具有維持其原始來源——動詞性質的特徵，這就叫做to不定詞的「維持動詞性質現象」。好像在那裡聽過吧？當然！在前面的動名詞章節中就已經出現過了。

由動詞變形的to不定詞仍舊維持動詞的性質，這點與動名詞非常相似，to不定詞具有主詞的含義，受詞或是補語、主動、被動、接受副詞的修飾等，維持動詞的性質的功用。

1. 在to不定詞中也有主詞的含義

動名詞如果有主詞的含義時，前面要寫上所有格吧？**to不定詞如果有主詞的含義時，就要寫上「for + 受格」**。另外在表達人感情的形容詞，要寫「of + 受格」，但在多益考試中，從來沒有出現使用這種介系詞of的問題。

好，我們現在直接來解下面的題目，感受一下考試的感覺吧。

1 It's a way (**for** / with) **a man to express** his anger.

在這個句子中表達憤怒的主體是a man，這就叫做有主詞含義的to不定詞。由上可知，受格名詞a man前面要加上介系詞for。

> **1** 那是一個方法／讓男人／表現自己憤怒。

2 It is possible **for** (**him** / his) **to submit** the report on time.

這是在問to submit的含義上主詞是什麼，這種情況，在介系詞for的後面加上受格就可以了，因此括號要填入的答案就是him。

> **2** 有可能／他提交／報告／按時。

2. to不定詞也有受詞或是補語

與動名詞的狀況相同，**被to不定詞所使用的動詞，要看它是第幾大句型動詞之後，再看後面要加上受詞或是補語**。這應該比要把在Chapter 03中所學的內容都背起來容易吧，我們直接來解決2個問題吧。

1 **To become** (**successful** / success) is his only wish.

> **1** 變得成功／是他唯一的希望。

在to不定詞中使用的become是第2大句型的動詞，因此後面需要加上形容詞補語，括號內的答案要填入successful。

2 Arriving (late / lately) will cause a serious problem.

2 遲到／會引起／嚴重的問題。

當作主詞使用的arriving是動名詞，動名詞arrive是第1大句型動詞，所以後面不需要有受詞或是補語，而是需要加上副詞。但late和lately都具有副詞的功能，再仔細解析的話，晚（late）到比起最近（lately）到的意思更符合句子的意思，因此括號內所要填入的答案就是late。

3. to不定詞也有主動與被動

如果在to不定詞中，使用的動詞是第2大句型的動詞，句子後面就需要形容詞補語，如果是第3、4、5大句型動詞，句子後面就需要受詞。萬一沒有受詞呢？這樣的狀況當然就是被動式了，所以要用to be p.p.來表示。來，繼續解下面的題目吧。

1 To love somebody is bitter but **to (love / be loved)** is sweet.

1 愛某個人／很痛苦／但／被愛／甜蜜的。

括號後面沒有受詞，所以是被動式，因此to不定詞的被動式to be loved就是正確答案，請與最前面的to love比較看看，在它後面是否有接受詞somebody？

2 To build (a house / for a house) will take about two months.

2 蓋房子／需要／2個月左右的時間。

在to build中build是第3大句型動詞，後面要有受詞，因此名詞a house就是正確答案。如果是to be built被動型態，就不需要受詞，那介系詞子句for a house是正確答案的可能性就增加了。

4. to不定詞也有時態

這個情況也與動名詞類似，**to不定詞的時態與句子中的主要時態一致時，寫上不定詞（to + 原形動詞）就可以，如果是表達比主要時態更早、更前面的結果時，就要寫上完成不定詞（to have p.p.）。**

請看下面兩個例句，同時想一想要填入括號內的答案是什麼。

1 She seemed (to be / to have been) tired when I **met** her yesterday.

1 她看起來／好像很累／我昨天跟她見面時。

我與她見面和她看起來很累的時態是一致的，在這種情況寫上不定詞就可以。因此填入括號內最適合的答案就是to be。那再來看下一道題目吧。

2 She **seems (to be / to have been)** rich when she **was** young.

2 她看起來／好像曾經很有錢／在她小時候。

她看起來的是現在（seems），曾經是有錢人是在她小的時候，也就是過去的事情，兩個時態是不同的，在這種情況就要寫完成不定詞，因此填入括號內最適合的答案就是to have been。

5. to不定詞也可以得到副詞的修飾

就像具有動詞性質的動名詞會得到副詞的修飾，to不定詞也可以得到副詞的修飾。如同在Chapter 01中所學到的，此時副詞要擺在to不定詞的前面或後面，或是擺在受詞補語的後面

1 **To check** it **(thorough / thoroughly)**, we need your permission.

1 為了確認那個／徹底地／我們需要／你的許可。

to check後面是受詞it，因此句子是完整的。由上可知，在後面會出現的修飾副詞就是thoroughly，那最適合填入下面例句括號內的答案是什麼呢？

2 I decided **(not / none) to go** with you this time.

2 我決定了／不和你去／這次。

有說過to不定詞是被副詞修飾吧，not是副詞，而none是名詞，不能填入括號內。所以可以填入括號內的答案就是not。

> **怪物講師的祕訣**
>
> **1** to不定詞前面如果是空格的話，就要直覺想到「for + 受格」。
> **2** to不定詞後面如果是空格的話，先看不定詞的動詞是第幾大句型的動詞之後，再看要寫受詞或是補語。
> **3** 除此之外，還要再確認主動、被動、時態，另外可用副詞來修飾不定詞。

動名詞與to不定詞有很多相似點，但是也有一些相異點，如果把動名詞與to不定詞的「維持動詞性質現象」做比較的話，請看下表。

	動名詞	to不定詞
主詞的含義	（所有格）+ -ing	（for + 受格）+ to不定詞
需要受詞／補語	-ing to 不定詞	to不定詞 + 受詞／補語
可以是主動／被動	及物動詞-ing + 有受詞 being p.p. + 沒有受詞	to不定詞 + 有受詞 to be p.p. + 沒有受詞
可以表現時態	-ing（單純動名詞） ＊與主要時態一致 having p.p.（完成動名詞） ＊比主要時態更早的過去	to不定詞（單純不定詞） ＊與主要時態一致 to have p.p.（完成動名詞） ＊比主要時態更早的過去
修飾語－副詞 （否定時， 副詞是not）	（副詞）-ing + 受詞／補語 +（副詞）	（副詞）to（副詞）原形動詞 + 受詞／補語 +（副詞）

Quiz

Q1 To (meet / be met) the deadline, we have to work overtime.

Q2 I don't want to (handle / deal) those problems.

攻略法

37

to不定詞的名詞性用法

以動詞為基礎的to不定詞具有名詞、形容詞、副詞的作用，這個就叫做「詞性變形現象」。
因為動詞會變成名詞、形容詞或是副詞，首先我們先來了解to不定詞的名詞性用法。

要把動詞當作名詞使用的話，應該就想到動名詞了吧？to不定詞也是一樣。那共通點與相異點呢？當作主詞或補語時，沒有太大的差異，而且可以互相交換使用，但是如果當作受詞使用的時候，就要非常的注意使用方式了。我們來仔細觀察吧。

1. to不定詞當作主詞使用時

to不定詞或是動名詞在句子中當作主詞使用的時候，可以互相交換使用，因為解題的方法一樣，連維持動詞性質現象也都完全一樣。只是，to不定詞是以「it...to」這種形式的虛主詞、真主詞用法來使用，但動名詞幾乎不會這樣。

1 (To conduct / Conduct) a survey will help you find out what customers want.

> 1 實施市場調查／會幫你／了解／客戶所要的。

主詞是「實施市場調查」，因此要使用to不定詞，conduct只是一般動詞，不能直接使用。當然如果這時候to conduct換成conducting也是沒有問題的，另外這個例句也可以寫成It will help you find out what customers want to conduct a survey. It...to形式的真主詞、虛主詞用法的句子，由上可知，括號內可以填入的答案就是to conduct。

2 It is not easy (to meet / met) our customers' needs all the time.

> 2 不容易／滿足／我們客戶的需求／時常。

看到在句子最前面的It，就想到It...to形式的真主詞、虛主詞用法，如此可以輕易的解題，因為這種句子是把虛主詞it放到前面，把「to + 原形動詞」型態的真主詞擺到後面的句子，所以括號內可以填入的答案就是to meet。

2. to不定詞當作受詞使用時

如果要把動詞當作受詞使用的話，只要寫出動名詞或是to不定詞就可以

了。只是，在前面的章節所學到的只有「**MEGAPAS ID**」**動詞把動名詞當作受詞來使用**，其實也有一些動詞把**to不定詞當作受詞來使用**。更詳細的內容我們在後面會再做說明。在這裡先把**與未來有密切關聯的動詞與to不定詞很親近的這一特點**背起來。

來看下面兩個例句中要填入括號內的答案是什麼。

1 Building owners **are expected** (**having / to have**) their properties renovated regularly.

1 建築物的主人很期待／改建自己的不動產／定期性的。

動詞expect是「期待、希望」的意思，是與未來有關連的吧？這種動詞大都不會使用動名詞，而是使用to不定詞當作受詞使用，因此to have就是答案。

2 He (**refused / minded**) **to accept** those ideas from us.

2 他拒絕／接受／我們的那些意見。

在後面把to不定詞當作受詞使用的動詞是refuse。mind是常把動名詞（-ing）當作受詞使用的動詞，因此可以填入括號內的答案就是refused。

怪物講師的祕訣

1 及物動詞中把to不定詞以及名詞當作受詞來使用的動詞

（用小故事來幫助記憶）

「想要（want, wish, hope, expect）去旅行的孩子們不知道會不會同意（agree）會不會拒絕（refuse），詢問他們的意願（intend），把下定決心（decide）要去的孩子找過來做個承諾（promise）並讓他們制定計畫（plan）。」

＊全都帶有與未來相關的意義。

2 包含to不定詞的慣用表現（片語）

• fail to + 原形動詞：…無法
• try to + 原形動詞：…試著去
• happen to + 原形動詞：偶然…
• seem to + 原形動詞：似乎…（＝appear to + 原形動詞）

3 把動名詞或是to不定詞當作受詞使用的動詞

（用小故事來幫助記憶）

「愛情開始（begin, start）之後變得喜歡（like, prefer）最後說我愛你（love）之後再求婚（propose），但是最後知道是劈腿，變得討厭（hate）於是找了其他的男人（attempt），並和那個男人持續（continue）交往到現在。」

＊ 要記得愛情是有可能劈腿的（to, -ing）

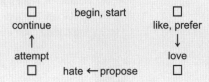

Q3 (There / It) was not easy for him to work in such a terrible condition.

Q4 He (agreed / enjoyed) to merge with our company.

▶ 解答在059頁

3. to不定詞當作名詞補語使用時

to不定詞很少被當作名詞補語來使用，因為名詞補語本身就很少被使用。**但如果真的要用的話，要先看有沒有和主詞具有同格關係**，解析題目的時候主要以「主詞…要做」解釋就可以了，這個時候，動名詞與to不定詞互相交換使用也是可以的。

1　My aim **is (to win / win)** the contract before January.

〈 1 我的目標是爭取到合約／在1月之前。

be動詞後面是補語的位置，分析之後，可知括號和主詞具有同格關係。因為「我的目標＝想要爭取的」，這就屬於to不定詞的名詞性用法。win是一般動詞，所以is不能放在後面，因此最適合填入括號內的答案就是to win。

2　The purpose of this meeting **is (to enhance / enhanced)** our productivity.

〈 2 這個會議的目的在於／提高／我們的生產力。

第2大句型動詞is後面是補語的位置。在這種情況下，to不定詞與主詞具有同格關係。enhanced是過去式動詞或是p.p.形式動詞，不能當作補語使用。加上後面的受詞our productivity不是被動，而是主動，因此填入括號內的答案就是to enhance。

怪物講師的祕訣

to不定詞很少被當作補語使用，因此請好好牢記下面的訣竅。

「The goal [purpose, aim, objective, plan] is to + 原形動詞」

目標 [目的、目標、目的、計畫] 是…。

38 to不定詞的形容詞性用法

to不定詞具有修飾名詞的形容詞作用，動詞擔任形容詞來修飾名詞主要有3大情況，在解決動詞具有形容詞功能的問題時，一定要馬上想起to不定詞、現在分詞（-ing）、過去分詞（p.p.）。

動詞修飾名詞的主要3大形式就是to不定詞、現在分詞（-ing）、過去分詞（p.p.）。現在分詞與過去分詞在下一個章節中會學習到，在這裡先簡單了解一下解題的方法。

1. to不定詞在名詞後面直接修飾

在原形動詞加上-ing寫成現在分詞，或是在原形動詞加上-ed寫成過去分詞（p.p.），也可以在原形動詞前面加上to寫成to不定詞，都具有像形容詞一樣修飾名詞的功能，但是現在分詞或過去分詞可以放在名詞的前後方，而to不定詞卻一定只能放在名詞的後方。我們來看看下面兩個例句吧。

1 **The (to write / writing / written) report** should be sent immediately. <1 寫完的報告／要被送出／馬上。

冠詞the以及名詞report之間是形容詞的位置。to write放在前面無法修飾名詞，也無法放在冠詞的後面。「被寫的報告」最符合句子的意思，因此p.p.型態的written是正確答案。這個題目不能以判斷有沒有受詞來解題，只能靠了解題目的意思來解答。

2 I have **a chance (to write / writing / written) the report**. <2 我有機會／寫報告。

I have a chance是完整的第3大句型句子（S + V + O），因此括號內就是修飾語的位置了，把前面a chance的意思解釋為「…的機會」會使句意自然，因此正確答案就是to不定詞的to write。

怪物講師的祕訣

to不定詞、現在分詞（-ing）、過去分詞（p.p.）的比較，在這裡主要討論的是to不定詞，但如果要解題的話，每次都要考慮現在分詞及過去分詞，所以在這裡先簡單的說明to不定詞和現在分詞（-ing）、過去分詞（p.p.）的相似點與相異點。

1 相似點
- 3個都具有修飾名詞的形容詞作用。

2 位置上的差異點
- 現在分詞（-ing）或是過去分詞（p.p.）可以放在名詞的前後方做修飾。
- to不定詞只能放在名詞的後面修飾。

3 意思上的差異點
- 現在分詞（-ing）的意思是「…中」，過去分詞（p.p.）的意思是「被…的」，to不定詞的意思則是「要…」。

4 主動、被動的差異點
- 現在分詞（-ing）是主動，過去分詞（p.p.）是被動。
- to不定詞是主動，to be p.p.是被動。

5 問題的解法
- 名詞前面如果是空格的話，就不能寫to不定詞，而是在現在分詞（-ing）與過去分詞（p.p.）兩個之中選擇一個。
- 名詞後面如果是空格的話，3種可以使用，因此就要看看句子的意思以及有沒有受詞了。

《講師的補充說明》
以下是與to不定詞搭配的名詞，除此之外的名詞大多都是與現在分詞（-ing）以及過去分詞（p.p.）搭配，只要記得下面粗體字的部分，會比較好記。

means to do 要做…的手段及 way to do 要做…的方法都不掩飾，right to do 做…的權力或是 authority to do 可以做…的權限，並且以 ability to do 符合自己能力的、effort to do 努力做…、plan to do 提前做…計畫的人會有好的 opportunity (chance) to do。

＊大部分都是帶有與未來有關連的名詞，這也是重要的提示。

2. be動詞在後面修飾主詞

be動詞是最具代表性的第2大句型動詞，後面主要是形容詞當作補語。如果把動詞當作補語來使用的話，就要使用形容詞型態的to不定詞、現在分詞（-ing）以及過去分詞（p.p.）。3種都可以使用，因此就要從句子的意思以及有沒有受詞來做判斷了。

1 The supervisor **is (to hire / hiring / hired) a few more people** in the near future.

> 1 那位主管／會聘用／多幾個人／不久的將來。

首先，後面有受詞a few more people，這個句子是主動式，因此被動型式的hired不能使用，剩下的2個都具有受詞的功能，但是了解一下句子的意思，因為有in the futrue這樣的副詞，因此to hire是最適合的答案，因為「be動詞＋to原形動詞」的意思是「預計…」。

2 The young man **is currently (to work / working / worked)** under my supervision.

> 2 那位年輕人正在做事／在我的監督下。

意思為「現在」的副詞currently是提示，to work是與未來相關的話，所以不可能是答案。work是第1大句型的動詞，但是沒有is worked這種形式的被動式，因此填入括號內的正確答案是working。

1 be 動詞後面有空格的情況，答案大概就是-ing或是p.p.。
　　只要了解句子的意思或是看看有沒有受詞就可以解題，也就是如果意思是「在…中」
　　而且有受詞的話，答案就是現在分詞（-ing）。如果意思是「變成…」而且沒有受詞的
　　話，答案就是過去分詞（p.p.）。

2 be 動詞後面是不定詞只表示未來的情況
　　預定、義務、可能、命運、意圖等單字，都是帶有與未來有關的意思時，to不定詞可以
　　是正確答案，但是這種型態幾乎沒有使用，因此成為答案的機率為零。

3 be 動詞後面是to不定詞的話不是當作形容詞就是當作名詞使用
　　He is to study English.（他預定要讀英文。）－形容詞用法
　　His aim is to study English.（他的目標是要讀英文。）－名詞用

3. 在第5大句型中當作受詞補語使用

和第2大句型補語相同，第5大句型補語主要都是形容詞。像這樣的話，
動詞被當作受詞補語使用時，就會變成to不定詞、現在分詞（-ing）、
過去分詞（p.p.），但是您還記得第3章的內容嗎？第5大句型的動詞
中，被當作受詞補語，而且可以當受詞補語使用的-ing或是p.p.就是
make、keep、find。帶有「使、要求、允許」意思的第5大句型動詞，只
能使用to不定詞了。那我們來看下面的題目吧。

1 They **allowed** us (**to stay** / staying) inside.

> 1 他們允許了／我們／待在裡面。

allow是帶有「使、要求、允許」意思的第5大句型動詞，所以當作受
詞補語的話就要寫成to不定詞，由上可知要填入括弧內的答案就是to
stay。

2 He **made** me (to stay / **stay**) inside.

> 2 他讓／我／待在／裡面。

make是使役動詞，因此在受詞me後面的受詞補語要寫成原形動詞，由
此可知要填入括弧內的答案就是stay。

1 make、keep、find + 受詞 + 受詞補語（＝形容詞、-ing、p.p.）
　　也可以是省略受詞補語的第3大句型

2 「使、要求、允許」動詞 + 受詞 + 受詞補語（to不定詞）
　　使：force（強迫）＝compel, persuade（說服、讓…）
　　要求：ask（邀請）、encourage（激勵、讓…）、require（讓…需要）、
　　　　　expect（期盼，第3、5大句型）、would like（期盼，第3、5大句型）
　　允許：allow（許可）＝permit, enable（讓…可能）
＊ANICAR動詞中，CAR也有對應這第5大句型的用法。
＊「使、要求、允許」動詞的受詞補語被寫成to不定詞是有原因的，那就是帶有與未來相關
的意思，所以請一定要記得在to不定詞中帶有與未來相關意思這一點。

攻略法 39

to不定詞的副詞性用法

這個單元要開始談to不定詞的副詞性用法，to不定詞在句子中可以當名詞、形容詞使用，但當副詞使用時，它的活用度是否比當作名詞使用的動名詞來得更高呢？

to不定詞在句子中可以當名詞、形容詞，當然還有副詞使用。以動詞為根本的to不定詞被當作副詞使用，是不是讓您感到有點意外？但是to不定詞事實上和副詞一樣，可以修飾動詞、形容詞或副詞，其中一定要**記得修飾動詞這一點。修飾形容詞或是副詞這點就當作記片語一樣，了解就可以了。**

1. to不定詞修飾動詞的時候

修飾動詞的就是副詞，**to不定詞和副詞一樣可以修飾動詞，意思為「為了…」。**另外因為是副詞，所以省略也沒有關係，副詞只有在完整的句子中才會使用。我們來看看下面的兩個問題吧。

1 **(To become / Became) acquainted with others**, you should introduce yourself first.

> 1 為了與其他人變得較熟／你應該先介紹你自己。

逗號（,）後面是完整的第3大句型。因此在逗號前面的副詞就算省略也沒關係，由上可知在逗號前面的to不定詞被當作帶有「為了…」意思的副詞使用，所以在括號中所要填入的答案就是To become。

2 He **wanted to go** outside (**playing / to play**) soccer.

> 2 他想要／去外面／踢足球。

內容上「為了…」這樣的意思很符合句意，因此在括號內要填入to play。「為了…」這種文法常常被用來修飾動詞「做什麼」吧？像這樣to不定詞修飾動詞，可以稱做**to不定詞的副詞性用法**。如果寫playing的話，意思就變成「做…中」，和語意是不是不同呢？

to不定詞被當作副詞使用的時候，主要解釋為「為了…」，位置大都放在完整句子的前後方。另外，這時的to不定詞可以寫成「in order to + 原形動詞」或是「so as to + 原形動詞」。在這裡的「為了…」表示未來。

to不定詞當作副詞使用的時候，是「為了⋯」的意思。

因為to不定詞當作副詞使用，所以寫在完整句子的前後方。另外在這個情況下，to不定詞可以寫成「in order to + 原形動詞」或是「so as to + 原形動詞」。

2. to不定詞修飾形容詞的時候

to不定詞也可以修飾形容詞，也可以當作副詞使用吧？在這種情況就當作片語「be able to + 原形動詞」來背是最簡單的（帶有未來的意思），那我們來看看下面的題目吧。

1　I **was** not **able (understanding / to understand)** his situation.

> 1　我無法理解／他的狀況。

只要記得「be able to + 原形動詞」的話，就馬上知道答案了吧？因為到形容詞able為止是以第2大句型結束，因此可以稱做副詞性的用法，但您不需要記這麼多，只要記得這個片語就好了，要填入括號內的答案就是to understand。

> 2　他準備／接手新的責任。

2　He **is (ready / difficult) to take** on new responsibilities.

「be able to + 原形動詞」型態的慣用表現出現了，但如果放入difficult後，整個句子的意思正確嗎？difficult是不能把人當作主詞來使用的形容詞。通常應該是寫成It is difficult for him to take on new responsibilities.，所以括號內要填入ready。

在多益考試中，常出現的「be able to + 原形動詞」的慣用表現

• be able to + 原形動詞	可以做⋯
• be ready to + 原形動詞	準備要做⋯
• be likely [liable, apt] to + 原形動詞	好像要做⋯
• be willing to + 原形動詞	願意要做⋯
• be sure [certain] to + 原形動詞	一定要做⋯

3. to不定詞修飾副詞的時候

當作片語來背是最簡單的，不需要想太多。句子的意思還是會帶有未來的傾向，請記得too...to、enough to。

1 Your answer is **too** difficult (**understanding / to understand**).

1 你的答案太難／對於理解
上。

這個句子是使用「太…以至於不能…」意思的「too...to」用法吧？這個
就是正確答案，另外讓您參考，動詞understand後面的受詞就是在內容
上最前面的主詞answer。句子的意思就是「你的答案太難，以至於無法
理解」，由上可知，要填入括號內的答案就是to understand。

2 He is qualified **enough** (**to be / being**) hired.

2 他有資格／充分的／足夠被
聘僱。

這是「enough to + 原形動詞」型態的to不定詞的副詞性用法，由上可
知，要填入括號內的答案就是to be。

怪物講師的祕訣

to不定詞的副詞性用法（全部都帶有未來的意思）。

1 為了做…（動詞修飾）
在完整句子的最前面或是最後面加上to不定詞幾乎都是這種用法。

2 「be + 形容詞 + to原形動詞」（修飾形容詞，把它當作片語來熟記）

- be able to + 原形動詞　　　　　　　可以做…
- be ready to + 原形動詞　　　　　　準備要做…
- be likely [liable, apt] to + 原形動詞　好像要做…
- be willing to + 原形動詞　　　　　　願意要做…
- be sure [certain] to + 原形動詞　　一定要做…

3 to不定詞修飾副詞的時候（把它當作片語來熟記）

- too + 形容詞（或是副詞）+ to原形動詞　　　太…以至於不能…
- 形容詞（或是副詞）+ enough to + 原形動詞　做得足夠可以…

攻略法 36　to不定詞的「維持動詞性質」現象

1 to不定詞前面需要介系詞的話？→ 了解意思之後，如果意思上是主詞的話，for就是正確答案。

2 to不定詞後面是空格的話？→ 隨著動詞的形式，以適合的受詞或是補語當作答案。

3 to不定詞的主動、被動如何區分？→ 第1、2大句型是主動，第3、4、5大句型要確認有沒有受詞。

4 to不定詞要完整的話？→ 如果上面3種情況都具備的話，就當作副詞的修飾語。

攻略法 37　to不定詞的名詞性用法

1 it是主詞的話，就選擇to不定詞當作答案，並且解析看看to不定詞是不是真主詞。

2 看到「去旅行的動詞」的話，就選擇to不定詞當作受詞。

3 如果aim、purpose、objective等主詞都帶有未來意思，選擇to不定詞當作補語。

攻略法 38　to不定詞的形容詞性用法

1 如果是ability、right、chance…等具有未來意思的名詞，就是to不定詞修飾，剩下的就是分詞修飾。

2 be to是「要做…」的意思，剩下的情況就是分詞是答案。

3 看到動詞make、keep、find的話，當作受詞補語形容詞的-ing、p.p.是答案。如果看到的是「要求、邀請、允許」動詞的話，to不定詞當作受詞補語。

攻略法 39　to不定詞的副詞性用法

1 **為了做…**（動詞修飾）

在完整句子的最前面或是最後面加上to不定詞，大都是這種用法。

2 **「be + 形容詞 + to原形動詞」型態的表現**（修飾形容詞）

• be ready to + 原形動詞（可以做…）

• be able to + 原形動詞（準備要做…）

• be likely [liable, apt] to + 原形動詞（好像要做…）

• be willing to + 原形動詞（願意做…）

• be sure [certain] to + 原形動詞（一定要做…）

3 **to不定詞修飾副詞的時候**（把它當作片語來熟記）

• too + 形容詞／副詞 + to 原形動詞（太…以至於不能…）

• 形容詞／副詞 + enough to + 原形動詞（做的足夠…可以…）

* 1 2 3 全都帶有未來的意思

例子 1

(A) to get
(B) getting
(C) gotten
(D) gets

① 把握問題的類型

③ 空格中要填什麼詞類？

The team leader used a loud voice _____ our attention when he announced the roles we were to assume.

② 把握提示

1 把握問題的類型
　　文法問題

2 把握提示
　　非限定動詞
　　（動狀詞）的位置

3 空格中要填什麼詞類？
　　to不定詞
　　（副詞性用法）

2　(A) reads
　　(B) read
　　(C) reading
　　(D) to read

When turning her computer on in the morning, Ms. Ramirez is advised _____ a lot of incoming e-mails every day.

1 把握問題的類型

2 把握提示

3 空格中要填什麼詞類？

3　(A) seen
　　(B) sees
　　(C) to see
　　(D) saw

It is my pleasure _____ that all of the shareholders are happy to support me in continuing my position as CEO.

1 把握問題的類型

2 把握提示

3 空格中要填什麼詞類？

4　(A) upgrading
　　(B) to upgrade
　　(C) upgrades
　　(D) upgraded

The hospital's staff agreed _____ the surgical department, but first they needed to find the necessary funding.

1 把握問題的類型

2 把握提示

3 空格中要填什麼詞類？

5　(A) to work
　　(B) wokers
　　(C) works
　　(D) working

In order to finalize the project and finish it on time, the staff will be required _____ extended hours.

1 把握問題的類型

2 把握提示

3 空格中要填什麼詞類？

6　(A) To make
　　(B) To have
　　(C) To become
　　(D) To permit

_____ healthy, Mr. Akita must bring his own food from home to eat for lunch in the employee dining room.

1 把握問題的類型

2 把握提示

3 空格中要填什麼詞類？

7　(A) to seeing
　　(B) to have seen
　　(C) to be seen
　　(D) to see

I went _____ a specialist doctor to have further tests done after listening to my family doctor's advice.

1 把握問題的類型

2 把握提示

3 空格中要填什麼詞類？

8　(A) to say
　　(B) to show
　　(C) to speak
　　(D) to look

Mr. Smith and Mr. Johnston used the teleconference room _____ to their colleagues in New York.

1 把握問題的類型

2 把握提示

3 空格中要填什麼詞類？

9　(A) In order to
　　(B) Due to
　　(C) Thanks to
　　(D) Owing to

_____ start the meeting, the chairman rose to introduce the guest speaker to the rest of the meeting participants.

1 把握問題的類型

2 把握提示

3 空格中要填什麼詞類？

10　(A) to confirming
　　(B) confirming
　　(C) confirmation
　　(D) confirm

The woman at the counter helped me _____ the dates and times of our bus tickets.

1 把握問題的類型

2 把握提示

3 空格中要填什麼詞類？

▶ 解答在059頁

101 CMOS Industries' annual aim is _____ its business in Europe and therefore intends to hire more employees.

(A) expanding
(B) expanded
(C) to expand
(D) expansive

102 Mr. Sanchez has hired an outside consulting firm _____ a deeper understanding of current consumer trends and preferences.

(A) to gain
(B) to remain
(C) to advise
(D) to appear

103 The best way _____ new products in this volatile market is to do careful and thorough market research.

(A) launching
(B) to launch
(C) launch
(D) to be launched

104 MCS Inc. _____ to gain the approval of several well-known technology review sites when they launch their new program.

(A) suggests
(B) postpones
(C) minds
(D) hopes

重要
105 To present the findings of their research, the doctors from St. Mary's Hospital have decided _____ a press conference.

(A) holding
(B) to hold
(C) to be held
(D) holds

106 In the current economic climate, because consumer spending is down, the company's only goal is to remain _____.

(A) solvency
(B) solvate
(C) solvent
(D) solve

高難度
107 Ms. Abramoff was forced _____ with her litigation after several threats of countersuits from her client.

(A) to cancel
(B) to remain
(C) to continue
(D) to proceed

108 The management reserves the right _____ all employees from using personal USB flash drives to prevent viruses.

(A) banned
(B) banning
(C) to ban
(D) to have banned

109 _____ is very cost-effective to put the cleaning contract out for tender instead of having the janitorial staff.

(A) That
(B) What
(C) There
(D) It

110 I was reminded _____ only the best companies in terms of investment opportunities excluding small tech-oriented start-ups.

(A) to watch
(B) watching
(C) watched
(D) to be watched

111 We held an information seminar _____ the mandatory medical tests that employees would be subject to.

(A) to notify
(B) to explain
(C) to occur
(D) to seem

112 The X-ray technician asked Mr. Asif _____ his foot so that she could get a better image of his healing bones.

(A) moving
(B) mover
(C) moved
(D) to move

113 Please be sure to _____ review your existing insurance policy before you sign up for the new health insurance.

(A) thorough
(B) thoroughly
(C) through
(D) though

重要
114 To be _____ in the job interview, you have to leave a lasting impression on the interviewers.

(A) success
(B) successive
(C) successful
(D) succession

115 We are pleased to _____ you that your application for our accounting position has been approved by the board of directors.

(A) notify
(B) notification
(C) notified
(D) notifying

116 Representatives of the customer satisfaction department have to have the ability _____ with demanding clients.

(A) dealing
(B) to deal
(C) deal
(D) dealt

117 As this meeting will be attended by all the upper executives, I was _____ to submit the report immediately.

(A) reminded
(B) wanted
(C) agreed
(D) predicted

高難度
118 All international orders _____ to arrive within 30 days of confirming the order, which is a common practice according to this contract.

(A) to expect
(B) expecting
(C) expect
(D) are expected

119 The unexpected interruption of the power supply makes _____ impossible for the employees to meet the production deadline.

(A) it
(B) that
(C) them
(D) how

120 The employees' strike for higher wages _____ the bank to lose some customers complaining about the inconvenience.

(A) forced
(B) refused
(C) informed
(D) registered

It's been documented that there is a correlation _____ a successful advertisement
                                                      121
and a promising product. However, how to make an advertisement _____ is a main
                                                                     122
concern before our product promotion bears fruit. _____ memorable is one of the
                                                          123
key qualities of a remarkable advertisement. In order to reach this goal, _____ in the
                                                                                 124
execution of an advertisement. You have to make your advertisement constantly appear in
public. Even still, it won't appeal to people at first, but they will get some impression about
it eventually. Since social media has developed rapidly, this is an avenue that enables us
to have a wide range of venues to advertise.

121 (A) among
    (B) beside
    (C) between
    (D) along with

122 (A) stand out
    (B) stand off
    (C) stand on
    (D) stand up

123 (A) Being
    (B) To been
    (C) Be
    (D) Been

124 (A) reputation plays a decisive role
    (B) recreation plays a decisive role
    (C) repetition plays a decisive role
    (D) relocation plays a decisive role

▶ 解答在062頁

Chapter 10 分詞
讓人頭痛的分詞解題法！

Review Test

回想在Chapter 09 學習的to不定詞，回答下列問題。

1 to不定詞前面有空格的情況？ ▶ ....

2 to不定詞後面有空格的情況？ ▶ ....

3 「to + 原形動詞」與「to be p.p.」的差異？ ▶ ....

4 修飾to不定詞的是？ ▶ ....

5 to不定詞成為主詞的話？ ▶ ....

6 要將to不定詞當作受詞的話？ ▶ ....

7 to不定詞被當成形容詞使用時？ ▶ ....

8 to不定詞被當成受詞使用時？ ▶ ....

Preview

1 分詞的特徵

很多人只要看到分詞就感到頭痛，簡單來說分詞就是為了**把動詞當成形容詞來使用**而改成**-ing或p.p.的型態**，可說是具有動詞性質的形容詞。**分詞有現在分詞（-ing）和過去分詞（p.p.）**，即是「**正在…**」、「**已經…**」。切記因為是形容詞，所以放在修飾名詞的位置。即使是扮演形容詞的角色，仍具有動詞的性質。若能征服分詞，在writing和speaking方面也大有助益。

2 分詞問題解法

若是修飾名詞的位置的情況，正確解答是分詞的機率很大。譬如「**正在…**」的話，現在分詞（-ing）就是解答；「**已經…**」的話，過去分詞（p.p.）就是解答。要清楚地知道受到修飾的名詞或是分詞之間的主動、被動關係。

正確答案｜ 1. 填「for＋受格」 2. 隨著為幾大句型動詞的不同，填入受詞或補語 3. 依後面是否有受詞來判斷 4. 副詞 5. 常出現虛主詞或真主詞 6. 一定要填入「去旅行的動詞」 7. 主要是在正前方有特定名詞，或是句子是第5大句型的時候。 8. 句子本身就已完成，或是以too...to這種片語表現的時候。

攻略法

40

to分詞問題的2個重點

具動詞性質的分詞與之前學習的動名詞或不定詞一樣，有「動詞性質維持現象」和「詞性變化現象」。

原來的根本是動詞，所以仍維持動詞的性質。-ing形態的現在分詞是「正在…」的意思；p.p.形態的過去分詞是「已經…」的意思，有主動和被動的差異，另有現在和過去的時態差異。這被稱為「動詞性質維持現象」，我們一邊解題，一邊來探討「動詞性質維持現象」吧！

1. 具有維持動詞性質的現象

分詞原本在句子中擔任形容詞的角色，原來的根本（詞性）是動詞。所以仍維持動詞的性質。-ing形態的現在分詞為「正在…」；p.p.形態的過去分詞為「已經…」，有主動和被動的差異，另有現在和過去的時態差異。這被稱為「動詞性質維持現象」。我們一邊解題，一邊來探討動詞性質維持現象吧！

1 The (**singing / sung**) **bird** always sits here in the morning.

括號為形容詞的位置。-ing或p.p.都可當形容詞，但是「唱歌的」比「變成歌的」更符合題意吧！因此括號內應填入singing。

2 We would like to hire more (**qualifying / qualified**) **applicants** this time.

括號是修飾後面的名詞applicants的位置。兩者皆為形容詞，但「有資格的」比「正給予資格」更顯得自然，所以p.p.形式的qualified為正確解答。不妨將qualified applicant整個詞彙記下來。

實際考試中出現現在分詞和過去分詞的機率很大，詳細地了解「動詞性質維持現象」選擇正確解答即可。

2. 詞性變化現象

我們無法用原形動詞修飾名詞，但若改成現在分詞或過去分詞就可修飾名詞。動詞轉變成形容詞使用，即為「詞性變化現象」。簡單來說，用

> **1** 那隻歌唱的鳥／總是／坐／在這／早晨。

> **2** 我們想採用／更有資格的應徵者／這一次。

動詞型態的單字來修飾名詞，不是-ing型態的現在分詞，就是p.p.型態的過去分詞。**若要表現正在主動做什麼的話，就使用現在分詞（-ing），欲表現依據什麼而「變成…」的話，即可使用過去分詞（p.p.）。**

1 **The (revise / revised) law** will be in effect from next month.

〈 1 被修改的法律／會從下個月 開始生效。

定冠詞the和名詞law之間為形容詞的位置。revise為原形動詞無法被當成形容詞使用，revised為p.p.形式的過去分詞可做為形容詞。因此括號中應填入revised，意為「被修訂的」。

2 I would like to see the **(visiting / visit) professor** as soon as possible.

〈 2 我想看／拜訪的教授／儘 快。

此題也一樣，定冠詞the和名詞professor之間為形容詞的位置。因此可做動詞和名詞使用的visit刪除，原為動詞的visiting是為了修飾名詞而轉成形容詞的分詞，本質為動詞也能做形容詞使用，我將它命名為「動形詞」。括號中應選擇visiting。

怪物講師的祕訣

目前為止所學的已經很足夠了。為了更進一步了解請看以下說明。

1 分詞意義上的主詞

a singing bird （唱歌的鳥）

→ 在此bird是singing意義上的主詞。

a revised law （被修訂的法律）

→ law不是受詞嗎？不是的，分詞所修飾的名詞是句中的主語。

2 分詞有受詞或補語

a bird singing a song （正在唱歌的鳥）

→ singing有受詞

a man becoming kind to women （轉變成對女人親切的男人）

→ become是第2大句型動詞，後面通常加上當作補語的形容詞。分詞也是維持句型，後面加上受詞補語。但分詞在名詞前面修飾的情況則不加受詞補語。

3 分詞有主動和被動

a man cooking some food （正在料理一些食物的男人）

a bird being cooked （正在被料理的鳥）

→ 皆為現在分詞，仍有主動分詞和被動分詞的區別。

4 分詞中也有時態

A man reading a book is James. （正在讀書的男人是詹姆士。）

A man having read the book is James. （讀完書的男人是詹姆士。）

→ 就算是相同的現在分詞，也是分為單純分詞和完成式分詞

5 分詞接受副詞的修飾

A man currently reading a book is James. （現在正在讀書的男人是詹姆士。）

→ 分詞是形容詞，雖然說形容詞可以受到副詞的修飾，但分詞本質是動詞，所以跟動詞一樣，受到副詞修飾的說明更具說服力。

＊由此已經給各位看了動名詞、to不定詞、分詞有「動詞性質維持」的5個證據。理論上是具有一致性的說明。

6 分詞的主動、被動關係

① 主動式分詞

主動式分詞具有下列主動和進行的意思

a running boy （正在跑步的男孩）

a crying baby （正在哭的孩子）

② 被動式分詞

被動式分詞有被動和已完成的意思

a revised plan （被修改的計畫）

an accepted proposal （被接受的提案）

Quiz ⋯⋯⋯⋯⋯⋯⋯⋯⋯⋯⋯⋯⋯⋯⋯⋯⋯⋯⋯⋯⋯⋯⋯⋯⋯⋯⋯⋯⋯⋯⋯⋯⋯⋯⋯

Q1 Newly (hiring / hired) managers must attend the information session this afternoon.

Q2 More items should be (producing / produced) to meet the demands.

▶ 解答在066頁

攻略法

41

分詞的位置固定

扮演形容詞角色的分詞在句子中的位置是固定的，可分成3種情況，首先把握3種情況的位置，接著考慮主動或被動，再選擇是現在分詞還是過去分詞即可。

只要是修飾名詞的位置都可看到分詞，也就是與形容詞位置相同。詳細介紹分成如下4個位置來說明。但不是只有現在分詞（-ing）和過去分詞（p.p.），還要考慮區分to不定詞才能正確解答。

1. 名詞的前面或後面

在名詞的前面可加入分詞，要用現在分詞還是過去分詞，應從句意上來做分析。切記不要以是否有受詞來做判斷，否則解答只會出現-ing，但名詞後面有空格時，解答有可能是分詞，也有可能是to不定詞。通常解答都是分詞，但如同之前在to不定詞單元中所學，像限定名詞ability to do一樣的to不定詞也可能是正確解答。若不是那種情況，分詞就是正確解答。這種情況下用解析句子意思或是否有受詞來判斷即可。（但在第1、第2大句型的情況下沒有受詞，只能解析句子的意思來作答）

1 My (**breaking / broken**) **nose** was bleeding.

> 1 我受傷的鼻子在流血。

不是「正在受傷的」鼻子而是「已經受傷」的鼻子，所以p.p.型態的broken為正確解答。這時將鼻子當成受詞，而選用-ing是錯誤的。分詞在前面修飾名詞的時候，只能以了解句意的方式來回答問題。

2 **My nose (breaking / broken / to break) by him** was bleeding.

> 2 我的鼻子／被他打傷的／正在流血。

雖然是分詞在後面修飾名詞的情況，但因為是「受傷的」鼻子，所以broken才是解答。用breaking來解說也不符合句子的意思，後面也沒有需要的受詞。要用to break修飾的話，前面的名詞必須是在to不定詞單元所學的特定名詞。現在沒有符合的答案！1和2的解答都是broken，但是位置都不同吧？通常分詞如同1是一個單字的話，則放在名詞前；若是像broken by him 由好幾個單字組合而成的話，則放在名詞之後。

```
冠詞
所有格
介系詞          +  [分詞] + 名詞 + [分詞或to不定詞]
動詞（不及物）
```

2. 在be動詞後面修飾主詞時

各位都知道像be動詞之類的第2大句型動詞，後面通常都會出現形容詞吧？-ing、p.p.、to不定詞的根本就是動詞，但具有形容詞功能，所以能出現在be動詞後面。我們常看到「be + -ing」或「be p.p.」，卻沒看過「to be 不定詞」吧？因為不會這樣使用。**在be動詞後以-ing或p.p.當作答案，觀察與主詞的動格關係或是有沒有受詞即可**。（大家都知道第1、2大句型中沒有受詞吧？）那麼我們來看題目吧！

1 They **are (reading / read) their own books** under a tree.

這是be動詞的形容詞補語位置，動詞read的過去式、過去分詞（p.p.）都是read。首先在這句子裡，被動的「他們被讀的」根本就不通，「他們讀」語意會較順暢，後面有受詞「their own books」，所以括號中應該填入主動的現在分詞reading。

2 The murderer **was (arresting / arrested / to arrest) by the police**.

be動詞後面當然是形容詞的位置囉！選項都是形容詞，所以要解析句子。不是殺人犯逮捕而是殺人犯「被」逮捕，所以被動式的過去分詞arrested為正確解答。由後面的by the police來看，被動式的過去分詞arrested是解答。使用to arrest的話，是表示「預計被逮捕」，意思不通。

> 1 他們正在讀／自己的書／在樹下。

> 2 殺人犯逮捕了／被警察。

怪物講師的祕訣

```
                    ┌ -ing＋受詞（正在…）
be動詞              │ p.p.（沒有受詞）（變成…）
（第二大句型）      │ to不定詞＋受詞（預定…）
                    └ to be p.p.（沒有受詞）（預定被…）
```

3. 被當成第5大句型受詞補語使用時

之前提過第5大句型的補語，通常都是放形容詞（參考Chapter 02和 03）。那麼扮演形容詞角色的-ing、p.p.、to不定詞都可以成為受詞補語 吧！還記得什麼情況下，只有-ing或p.p.（或形容詞）才能成為受詞補 語，什麼情況下，to不定詞才能成為受詞補語嗎？忘記的話請看Chapter 03。**若要判斷答案是現在分詞（-ing）還是過去分詞（p.p.），只需透過 句子解析或是判斷後面是否有受詞即可。（第1、2大句型中沒有受詞）**

1 I will **keep** the current assembly line (**to run / running**).

keep是第5大句型動詞，受詞補語通常會放-ing或p.p.，因此running是解 答。表示「組裝線繼續維持運轉」，使用具有現在進行式的-ing是合理 的。在這狀況之下，動詞run是第1大句型動詞，所以後面不需加上動 詞。

2 I **advised** them (**to keep / keeping / kept**) the house clean.

同樣都是第5大句型動詞，但是advise在受詞補語位置使用to不定詞。 （回想「使喚、請求、允許」動詞）因為「使喚、請求、允許」做某件 事，帶有未來式的to不定詞較為適合，因此解答為to keep。

上述內容整理

一主詞 + make [keep、find] + 受詞 + 形容詞 [-ing、p.p.]

一主詞 +「使喚、請求、允許」動詞 + 受詞 + to不定詞

Quiz

Q3 Despite some rumors, I found the movie (interesting / interested).
Q4 He got (confusing / confused) as he was not sure of it.

---

1 我會維持／現在的組裝線／ 持續運轉。

2 我勸告他們／維持／房子的 ／乾淨。

▶ 解答在066頁

攻略法

42

分詞構句解法

就算不大認識分詞構句，也常聽到分詞構句吧？太過深入探討只會把事情變複雜，接下來就介紹輕鬆破解分詞構句題型的祕技吧！

將「連接詞＋主詞＋動詞」改寫成「連接詞＋-ing」或「連接詞＋p.p.」即稱為分詞構句。詳細說明的話太過於複雜，在此就不深入說明。

完整的句子前後出現「連接詞＋-ing」或「連接詞＋p.p.」句型的情況，就可視為分詞構句。可以使用句子的意思解說，或用有無受詞來判斷該用-ing還是p.p.。簡單整理如下

> 分詞形態：連接詞＋S＋V＋OC, S＋V＋OC
>
> （連接詞）＋-ing [p.p.], S＋V＋OC

接下來，用實際解題來熟悉句型吧。下列括號中應選擇哪個解答？

1 (Breaking / Broken) by him, my **(breaking / broken)** nose was bleeding.

> 1 因他而斷／我被打斷的鼻子正在流血。

逗號（,）後面開始到my nose was bleeding為完整的第1大句型。前面提過連接在完整的句子前後的是分詞構句，不管有沒有連接詞都沒關係，逗號後的句子為「我被打斷的鼻子在流血」，所以一定要加入p.p.型態的broken。如果後面沒有受詞的話，就選擇p.p.。這個句子為了清楚地表達出分詞構句的概念，所以在逗號前後都寫出broken，其實只要在前面或後面寫一次即可。

2 While (browsing / browsed) your website, I noticed an error.

> 2 在瀏覽你的網頁時／我注意到了／一個錯誤。

看到括號前的連接詞while了吧？但句子卻沒有主詞，這就是分詞構句的證據。這時有無連接詞都可以，但如果有的話，就更可以清楚地表達。

因為是分詞構句，所以與後面句子的主詞連結看看，I是表示主動的browse，所以應該選擇現在分詞的browsing。

就像前面所出現的題目，省略主詞、改變動詞形態、簡化句子是分詞構句的功能。

怪物講師的祕訣

（連接詞）-ing [p.p.], 主詞＋動詞＋受詞補語，（連接詞）-ing [p.p.]

這種前後皆為分詞構句的情況，與主要句子的主詞連結之後了解句子的意思，如果是「正在…」的話就選擇-ing；若為「已經…」的話就選擇p.p.。當然也可以從有無受詞來判斷。只需留意第1，2大句型沒有受詞這一點。這時分詞位置也有可能為to不定詞，用「為了…」來解說最合適的情況下，正確解答不是分詞，而是to不定詞。

Quiz

Q5 If (renovating / renovated) within this week, the office will accommodate more staff.

Q6 (Situating / Situated) opposite our store, your store will easily attract customers.

▶ 解答在066頁

43 經常出題的分詞表現

下列出現的分詞表現是歐美人士常用的分詞表現，也經常出現在考試題目中。請經常大聲朗讀，牢記在腦海中。

下列的分詞若用理論思考，很容易會搞混，因此請反覆大聲朗讀，牢記在腦海中！這些東西不需用腦來記憶，應該要用舌頭來記憶。

1. -ing為解答的情況

可用理論來判斷，但皆為常見的用法，那就當作片語來背！首先來看看有現在分詞的2個例句，之後再介紹考試中常見的現在分詞表現。

1 The woman left **a lasting impression** on the interviewers.

2 We are currently trying our best to find **the missing child**.

以下是多益考試中常出現的現在分詞，這些分詞就像平常所使用的片語般記起的話就更好。

- a lasting impression　　　持久的印象
- missing luggage / child　　遺失的行李／孩子
- misleading information　　誤導的情報
- an existing facility　　　現有設施
- opening hours　　　　　營業時間
- preceding years　　　　　過去幾年
- an opposing point of view　反對意見（見解）
- rewarding discussion　　　有價值的討論
- encouraging remark　　　鼓勵的話
- challenging task　　　　　艱難的課題
- demanding customers　　　要求繁瑣的顧客
- overwhelming order　　　難以負荷的訂單

2. p.p.是解答的情況

下面幾乎都是慣用p.p.形態的過去分詞表現，大聲朗讀記憶吧！首先來

1 那個女人留下了／持久深刻的印象／讓面試官。

2 我們正盡最大的努力／為了尋找／那個失蹤的孩子。

看看有過去分詞的2個例句，之後再介紹考試中常出現的過去分詞表現。

1 Cash is the only **preferred means** of payment in our store.

2 In this case, **detailed information** must be provided for us.

以下是多益考試常出現的過去分詞。

- complicated problems   複雜的問題
- preferred methods / means 受歡迎的方法／手段
- dedicated employees   專心的員工
- experienced employees   有經驗的員工
- motivated employees   積極的員工
- qualified applicants   符合資格的應徵者
- distinguished scholars   傑出的學者
- informed decision   根據情報的決定
- detailed information   詳細的情報
- involved tasks   相關的事項
- merged companies   被合併的公司

2. 是形容詞還是分詞？

空格是形容詞的位置，若要在形容詞和分詞中選擇答案的話，很容易有形容詞一定是正確解答的錯覺。區分形容詞與分詞位置的方法如下。
——意思稍有不同的情況，分析各句子單字意思的差異。
——意思相似的情況，形容詞雖具優先權，但也有例外，所以參考下面的例句來解答。

1 The game was (**excitable / exciting**).

意思不同的情況，excitable意思為「容易興奮」，與句子的意思不符合。exciting意思為「吸引人的、有趣的」，與句子的意思相符合，因此解答為exciting。

雖然也可以用句子的意思來解答，但如果是常看到The game is exciting.（這遊戲很有趣。）這種英文句子的人，不需考慮就能作答，這就叫做慣例。

1 現金是唯一被採取的付款方式／在我們店裡。

2 這種情況／應該提供詳細的情報／給我們。

1 那個遊戲非常有趣。

2 Thank you for being so (**understandable / understanding**) in this situation.

2 謝謝你／非常體諒／這種情況。

understandable意思是「能夠理解的」，understanding意思是「有理解力的」。單字意思雖不同，但知道這類句子通常會使用understanding的人，就能輕易做答。形容詞understandable通常用在It is understandable that he sometimes makes mistakes.（能理解犯錯為人之常情。），因此括號中應選擇understanding。

5秒 解決出現頻繁的分詞的方法

以下分詞問題出現時，確實提高正確答題率的祕技

1 Before / After + -ing＋受詞, S + V（在…之前／之後）

When / While + -ing＋受詞, S + V（做…的時候、做…的期間）

Once / Unless / As + p.p. +（受詞）, S + V（一旦、變成…的話／如果不／如同）

2 主詞 + 動詞 + 受格補語 + -ing + 受詞（所以最後…）

3 名詞 + -ing + 名詞

→ 這種情況，-ing修飾前面的名詞。前面的名詞為主詞，後面的名詞為受詞

＊也有「名詞 + p.p. + 名詞」的句型，這就是前面的名詞與p.p.修飾後面的名詞的情況。

4 情緒動詞（excite, interest, embarrass, disappoint, bore, fascinate等）的情況

原則：名詞感受到那情緒的話使用p.p.，給那種情緒的話，使用-ing

要點：受到修飾的名詞為人的話則使用p.p.，若為事物則使用-ing

→ 這時情緒動詞後面的受詞也可省略，若以有無受詞或解析句子的意思來判斷的話，非常困難。

Quiz

Q7 The report (containing / contained) important information will be faxed to you soon.

Q8 As (suggesting / suggested), you should stay home during this emergency.

▶ 解答在066頁

攻略法 40-43　重點整理　　　　有系統的將本課學習內容，一目瞭然地整理吧

攻略法 40　to分詞問題的2個重點

1 **動詞性質維持現象**。-ing是主動，「進行」的意思；p.p.是被動，「完成」的意思。

2 **詞性變化現象**。本質是動詞，但扮演修飾名詞的形容詞角色。所以分詞的別名是「動形詞」，雖為動詞，但扮演修飾名詞的形容詞角色的意思。

攻略法 41　分詞的位置固定

1 **名詞的前後**：「分詞 + 名詞」或「名詞 + 分詞」

2 **第2形式補語位置**：「be動詞 + 分詞」

3 **第5大句型補語位置**：「第5大句型動詞 + 受詞 + 分詞」

4 **分詞句型**：「（連接詞）分詞 + 主詞 + 動詞」或「主詞 + 動詞,（連接詞）分詞」

攻略法 42　分詞構句解法

1 在中心主句前後修飾的分詞表現，即為分詞句型。

2 與主詞一起看，若為主動、進行的意思，則使用-ing；若為被動、完成的意思，則使用p.p.。

攻略法 43　經常出題的分詞表現

1 **解答為-ing的情況**

a lasting impression	持久的印象	missing luggage / child	遺失的行李／孩子
misleading information	誤導的情報	an existing facility	現有設施
opening hours	營業時間	preceding years	過去幾年
an opposing point of view	反對意見（見解）	rewarding discussion	有價值的討論
encouraging remark	鼓勵的話	challenging tasks	艱難的課題
demanding customer	要求繁瑣的顧客	overwhelming order	難以負荷的訂單

2 **解答為p.p.的情況**

complicated problems	複雜的問題	preferred methods / means	受歡迎的方法／手段
dedicated employees	專心的員工	experienced employees	有經驗的員工
motivated employees	積極的員工	qualified applicants	符合資格的應徵者
distinguished scholars	傑出的學者	informed decision	根據情報的決定
detailed information	詳細的情報	involved tasks	相關的事項
merged companies	合併的公司		

例子

1 (A) lead
  (B) leads
  (C) leading
  (D) leader

❶ 把握問題的類型

❷ 空格中要填什麼詞類？

As you probably know, it seems that the _____ cause of business failure is poor advertising.

❸ 把握提示

1 把握問題的類型
  詞性問題

2 把握提示
  空格前面是冠詞，
  後面是名詞

3 空格中要填什麼詞類？
  形容詞

---

2 (A) Surprising
  (B) Surprised
  (C) Surprise
  (D) Surprises

_____ by the high ticket prices, many of the museum's visitors were reluctant to enter the place.

1 把握問題的類型

2 把握提示

3 空格中要填什麼詞類？

---

3 (A) motivating
  (B) motivate
  (C) motivation
  (D) motivated

Reports show that shoppers _____ by store discounts will often spend more money, which seems unreasonable.

1 把握問題的類型

2 把握提示

3 空格中要填什麼詞類？

---

4 (A) Following
  (B) Followed
  (C) Follow
  (D) To follow

_____ this holiday weekend, I'll announce a great plan to give a boost in our overseas sales.

1 把握問題的類型

2 把握提示

3 空格中要填什麼詞類？

---

5 (A) import
  (B) imported
  (C) important
  (D) importing

Goods _____ from overseas often cost more than domestic goods, although their quality does not meet our expectation.

1 把握問題的類型

2 把握提示

3 空格中要填什麼詞類？

6 (A) blanketing
   (B) blankets
   (C) blanketed
   (D) blanket

The runway, _____ with snow, was unable to support air traffic all day long despite their dedicated efforts.

1 把握問題的類型

2 把握提示

3 空格中要填什麼詞類？

7 (A) stolen
   (B) stole
   (C) stealing
   (D) steals

There was shocking news that the police arrested five young boys for possession of _____ electronic equipment.

1 把握問題的類型

2 把握提示

3 空格中要填什麼詞類？

8 (A) applied for
   (B) applied to
   (C) applying to
   (D) applying for

A short confidential memo was sent to all employees _____ job promotions, which aroused more interest.

1 把握問題的類型

2 把握提示

3 空格中要填什麼詞類？

9 (A) reducing
   (B) reduced
   (C) to reduce
   (D) reduction

According to the new safety regulations, we must keep the waiting time _____ at security checkpoints.

1 把握問題的類型

2 把握提示

3 空格中要填什麼詞類？

10 (A) dedicating
   (B) dedication
   (C) dedicate
   (D) dedicated to

Smith Glue Supply, Inc., constructed two new factories _____ producing glass bottles.

1 把握問題的類型

2 把握提示

3 空格中要填什麼詞類？

▶ 解答在066頁

101 President Patel promised to increase the export of automobiles _____ domestically.

(A) to manufacture
(B) manufacturing
(C) as manufactured
(D) manufactured

高難度
102 _____ to become the top food provider in the nation, Alliance Foods expanded its distribution chain by twenty percent.

(A) Striven
(B) Strive
(C) Striving
(D) Strove

103 Experts in this field predict _____ demand for clothing produced in "cruelty-free" factories in the near future.

(A) increasing
(B) increases
(C) to increase
(D) increase

104 Job applicants _____ advanced skills useful for the position will have a greater chance of being hired.

(A) displayed
(B) have displayed
(C) displaying
(D) display

105 Mr. Harrison has demonstrated his expertise in managing sales professionals _____ with pushing the company's most expensive products.

(A) been tasked
(B) tasks
(C) tasking
(D) tasked

106 The president today warned the country of upcoming economic difficulties _____ the nation's war effort.

(A) related to
(B) related
(C) relating
(D) relation

高難度
107 _____ its plans to merge with its strongest competitor, Tropical Gear will counter the demand for fashionable eyewear.

(A) Announces
(B) Announcing
(C) To announce
(D) Announcement

重要
108 Although she had little experience working with computers, Ms. Lopez is often able to assist customers _____ technical support.

(A) require
(B) requiring
(C) requirement
(D) required

109 The police chief stated today that the city's greatest problem is the _____ trend of auto theft.

(A) risen
(B) raised
(C) rising
(D) raising

110 Mr. Ben Clinton apologized to those _____ the conference room for delaying the meeting.

(A) waiting
(B) waiting for
(C) waiting on
(D) waiting in

111 Tourists to New York City during the winter months find the city's holiday decorations _____.

(A) amazing
(B) amaze
(C) amazement
(D) amazed

112 The department store has recently installed _____ doors in an effort to conserve energy costs.

(A) revolve
(B) revolution
(C) revolved
(D) revolving

113 Having _____ the research project successfully, the R&D department could focus on another.

(A) finish
(B) finishing
(C) finished
(D) been finished

重要
114 Please find the _____ forum agenda and the itinerary and let us know at least a month in advance to cancel for any reason.

(A) enclosing
(B) enclose
(C) encloses
(D) enclosed

115 The newly released movie showed satisfying ticket sales at the box office for the first week and then the figures suddenly dropped to _____ levels.

(A) disappointing
(B) disappoint
(C) disappointed
(D) disappointment

116 _____ belongings can be traced more quickly and efficiently if a complete description can be reported.

(A) Miss
(B) Missed
(C) Missing
(D) To miss

117 Our language institute _____ in offering customized intensive courses is widely recognized for achieving the best results possible.

(A) specializes
(B) specialized
(C) special
(D) specializing

118 All attendants _____ in the conference room after the presentation are encouraged to fill out the survey form.

(A) remain
(B) are remaining
(C) remained
(D) remaining

119 Unless otherwise _____, you must abide by the existing rule to meet the production schedule even if you have to work late.

(A) contracted
(B) contract
(C) contractor
(D) contracting

120 We have always done our best to keep our investors _____ of the ever-changing market conditions.

(A) informing
(B) inform
(C) informed
(D) information

▶ 解答在069頁

Giant Supply, one of our main raw material suppliers, _____ with us for four years.
121
Currently they have officially notified us that they are going to raise the price by 5%, and
they may consider _____ additional 2% by the end of the year 2018 due to their
122
self-claimed increasing production costs. _____ an evaluation carried out by our
123
Accountant Department, we are unable to figure out the exact factors that have caused
their higher production costs since the price of international crude oil keeps decreasing,
and the labor cost in the place where their company is located has stayed stable.

_____ This termination will be effective in four working days. Orders in progress will
124
be either cancelled or terminated unless Giant Supply officially withdraws their previous
notification.

121 (A) has cooperated
(B) have cooperated
(C) had cooperated
(D) has been cooperated

122 (A) raise
(B) to raise
(C) raising
(D) raised

123 (A) Before
(B) As soon as
(C) Until
(D) After

124 (A) Nevertheless, we have determined to terminate our cooperation with Giant Supply
(B) In spite of this, we have determined to terminate our cooperation with Giant Supply
(C) After all, we have determined to terminate our cooperation with Giant Supply
(D) Therefore, we have determined to terminate our cooperation with Giant Supply

▶ 解答在069頁

Part 04
簡單易懂的連接詞和介系詞

名詞子句連接詞

展開時間的名詞連接詞的題型！

Review Test

我們在Chapter 10提到分詞扮演著形容詞角色，我們來回憶一下吧。

1 分詞的種類與其型態？　　　　▶ ....

2 現在分詞的意思是？　　　　　▶ ....

3 過去分詞的意思是？　　　　　▶ ....

4 如何區分現在分詞和過去分詞？　▶ ....

5 分詞的擺放位置為何？　　　　▶ ....

6 主要使用現在分詞的分詞詞彙為何？ ▶ ....

7 主要使用過去分詞的分詞詞彙為何？ ▶ ....

8 感官動詞如何使用？　　　　　▶ ....

Preview

1　名詞子句連接詞的特徵
　　名詞子句就是含有S（主詞）和V（動詞）的子句，且在句中扮演著主詞、受詞、補語的
　　角色。名詞子句一般位在主詞、動詞的受詞、介系詞的受詞或補語等位置，其連接詞大
　　部分都以what、that開頭。看似複雜，但只要記得「名詞」，就很簡單了。

2　名詞子句連接詞的解題法
　　❶ 確認句中名詞子句會出現的4個地方
　　❷ 確認句子中是否已有主詞、動詞
　　❸ 最後要翻譯出來

正確答案｜　1. 現在分詞（-ing）和過去分詞（p.p.）　2. 正在…中　3. 已經…　4. 翻譯出意思和確認是否有受詞　5. 名詞的前後、第2大和第5大句型的補語　6. when, while, before, after的後面　7. once, as, unless　8. 修飾人用p.p.，修飾事物用-ing

攻略法

44

解名詞子句題型的方法

簡單來說，名詞子句具備了「主詞（S）+動詞（V）」元素，扮演著名詞的角色。你說你不懂是什麼意思嗎？看完下面的例句和說明後，你就懂了。

1. 名詞子句的定義

只要具有「**主詞（S）＋動詞（V）**」型態的就叫做子句（clause），這時的子句也是「一段文章中的一句」。**名詞子句在句中可當主詞、受詞、補語，由「名詞」和「子句」組成的。別想得太難！「雖說是子句，但扮演著名詞」這樣想就簡單多了吧！**此外，也需要一個能連接子句和文章的連接詞，這就叫做名詞子句連接詞，最具代表性的有what, that, whether。

1　**(What / Because) I need is** just you.

動詞is的前半部分是名詞子句，連接名詞子句的連接詞應該選What。本句的意思是「我所需要的東西」，若是接Because，就變成副詞子句，也不能有is的主詞出現了。

1　我所需要的／就是你。

2　**I know (that / about) you are telling a lie.**

句中有兩組「S + V」的子句型態（I know和you are telling a lie），所以括弧內的答案必須是連結兩個句子的連接詞。about是介系詞，不能連結兩個句子，即使覺得翻譯出來的意思很通順，也無法選為解答。that以後就是名詞，也是動詞know的受詞。括弧內的正確答案就是that。

2　我知道／你正在說謊。

3　We **wondered (that / whether) we could finish it on time or not.**

雖然兩個都是名詞子句連接詞，能和wonder「很好奇」搭配的只有表示「是不是…」的連接詞「whether」。如果是接「that」，意思就變成「…的這件事」，整句話變得很奇怪了。

3　我們很好奇／我們是否可以準時結束掉那件事。

重新整理一下，**所謂的名詞子句就是「主詞（S）＋動詞（V）」一起組成的句子，在文中扮演著主詞（S）、受詞（O）、補語（C）**。不過要注意「主詞＋動詞」在文中是扮演主詞、受詞、補語，所以不要忘了

文中會有另外使名詞子句成為主詞、受詞、補語的主詞和動詞。簡單來說，就是需要有連接詞，**像這樣連接整組「主詞（S）＋動詞（V）」的連接詞就叫作名詞子句連接詞。**

2. 名詞子句的4種樣貌

名詞子句擁有4種不同的樣貌，可當主詞、動詞的受詞、介系詞的受詞和補語。要將句子的意思翻譯出來，才能知道是否為名詞子句，還有該在哪邊放入名詞子句連接詞。而分析的基本原則就是我們在Chapter 03裡學到的5大句型。想學好連接詞，一定要先把5大句型牢記在心裡。

(1) 名詞子句當作主詞時

What students want is just higher scores.

> 學生們希望的／只是更高的分數。

後面第二個動詞is的主詞是前面的what students want，這就是名詞子句的主詞角色。

(2) 名詞子句當作及物動詞的受詞

I **know** that he doesn't know it.

> 我知道／他不知道這件事。

know是第3大句型的動詞，that後面的單字就是扮演著受詞的名詞子句。所以如果基本5大句型沒學好的話，學習此單元會感到吃力。

(3) 名詞子句中當作介系詞的受詞

I don't have any information **about what they will do next**.

> 我沒有／任何資訊／有關於他們下次將要做什麼的。

例句what以下的整段句子，都是依附著about，這句話翻為「有關於他們將要做什麼的」的意思。這就是名詞子句當作介系詞的受詞。

(4) 名詞子句當作主格補語時

The reason why they were fired **is that they made too many mistakes**. < 他們被解雇的理由／是他們犯了太多失誤。

that以下的句子是名詞子句，也是第2大句型動詞is的補語。請看下面兩點。

第一、一般補語雖然是形容詞，但子句型態（S＋V）的句子當作補語時，100%是名詞子句，和主詞是同等關係。而形容詞子句絕對不能當作補語使用。

第二、結論「S＋V」是補語的時候，100%是名詞子句，並稱為第2大句型動詞的補語。

上述就是名詞子句在文中的4種角色。了解名詞子句的理論固然重要，但更重要的是平時要多接觸名詞子句，累積自己的實力到一看到文章，就能馬上自然而然地反應出「啊！這裡就是名詞子句啊！」。**但是名詞子句不一定會在句中當主詞、受詞或是補語，依據連接詞的特性會有些不同。**

怪物講師的祕訣

名詞子句連接詞位置的特徵
1 主詞：第二個動詞是限定動詞。注意，別和連接詞子句裡的動詞混淆。
2 及物動詞的受詞：及物動詞後面的一整個句子是受詞。
3 介系詞的受詞：介系詞也有受詞。後面的整個句子是受詞。
4 主格補語：為名詞補語，和主詞為同等關係。

Quiz

Q1 It is uncertain (whether / because) they will approve it or not.
Q2 I asked him (what / regarding) he wanted to do during his vacation.

▶ 解答在073頁

攻略法 **45**

名詞子句連接詞的種類

名詞子句連接詞有很多種，要了解各種連接詞的特性，才有辦法區分。來吧！深呼吸做好心理準備後，一起來看下面的說明吧！

前面提到4種名詞子句所帶出的連接詞，來看看是哪些，且它們的特性是什麼。

1. 名詞子句連接詞what和that

這是出題機率相當高的名詞子句連接詞。**如果說句子組合的要素都完備的話（也就是說具備了主詞、受詞、補語…等），就使用that；不夠完整的話（也就是說沒有主詞、受詞、補語…等），就使用what。**

1 (What / That) he fired her was known to everybody.

> 1 他解雇她的事／被所有的人知道了。

he fired her是完整的第3大句型（S＋V＋O），所以正確答案是that。在這裡that he fired her是名詞子句，當作動詞was的主詞。

2 (What / That) I expected from him was quite resonable.

> 2 我對他的期待／是非常合理的。

動詞was的整個前半部分是主詞，expect是第3大句型的動詞，但後面沒有受詞，屬於不完整的句子，所以要選擇what為解答。這時what開始到him是名詞子句，動詞was的主詞。

3 We will **announce (that / what) he will be promoted.**

> 3 我們將要發表的是／他即將要升遷。

announce是需要接受詞的及物動詞，所以announce以後的句子是被當作受詞的名詞子句。he will be promoted中的promoted雖然是及物動詞，但屬於被動態，後面不需要有受詞，所以括弧後面屬於完整句子，that為正確解答。

連接詞that或是what以後的句子都是解釋為「…的」，所以無法以翻譯解釋來區分；兩者皆可套用於4種名詞子句公式內，也無法用位置來做區分。雖然已經強調很多次，不過還是要再次提醒，「括弧後面是完整的句子時，就使用that；不夠完整的話，就使用what」。

名詞子句連接詞的位置和特徵

1 名詞子句連接詞that

與關係代名詞that不同。（請參考Chapter 12）

- 關係代名詞that前面要有先行名詞，後面接不完整句。

- 名詞子句that前面沒有先行名詞，後面需接完整句。

2 將that子句當作受詞的動詞

主張：argue, assert, declare, emphasize, insist, request, maintain...

說：say, state, tell, explain, indicate, predict...

想：believe, think, know, note...

出現（發現）：demonstrate, discover, find, reveal...

＊這些動詞的後面大部分會出現that、say that、believe that等，練習時直接發出聲音邊唸邊記憶，可加速熟悉用法。

3 名詞子句連接詞what

這裡的what和後面會學到的疑問句的意思不一樣

- 名詞子句連接詞what指「那東西」，和疑問詞的「什麼」意思不同。

- 雖然與that意思不一樣，但兩者都是名詞子句連接詞，後面都是接不完整句。

（疑問詞what後面必須接完整的句子。）

- what不能解釋為關係代名詞。因為關係代名詞是形容詞子句連接詞，而what不是形容詞子句連接詞。what僅是名詞子句連接詞。

《講師的補充說明》

和前面先行名詞同等關係的that

上面有提到，關係代名詞that的前面有先行名詞，後面出現的不完整句；名詞子句連接詞that前面沒有先行名詞，句子是完整句。不過也有可能兩種特性同時存在著，the fact that（…的事實）、the rumor that（…的傳聞）、the news that（…的消息）、the truth that（…的事實）。

這時前面和關係代名詞一樣出現了先行名詞，但是後面卻是接著完整句，這點又好像是名詞子句吧？真是讓人摸不著頭緒。此時的that嚴格來說，是名詞子句連接詞。

因為它和前面的先行名詞屬同等關係，that以後的句子和先行名詞同樣是名詞角色的名詞子句，因此that後面是接著完整句。像這類的表現the fact that已經是慣用語句，能熟記是上上策。

Quiz

Q3 I want to know (that / what) customers want.
Q4 The fact is (what / that) he knows every little detail.

▶ 解答在073頁

2. 名詞子句連接詞whether和if

這兩種連接詞皆可使用在名詞子句和副詞子句，**若要細分，whether常被使用於名詞子句；if常被使用於副詞子句。**

1 (If / Whether) he will be transferred or not is not sure.

名詞子句在這裡扮演著動詞is的主詞，因為whether常被使用於名詞子句；if常被使用於副詞子句，所以正確答案是whether。

1 不確定他是不是要調職。

2 (Whether / If) to buy it or not depends on the situation.

有看到括弧後面的to不定詞吧！請記住喔！能和to不定詞一起出現的連接詞就是whether，沒有if to do的表現方式，所以正確解答是whether。

2 要不要買那個／取決於／情況。

如同前面的例句，名詞子句連接詞whether和if的用法很容易搞混。上面也提到，兩者都能使用於名詞子句和副詞子句，因此將兩者的區分法整理如下面的表格，若能了解下面的表格，whether和if的題目答題準確率就能達到100%。

	whether	if	注意事項
名詞子句 是名詞子句時， whether為正解	是不是…	是不是…	無法用翻譯解釋的方式做區分
	用在完整句	用在完整句	追究是否為完整句會浪費時間
	用在名詞子句4種型態	if子句僅使用在及物動詞後面→主詞+及物動詞 if S + V + O（或C）	可依據出現的位置做區分
	可自由變形。 whether S + V (or not) = whether (or not) S + V = whether to 原形動詞(or not) = whether (or not) to 原形動詞 = whether A or B（關係連接詞）	if子句不可變形，僅能是if S + V (or not)	後面出現to不定詞或是or not，whether就極可能是答案，if絕非是答案。
副詞子句 是副詞子句時，if為正解。	不論是不是…	如果…的話	whether是名詞子句時，主要子句不完整（whether是S、O、C，所以拿掉的話，句子不完整）
	使用在完整句	使用在完整句	
	即使沒有whether子句，主要子句也是完整的。（因為是副詞子句）	配合4種假設法，須注意時態。因此需要注意動詞部分。	
	不使用在副詞子句	不使用在名詞子句	

Quiz ....

Q5 I wonder (if / what) he will approve it.

Q6 I asked (whether / that) we could finish it on time.

▶ 解答在073頁

3. 疑問詞（wh-、how）開頭的名詞子句

「疑問詞 + S + V」能使用在名詞子句的4個句子型態中，也可以當作名詞子句的一種。也可將「疑問詞 + S + V」寫為「疑問詞 + to不定詞」的型態。

疑問詞大略可以分成下面三種。
- 疑問代名詞：who / whom, what / which
- 疑問形容詞：whose, what / which
- 疑問副詞：when, where, why, how

1 I wonder (whom / where) you want to work.

括弧以後的句子是名詞子句，當作動詞wonder的受詞。括弧後面「主詞 + 動詞 + 受詞」是完整的第3大句型。（work是第1大句型的動詞，後面不需要受詞）因為是完整句子，正解為當作副詞使用的疑問副詞where。

2 (Who / When) will get the prize remains to be seen.

動詞remains的前面是當作主詞的名詞子句，will沒有主詞，因此正確答案就是可以當主詞的疑問代名詞who。when是疑問副詞，只能使用在完整句。

簡單來說，**句子是不完整句的話，答案就是疑問代名詞；如果是完整句的話，答案就是疑問形容詞或疑問副詞。若用在修飾名詞，請選疑問形容詞；若是修飾動詞、形容詞或副詞時，請選疑問副詞為解答。**

3 I can't understand (what / why) you are trying to say.

括弧以後是動詞understand的受詞子句，受詞子句中的動詞say以後沒有受詞，屬不完整句，因此解答應選疑問代名詞what。

4 I inquired of him (which / where) to stay.

動詞inquire需要有受詞，我們有說過「疑問詞 + S + V」的名詞子句可用「疑問詞to不定詞」取代，此例句正應用此方法。這裡的stay是「停留」的意思，屬第1大句型動詞，本身就是個完整句，因此正確答案為where。where to stay翻譯出來是「要在哪裡停留」，語意自然，若是which to stay翻譯出來是「要停留什麼」，完全不知所云

5秒 解決疑問詞題型的方法

1 句中沒有主詞、受詞、或是補語時→解答為疑問代名詞

- 代表人時→解答為who或whom

  → 如果沒有主詞或補語，解答為who；如果沒有受詞，解答為whom

- 代表事物時→解答為what或which

  → 沒有主詞、受詞或補語時，兩者皆可使用

  → 如果是選擇動詞（choose、select）時，解答為which；除此之外的其它情況解答為what

2 句子是完整句時→解答為疑問形容詞或疑問副詞

3 「受詞〔名詞補語〕S＋V」的型態時 → 解答為疑問形容詞

疑問形容詞在前面修飾受詞或名詞補語，所以如果受詞或名詞補語出現在前面的話，解答就是疑問形容詞。

4 單純的「S＋V＋O（或C）」時 → 解答可為疑問形容詞、疑問副詞

這時後面的主詞接代名詞、冠詞或是所有格，解答為疑問副詞的可能性很高；如果是只有名詞的話，解答很可能是疑問形容詞。這時解釋為誰的（whose）、什麼（what）、何者（which）較為合理。

5 疑問副詞的判別→用翻譯解釋的方式。何時（when）、何處（where）、為何（why）

「how S＋V」時，how大部分都解釋為「如何」，如果是「how 形容詞（副詞）S＋V」則解釋為「多麼」。

《講師的補充說明》

1) 疑問代名詞

想知道的部分（＝疑問）是主詞、受詞或補語時而詢問的話。（who 誰、whom 誰（受詞）、what 什麼、which 哪一個）

2) 疑問形容詞

想知道的部分（＝疑問）修飾名詞時而詢問的話。（whose 誰的、what 什麼、which 哪一個）

3) 疑問副詞

想知道的部分（＝疑問）修飾動詞、形容詞、副詞時而詢問的話。（when 何時、where 何處、why 為何、how 如何；多麼）

Quiz

Q7 I wonder (how / what) to do it.

Q8 Her hometown is (when / where) her son was brought up.

▶ 解答在073頁

4. 複合關係詞

複合關係詞的出題機率不高，急於學習其它部分的學習者可以跳過這部分。如果是想要拿高分的話，那就不能漏掉任何一部分。

1 I don't care (whatever / whosever) he may say.

動詞care的受詞是括弧後面的名詞子句，名詞子句內的動詞say後面沒有受詞，是不完整句，此時答案是複合關係代名詞whatever。

2 We welcome (whoever / whomever) comes first.

動詞welcome的受詞是名詞子句，名詞子句的動詞comes沒有主詞，因此答案要選可以當主詞的whoever。whomever是受詞格，複合關係詞的種類整理如下頁，仔細看的話，可以發現名詞子句連接詞，只有複合關係代名詞和複合關係形容詞。**如果是完整句的話，使用複合關係形容詞；如果是不完整句的話，則是複合關係代名詞。**

1 我不在乎／他可能說什麼。

2 我們很歡迎／不論是誰先來。

(1) 複合關係代名詞

whoever, whomever, whatever, whichever

→ 名詞子句，副詞子句連接詞

(2) 複合關係形容詞

whosever, whatever, whichever

→ 名詞子句，副詞子句連接詞

(3) 複合關係副詞

whenever, wherever, however

→ 副詞子句連接詞，不常使用於名詞子句連接詞

5秒 解決複合關係詞題型的方法

複合關係詞總整理

1 名詞子句

句子屬不完整句時，是使用複合關係代名詞；完整句時，使用複合關係形容詞。如果是人的話，使用whoever（主格、補格）或whomever（受格）；是事物時用whichever；其餘的就選擇whatever。

2 副詞子句

複合關係詞皆可使用，句子屬不完整句的話，須使用複合關係代名詞。當然，人和事物須區分清楚。後面的主詞或代名詞有接冠詞或是所有格的話，填入疑問副詞；如果只有名詞時，複合關係形容詞為正解的機率較高。如果是解釋為「不論是哪一種人」即使用whoever；若是解釋為「不論是什麼事」或「不論是什麼東西」時，就填入whatever或whichever。

Quiz ....

Q9 (Whoever / Whomever) she dismisses is not important in this case.
Q10 I don't care (whomever / whatever) he collects.

▶ 解答在073頁

攻略法 44　解名詞子句題型的方法

1 名詞子句和名詞子句連接詞的定義

名詞子句是「主詞 + 動詞」，在句子中被當作主詞、受詞、或補語使用。

所謂的名詞子句連接詞，是「主詞 + 動詞」和另一組「主詞 + 動詞」做連接的連接詞。

2 名詞子句連接詞的4種樣貌

1)（名詞子句連接詞 S + V1 + OC）+ V2 + OC —— 句子的主詞

2) S + 及物動詞 +（名詞子句連接詞 S + V + OC）—— 句子的受詞

3) S + V + OC + 介系詞 +（名詞子句連接詞 S + V1 + OC）—— 介系詞的受詞

4) S + 第2種句型動詞（一般為be動詞）（名詞子句連接詞 S + V1 + OC）—— 補語

＊須根據名詞子句連接詞來區分完整句和不完整句。

攻略法 45　名詞子句連接詞的種類

1 名詞子句連接詞that和what

不需翻譯解釋句意，只要觀察句子屬於完整句或是不完整句。是完整句的話，選擇that；不完整句的話，選擇what為解答。

2 名詞子句連接詞whether和if

是名詞子句的話，選擇whether為答案；若屬副詞子句的話，選擇if為解答，副詞子句if須特別注意時態。

3 疑問詞開頭的名詞子句

句子是不完整句的話，答案是疑問代名詞；如果是完整句的話，答案是疑問形容詞或疑問副詞。若是用在修飾名詞，請選疑問形容詞；若是修飾動詞、形容詞或副詞，請選疑問副詞為解答。

4 複合關係詞

- **複合關係代名詞**：whoever, whomever, whatever, whichever（名詞子句、副詞子句連接詞）

- **複合關係形容詞**：whosever, whatever, whichever（名詞子句、副詞子句連接詞）

- **複合關係複詞**：whenever, wherever, however（大部分是副詞子句連接詞）

例子

1　(A) what　　❶ 把握問題的類型
　　(B) how
　　(C) whose
　　(D) whoever
　　　　　　　　　　　　　❷ 把握提示
The research team conducted a study to find out _____
the consumers use the company's products.　　❸ 空格中要填什麼詞類？

1 把握問題的類型
　文法題
2 把握提示
　座格後的句子完整性
3 空格中要填什麼詞類？
　連接詞

2　(A) that
　　(B) whom
　　(C) when
　　(D) what

It is not surprising at all that _____ most workers in our division look for in a lunch menu is low-priced items.

1 把握問題的類型
2 把握提示
3 空格中要填什麼詞類？

3　(A) what
　　(B) that
　　(C) why
　　(D) whatever

The accountant's small but inexcusable mistake was _____ she did not properly record all of the travel expenses.

1 把握問題的類型
2 把握提示
3 空格中要填什麼詞類？

4　(A) whichever
　　(B) whether
　　(C) why
　　(D) that

Ms. Lee had to decide _____ she would announce her retirement or report it privately to her boss.

1 把握問題的類型
2 把握提示
3 空格中要填什麼詞類？

5　(A) whatever
　　(B) whenever
　　(C) whomever
　　(D) however

In my opinion, _____ health insurance plan you choose will certainly be better than having no insurance.

1 把握問題的類型
2 把握提示
3 空格中要填什麼詞類？

6 (A) who
(B) how
(C) if
(D) that

After her interview, Samantha was hopeful _____ she would be hired for the position soon.

1 把握問題的類型

2 把握提示

3 空格中要填什麼詞類？

7 (A) whether
(B) whom
(C) whenever
(D) wherever

Passengers are reminded to remain quiet _____ there is an announcement from the pilot.

1 把握問題的類型

2 把握提示

3 空格中要填什麼詞類？

8 (A) Who
(B) That
(C) Whoever
(D) If

_____ would like to make a purchase through this website should fill out an order form.

1 把握問題的類型

2 把握提示

3 空格中要填什麼詞類？

9 (A) if
(B) what
(C) although
(D) that

Due to the deadline, Ms. Tomlin would like to know _____ any employees need the new equipment.

1 把握問題的類型

2 把握提示

3 空格中要填什麼詞類？

10 (A) why
(B) when
(C) what
(D) and

You will certainly know _____ the ferry boat arrives because you will hear the loud steam whistle.

1 把握問題的類型

2 把握提示

3 空格中要填什麼詞類？

▶ 解答在073頁

高難度

101 For two years, the product warranty guarantees free repairs for _____ may happen to the item.

(A) however
(B) who
(C) if
(D) whatever

102 Dr. Juarez cautioned _____ continued tobacco use may result in negative effects on the body, particularly the lungs.

(A) that
(B) what
(C) whose
(D) who

103 The quality control team is responsible for any complaints _____ there is a product design flaw.

(A) because
(B) why
(C) where
(D) when

104 Employees who believe they are eligible should let their managers know _____ they would like to apply for a pay raise.

(A) that
(B) how
(C) if
(D) who

105 Jerry did not understand _____ his corporate credit card was declined when he attempted to pay for a business lunch.

(A) why
(B) when
(C) where
(D) what

106 Job advertisements are typically posted _____ the most suitable candidates are likely to see them.

(A) whatever
(B) however
(C) wherever
(D) whenever

107 Travelers hoping to rent a car may be disappointed to learn that the selection of vehicles is limited to _____ is available at the time.

(A) this
(B) it
(C) whoever
(D) whichever

高難度

108 The year-end performance bonus would be awarded to _____ had the highest total sales figure for the year.

(A) what
(B) whoever
(C) whom
(D) whether

109 _____ to construct a new warehouse or rent an existing building in the industrial park was a major point of discussion in today's meeting.

(A) Whether
(B) Whatever
(C) When
(D) If

重要

110 The computer tech can determine _____ employee's computer originated the virus that attacked the company network.

(A) which
(B) that
(C) where
(D) whose

111 Most airlines keep a list of _____ luggage is lost or stolen and will attempt to contact those passengers soon after the flight.

(A) whenever
(B) whom
(C) that
(D) whose

高難度

112 The brochure handed to theater patrons explains _____ the tickets were more expensive than usual.

(A) whether
(B) what
(C) why
(D) which

113 A METRO spokesman said _____ the company is targeting 6 to 8 new stores a year over the next three to four years.

(A) what
(B) whether
(C) that
(D) concerning

114 In spite of the fact _____ the economic prospect of the future is very uncertain, we should do our best to meet our goal.

(A) that
(B) what
(C) which
(D) while

重要

115 Please be assured _____ your application form has been received and you will be notified of the final result as soon as possible.

(A) that
(B) what
(C) concerning
(D) of

116 _____ we can deal with this economic crisis will be covered in the upcoming board meeting.

(A) Although
(B) What
(C) How
(D) While

117 Chances are that you're _____ the value and reliability associated with our brand name.

(A) attracted
(B) attracts
(C) attracted to
(D) attractive

118 The question of _____ the special bonus will be given or not this month is still under discussion.

(A) if
(B) whether
(C) whose
(D) what

119 Recent economic reports _____ that the economy may not need much cooling considering current interest rates.

(A) tell
(B) indicate
(C) inform
(D) express

120 _____ we are worried about most is that we have to face the difficulty we have to overcome even in times we don't want to.

(A) What
(B) That
(C) Though
(D) Unless

▶ 解答在076頁

Questions 121-124 refer to the following notice.

To all sales representative

_____ we have received some reports referring to missing parts or components in our
121
orders, we have determined to implement a new system. Sincere apologies _____ this
122
will cause you any additional trouble.

- Hand in your orders with the approval of the department head to the Purchasing Department with the specific brand name of the part, scale, quantity, and any other necessary information relating to the part.

- All the parts are expected _____ within five working days. No urgent deliveries will
123
be processed.

- You must pick up the parts with the duplication of the original order. Any pick up of parts without a duplication of the original order is prohibited.

- The warehouse is responsible for receiving and storing all the ordered parts only.

_____
124

121 (A) Due to
(B) Owing to the fact that
(C) Owing to
(D) Because of

122 (A) unless
(B) until
(C) in case of
(D) if

123 (A) delivering
(B) being delivered
(C) to be delivered
(D) delivered

124 (A) Fixing and repairing parts are included.
(B) Packaging and delivering parts are available.
(C) Refunding and exchanging parts are also arranged.
(D) Returning and exchanging parts are excluded.

▶ 解答在076頁

形容詞子句連接詞
用先行名詞來解決形容詞連接詞！

Review Test

Chapter 11裡學到了名詞子句連接詞。還記得that、what、if這些連接詞嗎？我們來複習前一章學過的內容吧！

1 名詞子句的4個位置？　　　　　　　▶ ....

2 名詞子句連接詞that和what的差別是？▶ ....

3 「是不是…」的連接詞為？　　　　　▶ ....

4 if和whether可以是_____子句、_____子句的連接詞。　▶ ....

5 if主要使用於_____子句；whether主要使用於_____子句。　▶ ....

6 哪2個疑問代名詞是有表示人的意思？　▶ ....

7 複合關係詞中，┌ a. 句子為不完整句時 ▶ ....

　　　　　　　　└ b. 句子為完整句時　　▶ ....

Preview

1 形容詞子句連接詞的特徵
「主詞＋動詞」的型態稱作子句。一個子句在文章中，像形容詞一樣修飾著名詞，這時**稱作形容詞子句，這種子句帶出的連接詞叫作形容詞子句連接詞。**而接受形容詞子句修飾的名詞就是先行名詞。若是了解形容詞子句的話，就可以自由自在地運用子句。

2 形容詞子句連接詞的解題法
❶ 確認出現在形容詞子句前的「先行名詞」。
❷ 形容詞子句內的句子要素是否都具備，確認是完整句或是不完整句。
❸ 用翻譯的方式，確認先行名詞和形容詞子句是否自然地連接。

｜正確答案｜ 1. 主詞、動詞的受詞、介系詞的受詞、補語 2. 不完整句時，使用what；完整句使用that 3. whether S + V或whether to不定詞
4. 名詞、副詞 5. 副詞、名詞 6. who、whom 7. a. 複合關係代名詞 b. 複合關係形容詞（複合關係副詞是副詞子句連接詞）

解決形容詞子句題型的方法

形容詞子句是關係子句的一種，不過用名詞子句、形容詞子句或副詞子句這樣的說法，比關係子句讓人更容易理解。

什麼是形容詞子句呢？簡單來說，就是用來修飾名詞的子句型態「S + V」，就叫作形容詞子句。因此，形容詞子句前面必定有接受該**形容詞子句修飾的名詞，這個名詞又稱作「先行名詞」。**

1 The **manager** (who interviewed me) expressed his satisfaction.

　　　先行名詞　關係詞主格　　動詞1　受詞　　動詞2　　　受詞
　　　　　　　（形，連）

> **1** 經理／面試我的那位／表現出／他的滿意。

例句中的manager是先行名詞，who以後到me是形容詞子句，是「面試我的」的意思，當作形容詞修飾前面的名詞manager。主詞manager的主要動詞，是形容詞子句後的expressed。

2 The **manager whom I met** will notify me by the end of this week.

> **2** 經理／我見到的那位／會通知我／在這禮拜結束以前。

以例句1的方式為基礎，來試著分析例句2。manager一樣是先行名詞。whom I met是修飾manager的形容詞子句，可有可無。可是為什麼例句1是用who，例句2卻是用whom呢？因為例句1裡「面試我的人」是經理，經理是面試這個行為的主體，所以使用主格who。

另一方面，例句2中「我見到的人」是經理，經理不是主詞，而是受詞，所以使用受格whom。要依據先行名詞在形容詞子句裡扮演的角色，而決定使用who或是whom。

這類的句子看很多了吧？不過大概了解跟真正徹底了解是不一樣的。就算覺得是老生常談，也要一字不漏記到腦海裡，若是可以直接用英文表達的機會時，想想看該如何表達較適當。用這種決心學習的話，結果絕對會不一樣。

若要細分形容詞子句連接詞的話，如下頁的圖表。

先行名詞	關係詞選擇	完整、不完整與否
人	who (= that)	沒有主詞或補語（不完整句）
	whom (= that)	沒有受詞（不完整句）
	whose	該有的都有（完整句）
事物	which (= that)	主、受、補之中缺少其一（不完整句）
	of which	該有的都有（完整句）後面的the名詞
	whose	該有的都有（完整句）後面沒有the名詞或是所有格需有名詞
時間	when	該有的都有（完整句）
場所	where	該有的都有（完整句）
理由	why	該有的都有（完整句）
方法	how	該有的都有（完整句）

《講師的補充說明》

下列句型是省略了關係詞受格。

「先行名詞 + 主詞 + 動詞1 + 動詞2 + OC」或是

「先行名詞 + 主詞 + 動詞1 + OC+ 介系詞 + 動詞2 + OC」

＊關係副詞都可用that替換，但不常這麼使用。

＊如果先行名詞是前半段整個句子時，請選擇「逗號（,）+which」（,which）為答案。

＊有先行名詞時，這些單字就是形容詞連接詞；如果沒有先行名詞，這些單字就當作是名詞子句連接詞使用。

5秒 解決形容詞子句題型的方法

第一階段：先行名詞是人？→ 答案選who, whom, whose

　　　　　先行名詞是事物？→ 答案選which, of which, whose

　　　　　先行名詞是時間、場所、理由、方法？→ 答案選when, where, why, how

第二階段：句子是完整句時 → 答案選whose, of which, when, where, why, how

　　　　　句子是不完整句時 → 答案選who, whom, which

Quiz

Q1 The woman (who / which) visited us yesterday was Jane.

Q2 The part (who / which) was ordered a week ago is ready to be picked up.

▶ 解答在080頁

攻略法

47

容易混淆的形容詞子句題型

在攻略法46，建立了形容詞子句的基礎，不過若想要得到高分，並且在寫作和口說都有不錯的能力，也要努力將接下來的學習內容都變成是自己的東西。

想要得高分，就得要在花功夫。這裡蒐集了大部分的人都會混淆的形容詞子句，當然，光靠前面的攻略法46就夠解決大多數的題型，如果覺得接下來的內容很難理解的話，你也可以跳過不看。但如果是想要了解得更深入，也可以試著學習看看。

1. 到底是名詞子句呢？還是形容詞子句呢？

who、whom、whose、which、when、where、why、how等，這些都是在名詞子句連接詞單元裡學到的字，不過在這邊卻是當形容詞子句連接詞使用。簡單說明一下，若句中有先行名詞的話，就是形容詞子句；若沒有先行名詞的話，就是名詞子句。我們來看看下面兩個例句吧！

1 I don't know **the man who is sitting outside**.

2 I don't know **who is sitting outside**.

如同前面說的，例句1有先行名詞，所以是形容詞子句。例句2沒有先行名詞，所以是名詞子句。例句1的who是形容詞子句連接詞，或是關係詞代名詞；例句2的who是名詞子句連接詞，或是疑問詞。雖然解釋上有些不一樣，但最終還是看有沒有先行名詞。

2. 容易混淆的that整理

(1) that是名詞子句連接詞，還是形容詞子句連接詞？
連接詞that可以當名詞子句連接詞，也可以當形容詞子句連接詞。同樣**如果有先行名詞，就是形容詞子句連接詞；如果沒有先行名詞，就是名詞子句連接詞**，和上面一樣。

1 我不認識／那男生／坐在外面的那位。

2 我不知道／是誰坐在／外面。

差別在形容詞子句連接詞是使用在不完整句，名詞子句連接詞是和完整句一起使用。

1 I will suggest **one thing that you should do**.

2 I will suggest **that you should do it**.

1 我要提議／一項你必須要做的事。

2 我要提議／你必須要做那件事。

因為有先行名詞one thing，所以例句1的that以後是形容詞子句。這時that以後的動詞do沒有受詞，是不完整句。例句2沒有先行名詞，是名詞子句，這裡that以後是完整的第3大句型。想要再更深入探討嗎？剛剛說例句1是形容詞子句吧？若將that以後的句子刪掉的話，前面的句子也是第3大句型，也就是說，that後是用來當修飾句的形容詞子句，即使拿掉對句子也毫無影響。剛剛也有說例句2是名詞子句吧？這裡that以後是動詞suggest的受詞，如果把that以後的句子拿掉的話，就變成動詞suggest沒有受詞的句子。

(2) 形容詞子句中that和which的區別
連接詞that的優點是不論先行名詞是人，或是物品都可以使用，但還是有幾個需要注意的地方。其中最重要的就是不可使用在逗點（,）或是介系詞後面。這規則也僅限在形容詞子句中。（連接詞that用法相當廣泛，可用在名詞子句連接詞、形容詞子句連接詞、副詞子句連接詞、同格that、強調的that、指示代名詞、指示形容詞等。）

3 He was awarded a medal, **(which / that) surprised us all**.

4 We are throwing a party at a hotel in **(which / that) we met before**.

3 他領了／獎牌，這件事令我們全部都感到相當驚訝。

4 我們辦派對／在一間飯店裡／我們先前見面的地方。

例句3的逗號（,）後面是屬「關係代名詞的持續性」用法，這時必須使用括弧內的which，因為that不使用在持續性用法，無法使用於逗號（,）後面。那麼例句4的括弧該填什麼答案呢？答案是which。這例句中，which的前面有介系詞in、on、at，不過that前面不可有這類字出現。

怪物講師的祕訣

除此之外你必須要知道的that的用法

1 that不論先行名詞是人，或是物品都可以使用

2 和which不同的是，that不可使用在逗號（,）或是介系詞後面
　　→ 這規則也僅限在形容詞子句中，名詞子句或副詞子句不受限。

3 that也可使用在先行名詞是「人 + 物品」上

4 先行名詞前面是最高級或是有the only、the same時，要使用that。

接下來，看看下面例句是什麼子句，並且正確地解釋。

5 It is uncertain **when she will arrive with the news**.

5 不確定／她何時會到／帶著那個消息。

it是虛主詞，when以後是真主詞，在句中扮演著主詞的角色，也就是名詞子句。when在這裡解釋為「何時」。

6 The time will come **when you realize the true love**.

6 那時會來／你了解到真愛的時候。

在這裡，when似乎是副詞子句，但實際上是修飾前面先行名詞the time的形容詞子句。這個句子原本應該寫成The time when you realize the true love will come.，但如此一來，主詞（the time）和動詞（will come）相隔太遠，語意變得模糊，因此在這種情況下，會先將主詞和動詞寫出來，再把修飾句放在後面。一般不會把形容詞子句連接詞when直接翻譯出來，會翻譯出其修飾先行名詞的意思。

7 When she was young, she had the accident.

7 她小時候／她遭遇了意外。

when帶出的she was young是屬於完整的第2大句型，因此即使是拆開，也是完整的when子句，同時也是副詞子句。在這裡是「…的時候」的意思。

怪物講師的祕訣

1 who(m)、whose、which、when、where、why、how等，在修飾先行名詞時就叫作形容詞子句連接詞，或是關係詞，一般不會直接翻譯出來。

2 上述的單字若無先行名詞時，當做名詞子句連接詞或是疑問詞，解釋為：誰、誰的、哪一（個）、何時、何處、為什麼、如何（或是多麼）。

3 that可以使用在名詞子句（完整句）、形容詞子句（不完整句）、副詞子句（慣用句，參考副詞子句單元）等。

4 that不使用在逗號（,）或是介系詞後。

攻略法

48

掌握省略關係詞的方法

有了關係詞反而變得更複雜，即使省略了，讓句子變得更難掌握。現在讓我們來了解何時會
省略關係詞，和省略了關係詞後，該如何解讀句子。

1. 「關係詞主詞＋be動詞」的省略

有時會看到形容詞不在前面修飾名詞，反而出現在名詞後面。**這可能是
已經省略了「關係詞主詞＋be動詞」，看看省略之前的狀態，大部分
be動詞後面有形容詞或-ing、p.p.、to不定詞、介系詞子句等**。這是第2
大句型，be動詞是因需要而當作補語使用的動詞。此時關係詞子句當作
形容詞子句，修飾前面的先行名詞。不過即使沒有「關係詞主詞＋be動
詞」，後面的形容詞或-ing、p.p.、to不定詞、介系詞子句等，依然可以
當作是形容詞的角色，可用來修飾前面的先行名詞。如此一來，以後**名
詞後面有形容詞或-ing、p.p.、to不定詞、介系詞子句等修飾的情況時，
就可以試著放入「關係詞主詞＋be動詞」看看**。這樣就簡單明瞭吧！想
想看下面的例句的括弧內要放入什麼句子，並試著解釋看看。

The man (interested / interesting) in you will call you tonight.

先行名詞the man後面放入who is看看，有想到慣用句be interested嗎？如
果當作先行名詞the man後面，省略了who is的話，那麼括弧內當然就是
interested。

2. 關係詞受詞的省略

有時會看到名詞後面有主詞、動詞吧？這幾乎都是因為省略了關係詞受
詞。如果連這個都不知道的話，很難進一步學習。一定要記住，名詞後
面的「S＋V」是用來修飾該名詞的形容詞子句。

The task he (assigned / was assigned) to us was too complicated.

先行名詞the task後面省略了受詞格關係詞which，所以which可以算
是動詞assign的受詞。因為原本就是受詞，所以答案要選擇主動形的
assigned。

《講師的補充說明》
如果先行名詞後面，出現當
作主詞的名詞，看起來像是
名詞重複出現的錯誤文法，
或是沒有看到連接詞，一個
句子中出現了兩個限定動
詞，句子也看起來怪怪的，
不過這些都是正確的句子。
沒看到連接詞，是因為被省
略了，句子當然會出現兩個
限定動詞。

那男人／對你有興趣的／今
晚會打電話給你。

任務／他分配給我們的／太
複雜了。

3. 關係詞主格的省略

若為被省略的關係詞主格，意思就完全不一樣。因為原本的連接詞不見了，但句中的限定動詞依舊有2個，意思當然就變了。**關係詞主格除了當連接詞，同時也是主詞，所以省略的關係詞主格，就等於「省略了連接詞和主詞」。原本是限定動詞的就變成動狀詞，也就是-ing或p.p.型態的分詞構句了。**（請參閱Chapter 10）

就是這個！關係詞主格可以省略，原本是限定動詞的動詞1就變成了-ing或p.p.型態的動狀詞。關係子句原本是當作形容詞子句，修飾前面先行名詞，省略關係詞主格後產生的分詞（-ing、p.p.），也是形容詞的一種，可在先行名詞後面當做修飾用。

The man who hires me is the manager.
→ **The man hiring me** is the manager.

> 那男生／雇用我的／是經理。

關係詞主格who被省略後，原本的限定動詞hires變成動狀詞hiring。這在解釋或翻譯上完全沒問題，可多練習這些多元的表現方式。

4. 先行名詞的省略

疑問詞和that也可當作名詞子句連接詞使用。不過疑問詞和that也會出現在形容詞子句和關係詞子句中，知道是為什麼嗎？這是因為省略了先行名詞。**先行名詞的省略現象，也可直接套用在關係副詞**，我們來看看下面的例句吧。

The reason why he resigned so suddenly is still unknown.
→ **Why he resigned so suddenly** is still unknown.

> 他那麼突然地辭職的原因／還沒被知道。

第一個例句中why以後的句子，是修飾前面先行名詞reason的形容詞子句。這裡省略了先行名詞reason，從why開始到suddenly是名詞子句，當作動詞is的主詞。

5. 關係副詞的省略

the time when, the place where, the reason why, the way how等，在這些表現中，可省略先行名詞或關係副詞。省略這兩者其中一種都無所謂。但要注意的是，不能兩個同時都省略，且除了the way how以外，其餘的可以兩者都使用。the way和how必須要刪掉其中一個。請看下面的例句。

The area we intend to build a plant has not decided yet.

我們想建立工廠的地區／還沒有決定。

先行名詞area後面的關係副詞where被省略了，從we開始到plant都是修飾先行名詞area的形容詞子句。這裡要注意，如果名詞後面出現「S + V」，就是省略了關係詞受格或關係副詞。這時先行名詞如果出現時間、場所、原因或方法等以外的名詞時，是省略了關係詞受格的句子。後面的句子，也就是形容詞子句是沒有受詞的不完整句。但如果是時間、場所、原因或方法等名詞的話，就是省略了關係副詞，後面的形容詞子句是完整句。

怪物講師的祕訣

1. 句子結構是「名詞 + 名詞 + 動詞」時？→ 省略了關係詞受格
2. 名詞後面有形容詞類後置修飾時？→ 省略了「關係詞主格 + be動詞」
3. 如果只有省略關係詞主格時？→ 必須轉換成分詞構句法
4. 如果省略先行名詞，所有的關係詞？→ 變成名詞子句連接詞，此時是疑問詞
5. 關係副詞是？→ 先行名詞或關係副詞中可省略其中一項

Quiz

Q3 The service we (offer / are offered) to our customers is exceptional.
Q4 The report (detailing / detailed) the sales figures will be submitted.

▶ 解答在080頁

攻略法
49
複合關係詞題型的解題法

光是關係詞就夠複雜了，現在又來了個複合關係詞。很頭痛吧？但其實都是之前有學過的東西，不用感到太有壓力。

正確來說，複合關係詞不是形容詞子句。只是因為名稱上有關係詞這幾個字，才在關係詞單元中一起討論。**複合關係詞和一般的關係詞不一樣的地方是，它不是形容詞子句連接詞。那麼是什麼子句的連接詞呢？是名詞子句和副詞子句連接詞。**

1. 複合關係詞的種類

1 (Who / Whoever) will be promoted has not decided yet. ⟨ 1 誰會升遷／還沒有決定。

括弧應要填名詞子句連接詞，who或whoever兩者都可當作名詞子句連接詞使用，但含義不同。在句中who（誰）比whoever（不論是誰）更恰當。

2 The man (who / whoever) would be promoted did not attend the ⟨ 2 那男生／可能被拔擢的／沒 meeting. 有參加會議。

括弧內到promoted都是修飾先行名詞the man的形容詞子句。who是帶出形容詞子句的連接詞，whoever則是帶出名詞子句或副詞子句的連接詞，因此括弧內的正確解答是who。

從上面例句也可以看到，字尾有-ever的複合關係詞，本身就包含了先行名詞，因此不會另外有先行名詞。也就是說，一般關係詞和複合關係詞從有沒有先行名詞就可以判斷。如果有先行名詞，就是放一般關係詞；如果沒有先行名詞的話，就是使用字尾有-ever的複合關係詞。

如下，複合關係詞可分為以下幾大類。
- 複合關係代名詞：whoever, whomever, whatever, whichever
- 複合關係形容詞：whosever, whatever, whichever
- 複合關係副詞：whenever, whereever, however（沒有whyever這單字）

2. 各複合關係詞的使用時機總整理

總括來說，複合關係代名詞和複合關係形容詞，是被當作名詞子句和副詞子句連接詞使用，複合關係副詞主要被當作副詞子句連接詞使用。

1 (**Whosever / Whomever**) **book this is**, I need to borrow it.

括弧內的兩個連接詞都是副詞子句連接詞，因為括弧後面的名詞book需要有修飾的形容詞，所以答案必須要選複合關係形容詞whosever。

2 (**Whenever / Whatever**) **it is cold**, please wear warmer clothes.

2 如果很冷的時候／請穿上／更保暖的衣服。

兩者都可帶出副詞子句，但逗號（,）前面的句子是完整句，所以答案要選擇whenever。

到目前為止所學的複合關係詞整理如下。

(1) 複合關係代名詞（主格）→ 主詞空著時
- **名詞子句，主詞機能：**

whoever / whichever / whatever + 動詞1 + OC + 動詞2 + OC（主要子句）
主詞 + 及物動詞 + whoever / whichever / whatever + 動詞 + OC（受詞子句）
- **副詞子句，主詞機能：**

whoever / whichever / whatever + 動詞1 + OC, 主詞 + 動詞2 + OC
（是誰…也、某個東西…也都、不論什麼…也）

(2) 複合關係代名詞（受格）→ 受詞空著時
- **名詞子句，受詞機能：**

whomever / whichever / whatever + 主詞 + 及物動詞, 動詞2 + OC（主要子句）
主詞 + 及物動詞 + whomever / whichever / whatever主詞 + 及物動詞（受格）
- **副詞子句，受詞機能：**

whomever / whichever / whatever主詞 + 及物動詞, 動詞2 + OC（主要子句）
（是誰…也、某個東西…也都、不論什麼…也）<為受詞狀態>
*另外請記住，有時在及物動詞的位置會出現介系詞的受詞。

(3) 複合關係形容詞（修飾主詞）→ 包含後面的名詞，完整句
- **名詞子句，修飾主詞：**

whosever / whatever / whichever + 名詞 + 動詞1 + OC + 動詞2 + OC（主要子句）
主詞 + 及物動詞 + whosever / whatever / whichever名詞 + 動詞 + OC（受詞子句）
- 副詞子句，修飾主詞：

whosever / whatever / whichever + 名詞 + 動詞1 + OC, 主詞 + 動詞2 + OC
（不論是誰的…／不論是什麼的…／不論是何者的）

Chapter 12_ 形容詞子句連接詞 241

(4) 複合關係形容詞（修飾受詞）→ 包含後面的名詞，完整句

- **名詞子句，修飾受詞：**

whosever / whatever / whichever + 名詞 + 主詞 + 動詞1 + 動詞2 + OC（主要子句）

主詞 + 及物動詞 + whosever / whatever / whichever + 名詞 + 主詞 + 動詞（受詞子句）

- **副詞子句，修飾受詞：**

whosever / whatever / whichever + 名詞 + 主詞 + 動詞1, 主詞 + 動詞2 + OC
（誰的…受詞、什麼的…受詞、何者的…受詞）

(5) 複合關係副詞 → 需要有完整句，尤其是however是常出題

- **副詞子句，修飾動詞：**

whenever / wherever 主詞 + 動詞 + OC, 主詞 + 動詞 + OC
（無論何時、無論何地）

however + 形容詞、副詞 + 主詞 + 動詞 + OC, 主詞 + 動詞 + OC
（無論是…也都…）

怪物講師的祕訣

關係代名詞與關係副詞的差別，在它扮演的是名詞或是副詞。也就是說，空格的後面是完整句的話，答案就是複合關係副詞；如果是不完整句的話，答案就要選複合關係代名詞。

如同上面整理的內容，如果以是否為完整句為基準做區別的話，那麼連接詞也可以區分出來。我們一起來看看吧！

- 名詞子句 → 絕對只能使用複合關係代名詞和複合關係形容詞
- 副詞子句 → 皆為副詞子句連接詞，所以要選擇是完整或不完整句

複合關係代名詞或複合關係形容詞都是用在名詞子句和副詞子句，但是複合關係副詞只能當作副詞子句連接詞使用。

Quiz

Q5 (Whatever / Wherever) it takes to make it true, it must be done at once.

Q6 A label (which /whichever) shows the destination must be affixed to all parcels.

▶ 解答在080頁

攻略法 46　解決形容詞子句題型的方法

第一階段先看先行名詞 → 第二階段確認是完整或不完整句

1 先行名詞
- 人　　　　　　　　　　→ who, whose, whom
- 事物　　　　　　　　　→ which, of which(=whose)
- 人、事物共通　　　　　→ that
- 時間　　　　　　　　　→ when
- 場所　　　　　　　　　→ where
- 理由　　　　　　　　　→ why
- 方法　　　　　　　　　→ how

2 名詞 + [_____ + 不完整句] → 關係代名詞主格，答案的格式為受詞格

名詞 + [_____ + 完整句] → 關係副詞或關係代名詞，答案的格式為所有格

攻略法 47　容易混淆的形容詞子句題型

1 如果who(m), whose, which, when, where, why, how等，是用來修飾先行名詞的話，就是當作形容詞子句連接詞或是關係詞使用，不必另外作解釋。

2 如果上述單字前面沒有先行名詞，即為名詞子句或疑問詞，解釋為誰（主詞／受詞）、誰的、某（個）、何時、在哪裡、為什麼、如何（多麼）。

3 that可當作名詞子句（完整句）、形容詞子句（不完整句）、副詞子句（參照慣用語、副詞子句單元）使用。

4 逗號（,）後面，或是介系詞後面，答案可以直接屏除that。

攻略法 48　掌握省略關係詞的方法

1 省略關係詞受格 → 如果句子為「名詞 + 名詞 + 動詞」，即是第二個名詞前面省略了關係詞受格（不完整句）。

2 省略關係詞主格 + be動詞 → 形容詞類修飾後面的名詞

3 省略關係詞主格 → 一定要轉換為副詞構句

4 省略先行名詞 → 形容詞子句轉換為名詞子句的瞬間

5 「先行名詞 + 關係副詞」省略兩者其中之一 → 省略先行名詞時，成了名詞子句；省略關係副詞時，成了「名詞 + 名詞+ 動詞」，是完整句。

攻略法 49　複合關係詞題型的解題法

1 複合關係代名詞 → whoever / whomever, whatever / whichever（名詞子句，副詞子句）

2 複合關係形容詞 → whosever, whatever / whichever （名詞子句，副詞子句）

3 複合關係副詞 → whenever, wherever, however（一般為副詞子句，沒有whyever此單字。）

例子 1 (A) when — ① 把握問題的類型
(B) which
(C) who
② 把握提示
(D) whom

An e-mail will be sent to any employees _____ miss more than ten days of work, which is our company policy.
③ 空格中要填什麼詞類？

① 把握問題的類型
  文法題

② 把握提示
  座格後是不完整句

③ 空格中要填什麼詞類？
  連接詞

2 (A) where
(B) when
(C) which
(D) that

Factory workers often work on an assembly line, _____ they repeat a specified task throughout the day.

1 把握問題的類型

2 把握提示

3 空格中要填什麼詞類？

3 (A) when
(B) what
(C) that
(D) who

The train schedule _____ is posted online is subject to change without any prior notice, so always check it before boarding.

1 把握問題的類型

2 把握提示

3 空格中要填什麼詞類？

4 (A) which
(B) that
(C) when
(D) where

The board meeting will be held in the conference room in _____ the staff meetings are usually held.

1 把握問題的類型

2 把握提示

3 空格中要填什麼詞類？

5 (A) where
(B) when
(C) which
(D) that

Moviegoers at the Royal Palm Cinema, _____ is the oldest theater in the state, will receive a free gift with every ticket purchase.

1 把握問題的類型

2 把握提示

3 空格中要填什麼詞類？

6　(A) assist
　　(B) assisted
　　(C) assistances
　　(D) been assisted

Vice President Khan received a thank-you letter from an employee whom he had personally _____ many years ago.

1 把握問題的類型

2 把握提示

3 空格中要填什麼詞類？

7　(A) during
　　(B) of
　　(C) for
　　(D) about

Spring is the season _____ which most companies host their annual employee picnics in outdoor areas.

1 把握問題的類型

2 把握提示

3 空格中要填什麼詞類？

8　(A) be depended on
　　(B) be depended
　　(C) depend
　　(D) depend on

Investors are known to be the persons you can _____ for the early success of your new business.

1 把握問題的類型

2 把握提示

3 空格中要填什麼詞類？

9　(A) attracts
　　(B) attracting
　　(C) attractive
　　(D) is attractive

The Medieval Fair is a festival that _____ tens of thousands of visitors from around the country.

1 把握問題的類型

2 把握提示

3 空格中要填什麼詞類？

10　(A) to contact
　　(B) contacting
　　(C) should contact
　　(D) contacts

All job seekers who wish to apply for the position _____ Margaret Lee at the telephone number below.

1 把握問題的類型

2 把握提示

3 空格中要填什麼詞類？

▶ 解答在080頁

重要
101 Industrial Technologies, Inc. has released a new calculator in hopes of attracting students _____ plan to study advanced physics.

(A) whose
(B) who
(C) which
(D) what

102 The engineering firm that _____ the suspension bridge failed to consider the impact of heavy winds over the river.

(A) designing
(B) was designed
(C) design
(D) designed

103 The real estate market, which saw incredible losses in the previous year, _____ to be recovering due to the booming economy.

(A) looks
(B) looking
(C) look
(D) is looked

重要
104 Coach Cal Santiago, _____ gymnastics team has seen four Olympic gold medalists, announced his early retirement today.

(A) which
(B) who
(C) whom
(D) whose

105 Please be sure to forward all suspicious e-mails to the technical support department, _____ they will be examined for viruses in.

(A) where
(B) which
(C) that
(D) whom

106 Nancy, the founder, will never forget the day her small business _____ its first employee much to her joy.

(A) was hired
(B) hiring
(C) hired
(D) were hired

高難度
107 The much desired position of lead researcher was awarded to Franklin Howard, whom everyone in the department _____.

(A) admired
(B) admirable
(C) was admired
(D) admiration

108 Dr. Meharra will give a lecture on the topic of stem cell research, _____ has been the subject of great debate at the university recently.

(A) where
(B) who
(C) that
(D) which

109 The shipping invoice that _____ in the package does not match the contents of the package.

(A) inclusion
(B) was included
(C) included
(D) including

110 Because of the troubled economy, the accounting department is attempting to locate areas _____ the company can reduce spending.

(A) where
(B) of which
(C) in that
(D) when

收集了多益考試中常出的題目。請當作正式的考試，確認時間並解題。

111 The hour before the end of the work shift, _____ most employees are thinking of their evening plans, is the least productive time of the day.
(A) whatever
(B) where
(C) which
(D) when

112 The labor union guaranteed wage increases to all the _____ who participated in last week's strike.
(A) working
(B) worker
(C) workers
(D) works

113 My long-awaited aim is to create a place _____ students can use what they learned from their classes freely.
(A) when
(B) whom
(C) which
(D) where

高難度
114 The client that I talked _____ yesterday expressed his gratitude for receiving our excellent service.
(A) to him
(B) him
(C) to
(D) for

115 The employee _____ submitted the new innovative and creative proposals to the management will be transferred to headquarters.
(A) which
(B) whom
(C) what
(D) who

116 Banks must have sufficient funds in case clients withdraw their money altogether _____ they have deposited into the banks.
(A) that
(B) this
(C) what
(D) whoever

117 Those _____ want to go to the computer program seminar need to notify the personnel department of their names and titles.
(A) whose
(B) who
(C) whoever
(D) will

118 The new accounting manager will assume the responsibilities that _____ general accounting issues as well as bookkeeping.
(A) includes
(B) are included
(C) include
(D) including

119 Ms. White _____ the loyal customer expressed deep satisfaction will be awarded a bonus and a week-long leave.
(A) whose
(B) what
(C) to whom
(D) whom

120 The effect the advent of the Internet _____ on our society is quite impressive.
(A) has been had
(B) to have
(C) having
(D) has had

▶ 解答在082頁

To all the business owners in the high-tech industry:

The annual Technical Expo is approaching soon again. This session of the Technical Expo will _____ in the International Expo Center in Munich, Germany from August 6th to
    121
August 10th. There are countless worldwide leading high-tech companies _____. It's
                                                                            122
definitely an exceptional opportunity to meet potential customers or develop cooperation

with other companies. We offer a wide-range of decoration selections for your booth,

and our seasoned and _____ engineering team will assist you in installing the
                      123
lighting system, power supply, or any media system you may have. We also offer some

economical packages which include booth rental, basic booth decoration, and a two-day

local tour. For more information, _____, www techexpo.com. See you in Munich!
                                  124

121 (A) happen
    (B) take place
    (C) appear
    (D) occur

122 (A) take part
    (B) to take part
    (C) taking part
    (D) taken part

123 (A) profession
    (B) professionalism
    (C) professionalize
    (D) professional

124 (A) please go to our office
    (B) please call our toll-free number
    (C) please access our official website
    (D) please mail our office address

Review Test

複習一下Chapter 12所學的形容詞子句的連接詞吧！

1 先行名詞為人的時候，關係詞為何？　▶ _____

2 先行名詞為事物時，關係詞為何？　▶ _____

3 關係詞性格的選擇基準為何？　▶ _____

4 省略關係詞的5種情況為何？　▶ _____

5 複合關係代名詞用在哪一種句子裡？　▶ _____

6 複合關係詞是否具有形容詞子句的功能？　▶ _____

Preview

1 副詞子句連接詞的特徵

很多人以為只要有副詞子句就是完整的句子，但希望各位能夠更正確的了解，並不是副詞子句本身，而是主要子句必須完整。副詞子句可能會因為連接詞而讓句子完整，也可能不會。**副詞子句可以放在主要子句後面，也可以放在中間，但最重要的是主要子句必須完整。**清楚了解副詞子句連接詞的話，在句子完整的情況下，就可以表達讓步、理由、時間、條件、目的、結果等的意思。

❶ 副詞子句連接詞 + S + VS + V + OC（主要子句完整）

❷ S + VS + V + OC（主要子句完整）+ 副詞子句連接詞 + S + V

2 副詞子句連接詞問題解法

❶ 確認主要子句是否完整。

❷ 主要子句完整的話，選擇副詞子句連接詞。

❸ 副詞子句連接詞中，表示讓步、理由時，要看句意；表示時間、條件時，要考慮時態；表示目的、結果時，則看片語。

攻略法

50 副詞子句的重點

所謂的副詞子句是要完成主要子句，以衍生「連接詞S＋V」的型態，接在主要子句前面或後面，修飾或強調動詞的意思。此時要注意：主要子句必須完整。

很多人誤以為副詞子句是完整的句子，但其實副詞子句隨著副詞子句的連接詞，會影響句子的完整性。現在就來看下列的例句吧！

1 Although we finished it on time, it wasn't completely satisfactory.

> 1 雖然我們完成了／準時／但不是很滿意。

逗號（,）後的主要子句中，it是主詞，was是第2大句型動詞，satisfactory是形容詞補語，是一個完整的句子。所以從although到time是可有可無的副詞子句。although子句是第3大句型句子，although只有連接詞功能，所以句子必須要完整。

2 Whatever we want, we'd better make our best effort beforehand.

> 2 我們想要什麼／我們應該事前盡最大的努力。

we是主詞，had better是助動詞，make是第3大句型動詞，our best effort是受詞，為完整的第3大句型句子（beforehand是可以省略的副詞修飾詞）。因此whatever到want是可以省略的副詞子句。

5秒 解決副詞子句問題的方法

1 連接詞、介系詞、副詞的區分

「＿＿＿＿主詞＋動詞, 主詞＋動詞」的型態 → 用連接詞來回答

「＿＿＿＿名詞, 主詞＋動詞」的型態 → 用介系詞來回答

「＿＿＿＿, 主詞＋動詞」的型態 → 用副詞來回答

2 各種類型的連接詞中，副詞子句連接詞為答案的情況

＿＿＿＿主詞＋動詞＿＿＿＿主詞＋動詞＋受詞（或補語）

主詞＋動詞＋受詞（或補語）＿＿＿＿主詞＋動詞

3 副詞子句連接詞有許多個的情況 → 分析句子的意思之後選擇答案

Quiz

Q1 I can't trust him anymore (because / why) he always tells a lie.

Q2 We could fulfill all the orders (as / due to) we expanded our factory.

> ▶ 解答在087頁

攻略法

51

副詞子句連接詞的種類

簡單來說，扣除名詞子句連接詞和形容詞子句連接詞，剩下的全部都是副詞子句連接詞。具有跟副詞一樣修飾動詞、完成主要子句的特徵。

連接詞當中最多的就是副詞子句連接詞，**使用副詞子句的句子中，主要子句必須完整，並且修飾動詞，因此用解析句子意思的方式來區分最適合。尤其是出題頻率第一名——具有讓步和理由意思的的副詞子句，就必須要了解句子的意思才能解題。**

出題頻率第二高的就是用來表示時間和條件的副詞子句，主要是出現現在時態的型態。雖然在時態單元中學到，現在式代替未來式，現在完成式代替未來完成式是最主要的用法。但在此主要子句大多是使用未來或未來完成。

最後，**表示目的和結果的副詞子句大多包含that。that主要是用在名詞子句和形容詞子句，但也有用在副詞子句**。目的或結果的副詞子句的特徵是採用「so 形容詞（或副詞）that」或是「such 名詞 that」或「so that」等的型態。當作片語背起來的話，就可以輕易解題。那麼就來一邊直接解題，一邊熟悉考試的感覺吧。

1　**(Although / Because) he is rich**, he can't help all the poor people.

兩個都是副詞子句連接詞，所以要透過了解句子的意思來判斷。富有和無法幫助窮人是相反的上下文，用連接詞although比較適合。because是用於因果關係。

> 1　雖然他富有／他無法幫助／所有的窮人。

2　I decided to buy a new car **(since / even if) it doesn't start sometimes**.

兩個都是副詞子句連接詞，那就用了解句意的方式來判斷。汽車有時無法啟動是主要原因，結果是下定決心要買新車。像這樣是原因和結果關係的話，就要使用像because、as、since表示理由的副詞子句連接詞，所以答案是since。

> 2　我決定了／買新車／那台車無法啟動／偶爾。

3 (Due to / Because) **he is in despair**, we should help him.

＜ 3 因為他陷入了絕望／我們應
該幫助他。

括號後面是「S + V, S + V」，所以連接詞because是正確答案。

due to是介系詞，所以不是解答。像這樣詞性不同時，應該透過需要使
用什麼詞性來解題，而不是了解句子的意思。

千萬切記！最重要的不是副詞子句放在哪個位置，而是主要子句必須完
整。

4 You should ask her the reason (**as / which**) **she is responsible for it.** ＜ 4 你應該問她理由／因為她對
這有責任。

括號前為止是完整的第4大句型句子，副詞子句as用文法或文意來說明
都非常適合。即使which是形容詞子句，修飾先行名詞reason，但which
後面不應該有主詞或受詞，可是括號後面的句子是完整的第2大句型句
子，沒有可以放which的位置，所以答案是as。

現在就來看下列整理過的副詞子句連接詞，牢記重點。表格中有重要的
副詞子句，只要正確了解之後，就能打敗副詞子句連接詞。

	連接詞	介系詞
讓步	although, though, even if, even though	despite, in spite of, with all, for all
理由 （出題頻率第二名） （因為…） ＊用於分詞句子結構 的話，一定要省略	because, as, since, now that, seeing that, for（限 用於連接詞時）	because of, due to, owing to, on account of, in view of, thanks to
時間 （時態很重要）	…時候：when, while, as, at the time (when) 一…就…：as soon as, the moment (when) = the minute = the instant …之前／之後：before / after（介系詞、連接詞） 到…為止：until（介系詞、連接詞）	…的期間：during …在：at, on, in …直到…為止：by, until 經過…：through …結束：over

條件 （時態很重要）	• 如果…的話：if, provided [providing] (that), suppose (that), supposing (that), on condition that, assuming that • …如同…的：as long as, as far as,	• 預防…情況：in case of, in the event of • 沒有…的話：without, but for
條件 （時態很重要)	• 不做…的話：unless • 為了預防：in case (that), in the event (that) • 一旦…的話：once（限連接詞） • 考慮…的時候：given（介系詞、連接詞）當形容詞時是「給予的…」的意思，considering（介系詞、連接詞）	
目的 （為了…)	so that...can [may, will], in order that...can [may, will] （that可以是名詞子句、形容詞子句、副詞子句） ＊是副詞子句時，當作片語熟記。	to do, in order to do, so as to do
結果 （太…所以…)	so 形容詞／副詞 that，such 名詞 that ＊是副詞子句，當作片語熟記	參考Chapter 18
複合關係詞	whoever, whosever, whomever, whatever, whichever, whenever, wherever, however 等	參考Chapter 12
根據…	according as S + V, S + V	according to 名詞
好像…一樣	as if, as though	like 名詞

5秒 解決副詞子句問題的方法2

表示「太…所以導致…」意思的副詞子句的用法非常多,雖然之後在形容詞單元中會學到,先預習一下!

1 「so 形容詞／副詞 that...」vs.「such 名詞 that...」

so that中間大多放形容詞或副詞,such that中間放名詞。反過來看,依照是形容詞／副詞,或是名詞來選擇答案是so還是such。

(so是副詞,such是形容詞)

2 「so 形容詞 that...」vs.「so 副詞 that...」

不要管that後面,只要觀察前面句子需要形容詞還是副詞就可以了。請記得that之後是副詞子句,所以也可以省略。

3 「so 形容詞 a / an 名詞」vs.「such a / an 形容詞 + 名詞」

把這句型當作片語背起來!

4 such 形容詞 + 名詞(複數名詞,不可數名詞)

跟前一個句型一起以「such + 形容詞 + 名詞」來背

＊「so many 複數名詞」,「so much 不可數名詞」,使用so而不是such

Quiz

Q3 If customers (will buy / buy) more than two sets, they will get a free delivery.

Q4 He was (such / so) tired from working out that he went to bed early.

▶ 解答在087頁

攻略法 **52**

被誤以為是連接詞的副詞

這裡介紹的單字是具有好幾個詞性，且意思跟連接詞相似，很容易被搞混的副詞。知道正確的用法和差異是關鍵。

很多人知道英文單字的意思，卻不知道單字的詞性。有人覺得學英文不一定要了解詞性，但在這裡我必須要說，一定要了解詞性！

1. however

however可以當副詞，也可以當連接詞。隨著當副詞或是當連接詞，意思會變得不一樣，要記的重點也會不一樣。來看看下面的例句吧！

1 **However** efficient this system may be, we can't do all of them in a day.
  在這裡however是「不管怎樣…」的副詞子句連接詞，也就是複合關係副詞！
  efficient是放be動詞後面的形容詞補語！

2 **However**, I would like to meet you.
  = I, **however**, would like to meet you.
  在這裡however是副詞「然而」的意思，可以用「still」替換。

1 不管這個系統有多有效率／我們今天無法／把那些做完。

2 但是／我想要見到你。

however有連接詞和副詞兩種用法。當作連接詞的時候，就像例句1「不管怎樣…」的意思，這時however是複合關係副詞，形容詞或副詞要放在however後面。反之however當副詞使用時，有「然而」的意思，主要是用於與前面說的話相反時使用，類似意思的單字是still。下面有簡單的公式。

> However + 形容詞／副詞 + S + V, S + V
> → 這時however是有「不管怎樣…」意思的連接詞
> → 後面接形容詞或副詞
> However, S + V
> → 這時的however是有「然而…」意思的副詞
> → 這時可以用still代替

2. 中間有the的單字，大部分是副詞

在此匯集考試中常出現的單字，方便記憶。請注意！用句意說明的話，看起來會很像是連接詞，但請記得絕對不是連接詞，而是副詞。請看下面例句！

Nevertheless, he arrived on time.

因為在這句子中，nevertheless的詞性是副詞，不行用介系詞despite或連接詞although替換。整理單字中出現the的副詞如下。

otherwise	不那樣的話
nevertheless	儘管…還是…
furthermore = moreover	更、加上

3. th開頭的單字，大部分都是副詞

匯集整理讓您方便記憶。不要被句意誤導，要記得是副詞！看看下面例句吧！

He was tired, **so** he needed some time off.

這裡的so是連接詞，可以連接「S + V」與「S + V」，但是不行因為意思相似就換成副詞thus。這些th-副詞在主要子句加逗號，單獨使用。整理th開頭的副詞如下。

then	之後
there	那裡
thus	因此
therefore	所以
＊though 雖然是th開頭，但多做連接詞使用，不屬於此。	

4. meanwhile (= meantime)

在詳細說明之前，先看看例句

Meanwhile, he finished all the tasks.

儘管如此／他準時到達了。

他很疲倦／所以他需要休息一下。

在那段時間內／他做完所有的事情。

這裡的meanwhile詞性是副詞，不可以因為意思相近，就使用連接詞while來替換。與meanwhile相同意思的meantime是副詞，也是容易被混淆的副詞之一，意思是「在那期間」。再次提醒，連接詞while不可以跟副詞meanwhile搞混。

怪物講師的祕訣

1. however的核心 → 在句子最前面或中間獨立使用，意思是「然而」的副詞
   → 以文法「however 形／副 S + V, S + V」來使用時，為連接詞「無論…也」
2. 中間有the的副詞 → nevertheless, otherwise, furthermore
3. th開頭的副詞 → then, there, thus, therefore
4. 與連接詞while意思相近的副詞 → meantime, meanwhile

Quiz

Q5 (However / Although) humble one's house is, there is no place like home.

Q6 (Unless / Otherwise), I will contact them in person.

▶ 解答在087頁

攻略法

53

同時可當介系詞、連接詞、副詞的單字

這裡收集整理了有各種詞性、考試中常出現的單字。仔細閱讀的話，考試時就能不慌張，輕易解題。

如果各位是出題者的話，也會把可當做各種詞性使用的單字，當作出題題目吧？這是考試中常出現的問題。通常這類問題的解答，大都是容易混淆且具有不同詞性的單字。

1. before / after

before「在⋯以前」和after「在⋯之後」可以當介系詞使用，也可以當連接詞使用。當連接詞使用時，應該留意時間、條件副詞子句中的動詞時態。當作介系詞使用時，before可以改成prior to，after可以改成following。請記住，在before和after後面加上ing的話，就變成分詞句型。採取「Before / After -ing, S + V」的形態（參考前面學過的分詞句型）。現在就來看看下列的例句吧！

1 **Before** he retires, he will contact all the customers personally.
= **Before** retiring, he will contact all the customers personally.

> 1 退休前／他會聯絡／所有客戶／親自。

上面例句中的before是連接詞，帶出時間副詞子句，所以句子裡用現在式取代未來式，表現未來的意思。逗號（,）後面的主要句子，使用了未來式。

2 He read the material **before** 10 that night.
在這句子裡，before是放在名詞10前面的介系詞!

> 2 他讀那份資料／10點前／那天晚上。

2. since

since可以當連接詞使用，也可以當介系詞使用。解釋為「因為⋯」時是連接詞；解釋為「從⋯以來」的話就是介系詞。since被當成「從⋯以來」使用的時候，要接完成式，請小心注意時態（參考Chapter 06）。請看下列2個例句。

1 **Since** this is exceptionally well made, it will sell well.

這時since是解釋為「因為…」的連接詞，可以跟連接詞because互換使用。請注意since不能被當成介系詞。

2 **Since** his retirement, we **have had** a few problems.

這裡的since是解釋成「從…以來」的介系詞，通常都是完成式。像上面例句後面就出現現在完成式（have had）。像這樣since被當成連接詞「因為…」時，沒有限制時態，但被當成連接詞「…以來」和介系詞「從…以來」時，有時態上的限制。另外，這個句子中逗號的前面部分，可以改成連接詞用法since he retired。

3. until

until的用法並不難懂，不管是當介系詞或連接詞使用，都是翻成「到…為止」，只要記得有兩種詞性就好了。until後面通常會出現某個時間點。另外，until後面出現過去時間點的話，主要子句就採取過去完成式。until之後出現現在時間點的話，主要子句就用未來式。請看下列例句。

1 He **had been** in charge of this division **until** she **came** in.
    因為until後面是過去，所以主要子句是過去完成式！

2 I **will keep** my eyes on it **until** he **comes** back.
    因為until後面是現在，所以主要子句是未來式！

4. once

once可當連接詞也可以當副詞，很常被使用於條件副詞子句。當作連接詞使用時，意思是「一旦…的話」，引出條件副詞子句。當做副詞時，帶有「一回、一次」的意思，主要是跟過去動詞一起使用。看看下列例句吧！

1 **Once** you **complete** this form, you **will have to contact** us first.

這裡的once是連接詞「一旦…的話」的意思，因為是條件副詞子句，所以用現在式（complete）代替未來式。當然逗號後面的主句是未來式。

1 因為這個做得非常好／它會賣得很好。

2 在他退休之後／我們有／好幾個問題。

1 一直以來都是他負責／這個部門／直到她上任之前。

2 我會持續注意／它／直到他回來。

1 一旦你完成這表格的話／你要先聯絡／我們。

2 I once met the CEO at the factory.

2 我有一天遇到執行長／在工廠裡。

這裡的once是副詞「一次、一回」，因為是過去發生的一次事件，所以當然使用過去式（met）。另供參考，上面的句子若改成現在完成的經驗，就是I have once met the CEO at the factory. 可以改成這樣，但是在多益考試中不常出現這樣用法。

怪物講師的祕訣

1 before / after的詞性 → 介系詞或連接詞

2 since的詞性 → 當成「從…以來」時是介系詞或連接詞；當成「因為…」時是連接詞

3 until的詞性 → 介系詞與連接詞

4 once的詞性 → 當成連接詞時是「一旦…的話」，當成副詞時是「一次、一回」

Quiz

Q7 I easily passed the exam (since / although) he helped me.

Q8 Once he (will accept / accepts) the proposal, we will proceed as planned.

▶ 解答在087頁

攻略法 50-53　重點整理　　　　　　有系統的將本課學習內容，一目瞭然地整理吧

攻略法 50　副詞子句的重點

副詞可以放在句子的前後，主要子句必須是完整的句子

副詞子句連接詞 + S + V（完全或不完全由連接詞決定），S + V + OC（主要子句完整）

= S + V + OC（主要子句完整）+ 副詞子句連接詞 + S + V（完全或不完全由連接詞決定）

攻略法 51　副詞子句連接詞的種類

1 解說重要的副詞子句連接詞

讓步：although, though, even if, even though／理由：because, as, since

2 時態重要的副詞子句連接詞

時間：when, as soon as, before, after, until

時間：if, provided / providing, unless, in case (that), in the event (that)

3 片語重要的副詞子句連接詞

目的: so that, in order that／結果：so 形容詞／副詞 that, such 名詞 that

攻略法 52　被誤以為是連接詞的副詞

1 連接詞：However + 形容詞／副詞 + S + V, S + V（不管…還是）

副詞：However, S + V（但是）

2 otherwise 除此之外、nevertheless 儘管如此、furthermore 更、再加上

3 then 之後、there 那裡、thus 如此、therefore 為此

4 meanwhile (= meantime) …在…期間

攻略法 53　同時可當介系詞、連接詞、副詞的單字

1 before / after：「…以前／…以後」（介系詞和連接詞）

2 since：「從…以來」（介系詞和連接詞）常與完成時態使用

「因為…」（連接詞）這種情況沒有時態限定

3 until：「到…為止」（介系詞或連接詞）

4 once：「一旦…的話」（連接詞）；「一次、一回」（副詞）

Once S + V（現在／現在完成式）, S + V（未來／未來完成）→ 條件副詞子句

S + once + V（過去）→ 過去曾經有一次…。

例子

1 (A) until ① 把握問題的類型
(B) unless
(C) if
(D) since

The renters had not signed the contract _____ the real estate agent explained each section in detail. ③ 空格中要填什麼詞類？

② 把握提示

1 把握問題的類型
文法題

2 把握提示
過去完成，
解說差異

3 空格中要填什麼詞類？
連接詞

2 (A) before
(B) what
(C) if
(D) because

An emergency board meeting is expected to be called _____ the economic crisis has worsened.

1 把握問題的類型

2 把握提示

3 空格中要填什麼詞類？

3 (A) During
(B) When
(C) Since
(D) Therefore

_____ you call the billing department, please have your account number ready to speed up the process.

1 把握問題的類型

2 把握提示

3 空格中要填什麼詞類？

4 (A) prior to
(B) following
(C) while
(D) even though

For better service, hotel guests are encouraged to fill out a comment card _____ they are checking out.

1 把握問題的類型

2 把握提示

3 空格中要填什麼詞類？

5 (A) will be sold
(B) sold
(C) are sold
(D) sells

In spite of soaring interest, the art gallery will close once three of the ten paintings _____.

1 把握問題的類型

2 把握提示

3 空格中要填什麼詞類？

6 (A) assuming that
(B) since
(C) that
(D) unless

An interview will not be scheduled _____ the candidate has the proper skills and adequate experience.

1 把握問題的類型

2 把握提示

3 空格中要填什麼詞類？

7 (A) since
(B) even though
(C) so that
(D) although

The restaurant does not serve any meat _____ many of the local residents are vegetarians.

1 把握問題的類型

2 把握提示

3 空格中要填什麼詞類？

8 (A) why
(B) wherever
(C) whenever
(D) whether

The computer technician travels to provide technical support _____ his customers are located.

1 把握問題的類型

2 把握提示

3 空格中要填什麼詞類？

9 (A) So as
(B) Where
(C) As
(D) Whereas

_____ he is the building manager, Tom is responsible for maintenance and repairs to keep it well-maintained.

1 把握問題的類型

2 把握提示

3 空格中要填什麼詞類？

10 (A) that
(B) even though
(C) provided that
(D) so that

The train conductor looked down the track _____ he could see if passengers were still boarding.

1 把握問題的類型

2 把握提示

3 空格中要填什麼詞類？

▶ 解答在087頁

101 Alexander Petrokov's new film "Roses, Daisies, You" is expected to be a hit at the box office _____ it receives negative reviews.

(A) even
(B) where
(C) even if
(D) in order that

102 Purchase orders should be submitted to Alice Greeley _____ they have been approved by a manager.

(A) whatever
(B) even though
(C) whether
(D) in case of

103 _____ assemble the cars with faulty parts, workers should alert their floor manager if they notice a problem.

(A) Whenever
(B) Before
(C) Rather than
(D) To

104 The chemistry laboratory is equipped for students of all levels _____ they are beginners or advanced.

(A) though
(B) whether
(C) nevertheless
(D) either

105 To qualify for the discounted shipping rate, online shoppers must remember to place their order _____ the end of normal business hours.

(A) before
(B) if
(C) why
(D) since

106 Dr. Chung often travels to give lectures, and she enjoys seeing the local tourist sites _____ she visits a new city.

(A) after
(B) even if
(C) where
(D) whenever

107 The equipment rental store has a large supply of snow shovels _____ the region rarely receives snowfall.

(A) because
(B) even though
(C) otherwise
(D) since

108 The nation's banking industry saw significant quarterly growth _____ most industries have been struggling to make profits.

(A) whereas
(B) why
(C) because
(D) so that

109 Office manager Rachel Weber distributed an e-mail notification to all employees _____ the office computers were at risk to a virus attack.

(A) however
(B) though
(C) provided that
(D) as

110 The local symphony hosts _____ many summer festivals that it can raise money for local arts schools.

(A) so
(B) for
(C) such
(D) very

收集了多益考試中常出的題目。請當作正式的考試，確認時間並解題。

111 Aviator Skydiving, Inc., will continue to manufacture the highest quality sports equipment, _____ many consumers prefer low-priced goods.

(A) for
(B) although
(C) once
(D) rather than

112 Employees should contact the payroll department _____ they notice a discrepancy in their monthly paycheck.

(A) unless
(B) even if
(C) as if
(D) if

113 They spent a considerable amount of time researching the project; _____, they didn't attain desired results.

(A) however
(B) otherwise
(C) therefore
(D) moreover

高難度
114 In most cases, you'd better prepare some more dishes _____ there are unexpected visitors.

(A) once
(B) in case
(C) while
(D) whether

115 _____ we know, there is no shortage of companies doing business in China and doing it well.

(A) Although
(B) As
(C) Providing
(D) The moment

116 _____ you'd like to receive a new catalog from us, please submit your information by clicking the box below.

(A) Owing to
(B) Although
(C) If
(D) Should

117 The monitoring system will be purchased as requested _____ the application is approved by the CEO.

(A) although
(B) as soon as
(C) whether
(D) that

118 _____ the product is developed completely, there will be a few additional steps to proceed before launching it into the market.

(A) Therefore
(B) So that
(C) Whether
(D) Even if

119 The annual shareholders' meeting is _____ an important event that we must find a more agreeable venue right away.

(A) so
(B) very
(C) too
(D) such

120 _____ you need room service during your stay, please contact the receptionist at the front desk.

(A) Perhaps
(B) Whether
(C) May
(D) Should

▶ 解答在090頁

Moving Sale

There is a golden chance that you _____ a long time. To all the loyal customers of
                                      121

Sweet Home Furniture, we are having a moving sale to thank you all for your long-lasting

support. In order to expand our display space to _____ more furniture for you, we will
                                                   122

move to the center of the town. We would like to take this opportunity to serve you as a

good and reliable neighbor. EVERYTHING you can find on our racks will be on sale. We

will offer you a huge discount to _____ each deal. _____ through this weekend
                                   123   **124**

only, so do not hesitate to come around. You will find plenty of furniture and ornaments

discounted to extremely low prices. Don't miss out on this chance of a lifetime.

121 (A) has waited for
    (B) have been waiting for
    (C) have waited for
    (D) had been waiting for

122 (A) display
    (B) discount
    (C) disorder
    (D) dispatch

123 (A) sweet
    (B) sweetness
    (C) sweeten
    (D) sweetened

124 (A) The sale was held
    (B) The sale has been held
    (C) The sale had been held
    (D) The sale will be held

▶ 解答在090頁

對等連接詞
前後對應就是對等連接詞！

Review Test

Chapter 13學習副詞子句了吧！填滿空格，確認副詞子句內容。

1 使用副詞子句連接詞時，要注意的重點是什麼？ ▶ ....

2 副詞子句連接詞中，出題頻率最高的是什麼？ ▶ ....

3 在時間，條件副詞子句中，副詞子句使用…？ ▶ ....

4 目的，結果的副詞子句有哪些？ ▶ ....

5 連接詞功能的副詞有哪些？ ▶ ....

6 once的兩種意思和詞性是什麼？ ▶ ....

7 until的意思和詞性是什麼？ ▶ ....

8 once當作連接詞使用時，意思是什麼？ ▶ ....

Preview

1　對等連接詞的特徵

　　對等連接詞有and、but、or。與其他連接詞不同，**有省略意思相同語句的特徵。有時會看起來好像只有「S＋V」的情況，但其實有多種型態的面貌。**大部分的人會覺得「只要知道對等連接詞就是and或or，不就好了嗎？」而輕忽它。但是對等連接詞也有不可錯過的獨特性質。

　　例如，有時會討厭連續使用同樣的話吧？如果需要省略，這時可以使用的連接詞就是對等連接詞。這個單元裡我們將會介紹正確的對等連接詞使用方法。

2　對等連接詞的問題解法

　　❶ 觀察對等連接詞的前後，把兩邊變成平行結構。

　　❷ 前後都是相同構造的情況，首先選擇對等連接詞作句子解釋。

| 正確答案 | 1、主要子句要完整 2. 讓步，理由（用解説來區分） 3. 現在或是現在完成 4. so that...so 形容詞／副詞 that...such 名詞 that... 5. however, th開始的單字。有the的單字。meantime 6. 「從…開始」或「因為…」可以當作介系詞、也可以當作連接詞 7.「到…為止」或「到…時候為止」可以當作介系詞、也可以當作連接詞 8. 一旦…的話 |

攻略法 54
對等連接詞的特徵

對等連接詞和之前學習的連接詞稍微有點不同。我們來看看對等連接詞和其他連接詞有什麼不一樣吧！

使用其他連接詞的情況，「連接詞＋S＋V, S＋V」之中「S＋V」出現2次。但使用對等連接詞時，「S＋V」有可能出現2次，也有可能不一樣。先來看看對等連接詞有哪些。

and, but (= yet), or, as well as, than, plus 等

1. 對等連接詞前後一樣的內容可以省略

使用對等連接詞時，前後相同的內容可以省略。對等連接詞的前後構造都一樣。

1 I went to a party. I enjoyed it so much.

將這兩個句子簡短的分開來寫，看起來像是不懂英文的人寫的吧？稍微懂一點英文的人，會把兩個句子寫成像下面的例句。

2 I went to a party **and** I enjoyed it so much.

上面句子比起例句1更為乾淨俐落，意思傳達也更清楚。例句1像小學生的寫法，例句2看起來也是有點不自然。比起例句2的用法，如果用「我參加派對非常高興」來寫的話就更自然。這句話可以改寫成如下的句子。

3 I went to a party **and** enjoyed it very much.

比起例句1和2更通順吧！前面動詞的主詞是I，後面enjoyed前面沒有主詞吧？那是因為主詞I省略了。

此時會跟我們所知的連接詞的定義稍微不同。舉例來說，連接詞and連接兩個句子是「S＋V and S＋V」，就變成「S＋V and V」的型態，and後面重複的主詞（S）被省略。

1 我去派對。我很愉快。

2 我去派對／且我非常愉快。

3 我去派對／非常愉快。

這時要注意的是，像and、but（yet）、or的對等連接詞才可以這樣省略。現在就來看看除了主詞以外，連動詞也省略的情況。

4 She is **well-educated and** (she is) **polite** to seniors. ⟨ 4 她受到很好的教育／對長輩有禮貌。

省略括號部分之後，連接詞and前後形容詞well-educated和形容詞polite並列。兩者都是she is的形容詞，有主詞補語的功能。出題的時候會把polite的位置空下來，請你從名詞、形容詞、副詞中選擇答案。能看出polite前面的she is被省略的人，就會毫不考慮的選擇形容詞。

5 We will buy **a copier or** (**a printer / printing**). ⟨ 5 我們要買／影印機或印表機。

看到括號前面的及物動詞buy的受詞（a copier）吧？括號內應該填入可以成為buy的受詞的a printer。a printer前面省略了we will buy。printing是表示「印刷」的動名詞，雖然可以當成受詞，但不能成為buy的對象。而且後面也沒有受詞，所以不能填動名詞。很有趣吧？要不要再舉個例子？

6 **The manager and the applicant** (is / are) in a conference room to ⟨ 6 經理和應徵者／在會議室裡／為了終止契約。
close a contract.

在這情況下，只看the applicant的話，括號內應該會填單數型動詞is，但主詞是經理和應徵者，所以應該填複數動詞are。

怪物講師的祕訣

對等連接詞的特徵

為了把到目前為止學的內容更方便理解，整理的資料如下所示。

1 動詞＋對等連接詞＋動詞。

2 名詞＋對等連接詞＋名詞。

3 形容詞＋對等連接詞＋形容詞。

4 副詞＋對等連接詞＋副詞。

5 介系詞片語＋對等連接詞＋介系詞片語。

6 S＋V＋對等連接詞＋S＋V。

2. 3個以上相同單字陳列時，也使用對等連接詞

對等連接詞不只連結2個主詞或受詞，也有連結3個以上的情況。在這種情況，應該觀察句子構造，使用合適的詞類。**同樣的話出現3個以上時，並不是連續使用對等連接詞，而是只要在最後使用一次就可以了。**

1 She is **pretty**, **clever**, and (**honest** / honestly).

1 她很漂亮／很聰明／而且很誠實。

這個句子裡pretty和clever都是修飾主詞she的形容詞補語。但是如果補語就此結束的話，就不會出現（,）而是and。但是clever後面出現逗號，表示會再出現一個形容詞補語。因此and後面應該接形容詞補語honest。如果有人說因為是在句子的後面，應該選擇副詞的話，就表示不了解對等連接詞的原理。

2 I have a **report** to submit, **a letter** to mail, **and a call** (to make / makes).

2 我有／要提出的報告書／要寄的信／還有要打的電話。

乍看之下，a call好像是and後面的主詞，所以很有可能誤把動詞makes認為是正確答案。但仔細看句子結構的話，最前面的have是必須要有受詞的第3大句型及物動詞，後面出現的a report、a letter、a call都是它的受詞。此外，to submit、to mail、to make全部都是用來修飾前面名詞的to不定詞的形容詞用法。因此a call後面也要放to不定詞的to make。

接觸的句子多了，就能一眼看透句子整體結構。沒有人能從一開始就了解句子的結構。類似的句子看了數十遍、數百遍之後，就會不知不覺地產生看透句子架構的能力。

3. 對等連結詞and、but（yet）、or不能放在句子開頭

其他連接詞放在句子開頭，被寫成「連接詞 S＋V, S＋V」的型態，但是像and、but或or的對等連接詞不可以放在句子開頭。因為必須用於省略前後相同的意思的句子，如果放在句子最前面的話會很奇怪。

所以如果句子最前面的空格要填連接詞的話，像and、but、or的連接詞就可以直接去除。（so或for如果當作連接詞使用的話，也不可以放在句子開頭）

(Though, But) **she was** well qualified, **she failed** again to be promoted.

雖然她非常有資格／她升遷又再次失敗了。

因為逗點前後的2個句子都是「S + V」的句型，所以括號內是連接詞的位置。用句意來看的話，兩者好像都可以吧？但是像but這種連接詞是無法放在句子開頭的，所以括號內應該放though。

使用簡單的公式來整理上面的內容如下所示。

（不行放對等連接詞）S + V + 受詞（或補語），S + V + 受詞（或補語）

4. 其他對等連接詞

(1) as well as
通常「不只是A，B也是」或者「不論A，B也是」很常用B as well as A 的表現，這時as well as是對等連接詞。為什麼是對等連接詞呢？我們先來看看下面的問題吧！

1　He gave me **a hand as well as** (**advice / advisable**).

> 1 他給了／我／幫助／還有忠告。

句子中的give是第4大句型動詞，當然me就是間接受詞（IO）。a hand和advice是直接受詞（DO），a hand和advice是用as well as這個對等連接詞來連接的。因為是直接受詞，所以括號內當然是要放名詞advice。在這個例句中，advice前面省略了he gave me。另外，give a hand直譯是「給一個手」，就是幫助的意思。

2　The project is designed to **enhance domestic demand as well as** (**creating / create**) **more jobs**.

> 2 那專案被設計出來／為了提振國內需求／還有創造出更多工作職缺。

在這個句子裡，括號前面省略了the project is designed to。所以括號內應該填入原形動詞create。你問我是怎麼知道的？類似的句子看數十遍，數百遍當然就知道。如果不相信的話，就是你的損失。抱著「啊！我還沒看過十遍、百遍，那就看吧！一看再看！」心態的人才能成功。萬事皆是如此，英文實力在於勤勉、實在、努力！

(2) than

than是有介系詞的功能，也具有對等連接詞功能的單字。意思是「比…」。透過下面的例句，來看看介系詞than和連接詞than的差異。

1 The man is **more energetic than me**.

1 那個男人更熱情／比我。

than在這個句子裡是介系詞。介系詞後面通常是接受格名詞或代名詞，在這個例句中，than後面有受格代名詞me。

2 The project will be **harder** to accomplish **than we anticipated**.

2 那個專案更困難／達成／比我們預計的。

在這個句子裡than是連接詞功能。因為後面的句子有主詞（we）、動詞（anticipated），前面也有句子，所以需要加上連接詞。這個句子中than we anticipated是省略句子than we anticipated that the project will be hard中that以後的部分，意思是「這個計畫比我們想的更困難…」。

怪物講師的祕訣

1 對等連接詞的種類

and、but (= yet)、 or、as well as、than、plus等

2 對等連接詞的特徵

1 省略對等連接詞前後相同意思的句子。

→ 對等連接詞的前後只剩下相同意思和相同作用的句子。例如，對等連接詞前面是名詞的話，後面也是名詞；前面是形容詞的話，後面也是形容詞；前面是介系詞片語的話，後面也是介系詞片語；前面是「S + V」的話，後面也是「S + V」。

＊此時，前後相同單字的功能也一樣。假設對等連接詞的前面是主詞的話，後面也是主詞；前面是動詞的話，後面也是動詞；前面是補語的話，後面也是補語；前面是修飾語的話，後面也是修飾語。所以才被稱為對等連接詞。

2 一樣的句子出現3個以上的：採取A, B and C的型態。

3 and、but (= yet)、or 這些對等連接詞不能放在句子開頭。

4 其他對等連接詞：as well as、than、plus等。

Quiz

Q1 Customers as well as the government (ask / asks) us to let them know what the possible effect will be.

Q2 I saw him working out this morning and (walks / walking) down the street this afternoon.

▶ 解答在093頁

相關連接詞的原理

攻略法 **55**

是考試中常常出現的部分。雖然可以當作片語來背，但應該要知道正確的原理，對英文作文或會話才有很大的幫助。

兩個以上的單字位置分開，相互關係緊密，有連接詞作用，所以被稱為**相關連接詞**。下列的both A and B、either A or B等就是代表性的相關連接詞。

> both A and B
>
> between A and B
>
> not A but B
>
> not only (= just) A but (also) B (= B as well as A)
>
> neither A nor B
>
> either A or B

1. 相關連接詞有對等連接詞的特性

在相關連接詞both A and B和between A and B當中，and前面的A是句子的主詞，且是名詞的話，用對等連結詞and連結的B，該怎麼辦？因為必須跟A是「對等的位置＝對等」的平行結構，所以B也是名詞。萬一A是形容詞受詞補語的話，B也必須是形容詞受詞補語。

1 We plan to make this city **highly attractive and environmentally (friendly / friend)**.

1 我們正在計畫／將這個都市／變得非常有魅力／並且環保。

對等連接詞and後面的environmentally，跟前面的highly一樣是副詞，所以括號內應該放跟attractive一樣的形容詞受詞補語。但是選項沒有形容詞？friendly雖然看起來很像加上副詞語尾-ly的副詞，但卻是有「親切的、友好的」意思的形容詞。

2 You must **neither violate the rules nor (disturbing / disturb) other colleagues**.

2 你不能違反規則／也不能妨礙其他同事。

看到neither A nor B的相關副詞了吧，請切記nor後面的you must被省略了。因此括號內應該放跟原形動詞violate一樣的（對等的）原形動詞disturb。

2. 相關連接詞問題應該找到夥伴

就像有both就有and，有neither就有nor，相關連接詞的問題只要找到夥伴就可以解答了。

1 The reason I don't buy it is (**both / not**) **because of price, but because of its quality**.

出現在後面的but的夥伴是什麼呢？當然是not囉！所以答案就是not。

2 We accept any applications if they are submitted (**either / and**) **by mail or in person**.

只要知道either A or B這個對等連接詞的話，當然就能解決問題囉！

3. 相關連接詞的單複數一致

The inspectors as well as I (**was / were**) **surprised at the horrible scene**.

B as well as A是從後面開始解說「不但A，而且B也」，焦點是放在B，所以動詞的單複數要配合B來決定。因此括號內要放were。像這樣用語意來讓單複數一致就是「語意法」。但是相關連接詞either A or B或neither A nor B的情況，是以採取找出離動詞最近者，決定單複數的「近者一致法」，決定B的單複數。

怪物講師的祕訣

1 對等連接詞問題解法

對等連結詞的前面或後面有空格的話，想一想被省略的句子，用同樣架構的句子來作答，空格的前面或後面架構一樣的話，選擇對等連接詞來作答。

2 相關連接詞問題解法

第一，當作片語熟記。

第二，將A與B的架構調整成一樣（一樣的詞性，相同作用的對等架構）。

第三，如同Chapter 04所學的方式確定單複數（在主詞位置的情況）。

Quiz

Q3 There must be no wide gap between the incomes of the learned (and / or) the experienced.

Q4 The semi-conductor market is not only highly competitive but also very (hardly / hard) to predict.

▶ 解答在093頁

（右側譯文）

1 我不買那東西的理由／不是因為價格／而是因為品質。

2 我們收／任何履歷書／只要提出方法是／用郵寄或是親自傳遞的。

調查官們／和我都／嚇到了／在那可怕的情況下。

攻略法 54　對等連接詞的特徵

1 對等連接詞的種類

and, but (= yet), or, as well as, than, plus 等。

2 對等連接詞的特徵

1 對等連接詞前後相同的話省略。

2 出現3個以上相同的話：A, B and C型態。

3 像and, but (= yet), or的對等連接詞不能放在句首。

4 其他的對等連接詞：as well as, than, plus等。

攻略法 55　相關連接詞的原理

both A and B：A與B，兩者全都。

between A and B：A與B之間。

not A but B：不是A，而是B。

not only (just) A but (also) B：不只是A，B也是。

neither A nor B：不是A或B其中之一。

either A or B：A或B其中之一。

例子

1 (A) or   ❶ 把握問題的類型
  (B) and
  (C) so   ❷ 把握提示
  (D) yet   ❸ 空格中要填什麼詞類？

The advertising plan was _____ will be our top priority for an additional two weeks according to the marketing team.

1 把握問題的類型
  文法題

2 把握提示
  對等連接詞，
  解說差異

3 空格中要填什麼詞類？
  對等連接詞

2 (A) and
  (B) so
  (C) but
  (D) for

Our military is always prepared to engage in any war _____ defend our invaluable country, so don't panic.

1 把握問題的類型

2 把握提示

3 空格中要填什麼詞類？

3 (A) yet
  (B) or
  (C) and
  (D) nor

Ms. Mutumbo has not finished her report, _____ has she conducted the necessary research.

1 把握問題的類型

2 把握提示

3 空格中要填什麼詞類？

4 (A) for
  (B) so
  (C) and
  (D) but

Sales are important to company growth, _____ many experts argue customer service is more important.

1 把握問題的類型

2 把握提示

3 空格中要填什麼詞類？

5 (A) yet
  (B) nor
  (C) or
  (D) and

The Pillow Factory will either reduce costs _____ raise prices in order to increase profits.

1 把握問題的類型

2 把握提示

3 空格中要填什麼詞類？

6 (A) yet
(B) or
(C) and
(D) however

It is strange that young people are widely unemployed, _____ their spending continues to rise.

1 把握問題的類型

2 把握提示

3 空格中要填什麼詞類？

7 (A) but
(B) as well as
(C) or
(D) yet

Meeting your performance goals _____ customers' needs, you will be given a large bonus.

1 把握問題的類型

2 把握提示

3 空格中要填什麼詞類？

8 (A) but
(B) so
(C) and
(D) than

Many investors lost money on the stock market, _____ continued to profit from other investments.

1 把握問題的類型

2 把握提示

3 空格中要填什麼詞類？

9 (A) for
(B) nor
(C) yet
(D) and

All ticket sales are final, _____ they cannot be traded or refunded at any time.

1 把握問題的類型

2 把握提示

3 空格中要填什麼詞類？

10 (A) for
(B) but
(C) or
(D) and

The organizers of the trip reminded participants that they can pay in advance _____ choose to receive a bill.

1 把握問題的類型

2 把握提示

3 空格中要填什麼詞類？

▶ 解答在093頁

高難度

101 Jonathan's favorite form of acting is theater, _____ he plans to pursue a career in television and movie acting.

(A) so
(B) yet
(C) and
(D) for

102 The seminar's directors promise to deliver top industry speakers _____ provide networking opportunities to attendees.

(A) and
(B) as
(C) or
(D) while

103 Many believed Albert would certainly get a promotion, _____ his mother was the head of the human resources department.

(A) nor
(B) yet
(C) and
(D) for

高難度

104 The governor insisted that he had not accepted bribes while in office, _____ had he made secret deals with any companies.

(A) and
(B) but
(C) so
(D) nor

105 MegaNet Services is the top provider of high-speed Internet services in the country, _____ so it claims in its advertisements.

(A) or
(B) but
(C) so
(D) yet

106 A new political party may increase voter enthusiasm but also _____ great confusion in the political sphere.

(A) causing
(B) caused
(C) cause
(D) to cause

重要

107 The record company noticed consumers today prefer to purchase music electronically and _____ to focus on Internet music sales.

(A) decide
(B) decided
(C) decision
(D) decisive

108 President and CEO Brian Callahan announced that the company must cut production costs _____ risk going bankrupt.

(A) or
(B) yet
(C) nor
(D) and

109 Ms. Nakamura called her cable company to complain about the service, _____ admitted that she did not pay her bills on time.

(A) nor
(B) and
(C) yet
(D) so

110 Those who enter the photography contest should fill out an entry form _____ submit their top three photographs.

(A) but
(B) and
(C) or
(D) yet

111 The realtor showed Judy an apartment within _____ just around the business district in order for her to live near her workplace.

(A) or
(B) but
(C) however
(D) as well

112 The television commercial claims that the new vitamins will neither cause harmful side effects _____ interfere with other treatments.

(A) and
(B) or
(C) for
(D) nor

113 Management is the work of coordinating the individual tasks, analyzing current market trends and _____ for the future.

(A) to prepare
(B) prepare
(C) preparing
(D) preparation

114 Please wear your protective helmet at the construction site, _____ you might be seriously injured by accidents.

(A) and
(B) yet
(C) or
(D) so

115 Employees are encouraged to commute by subway _____ bus to help avoid the lack of parking spaces.

(A) or
(B) but
(C) either
(D) with

116 Last week we gave a presentation about the newly developed model _____ received optimistic reactions from the attendees.

(A) when
(B) but
(C) since
(D) and

117 Staff members are encouraged to meet and _____ the details of the proposed plan as often as necessary.

(A) discussing
(B) discusses
(C) discuss
(D) discussed

118 The reserved parking lots are mine and the _____, so no one can park here without my permission.

(A) supervisor's
(B) supervisor
(C) supervision
(D) supervising

119 The company plans to _____ and reorganize many of its stores to eliminate overlap in jobs and office functions.

(A) closely
(B) close
(C) closed
(D) be closed

重要
120 I am looking forward to the marketing workshop and _____ the urgent matter in preparation for launching the new product.

(A) discuss
(B) discussion
(C) discussing
(D) to discuss

▶ 解答在095頁

Dear Mr. Hank,

Please kindly find the the blueprint of the interior design _____ your new office in the attached file. As per our previous discussion, I have added more concealed space
121

which _____ behind some removable compartment boards for your storage needs.
122

Please advise me what color paint you prefer on the surface of those boards. I also put

a bathroom adjoining your personal office according to your _____. _____. You
123 **124**

may select what you need by putting a checkmark by the picture when you send me

your confirmation of the blueprint. Please take your time to examine the entire design,

and please feel free to let me know if there are any flaws or problems. I look forward to

receiving your feedback soon.

Sincerely,

Jack Crews

121 (A) to
(B) on
(C) for
(D) at

122 (A) are
(B) is
(C) was
(D) were

123 (A) reply
(B) response
(C) request
(D) reaction

124 (A) I also sent you a list of furniture
(B) I also sent you a carpenter of repairing furniture
(C) I also delivered you a piece of furniture
(D) I also dispatched some material for furniture production to you

▶ 解答在095頁

Chapter 15 介系詞
必須要和名詞搭配解題的介系詞題型！

Review Test

Chapter 14裡學到了對等連接詞。我們來複習一下學過的內容吧！

1 對等連接詞的前面或後面有空格時？　▶ ....

2 空格的前後是相同的句型構造時？　▶ ....

3 不能放在句子最前面的連接詞是？　▶ ....

4 和both搭配成對的相關連接詞是？　▶ ....

5 和neither搭配成對的相關連接詞是？　▶ ....

6 可和not only A but (also) B互換的相關連接詞是？　▶ ....

Preview

1 介系詞的特徵

各位都知道介系詞的後面要接名詞吧？這叫做介系詞片語，在句中扮演著形容詞或副詞的角色。幾項要點如下。

❶ 介系詞後面有名詞的話？　　　　　　介系詞片語

❷ 介系詞片語在句中扮演的角色是？　　形容詞或副詞角色（大部分都是當副詞）

❸ 介系詞和副詞子句一樣　　　　　　　表讓步、理由、時間、條件、目的、結果

我們為什麼要學介系詞呢？說來說去，就是名詞有時候會當做形容詞和副詞使用，這時最有用的工具就是介系詞了。名詞前若放介系詞的話，就成為「介系詞片語」，名詞就可當形容詞或副詞使用。

2 介系詞的題型解題法

❶ 先確認句中是否都具備了句子應有的要素。

❷ 如果句子應有的要素都存在了，後面還有名詞的話，前面加上介系詞即成為修飾語

❸ 看看後面的名詞，看看前面的動詞，選擇適當的介系詞。

介系詞的角色

別單純地只把at、in、on當作介系詞，要真正地了解介系詞的含義才可以喔！不管是什麼，基礎穩固後才能把其他東西往上疊。

介系詞又叫做前置詞，顧名思義就是放置在前面的意思，這也代表後面應該會有些什麼吧？介系詞的英文是preposition，也是「放置（position）在前面（pre）」的意思。那麼**介系詞的後面到底應該放什麼呢？答對了！就是名詞！**介系詞和名詞為一組所組成的，我們叫做「介系詞片語」。介系詞後面出現名詞的情況如下。

- 介系詞＋一般名詞
  例 on the desk 在桌上

- 介系詞＋代名詞受格
  例 between you and me 在你我之間

- 介系詞＋動名詞
  - 例 by -ing 藉由…；without -ing 沒有…

- 介系詞＋介系詞片語
  例：from around the world 從全世界開始
  　　except in the room 除了房間內之外

上面最後一個狀況，介系詞後面出現介系詞片語是例外中的例外。

5秒 解決介系詞題型的方法

1 介系詞題型中，選項(A)～(D)都是介系詞時，就以最快的時間去看後面的名詞。
（平時多練習考試中常出現的題型，考試時可以快速解題。）

1 如果後面的名詞不是常出現的名詞時，請先確認和前面的動詞是否為慣用詞。

Quiz

Q1 (As / Through) your manager, I order you to work extended hours tonight.

Q2 We should deal (with / for) their complaints as soon as possible.

《講師的補充說明》

1) 不接介系詞的名詞是必須用語，當作主詞、受詞和補語。有介系詞的介系詞片語是當作修飾語的形容詞或副詞。

2) 介系詞後面的名詞可說是介系詞的受詞。

＊for he和for him中哪一個對呢？for him是正確答案。是「為他」的意思，是受詞的意思。

▶ 解答在099頁

讓步和理由的介系詞題型

表讓步的介系詞和表理由的介系詞。最常見的就是介系詞接在名詞前面，不但表示讓步和理由，也有修飾動詞的效果。

1. 表讓步的介系詞

解釋為「儘管…」。最常出題的型態為連接詞的區分為主，這種題目只要看句中有幾個「S + V」就可以知道。**表示讓步意思的介系詞和連接詞都是出題頻率第一名。**

1　(**Despite / Although**) **his late arrival**, we will not postpone the opening ceremony.

> 1　即使他遲到／我們也不會延遲／開幕式。

只要知道括弧後面的his late arrival是名詞，就可以輕鬆解題了。空格就是要填介系詞，所以解答是despite。如果答案是連接詞although的話，後面必須是接「S + V」。

2　We should proceed with the project (**in spite of / though**) **the budget deficit**.

> 2　我們必須要進行／那個專案／即使預算赤字。

後面除了名詞（the budget deficit）以外就沒有其它，括弧內當然就是介系詞了。所以正確答案就是in spite of。而though是連接詞。請注意囉！介系詞in spite of在這裡是放在名詞「預算赤字」前面，修飾動詞proceed的。這是「儘管…還是要進行」，要修飾動詞「進行」proceed。這就是介系詞在句中扮演的角色。

下面整理了表示讓步的介系詞和連接詞。

讓步的介系詞	讓步的連接詞
主要是「介系詞 + 名詞, S + V」的型態，常見如下	主要是「連接詞 S + V, S + V」的型態，常見如下
despite（儘管…）	although（儘管…）
= in spite of	= though
= with all	= even if
= for all	= even though

2. 表理由的介系詞

表示理由的介系詞，在句中一般解釋為「因為⋯」，在此必須和連接詞做好區分。出題的頻率高居第二位。正確的詞性和正確的含義是解題的關鍵。

She has been committed to this task (**due to / now that**) **the imminent deadline**.

有看到括弧後面的名詞the imminent deadline吧！這裡是要放修飾名詞的介系詞，解答是due to。now that是連接詞後面要接「S + V」。

放在名詞前表示理由的介系詞，和帶出後面子句、也是表示理由的連接詞，用表格整理如下。

表理由的介系詞	表理由的連接詞
主要是「介系詞 + 名詞, S + V」的型態，常見如下	主要是「連接詞 S + V, S + V」的型態，常見如下
because of（因為⋯）	because（因為⋯）
= due to	= as
= owing to	= since
= on account of	= now that
= thanks to	= seeing that
= in view of	= for
	* since → 當作「自⋯以來」的意思時，可以當作介系詞，也可以當作連接詞使用

怪物講師的祕訣

1 了解「儘管⋯」和「因為⋯」單字的真正詞性和正確的含義是最大的解題關鍵。

2 具有「儘管⋯」含義的介系詞是？→ despite, in spite of ...

3 具有「因為⋯」含義的介系詞是？→ because of, owing to, on account of, due to...

4 也可當作連接詞使用的介系詞是？→ although, though, because, as, since...

Quiz

Q3 She could be elected as a vice president (due to / since) she has been devoted to the tasks.

Q4 (Despite / Although) the fact that he has been dedicated to the company, he was not promoted.

▶ 解答在099頁

攻略法 58 時間和理由的介系詞題型

名詞前面放介系詞時，是表示時間的副詞。常以「在…時，做…」的形式出現，修飾「做…」的動詞。我們來看看有哪些是表示時間的介系詞吧！

在開始學習和時間有關的介系詞之前，首先要能清楚時間點和時間的區別。時間點就是像下午3點、星期、9月等，有特定的時間；時間就是6個小時、3週、14年等，這類從時間點到時間點的時間。

1. 介系詞by和until

這兩者都有「直到…」的意思，使用在時間點的單字前，但by和until在使用上是有差別的。以某個時間點為基準，在該時間結束時使用介系詞by；直至某個時間點仍舊持續進行時使用until。by有期限的意味，until有持續的意味存在。

1　We should have postponed the picnic **(by / until) the end of this month**.

雖然這兩者都有「直到…」的意思，但是這題是郊遊延期到這個月底，有一直延期的意思，所以要使用until。

2　Can you finish your homework **(by / until) tomorrow morning**?

這題是到明天早上前做完作業，以「明天早上」為時間基準點，要使用有「期限」意味的介系詞by。括弧內使用介系詞until的話，就變成了「一直結束到明天」的意思，文意完全不通。

2. 介系詞for和since

在「時態」單元中有學到現在完成式中常使用for和since吧？此時for的後面接期間，since的後面接時間點。

主詞 + have p.p. ┌ since + 過去時間點名詞
└ since 主詞 + 過去式動詞
主詞 + have p.p. + for (= in 在…、over 經過…) + 用數字表現的期間

《講師的補充說明》

請這樣記！

by就是結束某個動作時使用的動詞（submit, return, receive, inform等）一起使用，until就是和動作持續進行的動詞（stay, wait, continue, remain, last）一起使用。

＊not A until B像慣用語般一起使用，須記下來。直接翻譯的話，有「直到B都不A」，但是用中文翻譯的話，須翻成「直到B才會A」才通順。

1 我們應該要延期／野餐／到這個月底。

2 你可以完成你的作業嗎／在明天早上以前？

during有時候和for被當作一樣的意思使用，兩者都表示「…期間」，後面接一段期間。那有什麼差異呢？**具體來說，for常使用在用數字表現的期間，像是for 3 years這類的；而during後面大部分會接表示期間的名詞，像是during my vacation。簡單舉例如下，**

- for a decade (= for one decade) 10年之間
  for over 10 years 超過10年的期間

- during the meal 吃飯的期間
  during the lecture 演講的期間

我們來看看介系詞的題型，熟悉一下實際在考場上的感覺吧！

I have studied this area (**for /since**) **last June**.

我一直研究這領域／從上個6月以來。

不論是for或是since都常被使用在現在完成式中，不過括弧後的last June是「過去的一個時間點」，所以正確答案是since。如果要使用for的話，括弧後面應該要接three years這類的期間用詞。

3. 介系詞throughout和through

這些字彙看起來很相像，是容易混淆的介系詞。**throughout後面出現期間時，有「這整個期間內」的意思；後面如果是出現場所，有「這場所到處都」的意思。**而另外一個單字through則是具有「透過…」的涵意，為使用在利用「手段或媒介」時的介系詞。來熟悉一下實際在考場上的感覺吧！

He worked (**throughout / through**) **the week** as the deadline was approaching.

他工作了／一整週／因為截止日即將到來。

括弧後有期間相關的the week，所以使用「這整個期間內」的throughout較恰當。另外使用在其他情況，如throughout the day是「一整天」、throughout the week「一整周」、throughout the month「一整個月」。

- throughout 從開始到結束
  - throughout the conference 整個會議
  - throughout the city 整個都市

- through 透過；手段或媒介
  - through e-mail 透過電子郵件
  - through the dealer 透過商人

4. 介系詞within和by

within是介系詞，「…以內」的意思，後面不只可以接期間，還可接能力、範圍等，基本含義有「在一定的範圍內」的意思。而by也是介系詞，有「到…為止」的意思，如同前面有出現until和by二者選一的題型，within和by二選一的題型也不少。我們來看看下面的題目吧！

You are free to ask for a refund (**within / by**) **60 days** of the original purchase.

你可自由地要求／退款／從原始購買日開始起算60日內。

括弧後的60 days不是特定的時間點，解釋為「60天以內」比「到60天為止」更恰當。如果括弧內是by的話，後面應當為Thursday、November這類的時間點型態的單字。

介系詞within的用法簡單介紹如下：

- …的內部
  - within the room 房間內

- …的範圍內
  - within view 看得到的地方內
  - within one's ability [capacity] …的能力內

- （時間、距離、數量、程度）…以內
  - within the next three years 往後的3年以內
  - within a radius of 100km 半徑100km內

《講師的補充說明》

within + 期間, by + 時間點

這兩個很多人會搞不清楚，這須靠平時多看句型累積。例如，畫出「60天」界線，若想要表現在這期間以內交回即可時，要使用介系詞 within 60 days。但是像是有定出「星期五」這類特定的時間點，若要表達到該時間點前須完成某件事時，要使用介系詞by。

- within two months 兩個月以內
- within this year 今年以內
- by September 到9月為止
- by the end of this month 到這個月為止

5. 介系詞before（= prior to）和after（= following）

before和after都是表示時間點的介系詞，before是「在…以前」，after是「在…以後」的意思。before和after除了當介系詞使用，也可當連接詞，但是prior to和following只能當作介系詞。

We had considered this matter (**before / prior to**) you contacted us.

我們考慮過了／這個問題／在你跟我們聯絡以前。

有看到括弧後面的「S+V」嗎？括弧內可以填入帶出子句的連接詞 before，不過不能使用prior to。

6. 時間介系詞at、on、in

時間相關的介系詞在日常生活中使用頻率最高，因此要了解正確的使用法，請看下面的題型。

The manager plans to meet you (at / on) 6:00 tomorrow.

經理預計要和你見面／明天6點。

tomorrow這類的時刻前放介系詞at，six twenty（6點20分）這類的時刻前也是使用介系詞at。on是使用在規模比時刻更大一些的日子或星期上。

時間介系詞中除了at、on以外還有in，其用法簡單整裡如下。

- **at + 時刻：at 7**
- **on + 日、星期：on June 2（日）、on Monday（星期）**
- **in + 月以上更大的範圍：in January（月）、in spring（季節）、in 2011（年）、in 21 C（世紀）**

at night（在晚上）、in the morning（在早上）等在規則以外的，要另外記下。

《講師的補充說明》

下面的單字前面不使用介系詞at、on、in，因為它們本身就是一個完整的副詞。（介系詞後面要接名詞；副詞後面可以沒有名詞，前面也可以不需有不定冠詞a、an或定冠詞the。）

本身就是完整的副詞，前面不需接介系詞或冠詞。如下：

last year, this year, next year, yesterday, today, tomorrow, tonight 等。

7. 條件介系詞in case of

表示條件的介系詞in case of和連接詞in case。在副詞子句連接詞的單元裡有提過，但是這些長得很像，很容易被誤用。可記得，只有一組「**S＋V**」的話使用介系詞，**兩組以上的話使用連接詞**。我們來看看下面的句子，括弧內要放入什麼字？

(In case / In case of) inclement weather, we'd better stay inside.

萬一有惡劣的天候／我們最好要待在／室內。

括弧後面馬上就接名詞，所以要使用介系詞，此題的正確解答為in case of。這裡要小心的是in case of當作介系詞，後面應當要接名詞；不過in case是連接詞，後面應當要接「S＋V」。後面有沒有of差很多。

我們將前面的內容整理成表格。

介系詞 + 名詞, S + V	連接詞 S + V, S + V
• in case of 萬一⋯的情況 　= in the event of ＊ given 考慮⋯時（介系詞、連接詞）	• in case (that) ⋯的情況 　= in the event (that)

怪物講師的祕訣

下面將容易混淆的介系詞兩兩整理，讓你更容易記憶。

1 by, until

　→ by是到⋯為止，有完成的意思。

　→ until是直到⋯，有持續的意思。

2 for, since

　→ 兩者都是用在現在完成式。

　→ for是用在表現數字的期間，since是用在時間點。

3 throughout, through

　→ throughout是在整個期間內，整個場所的到處。

　→ through用在表示手段或媒介。

4 within, by

　→ within用在期間、能力、範圍內。

　→ by用在到某個時間點為止。

5 before, after

　→ 可當介系詞，也可當連接詞。

6 at, on, in

　→ at用在時刻，on用在日子或星期，in用在月以上的時間。

Quiz ···

Q5 The key to success is to make a plan (in / within) the range of the alloted budget.

Q6 You have to notify us of the plan in advance (by / until) the end of this week.

▶ 解答在099頁

攻略法

59

場所介系詞的題型

使用在代表場所的名詞前的介系詞主要有兩大類。一種是表示靜止狀態的介系詞,另一種是表示移動狀態的介系詞。

是表示靜止狀態?還是表示移動狀態?這就是這次要學習的介系詞的重點。絕對不要覺得了解個大概就好,介系詞的題型最重要的就是要知道介系詞的正確概念。一起來看看下面的圖。

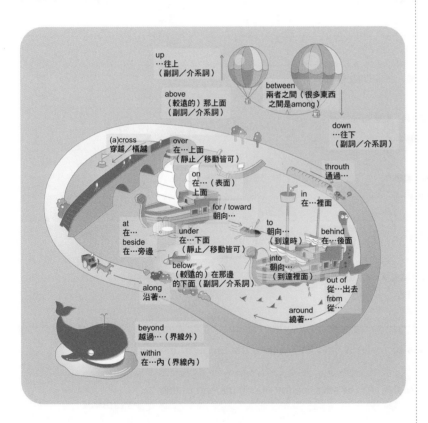

1. 使用於靜止狀態的介系詞

at, on, in, over, under (= beneath), above, below, by (= next), to (= beside), behind, between, among, beyond, within, opposite (= across from)

透過上面的圖了解後，我們再透過下面的例句具體了解用法。如果需要更多的例句，也可以利用字典。這些介系詞適用於靜止的狀態，請不要忘記了。我們一起來看看下面的例句吧。

1 The picture is hanging **on the wall**.

1 那照片掛在／牆上。

我們在講東西掛在牆上時，要使用好像把東西掛在某個東西的表面涵意的on。要記住喔！on是在把東西貼在某些東西表面時使用。

2 There is a convenience store **behind this building**.

2 有一家便利商店／在這個建築物後面。

介系詞behind有「在後面的」的意思，使用於靜止的狀態。

3 The museum is **opposite this building**.

3 博物館位在／這建築的對面。

opposite是形容詞，有「在對面」的意思，但也可像上面例句當介系詞使用。表示在對面的靜止狀態，此時也可與across from交替使用。

2. 使用於移動狀態的介系詞

for / toward, to, into, onto, out of, from, through, around / round, along, cross / across, up / down, over / under

這些介系詞都是適用於移動狀態的介系詞，請各位一定要下功夫透過圖片知道它們使用在何種情況。我們直接來看例句吧！

1 He is expected to leave **for Seoul**.

1 他預計／要離開／前往首爾。

有感受到離開前往首爾的移動感嗎？這樣的情況下要使用介系詞for，靜止狀態適用的in並不適用。來看看I live in Seoul.的情況，就可以很清楚了解介系詞in是使用在靜止狀態。

2 I took my wallet **out of my pocket**.

2 我拿出了我的皮夾／從我的口袋。

把原本在口袋中的皮夾拿出來外面，這句話也有明顯的移動意味，因此要使用out of。

3 He walked **across the street**.

3 他走路穿越街道。

橫越馬路讓人有感受到移動的感覺吧！這時要使用介系詞across，也可使用cross。**不過across from是使用於沒有移動的靜止狀態**，請區分清楚。

怪物講師的祕訣

表示場所或時間的介系詞題型的解題要領如下。

1 首先要確認是表示場所的介系詞，或是表示時間的介系詞。

2 如果是表示場所的介系詞，接下來要再區分是靜止性的介系詞，或是移動性的介系詞。

Quiz

Q7 He was standing (at / into) the door.
Q8 The fish jumped (on / onto) the board.

▶ 解答在099頁

攻略法

60

其他介系詞的解題法

到目前為止，我們學了讓步、理由、時間、條件和場所等相關的介系詞。在這裡也整理出其它重要介系詞，一起來看看。

有發現我們在介系詞的學習順序和副詞子句連接詞學習的順序很相似嗎？**差異僅僅在後面如果是名詞的話使用介系詞，如果是「S+V」的話使用連接詞**。副詞子句原本就是副，當然很相似囉！且兩者都是用來修飾動詞的。

1. 表示目的和結果的介系詞 so as to、in order to

兩者都是有「因為做…」或是「所以結果…」含義的介系詞，和**其他介系詞不一樣的是它們是使用原形動詞，是相當特別的例外情況。to不定詞的副詞用法中就是使用在目的和結果**。我們來試著解下面的題型吧！

He has to work hard (**that / so as to**) succeed.   < 他必須努力工作／為了成功。

括弧後面有原形動詞succeed，所以正確答案是so as to。如果that是答案的話，後面必須要接「S+V」，簡單整理如下表。

to（介系詞）+ 原形動詞, S + V	連接詞 S + V, S + V

• 目的：因為做…
 	
  to do = so as to do = in order to
 	
• 結果：非常…，所以結果…
 	
  to do = so 形／副 as to do
	• S + V so that S can [may, will]
	
	  原形動詞
	
	• S + V so 形／副 that S + V

其實在to不定詞的單元裡提過的部分，就是to不定詞副詞用法。對於表示目的的副詞子句很熟練，但是對於表示結果的副詞子句覺得很陌生吧？其實副詞子句的用法還有其它幾種，不過平時不常使用，只要熟悉常用的這兩種就可以了。

2.「除了⋯以外」含義的介系詞except

except是介系詞，有「除了⋯以外」、「⋯以外」的意思。不過except後面接when或that的except when、except that是扮演著連接詞的角色。好了，我們直接看下面的例句吧！

1　He is always kind **except some occasions**.

1 他一直都很親切／除了一些情況以外。

這句話是說，他除了某些情況以外其它時候是都很親切的意思。這時候except接在名詞some occasions前面，所以很明顯地是介系詞。

2　**Except when he is late**, he always uses this door.

2 除了遲到的情況以外／他總是走這道門。

遲到時擔心會引起其他人注意，所以從其它門偷偷進來，不過除了這個情況以外，都是從這道門進出的意思。有看到except when後面的「S + V(he is)」嗎？帶出非名詞的子句，這裡的except when是連接詞。

將except和except when / that整理如下。

- except：（介系詞，除了⋯以外。不使用於句子最前面。）

    = except for = excepting = but（皆為介系詞，除了except以外，其它皆可使用在句子最前面。）

- except that [when] S, S + V（可使用在句子最前面。）

- but for

    = without（介系詞，如果沒有⋯）

- excluding（介系詞，除了⋯以外。）

＊including和上面的介系詞意思相反，是「包含⋯」的意思，也是介系詞。

3.「關於⋯」含義的介系詞

最常使用於「關於⋯」和「對於⋯」的介系詞就是about，除此之外還有很多介系詞也可當作「關於⋯」和「對於⋯」使用。

We are going to hold a meeting **regarding this urgent matter**.

我們預計要開會／針對這個緊急的情況。

上面例句中regarding就是和about一樣，是「關於⋯」和「對於⋯」意思的介系詞。乍看似乎不太一樣，但是從後面接名詞this urgent matter看來，確實是介系詞無誤。

英文中，表示「關於…」和「對於…」意思的介系詞比想像中多。接下來要介紹的都是「關於…」和「對於…」意思的介系詞，請把握這次機會好好的把它們記起來。

下面把和about一樣有「關於…」和「對於…」意思的介系詞，整理成一個總覽。

about = concerning = regarding = as to = as for = with regard [respect, reference] to = in regard [respect, reference] to

＊as of和日期一起使用，有「從…開始」的意思，不要和as to和as for混淆了。

4. 使用在交通和通訊手段前的介系詞by

「搭計程車」、「搭巴士」、「打電話」等這類表示交通手段或是通訊手段的表現中是使用介系詞by。這時最重要的是，表示交通手段或是通訊手段的car、bus、taxi、train、plane、fax、telephone這類名詞前面不接冠詞，也不使用複數形，就原封不動直接使用就好了。

* 表示交通手段的表現（不接冠詞，也不使用複數型）
  - by car, by bus, by taxi, by train, by plane
  - You can come here by taxi. 你可以搭計程車來。

* 表示通訊手段的表現（不接冠詞，也不使用複數形）
  - by fax, by telephone

5. 「除了…以外、再加上」含義的介系詞

在英文中，名詞或名詞類前面接「除了…以外、再加上」的介系詞的情況相當多。下面介系詞就屬此類。

besides = in addition to = apart from = aside from = on top of

Besides helping others, he also tries to improve himself.

幫助其他人以外／他還花心思／想要提升自己的內涵。

6.「名詞 + of + 名詞」的表現

英文中很常出現「名詞 + of + 名詞」的表現，**特別是這些表現的主格、受格、所有格、同位格的相關題型常出現在考題中**。將這些歸類如下面簡單易懂的內容。

* 主格：a recent outbreak of a disease 最近發生的某種疾病
  → disease是主格

* 受格：the development of this city 這座都市的開發
  → this city是受格

* 所有格：the leg of this desk 這張桌子的腳
  → this desk是所有格

* 同位格：the aim of fulfilling his job 完成他的工作的目標
  → the aim = fulfilling his job

怪物講師的祕訣

在這單元學到的介系詞簡單整理如下：

1. 「為了做…」：to do = in order to do = so as to do
2. 「除了…以外」：except, excluding
3. 「關於…」：about, concerning, regarding, as to, as for
4. 表示交通、通訊手段：by train, by tax
5. 「除了…以外也」：besides, in addition to
6. 連結名詞和名詞的of：考題常出受格和所有格的關係。

Quiz

Q9 The customer tried to reach you (for / to) ask for a refund.

Q10 The satisfaction (of / for) customers is essential for our business.

攻略法

61 其他介系詞題型的解題法

整理出考試常出的介系詞慣用語，熟悉這類的表現有助於在考場上得高分。只要看到介系詞，就要把它們記起來。

下面介紹的介系詞是考題常出的慣用法，能整組記下來是最好不過。因為介系詞的題型常常會出現有既定用法的單字。

1. 考題常出的介系詞

• as	…身為（身分、資格）
• from now (on)	從現在開始
• (from) all over the world	從全世界
= (from) all around the world	
= throughout the world	
• reaction to	對於…的反應
• be founded with	訂立…的目標
• with very few exceptions	幾乎沒有例外
⟷ with some exceptions	有部分例外
• be comparable to / with	比較
⟷ compare A with B	比較A和B
• at the end of	在…之末
⟷ at the beginning of	在…之初
• demand for	對於…的需要（這裡的demand是名詞）
• access to	接近…（這裡的access是名詞）
• in the field of	在…的領域
• problem with	和…相關的問題
• make a deal with	和…往來
• a dispute over	和…相關的爭辯
• be ideal for	…是理想的
• information about / on	…相關的資訊
• be consistent with	在…有一貫性
• without having to do	沒必要做…
• contribution to	…做出貢獻
• a decrease in	…的減少（增加、減少都是用in可數名詞）
⟷ an increase in	

- effect on   對於…的影響
- experience in   經驗…
- influence on   關於…的影響
- problem with   和…的問題

2.「be動詞 + 形容詞類 + 介系詞」的組合

- be accustomed to   熟悉於…（= be used to -ing）
- be afraid of   害怕…
- be aware of   知道…
- be capable of   可以做…
- be dependent on   依賴…；依靠…（= be contingent on）
- be different from   和…不同
- be eligible for [to do]   有…的資格；有做…的資格
- be made of   由…製造
- be pleased with   因…而高興
- be responsible for   對…負責
- be responsive to   對…有反應；對…敏感
- be subject to   易受…

3.「不及物動詞 + 介系詞」的組合

- ask for 事物   要求（請求）…
- refer to 事物   參考…
- comply with 規定   依據（遵守）…
- deal with 事物   應付（處理）…
- interfere with 事物／人   妨礙（干涉）…
- aim at 事物   以…為目標
- search for 事物   找（搜尋）…

4. 其他主要介系詞表現

- according to   根據…
- by means of   利用…
- in charge of   負責…
- be in favor of   喜歡…
- instead of   代替…
- regardless of   與…無關
- under the control of   在…管制下
- under construction   施工中

攻略法 56　介系詞的角色

接在名詞前，用來當作該名詞的形容詞或副詞。常常也會被當做修飾動詞的副詞。

攻略法 57　讓步和理由的介系詞題型

讓步：despite, in spite of, with all, for all （儘管⋯）

理由：because of, owing to, due to, on account of （因為⋯）

＊讓步和理由的介系詞在翻譯解釋很重要，詞性的了解也相當重要。

攻略法 58　時間和理由的介系詞題型

1 **by, until**：有結束的感覺使用by；有持續的感覺使用until。

2 **for, since**：for後面接數字表示的期間；since後面接過去的時間點。

3 **throughout, through**：throughout有整個期間、整個場所到處的意思；through是用在手段、媒介。

4 **within, by**：within有在某界線以內的意思（期間、能力、範圍等）；by有直到某個時間點為止的意思。

5 **before (= prior to)和after (= following)**：before、after可當介系詞，也可當連接詞。

6 **at, on, in**：表示時刻用at；表示日子、星期用on；月以上使用in。

攻略法 59　場所介系詞的題型

靜止性的介系詞：at, on, in, over, under, above, below, behind, next to 等

移動性的介系詞：for, to, into, out of, across, up, down, around, along 等

攻略法 60　其他介系詞的解題法

1 **目的**：to do＝in order to do＝so as to do（為了做⋯）。

2 **「除了⋯以外」**：except, excluding 等。

3 **「關於⋯」**：about, concerning, regarding, as to, as for 等。

4 **通訊、交通手段**：by plane, by fax 等。

5 **「除了⋯以外也」**：besides, in addition to 名詞（或動名詞）。

6 **連結名詞和名詞的of**：考題常出受格和所有格的關係。

例子

1　(A) within　　❶ 把握問題的類型
　　(B) until
　　(C) by
　　(D) about
　　　　　　❷ 把握提示

Nonetheless, Sue was confident that she would be hired _____ the end of this year at the latest.　❸ 空格中要填什麼詞類？

1 把握問題的類型
　文法問題

2 把握提示
　空格後的
　時間點名詞

3 空格中要填什麼詞類？
　介系詞

2　(A) until
　　(B) across
　　(C) onto
　　(D) along

The artist's exhibition will continue _____ the beginning of next month, showing all of her recent works.

1 把握問題的類型

2 把握提示

3 空格中要填什麼詞類？

3　(A) through
　　(B) with
　　(C) by
　　(D) when

When you arrive for the interview, remember to bring a list of professional references _____ you.

1 把握問題的類型

2 把握提示

3 空格中要填什麼詞類？

4　(A) above
　　(B) past
　　(C) toward
　　(D) beside

Premier Office Design decided that its location one floor _____ its strongest competitor was no longer suitable.

1 把握問題的類型

2 把握提示

3 空格中要填什麼詞類？

5　(A) since
　　(B) during
　　(C) through
　　(D) for

Although the laboratory equipment has been tested _____ over six months, it didn't meet my expectations.

1 把握問題的類型

2 把握提示

3 空格中要填什麼詞類？

6 (A) within
(B) below
(C) down
(D) across

Because there is not a single bridge over there, the only way _____ the river is by ferry.

1 把握問題的類型

2 把握提示

3 空格中要填什麼詞類？

7 (A) by
(B) of
(C) for
(D) to

As you may have heard, the position is most suited for a job seeker with a passion _____ reporting the news.

1 把握問題的類型

2 把握提示

3 空格中要填什麼詞類？

8 (A) beneath
(B) from
(C) above
(D) outside

Most modern cities have a complex but convenient network of subway rails that run _____ the surface.

1 把握問題的類型

2 把握提示

3 空格中要填什麼詞類？

9 (A) Within
(B) Among
(C) Between
(D) Throughout

_____ those speaking at the conference will be Mark Leesburg, CEO of Star Dry Cleaning.

1 把握問題的類型

2 把握提示

3 空格中要填什麼詞類？

10 (A) toward
(B) onto
(C) after
(D) to

Please fax all correspondence _____ our head office in Venice just in case they need any evidence.

1 把握問題的類型

2 把握提示

3 空格中要填什麼詞類？

▶ 解答在100頁

101 The health and fitness facility, located _____ the corporate headquarters downtown, is open for any employee to use.

(A) inside
(B) throughout
(C) upon
(D) up

重要
102 All departments _____ the layout and design team are expected to submit their final revisions by the deadline on January 15.

(A) as
(B) because
(C) except
(D) once

高難度
103 Many worry that increasing the sales tax _____ an economic recession will be met with strong reactions from voters during the next election.

(A) during
(B) till
(C) between
(D) out of

104 Construction on the new facility stopped when it was discovered that endangered species were living _____ the near river.

(A) despite
(B) as
(C) along
(D) upon

105 Energy consumption across the nation has continued to rise _____ taxes and laws aimed at curbing usage.

(A) during
(B) between
(C) despite
(D) into

106 The president has announced plans to gradually increase taxes _____ the course of his term in office.

(A) while
(B) throughout
(C) around
(D) including

107 This letter is to inform you that our utilities have been billed twice the normal rate of every month _____ July, asking for your explanation.

(A) since
(B) outside
(C) on
(D) at

108 Three corporations will compete _____ one another for the ten-year maintenance contract from the state government.

(A) due to
(B) past
(C) around
(D) against

109 You can receive a credit to your account if your payment is received _____ the due date.

(A) before
(B) behind
(C) below
(D) beside

110 Please submit your invoice for the months of January _____ July to our corporate office at the beginning of August.

(A) around
(B) between
(C) over
(D) through

收集了多益考試中常出的題目。請當作正式的考試，確認時間並解題。

111 Ariel Graff was honored to stand on stage _____ two of her favorite writers as they each received the coveted Lexington Award.

(A) below
(B) above
(C) between
(D) across

112 All patients _____ health insurance will be required to fill out an additional form before receiving treatment.

(A) against
(B) without
(C) throughout
(D) into

重要
113 _____ unusually high demand, we couldn't increase our limited production capacity largely due to the regulation.

(A) In spite of
(B) On account of
(C) In case
(D) Now that

114 When you arrive at the airport, please go to the tourist information office because it will provide you _____ a free map.

(A) to
(B) for
(C) with
(D) about

115 The local government is considerably dependent _____ the income from the sightseeing of the provincial park.

(A) by
(B) on
(C) of
(D) at

116 Last quarter, the smart card company could cut its losses substantially thanks to a big jump _____ revenues.

(A) for
(B) over
(C) cross
(D) in

117 Most of the departments in this division remain open _____ noon on Saturdays.

(A) at
(B) by
(C) from
(D) until

高難度
118 Members will be notified _____ any amendments to these rules that may affect their rights or obligations.

(A) to
(B) at
(C) for
(D) of

119 According to the result of the sales report, the profits of our newly introduced items are far _____ our expectations.

(A) against
(B) beyond
(C) through
(D) toward

120 _____ the currently revised policy, we are not allowed to smoke inside the building.

(A) On
(B) Under
(C) Over
(D) According

▶ 解答在102頁

Questions 121-124 refer to the following article.

In a reference to current news, a few companies that _____ processed food products
                                                              121
were selling some contaminated food products on the market. This crooked way of

running their businesses has made a severe and considerable impact on citizens' health.

Some citizens have even started suffering from symptoms such as high fever, diarrhea,

and vomiting. _____ the authorities attempted to intervene in this incident to combat
             122
the spread of this contaminated food, the _____ number of afflicted citizens continues
                                          123
increasing. The owners of these companies have expressed their regret publicly in a press

conference and _____ in order to restore the confidence of their consumers. However,
              124
the boycott on their products is expected to continue into the future.

121 (A) trade down
    (B) trade off
    (C) trade in
    (D) trade up

122 (A) Now that
    (B) Since
    (C) Because
    (D) Though

123 (A) reporting
    (B) reported
    (C) report
    (D) reports

124 (A) increased the price of their products
    (B) enlarged the ad campaign of their
        products
    (C) recalled their products
    (D) changed the packaging of their
        products

▶ 解答在102頁

Part 05
句子內最基本的是
名詞和代名詞

名詞和冠詞

正確的位置是名詞和冠詞的重點！

Review Test

一起來確認Chapter 15中學過的介系詞。請在下面空格內填入適當的答案。

1 介系詞子句在句子中扮演的角色是？ ▶ ....

2 表示讓步的介系詞是？ ▶ ....

3 表示理由的介系詞是？ ▶ ....

4 表示時間的介系詞是？ ▶ ....

5 表示條件的介系詞是？ ▶ ....

6 表示目的、結果的介系詞是？ ▶ ....

7 表示場所的介系詞是？ ▶ ....

Preview

1 名詞的特徵

❶ 名詞在句子中可當主詞、受詞、補語。

❷ 名詞大致可分成可數名詞和不可數名詞。

❸ 在多益裡常出現名詞和名詞組成的複合名詞。真正了解名詞會出現的位置，以及多認識常出題的名詞的話，這部分就一點也不難了。

2. 冠詞的特徵

冠詞有不定冠詞a / an和定冠詞the，如字面意思不定冠詞就是使用在「沒有受限定的東西」上；定冠詞就是使用在「指定的東西」上。只要了解其中的差異就可以了。在句中名詞被當作必要的要素，可以使用在名詞、受詞或是補語等正確的位置上，名詞的前面依需要使用正確的冠詞就可以囉！

3. 名詞和冠詞的題型解題法

❶ 確認名詞的位置是否正確。

❷ 要能區分是可數、或不可數名詞

❸ 要知道和動詞的適切性，以及和形容詞的適切性，才可以解題。

|解答| 1. 形容詞，副詞 2. despite, in spite of 3. because of, due to, owing to, on account of 4. by / until, for / during, within / throughout, at / on / in等 5. in case of, in the event of 6. so as to do 是為了做…；so 形／副 as to do 是非常…所以… 7. 靜止（at, on, in, beside, between, above, below, over, under 等）；移動（for, toward, to, into, out of, from, over, under, up, down, around 等）

攻略法 62 找出名詞正確的位置

在Chapter 10中已經學過的內容！多益考題很常出現，但最重要的是，這也是英文作文或會話的基礎。趁這個機會把知識都變成自己的吧！

找出名詞正確的位置並不難，這邊只強調兩個重點。第一，這麼簡單的問題，盡量不要錯！第二，要盡快（5秒以內）解題！只要求這兩點。那我們來看看下面的說明吧！

1. 用角色區分──放在主詞、受詞（位在及物動詞或介系詞後面）、補語位置

名詞在句中可當作主詞、及物動詞的受詞、介系詞的受詞、第2大句型的補語、第5大句型的補語等。如同下面例句，除了名詞以外，也可當作名詞子句、動名詞、to不定詞等名詞類的主詞、及物動詞和介系詞的受詞、第2大句型和第5大句型的補語使用。

1 **What I want** is just a little break.（主詞）
   名詞子句當作主詞的例子。

2 I enjoy **being with others**.（受詞）
   動名詞當作受詞的例子。

3 The purpose is **to get rid of possible errors**.（補語）
   to不定詞當作補語的例子。

1 我想要的／只是一點喘息的空間而已。

2 我很享受／和其他人在一起。

3 目的是／消除／可能的失誤。

2. 看題目的空格前後文在5秒內找出名詞的位置

還記得「冠、所、介、動」嗎？是我們在Chapter 01中學過的內容，如果記不得的話，請複習過後再回來吧！接下來看看下面的題目。

The newly appointed (supervise / supervisor) who is strict will not forgive you.

新到任的那位監督者／很嚴格／不會原諒你的。

括弧位在「冠詞＋副詞＋形容詞」（the newly appointed）的後面，形容詞子句（who is strict）前面，所以是名詞的位置。因此括弧內應該要放入supervisor。（supervise是動詞）當然，也可以說是看句子的主詞來找解答，但是比起來，看括弧的前後文來解答的速度較快。

現在就把如同上面例子，可以一眼就看出句中名詞位置相關的內容整理如下。

- 冠詞 + 名詞
- 所有格 + （副詞）+ （形容詞）+ 名詞
- 介系詞 + 名詞
- 動詞 + 名詞（動詞為須與受詞搭配的及物動詞，是主動型態）

怪物講師的祕訣

空格內的解答可填入名詞的情況

1 如果是主詞、受詞、補語的位置時，就要先想到名詞。

2 記住「冠、所、介、動」後面是放名詞，這也不失為一個好方法。

Quiz ....

Q1 (Although / Whether) he will accept it depends on the situation.

Q2 The (applicant / application) which you submitted has not arrived yet.

▶ 解答在106頁

《講師的補充說明》

可在句子中當做主詞、受詞、補語的是？

可在句子中當做主詞、受詞、補語的，不是只有名詞而已。除了名詞以外，還有代名詞、動名詞和名詞子句等名詞類，都可以當作主詞、受詞、補語。

攻略法

63

區分可數名詞和不可數名詞

要將所有的名詞分成可數、不可數名詞不是一件簡單的事。要全部記下來也很難，再加上同時屬於兩邊的名詞也很多。但把代表性的不可數名詞記住以後，把其餘的當做可數名詞就簡單多了。

可數名詞就是像book、desk、boy、teacher可以用一、二、三…等去計數的名詞，這類的名詞有數（number）的概念。相反的water、milk或sugar無法一一細數，或是根本就不能算數量的名詞，就叫做不可數名詞。比起說是數，倒不如說是量的概念較恰當。**簡單來說，就是有數的概念的名詞，就叫做可數名詞；量的概念的名詞就叫做不可數名詞。**

1. 不可數名詞

不可數名詞就如同上面說明的，是具有量的概念的名詞。金（gold）、水（water）、沙（sand）等，這類名詞就是不可數名詞的代表。不過這些名詞幾乎不會出現在多益考題中，多益會常出像information這類商務用的名詞。

不可數名詞前面不能接a / an，也不能使用複數形字尾-s、-es，這一定要記住。因為不可數名詞無法計數，所以當然前面只能使用不定冠詞，無法使用其它如another、both、few、several、many等限定詞。**不可數名詞可以使用定冠詞the、所有格和little / much、other等**。

I couldn't find **a / an** (information / clue) to the problem.

看前面的不定冠詞a / an就可以知道括弧內應是可數名詞，所以括弧內的解答是clue。另外看括弧後面的介系詞to也可以選出正確解答，clue常常以clue to...（…的端倪、…的起頭）的型態使用。information是不可數名詞，所以不是正解。但怎麼知道clue是可數名詞？接下來介紹的名詞是不可數名詞，其餘的當作是可數名詞就可以了。

《講師的補充說明》

如果想知道是可數名詞還是不可數名詞的話？

查字典就可以知道。部分字典會標示，可數名詞會以（可），不可數名詞會以（不）做標示。但是大部分可數名詞還是會用C（= countable，可數），不可數名詞會以U（= uncountable，不可數）做表示。有些字典會在這邊會接上名詞noun，縮寫表示為CN、UN。也有些字典是同時標示C、U，這時先出現的表示代表主要的用法。

我無法找出／端倪／那問題點的。

多益常出的代表性不可數名詞，我們用下面的趣味性小故事讓你更簡單記住這些名詞。

> 「朋友寄了個mail（郵件）來，內容是有個小偷使用equipment（道具）打開了furniture（傢俱），但是發現居然一點money／cash（錢／現金）都沒有。所以就拿了其它貴重的advice（忠告）和information（資訊）替代，打包成baggage／luggage（行李）就逃出來的news（新聞）scenery（場面）。」

2. 可數名詞

可數名詞是具有數的概念，而非量的概念。可數名詞非常多，不像不可數名詞還可以區分背誦，所以沒有必要另外背。只要**記住上面的不可數名詞，其餘的大部分都是可數名詞，這樣記的話可以節省大量的時間。**

We need to install as **many (facilities / equipment)** as possible.

我們有必要設置／盡可能多一些的設備。

因為前面是限定詞many，所以括弧內的名詞就是複數型。不過equipment是不可數名詞，前面無法使用限定詞，如many。而且字尾也不可加-s、-es變成複數型。相反的，facility和equipment的意思有點類似，但是它不在上面的不可數範圍內，是可數名詞，前面可以放限定詞，且可以加-s、-es變成複數型。如同上面的英文例句所見，**可數名詞前面可有限定詞，也可以轉換成複數型。**

下面的可數名詞，是多益試題中常出現的模式。

(1) 指稱「人」的名詞
　　-er，-or結尾的名詞和critic（批判家）、representative（代表）、official（官員）等

(2) 「規則」相關的名詞
　　regulations（規則）、standards（標準）、codes（法規）、directions（方針）、steps（措施、處置）、procedures（程序）、measures（手段、方法、處置）

(3) 「增加或減少」相關的名詞（大部分後面的介系詞為in）
　　increase（增加）、hike（暴漲）、jump（劇增、激增）、rise（增加）、advance（發展）、decrease（減少）、reduction（削減）、decline（下跌）、drop（降低）、change（變化）等。

＊這些名詞除了reduction以外，其它也可當作動詞使用。當動詞時就不

使用a / an和介系詞。

(4) 「錢」相關的名詞（除了money、cash以外皆為可數名詞）
refund（退還）、price（價格）、account（帳戶）、credit card（信用卡）、bank（銀行）、cost（費用）、bill（帳單）、salary（薪資）、benefit（津貼）、bonus（紅利）、wage（月薪）、revenue（收益）、income（所得）、profit（利益）等

怪物講師的祕訣

下面的可數、不可數名詞互換後，連含義都改變了。請一定要特別注意。

- business：公司（可數）；事業（不可數）
- room：房間（可數）；空間（不可數）
- notice：通知書（可數）；通知（不可數）
- condition：條件（可數）；狀態（不可數）

因此必須要透過翻譯解釋，來確認單字是可數或是不可數。特別是condition很容易誤會，所以要牢牢記住下面的慣用使用方式。

- weather conditions 氣象條件
- economic conditions 經濟條件（可數名詞的例子）

這時很容易搞混的是-ment、-tion、-sion的字尾的名詞。具有這些字尾的名詞大都是可以是可數，也可以是不可數名詞。因此不要用可數、不可數名詞的角度去解題，必須要從其它的文法或是語彙去思考。

Quiz

Q3 We need (another / other) information before deciding what to do.
Q4 I decided to open (account / accounts) in your bank.

▶ 解答在106頁

《講師的補充說明》

何謂限定詞？

放在名詞前面，用來限定該名詞的意思。限定詞類型有不定冠詞a / an、定冠詞the、代名詞的所有格、指示形容詞this / that等等。因為限定詞的不同，名詞的單複數、可數、不可數也跟著不同，所以一定要好好記住。

- a / an + 可數單數

- the或所有格（my, this等）+ 單數、複數，不可數

- this / that + 單數和不可數

- these / those + 複數

- some / any + 單數、複數，不可數

- most / all + 可數複數和不可數

- every / each + 可數單數

- another / either / neither + 可數單數

- no + 單數、複數，不可數

攻略法

64

PART 5, 6 出題頻率

100%

80%

60%

40%

複合名詞的整理

「名詞 + 名詞」形成的複合名詞出現在題目中時，要怎麼分辨是不是答案呢？就只能硬背嗎？我們在這裡教你最簡單的解法。

名詞前面的空格大部分都是放形容詞。不過有時候名詞的前面，也會放名詞，因為有「名詞 + 名詞」形成的複合名詞。舉例來說，customer satisfaction是複合名詞「客戶滿意」的意思，所以如果出現＿＿＿＿＿＿ satisfaction的題目時，答案就是customer。這種時候空格內的單字到底是形容詞，還是名詞，實在很難分辨。除了將考試中常出現的複合名詞背下來以外，下面的例子讓你可以更輕鬆解題。

Our top priority was and will be **customer (satisfied / satisfaction)**.

> 我們最優先的課題／不論在過去或是未來都是讓客戶滿意。

如果你已經認識customer satisfaction這個複合名詞，可以毫不考慮就填入答案。括弧內不能是satisfied的理由是，customer是與人相關的可數名詞，雖然是可數名詞，不過前面沒有限定詞，也不是複數型吧？所以並非是可以用satisfied作後置修飾的一般名詞，而是像形容詞一樣修飾後面的satisfaction，所以括弧內適當的單字是 satisfaction。

該如何認出複合名詞呢？如同下面，複合名詞大致可分為兩大類，只要屬於其中一種就是複合名詞。

(1)「n2做n1」類型

舉例來說，「使客戶滿意」是satisfy customers，這裡的動詞satisfy變成名詞satisfaction後，動詞和受詞改變位置即成了「客戶滿意」的複合名詞customer satisfaction。這種類型的複合名詞和下面的例子，我們就叫做「n2做n1」。

* address verification　　　…住址確認
* baggage allowance　　　…行李重量限額
* building expansion　　　…建築物擴張
* project manager　　　…專案經理
* customer / client satisfaction　　　…客戶滿意
* money managment　　　…金錢管理

(2) 「為了n1的n2」

a form for application有「為了申請的表格」的意思，簡單來說就是「申請表格」的複合名詞，簡寫成application form。下面的例子也和「為了申請的表格」一樣，可以解釋為「為了n1的n2」。

- application form …申請表、申請書
- complaint form …客戶抱怨意見表
- parking lot …停車場
- replacement fee …更換費用

怪物講師的祕訣

複合名詞要注意的事項

1 n1是可數名詞或是不可數名詞都無所謂

→ customer satisfaction中，customer是可數名詞，但是前面沒有限定詞，也不是複數型。

2 會因為n2而決定整個複合名詞是可數、不可數名詞，或單數、複數狀態。

→ customer是可數名詞，但是satisfaction屬於有量的概念的不可數名詞，因此不能寫成a customer satisfaction。

3 大部分的n1不能是複數

→ 但是下面幾個狀況是例外，n1是複數型。

customs office 稅關、electronics company 電子公司、savings bank 儲蓄銀行、sales manager 業務經理、sports complex 綜合競技場

＊不過上面的複合名詞並非是依據n1，而是以n2來決定是可數、不可數名詞，或單數、複數狀態。

Quiz

Q5 Customers (satisfaction / satisfied) with our service will visit us again.

Q6 We have been committed to (customer / customers) satisfaction since our founding.

▶ 解答在106頁

攻略法

65

PART 5, 6 出題頻率

100%

80%

60%

40%

人相關名詞和事物相關名詞的區分

去報考多益看看吧！大部分的題目都能掌握到名詞的位置，但是考試都會給兩個名詞，這時又該怎麼選擇呢？

兩個都是名詞時，可以放在主詞、受詞和補語，也能被形容詞修飾，有時兩個的意思又似乎很像，但其實兩者意思大不同啊！所以能了解差異是解題最好的方法。

Strict (supervision / supervisor) is needed in this case.

需要嚴格的監督／在這情況。

supervisor是表示人的可數名詞。如果答案是supervisor的話，前面應該要有限定詞，或是本身是複數型，但是上面句子中並沒有，所以要選擇不可數名詞supervision。

人的名詞		事物的名詞
accountant（會計師）	→ ←	account（帳戶） accounting（會計）
applicant（申請人）	→ ←	application（申請、申請書） applying（申請）
member（會員）	→ ←	membership （會員資格／期間）
rival（競爭者）	→ ←	rivalry（競爭狀態）
advisor（顧問）	→ ←	advice（忠告） advising（忠告）
president（社長、總統）	→ ←	presidency （社長職位／社長任期）
attendee（出席者） attendant（出席者、隨員） flight attendant（空服員）	→ ←	attendance（出席）
interviewer（面試官） interviewee（受訪者）	→ ←	interview（面試） interviewing（面試）
assembler（組裝人員）	→ ←	assembly（組裝）
campaigner（社會運動家）	→ ←	campaign （戰役、社會運動、遊說）

Quiz

Q7 We need to hire additional (assemblers / assemblies) in our factory.

▶ 解答在106頁

解決詞彙問題有什麼祕密呢？有沒有覺得愈簡單的問題愈容易疏忽？只要掌握名詞詞彙，解題會變更簡單。

很多人看到出現了詞性一樣，但是意思卻不同的語彙時，都會先喘一口氣後，再迅速地從頭到尾看過後解釋出來。這樣的話，應該常常會感到時間不夠。如果是我就不會那樣做。各位很好奇我會怎麼做吧？

1. 主詞是空格時

如果主詞的位置是空格時，請盡速去看動詞，十之八九都會掌握到關鍵。我們來試著解下面的題目，感受一下實戰的感覺。

The (reservation / meeting) must be made in advance to get a better seat.

> 必須要事先完成預約／才能取得較好的位置。

大概解釋的話就是「被預約」或是「被開會」的意思，兩者好像都是正確答案吧？所以這題就不能用解釋意思的方式去解題。括弧內是主詞的位置吧？那麼剛剛說要看哪邊呢？沒錯！就是要看動詞。動詞是must be made，核心動詞就是make的被動態，所以句子的主詞應是make的受詞。這樣一來，適合make a _____的解答是make a reservation（預約），因此括弧內的正確答案就是reservation。名詞meeting的話，大部分都使用在hold a meeting（舉行會議）、arrange a meeting（安排會議）、attend a meeting（參加會議）等。

2. 動詞的受詞是空格時

如果受詞是空格時，什麼都不要想，直接去看動詞，能讓你更快解題。請看下面例句。

We will **notify the (interviewee / interview)** within next week.

> 我們將會通知／那位面試對象／在下週以內。

好久沒看到動詞notify了吧？ANICAR！還記得嗎？在Chapter 03學過了，這種動詞的受詞必須是人。interview不是人，所以正確解答是interviewee。

3. 補語是空格時

通常會把形容詞當作補語使用，但很少會把名詞當作補語使用。不過真的萬一在補語的位置中出現了名詞時，題目是第2大句型的話，選主詞；題目是第5大句型時，選擇與受詞是同格關係的名詞就可以了。一起來看看下面的題目吧！

ACE Holdings **has been a** (**leadership / leader**) in this field for a long time.

ACE Holdings公司是走在前端的領導者／在這領域中／有好一段期間。

has been是屬於第2大句型的be動詞，後面出現名詞補語。所以應該是與主詞是同格關係，與ACE Holdings公司的同格關係的不是leadership，而是leader。因此括弧內的答案是leader。

4. 接受形容詞修飾時

在形容詞和名詞結合的情況，也是要看合不合適，舉例來說，常會用fast food，卻沒人會使用quick food。一起來看看下面的題目吧！

Our **experienced** (**technician / technology**) will be of great help to you.

我們經驗豐富的技術人員／會有幫助的／對你。

experienced（有經驗的） 是與人相關單字合得來的形容詞，所以人相關單字technician是正確答案。名詞technology常被使用在the latest technology（最新技術）、advanced technology（先進技術、尖端技術）上。

5秒 解決名詞語彙題型的方法

1 主詞是空格時 → 觀察動詞。
2 動詞的受詞是空格時 → 觀察動詞。
3 補語是空格時 → 觀察和主詞或受詞是否一致。
4 接受形容詞修飾時 → 觀察和形容詞是否合適。

Quiz

Q8 You can have a comprehensive (knowledge / information) by attending this seminar.

Q9 We must compete with our (rivals / rivalries) in order to survive.

▶ 解答在106頁

5. 曾出題的名詞詞彙整理

多益考試常出現的名詞相關表現整理如下。平時多接觸這些表現方式，將它們都變成自己的基礎的話，在填空選擇題上會很有幫助。

• the master energy (plan)	綜合能源計畫
• renew their (subscription) to a magazine	延長他們的雜誌訂閱
• grant a 2 week (extension) on the loan	允許貸款延長兩週
• be appointed to head the (committee)	被任命領導委員會
• give a greater (opportunity) to do	提供更大的機會做…
• valuable (tools) for	為了…的珍貴工具
• a brief (interruption)	暫時中止
• reserve the (right) to change	擁有變換的權利
• due to unfavorable weather (conditions)	因為不利的氣象狀態
• the June (issue)	6月號
• a (lack) of knowledgeable salesperson	有知識的業務員的不足
• receive an (invitation) to attend	接到參加的邀請
• take (advantage) of	利用…
• safety (precautions)	安全預防守則
• respond to any (concerns) about	對於…的憂慮的回應
• in (conjunction) with	和…連結後
• have no (obligation) to pay	沒有付款的義務
• spend a large (proportion) of their income on	將他們所得的大部份花在…
• in a (statement) given yesterday	昨天發表的聲明書中
• accept our (apologies) for the delay	接受我們對於延遲的道歉
• face a serious (shortage) of teachers	面臨嚴重的教師資源不足的情況
• the (challenge) lies in	困難的是在於…
• eat lunch in the outdoor (area)	在戶外吃午餐
• require my immediate (attention)	需要我即時的關心
• offer new customers a twenty percent (discount)	給予新客戶20%的折扣
• keep better (records) of	好好的記錄下…
• participate in a (survey)	參加問卷調查

- a (division) of a company 一間公司的事業部
- (contributions) to 對於⋯的貢獻〔付出〕
- based on a number of (factors) 根據很多原因
- our (policy) is not to offer refunds 我們的政策是不能退錢
- a one-page (abstract) 一頁的摘要
- make a (difference) 差異化
- reschedule their (appointments) 重新與他們約時間
- in an effort to reduce (expenses) 為了降低費用
- in (retail) sales 在零售領域
- a significant (increase) in sales 業績上相當的提升
- The (pay) will be $100 薪資將為一百元
- a highly recommended (practice) 非常建議的訓練
- stay on the (market) 留在市場上（＝持續熱賣）
- request a refund or a (replacement) 要求退錢或退貨
- below is a (summary) of events 活動摘要在下面
- under the (supervision) of 在⋯的監督下
- accurate and timely (advice) 正確且時機恰當的忠告
- express their (appreciation) 表示他們的感謝
- the (job) description 工作描述
- are gaining (popularity) 人氣持續攀升
- take every (precaution) to ensure 為了達到確實而採取所有措施
- the (purpose) is to improve the quality 目的是提升品質
- make the task the highest (priority) 那件事被當作最優先的課題
- build customer (loyalty) 建立客戶的忠誠度
- successful (performance) by dancers 因為舞者而成功的表演
- devote more (time) to care for 奉獻了許多時間在照顧⋯
- use company (facilities) such as a swimming pool
  使用如游泳池這樣的公司設備
- be known for a high agricultural (output) 以高產量的農產品聞名
- address those (issues) 處理那些問題
- request a (copy) of 要求⋯的影本
- make a successful (transition) to 成功轉換成⋯
- lead a (discussion) 引起討論
- keep a comfortable work (environment) 維持舒適的作業環境
- celebrate a (release) of a product 慶祝產品的上市

攻略法

67

冠詞題型的解題法

冠詞有分不定冠詞a / an，和定冠詞the。冠詞本身不會單獨出現在多益題型中，但是為了追求更優秀的writing和speaking，還是有必要熟讀。

你真的了解出現在名詞前面的冠詞嗎？a / an是不定冠詞，使用於可數名詞，在指稱眾多東西中，不限定物品中的其一時使用。相反地，the是定冠詞，單數和複數可數名詞、不可數名詞都可以使用，主要使用在指稱某個物品時。

1. 使用定冠詞the的情況

簡單說，不論可數名詞或不可數名詞，**有限定某一東西或是有確定的一項東西時都可以使用**。很多時候，定冠詞the和所有格可以互換使用，但是所有格和冠詞不能同時使用。

1 **The money that I borrowed from him** must be returned.
  因為有指定是向他借的錢的「那筆錢」，所以使用定冠詞the。

2 **The employees in our western factory** showed very high productivity.
  因為有具體指出西部工廠的員工，所以使用定冠詞the。

> 1 那筆錢／我向他借的／一定要還。
>
> 2 員工們／我們西部工廠裡的／展現了／相當高的產能。

除此以外，還有像下面使用定冠詞the的情況。

(1) 放在最高級形容詞的前面
    the most efficient system（最有效率的系統）

(2) 放在扮演形容詞角色的序數（first, second, ...）的前面
    the first applicant（第一位申請人）

(3) 放在表示數量的名詞of後面
    one of the + 複數名詞、both of the + 複數名詞、some of the + 複數名詞 / 不可數名詞、many of the + 複數名詞、few of the + 複數名詞、several of the + 複數名詞、each of the + 複數名詞、(n)either of the + 複數名詞等。

2. 不使用冠詞的情況

如同下面情況，不使用不定冠詞a或an，定冠詞the。

(1) 學科名(-cs)

mathematics, economics, statistics, physics等

(2) by + 交通手段、通信

by car（坐汽車）, by train（坐火車）, by plane（坐飛機）, by taxi
（坐計程車）等
by fax（用傳真）, by e-mail（用電子郵件）, by telephone（用電話）
等

(3) play + 運動比賽（但play the + 樂器）

play soccer（踢足球）, play baseball（打棒球）等
play the piano（彈鋼琴）, play the guitar（彈吉他）等

(4) 星期、月、年度的前面

on Monday, in January, in 2018
→ on the Monday（×）

(5) 限定詞不可使用兩次（冠詞、所有格、any / some、every / each）

a my book（×）
→ a book of mine（○）

(6) per + 單數名詞

per night（每一晚）, per person（每一人）等

(7) 動名詞也不使用冠詞

the introducing many new items（×）
→ introducing many new items（○）

(8) 職責、身分或稱號

President Obama（歐巴馬總統）, Uncle Sam（山姆叔叔）, Waiter!
（服務生！）

3. 考題常出的冠詞表現

接下來要來看多益考題中常出現的冠詞表現。我們整理成三種情況，一
是使用不定冠詞a或an的情況，和使用定冠詞the的情況，還有完全不使
用冠詞的情況。請大家要睜大眼睛看清楚喔。

(1) 使用不定冠詞a / an的重要詞彙

in an attempt to do	想要試圖去做…
as a result of	如同…的結果
in an effort to	…的結果
at a higher price	用高價位
all of a sudden	突然
as a whole	整體來說
as a rule	通常
come to an end	結束
in a hurry	很匆忙地（＝end＝stop＝halt）
reach an agreement	達成協議
as a symbol of	為…的象徵
at a distance	遙遠地

(2) 定冠詞the的重要詞彙

be in the way	造成妨礙
on the contrary	和…完全相反
on the whole	整體來說
at the beginning [end] of	…的開始〔結束〕

(3) 完全不使用冠詞的情況

in error 因為失誤、in haste 匆忙地、in detail 仔細地、take care of 照顧、take advantage of 利用、until further notice 直到稍後有通知為止、keep track of 持續追蹤…、跟隨、take into account 考慮（＝take into consideration）

怪物講師的祕訣

1 是可數名詞？

這時a / an和the都可以使用。如果沒有特別指定是誰或是什麼東西，處在目標不明的情況時，使用不定冠詞a / an；如果是有具體指出目標時，使用定冠詞the。

2 是不可數名詞？

這時不可使用a / an。the是使用在有指出具體事物時使用，反之則不能使用。

Quiz

Q10 I accepted (an / the) advice that you gave me yesterday.

Q11 I sent an e-mail to you in (error / errors).

▶ 解答在106頁

攻略法 62　找出名詞正確的位置

1 名詞可以在句中當主詞、受詞和補語使用。

2 觀察空格前後，確認答案是否是名詞

　1 冠詞

　2 所有格 +（副詞）+（形容詞）+ 名詞 + 形容詞子句

　3 介系詞

　4 動詞（是及物動詞、主動型時）

攻略法 63　區分可數名詞和不可數名詞

1 可數名詞和不可名詞的區分

　－確認可數名詞前面是否有a / an這類的限定詞，或是是否為複數型。

　－不可數名詞不可以和a / an、複數形容詞或複數動詞一起使用。

2 代表性的不可數名詞（用小故事來記憶）

朋友寄了個mail（郵件）來，內容是有個小偷使用equipment（道具）打開了furniture（傢俱），但是發現居然一點money / cash（錢／現金）都沒有。所以就拿了其他重要的information（資訊、情報）替代，打包成baggage / luggage（行李）就逃走的news（新聞）scenery（場面）。

攻略法 64　複合名詞的整理

確認複合名詞是屬於「形容詞 + 名詞」，還是屬於「名詞 + 名詞」的方法

1 如果能解釋為「n2做n1」或是「為了n1的n2」的話，答案請選擇複合名詞。

2 除了幾個例外情況，n1不可使用複數形。

3 複合名詞的可數、不可數和單、複數形態決定於後面的單字。

攻略法 67　冠詞題型的解題法

1 使用不定冠詞a / an

僅能使用在可數名詞，沒有特別指定對象，且是初次談到目標物。

2 使用定冠詞the

可數（單、複數）名詞、不可數名詞都可以使用，不過只能使用在有指定的對象。

例子

1   (A) park   — ❶ 把握問題的類型
    (B) parks
    (C) parking
    (D) parked

    ❷ 把握提示

All employees may submit an application to the head of employee management for a company _____ space.

❸ 空格中要填什麼詞類？

1 把握問題的類型
  詞性題

2 把握提示
  複合名詞，
  翻譯解釋

3 空格中要填什麼詞類？
  名詞

---

2   (A) products
    (B) produce
    (C) product
    (D) production

Innotech Inc.'s new and improved line of _____ is expected to see the company come out ahead of its rivals this year.

1 把握問題的類型

2 把握提示

3 空格中要填什麼詞類？

---

3   (A) selection
    (B) selecting
    (C) choose
    (D) choosing

The _____ of food on the menu at the new upscale Italian restaurant will range from appetizers and salads to pizza and pasta.

1 把握問題的類型

2 把握提示

3 空格中要填什麼詞類？

---

4   (A) assistants
    (B) assistance
    (C) assistances
    (D) assistant

Anyone wishing to get any _____ in accessing our database should call our toll-free number.

1 把握問題的類型

2 把握提示

3 空格中要填什麼詞類？

---

5   (A) agent
    (B) agential
    (C) agency
    (D) agents

The International Management Team hopes to streamline our remittance procedures to pay overseas _____ quickly.

1 把握問題的類型

2 把握提示

3 空格中要填什麼詞類？

6 (A) number
(B) numbered
(C) numbers
(D) numbering

Please be advised that the airline will issue you a single e-ticket _____ that you can use for your connecting flights.

1 把握問題的類型

2 把握提示

3 空格中要填什麼詞類？

7 (A) regulation
(B) regulate
(C) regulations
(D) regulator

The main goal of this seminar is to raise awareness within the financial industry of the main issues surrounding new government _____.

1 把握問題的類型

2 把握提示

3 空格中要填什麼詞類？

8 (A) candidate
(B) candidates
(C) candidate's
(D) candidates'

Any _____ who have a lot of experience in customer service or reception will be favored for the position.

1 把握問題的類型

2 把握提示

3 空格中要填什麼詞類？

9 (A) possession
(B) possessing
(C) possessions
(D) possesses

Any confidential company documents in your _____ must be securely locked in your desk every night.

1 把握問題的類型

2 把握提示

3 空格中要填什麼詞類？

10 (A) flexible
(B) flexibly
(C) flexing
(D) flexibility

Thanks to technology, more and more people in the modern world enjoy the _____ of working from home.

1 把握問題的類型

2 把握提示

3 空格中要填什麼詞類？

▶ 解答在107頁

101 How a company contributes more to worker health care plans _____ becoming an important factor.

(A) are
(B) being
(C) is
(D) been

重要
102 Many large _____ in this country have formed an association to lobby the federal government for favorable legislation.

(A) manufacturers
(B) manufacture
(C) manufacturer
(D) manufacturing

103 Becscom Tools has a good reputation due to its _____ to sponsoring small and medium-sized sports teams.

(A) dedicated
(B) dedication
(C) dedicates
(D) dedicating

104 Please download, complete the proof-of-ownership documents and send them back to the company as an e-mail _____.

(A) attached
(B) attaching
(C) attach
(D) attachment

105 Scope Telecom's lack of _____ in providing a fast service to corporate customers has led to a class action against them.

(A) responsible
(B) responsibility
(C) response
(D) responding

106 Management has requested that every department construct a detailed action plan to address the current _____ in quality standards.

(A) declined
(B) declination
(C) declining
(D) decline

107 No e-mailed _____ for the vacancy will be accepted, so applicants are reminded not to send resumes and cover letters via e-mail.

(A) applicants
(B) applicated
(C) applications
(D) applicant

108 Creating a calm and relaxed working _____ is an important step in improving the productivity of any business.

(A) environmental
(B) environment
(C) environmentalism
(D) environments

重要
109 The warranty will expire after one year, but _____ to a discounted repair service can be obtained at the time of purchase.

(A) subscriber
(B) subscribing
(C) subscripts
(D) subscription

110 During negotiations with the shareholders association, he demanded the _____ to run the company as he wished.

(A) rightly
(B) right
(C) rightness
(D) rightful

111 The CEO is planning to establish a scholarship _____ to help the children of company employees gain a university education.

(A) funds
(B) funding
(C) fundable
(D) fund

112 Due to a _____ in commodity prices, many local manufacturers are worried about the future.

(A) hiked
(B) hiking
(C) hike
(D) hiker

113 _____ of the new office park will begin at the start of spring, which will alleviate the current parking problem.

(A) Construction
(B) Reservation
(C) Elevation
(D) Production

高難度
114 Airline passengers are expected to pick up and recheck all of their _____ before boarding their connecting flight.

(A) suitcase
(B) luggage
(C) baggages
(D) accommodation

115 Though not expected, the laboratory called today with the _____ of the DNA test.

(A) conditions
(B) exams
(C) finals
(D) results

116 Samantha Rose is the manager in charge of ordering _____ for the new office, so ask her.

(A) furniture
(B) supply
(C) equipments
(D) desk

117 After explaining her new design, the engineer will give a(n) _____ of the new technology to the audience.

(A) lecture
(B) exhibition
(C) circumstance
(D) demonstration

118 Bank tellers are given the _____ of ensuring that all transactions involving money going into and out of an account are accurate.

(A) responsibility
(B) productivity
(C) possibility
(D) novelty

高難度
119 Production volume is dependent upon not only the technical skill level but _____ in the quality of work.

(A) level
(B) durability
(C) consistency
(D) vacancy

120 A business lunch is a great opportunity to establish a _____ of working professionals whom you may wish to work with in the future.

(A) framework
(B) coursework
(C) network
(D) work list

▶ 解答在109頁

Questions 121-124 refer to the following notice.

To all the employees in the Domestic Sales Department:

First of all, I would like to express my sincere appreciation for your _____ and 121 contribution to your given tasks. The company would not be doing so well without your solid work. However, the recent waves of economic inflation have weakened our _____ in the computer software field. Our gross profit has dropped by more than 10% 122 three quarters in a row. For the effective operation of the company, I regret _____ 123 you that the Domestic Sales Department will be downsized. All the employees including team leaders, section managers, and contracted employees who started working at the company after March 1st, 2018 will be laid off with a full two-month salary severance package effective in seven working days. All the office supplies, facilities, equipment, and computers have to _____ after your last day at work. Your business e-mail accounts 124 and access to the database of the company will be terminated on your last day. Partial benefits of those who remain in this department will be reduced. Detail referring to this point will be announced in the near future. I am indeed disheartened to be making this announcement. Please feel free to contact the HR Department if you are unclear about anything or require any further assistance.

Jackson Kim
CEO
Golden Eye International Co.

121 (A) devote
(B) devotional
(C) devotion
(D) devoted

122 (A) compete
(B) competition
(C) competitiveness
(D) completive

123 (A) inform
(B) to inform
(C) informing
(D) informed

124 (A) be packed and stored
(B) be transported to another branch
(C) be left behind
(D) be donated to charity

▶ 解答在109頁

Chapter 17 | 代名詞
取代名詞的位置就是代名詞！

Review Test

我們在Chapter 16 學習了英文的中心──名詞，現在就來複習一下吧！

1 句子中名詞的位置在哪？　　　　　　　▶ ···

2 請填下列空格。

冠詞／所有格／介系詞／動詞 + ＿＿＿ + ＿＿＿ + 名詞 + ＿＿＿

3 請將下列畫底線的部分翻成英文，再次練習代表性的不可數名詞

「朋友寄了一封電子郵件寫說新聞報導有一個小偷利用工具打開了家具，但裡頭一

點錢／現金都沒有，因此把貴重的資訊當作贓物裝成行李帶了出來。」

4 無法與不可數名詞一起使用的？　　　　▶ ···

5 可數名詞一定要與＿＿＿一同使用改成＿＿＿。

Preview

1 代名詞的特徵

像I, you, he, she, we, they, it, this, that一樣，代替名詞來使用的詞類就是代名詞。代名詞分成如下的人稱代名詞、指示代名詞、不定代名詞、疑問代名詞、關係代名詞等。

- 人稱代名詞：I, you, she, they...
- 指示代名詞：this, that, such...
- 不定代名詞：any, some, one, another...
- 疑問代名詞：who, when, where, what, how, why, which...
- 關係代名詞：who, which, that...

其中疑問代名詞和關係代名詞，已經在名詞子句連接詞和形容詞子句連接詞單元中學過了，兩者都是具有連接詞功能的代名詞，其他代名詞就不具連接詞功能。

2 代名詞問題的解法

人稱代名詞須注意「格」，指示代名詞應注意單數和複數，不定代名詞應注意單數和複數，疑問代名詞應特別注意詞性。請看以下仔細的說明與介紹！

[正確答案] 1. 主詞，受詞，補語 2. 副詞，形容詞、形容詞子句 3. mail, news, equipment, furniture, money / cash, information, baggage / luggage 4. a / an，複數形字尾，複數動詞 5. 限定詞，複數

攻略法

68 人稱代名詞問題解法

如同字面意思是指人的代名詞。即：他（he）、你（you）、他們（they）等。好像是大家都知道的內容，但100%正確了解的人卻非常少。千萬別大略瀏覽，請仔細地讀一遍！

1. 人稱代名詞的5種變型

人稱代名詞（personal pronoun）**如同字面上意思是指人**（person）**的代名詞**（pronoun）。下列的表格很基本吧？首先熟記下列表格，詳讀細部說明！

人稱	單複數／性別		主格	所有格	受格	所有代名詞	反身代名詞	動詞例
第1人稱 說話者	單數		I	my	me	mine	myself	do, have
	複數		we	our	us	ours	ourselves	
第2人稱 聽話者	單數		you	your	you	yours	yourself	do, have
	複數		you	your	you	yours	yourselves	
第3人稱 第1、2 人稱之外	單數	男性	he	his	him	his	himself	does, has
		女性	she	her	her	hers	herself	
		中性	it	its	it	-	itself	
	複數 （人、 事、物）		they	their	them	theirs	themselves	do, have

2. 區分人稱代名詞的主格、所有格、受格

上列表格中，主格、所有格、受格常在考試中出現，尤其是所有格最常出現，所以一定要熟記所有格問題解法！簡單來說**動詞前面為主格，介系詞和及物動詞後面為受格，名詞前面為所有格**。看看下面的問題吧！

(We / Our) are well aware that **(his / he) plan will be revised** soon.

> 我們很了解／他的提案很快會被修改的事。

第一個括號為主詞位置，所以當然要選擇主格we。第二個括號後面的plan好像是動詞，所以可以選擇he，但是plan後面有動詞will be revised，所以這裡的plan不是動詞，而是名詞。那應該知道名詞前面要填所有格吧？所以第二個括號內應選擇his。

這時要注意的是所有格擺放的位置有幾個條件。第一,後面要有名詞（非代名詞）。第二,前面不可有冠詞或所有格。第三,應觀察是否為所需要素都具備的完整句子。

怪物講師的祕訣

1 選項全都是代名詞（he, his, him等）時,觀察空格的前後。

→ 主格 + 動詞 + 目/補（主格和所有代名詞皆可,由文意解說來區分）

主詞 + 不及物動詞 + 受格（受格、所有代名詞、反身代名詞皆可）

主詞 + 動詞 + 目/補 + 介系詞 + 受格（受格,所有代名詞,反身代名詞皆可）

所有格 + 名詞（一定要是完整句子。類似形容詞的作用）

2 選項為其他代名詞（he, she, it, they等）時

→ 解析句意,確認是否為代名詞所指的名詞。（單數、複數,人、事物,女人、男人）

Quiz

Q1 My report was rejected, but (he / his) was accepted.

Q2 He asked (me / myself), not knowing what to do.

3. 所有代名詞

所有代名詞有「…的」所有權的功能。因為**具有「…的」的意思,所有代名詞在句子中有代替主詞、受詞、補語的功能。**

所有代名詞是「所有格 + 名詞」的簡寫,可用在句子的主詞、受詞、補語位置,扮演名詞的角色。請看下面問題!

After I review **your proposal**, I can have some time to check out (**him / his**).

> 檢討你的提案之後／我能夠有時間／確認／他的提案。

him或his兩者都可做為受格,但從句意上解說的話,並不是確認「他」,而是確認「他的提案」才是正確的,所以括號中應選擇his。「所有格 + 名詞」組合而成的話,可簡化成所有代名詞his來使用。

所有代名詞的種類和型態如下

- mine 我的東西、yours 你的東西、his 他的東西、hers 她的東西、ours 我們的東西、yours 你們的東西、theirs 他們的東西
- Mr. Kim's 金先生的東西
- my supervisor's 我的主管的

怪物講師的祕訣

所有代名詞是答案的情況

1 主詞、受詞、補語位置是空格時

→ 若「…的」與句意不符時，需再做確認

→ 後面接名詞時不適用

2 使用雙重所有格時

→ a friend of my friends = a friend of mine

Quiz ⋯⋯⋯⋯⋯⋯⋯⋯⋯⋯⋯⋯⋯⋯⋯⋯⋯⋯⋯⋯⋯⋯⋯⋯⋯⋯⋯

Q3 (They / Theirs) was incredible in view of this difficult point.

Q4 The reserved seats are yours and (his / himself).

▶ 解答在114頁

4. 反身代名詞

後面連接-self的myself, yourself, himself, herself, themselves等就稱為反身代名詞。大家都知道反身代名詞與主詞是一致的，但單憑與主詞一致這一點並不充分，那麼還需與什麼條件相符呢？請看下列說明！

反身代名詞不只是主詞，還要跟動作的主體一致，也有「自己、主動地」的意思。 而反身代名詞，與主詞相符，也用純粹強調的意義。

They allowed **me** to go **by** (**themselves /myself**).

他們准許／我／出去／我自己一個人。

這一題很容易看到they就選擇themselves，但在前面說過什麼？反身代名詞與動作的主體要一致吧。上面句子中動詞go的主體是me，by oneself修飾go。因此句子中與受詞me一致的myself即為正確解答。**以上說明的反身代名詞的用法，常被稱做成為介系詞（by）之受詞的反身性用法。而且這種情況下，因為反身代名詞myself是受詞，所以無法省略。**

但是反身代名詞用在強調的情況時，反身代名詞是扮演副詞的角色，可以省略。例如，He himself solved the problem.（他獨自解決了問題。）中himself就是使用反身代名詞的強調用法，這種情形下himself也可省略。

人稱代名詞中具有可有可無的性質，只有所有格和反身代名詞。所有格扮演像形容詞的角色，反身代名詞扮演副詞的角色。

怪物講師的祕訣

反身代名詞為正確解答的情況

1 像片語來使用的類型

by oneself（自己／最常出現）、for oneself（主動／利用自己的力量）

2 動詞或介系詞的受詞為動作的主體的情況（反身性的用法）

例 She saw herself in the mirror.
（她看見了／自己的模樣／從鏡子中。）

3 句子完整，用來強調語氣的情況（強調性用法）

例 The woman herself accepted his idea.
（那女人她接受了／他的想法。）

Quiz ....

Q5 They wanted to do the work (theirs / themselves)

Q6 She asked me to work overnight by (herself /myself).

▶ 解答在114頁

攻略法

69

指示代名詞與指示形容詞問題解法

如同字面上的解釋，扮演指示某種名詞角色的代名詞和形容詞。讓我們一起來看看指示代名詞、指示形容詞有哪些？如何使用？及考試出題重點為何？

不論是人或是事物，當想要表示「這個」、「那個」或是「這⋯」、「那⋯」的時候，就可使用指示代名詞或指示形容詞。this和that及複數型態的these和those就是代表性的例子。整理幾個需要注意的重點。

1. 指示代名詞和指示形容詞

指示代名詞和名詞一樣，用在主詞、受詞、補語位置。指示形容詞為形容詞的一種，所以可修飾名詞。此時須注意的是名詞與單、複數相符合。

1 **That is** my car.（指示代名詞）
   不可寫that are！

2 **That car** is mine.（指示形容詞）
   不可寫that cars！

1 那是我的車。
2 那台車是我的。

不論是使用指示代名詞或指示形容詞，this或that與單數動詞一起使用，these或those與複數動詞一起使用。

2. 指示形容詞被當成限定詞使用

之前在名詞單元學過限定詞了吧？所有格（my, his等）、指示形容詞（this, that, these, those等）、some, any, every, each, another, either, neither, no等等。但這些限定詞在名詞前面不可連續出現兩次。也就是，若有冠詞或所有格的話，不可以用指示形容詞修飾名詞。

a my book （不可以）
a book of mine (= my book) 可以！
his these pencils（不可以）→ these pencils of his（可以）

3. 空格後面有of的話，只有that of或those of才是正確解答

這是什麼意思？簡單來說，this of或these of是絕對不會使用的表現。在 that of和those of中只需留意單數、複數來選擇答案即可。看看下面例句 就能理解。

The door of my house is bigger than (**this / that**) **of your house**. ⟨ 我家的門／更大／比你家的 那個（門）。

在括號中，是表示前面出現過的door的指示代名詞that的位置。為了避免 重複，因此使用that代替the door，這時絕對不用this of型態，而是用that of型態。英文通常是先講近的東西再說遠的東西，因此包含表示近的事 物指示的this of或these of，是不可能出現在句子的後半部分。

所以這種情況下，通常答案不是that of就是those of，上面句子前面的 door是單數，所以應選擇that of，前面若是出現doors複數的話，就應該 選擇those of。

4. 表示「做…的人們」的「those，anyone，everyone + 形容詞類」

在這種型態的表現中不使用this, that, these。「做…的人們」是複數，當 然this和that就不行。「做…的人們」大部分都是指位於比較遠的地方的 人，所以these也不可以使用。看看下面的例句吧！

(**Those / Anyone**) interested in this position **needs** to contact me first. ⟨ 不管是誰／對這個職位有興 趣的／需要先連絡我。

those與anyone兩者意思相似，也都受到interested修飾，但是後面的動詞 needs是單數動詞！因此括號內應填入單數名詞的anyone。

下面表格中所列出的詞類若出現在後面的話，答案就是those, anyone, everyone其中之一，只需留意單數（anyone, everyone）與複數（those） 就可以了。

```
those (who are)  + 形容詞, 介系詞片語, -ing / p.p.

          those + 形容詞

          those + 介系詞片語

          those + -ing / p.p.
```

怪物講師的祕訣

1 this, that, these, those通常要留意單數、複數。

2 後面若接of的話，答案通常是 that, those只需留意單、複數。

3 若為「做…的人」的話，答案則為 those, anyone, everyone。

Quiz

Q7 This (type / types) of person will not benefit your company much.

Q8 (Whoever / Anyone) who comes first will have it.

▶ 解答在114頁

《講師的補充說明》

this, these, those只能當指示代名詞和指示形容詞。但是that除了指示代名詞和指示形容詞之外，還可以當連接詞使用，當連接詞使用時就不需留意單數、複數。that只有當指示代名詞和指示形容詞使用時才和單數、複數有相關。

＊參考that可當作名詞子句，形容詞子句，副詞子句連接詞。

70 不定代名詞問題解法

與前面所學的指示代名詞不同，不定代名詞並不固定，即為可代替任何東西的代名詞。

1. 不定代名詞的概念與種類

不定代名詞就如同字面上的意思，表示沒有一定（indefinite）事物的代名詞。another, other, the other, most**等為代表性的不定代名詞。**注意單、複數及何時使用，把下面的表格背熟。搭配字典一起學習的話會更好。

1 If you need **an umbrella**, go and ask (**one / another**).

如果需要雨傘的話，就去要看看吧？要什麼？當然是要把傘！沒有指定說是這個（this）或那個（that），所以括號內應該要選擇表示不確定的（indefinite）的不定代名詞one。another雖然也是不定代名詞，但another是「另一個」的意思，與句子意思不符。

2 **Of the three, two** are acceptable but (**other / the other**) isn't.

總共3個當中（of the three），扣掉2個就只剩下一個吧？如前面所說，在多個當中指定最後所剩下的一個的時候，在other前面加上定冠詞the形成the other。因為是限定的，所以加上定冠詞the。所以括號內的解答為the other。

請看下列表格！為了幫助理解用圖案做了整理。

	1個	one （隨便一個──很多個當中）
	2個	one （隨便一個）/ the other （最後一個）
	2個	one （隨便一個)/ another （另外一個）
	很多時	one （隨便一個）/ the others （剩下的其他）
	很多時	one （一個）/ others （其他的──有剩的時候）
	很多時	some （幾個）/ the others （剩下的全部）
	很多時	some （幾個）/ others （其他的──有剩的時候）

1 需要雨傘的話/去要求/一個。

2 三個當中/兩個是可以接受的/但是/剩下的一個卻不行。

2. 不定代名詞與單、複數

不定代名詞的單、複數很容易混淆，所以一定要仔細地確認冠詞。那麼直接來解題吧！

(Another / Other) information is desperately needed in this case.

非常需要其他情報／在這種狀況下。

首先要知道後面接的information為不可數名詞，another只可以用在可數單數名詞前面，所以不可放到括號內，可以填入括號內的就是other。為了方便理解，將可當不定代名詞和不定形容詞的another、other、the other的用法，整理成了如下的表格。

	為形容詞時	為名詞時（尤其是當主詞時）
another （視為不定冠詞a / an）	another +單數可數名詞 + （單，動） another + 不可數名詞（X）	another + （單，動）
other （視為沒有a / an、the）	other + 單數可數名詞（X） other + 複數可數名詞 + （複，動） other + 不可數名詞 + （單，動）	other + （複，動） other不具名詞功能
the other （視為定冠詞the）	the other + 單數可數 + （單，動） the other + 複數可數 + （複，動） the other + 不可數名詞 + （單，動）	the other + （單，動） the other + （複，動）

（單，動＝單數動詞，複，動＝複數動詞）

3. 指「大部分的…」不定代名詞most

若要使用「大部分的…」的話，只要在下一頁整理好的各種表現中選擇其中的一個使用即可。雖然只有極小的差異，但是只要一個冠詞、單數、複數就能決定對錯，所以要詳細地多看幾遍。這些也是考試中常出現的考題。

(Almost / Most) all the houses are unoccupied.

幾乎所有的房子都是空的。

在句子括號之後到houses是「幾乎所有的房子」的意思。「幾乎所有的」英文是almost all，所以正確答案是almost。由兩個單字組成的這句話與most的意思相近。如果上面的英文要用most來表現的話，只要寫成most of the houses或most houses就可以了。

與不定代名詞most（幾乎所有的事物／人）一起使用的用法

- most of the + 名詞（可數複數，不可數）→ 若只有of或只有the則不行
- most of 所有格 + 名詞（可數複數，不可數）→ 所有格可以代替the
- most of them → 若為像them的代名詞時，不可填the或所有格
- most + 名詞（可數複數，不可數）→ of the省略
- almost all + 名詞
- almost all the + 名詞

4. 不定代名詞相關片語

在看有不定代名詞的片語之前，先看個題目吧！

The couple never had a chance to discuss it **with (each other / one another)**.

couple是一對男女，上面英文翻譯是兩人沒有互相討論的機會。**兩人用「互相」來表現時使用**each other。

- each other 兩人之間互相，one another 三人以上互相
  兩者的意思皆為「互相」，但詞性為名詞！
- one after the other 兩人輪流，one after another 三人以上輪流
  兩者的意思都是「輪流」，但詞性為副詞！

5秒 解決不定代名詞的方法

1️⃣ 首先提到的任何一個 → one
2️⃣ 提到一個之後再提到一個的話 → another
3️⃣ 首先提到的少許幾個 → some
4️⃣ 提到少許的幾個之後，再說到幾個的話 → others
5️⃣ 不定代名詞通常要考慮單、複數問題

Quiz

Q9 (Another / Other) information is needed for us to process your application.

Q10 I tried to understand (most of / most) the contents.

▶ 解答在114頁

攻略法

71

疑問代名詞、疑問形容詞、疑問副詞

「疑問詞 V＋S？」型態的疑問句被稱為直接疑問句。但是在多益的Part5、6考題不出直接疑問句。通常出題都是把「疑問詞 S＋V」型態的間接疑問句當作名詞子句來出題。

首先，疑問詞可分為下列3大種類。

- **疑問代名詞**：who / whom, what / which（名詞，有主詞、受詞、補語作用）
- **疑問形容詞**：whose, what / which（形容詞，修飾名詞）
- **疑問副詞**：when, where, why, how（副詞，修飾動詞，形容詞，副詞）

1 I asked him (what /where) he would do after 7:00.

括號之後的句子是當作動詞asked的直接受詞的名詞子句，所以括號內應選擇名詞子句的連接詞what。

2 I don't know (how / whom) to play the piano.

括號後面的句子是know的受詞，括號內應該放入連接名詞子句的連接詞。但是to play的有受詞（the piano）句子完整，所以括號內應填how。

疑問詞有下列功能 。
－在直接疑問句中只有名詞、形容詞、副詞功能
－在間接疑問句當中有「連接詞＋名詞」、「連接詞＋形容詞 」、「連接詞＋副詞」作用。尤其是用來當名詞子句連接詞
－名詞子句時，也可以把「疑問詞 S＋V」 換成 「疑問詞 to 不定詞」

> 1 我問他／他想做什麼／7點之後。

> 2 我不知道／如何演奏／鋼琴。

5秒 解決名詞題型的方法

1 是名詞子句嗎？→ 選擇名詞子句連接詞。

2 有看到inquire, ask, don't know, not sure嗎？→ 選擇疑問詞。

3 是沒有主詞、受詞、補語的不完全句子嗎？→ 選擇疑問代名詞。

4 是完整的句子，用來修飾名詞嗎？→ 選擇疑問形容詞。

5 是完整的句子，用來修飾動詞、形容詞、副詞嗎？→ 選擇疑問副詞。

✎ Quiz

Q11 The man bought a building (which / where) was a little bit expensive.

Q12 I actually don't know (which / where) one to buy.

▶ 解答在114頁

攻略法 68　人稱代名詞問題解法

1. 人稱代名詞

1 主格 + 動詞 + OC（主格和所有代名詞中使用語意來區分）

2 主詞 + 及物動詞 + 受格（受格、所有代名詞、反身代名詞皆可）

3 主詞 + 動詞 + OC + 介系詞 + 受格（受格、所有代名詞、反身代名詞皆可）

4 所有格 + 名詞（一定要是完整句子。可放形容詞）

2. 所有代名詞

1 答案可以放在主詞，受詞，補語位置

2 確認與「⋯的」句意是否相符

3 後面又有名詞時，不可使用

3. 反身代名詞

1 受詞作用的反身用法

2 強調修飾語的強調用法

3 by oneself 自行（最常出題，解釋為「獨自」，與行為主體一致時使用。）

攻略法 69　指示代名詞和指示形容詞問題解法

1 出現this / that，these / those時確認單、複數。

2 如果意思是「做⋯的人」的話，those是正確解答。

攻略法 70　不定代名詞問題解法

1 出現one, another, other的話，確認單、複數。

2 翻譯成「大部分的⋯」的話，most或almost就是正確解答。

攻略法 71　疑問代名詞、疑問形容詞、疑問副詞

1 要知道各疑問詞的詞性和功能。尤其應該清楚用在名詞子句和形容詞子句時的差異。

2 疑問詞種類

- **疑問代名詞**：who / whom, what / which（因為是名詞、有主詞、受詞、補語的作用）

- **疑問形容詞**：whose, what / which（因為是形容詞，所以用來修飾名詞）

- **疑問副詞**：when, where, why, how（因為是副詞，所以用來修飾動詞、形容詞、副詞）

例子

1 (A) she
   (B) her
   (C) their
   (D) his

① 把握問題的類型

② 把握提示

Ms. Benoit insisted that _____ assistant be present at all meetings as she needed all the details.

③ 空格中要填什麼詞類？

1 把握問題的類型
   文法問題

2 把握提示
   修飾語．
   所有格的解說

3 空格中要填什麼詞類？
   所有格代名詞

2 (A) its
   (B) them
   (C) your
   (D) it

Please remove your passport from the protective case and present _____ to the security agent.

1 把握問題的類型

2 把握提示

3 空格中要填什麼詞類？

3 (A) he
   (B) himself
   (C) that
   (D) his

A few minutes ago, George called to verify that the fax messages _____ sent earlier had been received.

1 把握問題的類型

2 把握提示

3 空格中要填什麼詞類？

4 (A) anything
   (B) nobody
   (C) something
   (D) everybody

Albert Mills, owner of Mills Publishing, sent a memo inviting _____ at his company to a summer family picnic.

1 把握問題的類型

2 把握提示

3 空格中要填什麼詞類？

5 (A) neither
   (B) both
   (C) either
   (D) each

The two diplomats agreed to the terms of the treaty, though _____ was completely satisfied.

1 把握問題的類型

2 把握提示

3 空格中要填什麼詞類？

6 (A) what
(B) who
(C) whose
(D) whom

Even after careful consideration, the panel of judges could not determine _____ had submitted the winning entry.

1 把握問題的類型
2 把握提示
3 空格中要填什麼詞類？

7 (A) few
(B) someone
(C) one
(D) any

Many employees applied for the position last week, but only _____ of them will get the promotion.

1 把握問題的類型
2 把握提示
3 空格中要填什麼詞類？

8 (A) our
(B) ours
(C) their
(D) theirs

The architects were asked to design the new building according to _____ own preferences.

1 把握問題的類型
2 把握提示
3 空格中要填什麼詞類？

9 (A) they
(B) their
(C) them
(D) themselves

While working, each factory worker must be given a pair of safety goggles and a hard hat for _____ own safety.

1 把握問題的類型
2 把握提示
3 空格中要填什麼詞類？

10 (A) he
(B) who
(C) his
(D) him

Although Karl is a professional music critic, _____ refuses to review jazz albums for unknown reasons.

1 把握問題的類型
2 把握提示
3 空格中要填什麼詞類？

▶ 解答在114頁

101 Some senior executives receive the highest salaries, though _____ may also earn more through bonuses and sales.

(A) others
(B) other
(C) another
(D) the other

重要
102 As a family dentist, Dr. Patterson decided to design _____ waiting room in a way that is comfortable and inviting to people of all ages.

(A) he
(B) him
(C) his
(D) himself

103 Before contributing money toward an investment fund, you should first determine what _____ financial goals are.

(A) their
(B) my
(C) our
(D) your

104 The accounting team _____ conducted an extensive investigation to determine which expenses could be reduced over the coming year.

(A) itself
(B) it
(C) its
(D) which

105 New employees should keep in mind that _____ learned while on the job could become useful at a later time.

(A) whichever
(B) whatever
(C) anything
(D) nothing

106 Although _____ was discussed at the meeting, the various agents and representatives were unable to reach any conclusions.

(A) many
(B) few
(C) several
(D) much

107 Moments before his meeting with Ms. Sanchez, Julio remembered that _____ had forgotten to bring the notes for his demonstration.

(A) she
(B) he
(C) who
(D) they

重要
108 _____ who brought in the most money at the box office usually wins the Film Award for best actors and actresses.

(A) Anyone
(B) That
(C) Those
(D) Whoever

109 The car rental specialist will contact them to identify what their travel needs are and determine how to accommodate _____.

(A) them
(B) theirs
(C) themselves
(D) their

110 The warranty provided with this machine does not cover everything, but covers _____ of the problems you may encounter.

(A) all
(B) almost
(C) both
(D) most

收集了多益考試中常出的題目。請當作正式的考試，確認時間並解題。

111 The audience stood and cheered as
_____ watched the closing scene of
the blockbuster action movie.

(A) he
(B) they
(C) it
(D) anyone

112 _____ customers who wish to receive
a discounted rate on furniture should use
the coupon code provided below.

(A) Those
(B) Who
(C) These
(D) Anyone

113 _____ economists expect that the
Korean economy will recover from the
economic recession in the near future.

(A) The most
(B) Almost
(C) Most of
(D) Most of the

114 The supervisor of the purchasing
department contacted all of the suppliers
_____ to have a meeting on the raw
materials.

(A) she
(B) her
(C) herself
(D) hers

115 The man asked the woman sitting next to
_____ not to forget to return the call
to the preferred customer.

(A) him
(B) himself
(C) her
(D) herself

116 You can see only the limited items in our
retail store, because _____ products
are stored in our warehouse.

(A) the others
(B) another
(C) others
(D) other

117 Unless you bring your own umbrella, you
may take _____ from the reception
desk with no need to return it.

(A) other
(B) another
(C) the other
(D) one

高難度
118 All of our subsidiaries try to attain this
year's sales goals, almost all of _____
are limited by many unexpected factors.

(A) them
(B) whom
(C) which
(D) theirs

119 His car and _____ are the same
model and have the same color, so
we can distinguish them only from the
registration plate.

(A) my
(B) I
(C) me
(D) mine

高難度
120 On the recommendation of a colleague
of _____, he could attract some new
clients and generate more incomes.

(A) his
(B) himself
(C) him
(D) he

▶ 解答在117頁

Dear Mr. Hanker,

We would like to take this time to express our appreciation for your attendance of the interview which _____ on December 4th, 2017 for the position of Chief Engineer
121
at our company. However, we regret to notify you that we will not be offering you the position. We were impressed _____ your comprehensive study referring to utilizing
122
solar energy in your academic years and admired your enthusiasm in the field of solar energy. Nevertheless, the position of Chief Engineer is a position which requires plenty of practical working experience. The Chief Engineer needs to _____ many unexpected
123
technical problems he may have encountered _____. Your lack of practical working
124
experience according to your CV is thus our chief concern. You are always welcome to attend the interviews in the future for other open posts. We wish you the best of luck on your continued job hunting.

Regards,
Sally Fields
HR,
Sun Power Co.

121 (A) holds
(B) is held
(C) was held
(D) has been held

122 (A) on
(B) about
(C) by
(D) of

123 (A) work with
(B) come with
(C) cope with
(D) accompany with

124 (A) while they are performing their duties
(B) while they are having their annual leave
(C) while they are dealing with private matters
(D) while they are taking their coffee break

▶ 解答在117頁

Part 06
修飾和特殊句型

形容詞
只要知道出題的單字和位置就好！

Review Test

在Chapter 17學習了代名詞。一邊回答下列問題，一邊再次確認在Chapter 17學習的內容。

1 人稱代名詞有哪些？　　　　　　▶ ....

2 人稱代名詞she的所有格？　　　　▶ ....

3 所有代名詞在句子裡的位置？　　▶ ....

4 複數的指示代名詞有哪些？　　　▶ ....

5 another後面接單數還是複數？　　▶ ....

6 疑問代名詞在句子裡的作用是什麼？　▶ ....

7 those who怎麼解釋？　　　　　　▶ ....

Preview

1　形容詞的特徵

　　形容詞具有在某個名詞前後修飾的作用，也能用在介系詞片語、非限定動詞、形容詞子句。形容詞出現在單字問題時，都是出一些高難易度的問題。透過這一章節，學習形容詞的正確位置和特定形容詞的正確用法，也可以知道解決形容詞問題的訣竅。

2　形容詞問題解法

　　❶ 形容詞的位置1：冠詞，所有格，介系詞，動詞 ＿＿＿ + 名詞

　　❷ 形容詞的位置2：第2大句型或第5大句型的補語位置

　　❸ every, all等決定單、複數

　　❹ 形容詞問題利用觀察「受到修飾的名詞意思是否相呼應」來解答

攻略法

72

形容詞的正確位置

雖然在Chapter 01已經學過了，但這是相當重要的內容，所以就當作再複習一次作重點整理。對沒有印象的讀者來說，就當作反省「我只有大略讀過，沒有熟讀」的機會。

基本上**若空格是修飾名詞的位置，形容詞就是正確解答**。但只知道這樣就太可惜了。首先記得「**名詞的前後**」和「**第2和第5大句型的補語位置**」，請仔細閱讀下列內容。

1. 基本形容詞的位置

> 冠、所、介、動 +（形容詞）+ 名詞 +（形容詞子句）

1 **My conclusion** is that we should work hard.
所有格my的後面是conclusion。

2 **Applicants who are qualified** will be hired.
形容詞子句修飾前面的先行名詞applicants。

1 我的結論是／我們應該努力要做事。

2 申請者們／有資格的／將被雇用。

這些是Chapter 01學過的內容吧？冠詞或所有格、介系詞、及物動詞（冠、所、介、動）等的後面一定會出現名詞，在中間可能會有形容詞。形容詞是修飾語，即使省略了也不會對句子架構造成影響。當然有時也會在形容詞位置出現名詞，即「複合名詞」。

2. 形容詞當作補語使用時的位置

> 第2大句型動詞be（become, remain）+（副詞）+ 主詞補語（形容詞）
> 第5大句型動詞make（keep, find）+ 受詞（名詞）+ 受詞補語（形容詞）

1 **The orders** remain **constant**.
用第2大句型動詞remain的主詞補語（形容詞）修飾主詞the orders。

2 I found **your story interesting**.
用第5大句型動詞find的主詞補語（形容詞）修飾受詞your story。

1 那些訂單／繼續存在。

2 我覺得／你的故事／很有趣。

都是Chapter 01和03中學過的內容。再次強調，形容詞和名詞都可以當**第2大句型和第5大句型的補語，但大部分都是形容詞**。

因此第2大句型的代表性動詞be, become, remain後面，大部分都是用形容詞修飾名詞主詞。像make, keep, find這些第5大句型動詞，在受詞後面通常會出現形容詞，-ing / p.p.當作受詞補語。那是為了修飾受詞。**第3大句型偶爾也會在受詞後面加上形容詞，第3大句型在受詞後面加上形容詞是可選擇的，但第5大句型當中，受詞後面加上形容詞卻是一定要有的**。這就是不同的地方。

3. 出現多個形容詞時

形容詞 + 形容詞 + 名詞

形容詞, 形容詞 + 名詞

形容詞 and 形容詞 + 名詞

1 a **creative original idea**
creative位置不可以跟副詞搞混

2 a **creative, original idea**
把名詞放在creative位置上的話，與後面的名詞idea有衝突

3 **interesting** and **informative workshops**
連接詞前後的形容詞修飾workshop

1 創意且獨創的想法
2 創意且獨創的想法
3 有趣又有益的研討會

通常都是「副詞 + 形容詞 + 名詞」的組合，但在這裡形容詞出現了2次。這種情況下就要了解句意來作答。也就是說，如果是副詞修飾形容詞的話，就使用「副詞 + 形容詞 + 名詞」的組合；如果兩個單字都是修飾後面的名詞的話，就使用「形容詞 + 形容詞 + 名詞」的組合。另外要記得不同於「形容詞 + 形容詞 + 名詞」的結構，還有「形容詞, 形容詞 + 名詞」和「形容詞 and 形容詞 + 名詞」（留意and）的結構。

4. 形容詞在後面修飾名詞時

基本上形容詞只有一個的話，是放在名詞前面，但是出現2個以上的話，就放在名詞後面。

1 a **kind man**
形容詞kind放在名詞man前面

2 a **man kind only to women**
修飾語太長所以就放到名詞a man後面

1 親切的男人
2 只對女人親切的男人

5. 慣用的形容詞放在後面的情況

下面的例句是慣用表現，將形容詞放在名詞後面的情況。這種表現很難用理論來解釋，不妨當作片語背起來。

1 three miles away, 10 years old
2 -thing / -body / -one ＋ 形容詞, 名詞 ＋ -able / -ible

5秒 解決形容詞問題的方法

1 冠、所、介、動後面有名詞，前面有空格的話？ → 答案是形容詞。

2 be, become, remain後面補語位置是空格的話？ → 答案是形容詞。

3 make, keep, find後面的受詞補語是空格的話？ → 答案是形容詞。

4 形容詞出現2次的話，形容詞放在名詞後面。

Quiz

Q1 We would like to hire a (professional / professionally) financial consultant.

Q2 The information should be kept (confidential / confidentially).

▶ 解答在120頁

攻略法 73 形容詞的單複數

形容詞也有單複數的說法很令人驚訝吧？考試中常出現的形容詞與後面名詞的單、複數有很大的關連，因此只要看到這些形容詞，就能分辨名詞是單數還是複數。

很多人在多益考試中，碰到答案選項（A）到（D）都是形容詞時，無法正確解答。在這種情況下，只要分辨是單數還是複數就能輕易做答。請詳讀下列形容詞相關內容。只有一眼就能看出是單、複數的人才能得到高分。

1. 與複數可數名詞一起使用的形容詞

both, several, few, a few**這些形容詞，是用在複數名詞前面的形容詞**。所以這些形容詞的後面通常都是出現複數可數名詞。反過來說，後面如果是複數名詞的話，那麼前面的空格就要放這種形容詞。

1 Both pictures were displayed at the museum.
both後面的名詞pictures是複數，後面的動詞were也是複數。

2 A number of factors are being considered.
a number of後面也是接複數名詞。

千萬別忘記看到下列形容詞的話，後面要接複數可數名詞。not a few或quite a few是「不少」的意思。很容易混淆，所以千萬要熟記！

- both　　　　　兩者都
- several　　　　好幾個的
- few　　　　　幾乎沒有
- a few　　　　　幾個
- not a few　　　不少 (= quite a few)
- many　　　　　很多 (= a large [good, great] number of = a great many)

1 兩幅畫都被展示／在博物館。

2 很多要素被考慮在內。

2. 與單數可數名詞一起使用的形容詞

every, each, another, either這些形容詞，都是放在單數可數名詞前面的形容詞。因此只要看到這些形容詞的話，就可以聯想到後面一定會出現單數可數名詞，當然動詞也會是單數動詞。

Every employee must attend this meeting.

every後面一定接單數名詞。

所有員工都應該出席／這個會議。

下列單字是後面一定接單數名詞的形容詞。**尤其every和all一樣，是「所有」的意思，但是後面一定是接單數名詞，而不是複數名詞。絕對不可以忘記。**

- every　　　所有（後面接單數名詞）
- each　　　各（後面接單數名詞）

＊只有respective雖然意思是「各」的形容詞，但是後面接複數名詞。

- another　　另一個
- either　　　兩個的其中一個
- neither　　不是兩者之中任一個
- this　　　　這…
- that　　　　那…

3. 與不可數名詞一起使用的形容詞

像much、little不是表示數而是量的形容詞，當然不可以放在可以數的可數名詞前面。（不可數名詞在名詞單元中學過了吧？）

Much advice is needed in this case.

advice是無法數的不可數名詞。

需要很多建議／這種情況下。

放在不可數名詞前面的形容詞如下。**many, few放在可數名詞前面，much, little放在不可數名詞前面。**

- much　　　　很多 (= a great deal of = a good deal of = a large amount of)
- a little　　　一點
- little　　　　不到一點點的
- not a little　　不少 (= quite a little)

4. 其他的複合形容詞

下列形容詞在多益考試中，主要是以單、複數問題出現。雖然有點複雜，但可藉這次機會正確地了解。

We needed **a lot of information**.

我們需要／很多情報。

information是不可數名詞，說「很多情報」的時候，前面不可以加上many，也不能在字尾加上複數字尾-s寫成informations。通常是使用much寫成much information。不然就像上面的例句，用a lot of取代much。a lot of可以放在可數名詞，也可以放在不可數名詞前面，非常方便。

- a lot of＋**複數可數名詞／不可數名詞**：很多
  → 不可以放單數可數名詞
- most＋**複數可數名詞／不可數名詞**：大部分
  → 放單數可數名詞顯得奇怪
- all＋**複數可數名詞／不可數名詞**：全部
  → 不可以放單數可數名詞
- some / any＋單數名詞：怎樣的
  some / any＋複數名詞：幾個的
  some / any＋不可數名詞：稍微的
- some / any of the＋複數名詞／不可數名詞：稍微的
  → 不可以放單數可數名詞

怪物講師的祕訣

1. 跟複數名詞一起使用的形容詞 → both, several, few, many, a number of
2. 跟單數可數名詞一起使用的形容詞 → every, each, another, either, neither, this, that
3. 跟不可數名詞一起使用的形容詞 → much, little
4. 可用於複數名詞、不可數名詞的形容詞 → a lot of = lots of = plenty of, most, all
5. 單數、複數、不可數名詞都可以使用的形容詞 → some / any

Quiz

Q3 (Every / All) the applicants seemed to be so qualified as to be hired.

Q4 (Some / Either) of the candidates were permitted to express their views.

▶ 解答在120頁

攻略法

74

有文法重點的形容詞

下列形容詞有文法的重點，應試時有幾點需要注意。準確地檢視重點就能輕易找出解答。

1. every的2種用法

every被翻成「所有」時，後面一定接單數名詞。但當作「每個…」使用時，像every five years（每5年）後面就要接複數名詞。這2種情況都是形容詞。

1 **Every part** in this machine <u>is</u> durable.
　　在這裡every是「所有」的意思，後面要接單數可數名詞！

2 **Every two years**, we hold a ceremony for our donators.
　　這裡的every是「每…」的意思，要留意後面名詞的單、複數！

1 這個機器所有的零件／都很堅固。

2 每2年／我們舉行典禮／為了我們的捐獻人。

怪物講師的祕訣

every two years 每兩年，兩年一次

= every second year = every other year = every alternate year

＊every後面接two, three數詞的時候，後面可能會接類似years的複數型態。

　但是如果every後面接類似second, third這種序數，後面一定要放單數名詞。

＊every few years是「好幾年一次」的意思。

＊every在這裡雖然是形容詞，但是every...years整體是當作副詞使用。

2. 顯示數字的形容詞的2種用法

(1) 數量很多不可數的情況

hundreds of spectators

數百位的觀眾

這時應該注意hundreds的複數語尾-s以及後面的介系詞of。前面不可以放two, three等。因為數量非常多，與能用正確數字的表現不相符。

• dozens of 數十個的 / thousands of 數千個的 / millions of 數百萬個的

(2) 正確數字的情況

three hundred spectators 300名觀眾

這時three hundred（300名的）有修飾後面名詞spectators的形容詞功能，所以不用加上複數型語尾的-s，後面也不用加上介系詞of。

把單字改成形容詞的代表性字尾整理成下列表格。

-ous, -ic, -ical, -ive, -ful, -less, -able / -ible, -ish	dangerous 危險的 economic 經濟的 economical 節省的 competitive 競爭的 careful 小心的 hopeless 絕望的 understandable 能理解的 sluggish 懶惰的
-ing / -ed, -ate （也用在動詞） -al （也用在名詞）	interesting 有趣的 interested 感興趣的 delicate 精美的 normal 正常的
-y, -ory, 名詞 + -ly （副詞是形容詞 + -ly）	sunny 陽光和煦的 preparatory 預備的 friendly 親近的

Quiz ·················

Q5 (Every / Once) a week, you'll have to check it out by yourself.

Q6 (Dozen / Dozens) of orders were canceled due to an unknown reason.　解答在120頁

Chapter 18_ 形容詞　**357**

副詞子句「太⋯以至於⋯」

學習副詞子句的時候曾經出現過吧！如果不是記得很清楚的話，再回頭快速讀過一遍吧！

1.「so + 形容詞／副詞 + that」和「such + 名詞 + that」

1 She is **so qualified that** she will be hired soon.

「so that」中間應該放形容詞「qualified」，因為是前面的第2大句型動詞is補語的位置。另外，so在這裡是修飾形容詞qualified的副詞。

> **1** 她很有資格／所以她／被雇用／很快地。

2 She had **such energy that** she will be hired soon.

看到在such that中間的名詞energy了吧？因為是前面have（有，第3大句型動詞）的受詞補語位置。在這裡such是修飾名詞energy的形容詞。

> **2** 她有那種活力／很快就會被雇用。

so that和such that都是「太⋯以至於⋯的意思」。多益考試中，通常考題都是在so或such的位置、連接詞that的位置出現空格，有時候考題也會在so that和such that出現空格。so是副詞，所以so that中間主要放形容詞或副詞。因為such是形容詞，所以such that中間主要是放名詞。當然有時也會在so或such的位置出題。如果是出現「____ 形／副 that」句型的話，答案就是so；如果是出現「____ 名詞 + that」句型的話，答案就是such。

2.「so + 形容詞 + that」和「so + 副詞 + that」

so that之間可以放形容詞和副詞。**常常會出現兩者當中哪一個比較合適的問題。**這時觀察前面，如果需要形容詞的話就放形容詞，如果需要副詞就放副詞。

The director made this movie **so (interesting / interestingly) that** it attracted many people.

> 那個導演製作的／這部電影／很有趣／以至於吸引了／很多人。

made是第5大句型動詞，所以括號內應該放受詞補語的形容詞interesting，當然是用來修飾前面的受詞movie。另外，在so that句型中that之後是副詞子句。沒有that之後的子句，整個句子還是完整的句子。（參閱Chapter 13）

3.「so + 形容詞 + a / an 名詞」「such + a / an + 形容詞 + 名詞」

意思為「太…以至於…」，請看一下位置。如果**句型是「＿＿＿ + 形 + a / an + 名」的話**，so**就是解答**；如果句型是「＿＿＿ a / an + 形 + 名」的話，such**就是解答**。這個順序一定要記下來！

1 The person is **so qualified an applicant that** he will be hired.
「so + 形容詞 + a / an 名詞」

2 The person has **such a great qualification that** he will be hired.
「such + a / an + 形容詞 + 名詞」

再次強調是「so + 形容詞 + a / an + 名詞」、「such + a / an + 形容詞 + 名詞」。

1 那個人是很有資格的應徵者／他會被雇用。

2 那個人有很傑出的資格條件／他會被雇用。

4.「such + 形容詞 + 名詞」（複數名詞，不可數名詞）

「such + a / an + 形容詞 + 名詞」句型中有a / an後面當然接單數名詞。但是後面接複數名詞或不可數名詞時，就不可以用a / an。所以遇到這種情況的話，就去掉such後面的不定冠詞a / an，用「such + 形容詞 + 名詞」的句型來表現。除了「so + 形容詞 + a / an 名詞」和「such + a / an + 形容詞 + 名詞」之外，再多背一個「such + 形容詞 + 複數名詞」就可以了。

They hired **such great applicants that** there was no opening at all.
用「such + 形容詞 + 複數名詞」的文法來表現

《講師的補充說明》

so many複數名詞、so much不可數名詞的情況，不能用such要用so

so many problems 本來就很多問題

so much money 本來就很多錢

他們雇用了／很多的應徵者／所以完全沒有／空位置／一點都。

怪物講師的祕訣

1 so that中間放形容詞或副詞，such that中間放名詞。

2 把「so + 形容詞 + a / an 名詞」和「such + a / an + 形容詞 + 名詞」文法背起來。

3 把「such + 形容詞 + 複數名詞 / 不可數名詞」也背起來，只有so many複數名詞或so much不可數名詞是例外。

Q7 They proposed (so / such) a nice idea that we agreed sooner than expected

Q8 They proposed an idea so (unexpected / unexpectedly) that we were embarrassed.

▶ 解答在120頁

怪物講師的祕訣

解決形容詞單字問題的方法

很多人遇到形容詞單字問題時,都會把答案選項(A)到(D)的形容詞放到空格裡試圖了解句意。但是那樣很花時間,形容詞在句子裡是修飾名詞的作用,所以出現形容詞單字問題時,把握形容詞和修飾名詞的關係就可以輕鬆解題。

攻略法 76 形容詞單字整理

將過去多益考試中常出現的形容詞單字做總整理，單獨記下括號內的形容詞是沒意義的。將整句完全背起來，才能看到題目就馬上回答。

＊下列是近幾年在多益考試中常出現的形容詞。

• be (emphatic) about	強調…（＝ have an emphasis on）
• be (eligible) to do	有資格…（cf. be eligible for 名詞）
• consider our company (progressive)	認為我們公司是很先進的
• in (chronological) order	依照年代順序（＝ chronologically）
• (protective) clothing	防護衣
• run (short)	變少（＝ run out of …耗盡、不足）
• it is not (economical) to replace something	更換什麼是很不經濟的
• (available) to all members at no extra cost	所有會員不需另外付費就可使用的
• (experienced) and dynamic employees	經驗豐富且活力十足的員工們
• the information should be as (specific) as possible	情報要盡量詳細
• remain (contingent) on	依存…、取決於…
• become (operational)	被操作
• the (diverse) tourist attractions	各種的觀光勝地
• be (likely) to do	有…可能（＝ be apt to do; be liable to do; tend to do）
• (dedicated) representatives	專注的代表們
• be (dedicated) to	獻身於…
• as (little) as $40	只不過是40美金的
• demonstrate (unwavering) commitment to	對…有堅定的承諾
• an (impressive) new line of cars	令人印象深刻的新車系
• (subsequent) events show that	一連串相關事情顯示了…
• for the fifth (consecutive) month	連續5個月

- their (creative) products　　　　　他們的創意產品
- (confirmed) reservations　　　　　已經確認的預約
- for the (upcoming) school year　　　即將來臨的新學年
- (formal) training　　　　　　　　正規的訓練
- (extensive) research　　　　　　　大範圍的調查
- (valid) receipts　　　　　　　　　有效的收據
- items that are (unclaimed)　　　　　沒被認領的東西
- (detailed) maps　　　　　　　　　詳細的地圖
- (consolidated) income statement　　統合所得報告書
- (established) companies　　　　　　基盤穩固的公司
- be (attractive) to　　　　　　　　被⋯吸引的
- the editorial is (enlightening)　　　那社論是啟蒙的
- without (written) consent　　　　　沒有書面同意
- physics is much too (demanding)　　物理學太困難
- (regular) assessment　　　　　　　定期評估
- (impressive) speed　　　　　　　　令人印象深刻的速度
- (visual) aids　　　　　　　　　　視覺輔助
- less (expensive) than　　　　　　　比⋯更便宜的
- (perishable) goods　　　　　　　　易腐爛的食物
- (comprehensive) testing　　　　　　綜合檢查
- take (quick) action　　　　　　　　採取快速的措施
- (financial) advisor　　　　　　　　財政顧問
- a (limited) number of　　　　　　　有限的⋯
- (environmental) hazards　　　　　　環境上的危險
- (combined) experience　　　　　　結合的經驗
- (finished) project　　　　　　　　完成的專案
- the noise was (disturbing)　　　　　噪音令人煩惱
- (accurate) information　　　　　　正確的情報
- be (capable) of -ing　　　　　　　能夠⋯（＝be able to do）
- (busy) telephone line　　　　　　　通話中
- be (pleased) to do　　　　　　　　很高興能夠⋯
- it is (likely) that ...　　　　　　　好像⋯
- lending service of books that are extremely (popular)

　　　　　　　　　　　　　　書的出借服務很受歡迎
- (frequent) inspections will ensure safety

　　　　　　　　　　　　　　經常調查的話就能確保安全
- he is highly (qualified)　　　　　　他非常符合資格
- the financial market is currently (unstable)

　　　　　　　　　　　　　　現在金融市場不穩定
- it is (beneficial) to hire an outside firm

　　　　　　　　　　　　　　雇用派遣人力非常有利

- (another) round of changes   又一次的變更
- the (near) elimination of a risk   幾乎消除的危險性
- conduct a (wide) range of surveys   實行各種範圍的調查
- seek (skilled) workers   徵求有技能的工人
- its (highest) level   最高的水準／高度（用widest就錯了）
- always (indicative) of a failure   總是顯示失敗的（reminiscent是錯的）
- cause (alarming) changes to   引起驚人的變化
- it takes (longer) than planned   所花時間比計畫的還要長
- be (scheduled) to travel   預計出差
- be fully (aware) of   非常了解
- have a (considerable) effect   有相當的影響力（considerate是錯誤解答）
- of (interest)   有趣的（= interesting）
- be (vulnerable) to damage   容易受損、容易損壞
- be (eager) to do   很想做…
- (specific) instructions   詳細的指南
- all loans are (due) today   所有的貸款到今天結束
- be (eligible) to receive   有資格接收
- the use of my credit card is (unauthorized)   我的信用卡沒有刷成
- they are my (close) acquaintances   他們是我認識的人
- be (accessible) through our website   可以透過我們的網站來使用
- serve as a (temporary) replacement   臨時替換（duplicate是錯誤答案）
- be (doubtful) that...   懷疑…
- make something (superior) to others   讓某個東西比其他東西更優秀
- his own (harshest) critic   對自己最殘酷的評論家
- be known as a (residential) area   為人所知的居住區
- services will be (available)   可以利用各種服務
- a (valued) member   親愛的會員
- through a (stringent) inspection process   透過嚴格的檢查程序

- accept our (sincere) thanks　　　　　接受我們真心的感謝
- due to (continuous) improvements in technology
　　　　　　　　　　　　　　　　　　持續的技術發展
- for a (limited) time only　　　　　　只能在有限的時間之內
- the (closest) station　　　　　　　　最近的車站
- because of (declining) sales　　　　因為銷售量減少
- (discontinued) appliances　　　　　停止販賣的家電產品
- (native) to the region　　　　　　　那個地區出身的
- be (nervous) about　　　　　　　　擔心…
- our supplies are (limited)　　　　　我們的備用品是有限的
- a single (comprehensive) book　　　單行本的綜合圖書
- be considered the (definitive) source　認為是決定性的資源
- be (grateful) for　　　　　　　　　對…感謝
- keep it in a (secure) location　　　　保管存放在安全的場所
- unlike (traditional) supermarkets　　跟傳統的超市不同
- on the basis of (previous) purchases　以以前的購買為基礎
- is currently (unavailable)　　　　　現在不可使用
- when something is (complete)　　　當完成什麼時
- before recommending an (appropriate) system
　　　　　　　　　　　　　　　　　　推薦合適的系統之前
- documents of a (confidential) nature　機密的文件
- build an (additional) parking lot　　增設停車場
- due to (unfavorable) conditions　　因為不公平的條件
- the case is (unique)　　　　　　　那種情況很特殊
- a (broad) familiarity with　　　　　很了解…
- any (improper) transaction　　　　任何不當的交易
- become / be (accustomed) to　　　對…變成習慣
- put (considerable) effort to　　　　對…付出了相當多的努力
- perform (routine) tasks　　　　　執行例行性的工作
- concern about the (inadequate) number　對不足夠數量的擔心
- a (lengthy) description　　　　　　繁瑣的說明
- (innovative) TV commercials　　　創新的電視廣告
- (extensive) public transportation systems　廣泛的大眾交通系統

攻略法 72　形容詞的正確位置

1 冠、所、介、動 +（形容詞）+ 名詞 +（形容詞子句）

2 第2類動詞be [become, remain] +（副詞）+ 主詞補語（形容詞）

3 形容詞 + 形容詞 + 名詞

　　形容詞, 形容詞 + 名詞

　　形容詞 and 形容詞 + 名詞

4 形容詞在名詞後面的情況？

　　形容詞的長度變長的情況：像a man kind only to women

　　本來就是放在後面的形容詞：像10 years old

攻略法 73　形容詞的單複數

1 使用複數名詞的形容詞 → both, several, few, many, a number of...

2 與單數可數名詞一起使用的形容詞 → every, each, another, either, neither, this, that...

3 與不可數名詞一起使用的形容詞 → much, little...

4 用於複數和不可數名詞的形容詞 → a lot of = lots of = plenty of, most, all...

5 單、複數不可數名詞都可用的形容詞 → some / any...

攻略法 74　有文法重點的形容詞

1 every的2種意思：所有（單數名詞）、每…（表示期間）

2 數百個的：hundreds of + 複數名詞

　　300個的：three hundred + 複數名詞

攻略法 75　副詞子句「太…以至於…」

1 「so + 形容詞／副詞 + that」和「such + 名詞 + that」

2 「so + 形容詞 + that」和「so + 副詞 + that」（把that前面變成完整句子）

3 「so + 形容詞 + a / an 名詞」和「such + a / an + 形容詞 + 名詞」

4 「such + 形容詞 + 名詞」（複數名詞，不可數名詞）

例子

1　(A) accessible —— ① 把握問題的類型
　　(B) access
　　(C) accessibility
　　　　　　　　　　　② 把握提示
　　(D) accessing

Confidential company records are only _____ to select employees due to security concerns raised by clients.

③ 空格中要填什麼詞類？

1 把握問題的類型
　詞性問題

2 把握提示
　be動詞後的補語

3 空格中要填什麼詞類？
　形容詞

2　(A) mildness
　　(B) mildly
　　(C) milder
　　(D) mild

The CEO has expressed _____ concern about the long-term viability of our international operations.

1 把握問題的類型

2 把握提示

3 空格中要填什麼詞類？

3　(A) thoroughly
　　(B) thoroughness
　　(C) thorough
　　(D) through

Even though the fair trade commission conducted an extremely _____ audit of company operations, no irregularities were found.

1 把握問題的類型

2 把握提示

3 空格中要填什麼詞類？

4　(A) regular
　　(B) regulate
　　(C) regulation
　　(D) regularity

By conducting _____ computer scans, employees can help prevent viruses from infecting the company network.

1 把握問題的類型

2 把握提示

3 空格中要填什麼詞類？

5　(A) account
　　(B) accountable
　　(C) accountability
　　(D) accounting

All employees of the corporation may be found legally _____ for revealing confidential information to third parties.

1 把握問題的類型

2 把握提示

3 空格中要填什麼詞類？

6 (A) unexpectable
   (B) unexpected
   (C) unexpecting
   (D) unexpectably

While annual vacation days are limited to 10 days per year, employees facing _____ situations may be granted leave.

1 把握問題的類型

2 把握提示

3 空格中要填什麼詞類？

7 (A) poised
   (B) poising
   (C) poise
   (D) poises

While the firm is in a period of consolidation, it remains _____ to enter several emerging markets in the Asia-Pacific region.

1 把握問題的類型

2 把握提示

3 空格中要填什麼詞類？

8 (A) retired
   (B) retiring
   (C) retirement
   (D) retire

New government legislation will necessitate an improvement in employee _____ benefits in all small and medium-sized companies.

1 把握問題的類型

2 把握提示

3 空格中要填什麼詞類？

9 (A) maliciousness
   (B) malicious
   (C) maliciously
   (D) malice

Any employee using company email to send _____ or threatening e-mails to fellow employees will face disciplinary action.

1 把握問題的類型

2 把握提示

3 空格中要填什麼詞類？

10 (A) troublesome
   (B) troubles
   (C) troubling
   (D) troubled

Due to the _____ state of the national economy, many excellent holiday packages are available at discounted prices.

1 把握問題的類型

2 把握提示

3 空格中要填什麼詞類？

▶ 解答在121頁

重要

101 Because the market remains _____, many leading economists are predicting a cut in interest rates by the Federal Reserve Bank.

(A) volatile
(B) volatileness
(C) volatility
(D) volatilizes

102 Due to their usefulness in business, smart phones and tablet PCs are becoming _____ among many professionals.

(A) ubiquitous
(B) ubiquity
(C) ubiquitousness
(D) ubiquitously

103 Despite slow growth during the first quarter, market watchers are _____ in their outlook for the latter part of the year.

(A) optimist
(B) optimistically
(C) optimistic
(D) optimism

104 Even though share prices are down, many potential investors find the market outlook _____.

(A) brightly
(B) bright
(C) brightness
(D) brighten

105 With proper procedures in place, any business can be assured of a _____ transition to a new management team.

(A) smoothly
(B) smoothed
(C) smoothest
(D) smooth

106 While learning to use new business tools can be _____ at first, employees often recognize their benefits.

(A) challenge
(B) challenging
(C) challengeable
(D) challenged

107 While consumers remain cautious, there are several _____ signs that the retail sector will soon pick up.

(A) positive
(B) positively
(C) positives
(D) positivity

108 There are _____ opportunities in developing countries for manufacturers looking to move their operations overseas.

(A) abound
(B) abundantly
(C) abundant
(D) abundance

109 _____ financial advisors have recently been handsomely rewarded for their willingness to help their clients.

(A) Profess
(B) Professionally
(C) Profession
(D) Professional

110 When first starting out in business, companies must be _____ to the changing needs of their customers.

(A) adaptability
(B) adaptable
(C) adaptation
(D) adapting

收集了多益考試中常出的題目。請當作正式的考試，確認時間並解題。

重要

111 With the rapid growth in data networks, many telecommunications companies are offering corporate clients _____ data downloads.

(A) unlimited
(B) unlimiting
(C) unlimitedly
(D) unlimitable

112 As companies grow in influence, they must take care not to appear to be _____ in the eyes of their supporters and allies.

(A) arrogance
(B) arrogantly
(C) arrogantness
(D) arrogant

113 The new library was constructed using _____ building materials in order to reduce the cost of shipping.

(A) efficient
(B) seasonal
(C) local
(D) national

114 If you have not been to our restaurant recently, please take a moment to look over our _____ menu.

(A) reordered
(B) redesigned
(C) rearranged
(D) restructured

115 Despite some difficulties, labor union talks ended amicably today, each side _____ with the final agreement.

(A) content
(B) friendly
(C) disappointed
(D) unhappy

高難度

116 The state-of-the-art train runs on _____ tracks powered by equal amounts of electromagnetic force.

(A) preparatory
(B) preliminary
(C) parallel
(D) perpendicular

117 In observance of local customs, our branches in China will close _____ during the last week of the lunar new year.

(A) late
(B) especially
(C) early
(D) prematurely

高難度

118 Guests at the reception will be served a _____ meal after the first keynote speaker delivers her address.

(A) complimentary
(B) supplementary
(C) sentimental
(D) complementary

119 The position offers a _____ salary in addition to a yearly bonus, a company car, and a personal assistant.

(A) disadvantageous
(B) competitive
(C) celebratory
(D) mediocre

120 Exhibitions of the artist's _____ series of paintings will be on display throughout the entire month of September.

(A) earliest
(B) least
(C) worst
(D) latest

▶ 解答在123頁

Lately, most people in this nation are threatened by the risk of contaminated food. It makes them _____ as to which foods are safe for their daily consumption. However,
121
there has been no further response from any authority or government department. I think we can _____ this issue from different aspects. First of all, as the costs for running
122
their businesses keeps increasing, business owners have no option _____ to reduce
123
their cost by using synthetic ingredients for the food production. Secondly, the average income has dropped and commodity prices are increasing dramatically; what's more, most people are purchasing inexpensive food. For meeting the market's demand, these food manufacturers use inadequate synthetic ingredients to lower their costs. Finally, the government monitoring system is not good enough. Therefore, these dishonest manufacturers are capable of selling contaminated food without being charged with endangering people's health. We now have to use some extreme measures to eliminate this problem or the health of everyone _____.
124

121 (A) confuse
    (B) confusion
    (C) confused
    (D) confusing

122 (A) look up
    (B) look after
    (C) look for
    (D) look into

123 (A) and
    (B) but
    (C) or
    (D) if

124 (A) will thrive constantly
    (B) will be improved successfully
    (C) will be impacted seriously
    (D) will be evolved continuously

▶ 解答在123頁

Chapter 19 副詞
句子的所有要素都具備的話，剩下的就是副詞！

Review Test

在Chapter 18學習了被當成第2大句型、第5大句型的補語，修飾名詞的形容詞。透過下列問題確認一下所學的內容吧！

1 形容詞的位置？　　　　　　　　▶ ....

2 a few跟哪種名詞一起使用？　　 ▶ ....

3 every和each跟哪種名詞一起使用？ ▶ ....

4 跟不可數名詞一起使用的副詞？　 ▶ ....

5 friendly的詞性是什麼？　　　　 ▶ ....

6 形容詞單字問題解法是什麼？　　 ▶ ....

Preview

1 副詞的特徵

　　副詞是呈現-ly形態，更正確地說明的話，就是「形容詞 + -ly」的型態。也就是說去掉-ly的話就是形容詞。但是請注意，並不是所有的副詞都是在形容詞後面加上-ly的型態。**像lovely，是在名詞love加上-ly變成，且不是變成副詞，而是形容詞。**還有already, too, well, just, hard等不加上-ly的副詞。**通常「形容詞 + -ly」的副詞會出單字問題；而沒有-ly的副詞則會被出在文法問題。副詞在句子裡有修飾動詞、形容詞、副詞的功能，尤其是修飾動詞的情況最多。**

　　副詞的英文是adverb。（ad是「往⋯」，verb是動詞）除了副詞之外，還要知道有副詞功能的副詞類。這一章將會學到輕易解決副詞的正確位置、特殊的副詞出題重點、副詞單字問題的方法。

2 副詞問題解法

❶ 如果是修飾動詞、副詞或是副詞的位置的話，選擇副詞作答。

❷ 如果有好幾個特定副詞，乾脆就將出題重點背起來。

❸ 副詞單字問題大多是配合最接近的動詞來作答。

攻略法

77

副詞類的位置

在Chapter 01當中學過的內容。快速讀過Chapter 01內容之後，再慢慢地讀過下面的內容的話，會更容易理解。當然也有Chapter 01當中沒提過的內容。

原則上，**副詞是在第1～5大句型中所需的結構都具備之後，就變得可有可無的修飾語**。但是修飾語不是只有副詞，還有形容詞吧？因此句子結構完整時，副詞跟形容詞都看起來很像是正確解答。這個時候只要**解析句意，修飾名詞的話，就選擇形容詞；修飾動詞或形容詞或副詞的話，就選擇副詞**。來看看下列例句！

I need to propose **an idea (acceptable / acceptably)** to the committee. ◁

> 我必須提案／一個想法／讓委員會能接受。

到括號前的idea為止是完整的第3大句型句子。那麼後面有可能會出現修飾語副詞或形容詞。利用說明來判斷答案即可。上面的英文中與其使用「值得接受地」副詞來修飾動詞，不如用「值得被接受的」想法修飾前面的名詞反而更自然。因此括號內應該填入acceptable。

怪物講師的祕訣

仔細整理副詞在句子裡的位置

1 動詞組合之間的話是副詞位置

- 助動詞 + 副詞 + 原形動詞
- have + 副詞 + p.p.（過去時態）
- be動詞 + 副詞 + -ing／p.p.（進行式／被動態）
- 副詞 + to + 副詞 + 原形動詞 + 受詞／補語 + 副詞
- 副詞 + 動名詞 + 受詞／補語 + 副詞

2 如果是第2大句型和第5大句型補語的形容詞前面的話，就是副詞的位置

像be動詞第2大句型的動詞 + 副詞 + 形容詞類

像make這種第5大句型動詞 + 受詞（名詞）+ 副詞 + 受詞補語（形容詞）

3 如果是修飾名詞的形容詞的話，就是副詞的位置

冠詞／所有格／前置詞／及物動詞 + 副詞 + 形容詞 + 名詞

Quiz

Q1 The company is (financial / financially) sound.

Q2 The man is a (professional / professionally) financial consultant.

▶ 解答在127頁

應該知道的副詞的文法特徵

請熟讀下列介紹副詞的文法特徵，這些副詞出現時，必須透過了解語意的方式才能解題。

出現與every相關的問題時，只知道意思「所有」是沒有用的。every的意思雖然是複數，但是應該要知道在**文法上是被當作單數來使用的特徵**。整理具有獨特文法特徵的副詞，如下所示。

	詞性：意思	確認重點
still	副詞：仍然	時態：現在式、現在進行式
	副詞：然而	句子：主要肯定句　　例外：否定句寫成still not
yet	副詞：還沒 連接詞：但是	副詞：have not yet p.p.（主要用在現在完成式） 　　→ 主要和not一起使用 　　→ have yet to（還…不是…） 連接詞：S + V, yet S + V（和but一樣的對等連接詞）
once	副詞： 一時、何時 連接詞： 一旦…的話	副詞：S once V（和過去式一起使用） 連接詞：once S + V（現在式／現在完成式）， （未來式／未來完成式）→ 時間，條件的副詞子句
besides	副詞： 再加上 介系詞： 再加上	副詞：besides, S + V（或者是S, besides, V） 　　→ 同義詞：in addition 介系詞：besides + 名詞 + 動名詞 　　→ 同義詞：in addition to
just	副詞： 現在正…	have just p.p. 剛剛正要… just...when …當正要… just as...as 只要像…（參考Chapter 20） just before... …之前，just after... …之後
ever	副詞：何時	hardly ever 幾乎不…（跟否定詞一起使用） have ever p.p. 何時曾經做過… ever since 從那以來何時…
already	副詞： 已經、早已	have already p.p. ... 已經做了… → 肯定句：與完成式一起使用

Quiz

Q3 (Beside / Besides), we have to devise a plan within a week.

Q4 I have not (still / yet) found out the exact reason.

▶ 解答在127頁

攻略法

79

數字前面常出現的副詞

跟數字一起使用的副詞，是多益考試中常出現的副詞。曾經連續好幾個月出現在考題。一定要背下來喔！

請先記住數字是形容詞這一點，所以數字前面通常放修飾形容詞的副詞。但並不是任何副詞都能用。在解說上另有適合的副詞。來看看下列例句吧！

1　They offer **up to 30** percent discount.
　up to是有「到…為止、最多到…為止」表示程度的副詞

2　**Only 10** employees attended the party.
　only是有「只有…」表示程度的副詞

上面看到數字30、10旁邊的up to和only不像是副詞，但是卻有副詞的作用。如同前面所提的，因為數字是形容詞，修飾形容詞的是副詞。與數字一起使用的副詞如下。

- **幾乎**：almost, nearly, approximately, roughly, around, about...
- **最多／最少**：a maximum of 數字 = up to 數字 / a minimum of 數字
- **只有**：only
- **以上**：more than (= over)
- **以下**：less than (= below)

1　他們提供／最多百分之30的折扣。

2　只有10名的員工／參加／那個派對。

怪物講師的祕訣

看到數字時，選擇下列副詞作答

- 幾乎：almost, nearly, approximately...
- 以上：more than (= over)...
- 以下：less than (= below)...

Quiz

Q5 It took (approximate / approximately) eight hours.

Q6 There were (more than / more) two thousand visitors.

▶ 解答在127頁

其他一定要記得的副詞

下列介紹出題頻率相當高的副詞，無論是每個副詞的意思、出題重點，都必須要熟記！

1. 集形容詞和副詞為一身

英文單字中，有幾個單字是名詞又是動詞。這些單字並沒有其他的形容詞或副詞型態，所以不要被副詞語尾-ly這個陷阱所騙。來看看下面的問題吧！

I **have (long / longly) waited** for her answer.　　　　　< 我等了很久／她的回覆。

have p.p.之間是副詞的位置，但是沒有longly這個單字。因為long這個單字可以當作副詞，也可以當作形容詞，所以上面的括號內要選擇long。

形容詞和副詞是一樣的單字中，尤其是下面4個單字最常出現在考題裡。雖然沒有幾個，但是一定要記起來。

	形容詞	副詞
fast	很快的	很快地
early	早的	很早地
long	長的	長久地
far	遠的	遠地

2. 形態上很容易混淆的副詞

英文單字中只要加上-ly就成為副詞，也有幾個去掉-ly之後，能夠成為形容詞或副詞的特殊單字。應該正確掌握這些單字加上或去掉-ly時的詞性和意思。多益考試出題老師最喜歡考的就是這種單字。來看看下面的問題吧！

The company will redesign its **(high / highly) successful model**.　　　< 那個公司會再次設計／它們非常成功的典範。

括號後面接了successful，那麼就是修飾形容詞的副詞位置！high

和highly都能當副詞使用，比起「高（high）」的成功典範，「很（highly）」成功的典範更順暢吧！

不加上副詞語尾-ly的時候，形容詞和副詞一起使用，但是加上副詞字尾-ly的話，就變成其他意思的副詞單字，整理如下。

① hard （副）努力地；（形）困難的
　　hardly （副）幾乎不是…
　　- work hard 認真工作、 it is hard to do 很難…
　　- hardly understand 幾乎無法理解

② near （副）近；（形）鄰近的
　　nearly （副）幾乎
　　- live near 住的很近、the near future 不久的未來
　　- nearly five hours 幾乎5個小時

③ high （副）高；（形容詞）很高的
　　highly （副）非常 (= very)
　　- aim high 訂很高的目標、high altitude 很高的高度
　　- highly successful 非常成功地

④ late （副）晚；（形）亡故的
　　lately （副）最近 (= recently)
　　- come late 晚到、the late Mr. Kim 已逝的金先生
　　　He was late. 他遲到了。
　　- We have been in trouble lately. 我們最近有問題。

⑤ just （副）現在才；（形）公正的
　　justly （副）公平地
　　- has just come 現在才來、a just decision 公正的判決
　　- deal justly with 公平地交易

⑥ close （副）近；（形）鄰近的
　　closely （副）詳細地、緊密地
　　- sit close 坐得很近、close to the school 鄰近學校的
　　- closely examine 詳細地檢驗

⑦ most （副）最、最好（最高級）；（形）大部分的、最多的。
　　mostly （副）大部分
　　- most boring 最無趣的、most people 大部分的人

- I don't do anything particular mostly. 我通常不做特殊東西。

3. 考試中常出現的副詞

這裡介紹的**副詞單字都是常出現在多益考試的單字。將副詞分類整理成程度副詞、焦點副詞、對等副詞、增減副詞**。熟記各類副詞，考試時選擇適當的副詞填寫。來解題吧！

The sales in overseas area **increased** (**markedly / prominently**). 海外的銷售／顯著增加了。

歷屆考古題中，屬於困難度很高的問題——「有顯眼地、引人注目的」意思的副詞markedly，是在什麼大幅增加或減少的時候使用。另外副詞prominently是常常跟動詞「展示」display一起使用的副詞。

將考試中常出現的副詞分成了程度副詞、焦點副詞、對等副詞、增減副詞4大類。

- 程度副詞：heavily 猛烈地、badly 非常、well below 比⋯還低、well over 更多的、well ahead of 更先、well in advance 更早
- 焦點副詞：only 只有⋯、even 甚至、just 正好、 exactly 正確地、particularly 特別 (= especially)
- 對等副詞：also（放在句子中間任何地方）、too（放肯定句最後面）、either（放否定句最後面）（全部都是「也」的意思）
- 增減副詞：increasingly 漸漸地更、dramatically 顯著地、significantly 相當地、rapidly 很快地、substantially 相當地 (= considerably)、remarkably 顯眼地 (= noticeably)、remarkedly 引人注目地

4. 副詞too的各種用法

副詞too是用法很多的副詞，不需要知道全部的用法，但下列的用法一定要謹記在心！這些副詞雖然是寫成「副詞 + 形容詞」的型態，但是本身也當成名詞。

(1) 當作「太」意思使用的副詞too
副詞too後面加上表示數或量的many, few, much, little等的話，表示「太」。當然是修飾形容詞的副詞

- too much money　　　太多的錢
  too many participants　太多的參加者
- too little courage　　不足的勇氣

《講師的補充說明》
much too + 形容詞／副詞 + to：太⋯，太⋯。（也能跟too far互換使用）

This question is much too difficult to me. 對我來說／這個問題太難。

too few respondents	太少的回覆
much too expensive	太貴的
far too abruptly	太突然

重點在於too much或too little後面接不可數名詞，too many或too few後面接可數的複數可數名詞

(2) too 也用來表示「太⋯，所以無法⋯」的意思
副詞too常常被寫成「too + 形容詞（或副詞） + to do」的型態，有「太⋯，所以無法⋯」的意思

He is **too tired to** get up early.
too是修飾後面形容詞的tired的副詞！

< 他太累了無法早起。

與上面例句相反，表示「太⋯所以能夠⋯」的文法是「形容詞／副詞 enough to do」。 enough在這裡是用來修飾前面的形容詞或副詞。所以叫做後置修飾副詞。只有寫成「enough + 名詞」型態的時候，enough是修飾名詞的形容詞。

(3) 用在「此外，也⋯」的too
副詞too放在句子的最後面，表示「此外，也⋯」的意思，跟also的意思差不多。肯定句要用too，否定句時要用either取代too。

1 He knows it **too**.
    too放在肯定句句尾！

2 He doesn't know it **either**.
    否定句時要用either取代too！

3 He **also** knows it.
    also用在肯定句，寫在動詞旁邊！

< 1 他也知道那個。
   2 他也不知道那個。
   3 他果然也知道。

378

5. 準否定詞 hardly

基本上否定詞都是副詞，not, never, hardly**也是如此。（no和none是例外）**在這裡要介紹的是，否定意思中出題頻率最高的準否定詞hardly。所謂的準否定詞，是比起表達確實地「不是～」的完整否定詞not，never，稍微弱一點的「幾乎都不…」的意思。因為是副詞，所以被用來修飾動詞、形容詞、副詞，但用來否定動詞。

1　He **is hardly concentrating** on this matter.

2　They **will hardly have** a chance to do that.

hardly本身就有否定的意思，不能和not或never一起使用。所以主要是放在be動詞或助動詞後面，也用在一般動詞的前面。常用的準否定詞除了hardly之外還有scarcely, seldom, rarely等。

另外還有一個要與準否定詞hardly一起熟記的一點，hardly常常以hardly ever（幾乎不是…）的型態出現。這時ever**用來強調**hardly**的意思**。

1 他幾乎沒有專心／在這個問題上。

2 他們幾乎沒有機會／做那件事。

怪物講師的祕訣

1　集形容詞和副詞於一身： fast, early, long, far

2　容易混淆的副詞：high（形）高的、（副）高；highly（副）非常

3　常用的副詞單字組合一起背起來的話更好

　　markedly increase 顯著地增加

　　prominently display 引人注目的展示

4　副詞too也用做「太…」、「太…所以無法…」、「又…」的意思

Quiz

Q7 We can finish it (well / very) in advance.

Q8 This is efficient and attractive, (too / either).

▶ 解答在127頁

攻略法

81

多益考試中出現過的副詞

考古題是準備考試最棒的資料。再次強調，最好要把單字背下來。這樣其他部分在考題中出現時就可以馬上回答。

- it is (absolutely) essential that...   做…是必須的
- has (yet) to do   還不…
- remind (again) that...   再次提醒…
- drop so (suddenly)   突然掉下
- at (approximately) 9:00 a.m.   大約是早上9點
  (= about)
- (temporarily) be using this office   臨時使用這個辦公室
- I am writing (again) to do   為了…再次寫信
- (highly) successful   相當成功
- bring them (immediately)   馬上拿過來
- I can travel (directly) between A and B   我可以直接往來A和B
  (= completely)
- the (unbearably) high temperatures   無法忍受的高溫
- (absolutely) free of charge   完全免費的
- (currently) looking for   現在正在尋找
- (especially) considering that...   尤其是考慮…的話
- (currently) not accepting any submissions   現在不接受任何提交
- begin (promptly) at 8 a.m.   準時早上8點開始
- (consistently) late   習慣性遲到
- working (primarily) on   主要做…工作
  (= mainly)
- (already) fully booked   已經預約滿的
- (completely) free of charge   完全免費

- move (quickly) to do 為了…快速移動
  (= swiftly)
- more (easily) than before 比以前更輕易
- (presently) under construction 現在建構中的
  (= now)
- pursue potential clients (aggressively) 積極尋找潛在顧客
- fill out the form (completely) 完整地填寫表格
- will (undoubtedly) be promoted 一定會升職
- be written (clearly) 明確地填寫
- (unfairly) raise the rent 不公平地提高房租
- (consistently) provide 持續地提供
- an (increasingly) popular hobby 漸漸變得有人氣的興趣活動
- follow the directions (carefully) 小心地遵循指示事項
- (well) below the average list price 比平均訂價還低
- drive very (cautiously) 非常小心駕駛
  (= carefully)
- discounts are available (exclusively) to members
  折扣只適用於會員
- have (already) received the invitation 已經收到邀請函
- (directly) reflect the price 即時反映價格
  (= immediately)
- draw (randomly) 隨機抽選
- reassure them (politely) 慎重地保證
- cost (significantly) less than before 比以前花更少的錢
- (almost) entirely dependent on 幾乎完全依賴
- (far) too expensive for the quality 跟品質對比太貴
- respond quite (differently) to 對…呈現相當不同地反應
- (finally) release the results 最終發表結果
- be inserted (correctly) 正確地插入
- (favorably) view 善意地眼光來看
- upgrade and innovate (continually) 持續地升級和革新

- proceed (slowly)　　　　　　　慢慢地進行
- grip the road (firmly)　　　　　（輪胎）緊緊抓住地面
- (accidentally) discover　　　　偶然發現
- the crop is ripening (nicely)　　穀物即將成熟
- increase (markedly)　　　　　　急遽增加
　　　　　　　　　　　　　　　　(= dramatically, rapidly, sharply)
- be replaced as (quickly) as possible
　　　　　　　　　　　　　　　　盡快更換
- (immediately) upon arriving　　一抵達就馬上…
- unless (otherwise) noted　　　　不另外提到的話
- (up to) three...　　　　　　　　最多到3個…
- (widely) admired　　　　　　　廣為推崇的
- (partially) obscures the driver's sight
　　　　　　　　　　　　　　　　駕駛視野有部分被遮住
- (nearly) 5 percent　　　　　　幾乎百分之5
　　　　　　　　　　　　　　　　(= almost)
- work incredibly (hard)　　　　驚人地努力工作
- take the customers' privacy (seriously)
　　　　　　　　　　　　　　　　尊重顧客的個人隱私
- (shortly) before　　　　　　　…不久之前
　　　　　　　　　　　　　　　　（shortly after …不久之後）
- (technically) impossible　　　　技術上不可能的
- shortly (thereafter)　　　　　　不久之後
- speak (quietly)　　　　　　　　小聲地說
- wrap the items (securely)　　　牢固地包裝
- (officially) open the store　　　商店正式開張
- the customers return (regularly)　顧客定期地光顧
- (happily) refund your money　　欣然地退錢
　　　　　　　　　　　　　　　　(= gladly)
- change (considerably)　　　　　相當地改變
　　　　　　　　　　　　　　　　(= significantly, substantially)
- call (ahead) for reservation　　為了預約打電話
　　　　　　　　　　　　　　　　(= in advance = beforehand)
- be distributed (equally)　　　　平均地分配

- (recently) issued summary　　　　　最近發表的總結
- be on sale for not (quite) ten hours　販售不到10個小時
- designed (exclusively) for kids　　專門為孩子們設計的
- (respectfully) decline your order　正式地拒絕您的訂單
- (just) as reliable as the old one　跟以前一樣值得信任
- (shortly) after　　　　　　　　　之後
　　　　　　　　　　　　　　　　(= soon, briefly)
- (confidently) predict　　　　　　有信心地預測
- not (knowingly) made false statements　在不知情的情況下做出假的
　　　　　　　　　　　　　　　　陳述
- work (diligently)　　　　　　　　勤奮工作
- be delivered (promptly)　　　　　迅速地配送
　　　　　　　　　　　　　　　　(= swiftly)
- knowledgeable, friendly, and, (above all), enthusiastic
　　　　　　　　　　　　　　　　博學、親切而且最重要的是
　　　　　　　　　　　　　　　　熱情
　　　　　　　　　　　　　　　　(= mainly)
- explain (in detail)　　　　　　　仔細地說明
- be (presently) being renovated　現在正在改造
- report (directly) to the president　馬上向總裁報告
- (fully) appreciate the value　　　完全重視價值
- has (already) become the best-selling item　已經成為最暢銷的產品
- (initially) resisted the plan　　　剛開始的時候反對計畫
- the price seldom (directly) reflects the cost of delivery
　　　　　　　　　　　　　　　　價格幾乎不會反映在運費上
- be drawn (randomly)　　　　　　隨機抽獎
- reassure the parents (politely)　讓父母安心
- watch exchange rates (closely)　密切地觀察匯率
- be considered (individually)　　分開考慮
　　　　　　　　　　　　　　　　(= separately)
- were (completely) satisfied with our service　對我們的服務完全滿意
　　　　　　　　　　　　　　　　(= totally)

- not (necessarily) lead to better quality 　　不一定變成更好的品質
- has (hardly) been used 　　幾乎不被使用

　　(= barely)

- are (conveniently) located 　　位置便利
- (quickly) gained popularity 　　馬上受到歡迎
- climb (dramatically) 　　急遽爬上
- in an (increasingly) competitive market 　　在競爭逐漸變激烈的市場
- take effect (immediately) 　　即刻生效
- rumors have been circulating (lately) 　　最近流傳的謠言

　　(= recently)

- are more (easily) found 　　更容易被發現
- (eventually) need to be demolished 　　結果被拆除
- (voluntarily) recall 　　自發性回收
- react (calmly) to any emergency 　　不管在任何情況下都沉著應對

- were (cordially) invited 　　誠摯地邀請
- most (closely) matched 　　最適合的
- the most (frequently) visited 　　頻繁被訪問的

　　(= often)

- will have (just enough) time to do 　　有充分的時間
- (personally) welcome 　　親自歡迎
- (particularly) important 　　特別重要的
- (tightly) fastened 　　繫緊（安全帶）
- (completely) support the bill 　　完全支持那個法案
- argued (persuasively) 　　有說服力的主張
- be made (separately) 　　分開製作
- be based (primarily) on 　　主要根據…

　　(= mainly, especially)

- be (primarily) caused by 　　主要是因為…
- (patiently) wait 　　有耐心地等待

攻略法 77　副詞類的位置

首先確認句子的主要要素之後，副詞最後放進句子裡。

副詞類／分詞結構，（形）主詞＋形／副＋動詞＋（副）形＋受詞／（副）補語（＝形）＋副／形

攻略法 78　應該知道的副詞的文法特徵

still	副詞：仍然 副詞：但是	besides	副詞：加上 介系詞：加上
yet	副詞：還沒（還未發生的事） 連接詞：但是	just	副詞：現在才
		ever	副詞：何時
once	副詞：一時、何時 連接詞：一旦…的話	already	副詞：已經、早已

攻略法 79　數字前面常出現的副詞

1 幾乎：almost, nearly, approximately, roughly, around, about

2 最多／最少：a maximum of 數字 = up to 數字 / a minimum of 數字

3 才：only

4 以上：more than (= over)

　以下：less than (= below)

攻略法 80　其他一定要記得的副詞

1 形容詞與副詞一體：fast, early, long, far ...

2 形態上容易混淆的副詞：hard, near, high, late, just, close, most ...

3 考試中常出現的副詞：程度副詞、焦點副詞、對等副詞、增減副詞

4 副詞too的各種用法：太、太…所以、無法…又

5 準否定詞：hardly, scarcely, seldom, rarely ...

例子 **1** (A) even   **①** 把握問題的類型
(B) only
(C) yet
(D) still

② 把握提示   **③** 空格中要填什麼詞類？

Although the meeting had not been scheduled _____, several employees were beginning to prepare their presentations.

1 把握問題的類型
文法問題

2 把握提示
not yet

3 空格中要填什麼詞類？
_副詞_

---

2 (A) easily
(B) readily
(C) steadily
(D) measurably

You should remember that our office policy does not change _____ without a strong reason.

1 把握問題的類型

2 把握提示

3 空格中要填什麼詞類？

---

3 (A) equally
(B) mostly
(C) partially
(D) fully

The studio demands a strong work ethic and expects actors to be _____ prepared before taping begins.

1 把握問題的類型

2 把握提示

3 空格中要填什麼詞類？

---

4 (A) finance
(B) financial
(C) financed
(D) financially

It is said that renting a house can be a _____ wise decision if interest rates on home loans are high.

1 把握問題的類型

2 把握提示

3 空格中要填什麼詞類？

---

5 (A) time
(B) timely
(C) timeless
(D) timing

We require that submissions be submitted _____ so that our contractors can arrange a schedule.

1 把握問題的類型

2 把握提示

3 空格中要填什麼詞類？

6   (A) almost
      (B) quite
      (C) hardly
      (D) nearly

The audience found the documentary to be _____ entertaining, and they applauded in the end.

| 1 把握問題的類型 |
| 2 把握提示 |
| 3 空格中要填什麼詞類？ |

7   (A) recently
      (B) relatively
      (C) really
      (D) regretfully

The banquet on this Friday afternoon will feature speakers who have _____ retired from journalism.

| 1 把握問題的類型 |
| 2 把握提示 |
| 3 空格中要填什麼詞類？ |

8   (A) certain
      (B) certainty
      (C) ascertain
      (D) certainly

The strong partnership of Acme Supply Co. and Beta Production, Inc., will _____ create large earnings for shareholders.

| 1 把握問題的類型 |
| 2 把握提示 |
| 3 空格中要填什麼詞類？ |

9   (A) high
      (B) highly
      (C) highness
      (D) higher

Despite its tragic ending, readers whom I met enjoyed the novel's _____ creative use of language.

| 1 把握問題的類型 |
| 2 把握提示 |
| 3 空格中要填什麼詞類？ |

10 (A) sometimes
      (B) always
      (C) rarely
      (D) frequently

The plant manager himself set an example for his employees by _____ missing a day of work.

| 1 把握問題的類型 |
| 2 把握提示 |
| 3 空格中要填什麼詞類？ |

▶ 解答在128頁

重要
101 The most _____ friendly solution is to use alternative energy as much as possible, such as solar or wind power.

(A) environmentally
(B) environment
(C) environmental
(D) environments

高難度
102 The committee debated for hours and hours, slowly and _____ poring over every detail of the proposal.

(A) destructively
(B) demonically
(C) demonstratively
(D) deliberately

103 Regal Energy Service promises to deliver power _____ every day of the year, with zero interruptions to your service.

(A) tirelessly
(B) continuously
(C) discontentedly
(D) repeatedly

104 No one knows how successful he is; _____, he will be remembered forever as an amazing talent.

(A) therefore
(B) but
(C) however
(D) yet

105 Dr. Giuliano was _____ finished with the procedure when his attention was diverted by an emergency patient rushing into the hospital.

(A) near
(B) nearer
(C) nearness
(D) nearly

106 Attorney Padma Singh is famous for _____ founding a charity for underprivileged citizens to receive free legal representation.

(A) aggressively
(B) aggressive
(C) aggression
(D) aggravate

107 Shipping invoices should be submitted _____ to Chief Carlsberg in the warehouse prior to finalizing an order.

(A) direct
(B) directly
(C) direction
(D) directive

108 Although the aerospace program had plenty of capable engineers, the head of the department _____ desired someone with a more creative vision.

(A) too
(B) even
(C) once
(D) still

109 Banking services on, before, and after December 25 will be suspended _____ in honor of the Christmas holiday.

(A) meanwhile
(B) frequently
(C) temporarily
(D) permanently

110 Due to interoffice difficulty, all outbound correspondence must _____ be approved by a manager before sending.

(A) just
(B) especially
(C) first
(D) finally

111 The two nations arrived at a settlement peacefully after _____ two weeks of negotiations.

(A) approximate
(B) most
(C) near
(D) more than

高難度

112 Radio host John van Gusten _____ interrupted his guest in order to prevent certain information from being broadcast.

(A) intentionally
(B) graciously
(C) gracefully
(D) interrogatively

重要

113 _____ we started using the newly introduced software system in our office, the efficiency of our work has increased significantly.

(A) While
(B) Since
(C) Once
(D) Even though

114 You should understand that this is an important matter and should be dealt with _____.

(A) prompt
(B) promptly
(C) promptness
(D) prompting

115 Only one month has passed since this book was published, and yet it has _____ become a hot selling item in the market.

(A) yet
(B) still
(C) already
(D) otherwise

116 Once _____ available to authorized members, the fantastic cafe will be open to the public as of August 15.

(A) exclusively
(B) exclusive
(C) excluding
(D) excluded

117 Prices have dropped by _____ 30% in the previous quarter partly due to the increased competition in the market.

(A) nearly
(B) near
(C) nearing
(D) nearer

118 Our soon to be released cleaner for cars makes it much _____ to keep them shiny than the old one.

(A) more easily
(B) easier
(C) easiest
(D) most easily

119 The candidate is making the public _____ interested in participating in this year's election mainly due to his intriguing personality.

(A) increasing
(B) increasingly
(C) increased
(D) increases

120 The basic grammar is _____ the best course among other lectures we have been offering for this semester.

(A) definitely
(B) definitive
(C) define
(D) definition

▶ 解答在130頁

By general acknowledgement, the life of human beings is benefited _____ new

    121

technological inventions. They enable our lives to be easier, _____, and more

    122

comfortable. However, they may result in unpredictable consequences in our future life.

For one thing, most of the new inventions are only tested under laboratory conditions. It

seems uncertain they will always work well since our living environment varies over time.

We may _____ some problems with them in the future. Secondly, most of these new

    123

technological inventions are invented by prosperous corporations. Profit is their main

concern; therefore, it will be possible for us to be in a situation where we won't have

sufficient after-sale assistance should a new invention go wrong. Finally, for any particular

invention, there's often something new on the market with similar features. It will result in

an inflated price to constantly renew inventions just _____. All in all, rolling out new

    124

technological inventions seems to be a double-edged sword for consumers.

121 (A) to
    (B) on
    (C) of
    (D) from

122 (A) smart
    (B) smartness
    (C) smarter
    (D) more smart

123 (A) come about
    (B) come after
    (C) come across
    (D) come around

124 (A) because new things keep coming out
    (B) so that new things keep coming out
    (C) due new things keep coming out
    (D) accounts for new things keep coming
        out

比較級和倒裝句
主詞和動詞的位置對調？

我們來一起複習Chapter 19學過的內容吧！

1 我們要怎麼確定空格內是副詞？ ▶ ....

2 副詞類的種類有？ ▶ ....

3 once當作副詞使用時的意思是？ ▶ ....

4 數字前面常使用的副詞是？ ▶ ....

5 請說說看high和highly的詞性和涵意？ ▶ ....

Preview

1 比較級和倒裝句的特徵

首先我們要知道，只有形容詞和副詞才有原級、比較級、最高級。如果沒有比較的對象，就是使用原級；有一個比較的對象就是比較級；如果有多個比較對象，就是使用最高級。

考題中常出現的形式是省略了if的倒裝句，或是否定句出現在句子最前面。我們在這一章要熟悉比較級和最高級的差異與用法，以及熟悉多種倒裝句的表現方式。

2 比較級和倒裝句的解題法

❶ 先觀察是否有比較對象

❷ 一般來說，句子最前面有出現has、were、did、should就是假設法的倒裝句；如果是出現never、hardly就是否定句的倒裝。

攻略法

82

比較級的基本理解

比較級？這不是就只是用more或-er、than來做比較時使用嗎？別想得太簡單！比較級的句子裡也有許多你不得不知道的要點。

首先我們要知道原級、比較級、最高級這三種用語。**原級、比較級、最高級是只有形容詞和副詞才有的**。原級、比較級、最高級不存在於動詞或名詞中。

1　He is **tall**.

無比較對象，所以是原級。

2　He is **taller**. (×)

因為沒有比較對象，使用比較級的taller顯得突兀！

上面第2個例句要改成He is taller than my father.（他比我的爸爸高。）才是正確的句子，那麼看看下面的句子是怎麼樣呢？

3　He is the **tallest**. (×)

因為沒有比較對象，使用最高級的tallest顯得突兀！

上面的例句應該要寫成He is the tallest among us.（他是我們之中最高的。）將上面的內容簡單整理如下。

- **如果無比較對象** → 原級
- **如果有一個比較對象** → 比較級
- **如果有多個比較對象** → 最高級

> 1 他很高。
> 2 他比較高。

> 3 他最高。

5秒 解決比較句的題型的方法

1 先確認空格內是形容詞還是副詞。

2 如果無比較對象是原級，如果有一個比較對象是比較級，如果有多個比較對象是最高級。

《講師的補充說明》

有時候會看到像more money（更多錢）名詞前面接著比較級的句子，這是將形容詞much（多的）的比較級more放在名詞前，並非是把money變成比較級。（以後別再說名詞也可以有比較級囉！）

Quiz

Q1 The updated text has (more / most) errors than the original version.

Q2 The system is the (most / more) efficient one that I have ever used.

▶ 解答在133頁

攻略法

83 比較級和最高級的變化

大家應該都大概了解比較級和最高級，但能真正了解透徹的人卻很少。我們來趁這個機會好好了解比較級和最高級的變化吧！

PART 5, 6 出題頻率

100%

80%

60%

40%

1. 規則變化

這邊簡單做個說明。**大部分較短的形容詞或副詞，在字尾加-er、-est即可；如果是較長的形容詞或副詞，可以在前面使用**more、most。不過英語的表現很相似，必須要能在極短時間內去判斷要接-er、-est，還是要接more、most，否則不論時間寬裕或是緊迫，也沒人會有閒暇時間去分辨這是2音節或3音節的單字。

比較級和最高級的變化一覽表

種類	類型	單字後接的字尾
形容詞／副詞	比較級	-er
2音節以下	最高級	-est

種類	類型	單字前
形容詞／副詞	比較級	more...
部分2音節，3音節以上	最高級	most...

舉例來說，new的比較級和最高級分別是newer和newest，一般不使用more new和most new，因為它是單音節。不過像是important就不會變化成importanter和importantest，會使用more important、the most important。因為這是3音節的單字。

2. 不規則變化

如同動詞有規則變化（-ed）和不規則變化（take-took-taken）般，比較句也有分成規則變化和不規則變化。不規則變化的形容詞和副詞不多，希望大家都可以背下來。我們將不規則變化的形容詞和副詞整理如下。

- good 好的（形容詞）-better（形容詞、副詞）-best（形容詞、副詞）
  well 好好地（副詞）；健康的（形容詞）
- bad 壞的（形容詞）-worse（形容詞、副詞）-worst（形容詞、副詞）
  ill 生病的（形容詞）；差勁地（副詞）
- many 多的（形容詞＋可數名詞）-more（形容詞、副詞）-most（形容詞、副詞）
  much 多的（形容詞＋不可數名詞）（more、most可數名詞和不可數名詞皆可使用）
  ＊用於修飾名詞時，more / most是形容詞；用在形容詞或副詞做比較級和最高級句子時，more / most是副詞。
- little 少的（形容詞＋不可數名詞）-less（形容詞、副詞）-least（形容詞、副詞）
  ＊few-fewer-fewest意思一樣，但是使用在可數名詞前面。
- late 晚的（時間）-later 較晚的 -latest 最近的
  後面的（順序）-later 後半部的 -latest 最後的
- low 低的（形容詞）-lower 更低的 -lowest 最低的
  ＊lower是有「降低…」意思的及物動詞，這時與比較級完全無關。

怪物講師的祕訣

1 要使用比較級或最高級時，有規則變化和不規則變化的區分。

2 規則變化是-er、-est或是 more...、most...。
不規則變化需要另外背誦，一定要熟悉正確的用法。

✏ **Quiz** ....

Q3 I found the (latter / later) part of the movie too predictable.
Q4 This version is (recenter / newer) than the one you showed me.

▶ 解答在133頁

有比較對象的比較級和最高級

一再強調，不論是比較級或最高級，一定是有比較對象時使用。沒有比較對象時，不能使用比較級和最高級句型。

前面有提過，如果無比較對象是原級；如果有一個比較對象是比較級；如果有多個比較對象是最高級。但有時候，句子中會省略比較的對象。

舉例來說，He has an elder sister, but he is taller.（他有一個姊姊，但是他比較高。）誰比較高呢？當然是than his sister。像這種是從句子中可以得知來龍去脈，所以省略了than his sister。一定會有人問這裡沒有than，為什麼會是比較級呢？

Compared to last year, we'll have (**many / more**) attendees.

和去年比較／我們將會有更多的出席者。

因為前面已經有了和去年比較的句子，所以要使用比較級的more。動詞compare本身就有比較的意味，很多句子會像這樣和比較級一起使用。

比較級和最高級的概念如下。

❶ 比較級和最高級一定要有比較的對象
（必須要看得到或是透過內容得知。）

❷ 比較級大部份會使用than表現。

❸ 所以有than就是比較級，有比較級的話要找出than。

5秒 解決比較題型的方法

1 如果無比較對象 → 正解是原級。

2 如果有一個比較對象 → 正解是比較級。

3 如果有多個比較對象 → 正解是最高級。

Quiz

Q5 I have a brother and he is (old / older) than me.

Q6 I like coffee more (that / than) tea.

▶ 解答在133頁

攻略法

85

拉丁語的比較級（-or字尾的形容詞）

有些比較級較特殊，有些形容詞和副詞使用to來取代than。這些大部分都是拉丁語過來的單字，就當作是慣用語記下來就行了。

英語中有很多單字都是從拉丁語演變來的。這些從拉丁語中演變而來的單字，在轉換成比較級在字尾不使用-er，而是使用-or。而且更重要的是，-er搭配使用than，但是-or是使用to。

This system is **superior to** the old one.
superior後面使用to來取代than。

我們將這類用法的拉丁語系統整理出來如下。

- superior to　　　比…更優秀的
  inferior to　　　比…更劣等的
- senior to　　　比…更老的
  junior to　　　比…更年輕的
- prior to　　　比…更早（= earlier than）

這系統優於／舊系統。

《講師的補充說明》

prefer A to B
（比起B，更喜歡A）

prefer本身是動詞，並非是比較級。只是使用這個動詞時，最大的特徵是後面要使用to，不可使用than，這就是拉丁語的比較級。

怪物講師的祕訣

1　看到比較級的話，使用than；看到than的話，使用比較級。
2　-or結尾的形容詞使用to，看到to使用-or。

Quiz

Q7 He is 5 years (senior / older) to me.
Q8 I prefer coffee (than / to) tea.

▶ 解答在133頁

最高級的兩大要點

比較的對象有三個以上時，不使用比較級，要使用最高級。不過在最高級文法裡，冠詞和比較對象是最重要的兩個要點。

1. 形容詞的最高級使用the（副詞的最高級不使用）

1 She is **the fastest** runner in this area.

這裡的fast是形容詞，有「快的」的意思，要使用定冠詞the。

2 She runs **fastest** among us.

這裡的fast是副詞，副詞的最高級不使用定冠詞the。

怎麼會這樣呢？**形容詞最高級是「…當中最…的」的意思，修飾特定的名詞，所以要使用定冠詞the。如同字面上的意思，因為有限定的對象。**那難道副詞就沒有限定對象嗎？不是這樣的。是冠詞後面有名詞才需要使用，**但是副詞後面沒有名詞嘛！**所以**理所當然地就不使用冠詞了。**大部分的學生不知道其中的原因，就以為最高級通通都要加上定冠詞the，千萬不要這樣做。一定要記住，文法中沒有「冠詞＋副詞」。

但是萬一出現了「＿＿＋副詞最高級＋形容詞＋名詞」的題目該怎麼辦？空格在副詞的最高級前面，不是不能填定冠詞the嗎？不是這樣的。有看到後面的名詞嗎？這裡當然要填冠詞了。來看看下面的例句，可以讓你更了解。

3 It was probably **the most eagerly awaited scene change** in the history of the Royal Opera.

most eagerly修飾後面的awaited，awaited又再修飾後面的名詞scene change！

副詞eagerly前面有最高級most。副詞前面是最高級，所以就不能使用定冠詞the嗎？不是這樣的。看看後面，有名詞scene change，所以這裡可以使用定冠詞the，變成the most。

1 她是最快的跑者／在這個地區裡。

2 她跑得最快／在我們之中。

3 那大概是最令人期待的場景變化了／在皇家劇場的歷史裡。

2.最高級也要有比較對象

和比較級一樣，沒有比較對象只有He is the strongest.的表示，看起來好像哪邊不太對。因為最高級的意思是「在…之中最…」，必須要有比較的對象。**因為是最高級，所以要有多個比較對象，如果只有單一比較對象的話，頂多只能使用比較級而已**。下面是最高級的例句，請各位觀察一下什麼是多個比較對象。

1 This machine is **the most efficient** (machine) **I have ever encountered**.
  括弧內的machine和前面的machine重複，可以省略！

2 **Of all the samples**, this is **the most affordable** (sample).
  括弧內的sample和前面的sample重複，可以省略！

3 This product is **the most popular** (product) **in the world**.
  括弧內的product和前面的product重複，可以省略！

將上面的內容簡單整理如下。
• the + 最高級 + 名詞 + 主詞 + have p.p.（現在完成式，到現在為止…之中最…的）
• the + 最高級 + 名詞 + of / among (all) 複數名詞（…之中最…的）
• the + 最高級 + 名詞 + in + 場所（範圍，…之中最…的）

＊很多句子在內容上也都會省略名詞，所以別再問為什麼冠詞後面沒有名詞囉，因為被省略掉了！

5秒 解決最高級題型的方法

1 是否出現多個比較對象？→ 如果是的話，答案請選最高級。
2 最高級前面必須要有定冠詞the或是所有格，但是副詞後面不出現名詞，因此不使用the。

Quiz

Q9 He is the (good / best) student in this class.
Q10 He did it (well / best) among the participants.

▶ 解答在133頁

1 這個機器是最有效率的機器／那個是我所見過的。

2 所有的樣品中／這個是／價格最適當的樣品。

3 這個產品是最熱門的產品／在這個世界上。

攻略法 **87** 比較句和冠詞

前面有稍微介紹過比較句和冠詞，但是在這邊我們再來複習一下，並且做更深層的討論。

請記住！基本上我們都是假設比較句和冠詞後面是有名詞的。因為後面沒有名詞的時候，一直去看副詞的原級、比較級、最高級有沒有冠詞是很浪費時間的。首先我們將比較句和冠詞的關係用圖表表示如下。

種類	不定冠詞（a / an）	定冠詞（the）
原級	可使用（可數單數）	可使用 （可數單、複數或不可數名詞）
比較級	可使用（可數單數）	原則上不可使用
最高級	不可使用	可使用 （後面有名詞時）

形容詞或副詞的原級前面可使用不定冠詞、定冠詞。不論到哪邊後面都有名詞的名詞。如同前面提到的，最高級後面有名詞的話（即使是省略）要使用the，不可使用a / an。因為最高級有限定對象，因此要使用定冠詞。如同上面圖表所示，**原則上比較級的前面不使用定冠詞，不過還是會有例外。即使是比較級，也會有像下面的例外需要使用定冠詞的例外時候**。因為是特例，要記在腦海中喔！

1. the 比較級, the 比較級

The happier we make our customers, **the more** money we make.

我們讓客戶更高興／我們可以賺更多錢。

原則上比較級的前面不使用定冠詞，但這情況還是要破例使用the。再深入了解的話，為什麼句子中前面不是the more happily，而是the happier呢？這是因為後面出現的make是第5大句型的動詞，所以要使用受詞和受詞補語。受詞是our customers，那麼受詞補語呢？形容詞受詞補語happier跑到句子最前面去了。

不過為什麼受詞補語不在受詞的後面，卻跑到句子的前面去了呢？如果是在受詞後面，哪裡會出「the 比較級, the 比較級」的句型呢！

逗號（,）後面the more money又是為什麼呢？逗號後面的make是第3大句型的動詞，所以the more money就成了make的受詞。make money有「賺錢」的意思，不過應該是只有more到前面去就好了，為什麼連money都跑到前面去了呢？因為much money、more money是一起使用的字組，通常是不拆開的，所以才會一起跑到前面去。

2. 句中有出現of the two時

of the two或between the two用來表示「兩者之中」時，應該是使用在原級、比較級和最高級的哪一個呢？答對了！就是**使用在比較級**。兩者中「⋯更⋯」比兩者中「⋯最⋯」更自然。**不過重要的是，這時候比較級前面是使用the**。為什麼呢？因為我們在表示「兩者中一個更⋯的」的時候，有限定出「更⋯的」的緣故。把這些當作是慣用語背下來吧！

Of the two candidates, **the former** is the more qualified (candidate).
前者是the former，後者是the latter。後面的candidate有重複，可以省略！

> 兩個候選者中／前者是更有資格的候選者。

怪物講師的祕訣

1 看到a / an時，答案請選擇原級和比較級（看有無比較對象決定）。

2 看到the時，答案請選擇原級和比較級（看有無比較對象決定）。

3 請記住「the 比較級, the 比較級」是例外。

Quiz

Q11 The more books you read, the (wiser / more wisely) you become.

Q12 The (much / more) I work with him, the better I know him.

▶ 解答在133頁

原級比較和強調句

「如同…程度」的英文要怎麼表示呢？這時通常會使用as...as...來表達。但是「as...as...」又有許多微妙的變化，一定要觀察入微。

說到比較級，大家會想到-er、more、than這些關鍵字。除此之外，**less、as有時會被用來使用在比較級句型裡**。下面三個種類都可算是比較級。

• more...than...（比…更…的，優等比較——比…更好。）
• less....than...（比…較差的，劣等比較——比…更差。）
• as...as...（像…一樣…，對等比較——比較過後兩者程度相當。）

1. as...as...句型的空格題型

(1) as...as...句型
考題常出的模式是前面或後面的as只寫一個，空格內讓考生填入另一個as。我們來看看下面的題目吧！

He is **as** qualified (**as**, **than**) I (am qualified).
前後要填入as，括弧內的am qualified可以省略！

> 他具有和我相當的資格。

(2) as和as之間放入原級的題型
還有另一種題型是**前後的as都有出現，讓考生選擇中間空格應該是填入原級、比較級或最高級**。as和as之間是放形容詞或副詞，動詞和名詞等絕對是No！因為本身就是原級的比較，所以形容詞或副詞都是要選用原級，因此比較級和最高級也是絕對No！我們來看下面的題目。

This is **as** (**larger / large**) **as** that.
as...as的句型中要使用原級，因此括弧內是large。

> 這個和那個一樣大。

(3) as 和 as 之間要放入形容詞或副詞的題型
第二個as以前的句子是不完整句時，使用形容詞；是完整句的話，使用**副詞**。我們來看下面的題目。

We find this **as (useful / usefully) as** those.

我們知道／這個和那些一樣有用。

find屬於第5大句型的動詞，所以this是受詞，括弧內的答案是受詞補語。受詞補語就是形容詞，所以正確答案是useful。

(4) as 形容詞 + 名詞 as
原則上原級比較的句型as...as之間要放形容詞或副詞。前面有形容詞時，也可以放入名詞。一起看下面的例句。

We have **as many employees as** your company.
名詞employees前面有many。

我們的員工數／和你們的公司一樣多。

(5) as...as 前面要放什麼的題型
在強調as...as句型時，前面可以用just。（請參閱Chapter 19副詞單元中的just部分）我們來看下面的題目。

He runs **(just / very) as** fast **as** she (runs).

他跑得就和她一樣快。

強調as...as句型的副詞就是just。可以假設成把just的位置改成空格，very和just中做選擇的題型，當然就是選擇just啦！

2. 強調比較級和最高級的副詞總整理

可以用一些單字放在比較級或最高級的前面來表示強調。**比較級或最高級是利用形容詞或副詞組成，所以如果要修飾或強調的話，當然就是要用副詞。**我們來看下面的題目。

The weather is **(by far / even) the best**, so we can have our lunch outside.

天氣是最近這段期間內最好的／所以我們可以吃午餐／在戶外。

有看括弧後面的最高級the best吧？強調最高級的部分就是by far。even則使用在強調比較級，因此上面題目的括弧內要放入by far。

我們將強調原級、比較級、最高級的副詞整裡如下。

- 原級修飾（形容詞／副詞、p.p.型的形容詞）：very、so、quite、
extremely、pretty等
- 比較級修飾：even（更）、still（更）、a lot（多）、a little（一點）等
- 比較級／最高級修飾通用：far、much等
- 最高級修飾：by far、only等

怪物講師的祕訣

1 看到as放入as。（原級比較或是對等比較句）

2 as...as之間放入形容詞或副詞的原級。

3 看到very、so、quite等，答案請選原級。

4 看到even、still等，答案請選比較級。

5 看到by far、only等，答案請選最高級。

Quiz ....

Q13 This radio works as (efficiently / efficiency) as the latest one.

Q14 This is (so / even) durable that we can use it frequently.

▶ 解答在133頁

攻略法

89

倒裝句

句子不是任何時候可以倒裝，只有發生下面幾種情況才可以。最重要的是要多看、多練習倒裝句，才能在短時間找出答案。

英文句子的順序一般都是「S + V」，但是很少有**「V + S」的情況**，這種情況叫做倒裝句。舉例來說，There is a book.（有一本書。）這個句子就是最代表性的倒裝句，因為主詞a book在動詞is的後面。到底在什麼樣情況句子才會變成倒裝句呢？**英文句子倒裝的情況，主要分成下面兩大類，一是假設法中省略if時，二是把想要強調的句子放到句子最前面時。**

1. 假設法中省略if時（參閱Chapter 07）

假設法中省略if時，主詞和動詞間會出現倒裝。這是在Chapter 07裡學過的內容，我們藉由看下面的內容，來恢復記憶吧！也請用最快的速度再回去Chapter 07複習一下。

我們將假設法中省略if後，主詞和動詞就會倒裝的情況整理如下。

❶ 假設法過去完成式的倒裝句
had 主詞 p.p., 主詞 + would [should, could, might] + have p.p.
（如果…了的話，應該…）

❷ 假設法過去式的倒裝句
were 主詞 + 補語, 主詞 + would [should, could, might] + 原形動詞
（如果…，應該會…）

❸ 假設法未來式的倒裝句
should 主詞 + 原形動詞, 原形動詞（祈使句）
（如果…，請…）

《講師的補充說明》

要倒裝有be動詞或助動詞的句子時，把be動詞或助動詞放到句子最前面即可倒裝。但是沒有be動詞或助動詞，只有一般動詞時，依據句子的時態選擇助動詞do、does、did後放到句子最前面，再將原本的動詞改成原型即可。

2. 把想要強調的句子放到句子最前面時

這類的倒裝句已經像是個慣用方式固定不變了，因此最好的方式就是平時每次接觸到這類慣用表現時，就把它們都背下來。

(1) 將否定詞放到句子最前面強調時

seldom、scarcely、hardly、never、no sooner這類的否定詞，放到句子前面強調時，主詞和動詞之間就會發生倒裝。

1 Seldom had he reviewed it **when** he found an error.
　要注意動詞的位置和時態！

上面例句有時候也會用hardly或scarcely取代seldom，用before取代when。

2 Never have I studied English so hard like this.
　這裡也是要注意動詞的位置和時態！

上面例句原本應該為I have never studied English so hard like this.，為了表示強調語氣，將否定詞never放到句子最前面，主詞I和動詞have位置對調後，形成了上面的倒裝句了。

(2) 將副詞、副詞片語和副詞子句等放到最前面強調時
不要以為隨便任何一個字都可以拿掉，隨便都可以倒裝。下面的例句都像慣用語般，已經是固定的表現了，請整個背下來吧！

1 Only recently did he realize it.
　did是倒裝句的助動詞，後面必須是原形動詞。

這個句子原本是He realized it only recently.或是He only recently realized it.，為了強調only recently，所以將only recently放到句子最前面。不過沒有be動詞或助動詞，只有一般動詞（realized），realized是過去時態，因此把助動詞配合數量或時態變成了did後，再放到句子最前面。

2 There is a challenging task waiting for you.
　這是there is開頭的的第1大句型！

(3) 把補語放在句子最前面強調時
把形容詞當做補語的第2大、第5大句型中，時常為了強調語氣，而把補語放到句子最前面。

---

1 （直譯）幾乎他無法檢查那個／當時發現了／失誤。

　（意譯）他一檢查那件事馬上就發現了一個失誤。

2 我從來沒有／像這次一樣這麼認真學習英文。

1 終於到了最近／他才覺悟。

2 有個辛苦的課題／等待你的。

這樣的表現方式把平凡且平淡的句子，變得更加洗練有修飾。另外，p.p.型的形容詞enclosed和attached，特別常使用在下面的句型裡。

1 A resume is enclosed.（第2大句型一般句，平淡無味）
  → **Enclosed** is a resume.（倒裝句，句型活用，有修飾）

2 You will find a message attached.（第5大句型一般句，平淡無味）
  → **Attached** you will find a message.（無倒裝，句型活用，有修飾）

第一個例句是使用be動詞的第2大句型，把p.p.型的形容詞補語enclosed放到句子最前面，主詞a resume和動詞is對掉的倒裝句。將第5大句型倒裝的第二個例句，把受詞補語attached放到句前，後面的主詞you和助動詞will維持「S＋V」的狀態。這些當做是常用的固定用法記下來即可。

5秒 解決倒裝句題型的方法

1 如果had、were、did、should出現在句子最前面，就是假設法的倒裝句。

2 否定詞出現在句子的最前面，也是倒裝句。

3 only副詞類和enclosed、attached等也都是倒裝句中常見的常客。

 Quiz

Q15 Only after I met you (did / and) I achieve the best result.

Q16 No sooner had he learned the fact (when / than) he was in despair.

▶ 解答在133頁

1 履歷表被密封著。
  被密封著的是／履歷表。

2 你會發現的／有附上留言。
  附上／你將會發現的／留言。

406

| 攻略法 82 | 比較級的基本理解 |

■ 如果無比較對象 → 原級　■ 如果有一個比較對象 → 比較級　■ 如果有多個比較對象 → 最高級

| 攻略法 83 | 比較級和最高級的變化 |

■ 2音節以下的形容詞、副詞 → -er, -est　■ 3音節以上的形容詞、副詞 → more..., most...

| 攻略法 84 | 有比較對象的比較級和最高級 |

■ 比較級和最高級一定有比較對象　■ 大部分的比較級會使用than

| 攻略法 85 | 拉丁語的比較級（-or字尾的形容詞） |

superior to 比…更優秀的 ←→ inferior to 比…更劣等的
senior to 比…更老的 ←→ junior to 比…更年輕的
prior to 比…更早

| 攻略法 86 | 最高級的兩大要點 |

■ the使用在後面有名詞的最高級　■ 最高級必須要有多個比較對象

| 攻略法 87 | 比較句和冠詞 |

■ the比較級, the比較級：愈…愈，漸漸…
■ of the two、between the two：使用於比較級，比較級前面要有the

| 攻略法 88 | 原級比較和強調句 |

• 原級修飾（形容詞／副詞、p.p.型的形容詞）：very、so、quite、extremely、pretty等
• 比較級修飾：even（更）、still（更）、a lot（多）、a little（一點）等
• 比較級／最高級修飾通用：far、much等

| 攻略法 89 | 倒裝句 |

■ 假設法省略了if時
■ 把想要強調的句子放到句子最前面時

例子

1 (A) more reliable   ① 把握問題的類型
   (B) as reliable
   (C) more reliably
   (D) most reliable   ② 把握提示

I want to make it clear that our shipping methods are _____ than any of our competitors.

③ 空格中要填什麼詞類？

1 把握問題的類型
　文法問題

2 把握提示
　than、be動詞

3 空格中要填什麼詞類？
　形容詞的比較級

---

2 (A) having been
   (B) having
   (C) has
   (D) have

To my surprise, not only _____ ticket sales risen, but prices are higher than ever before.

1 把握問題的類型

2 把握提示

3 空格中要填什麼詞類？

---

3 (A) anxiously
   (B) more anxious
   (C) anxious
   (D) anxiety

Never has the line manager been as _____ as he was today to schedule this weekly meeting.

1 把握問題的類型

2 把握提示

3 空格中要填什麼詞類？

---

4 (A) decides
   (B) decide
   (C) decided
   (D) has decided

Only after the local population had grown larger did the city government _____ to raise taxes.

1 把握問題的類型

2 把握提示

3 空格中要填什麼詞類？

---

5 (A) more important
   (B) importanter
   (C) importance
   (D) more importantly

The more complicated our society becomes, the _____ immigration becomes to our community.

1 把握問題的類型

2 把握提示

3 空格中要填什麼詞類？

6 (A) greater

(B) greatly

(C) great

(D) greatest

He is looking forward to solving the _____ challenges he has ever taken since he became a manager.

1 把握問題的類型

2 把握提示

3 空格中要填什麼詞類？

7 (A) speedy

(B) speedier

(C) speed

(D) speedily

In my assumption, the two-hour flight to Tokyo is much _____ and more efficient than the ferry.

1 把握問題的類型

2 把握提示

3 空格中要填什麼詞類？

8 (A) very

(B) more

(C) as

(D) most

With some encouragement, Alfred can become _____ talented as his older brother is in science.

1 把握問題的類型

2 把握提示

3 空格中要填什麼詞類？

9 (A) more

(B) less

(C) many

(D) much

Company profits grew as _____ as the stockholders had hoped, which led to the current success.

1 把握問題的類型

2 把握提示

3 空格中要填什麼詞類？

10 (A) slower

(B) as slow as

(C) slowness

(D) slowly

The shopping season coming to an end, workers are ready for _____, less frantic workdays.

1 把握問題的類型

2 把握提示

3 空格中要填什麼詞類？

▶ 解答在134頁

101 No sooner had they received numerous complaints _____ the software developers attempted to solve the problems.

(A) because
(B) when
(C) than
(D) such

102 Concerned about a shrinking market, the construction company built _____ homes this year and reduced the size of its staff.

(A) greater
(B) excessive
(C) less
(D) fewer

103 So positive were the sales results this year that the managers got _____ bonuses than they had in any year past.

(A) more sizable
(B) as sizable
(C) most sizable
(D) so sizable

104 So shaky is the world economy that foreign investments are expected to be _____ riskier than they were in the previous decade.

(A) single
(B) by far
(C) quite
(D) still

105 Given that sales have been _____ consistent this year due to the failing economy, many companies are scaling back production.

(A) less
(B) more
(C) as
(D) most

106 Not wanting to be out of touch with her employees, the company president's office was as _____ as any of her employees' offices.

(A) less modest
(B) most modest
(C) more modest
(D) modest

高難度
107 _____ he understood the shipping requirements, he would not have said such a silly thing in front of us.

(A) Did
(B) Should
(C) Had
(D) If

108 Never has Neil _____ such a grandiose exhibit before, so he took enough time to look around all of it.

(A) seen
(B) sees
(C) saw
(D) see

重要
109 If the goods you receive are less satisfactory _____ you expected, you may return them for a full refund at no extra shipping cost.

(A) when
(B) than
(C) while
(D) as

110 Knowing the flight would be _____ than usual due to the inclement weather, Heather took anti-nausea medicine before takeoff.

(A) bump
(B) bumper
(C) bumpy
(D) bumpier

收集了多益考試中常出的題目。請當作正式的考試，確認時間並解題。

111 Only after hearing about a potential job promotion did she begin working _____ than the other employees.

(A) efficiently
(B) more efficiently
(C) efficient
(D) more efficient

112 For your information, _____ are my resume and reference letters you can refer to if you need.

(A) enclosure
(B) enclosing
(C) enclosed
(D) enclose

113 The _____ a product becomes, the more errors it can have.

(A) sophistication
(B) more sophisticated
(C) sophisticate
(D) most sophisticated

重要
114 _____ higher proportion of total assets must be invested aggressively to make good use of this bullish market.

(A) Very
(B) Quite
(C) Still
(D) By far

115 To launch our product successfully, it might be a good idea to give consumers as _____ promotional offers as they want.

(A) much
(B) more
(C) many
(D) most

116 As its current marketing strategy is not as efficient _____ the old one, considerable losses are expected.

(A) as
(B) more
(C) than
(D) to

117 The newer, more efficient, and more powerful equipment is far _____ to the old one.

(A) super
(B) superior
(C) excellent
(D) better

高難度
118 Scarcely had Mr. Hilton _____ in for a transfer to another branch when an emergency meeting was held.

(A) has put
(B) putting
(C) puts
(D) put

119 The easy way of investing in the market is to spread the money in as _____ sectors as possible.

(A) little
(B) many
(C) much
(D) more

120 _____ our partner firm listened to our advice seriously, there wouldn't have been so many errors.

(A) Has
(B) Had
(C) If
(D) Unless

▶ 解答在136頁

Post-fact is a newly invented concept. It's not only a new word, but also a _____ of
                                                                                    121
an odd phenomenon. Now that the internet has been fully developed and is being used

widely, it is now a daily pattern for almost everyone to post their opinions, criticisms, or

judgments _____ various social network websites. However, _____ isn't equal
             122   123
to a fact. It's just your own thought which is based on your background, or previous

experiences. Through the widespread use of the internet, some people use these ways

to support your idea. When the amount of followers a person has reaches a considerable

number, then people start to believe that what he says is true rather than just see it as

someone's _____ idea. This phenomenon may result in severe consequences as the
             124
boundary between fact and opinion is blurred. This means we ought to be more cautious

about what information we accept as fact from the virtual world, and we have to think

about each piece of information rationally to avoid being misled.

121 (A) reflect
    (B) reflective
    (C) reflection
    (D) reflected

122 (A) in
    (B) on
    (C) at
    (D) with

123 (A) a well-documented theory
    (B) a sufficiently evident incident
    (C) a generally acknowledged phenomena
    (D) a subjectively personal idea

124 (A) careful
    (B) faithful
    (C) fanciful
    (D) thoughtful

▶ 解答在136頁

Part 07

快速解讀的
閱讀對應法！

學習法和問題類型的對應法

學習法

★ 平時多閱讀文章！

Part 7的題型是單篇閱讀測驗和多篇閱讀測驗。為了把對長篇文章的恐懼最小化和維持集中力的時間最大化，我們必須要接觸多元化的文章。比起做過的練習題數量，更重要的是，要透過多方閱讀培養豐富的詞彙能力和架構分析能力。

★ 充分活用網路、英語新聞和雜誌！

為了考多益，平時至少也要找些英語新聞、文章或字典來閱讀，這會比閱讀英文小說或是看美國連續劇更有幫助。常出現在多益裡的詞彙是international communication，也就是國際交流上常使用的內容，所以新聞文章（article）、廣告（advertisement）、信件或電子郵件（letter & e-mail）、公告（notice）、備忘錄（memorandum）、通知（annonucement）、簡訊（Message）、線上聊天（SMS）等是閱讀測驗常出的類型。這類的閱讀文章不好找，但是可利用網路搜索找出足以練習閱讀測驗的文章，當然能閱讀大量文章是最好的。

★ 語法請使用同義詞字典！

Part 7題目最常出現的題型之一就是文法，用不同的方式表現相同含義。這時使用同義詞辭典可以達到高效率，如同上面所說，也可以透過網路得到充分的資訊，多認識一些同義詞可讓你的語彙能力像雪球一樣愈滾愈大（snowball effect）。

Part7的閱讀學習法

閱讀測驗難道除了死背，就沒有別的方法了嗎？

1. Part 7 的問題構成

Part 7總共有54個題目，如下面由單篇和多篇閱讀測驗組成。

- 單篇閱讀測驗：29個問題（9-10篇文章）
- 多篇閱讀測驗：25個問題（5組文章）

聽力測驗進行45分鐘後即開始閱讀測驗，這時Part 5、6裡文法和語彙題有46題，接下來就是閱讀的部分，也就是Part 7。不過**請各位先做Part 7後，最後再來做Part 5、6。**

不論是誰，眼看著考試時間剩下20分鐘、10分鐘時，心中不免焦急萬分，像是Part 7這種長篇文章看也看不下去。考生也會因為不知所措而浪費了寶貴的10～20分鐘，這樣也很難拿到高分。

不過如果先解完Part 7後，將Part 5、6擺在後面，僅僅如此也能得到很大的效果。Part 5、6是由一篇篇短篇文章組成，解題解到後來時間即使剩不到10分鐘，也不至於到驚慌失措。甚至只剩1分鐘，也能解個2～3題。（Part 7是讀解型的題目，2～3分鐘基本上算是沒什麼幫助的時間吧？）所以在**做閱讀測驗的題目時，建議答題順序為Part 7 → Part 6 → Part 5較佳**。Part 6的閱讀測驗比Part 5稍長，因此才建議先做Part 6。**無論如何，結束聽力測驗後，一定要緊接著做Part 7！知道了嗎？**

來！一起來看看Part 7吧？總題數有54題，其中閱讀測驗之一的單篇文章題目有29題。單一文章的情況，每個文章都會有2～4題，整體來說一般有9篇文章。

大部分的考生們都抱怨Part 7時間不夠用。但只要提升實力，時間應該會夠用，依據上面的建議把聽力題目先做完後，依據Part 7 → Part 6 → Part 5的順序做題目的話，將更明顯感受到時間分配上會更游刃有餘。請一定要試試看！

2. 時間分配

（會因為考場有些微差異，以下時間皆是包含畫答案卡的時間。）

Part 1-4 聽力　　　　　　10：00 - 10：55分　（55分鐘，第1題～第100題）

Part 7 多篇文章閱讀　10：55 - 11：20分　（25分鐘，第176～200，每題組 5分）

Part 7 單篇文章閱讀　11：20 - 11：50分　（30分鐘，第147題～第175題，每題1分鐘）

Part 6 短文填空　　　　11：50 - 11：57分　（7分鐘，第131題～第146題，每題組1分45秒）

Part 5 單句填空　　　　11：57 - 12：10分　（13分鐘，第101題～第130題，每題26秒）

=總共120分鐘 + 考卷缺損檢查及direction的時間4分鐘，要答第101～110題

（手寫註記）55 min 內

（手寫註記）20 min 內

1 考試時間120分鐘以外，找出隱藏的4分鐘！

Part7在55分鐘內解完是最理想的（包含畫答案卡的時間。）想達到這樣的標準，必須要具備20分鐘內做完Part 5、6的實力。所以本書的前面一直在建議大家熟讀Part5、6，要訓練到平均每一題在30秒內解答。

不過事實上要在20分鐘內把Part5、6解決掉，不是一件容易的事。所以**將一些零碎的時間發揮最大的活用來解答Part5，這樣活用零碎的時間大概可以賺到4分鐘**。像這樣活用零碎時間的話，在其他考生只有20分可以解Part 5、6戰戰兢兢的同時，各位卻擁有24分鐘的時間，可以有比別人較寬鬆的時間做答Part 5、6。如此一來，Part 7的閱讀測驗部分結束後20分鐘（各位有24分鐘）左右的時間，來做Part 5、6就變得有可能啦。

2 分給Part 7 55分鐘！

依照上面的辦法，如果能在20分鐘（包含零碎時間共24分鐘）內做完Part 5、6的話，就可以有55分鐘解Part 7。Part 7總共有54個題目，每一個題目大約可以分配到1分鐘。如果有3題，就須在3分內；如果有5題就須在5分內讀完文章，包含做完題目。多篇文章閱讀測驗更需要花時間，所以單篇文章必須要在1分鐘以內做完。

總結說來，閱讀測驗100題的考試時間總共有75分鐘，因此在55分鐘內做完Part 7，其餘的20分鐘拿來做完Part 5、6，如此一來就萬事OK！請別忘了喔！時間剩太多也不好，時間不夠也不好。時間剩太多，也不會換成分數給你，因此不要管別人炫耀自己在考試時還剩多少時間，記得我們只看分數！請大家一定要熟悉我們這裡跟各位建議的時間管理要領，以後即使不看手錶也能把時間分配得恰恰好。最重要的是，要不斷地讓自己的身體熟悉時間管理的要領。

3. 為使Part 7得到高分的平時訓練

1. 累積背景知識

2. 透過閱讀培養單字量

* RFID是什麼，你知道嗎？ ◄─────────────

> 何謂RFID？Radio Frequency Identification的簡寫，是無線現金支付或是身分確認系統。（無線射頻自動識別系統）

對於考題出的閱讀測驗的背景有所了解的人，讀解速度才會快。RFID，你知道嗎？這是以前多益考題曾經出現過的字，當時考試結束後，一位考生這樣告訴我：「老師，有一題RFID我連文章都沒看，題目就都解完了。」托字典的福，對於RFID的背景說明很多、很詳細，所以閱讀測驗的文章沒有看也能一眼看到答案。

就是這個！在Part 7多累積背景知識的話，可以輕鬆解題。

這裡不是叫你把字典裡有關RFID的專門知識都背下來喔。是在告訴各位多接觸多益Part 7的例題文章，就可以在無形之中攝取並累積下五花八門的知識。

* 何謂real estate agent? ◄─────────────

> 不動產經紀人的意思。

擁有較強詞彙（單字量）能力的人，可以迅速地了解並接受文章的含義。
那要如何才能培養詞彙能力呢？要買單字書來背嗎？不是的，這樣累積的詞彙能力，就像沙灘上的城堡般地不堪一擊。最好的方式就是要靠平時邊閱讀時邊做整理的過程來累積。從實際文章中熟悉詞彙的話，該詞彙不論何時、以任何型態出現，也能馬上掌握它的意思。而且每次見到新的詞彙時，如果也能一起熟記字源和其他衍生出來的字，也是一個很好的方式，以這種方式來熟記單字，可以快速地兩倍、三倍的速度累積詞彙能力。

4. Part7解題的6大祕訣

1. 先看題目。
2. 此時先熟悉題目的類型。
3. 不必先看選項。
   （但是NOT／TRUE類型，或是推論型的題目須先看選項。）
4. 務必先確認文章內容可用選項內的何種單字替換。
5. 文章的最前面和最後面一定會各出一題。
6. 每篇文章作答結束時，須馬上畫答案卡。

1 先看題目

如果先看完題目，可依據題目的類型決定該挑哪一部分閱讀文章。當然，時間很充裕的人就不必挑著讀了，把文章全部讀完再解題也可以。不過大部分的人時間都不太夠，所以須要先看完題目，擬定適當的戰略。閱讀測驗的文章該看哪一部分，我們在題目類型的整理單元裡已經都整理好了。

2 先熟悉題目的類型

叫各位先看題目，不代表各位可以一個單字、一個單字地慢慢分析。在**多益考試中題目千萬不可以用分析的。必須要一眼就可以「啊！是這種題目類型！」**。舉例來說，What is this article mainly discussing?或是Why was this memo written?這類的題目出現時，看到的同時須馬上意會到「啊！這是問主題的題型！」，平時有記住題目的類型的話，在考場中是相當有利的。題目類型在下一個攻略將會另外詳細整理給大家。

3 不必先看選項（但是NOT／TRUE類型，或是推論型的題目須先看選項）

先看題目的叮嚀應該聽到不想聽了吧？那麼你是否連選項都先看了呢？其實沒有必要！因為即使先看了，在看文章時想不起來，還是得要再看一遍，**所以結論就是選項可以不必先看**。只要先看題目，依據題目的類型在文章中選取需要的部分閱讀後，再回到題目看選項選出正確答案，這是最有效率的解題辦法。

但是NOT／TRUE類型，或是推論型的題目須先看選項，會比較有幫助。這種類型的題目需要選項(A)到(D)一一和文章對照，所以先看過選項的話，就可很快地確認和文章是否適合。

4 務必先確認文章內容可用選項內的何種單字替換

在閱讀測驗的文章內使用的單字，不會一成不變地在選項答案中再度出現。所以選擇答案時，如果選擇的選項內有文章中出現過的單字時，十之八九是錯誤的。另外，在Part 7裡隨便看過就作答，反而會錯得更多。

中文不也一樣嗎？就算知道「ㄅㄆㄇㄈ」也是照著字發音念而已。但是只是照著念的話，也僅能說是朗讀而已，為了能讀並且了解長篇文章，平時就要多看、多讀閱讀測驗的文章。當然這種不是一天兩天就可以達成，所以平時就要投注時間和努力去累積實力。

所以**明明能閱讀文章、答案卻老是選錯的學生**，大多是不了解出現在選項的，其實是已經被改變過文章句子或單字，也就是所謂的同義語（paraphrasing），想真正了解同義異字的選項的話，詞彙能力歸詞彙能力，**平時多接觸些題目，就可以提升對同樣含義選項的理解能力**。

5 文章的最前面和最後面一定會各出一題

如果是找主題的題目類型，通常答案會出現在文章的最前面。找主題是出題率很高的題型。那麼文章最後面又是什麼呢？出題者都會希望考生可以把文章都看完，都費盡心思在出考題了，當然不會讓大家光看前面就都能解全部題目啦，所以都會在文章前後埋下伏筆，這是出題者的心理戰術。

所以**在閱讀測驗的文章最前面找主題；如果在文章的中間有解到一題的話，最後一題可以不用花太多精力在文章的中間部分找答案，看文章後面部分也可能解題**。這樣的解題要領在讓自己達到某些程度的習慣之後，將來會忽然發現自己以驚人的速度在長篇的文章內，循序地找到解答所在的地方。

6 每篇文章做答結束時，須馬上畫答案卡

舉例來說，如果一篇閱讀測驗有3個題目的話，3題都在考卷上作答後，將答案以「A、C、B」的方式記下來後，馬上在答案卡上畫記號。但是不是整個畫滿，是稍微做記號就好。

要小心避免發生因為一時失誤看錯一格，後面就全部錯的致命性錯誤。所以**每做完一篇閱讀測驗2到5個題目，就即時把答案畫到答案卡上，可減少失誤的機會**。

我的情況是單篇文章的題目都做完後，再一口氣把我之前在答案卡上稍微畫記號的答案畫滿。一方面是預防萬一失手畫錯答案，也是有讓自己在進入多篇文章前，稍微冷靜腦袋和心情的效果。實際上像這樣暫時的「上色學習」後，腦袋會變清晰，可集中在做多篇文章時的注意力，這是我的臨床實驗研究結果。

最後，多篇文章也是要分3階段畫答案卡。就是到176題都是要做完10題，再畫答案卡，到195題是每做完題目就畫答案卡，最後一個題組最後畫答案卡。這是我近6年以來，參加多益考試所找出的最佳方法。如果沒有自己的方法，又或者時間管理不佳的考生可試試看這方法，可看到很大的效果。

5. Part 7的2大煩惱

1 無法解釋翻譯的類型
　請用眼睛比較英文文章和中文翻譯，以及要如何翻譯？

2 可以翻譯，卻無法解題的類型
　試著各個題組以固定的時間作答（建議10個題組），養成仔細看題目的習慣。

1　無法完全翻譯！

若您還處在基礎的階段的話，請把文章和譯文同時攤開，一行一行對照解釋、翻譯。這樣一來邊「啊！原來這句話是這樣解釋的啊！」「啊！原來這個字組可以換成這樣說啊！」邊逐漸熟悉翻譯的方式。這裡要注意的是，不要被一個一個單字的解釋束縛。當細微部分的解釋累積到一定的實力時，會逐漸地更進一層樓。把重點放在閱讀測驗文章的整體流暢度，或是前後文的內容呼應較佳。

沒有人一開始就可以順利地一篇又一篇地翻譯長篇文章。這是必須通過能掌握整體流程的階段後，再透過更多的文章閱讀，逐漸累積出來的能力。但我們是在準備多益考試，而非翻譯練習，能夠完美的進行中英翻譯並非重點，重點在「理解文章」的內容。因此建議大家，首先還是要把焦點放在掌握文章整體的脈絡，認真地學習一個月後，就可以看到成效。

2 我能翻譯出來，但是無法解題！

能走出初級階段，是值得祝賀的事，不過怎麼覺得好像更加煩人了？倒不如連題目都翻不出來、看不懂，至少還可以說「啊！看不懂，可能無法解題了」，看得懂題目的內容，卻無法解題才是問題啊！又或者是題目翻譯完了，很有自信地認為是這個意思，也能解題了，偏偏看到答案又心猿意馬，這才真的是會讓人發瘋啊。

可以馬上告訴你，原因就是因為經驗不足。也就是說，雖然有英文的基礎，但還沒充分地接觸夠多的英文文章，閱讀測驗的題目也練習的不夠充分。請想想，我們中文考試裡也常有明明就了解題目在說什麼，要你馬上回答問題，卻答錯答案的情況。舉例來說，閱讀長篇的中文文章，如果題目問說「此篇文章整體屬於何種氣氛？」時，你回答「哲學的」，但正確答案卻是「辦公室嚴肅的氣氛」一樣。

所以**建議有這樣苦惱的考生們需要增加閱讀文章的量，還要培養細看內容的習慣**。平時閱讀文章的數量當然是愈多愈好，不過當然無法無上限地閱讀文章。若要提供指引的話，Part 7的54題為一個題組，至少要經歷過在時間內（55分鐘）做完10題組以上，並且還要徹底檢討的過程。

另外，**文章內的表現在選項內有經過些許轉換、變化時，要注意會有同義語出現的情況**。有些人會認為題目似乎是出得既偏頗、又冷門，應該是為了考試而出的題目，雖然可能大家覺得很討厭，但這裡要告訴大家，絕對不是這樣的！請想想看，多益不是為了職場人士所設計的考試嗎？在公司裡業務用的重要契約，中間有許多微妙的差異，如果誤解的話不就會招來極大的虧損嗎？如果出差錯的話，可能會被公司解雇。把這考試當作是避免發生問題所做的事前練習，心情應該會舒服一些。

6. 在Part 7最後的建議

Part 7的解題祕訣將會在下一個攻略裡告訴大家。不過請各位要記住的是，**在上面一大篇告訴各位鞏固基礎的方式，如果大家不願意照做的話，那麼即使多麼厲害的絕招還是沒有用**。基礎穩固的人，擁有解題祕訣就像是得到一對翅膀，可以盡情地翱翔在Part 7的上方。

各位！期待讀英文文章就像是在看中文文章般通順無阻，從下一個攻略開始，一起來細讀Part 7的作答具體方法。

專家的建議：真實考生的Part 7 研讀法

在3個月內讓你的分數從500分往975分Up！

○ TOEIC 成績確認／成績單分發

柳延錫的
2008年11月15日起2年內的成績。
最初線上成績單收受的期間與成績有效期間一樣。

成績單出次發行列印錯誤時，請於顧客服務中心網頁下留下發行錯誤相關文章後，
將於星期一（11月17日）早上9點以後盡速為您處理。
若是急件請利用成績單補發服務。

考試日期	准考證 編號	L/C	R/C	Total	Graph	Proficiency Description	成績單 初次發行	成績單 補發
2008.10.26	370693	480	495	975	▬▬▬▬ 975	▸確認	郵寄	申請
		會員您的第190回考試成績單初次發行方式已選擇使用郵寄方式寄送，將於成績公佈 後的97-10日送達。						

我的英文也不是很好，老師給了我這個機會，讓我在短期間內可以提升我的成績。希望對各位也有幫助。

Part 7要這樣學習！首先就**一天唸一課**。**掌握有哪些類型**後，會有許多幫助。要怎麼掌握呢？就是透過這些類型，去思考該如何解答實戰題目這類的問題。實際體驗過的結果就是這些題目真的很讚！成績也提升了不少。題目量其實不算很多，所以一定要**多複習幾次，類型分析也要一起進行**。

這部分結束後，**接下來就是要看實戰類型的書**。我是只看《全新制50次多益滿分的怪物講師TOEIC多益閱讀攻略＋模擬試題＋解析》和聽力篇這兩本而已。以我的情況來說，我光是《全新制50次多益滿分的怪物講師TOEIC多益閱讀攻略＋模擬試題＋解析》就**看了7遍**，聽力篇現在正在看第5遍。

一直反覆看實戰類型的書，別急著先要翻譯解釋出來。因為這樣一來就變成英文翻譯，不是掌握文章的內容了。請一定要**培養出掌握文章內容的能力**。複習時，要掌握各段落蘊含著哪些內容，看到哪些東西就可以找出答案，試著這樣重點式的學習。

以上這些大概就是Part 7的學習法，沒什麼特別的吧？剩下的就是各位的努力了。各位想想看，我只在3個月內就從500分提升到975分，我投入了多少的努力呢？是幾乎每天有16個小時都在唸書所得到的結果。我也希望各位能選擇好教材、好的課程，考到好成績。也感謝各位把我這篇微不足道的內容看完。

柳延錫敬上

各類型題目的解題法

知道題目類型就拿到一半的機會！

Part 7要先看題目，且依據題目的類型，要快速地找出對應方法。

1. 找主題的題目類型

1 What is the purpose [objective, aim] of this memo?

2 Why was this letter written?

3 What is the topic of this article?

4 What is the main idea of this report?

5 What does the notice mainly discuss? 討論

6 What made James write this letter?

  * What made = Why

1 這備忘錄的目的是什麼？
2 這信件為何而寫？
3 這文章的主題是什麼？
4 這份報告的主題是什麼？
5 這通知主要在討論什麼？
6 詹姆士為什麼要寫這封信？

上面就是找主題類型。在多益考試中，找主題的題型十有八九在文章的前半部份可以找到答案。這個一定要記住，**主題在前面尋找，特別是像下面的句子會把主題點出來，這就是重要的關鍵。**

→ 解法： 主題請在閱讀測驗文章的前面部份找。

找主題類型的問題裡，下面的表現方式就是找出解答的關鍵！

• Re: 或是 RE: → regarding（與…有關）的簡寫，暗示主題——在e-mail等裡

• Subject → 用「主旨」直接告訴大家主題內容的關鍵——在e-mail等裡

• 文章標題：→最上面的中間，用深色和較大的字體標示著——廣告文等

• in order to 原形動詞：→「為了…」的意思，表示文章的目的或是理由的關鍵，也可能以「so as to + 原形動詞」或是「to + 原形動詞」方式表現——信件等

• I'm writing in regard to...（正在寫與…相關的信）

• This is a letter to + 原形動詞（這是因為…而寫的信）

• I am pleased to + 原形動詞（因為做到了…而感到高興）

- I am writing to inquire [apologize, confirm]（我為了問／道歉／確認寫了封信）
  （一般寫在信件的開頭）

- This is in part due to （這是部分因為…）
  = Because S + V, S + V（直接說出主題的方式）

- 閱讀測驗文章第三句 → 在找主題的題目。如果文章裡沒有上述的關鍵，大部分
  讀完文章前面的第三句後，也可以找到答案（但是報導（article）類型的文章就
  不要這麼斷然確認答案，可以先從其他題目先做後，最後再來思考主題為何。）

2.「期望…的是？」的題目類型

1 **What** does Richards Street **want [= require, ask]** Emilie Green **to do**?

2 **What** should employees **do** if they wish to get reimbursed?

1 理查・史崔想要艾蜜麗・葛林做什麼？

2 如果職員們希望得到賠償的話，需要做什麼？

What...want [require, ask]...to do? **「期望…的是？」這類型的特徵，大部分答案都會出現在文章的最後**。這類型的問題出現時，在閱讀測驗的文章後半部裡找出下面的表現，就可以找出答案。

→ 解法：要求的事項在文章的後面部份。

「期望…的是？」這類型出現下面的表現方式就是解答！

- 命令句 →「Please + 原形動詞」型態，「請做…」是直接表現

- I want you to do（希望你做…）→ 也可用would like取代want

- You are asked to do （你應該要…）→ 可用required、obliged、advised取代asked

- You had better + 原形動詞（最好可以做…）→ 直接命令句，常見用You'd better 簡寫

- Could [Would] you please...?（能幫我做…嗎？）謙遜地請求

- It might be better if you...（如果能幫我…的話，那就好了）禮貌性地請求

- Why don't you...?（你覺得做…如何呢？）勸誘

- I would be grateful if you（如果你做…的話，我會感到感謝）→ 非常慎重地請求

3. 找key word的題目類型

1 What is the subscriber asked to do **by Friday**?

2 What is the **main duty of James Buchanon**?

3 How much can be **saved** from the **total amount of $32,000**?

1 訂閱者要求到星期五前要做什麼？

2 詹姆士‧布坎南的主要職務是什麼？

3 能從總額3萬2千元中省下多少？

這是考試最常出的類型。看到題目時，**要先記下題目的**key word**，然後邊讀閱讀測驗的文章時，就可以「啊！這是和第幾題有關！」邊找出答案**。如果不這樣，要先認真看完文章後，再去看題目，然後又再去看文章找答案，這樣一來，又陷入了時間不夠的老問題裡了。

那麼要怎麼看出題目的key word呢？大部分的key word都是動詞或是名詞。動詞和名詞在英文句子裡傳達重要的訊息，裡面也包含了文章的重要核心資訊，所以最重要的就是要留意動詞和名詞。除此之外，**數字或是字母大寫等也都扮演著**key word**的重要角色**，所以問題裡如果有數字或是大寫字母，若能找到閱讀測驗的文章裡和問題相對應的數字或大寫字母，應該就可以解決問題了。要在全都是英文字母的文章裡，找出數字或是大寫字母不是一件難事。

→ **解法：有問題出現過的**key word**的地方就是關鍵！**

遇到找key word的類型，試著用眼睛去搜尋題目裡的核心動詞或名詞，又或者是數字或大寫字母，就可以輕易解題。

4. NOT / TRUE的題目類型

1 What is NOT a thing that participants can anticipate?

2 What is TRUE according to the job requirement?

1 什麼是參加者不能期待的？

2 如果依據工作資格，哪一個是真的？

這就是題目裡有大寫NOT「不是…的是？」，或是TRUE「哪一個是事實？」的問題類型。這時**別和其他類型一樣看完問題就去看文章，要連問題的選項都看完，並記住以後才去看文章**，要這樣才方便和文章內容做對照。此時，如果選項和文章都差不多的話，很多選項都在小地方設有陷阱，必須要小心。特別是選項內容在文章內從未出現過，又或者是雖然有出現過，但內容和文章內容不一樣的，千萬別純粹因為自己的直

覺判斷，就決定它是答案。像這樣自己判斷，或是憑直覺去解題的話，答對率是很低的。

所以在NOT / TRUE的題型，建議初學者還是要多注意有標點符號和使用記號的部份，這祕訣在廣告文裡是相當受用的。因為NOT / TRUE類型中，常出現有很多逗號表示有列舉許多東西，或是標上記號表示列舉等題目。找出這些部份，一一對照選項也能找出答案。

NOT / TRUE的題型是初學者很難拿分數的類型之一。多益Part 7必須要用相當少的時間，幾乎是要每段文章只能花一分鐘解題。且在解NOT / TRUE的題型時，必須要避開各種陷阱，找出正確的解答，是很容易陷入迷思的題目類型。**對初學者來說，直接跳過NOT / TRUE的題型也不失為一種方法。**

→ **解法：**NOT / TRUE的類型一定要連問題的選項都要看完後，才能與文章對照。**特別是廣告文的情況，答案常常在逗號很多或是羅列的部份裡可以找到。**

5. 找場所、職業和文章對象的類型

1 Where can this advertisement be placed?

2 Who is the intended reader of this article?

1 這廣告是刊登在哪裡？

2 誰是這篇文章預設的讀者？

文章的背景場所在哪、作者的職業是什麼、或是這篇文章是以誰為對象…等，這些可以看成是同一種類型。因為場所可以顯示作者的職業或是對象的身分。（假設場所是餐廳，一個當醫生的角色就幾乎不會出現在這裡。）當然文章裡不會具體說出這裡是哪裡，誰的職業是什麼，這篇文章是以誰為對象而寫的。那我們該怎麼判斷呢？

有些**特定的單字會成為重要的端倪**。例如luggage（行李）、check in（登錄）、boarding pass（登機證）、customs（海關）等單字出現的話，解答可以聯想到airport。即使出現這樣的題目，也可以在閱讀完文章後順利解答。而且這個技巧在聽力測驗也可以適用。

→ **解法：**遇到找場所和職業類型的題目時，**找出特定詞彙即可找到端倪輕鬆解題。**

6. 確認收件人和寄件者的類型

> • Who most likely is the sender of this e-mail?

問信件或是e-mail裡的收件人和寄件人的題目很常見。這時文章裡稱作I的就是寄件人，稱呼為you的就是收件人。在信件上方和下方就可以找出信件的寄件人和收件人的資訊。

→ **解法：遇到問收件者或寄件人的題型，信件或是e-mail的上方和下方可以找到寄件人和收件者的資訊，這時稱作I的就是寄件人，稱呼為you的就是收件人。**

7. 問一起寄送物品的類型

> **1** What is with this letter?
>
> **2** What is enclosed with this <u>estimate</u>?

1 和這封信一起的東西有什麼？

2 和這報價單一起封起來的東西是什麼？

這種題型常出現在信件、e-mail或通知文裡。若是出現這類型的題目時，馬上看**文章的前面或後面（特別是後面）裡出現的**enclosed（封入的）、attached（附件的）、send along（一起寄出）**等表現方式**。這樣會比別人快一步找到答案。

→ **解法：找出閱讀測驗的文章後面enclosed、attached的表現方式。**

8. 找同義語的類型

> • What is the closest in meaning to the word 'amenities' in line 7 of the second paragraph?

哪一個答案和第二段第七行的「amenities」意思最接近？

在閱讀測驗裡，一般會出現1到2個這類型的問題。這時**和整體內容無關，只要知道這單字本身的意思就可以解題**。也就是說文章裡出現amenities（舒適的設施）的話，選擇選項中的comfort（舒服）就可以了。

一般來說，大部分如果文章裡使用的詞彙很簡單的話，選項的詞彙就會很艱澀；如果文章使用的詞彙較困難的話，答案的選項就會比較簡單。平時透過英英字典多多累積同義字和反義字，在這裡會有極大的幫助。

舉例來說，單字leave有「離開」、「留下」和「休假」等多種意思，像這樣有多種意思的英文單字要找同義字時，必須要確認這單字在文章內所使用的意思，然後在選項中找出正確的答案。

→ 解法：找同義字的類型有兩種，一種是單字本身很困難，與文章無關，要找出和該單字同意思的答案。另一種是單字本身不難，但有多種意思，要找出與文章內所使用的意思相同意義的單字。平時透過英英字典學習同義字、反義字可看到很大的效果，而英英字典在英語學習中也有多方面的獲益效果。請多加利用。

9. 推論型

• What can be inferred from this article?

從這文章內可推論出什麼？

這是不容易回答的題目類型。因為閱讀測驗文章裡的敘述都拐彎抹角，用題目的選項來提示，但**選項裡包含了幾乎全部的文章內容，要選出答案真的要耗盡心思和花費許多時間。**

所以**建議初學者們如果遇到這類的題目，先跳過去做其他的題目。等到有中級以上的實力後再來挑戰**。而且這題型的選項都要一一細讀後，選出與文章內容一分不差的答案，偏偏大部分的選項在乍看之下，都好像是正確解答，但再仔細看，又會在一些小地方發現差異。

→ 解法：推論型的題目都要選出與文章內容完全符合的選項，即使有一丁點內容和文章不符合就無法成為解答。這類型的題目一定要先看完選項後，再來看文章。

10. 多篇文章對照類型

• Comparing the two articles, what is NOT true?

比較兩篇文章後，哪一個不是事實？

一個題組有5個問題，通常會有一個問題是必須要閱讀完每篇文章，融會貫通後才能解答的高層次題型。**這種類型是要成為閱讀測驗達人以後才有辦法做的類型，所以建議初學者先跳過去做其他的題目**。想緊抓這題目跟它拼的話，也只是浪費時間，讓自己的壓力更大而已，對精神上反而更不好。

如果是已經做過很多閱讀測驗的人，看到這種多篇對照類型的題目就可以馬上知道，「啊！這種就是要將第一篇和第二篇（或第三篇）文章作

聯繫後才能解的題目！」沒錯！做這種題目的關鍵就是要快速地且正確地找出可以聯繫多篇文章的環節。

→ 解法：遇到多篇對照類型的題目時，**建議初學者先跳過去做其他的題目。注意第3、4題，一定要找出可聯繫上下篇文章的環節，正確地判斷後快速解答。**

11. 十有八九的答案就在轉換語句中

• By the way	不過
• However	可是
• Unfortunately,	不幸地
• I'm afraid that...	對that以下表遺憾

在經驗上，**文章內出現上面的表現時，那附近至少會隱藏著一個解答。**因為和前面說的不一樣，而又是說話者真的很想做的部份。在出題者的立場上，是想測試考生們到底有沒有消化這部份的內容。

→ 解法：**出現轉換語句的however、unfortunately時，後面有解答！**

12. 同義詞（paraphrasing）

在閱讀測驗的文章裡使用過的話，絕對不會原封不動地再度出現在答案選項裡。所以常常看得懂文章卻找不到答案的人，一定要注意paraphrasing的部份。也就是說，**文章內出現的表現（phrase）在選項裡找出類似（para）的答案。**

→ 解法：**請留意paraphrasing。選項大部分都是轉換成其他的表達方式了。**

❶ **意義的擴大和縮小**
　→ 閱讀測驗裡的He likes soccer.在選項裡變成了He likes sports.。

❷ **簡單的單字和艱澀的單字之對比**
　→ 閱讀測驗裡的outfit（全套裝備、全套服裝）在選項裡變成了clothes（衣服、衣類）。

❸ **活用同義字、反義字的paraphrasing**
　→ 平時多使用英英字典會得到許多幫助。

下面會介紹paraphrasing代表性的例子，別忘了**在閱讀測驗中出現的用法，都會以這種同義的狀態出現**。英英字典在提升paraphrasing的實力時是一個不錯的工具。

閱讀測驗的表現	paraphrasing的表現
chicken 雞	▶ poultry products 家禽類（雞、鴨等）製品
limousine service 接送服務	▶ transportation service 運送、交通服務
dry-cleaning service 乾洗服務	▶ laundry service 洗衣服務
regular price 定價	▶ usual price, sticker price 定價
uniform 制服	▶ clothes which must be worn by employees on duty 工作場合裡給員工穿的衣服
books 書	▶ reading materials 閱讀的東西
submit 提出	▶ hand in = turn in 提出
I, you （信件、e-mail等）	▶ I = 確認是寄件者資訊 you = 需再確認收件人資訊
name 任命	▶ hire = employ 提出
stockholders 股東	▶ shareholders 股東
want to come back 期望再回來	▶ readmission 重新接納
two months 兩個月	▶ over a month 一個月以上
everyday 每天	▶ daily, once a day 一天一次
every week 每週	▶ weekly, once a week 一週一次
every month 每月	▶ monthly, once a month 一個月一次
every quarter 每季	▶ quarterly, once a quarter 每季一次
every year 每年	▶ yearly = annually, once a year 一年一次

13. 簡訊及即時通訊常用縮寫類型

簡訊及即時通訊比起一般商業書信或email雖然較為輕鬆，但是有其常用詞彙縮寫，像是：

❶ **AFAIk = as far as I know 就我所知**
AFAIK, he won't show up. 就我所知他不會出現。

❷ **ASAP = as soon as possible 儘早**
I need the data. A.S.A.P. 我需要資料，愈快愈好。

❸ **B4 = before 之前**
Can we meet B4 noon? 我們可以在中午前見面嗎？

❹ **BFN = by for now 先這樣**
BFN. See you tonight. 先這樣，今天晚上見。

❺ **BRB = be right back 馬上回來**
BRB. I need to talk to John first.
馬上回來，我必須先跟約翰說個話。

❻ **BTW = by the way 順便一提**
By the way, who's the lady doing exporting in Hong Kong that talked to us last week?
順便一提，那位上星期跟我們說在香港做出口的女士是誰？

❼ **CU = see you 再見**

❽ **FYI = for your information 讓你知道一下**
For your information, I reschedule my appointment with Chairman Lee. 讓你知道一下，我重新安排了跟李董事長的會面時間。

❾ **GTG = got to go 該走了**
GTG. My phone is ringing. 該走了，電話在響。

❿ **IMO = in my opinion 依我看**
IMO, we are very likely to succeed. 依我看，我們很可能成功。

⓫ **LOL = laugh out loud 大聲笑**
LOL! This is interesting. （大笑！）太有趣了。

⓬ **PLZ = please 請**
Phone me PLZ. 請打電話給我

⓭ **PPL = people**
PPL are expecting the launch of our new product.
人們很期待我們新產品的上市。

⓮ **TY = thank you.**

TY. I appreciate very much. 謝謝，我很感激。

⓯ **U = you**

U are what we are looking for. 我們找的就是你。

簡訊及即時通訊，因為講求快速，所以經常使用縮寫或是表情文字（emoji）來表達，而不完整拼出一個字，**解題技巧為從上下文去探究縮寫字彙的意思。**

例如，PLZ let's reschedule our meeting.看到reschedule就了解必須重新安排時間，可以進一步了解PLZ = please。另外**縮寫字大多以發音為原則**，多唸幾次PLZ就會發出please的音。如果縮寫字並非考題中的關鍵點，也可以稍稍略過，直接看懂簡訊或即時通訊中重要訊息即可，在此只要懂let's reschedule our meeting，PLZ看不懂，不會嚴重地影響對內容的理解。

14. 詢問句子插入位置

必須了解要插入句子的意思，再運用邏輯整體理解，找出適當插入位置，節省閱讀時間，加快速度。

每個句子在段落中都有功能性在，可以依據邏輯功能大略分成三類：

❶ **主題句**（topic sentences）

❷ **支持性論述**（supporting arguments）

❸ **轉折句**（transition sentences）

❹ **結論句**（concluding sentences）

1 主題句

→ **重點：說明討論或提供立場，吸引讀者注意。**

> **1** A great leader requires several characteristics.
>
> **2** Pets help us live longer because with a pet, you will feel better.
>
> **3** With this carbon emission calculator, companies can calculate greenhouse emission they emit.
>
> **4** Here are effective marketing strategies for small companies on a tight budget.
>
> **5** Benefits for us to travel include finding a new purpose in life and at work.

1 偉大的領袖需要有一些特徵。

2 寵物讓我們更長壽，因為養寵物，會讓你感覺更好。

3 使用這個碳排放計算器，公司可以計算他們所排放的溫室氣體。

4 這些有效的行銷策略，對小型並且預算較緊縮的公司很有幫助。

5 旅行的好處包括找到生活與工作的新意義。

主題句為新的想法，通常使用主動語態與現在式。

2 支持性論述

→ **重點：根據場景與邏輯，判斷句子是否用來提供更多資訊及範例等做為支持用。**

常使用的範例句子如下：

• **統計結果**

Slow traffic speed reduces the number of car accidents each year.

速度較慢的交通減低了每年車禍數字。

- 範例

Working for longer hours does not add up to productivity since your brain can only focus for a certain period of time.

長時工作不表示會增加生產力，因為你的大腦只能在特定時間內保持集中力。

- 專家意見

Many business leaders said they would not have been so successful if they had not learned local languages.

如果之前沒學過當地語言，許多商業領袖都說他們現在不會這麼地成功。

3 轉折句

→ 重點：轉折句會由一定的次詞片語或副詞所帶領。

- 表示同意及補充意見

not only... but also 不僅…也…   similarly 相同地

additionally... 此外   by the same token 同樣地

moreover, furthermore 再者

- 表示反對及不同

although... yet 雖然…但是   at the same time 同時

on the contrary 相對地   whereas 儘管

despite, in spite of 儘管…

- 表示因果和目的

in the event that 在…時   owing to 因為

provided that 但是   in view of 因為

for the purpose of 基於…目的

- 表示強調

in other words 換句話說   notably 特別是

that is to say 也就是說   in this case 在此情況下

namely 即

- 表示時間順序

at the present time 目前來說   until now 到目前為止

hence 因此   shortly 不久之後

all of a sudden 突然   whenever 不論何時

- 表示空間

  here 在此　　　　　　　　adjacent to 鄰近

  behind 之後　　　　　　　opposite to 對面

  in the center of 中心處

依據句子的描述判斷是否為轉折功能，再放入適當位置。

4　結論句

→ 重點：結論句的特色為摘述論點、重覆之前提過的重要概念和單字與使用結論用語結束段落及文章。

- 摘述論點

  A strong ethics is important for companies.

  強力的倫理對公司很重要。

- 重覆之前提過的重要概念

  Our worldwide community contribution activities demonstrate our global corporate citizenship.

  我們全世界的社區回饋活動展現了我們的全球公民身份。

- 使用結論用片語

  Finally, we cannot generalize individual's learning.

  我們不能概化每個人的學習。

  It is agreed that workers deserve the right to work safely.

  大家都同意勞工應該有安全工作的權利。

- 作為結論用的片語還包括：

  as a result... 因此…　　　　it can be seen that 可以視為

  therefore... 因此…　　　　　the evidence suggests that 證據顯示

  otherwise... 否則…

因為已經是結論，通常不會再有細微的資訊和數字出現，常見的是**總結及重覆之前提過的重要資訊和概念**。

多閱讀，提升理解力，確實了解句意，並且依據上下段落中的邏輯，才有辦法適時地將句子放入正確位置。

信件和電子郵件

信件（Letter）

★ 信件的閱讀測驗內容

❶ 委託（委託演講或是講課）

❷ 拒絕或接受委託

❸ 通知文（受獎、合併案、會議、瓦斯或水管的檢查確認等）

❹ 抱怨文（訂購商品的延遲到貨、申請書的錯誤、店員態度）

❺ 抱怨文的回信（對於抱怨的處置措施）

❻ 催繳文（應繳金額超過期限未支付）

❼ 投履歷時的附件資料

❽ 錄取通知（確認工作條件等）

★ 信件的出題內容

❶ What is mentioned in the letter? 信件中提及什麼？

❷ What is NOT mentioned in the letter? 信件中未提及什麼？

❸ What is the main purpose of this letter? 此封信的主要目的為何？

電子郵件（E-mail）

★ 電子郵件的閱讀測驗內容

❶ 會議結果、公司內部的聯絡事項

❷ 訂購和寄送的確認事項

❸ 與銀行往來等的聯絡

★ 電子郵件的出題內容

❶ What can be inferred from the e-mail? 從電子郵件中可以推論什麼？

❷ What is mentioned in the e-mail? 電子郵件中提及什麼？

❸ What is NOT mentioned in the e-mail? 電子郵件中未提及什麼？

❹ What does A suggest B do? A對B建議了什麼？

攻略法

92

信件（Letter）

Part 7絕大部分都是信件或電子郵件！

信件和電子郵件在多益考試Part 7裡佔了將近45%的出題比例，也就是說只要徹底了解信件和電子郵件的出題型態，做好準備，就能拿到Part 7的大部分分數，所以信件和電子郵件是在閱讀測驗中最重要的部份。

首先，我們先來看信件。信件的最上方是寄件人的住址，下面是收件人的姓名、職銜和住址等，這樣的標示形式是信件類型的特有格式，所以清楚了解信件的特有格式是非常重要的。

1. 信件文章的類型

信件類型的閱讀測驗會出何種文章呢？先了解信件中會出現什麼樣的文字，可以加快解題速度。盡可能接觸各種類型的信件型文章，雖然將讀過的類型都輸入到腦海中，但是還是要節省時間吧！我來幫你節省時間。**一般信件分為公司對公司、公司對個人、個人對個人…等，一般來說，個人對個人的格式不會出現在題目中。**

1 公司對公司信件

產品說明、大會或座談會等活動內容、錯誤訂正、事故、要求、公司與交易所間的業務內容…等等。

2 公司對個人信件

委託求職、選擇人員、檢查、產品或費用、服務等的抱怨問題、合約終止及延長、產品優惠購買的內容、升遷內容、新業務的訊息、慈善活動的募款、訂購物品及寄送相關疑問…等等。

2. 信件文字的類型

1 詢問信件的主題或目的類型（引導部分）

• I'm writing in regard to...
• This is a letter to...
• I am pleased to...
• I am writing to inquire / apologize / confirm...

寫封與…相關的信件給您。

這是為了…的信件。

我很高興…。

為了詢問／道歉／確認而寫
了這封信。

2 詢問收件人和寄件人的類型

從信件的上方和下方可以得到收件人和寄件人的住址，這時候一定要寄
記信件中的I是寄件人，you是收件人。如果直接提到名字時，那就不是
I，也不是you的第三人了。

3 詢問信件中提及的人物的類型
4 詢問細部資訊的類型
5 需透過推論解決的類型

3. 信件內文字的處理要領

1 須確實區分寄件人和收件人！（名字、職銜、I和you的關係等）
2 閱讀選項以外的題目後，記住key word。
3 先熟悉問題類型後，馬上找出在信件中出現的位置。
4 信件最前面和最後面的客套話可以省略不看。

4. 怪物講師的解法

請依照下一頁的指示事項的編號順序解解看。記住，一定要先看題目。
大部分的信件類型都可以照下面的解法進行。

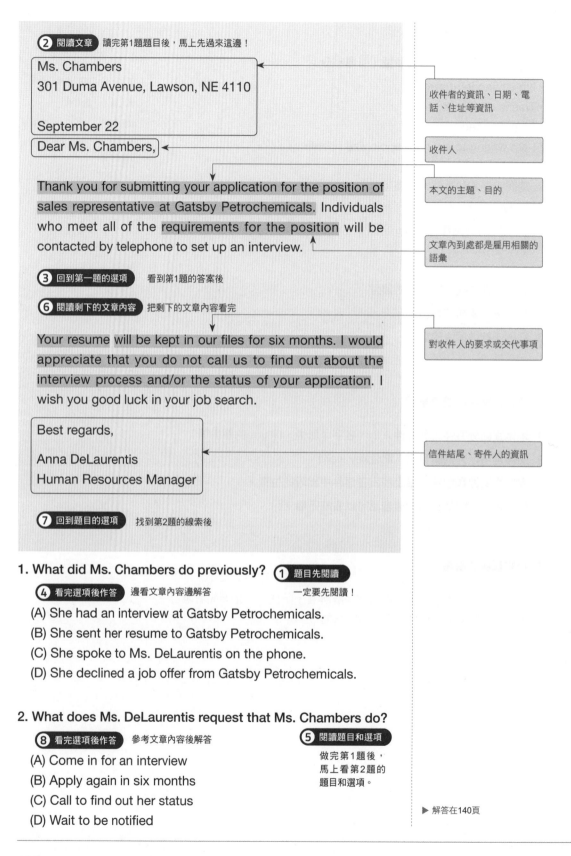

② 閱讀文章　讀完第1題題目後，馬上先過來這邊！

Ms. Chambers
301 Duma Avenue, Lawson, NE 4110

September 22

收件者的資訊、日期、電話、住址等資訊

Dear Ms. Chambers,

收件人

Thank you for submitting your application for the position of sales representative at Gatsby Petrochemicals. Individuals who meet all of the requirements for the position will be contacted by telephone to set up an interview.

本文的主題、目的

文章內到處都是雇用相關的語彙

③ 回到第一題的選項　看到第1題的答案後

⑥ 閱讀剩下的文章內容　把剩下的文章內容看完

Your resume will be kept in our files for six months. I would appreciate that you do not call us to find out about the interview process and/or the status of your application. I wish you good luck in your job search.

對收件人的要求或交代事項

Best regards,

Anna DeLaurentis
Human Resources Manager

信件結尾、寄件人的資訊

⑦ 回到題目的選項　找到第2題的線索後

1. What did Ms. Chambers do previously? ① 題目先閱讀

④ 看完選項後作答　邊看文章內容邊解答　　一定要先閱讀！

(A) She had an interview at Gatsby Petrochemicals.
(B) She sent her resume to Gatsby Petrochemicals.
(C) She spoke to Ms. DeLaurentis on the phone.
(D) She declined a job offer from Gatsby Petrochemicals.

2. What does Ms. DeLaurentis request that Ms. Chambers do?

⑧ 看完選項後作答　參考文章內容後解答　　⑤ 閱讀題目和選項

做完第1題後，馬上看第2題的題目和選項。

(A) Come in for an interview
(B) Apply again in six months
(C) Call to find out her status
(D) Wait to be notified

▶ 解答在140頁

5. 讓Part7變簡單的句子分析

> **1** Individuals who meet all of the requirements for the position will be contacted by telephone to set up an interview.

符合那職位所有資格的人們／將會接到電話通知／來安排面試。

本文的限定動詞是什麼？是meet還是will be contacted？還是set up？前面雖然有學過，這邊還是再提醒句子的限定動詞只能有一個。剩下的是連接詞子句的動詞，或是動狀詞。在這邊有幾個連接詞呢？是的，沒錯。主格關係代名詞who一個。Individuals是先行名詞。主詞（Individuals）的動詞，也就是限定動詞在哪裡？後面的will be contacted就是限定動詞了。

Individuals / who meet / all of the requirements / for the position /
　主詞　　　主詞 關係詞　　　　受詞　　　　　　　受詞介系詞子句
will be contacted / by telephone / to set up an interview.
　限定動詞（被動）　　　介系詞子句　　　to不定詞（副詞的用法）-動狀詞

> **2** I would appreciate that you do not call us to find out about the interview process and/or the status of your application.

我會很感謝／你不要打給我們／來了解面試過程／或者你的申請狀況。

這個句子看起來很長吧？但是本句是可以整理為「主詞＋動詞＋受詞」的第3大句型。主詞是I，限定動詞是would。決定了主詞和動詞，現在只剩下受詞了。別太驚訝。appreciate後面的that子句，整個都是受詞。這邊的that是扮演名詞角色的名詞子句連接詞，把to find out當作是修飾動詞call的to不定詞的副詞用法即可，解釋為「為了…」。

I / would appreciate / that you do not call us / to find out /
主詞　　　限定動詞　　　名詞子句 連接詞 完整句　　　to不定詞
about the interview process / and/or / the status of your application.
　　　介系詞子句　　　　　　對等連接詞　　　　　名詞

Chapter 22_ 信件和電子郵件　**441**

(1) Single Passages

Questions 1-2 refer to the following letter.

Personnel Director
Metatron Software
Route de Moncor 14 - PO Box 49
Switzerland

Dear Sir or Madam,

I am writing to express my interest in the position of senior programmer posted on Metatron's website. As I indicate on my enclosed resume, I previously worked for over 10 years as a programmer at O.G.Soft, where I was involved in the development of many of its applications. Among other projects, I was the primary designer on its best-selling spreadsheet software CalQLate. In addition to overseeing a team of software programmers, my duties at O.G.Soft included programming new applications, maintaining and updating existing software, and quality testing.

I look forward to discussing this employment opportunity with you in person. Thank you for your time and consideration.

Sincerely,

Cecil Vyse
Cecil Vyse

---

1 What is indicated about CalQLate?

(A) It took 10 years to develop.
(B) It is sold out.
(C) It was commercially successful.
(D) It was produced by Metatron.

2 In which area does the writer NOT have experience, according to the letter?

(A) Marketing computer accessories
(B) Managing employees
(C) Conducting quality tests
(D) Creating software

▶ 解答在140頁

Questions 3-5 refer to the following letter.

Von Dreyer Medical Supply
Markplatz 7, 74072 Heilbronn, Germany

October 19, 2017

Mr. Adrian Coyne
Northview Apartments 388
400 Ritalynn Circle
Norman OK 73019-0390

Dear Adrian,

As discussed following your interview on October 15, we are pleased to offer you a one-year contract of employment at Von Dreyer Medical Supply. The position will commence on November 1 and continue until October 31 next year.

The yearly salary for the position is $42,000. In addition to public holidays, you are entitled to two weeks' paid vacation. You will also receive medical and dental coverage.

On your first morning at work, please report to Chad Finn in the personnel department at 9:00. He will explain the benefits and working conditions in detail and provide a copy of your contract for your files. You will also be expected to sign a confidentiality agreement, which will be prepared for you by Chad.

We look forward to having you on the team.

Maureen Hughes
Maureen Hughes
Vice-President of Operations

3 When will Adrian begin working at Von Dreyer?

(A) October 15
(B) October 19
(C) October 31
(D) November 1

4 What is NOT stated in the letter?

(A) The duration of Adrian's contract
(B) The amount of vacation time Adrian will receive
(C) The department Adrian will work for
(D) The benefits Adrian will receive

5 What will Adrian have to do on the first day, according to this letter?

(A) Agree to keep company secrets
(B) Submit a personnel report
(C) Receive a medical check-up
(D) Prepare a presentation

▶ 解答在140頁

(2) Double Passages

Questions 6-10 refer to the following invitation and letter.

You are invited to join
James Leem, personal investor and
Chief Executive Officer at JL Financial,
for a Black Tie event
at the Pink Horizon Inn and Spa
on the banks of the PacificOcean.

Guests will enjoy an internationally-acclaimed three-course meal,
after which they will be treated to
a sunset cruise on the ocean.

For those who would like to stay the night,
one night's accommodation for two
has been reserved for each guest.
Each couple will also receive a voucher for the spa,
all courtesy of Mr. Leem.

This evening is for Preferred Clients only:
thank you for referring over 10 new clients to Mr. Leem this year.

Kindly RSVP by June 21
to Mr. Leem's secretary.

Ms. Jasmine Park

JL Financial

135-283 Seoul

KOREA

Dear Ms. Park,

Thank you for the invitation to Mr. Leem's Black Tie event. I must say I was quite surprised to receive it. It is the first time I have been recognized in this way by an investment banker. It will certainly encourage me to remain a "Preferred Client." Smart business move!

Unfortunately, I am unable to attend the event due to a prior business engagement. Because I am the sole proprietor of my business, I am kept quite busy, and I will be out of the country the night of the event. My wife is also sorry she will miss out the evening and cannot see Mrs. Leem.

I wonder if we will be invited next year to make up for our absence this year. I would be honored to attend another time, if this is the sort of thing Mr. Leem does regularly. In future, I need at least two months' notice instead of three weeks in order to make a commitment to an event such as this one.

Thank you again for the invitation. We are pleased with our decision to invest with Mr. Leem and look forward to meeting you in the future.

Regards,

Daniel Sujek

President, Sujek Consulting

6 What is the purpose of the event?

(A) To thank clients for their business
(B) To attract new customers to invest
(C) To celebrate James Leem's success
(D) To recognize referrals made by clients

7 What can be inferred about the event from the letter?

(A) It is a unique way to grow business.
(B) It includes only sole proprietors.
(C) It is being poorly organized.
(D) It only happens once every year.

8 Why is Daniel Sujek unable to attend?

(A) He has a business meeting.
(B) His wife cannot attend.
(C) He will be out of town.
(D) He did not have enough notice.

9 Who is Jasmine Park?

(A) James Leem's secretary
(B) Daniel Sujek's wife
(C) An investor at JL Financial
(D) The receptionist at Pink Horizon

10 Why is Daniel Sujek surprised by the invitation?

(A) It is the first time he has been recognized for referring clients.
(B) The invitation arrived only three weeks before the event.
(C) His wife is not normally invited to attend recognition events.
(D) Recognition events are not normally held at spa resorts.

▶ 解答在140頁

93 電子郵件（E-mail）

最近是E-mail的天下！

和信件常出現在多益Part 7的題目中的就是電子郵件。和信件差不多，不過硬要比較的話，電子郵件的形式比信件稍微不那麼格式化。**信件和電子郵件加起來幾乎佔了Part 7閱讀測驗的45%，屬常出類型**，請一定要熟悉。

最近Part 7的文章讓考生們很頭痛，電子郵件也是其中之一，內容本身雖不難，但是文章內容很多，讓閱讀的部份難易度上升，導致考生時間不夠用。

1. E-mail的主要內容

所有方面看來和信件都很類似，但相較之下不死板，語氣較為輕鬆、簡短的文字構成。也不像信件的客套話冗長，或幾乎沒有客套話，簡單來說就是內容較簡略。

1 公司對公司的E-mail
   商品廣告、道歉、活動訊息、錯誤訂正、要求等

2 公司對個人的E-mail
   委託求職、邀請、感謝、商品抱怨、契約中斷及延長等

2. E-mail的主要類型和表現

1 詢問主題或目的類型
   Re(regarding)或是Subject後面出現的主旨或引導文內容為基礎，詢問主題或目的。

2 詢問收件人和文中提及的人物的類型
   一定要確認寄件人和收件人。

3 有要求時

- Could / Would you please...?（能幫我…嗎？）
- 命令句（請…、去做…──動詞原形在句子最前面）
- It might be better if you...（如果你能…就更好了。）

4 下面表現（又稱轉換語句）後面常出現與解答有關的關鍵

- By the way...（不過…。）
- However...（可是…。）
- Unfortunately...（不幸地…。）
- I'm afraid that...（因為…感到遺憾…。）

5 輕鬆找出附件的東西

- Enclosed is + 名詞（…一起寄出）
- Attached is + 名詞（…已附件）

3. E-mail的處理方法

1 盡速掌握寄件人和收件人。（I是寄件人，you是收件人）

2 先看題目，先別看選項，依據類型別活用解題方式。

3 熟悉E-mail的主要表現方式，可以加速找到解答的速度。

4 題目問到細部內容時，最好可以記住題目。

4. 題目問到細部內容時，最好可以記住題目。

請依照下一頁的指示事項的編號順序解解看。記住，一定要先看題目。
大部分的信件類型都可以照下面的解法進行。

③ 回到第一題的選項 E-mail的目的出現了

⑦ 閱讀剩下的文章內容 把剩下的文章內容看完

Catalog No.	Description	Quantity	Cost per unit
FV-375	Fovex 2-person tent	1	$349.99
LS-83	Lista down sleeping bag	2	$95.00
		Sales Tax	$22.25
		TOTAL	**$467.24**

這樣的字又叫作invoice（發票的意思）

營業稅金

We expect to be able to fill your order within five business days. Since your order exceeds $100 before tax, shipping charges will be waived.

總計

多益常出現的內容

⑧ 做第2題 記住第2題的選項後看文章，看到內容出現第2題的線索後馬上停止閱讀，盡速作答。

付款方式

Payment will be billed to your credit card when the order is shipped. You will receive another e-mail at that time. If you have any questions about your order, please call 1-800-388-3888. Thank you for shopping at Wildriver Camping Supplies.

原來還沒寄出！

---

1. **What is the purpose of this e-mail?** **① 題目先閱讀**

④ 看完選項後作答 邊看文章內容邊解答 一定要先閱讀！

(A) To announce that an order has been shipped
(B) To confirm receipt of an order
(C) To cancel a shipment
(D) To explain a price change

2. **What is true of Mr. Oliver's order?** **⑤ 先閱讀題目和選項**

(A) Sales taxes have been waived.
(B) He must pay a $100 deposit.
(C) He placed it over the telephone.
(D) There is no delivery charge.

⑥ 回到閱讀測驗文章 須看完題目和選項後，記在腦中 ▶ 解答在143頁

5. 讓Part 7變簡單的句子分析

---

1 Wildriver Camping Supplies has received the order you placed on June 3 via our online store.

1 野溪露營用品社已收到／訂購單／你在6月3日透過我們線上商店下的。

不論是什麼樣的句子都要先找出主詞和動詞。主詞是Wildriver Camping Supplies，動詞是has received。the order是receive的受詞，那麼you placed以下要怎麼看呢？動詞place後面需要有受詞，不過怎麼沒看到受詞？而且主詞和動詞又出現了，但怎麼沒有連接詞呢？這裡需要的受詞關係詞（形容詞子句連接詞）。受詞關係詞可以修飾先行名詞the order，又可扮演place的受詞，並且連接兩個以上的「主詞＋動詞」的形容詞子句連接詞。這裡有個叫作the order的事物，應該要有受詞格關係詞that或which，不過已經省略掉了。後面出現的on June 3 或via our online store全都是介系詞子句。

Wildriver Camping Supplies / has received / the order / (which
　　　　　　主詞　　　　　　　　　　動詞　　　　受詞
or that) / you / placed / on June 3 / via our online store.
受詞格關係詞　主詞　動詞　　介系詞子句　　　　介系詞子句

---

2 Payment will be billed to your credit card when the order is shipped.

2 將會用你的信用卡付款／訂購的商品寄出時。

首先找出主詞和動詞。主詞是有名詞型字尾-ment的Payment，動詞是will be billed。不過後面出現了to your credit card介系詞子句和when連接詞子句，也就是動詞bill沒有受詞，因為這是被動式。像這種句子中主詞（We）不太重要，常常使用在被動式，when子句中的is shipped也是被動式。

Payment / will be billed / to your credit card / when /
　主詞　　　動詞（被動）　　　　介系詞子句　　　　副詞，連接詞
the order / is shipped.
　主詞　　　動詞（被動）

(1) Single Passages

Questions 1-3 refer to the following e-mail.

To: bhinton@worldnet.com
From: inge@barnabycommunications.com
Subject: Upcoming Work
Attachment: Projects.sht

Hi Brandon,

I hope this e-mail finds you well. My name is Inge Samuelsson. As you probably know, Sheila Campbell left Barnaby Communications last month, and I have taken over her position. According to Sheila's notes, you are the primary translator for outsourced projects, so I assume we'll be working together a lot.

We have a number of translation projects in the pipeline, and I'd like to give you the first chance at claiming them. Please consult the attached file which shows the projected due dates and estimated word counts of each assignment. Needless to say, the deadlines are likely to change, but hopefully not by too much. The English drafts of the first project will be assigned to translators next week. If you are interested in any of the projects or if you have any questions, please reply by e-mail by the end of the day tomorrow.

Best regards,

Inge Samuelsson,
Editor

---

1 Who most likely is Brandon?

(A) A freelance translator

(B) A prospective client

(C) A job applicant

(D) A project manager

2 What is included with the e-mail?

(A) A cost estimate for a project

(B) A document to be translated

(C) A tentative work timeline

(D) Inge Samuelsson's resume

3 What will most likely happen next week?

(A) Brandon will reply to Ms. Samuelsson's e-mail.

(B) Documents will be ready for translation.

(C) Inge Samuelsson will become the new editor.

(D) A finished translation will be submitted.

▶ 解答在144頁

Questions 4-6 refer to the following e-mail.

From: jbrownstein@slateru.org

To: stephanieh@pineplazahotel.com

Subject: Last weekend

Dear Stephanie,

I'd like to express my gratitude to you and your staff for all your help during our symposium last weekend. It was the first time our department hosted an event of this kind, and we were not as organized as we would have liked. We had to make a lot of last-minute rearrangements and requests for equipment, but your staff was always able to accommodate us.

I particularly appreciated the extra effort you yourself made to call other hotels and find extra rooms for the non-registered attendees. Several attendees complimented the food at the banquet. In short, the event was a great success, and that wouldn't have been possible without your outstanding service.

We hope to hold another, similar event next year, and assuming that the timing is not a problem, we will definitely be using your hotel's facilities again. I look forward to the opportunity to work with you again at that time.

Best regards,

Janet Brownstein

Department of Political Science

Slater University

4 What is the main purpose of this e-mail?

   (A) To thank a hotel for its service
   (B) To request some extra rooms for guests
   (C) To confirm a reservation
   (D) To complain about conditions in the hotel

5 What does Janet Brownstein say about the event?

   (A) She was disappointed in the food.
   (B) The symposium was too short.
   (C) Her department was rather unprepared for it.
   (D) There were fewer attendees than expected.

6 What did Stephanie do to assist Ms. Brownstein?

   (A) She prepared a speech.
   (B) She arranged additional accommodations.
   (C) She called the attendees.
   (D) She repaired some equipment.

▶ 解答在144頁

(2) Double Passages

Questions 7-11 refer to the following notice and e-mail.

Notice to All Residents of Skyline Condominium

April 24

As a result of last month's vote, three new rules have been added to our Condominium Agreement. You can find a description of the rules that have been approved below:

1. Any guest visiting the building who requires a parking space for over one week must pay a fee of $5 per day.

2. Any renovations requiring electrical or plumbing changes must be approved by the newly appointed Condominium Inspector prior to the commencement of the renovations.

3. All windows must be closed and locked if your suite is vacant for a period of 48 hours or more.

Each resident is asked to sign the attached form and return it to the President of the Resident Council in Suite #313 before the end of April.

The changes will be considered in effect starting May 1. Any resident who does not follow these rules will be fined $150 per offense.

Sincerely,

Stacey Partel
President, Resident Council
Skyline Condominium

Date: May 3

From: Hans Schoenberg <hans@schoenbergmedia.co>

To: Stacey Partel <spartel@skyline.com>

Subject: Window Fine

Dear Ms. Partel,

I would like to request that the fine I received in the mail be waived.

I have been away on business for the past three weeks and only returned home today. I did not receive the notice that the rules of our Condominium Agreement had been updated until today.

Prior to my departure three weeks ago, I had arranged for a friend to come into my suite and open the windows over the weekend to let in some fresh air. I made these arrangements before the changes to the Agreement took effect. Therefore, I ask that you reconsider the fine and treat it as a notice for future offenses. I assure you I will have no difficulty obeying the rules.

Thank you for your understanding.

Sincerely,

Hans Schoenberg

Suits #405

7 Why is the Condominium Agreement being changed?

(A) The President wanted to increase security.
(B) Residents voted to add more rules.
(C) The condominium hired an Inspector.
(D) The residents complained about fines.

8 What is each resident asked to do?

(A) Email the Condominium Inspector
(B) Pay the $150 fine to the President
(C) Acknowledge receipt of the changes
(D) Send a notice to those who break the rules

9 Who is Hans Schoenberg?

(A) The Condominium Inspector
(B) A member of the Resident Council
(C) A guest
(D) A resident

10 Why is Hans Schoenberg writing to Stacey Partel?

(A) To request she withdraw the fine for leaving windows open for 48 hours
(B) To ask to receive a copy of the changes to the Condominium Agreement
(C) To give her notice that he will be out of town for three weeks on business
(D) To arrange for the Condominium Inspector to look after his suite

11 What does Hans ask Stacey to do?

(A) He asks her to change the fine into a warning.
(B) He requests that she alter the new rules.
(C) He demands to be part of a second vote.
(D) He threatens to file a complaint.

▶ 解答在144頁

公告文（Notice）

★ **公告文的出題類型**

❶ 停車場及內部餐廳等公司設施的改建及改建時間，以及這段期間的應對方法

❷ 給薪休假、出差費用等與經費處理相關的公司類規定確認及變更

❸ 公共機關成為贊助者的活動公告

❹ 公司活動的時間、申請方法、結束日的公告

❺ 文化及運動設施等地臨時休館或是開館，關於變更使用方法的公告

★ **公告文被出題的閱讀內容**

❶ What can be inferred from the notice [memo]?
   透過公告（備忘錄）可以推論的是什麼？

❷ What is mentioned [described / stated / written / included / true /
   indicated / suggested / implied] in the notice [memo]?
   公告（備忘錄）中提到什麼？

❸ What is NOT mentioned [described / stated / written / included / true /
   indicated / suggested / implied] in the notice [memo]?
   公告中（備忘錄）沒有提到什麼？

❹ When will the new company cafeteria be completed?
   公司新的餐廳何時完工？

❺ Where can people find more information?
   人們在什麼地方可以找到更多資訊？

攻略法

94

公告文
（Notice and Announcement）

只要了解固定的類型就可以輕易解決的公告！

公告文沒有特別訂定的形式，且內容幾乎都很相似。在公司的情況，大多是有新人或是有人辭職的內容，或是某種變更事項（薪水、醫療保健、電腦系統）等。如果官方公文的話，會出現道路的補修，為了特定活動的志願者之募集公告。

因為公告的主要目的就是要讓某個事實可以廣泛讓人知道。大部分是公司或是官方單位等團體，或是其它團體或是要傳送給個人了解這幾類。
memorandum（備忘錄，簡寫成memo）也是公告的一種。

1. 公告的種類

在多益Part 7中，最常以與下面的公告閱讀內容來出題。

> 道路補修、公共設施新建、改建、募集志願者、公司或是學校等機關的活動日程、著作權相關的公告、產品不良的回收說明、公司內所提供的額外福利說明、房東向租客公佈的公告、信用卡公司向會員們公佈的公告、購買商品更換或是退錢的說明等。

2. 公告文的主要類型

1 問主題的類型

- What is the main objective of this notice?

- What is being notified?

2 掌握細部事項的問題

- What is NOT mentioned as a safety precaution?

3 推論問題

- What should residents do if they wish to get reimbursed?

4 關於公告文的對象或是被要求的行動而詢問的問題

- For whom is this notice most likely intended?

1 這個公告文主要的目的是？什麼正在被公告？

2 做為安全預防守則，什麼沒有被提到？

3 萬一居民們希望得到賠償的話，該做什麼？

4 這個公告是以誰為對象？

3. 公告文的處理技巧

1 誰、向誰、要傳達什麼是最重要的關鍵。

2 以個人或是團體為對象的請求、命令、指示、邀請、委託。

3 主題或是目的，在標題或是閱讀內容的前半部會出現。

4 有幾種細部事項的情況，以NOT / TRUE類型出現，因此要仔細地對照。

4. 怪物講師的解法

請依照下面的指示事項中所提供的號碼順序解題看看。一開始一定要先閱讀題目。

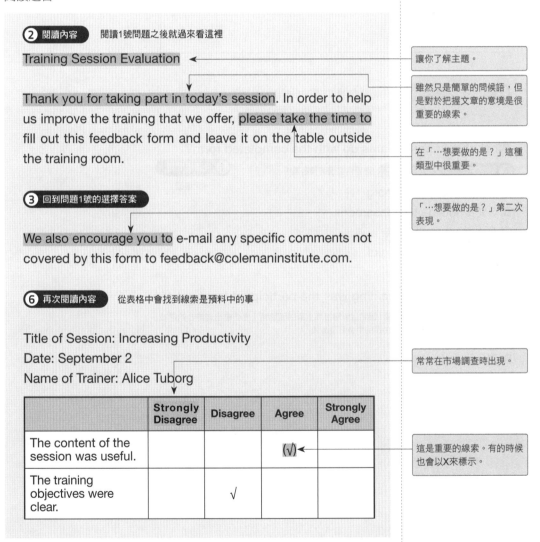

② 閱讀內容 閱讀1號問題之後就過來看這裡

Training Session Evaluation ← 讓你了解主題。

Thank you for taking part in today's session. In order to help us improve the training that we offer, please take the time to fill out this feedback form and leave it on the table outside the training room.

> 雖然只是簡單的問候語，但是對於把握文章的意境是很重要的線索。

> 在「…想要做的是？」這種類型中很重要。

③ 回到問題1號的選擇答案

We also encourage you to e-mail any specific comments not covered by this form to feedback@colemaninstitute.com.

> 「…想要做的是？」第二次表現。

⑥ 再次閱讀內容 從表格中會找到線索是預料中的事

Title of Session: Increasing Productivity
Date: September 2
Name of Trainer: Alice Tuborg

> 常常在市場調查時出現。

	Strongly Disagree	Disagree	Agree	Strongly Agree
The content of the session was useful.			(√)	
The training objectives were clear.		√		

> 這是重要的線索。有的時候也會以X來標示。

The training was held in a suitable location.	√			
Training materials were appropriate.			√	
The trainer was professional and his/her style was conducive to learning.				√
Activities conducted during the training were appropriate and helpful.			√	
Overall, the training was worth my time.			√	

7 閱讀內容後選擇答案　要從表中選擇最不滿意的部分，因此就要參照Strongly Disagree

1. What should participants do with the completed form?

4 閱讀答題選項之後選擇答案　邊看內文邊選擇答案　　**1** 先讀過問題 一定要讀！

(A) Hand it to Alice Tuborg

(B) Set it outside the classroom

(C) Submit it via e-mail

(D) Leave it on their desks

2. What aspect of the training was the participant least satisfied with?

5 先讀過題目　第1個問題解題後馬上再閱讀問題。應該會出現符合的選項，在表格中會發現線索

(A) The materials

(B) The location

(C) The instructor

(D) The activities

▶ 解答在148頁

5. 讓Part 7變簡單的句子分析

> 1 In order to help us improve the training that we offer, please take the time to fill out this feedback form and leave it on the table outside the training room.

1 為了幫助我們改善／我們提供的訓練／請花些時間填寫意見表／並把它放在訓練室外面的桌子上。

首先要找看看主詞與動詞，最前面的In order to部分是帶有「…為了」意思的副詞子句。在In order to後面出現的help us improve the traning中，把help看作是第5大句型動詞，us看作是受詞，而後面的improve看做是第5大句型受詞補語即可。因為help是把原形動詞當作受詞補語來使用。逗號（,）後面的主要子句（獨立子句）看不到主詞。please take之後是命令句。take當作動詞，the time當作受詞，從to fill到form為止，是修飾前面的名詞time的to不定詞的形容詞性用法（解釋為「要做…」）。另外在對等連接詞and後面，會出現與動詞take在相同位置所使用的動詞leave，以及出現出現受詞it。也就是說，take和leave都是句子的動詞。

In order to / help / us / improve the training / that we offer, /
　= To　　　動詞　受詞　　受詞補語（原形動詞）　　　關係子句
please / take / the time / to fill out this feedback form / and /
　副詞　　動詞　　受詞　　　　to不定詞的形容詞用法　　　　對等連接詞
leave / it / on the table / outside the training room.
動詞　受詞　介系詞片語　　　　介系詞片語

> 2 We also encourage you to e-mail any specific comments not covered by this form to feedback@colemaninstitute.com.

2 我們也建議／以電子郵件寄出／不包括在這張表格中的明確的意見／電子郵件地址feedback@colemaninstitute.com

主詞是we，動詞就變成encourage。encourage是第5大句型動詞，因此to不定詞就變成受詞補語。另外就算變成to不定詞，e-mail這個單字還是帶有動詞詞性，因此後面就必須要有受詞（any specific comments）。

We / also / encourage / you / to e-mail / any specific comments /
主詞　副詞　動詞（第5大句型）受詞　受詞補語　　　受詞（動詞e-mail的）
not covered / by this form / to feedback@colemaninstitute.com.
介系詞子句　　　介系詞片語　　　　　介系詞片語

(1) Single Passages

Questions 1-2 refer to the following memorandum.

Attention: All Staff
Subject: New office stationery

The company's new logo is expected to be approved by the board at its meeting on February 10. Some changes to the original design were suggested at the previous board meeting, and the design company is working on those.

We realize that the finalization of the new logo has taken longer than expected, and that some of you are concerned about running out of the current stationery. We will be holding off ordering new stationery until after the new logo has been approved, in order to avoid wasting money on supplies we will likely not use. In the meantime, please do your best to minimize the use of letterhead paper, envelopes, business cards, notepads, etc.

Rachel Silverman
Office Manager

1 What did the board do at its previous meeting?

(A) It approved the new logo.
(B) It decided to hire a new design firm.
(C) It recommended changes to the logo.
(D) It voted to reduce stationery use.

2 What are some employees worried about?

(A) The stationery is too expensive.
(B) They might not have enough stationery.
(C) The board will not approve the logo.
(D) The stationery will not be used.

Questions 3-6 refer to the following memorandum

From: Janice Friedman
To: All Staff
Subject: Work flow during my absence

As you know, I'll be going on maternity leave for six months, starting October 1, and I want to make sure that everyone has a clear understanding of the work arrangements during my absence.

Danielle Danvers, whom you remember from when she worked here at the Omni Institute, will be stepping in to coordinate the editing and publication of research reports. Danielle now has her own company, Danvers Media, and she has edited many of our past publications. Draft texts should be sent to her by e-mail for editing. She will then forward them to Xavier Marquez for translation and to Celia Kane at Coleman Design for layout.

I've asked Conrad Wong, a graduate journalism student at Freeman University, to assist with the writing of press releases. Conrad will be working in the Omni Institute's office three days a week.

I'm confident that you will enjoy a productive working relationship with both Danielle and Conrad, and that you will extend them every courtesy while I'm on leave. Please let me know if you have any questions or concerns.

3 What is indicated about Danielle Danvers?

(A) She has published a book.
(B) She is a graduate student.
(C) She is taking a six-month leave.
(D) She is a former employee of the Omni Institute.

4 Where will Conrad Wong be working?

(A) Freeman University
(B) The Omni Institute
(C) Danvers Media
(D) Coleman Design

5 Who will edit draft text?

(A) Conrad Wong
(B) Janice Friedman
(C) Celia Kane
(D) Danielle Danvers

6 What will be Xavier Marquez's responsibility?

(A) Sending e-mails to Janice Friedman
(B) Writing press releases
(C) Translating research reports
(D) Designing the layout

▶ 解答在148頁

(2) Double Passages

Questions 7-11 refer to the following notice and letter.

Swimming Pool Closure

The Jaymes D. Finn Swimming Pool will be closed for regular cleaning and maintenance September 1 to September 12.

This is a yearly closure done to clean the facilities, including all pool accessories, the pool deck, and life saving equipment.

All swimming classes are cancelled during the time of the pool closure. They will recommence on Monday, September 13.

Note: Locker rooms will remain open during the pool closure, but all lockers will be cleaned. We recommend you not leave any personal items in the lockers. All locks will be removed in order to complete the cleaning, and items left behind will be brought to the Lost and Found. We do not take any responsibility for lost or stolen items.

Thank you for your cooperation!

Pool Management

Mandjit Wolowitz
Jaymes D. Finn Facility
49 Dean Avenue
Boise, ID
50002
September 23

Dear Ms. Wolowitz,

I arrived at the Jaymes D. Finn Swimming Pool today to learn that my locker has been emptied and my belongings are missing.

When I reported the theft to the front counter, your staff informed me that notices had been posted around the facility to remove one's personal belongings for yearly cleaning. I have been out of town for the last month, so I never saw the notices.

The fact that my locker was cleaned would not have bothered me if it wasn't for the fact that my items are now missing. Your front desk staff was unable to locate my towel, running shoes, and shampoo. It seems someone claimed my items as his or her own and took them.

I am therefore writing to inform you of my dissatisfaction with the management of the pool closure. Notices are a great way to make announcements, if you can be assured that all your members will see the signs. As a membership holder, I would have thought that I would receive a special notice, or perhaps a phone call, to inform me to empty my locker. I would have gladly emptied my locker before my holidays if I had known I would need to.

I look forward to hearing from you.

Sincerely,

Frank Lee

7 What is suggested in the notice?

(A) The pool is an old facility that requires maintenance.

(B) The closure is a last-minute announcement.

(C) The locker rooms are not being cleaned.

(D) There is nothing unusual about the closure.

8 Why should personal items be removed from the locker room?

(A) To facilitate the cleaning of lockers

(B) To encourage cleanliness

(C) To accommodate new lockers

(D) To detract thieves from stealing

9 From where were Frank Lee's items stolen?

(A) The locker room

(B) The pool deck

(C) The Lost and Found

(D) The front counter

10 Why did Frank Lee NOT empty his locker?

(A) He did not have time to collect his belongings.

(B) He thought members would receive telephone calls.

(C) His items were stolen before he could remove them.

(D) He did not visit the facility in the last month.

11 What is suggested about the pool closure?

(A) Management did not properly communicate information.

(B) The two-week closure did not give members time to clear lockers.

(C) The cleaning should have happened in the summer time.

(D) The front desk staff should not have given away Frank's items.

▶ 解答在148頁

資訊文
（Information & Instructions）

只在一定類型中出現的資訊文！

資訊文與公告文一樣，出現的內容幾乎是固定的。由此可知只要熟記類型的話，**只要看到題目大概就可以猜出閱讀內文大部分的內容。**

資訊文是要告知很多人關於特定的活動情報的文章，因此是找出主題或是找出細部資訊的疑問類型。

1. 資訊文的種類

1 產品資訊：使用說明書、注意事項等

2 活動資訊：講座、研討會、展示會等費用及利用時間資訊

3 公司資訊：人事異動、意見募集、教育訓練資訊、安全方針、設施維修資訊等

4 其他資訊：變更事項、制度資訊、公共場所的變更事項資訊、藥物服用方法等

5 會議記錄（minutes）：會議內容簡略說明及後續處理資訊等

6 提醒文（reminder）：各種預約的確認、注意及叮嚀事項資訊等

7 電話訊息（notes）：電話內容的傳達

2. 資訊文的疑問類型

1 詢問目的、理由的類型

• What is the purpose of this information?
• What are the guests asked to do?

1 這則資訊的目的是什麼？
客人們被要求做什麼？

2 找出細部資訊的類型

• What information is being given about the item?

2 關於這個商品的哪種相關情報被告知？

3 其他類型

以誰為對象的問題。就算本文中沒有出現，需要利用整體閱讀內容去推

測，是有點困難的類型。

• For whom is this information intended? 3 這個資訊是以誰為對象？

3. 資訊文處理技巧

1 因為內文很短，所以先閱讀過問題之後在本文中找出答案是最好的方式。特別是要抓到抓到key word。

2 這個類型需要注意的是誰要轉達給誰什麼東西。這是問題的核心，因此只要可以了解這個部分的話，幾乎所有的問題都可以迎刃而解。

4. 怪物講師的解法

請依照下面的指示事項中所提供的號碼順序解題看看。一開始一定要先閱讀題目。

看起來是說明使用方法的閱讀文章。

③ 閱讀內文 讀過第2道問題之後就趕快回來！

是非常仔細的藥物服用方法。

Directions for Use: Adults and children over 13 years old, take 1-2 pills with a glass of water, every 3-4 hours, up to 4 times per day. Do not exceed 8 pills per 24-hour period. If you accidentally consume more than the recommended dose, see a physician as soon as possible, even if there are no noticeable side effects.

這個非常重要。因為用錯的話會發生大事。

Caution: If symptoms persist for more than 7 days, see a doctor.

④ 回到第2道問題

⑥ 繼續閱讀內文

Prolonged use of this medication is not advised. Individuals who have high blood pressure, heart disease, or other chronic illness, pregnant women, the elderly, and anyone taking other medication should receive a doctor's permission before taking the product. Regular use may cause drowsiness or sweating.

副作用的例子。

Chapter 23_公告文和說明文 **469**

7 回到第1道問題

Avoid consuming alcohol, driving, and activities requiring quick reaction while on this medication.

應該要避免的行動。

1. What is mentioned as a possible side effect of this medication?

1 先閱讀問題
一定要讀！

(A) Difficulty in sleeping

(B) High blood pressure

(C) Tiredness

(D) Dizziness

8 選擇問題的答案　與閱讀內文做比較之後再解題

2. Under what circumstances should a doctor be consulted, according to the instructions?

2 先閱讀問題
一定要讀。也有閱讀內文全都讀過才出現答案的狀況。

(A) If the user sweats more than usual

(B) If the user takes eight pills in a day

(C) If the user has not gotten better after a week

(D) If the user drinks alcohol while on medication

5 解題　與內文做比較之後再解題

▶ 解答在151頁

5. 讓Part7變簡單的句子分析

1 If you accidentally consume more than the recommended dose, see a physician as soon as possible, even if there are no noticeable side effects.

1 錯誤服用的狀況／超過建議用量／請找醫生／盡快／就算沒有明顯的副作用。

這個句子是出現if的條件子句與主要子句，另外在最前面再次加上了附加說明用的條件子句。在這裡必須要注意的就是隨著子句的增長，連接詞的數量也會增加。if子句的主詞是you，動詞是consume，受詞是more than the recommended dose。accidentally是修飾動詞consume的副詞。第一個逗號（,）後面的主要子句是沒有主詞的命令句。as soon as possible（儘速）請當作一個單字來熟記。一開始解釋的順序如下所示。「萬一你要做⋯的話，就去做⋯，就算沒有⋯ 」。

If / you / accidentally / consume / more than / the recommended
　　主詞　　　副詞　　　　動詞　　　　　　　　受詞
dose, / see / a physician / as soon as possible, / even if /
　　　　動詞　　補語　　　　　副詞片語　　　　　連接詞
there / are / no noticeable side effects.
　副詞　動詞　　　　　主詞

2 Avoid consuming alcohol, driving, and activities requiring quick reaction while on this medication.

2 請避免／喝酒、開車／以及其他／需要快速反應的活動／服用這個藥的時候。

看到沒有主詞且原形動詞avoid出現在句子最前面，就可以判斷這個句子是命令句。句子全部的動詞只有avoid一個，把while之後的部分看成副詞子句即可。首先avoid是把動名詞當作受詞的動詞，因此在後面的動名詞會出現consuming和driving。activities也是把名詞當作動詞avoid的受詞。後面的requiring quick reaction是在後面，修飾先行名詞activities的分詞，或者看做是省略「主格關係代名詞＋be動詞」（which are）的形容詞子句。

Avoid / consuming alcohol, / driving, / and activities / requiring
　動詞　　　　受詞1　　　　受詞2　　　受詞3
quick reaction / while on this medication.
　分詞（形容詞子句）　　　　　連接詞

(1) Single Passages

questions 1-3 refer to the following notice.

Important Notice

You may have noticed recently that your tap water appears somewhat cloudy. We'd like to assure all our tenants that the water is still perfectly safe to drink. The cloudiness is due to higher than normal levels of rainfall in the Gulf Mountains area. The heavy precipitation has caused the rivers that supply the city's water to flow faster than usual. As a result, there is a greater amount of sediment being carried into the water supply tanks. This sediment is what causes the water to appear cloudy.

As a precaution, the city has tested the water to check that the drinking quality is acceptable. Health officials have indicated that there is no risk involved in drinking it or using it for other purposes, and there is no need to boil the water before use.

If the government does issue a water safety advisory at some point, we will put notices in your mailboxes immediately.

Regards,

The management
Jersey Heights Apartments

---

1 Who is this notice aimed at?

(A) Government workers
(B) Water plant inspectors
(C) Apartment residents
(D) Health officials

2 What has caused the water to become cloudy, according to the notice?

(A) Pollution
(B) Heavy rainfall
(C) Low water levels
(D) Damaged supply network

3 What is indicated about the water?

(A) It is safe for drinking and other uses.
(B) It should be boiled before use.
(C) It will be temporarily unavailable.
(D) It was bottled in the Gulf Mountains.

Questions 4-7 refer to the following advertisement.

Toronto Indo-Canadian Society (TICS)

General Information
TICS provides a variety of cultural, educational and support programs for Indian immigrants to Canada in the Toronto area. We also host many monthly events, which are open to the public at no cost. To work as a volunteer in any of our programs, you must first register as a member of the society. Contact Deepa Jhabvala at the provided phone number to volunteer.

Upcoming Monthly Events
Group city hike – enjoy visiting parks in and around Toronto. Trails are easy and take 1-2 hours. Meet at TICS Center, April 10 at 11:00 A.M.

Book sale – buy used paperbacks and hardcover books at TICS Center, April 30, 10:30A.M.-1:00P.M. Donations will be accepted throughout April. Proceeds benefit the Indian Health Initiative's campaign to provide free immunizations to rural children.

Volunteers needed
Kitchen helpers – learn about Indian cooking and provide delicious meals for seniors in our community meals program.

Language education – help immigrants from all over the world learn English in our fun language program.

---

4 What can only members of the society do?

(A) Study English at TICS Center
(B) Shop at the book sale
(C) Work for the community meals program
(D) Join the group city hike

5 What will take place on April 10?

(A) Language lesson
(B) A cooking class
(C) A book sale
(D) An organized walk

6 Why should someone contact Deepa Jhabvala?

(A) To order a book
(B) To take a cooking class
(C) To renew a visa
(D) To teach language

7 What is indicated about the book sale?

(A) Only hardcover books will be accepted.
(B) Sales will be donated to charity.
(C) Purchases may be made all month.
(D) Unsold books will be sent to India.

▶ 解答在152頁

(2) Double Passages

Questions 8-12 refer to the following memorandum and instruction.

Memorandum to all staff at Setagaya Database Management

June 10

Dear staff,

Since the installation of our new alarm system last week, the third floor alarm has been set off three times. It seems employees don't carry their employee cards with them when they travel to offices on different floors!

While the problem has been easily explained to the police, who have been called each time, Management feels the ringing alarm is disruptive to the workday and is causing stress and anxiety in the office. Everyone seems to be waiting for the next person to set off the alarm!

I have attached instructions to this memo. Please review them carefully and make sure you are familiar with how to disarm the alarm. If further problems occur, we will hold a training session with Richfield Security on Friday. Notice will be sent by e-mail.

Please address any questions to me.

Kazue Morioka
Administrative Assistant

New Security Code Instructions

For Employees of Setagaya Database Management

Upon entering the building:

1. When you open the door, you will hear the alarm pulse quietly. Walk into the main office. The alarm box is located to the right of the doorway.

2. Enter the unique employee code that has been assigned to you. Do not share this code with anyone, not even other employees. If you accidentally enter the wrong code, you have 10 seconds to CLEAR the original number and enter the correct code. Failure to do so will set off the alarm, and the police will be notified automatically.

3. Next, you are required to swipe your employee card. The system will verify that your card matches your unique security code. If they do not match, the alarm will sound instantly, and the police will be called. In the case of a problem, we are able to detect who touched the alarm by connecting the employee code to the employee card.

Remember: If you incorrectly enter the information and the police are called, you will be required to show business identification and provide the answer to a security question. Management has given Richfield Security a different question for each employee based on our personal knowledge of each of you. You will not know your own security question until you are asked it by a member of Richfield's response team! This secrecy is to eliminate the possibility of accidentally passing on your security question to a criminal.

Special Note: Each floor of the building is equipped with a separate alarm system.

Upon leaving the building:

1. Enter your security code.
2. Provide your fingerprint.
3. Exit the building within 30 seconds or the alarm will sound.

8 Why have the police been called to Setagaya Database Management?

(A) Employees failed to disarm the alarm system.

(B) They are testing the security system.

(C) Management failed to deliver instructions to staff.

(D) Several attempted robberies set off the alarm.

9 What are staff members asked to do?

(A) Memorize their security codes

(B) Carry their employee cards

(C) Study how to use the alarm

(D) Sign up for a training session

10 Why has the alarm on the third floor sounded?

(A) Staff members have forgotten their employee cards.

(B) Third floor employees have not received training.

(C) Management failed to explain how to turn off the alarm.

(D) Employees have forgotten their security codes.

11 According to the instructions, why must the security card be swiped?

(A) To maintain maximum security

(B) To ensure each floor is protected

(C) To track which employee set the alarm

(D) To reassure staff the alarm has been set

12 Why are staff members not made aware of their security questions?

(A) To deter robbers from entering the building

(B) To maintain secrecy among staff members

(C) To allow the police to investigate employees

(D) To add an increased level of security

▶ 解答在152頁

新聞文章、廣告和各種表格

新聞文章（Article）

★ 新聞文章出題的內容

❶ 公司合併等原因、人事異動的發表、重要職位、新就職者的經歷介紹

❷ 受獎者新聞以及受獎者的經歷介紹

❸ 天氣預報及受到氣候影響的公司新聞

❹ 在家辦公的優點與缺點

❺ 競爭對手的網頁以及和售價金額的比較

❻ 新軟體商品的測試使用時間與銷售比較

廣告（Advertisement）

★ 廣告出題的內容

❶ 飯店、餐廳、旅行社套裝行程的預約折扣、募集會員廣告、打折活動廣告

❷ 百貨公司、健身房、園藝用品、家具店、電子產品專賣店、書店的開幕及歇業、打折活動

❸ 以老闆或是新進員工為對象的各種講習會議

❹ 不動產的買賣與租貸

❺ 銀行的網路銀行資訊

表格（Form）

★ 表格出題的內容

❶ 飯店、餐廳、套裝行程、健身房、汽車租借、與商品相關的問卷調查

❷ 銷售業績的圖表

❸ 動物園、植物園、水族館、美術館、圖書館、展示會等開館、開園時間及票價表

❹ 訂單、訂購申請單的樣式

❺ 行程表的時間與活動

❻ 商品券、入場券、電話卡的購買方式

96 新聞文章（Article）

希望新聞文章不要佔太大的出題比重！

最近常聽到學生們在抱怨Part 7變得很難，一直持續在考試的我也覺得Part 7的難度比之前高，特別是新聞文章（article）出題的比重變高，是其中一個原因。最近article不停地出現在多益考試中，**感覺article與信件、e-mail一起成為Part 7的代表性主題，只要出現三四篇文章題組，整個Part 7的難易度也會提升。**

article是要傳達讀者新消息或是事實的文章。是**多益閱讀內文當中量最多而且單字也最難的文章類型，對於剛開始學習的人來說，也是最難的類型。**由上可知，如果初學者看到在問題中有出現refer to the following article（與以下文章有關）的時候先跳過，從其它比較簡單的類型開始解題會比較好。

1. 新聞文章的種類

1 **報導文章**：公司的合併、結構調整、政府政策、公共系統變更、事故報導、產品回收等

2 **經濟文章**：新產品開發、出口進口相關、貿易、物價上漲或下降消息等

3 **解析文章**：特定公司或是產業的展望以及相關說明，環境或是特定地區相關的文章等

4 **採訪文章**：特定的人或是對於特定產業的採訪文章、書評、電影、公演相關的文章等

2. 新聞文章的問題類型

1 **帶有目的或是主題的類型**：通常會在文章最前面出現。雖然也有在文章的後半段才出現的情況，但是在這種情況，要尋找主題是屬於非常難的類型。

2 **找出與文章相關人物的類型**

3 **找出細部資訊的類型**：以問題內容當作線索，快速找出在閱讀內文中對應的部分來解題是最好的方法。這就是所謂的找出key word。

4 **詢問文章出處的類型**

3. 新聞文章的處理技巧

1 因為文章本身很難，因此要記憶文章的內容是很困難的。

2 通常在文章的前半部會出現主題或是目的，看文章前半部的話可以了解整篇文章的動向。

3 新聞文章大都是依據5W1H原則編寫。所以把握句子的結構會更容易解題。

4. 怪物講師的解法

請依照下面的指示事項中所提供的號碼順序解題看看。一開始一定要先閱讀題目。

②閱讀內文 讀過第1道問題之後馬上回來看！

Eating to Lose Weight

標題是了解主題的最好提示。

Are you trying to lose weight, without sacrificing all the foods you love? Here are some simple guidelines for reducing the amount of calories you take in without changing your diet significantly.

請再次確認一次主題。

1. People who have a bowl of soup or a green salad about 30 minutes before dinner take in roughly 10 to 20 percent fewer calories than those who don't. Eating soup or salad partially fills you up, meaning that you won't want to eat as much of the main course.

句中説「先喝湯與吃沙拉比較好」！

③再次回到問題1的答案選項 主要的句子a bowl of soup出現

⑥再次閱讀內文

2. People tend to eat everything on their plate. If you use a smaller dish, then you won't have as much food to begin with eating. Avoid the urge to have a second helping.

句中説「使用小的碗」。

句中說「分兩次用餐」。

3. Split your dinner into two equal portions, eating one at your usual mealtime, and the other two to three hours later. Because you are eating at regular intervals, your body will not have a chance to grow hungry or crave unhealthy snacks.

⑧ 2號問題解題　以第2道問題的答案選項內容當作基礎，找出正確答案的線索的時候，進行解題並且與內文對照。

1. When should people eat a bowl of soup, according to the information?

① 先閱讀問題

一定要讀

(A) Every two or three hours

(B) About half an hour before a meal

(C) With a meal

(D) In the morning

④ 閱讀答案選項之後找出答案　邊看內文的內容，邊找出答案

2. What is NOT suggested as a way to lose weight?

⑤ 先讀過問題與答案選項　這個類型是必須要反覆閱讀內文與答案選項。是最難也是最耗時間的問題。

(A) Splitting a meal in half

(B) Eating a green salad

(C) Using smaller dishes

(D) Reducing sugar intake

3. The word "crave" in the last paragraph, line 4 is closest in meaning to _____.　⑨ 閱讀答案選項和作答

(A) desire

(B) dislike

(C) humiliate

(D) dig

▶ 解答在155頁

5. 讓Part 7變簡單的句子分析

> 1 People who have a bowl of soup or a green salad about 30 minutes before dinner take in roughly 10 to 20 percent fewer calories than those who don't.

1 人們／吃了一碗湯及綠色蔬菜沙拉／在晚餐前30分鐘／大約減少攝取百分之10-20的卡路里／比起沒有這麼做的人。

句子看起來有點長，但是是以「主詞 + 動詞 + 受詞」組成的典型第3大句型的句子。people是主詞，who之後到dinner為止是修飾主詞people的主詞關係代名詞子句，後面的take in是依附主詞people的限定動詞。take in後面有出現幾種的修飾片語，受詞是calories。而且than是連接子句的對等連接詞。句子最前面的those who解釋為「做…的人」，使用複數，所以在who後面的動詞不是dosen't 而是don't。

People / who / have / a bowl of soup or a green salad /
　主詞　　主詞關代　動詞　　　　　　受詞
about 30 minutes / before dinner / take in / roughly /
　　介系詞片語　　　　介系詞片語　　限定動詞　副詞
10 to 20 percent fewer calories / than / those / who / don't.
　　　　　受詞　　　　　　　　　　對等連接詞　主詞　主詞關代　動詞
* 句子最前面的have a bowl of soup or green tea 省略

> 2 Eating soup or salad partially fills you up, meaning that you won't want to eat as much of the main course.

2 吃沙拉與喝湯／會讓你有飽足感／代表／你不會想要吃／太多主食。

這個句子的主詞是Eating soup or salad。另外動詞是fills，這裡的fill up是片語的表現，意思是「讓…飽足」。如果這個片語的受詞是you、him、me這種代名詞的時候，在fill與up之間就會插入代名詞。問題是在後面的部分，這裡的meaning是什麼？meaning是承接前面的句子，也可以寫成which means。把它看成是一種分詞子句即可。意思就是「句子前面的部分就代表that之後部分的意思」。後面的句子中as much的意思就是「相同」。意思就是吃了較少「相同份量」的湯與沙拉。

Eating soup or salad / partially / fills you up, / meaning /
　主詞（動名詞）　　　　　副詞　　　動詞子句　　　分詞
that you won't want to eat / as much / of the main course.
　　　　名詞子句　　　　　　　分詞　　　　介系詞片語

(1) Single Passages

Questions 1-4 refer to the following article.

Smokers are less likely to show up for work than their non-smoking counterparts. That's the conclusion of a new Danish study published in the medical journal *Side Effects*, which reports that smokers average seven more days of sick leave per year than non-smokers.

Over 12,000 people in seven countries took part in the 10-year survey, which compared smokers and non-smokers on a number of issues, including work absences, hospitalization times, diet, and personal finances. Overall, people in the survey took an average of 12 days of sick leave each year. The average was 16 days for smokers and nine for non-smokers. Among countries surveyed, the number of working days lost each year due to sickness was highest in Denmark(18) and lowest in the United States(10).

The study also found that smokers are more likely to be obese and have chronic health problems. Jens Gronkjaer, the author of the study, says, "On one level, the data shows what we already know - smoking is bad for individual health. But it also shows there are secondary effects that we usually don't consider, like a negative impact on productivity."

1 What was one purpose of the survey?

   (A) To measure the impact of smoking on workplace attendance

   (B) To evaluate anti-smoking laws

   (C) To compare the effectiveness of different diet programs

   (D) To study programs for preventing obesity

2 What issue was NOT addressed by the study?

   (A) Eating habits

   (B) Time spent in hospitals

   (C) Time spent away from work

   (D) Fitness routines

3 How many days of sick leave does the average smoker take per year, according to the study?

   (A) 9

   (B) 10

   (C) 16

   (D) 18

4 What does Jens note about the findings?

   (A) All of them were surprising.

   (B) Some of them were known beforehand.

   (C) They contradicted earlier studies.

   (D) The results were inconclusive.

▶ 解答在156頁

Questions 5-8 refer to the following article.

Fifty years ago, Plimpton's Main Street was a bustling shopping district, lined with shops and crowded sidewalks. All of that changed as families began moving to the suburbs. As the town's focus of commerce shifted to the outskirts, business owners and shopkeepers eventually abandoned Main Street. Now, the Plimpton municipal government has introduced a $20 million redevelopment program called the Main Street Initiative, in the hope of revitalizing the downtown area.

The money will go to repaving the streets, replacing the old asphalt sidewalks with new brick ones, creating a series of parks and gardens, and restoring several historic storefronts. The plan also provides special tax reductions for businesses that choose to rent or buy space downtown. To encourage shoppers to return to the center of town, fees will be waived at all public parking lots on weekdays after 5:00 P.M., as well as on weekends and public holidays. "My fondest childhood memories were of shopping downtown with my family," says George Hucklebuck, mayor of Plimpton. "The initiative will help restore a sense of community to our great town."

5 What will NOT be financed by the city government?

(A) The paving of streets
(B) The restoration of buildings
(C) The creation of parks
(D) The installation of traffic lights

6 What is one of the aims of the Main Street Initiative?

(A) To promote driving safety
(B) To encourage businesses to open downtown
(C) To publicize a history museum
(D) To build a highway through Plimpton

7 When will people have to pay for downtown parking?

(A) On weekday mornings
(B) On weekday evenings
(C) On Saturdays and Sundays
(D) On public holidays

8 Who is George Hucklebuck?

(A) A local shopkeeper
(B) A land developer
(C) A political leader
(D) A real estate agent

▶ 解答在156頁

(2) Double Passages

Questions 9-13 refer to the following e-mail and article.

Date: September 30
From: Daniel Audain <d_audain@cityglobe.co>
To: Madison Mathens <madison@mathensbooks.com>
Subject: Article for City Globe

Dear Madison,

Thank you again for meeting me for an interview the other night. I enjoyed hearing your thoughts on your award-winning book "Truth", especially now that it has sold its millionth copy and won the City Globe Reader's Choice award. What a tremendous success for a brand-new writer from our little city. To think we've known each other for years, and you were a hidden talent!

I've written a draft of the article, but I wanted to verify a few things. When did you decide to start the book: were you in France, or was it when you got home? Also, were you alone or were you traveling with someone?

Again, thank you for taking the time to meet with me. I know our readers will be thrilled to learn more about the author behind their favorite book of the year!

Congratulations!

Daniel Audain
Writer, City Globe

The Truth behind Madison Mathens
A Reader's Choice Profile

By Daniel Audain

Madison Mathens is not your typical author; she did not spend a lifetime perfecting her craft or even dreaming about being a writer!

At 68 years old, Madison, a retired seamstress, only recently decided she wanted to be a writer. On a solo trip to France two years ago, she stopped in the village of Avignon to explore a market and twisted her ankle. Unsure how badly she'd hurt herself, she sat down on a park bench and watched the people mingle in and out of the marketplace. Sitting there, she took pictures of the scene in front of her and listened to the stories she heard as people walked by. Unknown to her, she had started the research for her first book.

When she returned home from France, she tried to match the photos she'd taken to the stories she'd recorded. She soon realized she was looking at the rough draft of a book on a group of people, whose stories come together for one day, and then move on forever.

Moments after this realization, Madison started crafting her best-selling novel, *Truth*. "I just realized I could do it," she said, incredulous that her spontaneous idea has led to such widespread success. "I'm amazed that a twisted ankle and an old camera brought me the inspiration I was waiting for my entire life! I used to want to be a pianist, but I never even took lessons. Who knew my hidden talent was writing?"

For now, Madison is enjoying the acclaim of her first book. She currently has no plans to publish a second but remains open to the possibility. "I spend a lot of time on park benches," she said laughing. "Just in case!"

9 Why did Daniel email Madison?

(A) To arrange an interview for a newspaper

(B) To clarify information from an interview

(C) To email a draft of an article on Madison

(D) To tell Madison her novel won an award

10 What can be inferred from the e-mail?

(A) Daniel had difficulty contacting Madison.

(B) Madison's book is an international bestseller.

(C) Daniel and Madison are acquaintances.

(D) Daniel aspires to write a novel.

11 Why is Madison featured in City Globe?

(A) She wrote a book that won an award.

(B) She published her first novel at age 68.

(C) She is a famous seamstress.

(D) She promotes traveling to France.

12 What incident led Madison to write her book?

(A) She took photographs.

(B) She took a piano lesson.

(C) She traveled on her own.

(D) She hurt her ankle.

13 What is NOT one of Madison's talents?

(A) Sewing

(B) Photography

(C) Piano

(D) Writing

▶ 解答在156頁

攻略法

97

廣告（Advertisement）

可以快速解決的類型，就是廣告！！

廣告（advertisement）比前面的新聞文章（article）的內容更容易，相對的可以快速地解題。以最快的速度以及使用正確方法來解題是重要關鍵。廣告通常會出題1~2篇。廣告最主要分為廣告有形商品的產品廣告，以及無形的商品，像是旅遊或是徵人廣告。不管是有形的還是無形的廣告，以在日常生活中常常接觸的產品或是服務相關的廣告居多。

1. 有形廣告與無形廣告

有形的廣告與無形的廣告主要介紹的內容如下所示。

1 **有形的廣告**：電子產品、藥品、車輛、年度會員券、不動產、訂閱定期的雜誌等

2 **無形的廣告**：徵人、旅遊商品、公演、研討會等

2. 廣告的主要類型與問題

以下是廣告內文的代表性類型別的問題。

1 **詢問廣告的目的與對象的類型**

What is the purpose of this advertisement?

2 **詢問廣告產品的具體性事實的類型**

What is true about the advertised product?

3 **詢問宣傳公司、工作、應徵者等的類型**

What position is being advertised?

4 **詢問應徵資格及應徵方法的類型**

What are the qualifications required?

1 這個廣告的目的是什麼？

2 關於廣告產品的事實是什麼？

3 廣告什麼樣的職位？

4 被要求的資格條件是什麼？

3. 廣告文的處理技巧

1. 廣告主旨會出現在最上面。廣告文不用以具備「主詞 + 動詞」的敘述型完全句子來表現，而是透過簡短的表現，達到快速傳達意思的效果。因為這個緣故，你需要熟悉這種簡短結束的表現。特別是在題目中，就要大概了解到這個廣告要說什麼。

2. 只讀選項答案之外的問題，找出想要知道的資訊大概的位置。

3. 最上面的標題以及文章最後面的部分最常被出題，因此要特別注意這兩個部分。

4. 必須要尋找key word以及熟悉paraphrasing。

4. 怪物講師的解法

請依照下面的指示事項中所提供的號碼順序解題看看。一開始一定要先閱讀題目。

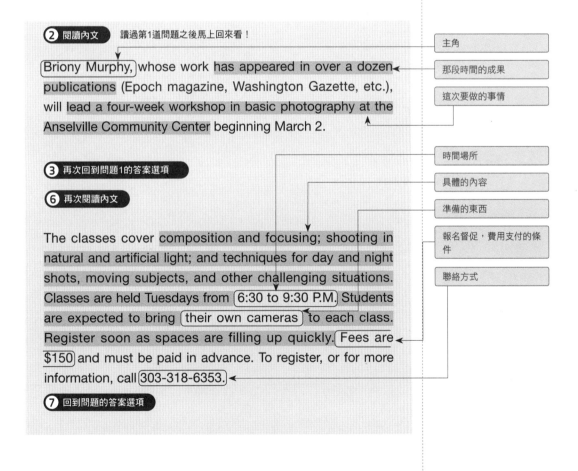

② 閱讀內文　讀過第1道問題之後馬上回來看！

主角

Briony Murphy, whose work has appeared in over a dozen publications (Epoch magazine, Washington Gazette, etc.), will lead a four-week workshop in basic photography at the Anselville Community Center beginning March 2.

那段時間的成果

這次要做的事情

③ 再次回到問題1的答案選項

⑥ 再次閱讀內文

時間場所

具體的內容

準備的東西

報名督促，費用支付的條件

聯絡方式

The classes cover composition and focusing; shooting in natural and artificial light; and techniques for day and night shots, moving subjects, and other challenging situations. Classes are held Tuesdays from 6:30 to 9:30 P.M. Students are expected to bring their own cameras to each class. Register soon as spaces are filling up quickly. Fees are $150 and must be paid in advance. To register, or for more information, call 303-318-6353.

⑦ 回到問題的答案選項

1. What will Briony Murphy do, according to the advertisement?

(A) Exhibit her work

① 先讀問題

一定要看！並記憶主要的內容！

(B) Conduct a photography course

(C) Submit a magazine article

(D) Move to Anselville

④ 讀答案選項之後選擇答案

邊看內文的內容，一邊解題

2. What can be inferred about the workshop?

(A) It is free of charge.

⑤ 先讀問題與答案選項

(B) It focuses only on daytime photography.

(C) Cameras will be provided for students.

(D) Only a limited number of students can register.

⑧ 讀答案選項之後選擇答案

▶ 解答在159頁

5. 讓Part7變簡單的句子分析

1 Briony Murphy, whose work has appeared in over a dozen publications, will lead a four-week workshop in basic photography at the Anselville Community Center beginning March 2.

1 布萊妮‧莫菲／作品出現在／超過12個出刊物／將帶領／4個禮拜的研討會／關於基本攝影技術／在安結比社區中心／從3月2日開始。

這個句子的主詞是Briony Murphy，限定動詞就是後面的will lead。另外動詞lead的受詞是a four-week workshop。剩下的部分都可以看成修飾語片語。whose是所有格關係代名詞，前面出現的Briony Murphy就變成是後面名詞work所有的意思。這是所有格關係代名詞的特徵。最後面的beginning之後的部分就是意思為「從3月2日開始」的副詞語句。

Briony Murphy, / whose / work / has appeared / in over a dozen
主詞　　　　　所有格關係詞　名詞　　　動詞　　　　介系詞片語
publications, / will lead / a four-week workshop / in basic
　　　　　　　限定動詞　　　　受詞
photography / at the Anselville Community Center /
介系詞片語　　　　　　　　介系詞片語
beginning March 2.
　　副詞

2 Students are expected to bring their own cameras to each class.

2 學生們應該要帶自己的相機／去每堂課。

首先句子的主詞是students，動詞是are expected。但是在動詞expect前面會有be動詞，後面會有to。expect是被當作代表性第5大句型的動詞，被當作受詞補語時要使用to不定詞。把這個部分改成原來主動式句子的話就如同後面的句子。We expect students to bring their...。把內容上大家都知道的主詞刪除寫成被動式。把be expected to綁在一起當作片語來看會比較方便。而且to bring是動詞expect的受詞補語，因為to不定詞具有與動詞相同的性質，所以後面要採用their own cameras的受詞。

Students / are expected / to bring / their own cameras / to each class.
主詞　　　動詞（被動）　to不定詞　　受詞　　　　介系詞片語

(1) Single Passages

Questions 1-3 refer to the following advertisement.

Portable music players allow you to enjoy your favorite tunes while walking on the street, sitting in an airplane, or working at your desk. But while it's easy to bring your music with you, it's not so easy to avoid background noise. That's why Resonance Audio Inc. has developed our exclusive NB (Noise-Block) headphones.

Our NB headphones provide you with the ultimate listening experience. Our revolutionary noise-blocking technology cuts background noise by 70%, which is at least 20% more than any other brand on the market. Resonance Audio Inc. is a leader in sound quality, and these new headphones live up to our high standards.

NB headphones have been designed with your comfort and convenience in mind. They have a compact shape, making them easy to carry or put in your bag. The soft padding around the earpieces allows you to wear them for hours without discomfort.

Visit www.rai.com to learn more. Order now and you can try NB headphones risk-free for 30 days – if you are not completely satisfied, we will give you a full refund.

1 What kind of product is being advertised?

(A) A portable music player
(B) A pair of headphones
(C) A home stereo system
(D) An article of clothing

2 What is stressed as an advantage of the product over other brands?

(A) Its ability to reduce noise
(B) Its attractive design
(C) Its reasonable cost
(D) Its compact size

3 What is NOT a feature of the product?

(A) Comfortable padding
(B) Excellent sound quality
(C) A carrying case
(D) A guarantee

▶ 解答在159頁

Questions 4-8 refer to the following advertisement.

Vizio TV - Television for you!

At Vizio, we have a variety of cable television combination packages to choose from, including our Entertainment, Sports, or Value Combo Packs. Just added this spring is our brand-new Family Combo. These combos offer greater savings for you and ensure that you get all the programs you want.

Additionally, subscribe by April 30 and take advantage of these special promotions!

- A subscription to Vizio's cable Internet service, the highest speed Internet connection in the country, for only $10 per month, down from our usual price of $20
- No first-time yearly membership charge (save $29!)
- Free cable installation
- A complimentary monthly TV guide

To order your Vizio cable package, call us today at 858-677-9898, or visit our website at www.vizio.com.

Combo Packages Available from Vizio TV

Package	Specialty Channels Included	Total Channels	Monthly Fee
Basic*	none	18*	$25
Sports Combo	Baseball, Basketball, Football, and Hockey channels	24	$30
Entertainment Combo	Musico TV, The Movie Network, Variety Vision	30	$35
Family Combo	The Learning Network, Family Entertainment, Nature TV	45	$40
Value Combo	All specialty channels	61	$65

*The Basic package includes all the major U.S. networks as well as News 24, Weather Spotlight, and a variety of local channels. The basic package is included in all other combos.

4　What is NOT included free of charge when signing up by April 30?

(A) Internet service

(B) One year's membership

(C) Cable installation

(D) A TV guide

5　The word 'offer' in paragraph 1, line 3 is closest in meaning to

(A) make available

(B) negotiate

(C) suggest

(D) leave out

6　How much does Vizio's newest package cost per month?

(A) $30

(B) $35

(C) $40

(D) $65

7　Which of the following options includes the fewest channels?

(A) The Sports Combo

(B) The Entertainment Combo

(C) The Family Combo

(D) The Value Combo

8　What is included in all packages?

(A) Weather Spotlight

(B) Variety Vision

(C) Nature TV

(D) The Learning Network

▶ 解答在159頁

(2) Double Passages

Questions 9-13 refer to the following advertisement and e-mail.

Wanted: Late Night Delivery Person

Pizza Palazzo's downtown location is seeking a flexible, late night delivery person. The successful applicant agrees to be on-call four nights a week for potential deliveries from 10 p.m. to 4 a.m.

The position starts at $10 an hour for every hour or partial hour a call is answered, with an increase to $12 after three months. For every hour no call is received, the applicant will receive $5 an hour. If the successful applicant possesses previous experience in this field, the starting wage will be $13 with an increase to $15 after three months.

Pizza Palazzo recognizes the challenges associated with working an ambiguous, overnight schedule and therefore offers a competitive salary and benefit package (available after six months of employment). No other pizza place in town offers benefits!

Applicants must have 24-hour access to a telephone and vehicle and must possess a valid driver's license. You must also agree to monthly car inspections, paid for in full by Pizza Palazzo.

To apply: e-mail monica@pizzapalazzo.com

Make sure to include contact information for two managers from other jobs you have held.

Date: November 14
From: Monica Palazzo <monica@pizzapalazzo.com>
To: Reginald DuFour <rdufour@myemail.co>
Subject: Paperwork

Dear Reginald,

We are delighted that you have accepted our job offer of being our newest on-call, late night deliveryman for our downtown store. We hope you will be very happy here.

I was wondering if you would be available to come in tomorrow around 5 p.m. to fill out some paperwork related to your pay. We should also schedule your vehicle's check-up, but that can wait until next week.

When I told the staff that we had finally hired a suitable nighttime driver, they were thrilled! Some of our staff have been working late and coming in early in order to keep up with our quickly increasing orders. Everyone was also happy that you have previous experience delivering pizza. They thought you might be able to offer some suggestions about how to improve our late night service!

Let me know if you are able to come in tomorrow.

Monica

9 Why does the ad say the wages are competitive?

  (A) To reward the uncertainty of on-call work
  (B) To attract experienced employees
  (C) To compete with other pizza restaurants
  (D) To offset costs of the vehicle inspections

10 What are interested applicants asked to do?

  (A) Apply in person downtown
  (B) List two previous employers
  (C) Inspect their vehicles
  (D) Itemize their availability

11 Why did Monica Palazzo send this email?

  (A) To offer Reginald a job
  (B) To arrange an appointment
  (C) To schedule a car inspection
  (D) To check Reginald's references

12 How much will Reginald earn when he starts at Pizza Palazzo?

  (A) $10
  (B) $12
  (C) $13
  (D) $15

13 What can be inferred about Pizza Palazzo from the e-mail?

  (A) The location has changed.
  (B) There is a new owner.
  (C) Late delivery is a new service.
  (D) Business is growing.

攻略法

98

各種表格（Forms）

如果在Part 7中出現這種問題！

這是在Part 7閱讀類型中，最容易掌握的類型。在各種表格類型中，出題頻率最高的就是問卷調查、邀請函、發票、日程表、價格表等。表格與其他的類型比較起來，閱讀的內文較短，對於節省時間上有很大的幫助。對平常熟悉這種樣式的人來說，是非常簡單的問題，但是對於不熟悉的人，理解較困難，也需要花很久的時間才能掌握。平常好好把多益考試中常出現的商務樣式，依照類型別來整理記憶的話，在考試的時候會有很大的成效。

1. 各種樣式的種類與主要內容

1 種類
調查問卷、發票、日程表、價格表、邀請函、產品使用說明書、廣告用宣傳單、表格、圖表、統計圖表、圖示圖表等

2 主要內容

❶ 調查問卷：問題有好幾個，但實際要確認的內容是最重要的

❷ 出入境申請書：個人資訊、出境或是入境的目的、攜帶物品、注意事項等

❸ 旅遊行程表：顧客姓名、旅行社名稱、旅遊日期、目的地、交通方式、時間表等

❹ 其他：產品說明書、料理方法、診療卡片、生產相關圖表等

❺ 電話紀錄：接電話與打電話的人、紀錄的時間、轉達的內容等

2. 各種樣式的問題類型

1 NOT / TRUE 類型：一一對照本文的資訊之後決定答案
What is NOT mentioned as a means of payment?

2 找出 key word 類型：掌握問題的 key word 後在文中快速找出答案
What information is included in the form?

> 1 沒有提到的付款方式是？
>
> 2 在這個表格中包含什麼樣的資訊？

3. 處理各種表格的技巧

1 在問題中快速找到key word後，再從內文找出可以成為答案的資訊。

2 平常就要熟悉觀察表格的方法。表格的內文通常都不多，也不太會有困難的單字，只要好好熟記觀察表格的方法，就可以在考試中輕鬆的解題。

4. 怪物講師的解法

請依照下面的指示事項中所提供的號碼順序解題看看。一開始一定要先閱讀題目。

讓你了解主題

City Circuit Buses
See Scottsville at Your Own Pace ◄— 意思就是依照你的心情決定速度

	One-Day Pass	Two-Day Pass
Adult (Ages 21 and over)	$30	$50
Student (Ages 12-20)	$24	$40
Child (Under 12)	$15	$25
Senior (65 and over)	$24	$40

② 1號問題的解題 快速的掌握問題1與圖表有沒有關聯，確認對應的部分之後解題。

④ 再次閱讀內文 一邊確認問題2的內文，一邊一一地刪除答案選項，當每次出現一些線索的時候，再看答案選項確認答案。

巴士上是開放式

City Circuit Buses are the best way to tour Scottsville's many sights. Our open-air buses offer you great views of the city's Harbor District and Old Town, and the narrated ◄— 有負責解說的導遊 commentary (available in six languages) will explain the history and importance of key landmarks. Get off anywhere you like and get back on at any bus stop marked with the City Circuit symbol.

Buses depart every 15 minutes between 9:30 A.M. and 4:30 P.M. during peak season (April-October). During the off-season (November-March), departures are every 30 minutes, with the last bus leaving at 4:00 P.M.

⑤ 2號問題的解題 把問題2的答案選項與內文做比較，選出正確答案

1. How much is a two-day pass for a 17-year old? ① 先讀問題

一定要讀！

   (A) $24

   (B) $30

   (C) $40

   (D) $50

2. What is indicated about the tours? ③ 先讀問題

這個問題的類型是要
看內文才能解題

   (A) They offer commentary in several languages.

   (B) They take 30 minutes to complete.

   (C) They depart with the same frequency year round.

   (D) They are not run in winter.

▶ 解答在162頁

5. 讓Part7變簡單的句子分析

> 1 Our open-air buses offer you great views of the city's Harbor District and Old Town,

1 我們的露天巴士提供／給各位／美麗的風景／市區的港口區域以及舊城鎮的，

主詞是Our open-air buses，限定動詞是offer。而且依附於動詞offer的受詞就變成you。因此you後面的great views of the city's Harbor District and Old Town是什麼呢？因為offer是第4大句型動詞，使用直接受詞（向…）與間接受詞（做…）兩個受詞。意思就是「向…做…」。

Our open-air buses / offer / you / great views of the city's Harbor
    主詞   動詞 間接受詞   直接受詞
District and Old Town,

> 2 During the off-season (November-March), departures are every 30 minutes, with the last bus leaving at 4:00 P.M.

2 淡季（11月到3月）的時候／以30分鐘為單位出發／末班巴士下午4點出發。

在上面的句子中，最前面出現的During是什麼呢？看到後面出現的名詞the off-season之後就知道是介系詞了。像這樣介系詞during後面會接著表示時間的名詞。之後在（,）後面出現的是在主要子句中的主詞departures以及動詞are。are是帶有「在、存在」意思的第1大句型動詞，every 30 minutes是帶有「每30分鐘」意思的副詞。（把在英文中與時間有關的表現幾乎都看成副詞即可。）而且後面是以介系詞片語擔任補充前面內容的角色。在這裡leaving是現在分詞，用來修飾正前方的bus。

During / the off-season, / departures / are / every 30 minutes, /
介系詞   名詞（介系詞片語）   主詞   動詞   副詞
with the last bus / leaving / at 4:00 P.M.
    副詞   分詞   介系詞片語

Questions 1-2 refer to the following receipt.

DELI-MART

400 Granger ST, Bentner, IL 10922
Tel : (555) 763-4481

12 January 2:25 P.M.
CASHIER: Sara

White grapes (0.53 lbs @ $4.00/lbs)	$2.06
Ground pork (1 pack @ $4.49/pack)	$4.49
Green onion (1 pack @ $0.99/pack)	$0.99
Carrots (1 pack @ $1.33/pack)	$1.33

subtotal: $8.87
sales tax: $0.00
Total due: $8.87

cash: $20.00
change: $11.13

Returns are accepted within 3 days of original purchase, as indicated above.
Food purchases must be returned within 24 hours. Only products in their original
conditions may be returned.

Thank you for shopping at DELI-MART

---

1 What information is included in the receipt?

(A) The time of purchase
(B) The customer's name
(C) A delivery location
(D) The store's business hours

2 What can be understood about the purchase?

(A) Sales tax is applicable to groceries.
(B) The ground pork is sold by weight.
(C) The customer paid with a check.
(D) None of the items may be returned after 24 hours.

Questions 3-6 refer to the following review.

The French consume more fattening, high-cholesterol food like beef, cheese, cream, and butter than most cultures, but the heart disease rate is among the lowest in Europe. This unexpected fact is the basis for Owen Shipley's new book, *The French Paradox.*

Scientists believe that wine is the key. Red wine can reduce the risk of heart disease, and the French are certainly known to enjoy a glass of wine with their meals. But in The French Paradox, Shipley, who is a noted wine critic-argues that red wine is not the only reason. He points to many other aspects of the French lifestyle which result in healthier citizens. For instance, the French are much more likely than North Americans to buy their groceries fresh from the market each day, rather than buying in bulk from a superstore. They are also more willing to pay more for better quality products—like fine chocolate instead of mass—produced junk-and eat fast food less often.

Shipley's book is an easy read packed with interesting facts and information. *The French Paradox* has plenty of good advice for anyone struggling to balance a love of eating with a healthy body.

3 What is Owen Shipley's field of expertise?

(A) Cooking
(B) History
(C) Wine
(D) Science

4 What does the article state is more common in France than elsewhere?

(A) Eating foods in high cholesterol
(B) Fast food consumption
(C) Heart disease
(D) Buying bulk groceries

5 What does Owen Shipley claim in his book?

(A) Wine does not reduce the risk of heart disease.
(B) It is healthier to eat fresh food from a market.
(C) Chocolate can have a negative impact on health.
(D) Food in North America costs more than in France.

6 What kind of information can be found in *The French Paradox*?

(A) Recipes for French cuisine
(B) Tips for a healthier lifestyle
(C) Wine recommendations
(D) Advice on cultural etiquette

▶ 解答在163頁

(2) Double Passages

Questions 7-11 refer to the following invoice and e-mail.

Invoice – June 5

Flowers shipped to:

Janessa Sampson

1450 Santa Anna Avenue

Los Angeles, CA

90003

Order taken: May 19

Delivery Date: June 2

Please send payment to:

Daisy Chain Flower Shop, 25 Lavalle Boulevard, Los Angeles, CA, 90001

Items

Quantity	Description	Unit Price	Net Amount
2	Large flower arrangement (assortment of white flowers)	$175	$350
5	corsages (lily)	$10	$50
1	bouquet (lilac)	$40	$40
1	delivery	$25	$25

Discount Code: B7SIK91   Applicable Discount: $30

Discount Code: H71029F   Applicable Discount: $15 (shipping)

Total Bill of Sale: $420

Thank you for your business!

For questions or inquiries, please call Daisy Chain at 555-587-1029. Orders not paid within 10 business days will be charged a penalty of $5 per day.

Date: June 24

From: Janessa Sampson <jsampson@newmail.co>

To: Celeste Chain <celeste@daisychain.com>

Subject: Invoice

Dear Celeste,

I received your invoice today for the flowers I ordered last week.

On the invoice, you listed one bouquet of lilacs, which is indeed what I ordered, except that I received tulips instead! I wasn't upset because I love tulips as well, but I was wondering if there is a price difference. If not, I am happy to pay the amount listed, but if there is a difference in price, I would appreciate a new invoice reflecting the change.

The guests at my dinner party were in awe of the beautiful flowers! My aunt particularly loved the lilies. Your work is always well received among my guests.

Oh, and thank you for applying the white flower discount; you had mentioned the promotion was over, so I appreciate that you extended it for me.

Let me know about the price adjustment, if there is one!

Janessa

7   When did Janessa Sampson receive her flowers?

(A) May 19
(B) June 2
(C) June 5
(D) June 15

8   What is Janessa asked to do?

(A) Pay the invoice
(B) Call for clarification
(C) Arrange a shipping date
(D) Verify the order

9   Why did Janessa email Celeste?

(A) To arrange a delivery date
(B) To verify an item on the invoice
(C) To inquire about a type of flower
(D) To thank her for the discount

10 Why did Janessa receive a $30 discount?

(A) For receiving the wrong flowers
(B) For renting large vases
(C) For emailing Celeste
(D) For ordering white flowers

11 What does Janessa suggest in the e-mail?

(A) She has ordered flowers from Daisy Chain in the past.
(B) She prefers white flowers to purple ones.
(C) She is unsatisfied with the cost of flowers.
(D) She will not order flowers from Daisy Chain in future.

▶ 解答在163頁

簡訊和線上聊天

簡訊（Message）

★ 簡訊的出題類型

❶ 公司內部公告簡訊：給內部員工的活動訊息、規定。

❷ 公司外部溝通簡訊：公告、廣告、感謝、促銷等。

★ 簡訊被出題的閱讀內容

❶ What is the main purpose of this text message? 簡訊的主要功能為何？

❷ What has been announced in this text message? 簡訊公告了什麼？

❸ Who sent this text message? 誰是傳送簡訊的人？

❹ Who is the recipient of this text message? 誰是簡訊的接收者？

❺ When is this text message sent? 簡訊何時發出？

❻ Why is this text message sent? 為什麼傳送簡訊？

線上聊天（SMS）

★ 線上聊天的出題類型

❶ 公事：內容五花八門，只要跟工作有關皆可能出現。聊天人數不受限，可以一對一，也可以多對一，甚至為群組聊天。

❷ 非公事：同事與同事，朋友及家人之間，比較非正式的閒聊。

★ 線上聊天被出題的閱讀內容

❶ What is the main purpose / issue of the online chatting?
線上聊天的主要目的／議題為何？

❷ For whom is the online chatting mostly intended? 主要聊天對象有誰？

❸ What is / is not mentioned / discussed? 有／未提及／討論到的？

❹ What should your coworkers do if they want to help?
如果同事需要協助，應該怎麼辦

攻略法

99

簡訊（Messages）

2018改制後出現的新題型！

多益於2018年改制之後，在Part 7的閱讀文章中，新增了簡訊、線上聊天這類的閱讀題材，這樣的改變，讓多益考試更加貼近生活中會碰到的場景。多益中的簡訊題簡訊以溝通為主要目標，讓接收方能馬上了解其內容，因此考生應該利用此特性，快速瀏覽對話內容，找出對話的主要目的和關鍵訊息。

1. 簡訊的內容

相較於信件與email，簡訊通常為一個畫面的長度，較為簡短，目的也比較直接了當，常會省略稱呼，傳簡訊者的署名常位於簡訊一開始或結束位置。

1 公司內部公告簡訊：給內部員工的活動訊息、規定。

2 公司外部溝通簡訊：公告、廣告、感謝、促銷等。

2. 簡訊的主要類型和表現

1 詢問簡訊目的

What is the main purpose of this text message?

What has been announced in this text message?

Who sent this text message?

Who is the recipient of this text message?

When is this text message sent?

Why is this text message sent?

1 簡訊的主要功能為何？
簡訊公告了什麼？
誰是傳送簡訊的人？
誰是簡訊的接收者？
簡訊何時發出？
為什麼傳送簡訊？

2 推論問題

Why would employees get vaccinated against the flu?

What would employees do if they would like to get the flu shot?

How does flu vaccine work?

2 為什麼員工必須施打流感疫苗？
如果員工願意施打流感疫苗，應該怎麼做？
流感疫苗的成效如何？

3 評論性問題

In our opinion, who should/should not...?

It is important...

4 公告

CX8732 will depart at SFO at 00:50.

（使用句型：... will 將…）

This is to remind you that your flight will be delayed and the new departure time is at 8:05.

（使用句型：this is to... 這是要…）

If you have any problems concerning this policy, please let us know.

（使用句型：if... 如果…）

5 請求協助

We ask you that you check out by 11 am so that we can prepare the room for other guests.

（使用句型：We ask you that..., so that... 我們請您…以便…。）

6 感謝

Thank you for shopping with us.

（使用句型：thank you for... 感謝…）

7 連接用詞

As far as I know...（就我所知）→等於AFAK

at the moment...（現在）→等於ATM

You are（你…）→等於U R

3 我們認為，誰…？
…很重要。

4 CX8732班機將於00:50於舊金山機場起飛。
這是要通知您，您的班機將會延遲，新的登機時間是8:05。
如果您對於此政策有任何問題，請告知我們。

5 我們請您在早上11點退房，以便我們為其他房客準備房間。

6 謝謝您的惠顧。

3. 簡訊的處理方式

1 快速瀏覽了解簡訊發送與接收對象和目的。

2 先看題目，依據題目類型，再尋找答案。

3 了解簡訊的呈現結構，快速找到答案。

4. 了解簡訊的呈現結構，快速找到答案。

請依照下面的指示事項中所提供的號碼順序解題看看。一開始一定要先閱讀題目。

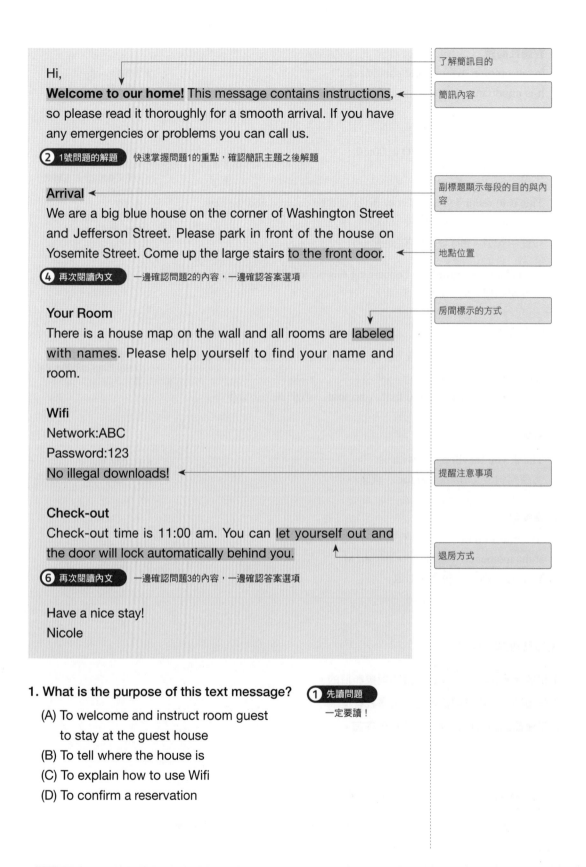

Hi,

Welcome to our home! This message contains instructions, so please read it thoroughly for a smooth arrival. If you have any emergencies or problems you can call us.

了解簡訊目的

簡訊內容

2 1號問題的解題　快速掌握問題1的重點，確認簡訊主題之後解題

Arrival

副標題顯示每段的目的與內容

We are a big blue house on the corner of Washington Street and Jefferson Street. Please park in front of the house on Yosemite Street. Come up the large stairs to the front door.

地點位置

4 再次閱讀內文　一邊確認問題2的內容，一邊確認答案選項

Your Room

房間標示的方式

There is a house map on the wall and all rooms are labeled with names. Please help yourself to find your name and room.

Wifi

Network:ABC
Password:123
No illegal downloads!

提醒注意事項

Check-out

Check-out time is 11:00 am. You can let yourself out and the door will lock automatically behind you.

退房方式

6 再次閱讀內文　一邊確認問題3的內容，一邊確認答案選項

Have a nice stay!
Nicole

1. What is the purpose of this text message?

1 先讀問題

一定要讀！

(A) To welcome and instruct room guest
to stay at the guest house
(B) To tell where the house is
(C) To explain how to use Wifi
(D) To confirm a reservation

2. Where should the guest park? ③ 先讀問題 找到關鍵字，
就可以對照內文答題

(A) At the corner of Washington and Jefferson Street

(B) In front of Yosemite Street

(C) In front of the park

(D) Wherever is suitable

3. How can the guest check out? ⑤ 先讀問題 找到關鍵字，
就可以對照內文答題

▶ 解答在166頁

(A) To take the key out and lock the door

(B) To leave the key in the room and leave

(C) To leave the door open and go out

(D) To return the key to the owner of the guest house in person

5. 讓Part 7變簡單的句子分析

> 1 There is a house map on the wall and all rooms are labeled with names.

1 牆上有房子地圖／所有的房間／都有標上姓名。

分析句子前要看清楚句子的結構，基本上這是兩個由對等連接詞and 連接而成的句子，也就是There is a house map on the wall + and + all rooms are labeled with names。這兩個句子都是形容物體的狀態，所以主詞都不是人，後面的be labeled with為被動語態的句子。句子與句子之間要有連接詞連接。

> 2 You can let yourself out and the door will lock automatically behind you.

2 你可以／自行離開／門／會／自動上鎖／在你之後。

一樣是利用對等連接詞連接的兩個句子：You can let yourself out +and+ the door will lock automatically behind you.。第一個句子使用的是使役動詞let的句型，let oneself + 原形動詞（let yourself out 走出去）。接著，雖然主詞是door，但這裡不使用被動式，而使用the door will lock automatically。

You / can let / yourself out / and / the door / will lock /
主詞　使役動詞　反身代名詞　　連接詞　　主詞　　　動詞
automatically behind you.

Questions 1-3 refer to the following message.

Dear Customers,

The great news is you can easily customize your billing notifications online. Once you're logged in, please follow these steps:

At the top of the page, select the my Profile.

Click the Select button and choose your wireless account.

Scroll down to the Billing Notifications section and select Edit.

You may opt in or out of each type of listed billing notification for either text messages or emails.

Select Save Changes to save your updates and then you complete the setting.

We greatly appreciate you use our services!

Please let us know if this resolves your issue.

Yelta, TSMA Community Specialist

1 Who most likely will receive this text message?

(A) Customers of TSMA
(B) Suppliers of TSMA
(C) Prospects of TSMA
(D) Employees of TSMA

2 What is included with this text message?

(A) Information about order tracing
(B) Information to confirm order
(C) Information to trace shipment
(D) Information to set up billing notification

3 What has been instructed as the last step of customizing billing notification?

(A) Scroll down the billing notification.
(B) Opt in and out the type of billing notification.
(C) Save your setting.
(D) Select Edit.

Questions 4-6 refer to the following text message.

Dear Customer,

Your ABC Friend Card is going to expire by the end of December. You only need to purchase USD 300 to upgrade your membership to the next level. After upgrading, you are eligible for choosing a free gift on your next visit to us. Thank you for being our valued customer. We are grateful for the pleasure of serving you.

4   What is the purpose of this text message?

(A) To thank the customer

(B) To confirm customer information

(C) To promote and encourage the customer to update his/her membership to the next level

(D) To discontinue the membership

5   What would the customer do if he/she wish to choose a free gift on next visit?

(A) Purchase a single item at the price less than USD 200

(B) Make an additional purchase at the price higher than USD 300

(C) Apply for a new membership

(D) Do nothing

6   When will the membership become ineffective?

(A) The end of January

(B) The end of the year

(C) The end of July

(D) The end of summer

▶ 解答在166頁

(2) Double Passages

Questions 7-11 refer to the following text messages.

Dear participants,

We will change venues for both opening ceremony and dinner banquet to International Banquet Hall on 2F of Hotel Aloha. The opening ceremony will start at 18:00 and dinner banquet at 18:30. Shuttle buses are arranged to pick you up at the train station and airport. Our staff will guide you to take the shuttle bus to the hotel. The first shuttle bus will departure at 17:40.

If you miss the first shuttle bus, please wait for the next one at 18:10. If you miss both shuttle buses, you need to go to the hotel on your own. Thank you for your participation. If you have any question, please contact me at 612-356-7654, Ms. Umi. This text message is sent by the system and do not reply it directly.

7 What has been changed according to this text message?

(A) The venues for opening ceremony and dinner banquet

(B) Departure time of shuttle bus

(C) The venues for the conference

(D) Meeting time at the train station and at the airport

8 What time should a participate take the shuttle bus?

(A) 18:00 or 18:30

(B) 17:40 or 18:10

(C) 18:00

(D) 18:30

9 If a participant needs a help, whom he/she should contact?

(A) Reply the text message directly

(B) Call the hotel

(C) Call someone at the venues

(D) Call Ms. Umi

10 Where can a participant take the shuttle bus?

(A) The hotel

(B) The park

(C) The train station or the airport

(D) Call Ms. Umi

11 If a participant misses the departure of shuttle buses arranged, what should he/she do?

(A) Go to the hotel by taxi

(B) Wait for another shuttle bus to come

(C) Call Ms. Umi

(D) Call the hotel

▶ 解答在166頁

100 線上聊天（SMS）

2018改制後出現的新題型！

線上聊天為二或多人使用手機、平板、桌機或其他行動裝置進行的溝通對話，沒有特定形式與主題，在廣為使用的今日，為了省事及省時間，常利用發音進行縮寫，甚至使用emoji和聲音內容。

1. 線上聊天的主要類型

1 公事：內容五花八門，只要跟工作有關皆可能出現。聊天人數不受限，可以一對一，也可以多對一，甚至為群組聊天。

2 非公事：同事與同事，朋友及家人之間，比較非正式的閒聊。

2. 線上聊天文字類型

1 **線上聊天的主題**

What is the main purpose / issue of the online chatting?

2 **線上聊天對象**

For whom is the online chatting mostly intended?

3 **確認細節**

What is / is not mentioned / discussed?

4 **推論問題**

What should your coworkers do if they need help?

1 線上聊天的主要目的／議題為何？

2 主要聊天對象有誰？

3 有／未提及／討論到的？

4 如果同事需要協助，應該怎麼辦？

3. 線上聊天題型的答題技巧：

1 先閱讀及熟記題目。

2 由題目去找問題答案，確認問題。

3 如果為推論問題，就題目去瀏覽及了解聊天對象、內容要旨。

4. 了解簡訊的呈現結構，快速找到答案。

請依照下面的指示事項中所提供的號碼順序解題看看。一開始一定要先閱讀題目。

Alex Jones:	We found the light in the front is out of order. [4:39 pm]	了解主旨

② 1號問題的解題　　快速掌握問題1的重點，確認簡訊主題之後解題

Michael Wong:	Is it the problem found in Machine ABC? [4:40 pm]	
Alex Jones:	Yes.　　　　　　　　　　　　　　　　[4:43 pm]	
Eric Forbes:	Indeed, before Alex, Richard brought the issue of failure of light bulb to the client. [4:45 pm]	之前與問題有關的經驗
Alex Jones:	Yes. We reported to the client again. Changing the light bulb is easy, but we need to shut down the system for about five minutes.　　　　　　　　　　[5:00 pm]	問題必須進一步解決
Michael Wong:	That will become an issue. It is peak time now because everyone rushes to get off from work before 6:00 pm. Eric, ask him whether we can work on the machine tonight?　　　　　　　　　　[5:10 pm]	面對的困難和原因
Eric Forbes:	Surely and I will get back to you soon. [5:12 pm]	後續的程序
Michael Wong:	Thank you very much for your help.　[5:15 pm]	
Alex Jones:	Then you will need to find someone else to do this replacement since I have scheduled work tonight.　　　　　　　　[5:30 pm]	小總結與問題解決的進一步線索

④ 再次閱讀內文　　一邊確認問題2的內容，一邊一一刪除答案選項，每次出現線索的時候，再看答案選項確認

1. What is the issue? 一定要讀！

   (A) No one is available to do the replacement.

   (B) Everyone is rush to get off from work before 6:00 pm.

   (C) There is a light bulb failure found.

   (D) Alex has scheduled work.

2. If the replacement work is confirmed, ③ 先讀問題 這個問題的類型是要看完內文才能解題   ▶ 解答在168頁
   who should take charge of it?

   (A) Alex Jones

   (B) Michael Wong

   (C) Eric Forbes.

   (D) We do not know since a person shall be found to do the work.

5. 讓Part 7變簡單的句子分析

> **1** It is peak time now because everyone rushes to get off from work before 6:00 pm.

1 因為每個人／都忙著要在／下午6:00前下班／尖峰時間／現在。

拆開來看為「It is peak time now + because + everyone rushes to get off from work before 6:00 pm.」。這是由because連接詞所連接的兩個子句，because之前的子句可以獨立構成句子，但是because之後的子句，因為說明第一個子句的原因，所以在語意和文法上皆無法單獨存在。

這個句子中的because 也可以放置在句首，變成：Because everyone rushes to get off from work before 6:00 pm, it is the peak time now.

※注意because 放在句中時，前面不可有,（逗點）。

> **2** Then you will need to find someone else to do this replacement since I have scheduled work tonight.

2 你必須／找其他人／來做更換工作／因為／我有排程工作／今晚。

拆開來看為「Then you will need to find someone else to do this replacement + since+ I have scheduled work tonight.」。since為「既然」的意思，這個句子一樣可以把since放到句首，變成：Since I have schedule work tonight, then you will need to find someone else to do this replacement.

※兩個重點要提醒：since在句中時，前面不可有逗點；then是副詞，不是連接詞，不可以直接拿來連接句子。

(1) Single Passages

Questions 1-3 refer to the following online chatting.

Vincent Murry:	We have been waiting for the client for a couple of hours.	[11:32 am]
Roger Woods:	What? You told me that you have the meeting at 9:00 in the morning. It's almost lunch time.	[11:34 am]
Lilly Wen:	I will call Mr. Brown again.	[11:34 am]
Vincent Murry:	Thank you, Lily. Can you talk to his secretary Lisa to find out when he will be here?	[11:36 am]
Roger Woods:	I think you had better have someone wait there and begin to take turns eating lunch if he does not show up 15 minutes later.	[11:40 am]
Vincent Murry:	We will not going anywhere before Lilly confirms when Mr. Brown will arrive.	[11:42 am]
Lilly Wen:	I talked to Lisa already and she said some emergency occurred and Mr. Brown has to take care of it in person. He will be there around 13:00. He is very sorry for making you guys waiting for long hours.	[11:45 am]
Vincent Murry:	Roger, I think you are right. It is time for early lunch now.	[11:46 am]

1 What happened as indicated in the passage?

(A) The client came on time.

(B) The client did not show up on time.

(C) The client treated Vincent Murry and his people for lunch.

(D) The client refused to see them.

2 What would Vincent Murry and his people do?

(A) They left and leaved a note.

(B) He directly called the client's secretary.

(C) They went for lunch.

(D) They will take turns to have lunch and request the client's secretary to call back.

3 Why did Mr. Brown fail to see Vincent Murry on time?

(A) He needed to take care something emergent in person.

(B) He was ill.

(C) He forgot the meeting.

(D) He was angry to see them.

Questions 4-6 refer to the following online chatting.

Mandy Chen:	Ms. Foster, are you on your way to the office?	[10:45 am]
Christine Foster:	Yup, I am almost there.	[10:45 am]
Mandy Chen:	Great. Mr. Machchan from India is here now; his flight arrived earlier.	[10:46 am]
Christine Foster:	Show him the new product catalogue we have.	[10:47 am]
Mandy Chen:	I did. He has some questions.	[10:48 am]
Mr. Peter Smith:	I am there with him. But he requested to talk to you.	[10:50 am]
Christine Foster:	Give me some more minutes and I will be right there.	[10:51 am]
Mandy Chen:	I put him on the telephone now. Do you have a minute to talk to him?	[10:53 am]

4 Where was Christine Foster?

(A) She was on her way back to office.
(B) She was at a meeting.
(C) She was home.
(D) She was at a restaurant.

5 Who was with Mr. Machchan?

(A) Peter Smith
(B) Christine Foster
(C) Mandy Chen
(D) Mr. Machchan was alone.

6 What was the intention to show Mr. Machchan the new product catalogue?

(A) To kill time
(B) To disturb him
(C) To promote
(D) To entertain him

▶ 解答在169頁

(2) Double Passages

Questions 7-11 refer to the following online chatting.

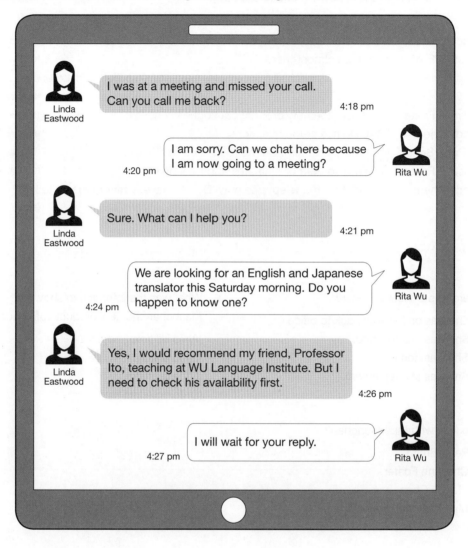

Linda Eastwood: I was at a meeting and missed your call. Can you call me back? 4:18 pm

Rita Wu: I am sorry. Can we chat here because I am now going to a meeting? 4:20 pm

Linda Eastwood: Sure. What can I help you? 4:21 pm

Rita Wu: We are looking for an English and Japanese translator this Saturday morning. Do you happen to know one? 4:24 pm

Linda Eastwood: Yes, I would recommend my friend, Professor Ito, teaching at WU Language Institute. But I need to check his availability first. 4:26 pm

Rita Wu: I will wait for your reply. 4:27 pm

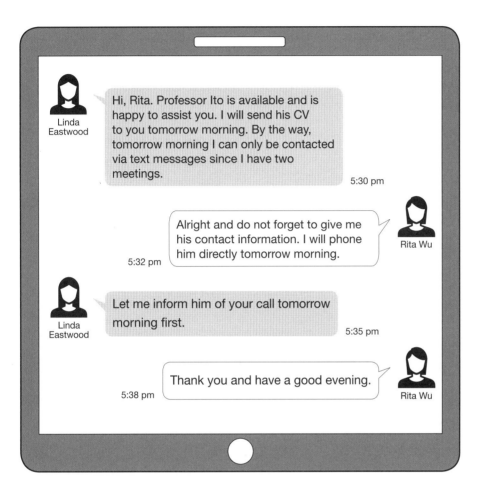

Linda Eastwood: Hi, Rita. Professor Ito is available and is happy to assist you. I will send his CV to you tomorrow morning. By the way, tomorrow morning I can only be contacted via text messages since I have two meetings. 5:30 pm

Rita Wu: Alright and do not forget to give me his contact information. I will phone him directly tomorrow morning. 5:32 pm

Linda Eastwood: Let me inform him of your call tomorrow morning first. 5:35 pm

Rita Wu: Thank you and have a good evening. 5:38 pm

7　What could Linda Eastwood help?

(A) To go to a meeting
(B) To set up a time to talk
(C) To find a translator
(D) To call Rita back

8　Could Linda Eastwood help?

(A) Yes, she could be the translator.
(B) Yes, she would recommend her friend.
(C) Yes, she would place a classification.
(D) Yes, she would ask her friend to recommend someone else.

9　What would Rita Wu do at the first place?

(A) Contact Professor Ito immediately
(B) Wait to see whether Professor Ito is available
(C) Call Professor Ito
(D) Talk to Professor Ito at a meeting

10　What is a CV?

(A) A life course
(B) A business card
(C) A application letter
(D) A purchase order

11　In the end, what was agreed?

(A) Professor Ito would call Linda Eastwood.
(B) Professor Ito would be informed of Rita Wu's phone call tomorrow first.
(C) Professor Ito would be requested to come to two meetings.
(D) Professor Ito would be requested to text Rita Wu.

▶ 解答在169頁

雙篇閱讀（Double Passages）

★ 在雙篇閱讀出題的內容

❶ 「郵件或是信件」＋「回信郵件或是信件、傳真」

❷ 「郵件或是信件」＋「問卷調查表、訂單、請款單、文章、保證書」

❸ 「廣告」＋「廣告」

❹ 「廣告」＋「郵件、信件、保證書」

❺ 「徵人廣告」＋「申請者履歷表」

❻ 「徵人廣告」＋「徵人廣告」

❼ 「履歷表」＋「履歷表」

❽ 「表格」＋「表格」

❾ 「文章」＋「公司內部文件、表格」

❿ 「保證書」＋「保證書」

★ 在雙篇閱讀出題的內容

❶ 文章中有敘述那些關於 A 的事情？

❷ A 寄出信件〔郵件〕的理由？

❸ According to the A 依據A的話

→ 在A的位置可以插入廣告、表格、信件、郵件、傳真、備忘錄、公告、方針、新聞文
　章等。由上可知，看到A的話，就可以馬上知道要閱讀那些內文後解題。

攻略法

101

雙篇閱讀（Double Passages）

放棄雙篇閱讀就等於放棄高分！

就像Part 7最前面所說明的，聽力測驗結束之後就是要寫這種多篇閱讀，也就是先解176題到200題是最適當的。（約25分鐘以內）如果想說後面再來解題的話，就會一直趕時間而無法正確的了解內容。雙篇閱讀是把2篇閱讀內文變成一篇文章。舉例來說，一部分是某個公司的產品打折廣告要先推出的內容，另一部分就是直接購買產品的消費者滿意度以及出現抱怨的信件內容。

像這樣二到三篇閱讀所組成的多篇閱讀，在一個題組中會有5個小問題。從176題到200題為止總共有25題，因此總共會出現5個多篇閱讀的題組。如果從時間管理的層面來看，一個題組的閱讀內文以及5個小題的題目最多只能花費5分鐘的時間。絕對不可以超過。平常在做模擬測試的時候，使用碼錶來確認自己解題的速度。

1. 雙篇閱讀的類型

閱讀內文1	閱讀內文2
問題、疑問	說明問題的解決方法
與產品、服務相關的廣告	對於廣告的追加問題或是與內容不同的抗議
徵人廣告	求職詢問或是求職申請
新聞或是雜誌文章	對於誤報的更正要求
與產品、服務相關的客戶不滿	道歉及退錢、交換流程說明
公司政策、便利設施、福利說明	詢問或建議事項
商品廣告	保證書
購買產品、服務的客戶感謝信件	表示感謝的意思而贈送各種公演的入場券
公司內的支援要求	包含負責人、聯絡方式、負責業務等內容的表

2. 處理雙篇閱讀的技巧

1 了解雙篇閱讀上會出現如下的提示之後，把握問題的類型。

Questions 176-180 refer to the following advertisement and the letter.

了解了第一個內文是廣告，第二個內文是信件之後，想像一下廣告後面的信件的內容。當廣告後面接著信件的時候，大多是抱怨的信件。

2 看過兩三個問題之後，再閱讀一次本文，再看兩三個問題之後，再閱讀一次本文。因為一次把5個題目都看完並沒有太大的幫助，因為要記清楚每個問題是很難的。因此，如果是我的話，我會先看過兩三個問題再閱讀本文，當答案出現的話再進行確認。再次看過兩三個問題之後閱讀本文，再找出答案的這種方式最好。為什麼不要一個一個看問題的原因，就是問題順序不會與本文的順序一致。再次提醒，依我個人的意見，先看兩三個問題在從本文中找答案，再次看兩三個問題後，再次地從本文中找答案這種方式是最好的。

3. 怪物講師的解法

請依照下面的指示事項中所提供的號碼順序解題看看。一定要從閱讀題目開始，也有閱讀測驗的內文很多，就必須要把內文看過兩三次的情況，閱讀時間會比預期中花時間。

② 開始閱讀內文 以問題1為中心先記憶再快速地尋找答案。

Faraway Travel Limited
165 East 47th Street New York NY

To: Mel Goulet

From: Anika Reese

Re: Available Flight from New York to Miami

	Date	Airline	From	To	Departure	Arrival	Cost
Option 1	May 2	Eagle Air	New York	Miami	8:15 A.M.	12:15 P.M.	$400
Option 2	May 1	SR Airlines	New York	Atlanta	3:00 P.M.	4:30 P.M.	$300
		SR Airlines	Atlanta	Miami	5:45 P.M.	7:30 P.M.	
Option 3	May 1	Calico Air	New York	Miami	9:00 A.M.	1:00 P.M.	$450

⑥ 比較圖表與問題2之後找出答案

Notes: All fares includes a $100 fuel surcharge and a $50 Miami Airport maintenance charge.

③ 移動到問題1的答案選項 找出有重點句的地方

Please visit our website at www.farawaytravel.com for a full list of ticket conditions.

To: Anika Reese (areese@farawaytravel.com)
From: Mel Goulet (mg@crooners.net)
Date: April 25
Subject: Flight from New York to Miami

Dear Anika,

Thank you for your prompt response to my e-mail about flights from New York to Miami departing on or around May 1.

⑫ 選擇答案 第4題答案選項和第二段內文反覆地看，選出答案。

I understand that I have left my booking rather late, which means there are very few options left open to me. As we discussed in our previous exchange, it is important that I get to Miami earlier rather than later, in order to set up my company's booth at the International Car Show, which will start on May 3. Looking at the fax you sent me then, I think my best option would be the direct flight on May 1.

⑨ 移動到問題3 所有的線索都出現了

I would appreciate it if you could please reserve that flight and send me a confirmation e-mail as soon as possible so that I can make my payment.

I will be bringing along a number of samples for the trade show, so I was also hoping you might be able to tell me the luggage weight limits and extra luggage charges for that flight.

⑭ 與第5題答案選項比較之後選擇正確答案

Best regards,

Mel

1. What is indicated about the maintenance charge?

   (A) It is $150.
   (B) It has already been paid.
   (C) It has been added to the listed price.
   (D) It is refundable.

   ① 先閱讀問題
   一定要讀！

   ④ 先看文章內容解決問題

2. What is NOT true about the SR Airlines option?

   (A) It is the cheapest option.
   (B) It departs on May 1.
   (C) It arrives in Miami in the evening.
   (D) It is a direct flight.

   ⑤ 閱讀問題
   問題的類型要先看文章，再一個一個分辨類型。

   ⑦ 先看文章內容解決問題

3. What time will Mel likey depart for Miami?

   (A) 8:15 A.M.
   (B) 9:00 A.M.
   (C) 3:00 P.M.
   (D) 5:45 P.M.

   ⑧ 閱讀問題
   看看現在的內容有沒有延續到下一個段落。

   ⑩ 選擇問題的正確答案

4. What does Mel Goulet indicate in his e-mail?

   (A) He has previously contacted Anika Reese.
   (B) He will be traveling to Miami on vacation.
   (C) He has never been to Miami before.
   (D) He has already paid for his ticket.

   ⑪ 閱讀問題與答案選項　掌握到這裡與第二段文章有關係，移動到第二段文章。看過答案選項再與文章內容做比較的這一點，是很重要的。

5. What does Mel want Anika to do?

   (A) Book a rental car for him
   (B) Send him new departure dates
   (C) Inform him of an airline's baggage policy
   (D) Confirm a hotel reservation

   ⑬ 閱讀問題
   先了解問題中要求的部分是什麼，直接跳到第二段文章。

▶ 解答在172頁

4. 讓Part7變簡單的句子分析

1 I understand that I have left my booking rather late, which means there are very few options left open to me.

1 我了解／我讓我的預約延遲／表示／沒有很多選擇的機會／給我。

在上面的句子裡，主詞是I動詞就是understand。that之後是understand的受詞變成的名詞子句。因為是名詞子句，在that子句之後包含了所有的要素。出現逗號（,）之後關係代名詞which也出現了，這裡的which就是以持續性的用法來寫的關係代名詞，承接前面的句子（I understand...late），所以which means that...就代表了逗號前面部分以及there are後面部分的意思。另外在後面的left open是把第5大句型動詞leave當作被動式以及分詞來寫。

I / understand / that I have left my booking / rather / late, /
主詞　　動詞　　　　　　　名詞子句　　　　　　　分詞　　副詞
which means there are very few options / left open / to me.
　　　關係代名詞子句（持續性用法）　　　　　分詞　　介系詞片語

530

2 Looking at the fax you sent me then, I think my best option would be the direct flight on May 1.

◁ **2** 看之前你寄給我的傳真／我想／我最好的選擇就是直飛航班／在5月1日。

上面的句子中，最前面的looking之後到then為止是分詞語句。原本after（或是when）I looked at the fax...then這個句子，省略了after和主詞I，並把looked改成looking之後變成分詞語句。解釋為「看了…之後」。而且在後面出現的you sent部分中的動詞send是第4大句型動詞，因此要使用兩個受詞，但是前面的受格關係詞that可以省略。I think之後的that也被省略。

Looking at /	the fax /	you /	sent /	me /	then, /	I /	think /
分詞語句	受詞	主詞	動詞	間接受詞	副詞	主詞	動詞

my best option /	would be /	the direct flight /	on May 1.
主詞	動詞	主詞補語	介系詞片語

(1) Double Passages

Questions 1-5 refer to the following information and letter.

Ivory Towers Building Regulations

1. All bicycles must be parked in the bicycle-parking area to the right of the main entrance. Bicycles left on the sidewalk in front of the building or in the hallways will be removed by maintenance.

2. Ivory Towers' pool hours are from 9:00 A.M. to 9:00 P.M., Tuesday through Sunday. Children under the age of 18 must be supervised by an adult, and people using the pool are asked to keep their volume levels down out of respect for other tenants in the building.

3. Garbage must be placed in the appropriate containers in the garbage room located on the first floor of the building. Please ensure that container lids are firmly closed to prevent animals and pests from getting into them.

4. Pets are allowed, but must be kept under control at all times. Dogs must be kept on a leash on the premises, and other pets must be properly restrained or kept in cages when being taken into and out of the building.

July 19

Dear Mr. Franklin Mint,

I have been a tenant here at Ivory Towers for almost 15 years now, and for the most part I have been extremely satisfied with the way management has taken care of things.

I am writing to bring your attention to a potentially serious problem. I know that a new family with three children has moved into Unit 204. I work an early shift at my job, and am always in bed by 10:00. Recently, however, I have been awakened at night by these children making quite a bit of noise while using the swimming pool. This has happened several times now. I know that the regulations are posted at the entrance to the pool, but I am hoping that you, as superintendent of the building, could have a word with the family to make sure that they fully understand them. I imagine other tenants might feel the same as I do.

Thank you for your attention to this matter.

Sincerely,

Esther Smith
Apartment 301

1 Which topic is NOT covered in the regulations?

   (A) The swimming pool hours
   (B) The car park location
   (C) Garbage disposal rules
   (D) Transporting pets into the building

2 Where should bicycles be kept, according to the regulations?

   (A) In the hallway of the building
   (B) On the left side of the entrance
   (C) In the designated bicycle area
   (D) On the sidewalk in front of the building

3 What is indicated about the children in Apartment 204?

   (A) They return from school late at night.
   (B) They are using the pool after closing hours.
   (C) They park their bicycles in the hallways.
   (D) They have lived in the building for 15 years.

4 Who is Franklin Mint?

   (A) The superintendent of Ivory Towers
   (B) A parent of three children
   (C) The tenant of Apartment 204
   (D) The owner of the swimming pool

5 What is the purpose of the letter?

   (A) To request changes to the regulations
   (B) To register a complaint
   (C) To inform Mr. Mint of a new schedule
   (D) To welcome a new tenant

▶ 解答在173頁

Questions 6-10 refer to the following advertisement and letter.

Ming's Framing Center

Ming's Framing Center has just opened its third location!

To celebrate, we have lowered our prices for one week only: 25% off all orders over $75 and 35% off all orders over $125.

We offer a wide selection of wooden and metal frames in a variety of colors and textures –something to fit every kind of print. Our expert staff will help you choose a frame with the style and colors to make your print stand out.

Read more about our glass options:

Ming's Original Glass: The most cost-effective option, this glass is best in areas of low light. It is an all-around good quality glass that offers minimal reflection and quality protection from sunlight, while still allowing clarity to see the details in your print.

Non-reflective Glass: This glass is perfect for sunny rooms! The non-reflective coating allows your print to remain clear, even in sunny rooms. (Note: the non-reflective coating can be added to the Perfect Portrait glass for a small fee based on the size of the print.)

Museum Glass: This high-quality glass is suitable for great works of art or important family pictures you want to preserve. Not only is the glass non-reflective, it also protects prints against changes in temperature and humidity. This is our top-of-the-line glass, and while the price is high, you will not be disappointed with the results!

Perfect Portrait Glass: Finally, a glass that emphasizes fine details! This glass is thin, but just as durable as Ming's Original Glass. It is engineered to bring out fine details in pictures, and thus is perfect for portraits or for old images that have faded.

Elspeth Hanson

Ming's Framing Center

2031 Main Street

Cincinnati, OH

54100

Dear Ms. Hanson,

I wanted to thank you for all of your help choosing a frame and glass for my mother the other day.

It was my first time in Ming's, and I was impressed not only with the incredible selection of product, but also with the service. I was pleased when you told me that Mr. Ming insists that all his staff take decorating classes to learn about complementary colors. Your expertise was certainly appreciated.

My mother was so thrilled when she saw the framed portrait of herself as a young girl. I had found the old picture behind her couch, where it had become faded from the sun. But put behind the specialty glass you recommended, it seemed as though the details became clearer. My mother could even read the sign of the store in the background! She told me all about it – Anderson's General Store. They used to have 50 cent ice cream cones, she said.

Anyway, thank you for the positive experience of working with you. I will highly recommend Ming's services to my friends and family.

Sincerely,

Jacqueline Baker

6 Why is Ming's being promoted?

   (A) To announce a sale
   (B) To describe new inventory
   (C) To increase business
   (D) To advertise a new location

7 What is the advantage of Museum Glass?

   (A) It is the most cost-effective.
   (B) It has a non-reflective coating.
   (C) It brings out fine details in prints.
   (D) It protects prints in damp conditions.

8 Who Is Elspeth Hanson?

   (A) A customer at Ming's Framing Center
   (B) A staff member at Ming's Framing Center
   (C) A friend of Jacqueline Baker's
   (D) Jacqueline Baker's mother

9 What glass did Jacqueline Baker likely buy?

   (A) Ming's Original Glass
   (B) Non-reflective Glass
   (C) Museum Glass
   (D) Perfect Portrait Glass

10 What is Anderson's General Store?

   (A) A store owned by Mr. Ming
   (B) A store owned by Jacqueline Baker
   (C) A framing store
   (D) A store in a photograph

▶ 解答在173頁

三篇閱讀

三篇閱讀（Three Passages）

★ 在三篇閱讀出題的內容

❶ 「郵件或是信件」＋「回信郵件」＋「回信郵件」

❷ 「廣告或產品資訊」＋「訂單」＋「回件」

❸ 「廣告」＋「信件」＋「回信郵件」

❹ 「徵人廣告」＋「申請者履歷表」＋「信件」

❺ 「公告」＋「信件」＋「回信郵件」

★ 在三篇閱讀出題的內容

❶ 文章中的主題

❷ 推測接下來會發生的事情

❸ 選出正確的資訊

❹ 關於某項主題的資訊

❺ 同義字

攻略法

102 三篇閱讀（Three Passages）

2018改制後出現的新題型！放棄三篇閱讀就等於放棄高分！

多益於2018年改制之後，新增了三篇閱讀的題型。在Part 7的文章理解題中，將會有三組三篇閱讀，每組五個題目。

三篇閱讀聽起來很多，但可以把它想像成「把三篇短文變成一篇較長的文章」來閱讀，也可以把三篇短文視為一篇文章中的三個段落，關鍵在於連接不同文章中的相關資訊。例如：如果第一篇是給潛在買家的產品介紹，第二篇可能就是潛在買家對感興趣產品提出的相關問題，第三篇則是針對第二篇所提出問題的進一步答覆。

一定要快速瀏覽題目，找出答案，才不會在三篇閱讀上花費太多時間。

1. 三篇閱讀的類型

閱讀內文1	閱讀內文2	閱讀內文3
背景資料	問題、疑問	解決方法
廣告	資訊索取	資訊提供
徵聘	應徵	回覆
新聞稿發佈	相關要求	回覆
政策說明	釐清	回覆
公司支援要求	因應要求與提問	回覆

2. 處理三篇閱讀的技巧

1 因為閱讀內文1是三篇文章中的開頭與基礎，一定要快速瀏覽找出主旨和與其他兩篇內文的相關性。

2 了解問題與問題之間的關係，也可以幫助了解文章主旨。例如三篇閱讀如果屬廣告文章，即使問題的順序不一定會依照文章中的順序，branding（做品牌）、promotion（促銷）、sales revenues（銷售收入）等在問題中提及的關鍵字，也可以幫助考生了解三篇閱讀內文主旨與marketing 脫不了關係。

3. 怪物講師的解法

請依照下面的指示事項中所提供的號碼順序解題看看。一定要從閱讀題目開始，也有閱讀測驗的內文很多，就必須要把內文看過兩三次的情況，閱讀時間會比預期中花時間。

TRYOUTS FOR REBEL CHEERLEADERS
No Experience Required

Are you a young, vivacious, | 詢問同義字
and energetic woman looking for a challenge?

④ 閱讀句子 閱讀整個句子，並與答案選項相互確認

The local football team, the Graniteville Rebels,
is now looking to take on a few more cheerleaders.

No experience is necessary. | 需具備的條件
You just need to be willing to learn!

⑧ 閱讀內文 一邊確認問題3的內容，一邊一一刪除答案選項，每次出現線索的時候，再看答案選項確認

Don't hesitate.
Take advantage of this unique opportunity.

Tryouts will be next weekend, July 22nd and 23rd, from 9:00 a.m. to 6:00 p.m.

If interested, e-mail rebelcheerleaders@gmail.com. Please include a few head shots and body shots. We will contact you with your tryout time after we receive your e-mail with head and body shots.

Good luck!

Hello,

I saw the ad for open tryouts you placed in the Graniteville Daily. I am curious if it would be worth my time to show up. I am almost 35, and I am not in the best shape. I still look very pretty, but I worry my body is not good enough to be a cheerleader.

廣告刊載的地方

擔心的事項

2 1號問題的解題 快速掌握問題1的重點，確認廣告主題之後解題

10 閱讀內文 一邊確認問題5的內容，一邊一一刪除答案選項，每次出現線索的時候，再看答案選項確認

If you could be honest with me, I would appreciate it. I really would like to give it a shot, but please let me know if I am would just be wasting my time. Thanks so much.

詢問同義字

6 閱讀句子 閱讀整個句子，並與答案選項相互確認

Sincerely,
Melissa McCarthy

Hi Melissa,

Don't worry so much! The average age of the cheerleaders on the squad is close to 33. None of us are 18 years old or anything. We are more interested in enthusiastic women who want to give it their all. Based on your message, you seem like the perfect fit for us.

偏好的特質

And regarding your body, again, don't worry. We have a diet and exercise program we will put you on if you make the squad. We will also practice four times a week for the two months leading up to the football season.

Hope to see you at tryouts,

Beth King,
Head Cheerleader for Graniteville Rebel Cheerleaders

1. Where was the advertisement for the open tryouts posted?

   (A) In a newspaper

   (B) In a magazine

   (C) On a website

   (D) In a book

① 先閱讀問題

一定要讀！

2. Which word is CLOSEST in meaning to "vivacious"?

   (A) lively

   (B) humorous

   (C) athletic

   (D) experienced

③ 先讀問題與選項

先大略了解選項中的字義

3. Which one of the following characteristics is the Rebel
   Cheerleaders looking for in the women who are trying out?

   (A) Love to dance

   (B) Experience in cheerleading

   (C) Desire to learn

   (D) Knowledge of the Rebels

⑦ 先閱讀問題

這個問題的類型是要
看完內文才能解題

4. Which of the following phrases is CLOSEST in meaning to the
   phrase "give it a shot"?

⑤ 先讀問題與選項

先大略了解選項中的字義

   (A) make an attempt

   (B) hurt someone

   (C) create something

   (D) enjoy yourself

⑨ 先閱讀問題　　這個問題的類型是要看完內文才能解題

5. Why is Mrs. McCarthy worried about trying out for the Rebel
   Cheerleaders?

▶ 解答在176頁

   (A) She believes she is not physically in good enough shape.

   (B) She doesn't thinks she is pretty enough.

   (C) She believes she is not good-looking enough.

   (D) She doesn't thinks she have enough time to attend all the
   practices.

Questions 1-5 refer to the following announcement and letters.

Homeland Security Web Announcement

The Internet touches almost all aspects of everyone's daily life now. October is National Cyber Security Awareness Month(NCSAM), an annual campaign to raise awareness about the importance of cyber security. NCSAM is designed to engage and educate public and private sector partners with tools and resources needed to stay safe online. We ask that everyone participate in National Cyber Security Awareness Month.

Dear Colleges,

We are proud to announce that we have become a partner of National Cyber Security Awareness Month (NCSAM) this year. This is a growing global effort among businesses, government agencies, colleges and universities, associations, nonprofit organizations and individuals. Our purpose is to ensure all digital citizens have the resources needed to stay safer and more secure online while also protecting their personal information. At Alliance, we are commitment to cyber security, online safety and privacy of our customers. For more information about our participation in NCSAM, please launch on the company's website at www.alliancetrue.com.

Jack Sinatra

CEO of Alliance Company

A Letter from the Information Office

When we are conducting our business, emails and digital communication methods help us to contact our suppliers and customers. At the same time, our intellectual property, confidential communications and other private information have been threatened by malware.

The Information Office now would like to give you one essential tip to enhance email security: Avoiding accessing email via public computers or public networks. The convenience to check your emails also makes you a target for hacking. After joining the NCSAM this year, the Information Office of Alliance Company will periodically share tips on how individuals can work to take a part in activities related to NCSAM. We will keep you updated.

May Peterson
Director of Information Office

1　Which topic is not covered in the above announcements?

(A) Cyber security
(B) Hacking
(C) Labor rights
(D) Email security

2　According to Information Office, what should be prohibited?

(A) Using digital devices to contact customers
(B) Using mobile phones at work
(C) Supporting NCSAM activities
(D) Accessing emails related to work in public places

3　What is indicated about NCSAM?

(A) A campaign to celebrate the era of digitalization
(B) A campaign to enhance cyber security
(C) A campaign to improve the public and private partnership in digital industry development
(D) A campaign to foster protection of intellectual property

4　What is the purpose of the announcement of Homeland Security Website Announcement?

(A) To educate people what NCSAM is and ask for support
(B) To request people to protect themselves online
(C) To inform people of importance of digital tools
(D) To encourage people to use digital devices

5　What would malware and spyware do to our emails?

(A) To infect our system
(B) To help our system
(C) To diversify our system
(D) To protect our system

▶ 解答在177頁

實戰測驗

READING TEST

In the Reading Test, you will read a variety of texts and answer several different types of reading comprehension questions. The entire Reading Test will last 75 minutes. There are three parts, and directions are given for each part. You are encouraged to answer as many questions as possible within the time allowed.

You must mark your answers on the separate answer sheet. Do not write your answers in your test book.

PART 5

Directions: A word or phrase is missing in each of the sentences below. Four answer choices are given below each sentence. Select the best answer to complete the sentence. Then mark the letter (A), (B), (C), or (D) on your answer sheet.

---

101. The awards ceremony will begin right after the CEO arrives and will be _____ by his speech.

(A) accepted
(B) postponed
(C) proceeded
(D) followed

102. Glenda has always _____ enthusiastic about environmental protection and dedicated herself for charity work.

(A) is
(B) be
(C) been
(D) being

103. When reporting a traffic accident, remember to omit _____ details unless otherwise noted.

(A) incidental
(B) prerequisite
(C) decreased
(D) insufficient

104. As a section chief, Clara will have to find out what her workers need _____.

(A) urgent
(B) urgently
(C) more urgent
(D) urgency

105. It is essential that everyone _____ safety procedures in the event of an emergency.

(A) follow
(B) followed
(C) following
(D) be followed

106. Alex replied that his office is _____ between a pharmacy and a bakery on Redex Street.

(A) location
(B) locates
(C) located
(D) locating

107. We started to find _____ managers who have excelled in a variety of market environments over a long period of time.

(A) missing
(B) opposing
(C) experienced
(D) significant

108. A simple way to _____ funds would be to offer an incentive program for the donors.

(A) generate
(B) manufacture
(C) deliver
(D) contract

109. _____ the facility is quite new and durable, we intend to renovate our headquarters at the end of this year.

(A) Unless
(B) After
(C) Supposed
(D) Although

110. To meet your _____ needs, we are offering different types of shuttles, including hospital-based shuttles and corporate shuttles.

(A) physical
(B) individual
(C) absurd
(D) emotional

111. For the past _____ months they have been taking care of all new statistical information in the papers.

(A) several
(B) less
(C) another
(D) a lot

112. For people with food _____ and allergies, it is hard to choose a place to eat, not to mention finding fresh vegan dishes.

(A) sensitivities
(B) sensible
(C) senses
(D) sensation

113. We have to subject the redesigned car seat to the test to officially confirm that it is _____ strong.

(A) sufficient
(B) sufficiently
(C) more sufficient
(D) most sufficient

114. The conductor believed music is freely shared and able to build community, and that has _____ out to be true in the small village.

(A) spelled
(B) planned
(C) wiped
(D) turned

115. Seeing that Hansung Airlines is promoting specially discounted tickets, the major carriers are forced to be more _____ in their pricing.

(A) compete
(B) competition
(C) competitive
(D) competitor

116. _____ the roads were slippery, drivers should exercise their extreme caution to avoid traffic accidents.

(A) However
(B) Despite
(C) For
(D) Since

117. Your quick comments on our services are needed to make our company more customer-friendly _____ will assist us in serving you more efficiently.

(A) what
(B) so that
(C) which
(D) and

118. Original receipts must be presented to get reimbursed in order to _____ your spending while going on a business trip.

(A) reverse
(B) claim
(C) justify
(D) assure

119. Recently, the price of crude oil affecting each country's economy _____ moderately.

(A) to rise
(B) risen
(C) rises
(D) rose

120. Since the 1600s, when the city _____ as the region's commercial hub, the place has been a shopping destination.

(A) served
(B) serves
(C) had served
(D) serving

121. Please take note that there are two different maps in the Visitors Guide; _____ of these two will help you find your way around here.

(A) either
(B) all
(C) two
(D) none

122. Being the fifth largest transit system in the country, the commission provides an excellent source of _____ within the city.

(A) transformation
(B) transportation
(C) transmission
(D) transaction

123. If you are interested in these tours, arrive as early as possible because they are available on a first come _____ and often sell out.

(A) bias
(B) base
(C) basis
(D) basic

124. The firm has decided to offer all of its customers a weekly newsletter _____ free of charge.

(A) extremely
(B) absolutely
(C) exclusively
(D) additionally

125. The safety guidelines should always be put on the notice board to _____ the entire staff read and follow them.

(A) let
(B) allow
(C) advise
(D) get

126. This urgent project _____ he spent hours working needs additional help to finish on time.

(A) which
(B) what
(C) on which
(D) of which

127. Every safety _____ should be taken to ensure that they wear safety goggles.

(A) advice
(B) precaution
(C) idea
(D) place

128. _____ you desire for the oceanfront suites or mountain view suites, you'll find the best of both worlds in the resort.

(A) When
(B) Whether
(C) What
(D) Where

129. We are not only a restaurant that offers authentic meals, _____ a unique experience you will not find anywhere else.

(A) so
(B) or
(C) nor
(D) also

130. _____ did he arrive 4 hours late but he also forgot to bring the requested document.

(A) Not only
(B) In addition
(C) Besides
(D) No sooner

PART 6

Directions: Read the texts that follow. A word or phrase is missing in some of the sentences. Four answer choices are given below each of the sentences. Select the best answer to complete the sentence. Then mark the letter (A), (B), (C), or (D) on your answer sheet.

Questions 131-134 refer to the following article.

Owing to advances in medicine and new treatments, the mortality rate of some terminal diseases _____ significantly declined. Some figures indicate this
131.
considerable drop motivates not only some private corporations but also the government _____ willing to invest more capital into even further development
132.
of medication. Better still, some professional institutions devote a great deal to take care of patients who unfortunately contracted some chronic diseases to ensure they receive adequate medical care _____ their declining years. Meanwhile, well-
133.
developed medication also can lead to so-called medical tourism which means some foreigners travel to a given country to accept _____
134.

131. (A) have
(B) has
(C) had
(D) will have

132. (A) be
(B) being
(C) is
(D) are

133. (A) in
(B) on
(C) at
(D) from

134. (A) some education just because the country boasts an academic system.
(B) some entertainment just because the country boasts recreational facilities.
(C) some treatment just because the country boasts a good health care system.
(D) some training just because the country boasts a professional training program.

Questions 135-138 refer to the following article.

Strolling is an _____ relaxing activity, and it's also a highly recommended activity
135.
for relieving stress. For one thing, a slow walking pace allows our circulation system
to work slowly. Therefore, it leads to releasing our accumulated stress naturally.
_____, it's one of the effective ways for people who live and work in a city to
136.
eliminate their inevitable pressure. Moreover, some other leisure activities such as
playing sports, traveling, or even listening to music often cost money, but they don't
always work well to meet the goal of relieving people from their fatigue. However,
strolling costs people virtually nothing, _____ it enables them to feel comfortable
137.
and carefree. Finally, people are able to explore some fresh things by strolling.
Peoplo usually head for the office during weekdays and rarely notice minor changes
taking place around them. Strolling around may provide us with some eye-opening
experiences. In sum, _____, it's a good idea to go strolling.
138.

135. (A) excess
(B) excessive
(C) excessively
(D) excessiveness

136. (A) Take it into account
(B) On no account
(C) By one's own account
(D) By all accounts

137. (A) for
(B) or
(C) yet
(D) so

138. (A) since strolling has the above
drawbacks
(B) since strolling has the above
downsides
(C) since strolling has the above merits
(D) since strolling has the above flaws

Questions 139-142 refer to the following letter.

Dear Ms. Charlotte,

Regarding the freight issue you _____ in our conversation earlier today, it seems
139.
like you have a dire concern on the previous offer of the freight charge and the

contents of related services. _____ long term cooperation, we should clarify
140.
each aspect of the arrangement of the distribution to meet our common interests.

If it wouldn't bother you too much, I would like to know what your budget is for the

freight, what the requirements are for hiring an agency to handle your customs'

documents, and _____ your lead time needs to be for packaging. In summary,
141.
please send me your ideal price, requirement, and packaging time whenever you

need freight service at your convenience. _____
142.

Sincerely,

Allen Lin

139. (A) brought about
(B) brought forth
(C) brought up
(D) brought on

140. (A) To
(B) In
(C) By
(D) For

141. (A) how far
(B) how long
(C) how often
(D) how big

142. (A) I will contact you for further
discussion as soon as I will receive
your clarification.
(B) I will contact you for further
discussion as soon as I received
your clarification.
(C) I will contact you for further
discussion as soon as I receive your
clarification.
(D) I will contact you for further
discussion as soon as I receives
your clarification.

Questions 143-146 refer to the following advertisement.

Do you want to travel to the outback to enjoy natural wonders but are concerned about the inconvenience of local transportation? Do you want to immerse yourself in a pleasurable camping trip _____ an RV but have difficulty _____ one?
143.   144.
Do you want to have a car to run your personal business but do not have enough money to _____ one on your own? Budget.com has all the solutions for you. We
145.
are a car rental website that is a household name. We offer all kinds of vehicles for your every possible need. A four-door mini-van is just US$ 10.99 per day with full insurance, a fully functioning RV is just US$ 15.99 per day with full insurance, and a pick-up truck is just US$ 10 per day. _____ What are you waiting for? Just go
146.
online and search our official website.

143. (A) at
    (B) on
    (C) by
    (D) with

144. (A) to buy
    (B) buying
    (C) buy
    (D) bought

145. (A) process
    (B) profess
    (C) possess
    (D) progress

146. (A) The longest you rent the more discounts we offer.
    (B) The longer you rent the most discounts we offer.
    (C) The longer you rent the shorter discounts we offer.
    (D) The longer you rent the more discounts we offer.

PART 7

Directions: In this part you will read a selection of texts, such as a magazine and newspaper articles, letters, and advertisements. Each text is followed by several questions. Select the best answer for each question and mark the letter (A), (B), (C), or (D) on your answer sheet.

Questions 147-148 refer to the following note.

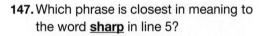

Open Casting Call!

Attention residents of Blacksburg. This is an opening casting call for the new film "Do You Love Me?" that is being filmed here in your lovely city. We are looking for people to be extras in several scenes we will be filming around the city. No acting experience is required. If you are interested, please arrive at 360 West Road on August 8th at 8:00 a.m. **sharp** for auditions. We need people of all body types, ages, and ethnicities, so do not worry that you are not the "type" of person we are looking for. Chances are you are exactly who we are looking for! We hope to see you on August 8th at 8:00 a.m.!

147. Which phrase is closest in meaning to the word **sharp** in line 5?

(A) With haste
(B) As soon as possible
(C) On the dot
(D) Over the moon

148. What does the word "open" in "open casting call" MOST LIKELY mean?

(A) Anyone is welcome to audition.
(B) There is no fee to audition.
(C) The auditions will be outdoors.
(D) The auditions will be viewed by others.

Questions 149-150 refer to the following text message chain.

149. Why does Carl Weathers say "that is a shame" at 12:32 p.m.?

(A) He wanted to join the meeting Leon was going to but could not.
(B) He hoped Leon would have lunch with him but Leon responded too late.
(C) He desired to discuss Leon's recent trip to Thailand with Leon, but Leon did not want to.
(D) He wished to hear from Leon about his vacation plans for Thailand, but Leon was unavailable.

150. Where will Carl Weathers and Leon Brown go after they meet tomorrow?

(A) They will go to Carl Weathers' office.
(B) They will go to Carl Weathers' neighborhood.
(C) They will go to a restaurant in the area around Carl Weathers' office.
(D) They will go to a Thai restaurant in the city that Carl Weathers believes is the most authentic.

Questions 151-152 refer to the following memo.

To: All Staff
From: Frank Lindell, General Manager
Date: March 22nd, 2017
Re: Unanswered Question about Maternity Leave from This Morning's Meeting

After checking with our CEO, I want to take this moment to address the question Nancy raised this morning. For those of you who forgot, she asked about the company's willingness to offer more maternity leave. As of right now, it is not government-mandated, and we currently offer ten day's paid leave for new mothers. Nancy wanted to know if it was possible to extend maternity leave from ten days to one month. She cited examples of other countries as well as other companies in our country that offer much more than ten days.

Well, our CEO said this is not something he can give a definite answer to right now, but he will consider the issue and bring it up at the board meeting next week.

Thank you, Nancy, for bringing this to my attention at the meeting.

151. Why has Frank Lindell written this memo?

(A) To inform the staff that the CEO has made a decision about maternity leave.
(B) To express his disappointment with the staff during the morning meeting.
(C) To thank Nancy for her contributions to the company.
(D) To tell the staff that the CEO is now thinking about updating the company's maternity leave policy.

152. What can be inferred from this memo?

(A) The maternity leave policy is not important to the company's CEO.
(B) Frank Lindell hopes the maternity leave policy will change.
(C) Nancy will quit if the maternity leave policy is not changed.
(D) There is a chance that the maternity leave policy will be changed.

Questions 153-154 refer to the following form.

Request for Leave of Absence

1. Name: Erika Walters
2. Employee Number: 24-4535433
3. Division: Finance and Accounting
4. Type of Leave

Purpose:
- ■ Employee illness/injury
- ☐ Employee medical/dental/eye examination
- ☐ Care of family member, including medical/dental/eye of family member
- ☐ Care of family member with a serious health condition
- ☐ Other

Date:

Date		Time		Total Hours
From	To	From	To	
5.5	5.26	09:00	17:00	120

5. Remarks: I have submitted documentation from my doctor relating to the car accident.
6. Official Action on Request:　■ Approved　☐ Disapproved

---

153. What is the reason for the application?

(A) Non-medical emergency
(B) Health problem of close relative
(C) Personal injury
(D) Business trip

154. What is NOT mentioned in the form?

(A) The applicant will be paid during the leave.
(B) The applicant will attach a doctor's note.
(C) The employee will be away for three weeks.
(D) The employee will work at the accounting department.

Questions 155-157 refer to the following text message chain.

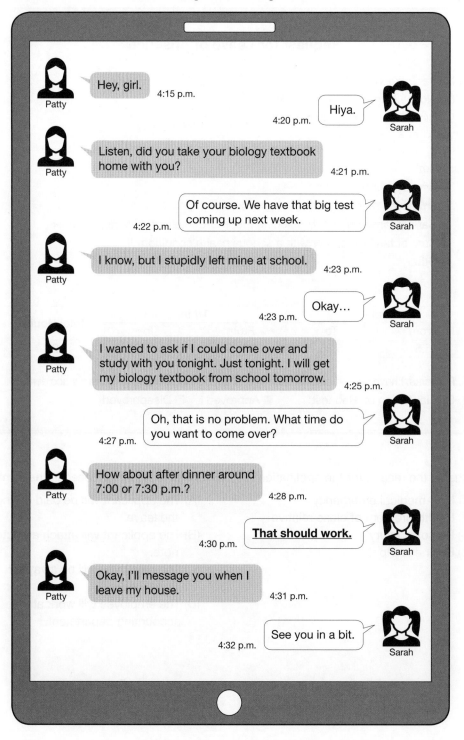

155. When is the biology test?

  (A) Tomorrow
  (B) This week
  (C) Next week
  (D) Next month

156. Why is Patty going over to Sarah's house?

  (A) To borrow Sarah's biology textbook
  (B) To get Sarah's help on the biology homework
  (C) To prepare for the biology test with Sarah
  (D) To play games with Sarah at her house

157. Which of the following phrases is closest in meaning to "**That should work**"?

  (A) That is okay.
  (B) That is useable.
  (C) That is enough.
  (D) That is agreeable.

Questions 158-160 refer to the following e-mail.

From: Lynne Buttler
To: All Downtown Business Association Members
Date: July 22
Re: New Operating Hours

The Downtown Business Association is recommending that stores in the main core remain open for two extra hours on Friday and Saturday night. On these evenings we expect to see stores open until around 8:00. This is to facilitate the increased volume in tourist traffic we have begun to see during the summer months. The evenings are especially busier as people come to enjoy the free entertainment available on the streets.

We have already received advance agreement from the Inner City Mall and hope to receive confirmation from all of you regarding this matter by May. The suggested dates during which to implement the new schedule are June 1st and September 4th.

If this presents a challenge for scheduling employees, you may consider opening your store two hours later than the normal opening time on the days mentioned above.

158. Why does the association want stores to change their hours?

(A) To diminish traffic in the downtown area
(B) To allow employees to listen to music
(C) To help travelers find accommodation
(D) To increase business in the summer

159. When are store owners asked to change their hours?

(A) Between May and September
(B) Between June and September
(C) Between June and July
(D) Between July and September

160. What can owners do to avoid staff scheduling problems?

(A) Open two hours later than normal
(B) Close their stores by 6:00 in the evening
(C) Inform employees as soon as possible
(D) Follow the hours used by stores in the mall

The Provincial Museum Special Exhibit

Rules for visitors

These rules apply to the special exhibit offered to the public between July 2 – August 23

1. Hours

Family Time: Monday-Friday 11:00 AM to 5:00 PM, Saturday-Sunday, 9:00 AM – 12:00 PM

Adults Only: Monday-Friday 9:00 AM to 11:00 AM, Saturday-Sunday, 1:00 PM – 5:00 PM

2. No photography or recording devices are permitted in the exhibits. Use of such a device may result in temporary confiscation.

3. Food and drinks are not permitted in the exhibit area.

4. Children under the age of 14 must be accompanied by an adult at all times.

5. Audio devices explaining each item in the exhibit are available at the registration desk for an additional charge. They must be returned before leaving the exhibit.

6. Some of the animated visual presentations may cause dizziness. This is usually remedied by remaining seated and shutting your eyes for a short time. Assistants are available on each floor of the exhibit to provide help when needed.

* Most visual presentations last approximately 20 minutes and start every half hour. Seatings for these are available on a first-come first-served basis.

161. When are children NOT allowed in the exhibit?

(A) Monday to Thursday 11:00-5:00
(B) Monday to Friday 9:00-11:00
(C) Friday 11:00-5:00
(D) During weekends and holidays

162. What should visitors do if they feel unwell when watching a video?

(A) Report to a manager
(B) Close their eyes
(C) Wait for twenty minutes
(D) Walk around the exhibit

163. What is NOT true according to the rules?

(A) Underage children must come with adults.
(B) Videos are shown every 30 minutes.
(C) Cameras can be used in some exhibits.
(D) Audio devices can be rented at the museum.

Questions 164-167 refer to the following notice.

The 3rd Annual Social Network Club Conference
Changing Paradigms
University of Phoenix, Phoenix, Arizona

November 19, 2011

The Social Network Club's main objective is to advertise media literacy, advocate standard technologies, promote ethical behavior, and share best practices. We bring together people from many professions, including journalists, publishers, communications professionals, and teachers. We are the people who develop and consume media and want to see the media industry evolve for everyone's benefit.

Registration will take place between August 2nd and November 4th. Early registration discounts will only be offered until September 1st.

Agenda

Time	Sessions
10:30	Session 1A: Online Social Networks

Edward Dutton: **Social Networks: Reconfiguring Access to People**

Will discuss effects from use of the Internet in many overlapping and interacting areas influenced by strategic decisions about the design and use of the technology.

12:00   Lunch

13:30   Session 2A: Businesses and Online Social Networks

Ronald Allan (Ciskan): **Social networking and business practice: A case study in the telecoms industry**

This talk will explore the reaction of an important technology company to the development and growth of social networking.

15:00   Session 2B: Rhonda Ward (Allan & Jacobs): **Social software in a hard world**

Rhonda Ward will share her experiences of using social platforms in an international professional services business, highlighting common pitfalls to avoid from a legal perspective.

16:00   Maryland Burgess: **Online encyclopedias: The potential of a peer production effort**

On-line encyclopedias are a phenomenal success. Through a process of trial and error, its capacity to adapt and improve itself is a model for how to organize information.

Join us and together we can create the future!

164. By when should people sign up for the event in order to get a better price?

(A) By the beginning of September
(B) By the end of October
(C) By November 4th
(D) By November 19th

165. Which talk would most likely cover the use of media in mobile phones?

(A) Reconfiguring access to people
(B) A case study in the telecoms industry
(C) Social software in a hard world
(D) The potential of a peer production effort

166. Which speaker would the participating teachers most likely find interesting?

(A) Edward Dutton
(B) Maryland Burgess
(C) Rhonda Ward
(D) Ronald Allan

167. Where does Rhonda Ward most likely work?

(A) At an educational institution
(B) At a law firm
(C) At a Web development company
(D) At an advertising firm

Everything, no matter how beneficial it seems, comes with pros and cons. Automobiles are an effective example of this point. No one can deny that automobiles, one of the most influential inventions in modern times, have drastically changed the way we live, and we must recognize that the changes have been advantageous and disadvantageous and not purely advantageous. It must be acknowledged that automobiles have caused serious problems in society, problems such as air pollution, traffic congestion, and fatal accidents. However, ---[1]---, automobiles have improved modern life immensely and will continue to have a profound influence far into the future.

Several reasons and examples can be used to demonstrate that the benefits of automobiles outweigh the drawbacks. Automobiles, ---[2]---, have revolutionized transportation worldwide. With their speed, they have been able to connect people in faraway places. What's more, they are comfortable and have made travelling—even travelling long distances—a cozy, enjoyable experience. They have removed many of the barriers, obstacles, and impediments to people's travelling plans. Therefore, in their convenience, automobiles have made people's lives easier. Also, ---[3]--- automobiles have made the world a more prosperous one. Large automobiles like trucks and vans have the capacity to carry huge amounts of products to every corner of a country, which in turn leads to cheaper costs for consumers.

With the advantages mentioned above, ---[4]--- automobiles can be seen to have greatly affected the world's social structure, living standards, and economic condition. Thus, it can be effectively argued that people's lives would be worse off if automobiles had never been invented.

168. What can be inferred from this passage?

(A) The author believes automobiles do more harm than good.

(B) Automobiles have been around for centuries and have played a minor role in the progress of human civilization.

(C) The world would not be what it is today if it were not for the invention of automobiles.

(D) The horrible traffic accidents that take innocent lives show that automobiles have overall been a bad invention.

169. Which of the following drawbacks to automobiles is NOT mentioned in this article?

(A) Dirty air

(B) Expensive to maintain

(C) Traffic jams

(D) Car crashes

170. Which of the following is NOT an advantage of automobiles mentioned in this article?

(A) Bringing places and people closer together

(B) Providing a more enjoyable way of life

(C) Promoting economic prosperity

(D) Helping people avoid their responsibilities

171. In which of the positions marked [1], [2], [3] and [4] does the following sentence best belong?

"despite these drawbacks"

(A) [1]

(B) [2]

(C) [3]

(D) [4]

The Business of Change

Tom Warner Consulting

With the rapid advances being made in technology, the demand for change in companies has never been greater. But despite the efficiencies these new solutions promise, integrating them into our work-flows presents challenges that consume time and resources at the front end. In summary, they require us to change in order to use them. And that is not easy.

At Tom Warner Consulting, we understand the demands being put on businesses to keep up with the flow. More importantly we know that the most crucial factor in realizing change in an organization is its personnel – and that specialization separates us from the others.

All of the people on my team are strategic thinkers with the capacity to achieve high standards in business improvement within a fast paced and competitive environment. Over two decades in business we are skilled in all aspects of change and transitional project management. We do all this while keeping your costs in check. We specialize in working with media and technology companies.

If you've hit a wall, your morale is low or your sales are off, contact me to set up an initial consultation to discuss the changes needed in your organization.

172. According to the advertisement, what do companies struggle with?

(A) Managing their human resources
(B) Changing their work schedules
(C) Developing useful software
(D) Making use of new technology

173. According to the advertisement, what is unique about Tom Warner Consulting?

(A) They only work with media companies.
(B) They know change is difficult.
(C) They have more than 20 years in business.
(D) They focus on people.

174. The word "capacity" in paragraph 3, line 1 is closest in meaning to

(A) ability
(B) tendency
(C) motivation
(D) drive

175. When would a company NOT require Tom Warner Consulting's services?

(A) If staff are unmotivated
(B) If costs are getting out of control
(C) If new technology is being introduced
(D) If you have an internal design team

Questions 176-180 refer to the following advertisement and mail.

STUDIO APARTMENT FOR RENT

Details: This spacious studio apartment is located on the fifth floor of a three-year old building that comes with hotel-style amenities. There is a 24-hour guard service, four elevators, a gym, a swimming pool, a KTV room, and more. The apartment comes with an air-conditioner, a television with cable, a kitchenette with a one-burner stove and a small refrigerator, a tasteful bathroom with a washer-dryer; and it is furnished with a desk, a sofa, and a bed. As a bonus, the apartment gets plenty of natural lighting and has an incredible view of the park across the street.

Total Area: 15 pings
Rent: $5,500 USD/month + $1,000 USD/month management fee (utilities included)
        with an **initial** security deposit of $11,000 USD
Contact: Mr. Carl Crews, ccrews@bigrealestate.com

Dear Mr. Crews,

I am writing to you because I am extremely interested in the studio apartment you listed for rent on Home Real Estate. Is it still available? I do have a few questions I am hoping you can answer. In terms of amenities, I did not see anything mentioned about parking and garbage. Are there car and scooter parking spaces to rent in the building's basement, and is there a garbage area? If I can rent parking spaces for my car and scooter, and there is a place to throw my garbage, then I can pretty much promise you that I will rent the apartment.

I look forward to hearing back from you. I would like to know when I could schedule a visit to the apartment. Is this weekend okay? I am free both Saturday and Sunday all day, so I can meet you at the apartment any time.

Thanks,
Bill Parker

176. Who is this apartment BEST SUITED for?

(A) A small family
(B) An extended family
(C) A single adult
(D) Young Couple

177. What is this advertisement for?

(A) Leasing an apartment
(B) Purchasing an apartment
(C) Subletting an apartment
(D) Renovating an apartment

178. What is the price Bill Parker must pay right away if he decides to move in?

(A) $1,000 USD
(B) $5,500 USD
(C) $11,000 USD
(D) $16,500 USD

179. What is NOT included with the apartment?

(A) A sofa
(B) An air-conditioner
(C) A chair
(D) A washer-dryer

180. Which word is CLOSEST in meaning to "**initial**"?

(A) Protected
(B) Advanced
(C) Beginning
(D) Final

Questions 181-185 refer to the following survey and report.

VTR International Rail

Dear Passenger,

Please take some time to answer a few short questions regarding your experience traveling with VTR. A completed survey qualifies each participant for a draw for an all-expenses-paid return trip for two to Whistler, BC. Please note there is a limit to one survey per person.

1. Which VTR service would you like to see improved or changed?

A ☐ Selection of on-board food   C ☐ Number of stops
B ☐ Attentiveness of train staff   D ☐ On-board entertainment

Comment:

2. How often do you travel with VTR rail?

A ☐ Several times per week   C ☐ Once per month
B ☐ Once per week   D ☐ Once per year or less

3. Please use the space below to make any other suggestions you may have.

VTR Survey Conclusions
Tuesday, September 6th, Vancouver

The purpose of this report is to share the findings of a survey that was conducted to learn about the needs and preferences of VTR Rail passengers. Once a year VTR conducts this survey with the hope of improving its services countrywide. The survey information was gathered from travelers from Thursday to Saturday during the last week of August, typically the busiest time of the year for VTR's operations. The survey forms were obtained the following Monday from the drop boxes located at each of VTR's main stations. More than 2,200 forms were completed.

For question 1, the majority of respondents selected choice C, with most commenting they would like to see fewer stops on express trains. A distant second was the request for entertainment. Question 2 revealed that the majority of participants travel frequently with VTR, with mostly options A and B selected.

Question 3 was open, inviting travelers to comment on items not included in the survey. Not surprisingly, the most common response to this was a desire for fewer cancellations. However, this is not something the company has a lot of control over; disruptions to travel usually occur as a result of factors such as severe weather during the winter months.

---

181. Who completed the survey?

(A) Travel consultants
(B) Customers
(C) Train station employees
(D Railroad engineers

182. What are survey respondents eligible for?

(A) A non-stop train to any destination
(B) Complimentary travel points
(C) A free trip to Vancouver
(D) A lottery for a round-trip vacation

183. On what day were completed survey forms gathered?

(A) Monday
(B) Tuesday
(C) Thursday
(D) Saturday

184. How often do most respondents travel with VTR?

(A) Once a day
(B) Once a week or more
(C) Once a month
(D) Less than once a year

185. What did most respondents say they want in question 3?

(A) More stops along the way
(B) To travel less during winter
(C) Free stays at affiliated hotels
(D) A reduction in travel delays

Questions 186-190 refer to the following notice and letters.

Shopper's Paradise
Exchange Policy

All our stores observe the following guidelines when it comes to customers wanting to exchange goods:

1. The receipt of the purchased goods must be presented when making an exchange.
2. Goods must be exchanged within thirty days of their purchase.
3. Goods cannot be taken out of their original packaging or have their tags or labels removed.

If any of these three points is not satisfied, then we will not exchange your goods. Thanks for your understanding, and we appreciate your patronage.

Ben Nesbeth, Owner and Founder of Shopper's Paradise

Hello,

My name is Marcha Gethart, and I have a question for you regarding your exchange policy. I recently purchased a microwave from your store on Lexington Avenue, and the very first time I plugged it in, it short-circuited or something and died. It has not worked at all, not even once. I am guessing it is a defective product. I certainly don't blame you or think you willfully sold bad merchandise.

I would like to exchange this dead microwave for another one of the exact same model that will hopefully work. My problem is that my husband threw away the microwave's packaging last night without telling me. Will I still be able to exchange this microwave for a new one without the box?

Thank you,
Martha Gethart

Dear Martha,

Thank you for your e-mail. We really appreciate you choosing to shop with us at Shopper's Paradise.

Regarding your issue, it is our policy to bring the original packaging of the item you wish to exchange with you when you visit one of our stores to make the exchange. However, as you say this microwave is defective and does not work, we should be able to waive this part of the exchange policy. Bring the microwave to your nearest Shopper's Paradise, show them your receipt and explain that the microwave is defective and that the packaging was mistakenly thrown out. The employees there should test the microwave, and if they find that it is indeed defective, they will allow you to exchange it for another one.

The packaging is a requirement for items that are in working condition but that customers **nevertheless** want to exchange. If you are unable to successfully exchange your broken microwave, please call me at 1-800-555-4242 ext. 901, and I will talk to the store employees on your behalf.

Sincerely,
Rebecca Lispe, Customer Service Representative
Shopper's Paradise

186. Which of the following is NOT necessary when a customer wants to exchange goods at Shopper's Paradise?

(A) Items remain in their packaging and have all their tags and labels.
(B) Customers exchange their items before thirty days have passed.
(C) Customers provide a valid reason for why they wish to exchange an item.
(D) A receipt of the purchased item or items be given.

187. What is Martha's problem?

(A) Her microwave is not suitable for her needs.
(B) She does not know where to go to exchange her defective microwave.
(C) She does not have the original box the microwave came in.
(D) She is not familiar with Shopper's Paradise's exchange policy.

188. What is Rebecca's solution to Martha's problem?

(A) Explain to the store employees that the microwave was defective all along.
(B) Bring the defective microwave to where Rebecca works.
(C) Take the defective microwave to a repair shop first.
(D) Have Martha's husband search for the microwave's packaging.

189. What can be inferred from the exchange between Martha and Rebecca?

(A) Martha and Rebecca are friends and see each other socially.
(B) Rebecca will personally help Martha exchange her microwave if need be.
(C) Martha will not be satisfied with the help Rebecca has offered.
(D) Rebecca wants to help Martha but will not be able to.

190. Which of the following words is a synonym for "**nevertheless**"?

(A) Despite
(B) However
(C) Therefore
(D) Ergo

Questions 191-195 refer to the following letters.

ATTN: All Department Managers

This Friday, November 23 at 3 pm there will be a company meeting for Department Managers. I would like all ten of you to prepare a five-minute PowerPoint presentation that includes the Current Sales-To-Date, the Forecast Annual Sales for this year and any anticipated discrepancies between the forecast and the reality, so that I can be up-to-date on the current company sales situation.

In addition, we are currently looking for Deputy Managers for both the Dental Sales Department and the Medical Supplies Department. As always, we would first like to consider promoting from within, so I ask that you put forth any members of your department that you feel would be a good fit for either of these positions.

The meeting is likely to run past five o'clock. If there are any more topics you would like to bring up, please email them to me first, and I'll confirm whether it will be possible to include them in the meeting.

See you all Friday,
Annabelle Foucher

Dear Ms. Foucher,

I wanted to request that we touch on current expenditures YTD for each department. I have a feeling that a couple of our departments are running over budget, and I'm wondering what we can do to balance the expenses.

In addition, I wanted to put forth Miriam Sloane for either of the Deputy Manager positions. She has been with the company for seven years, is always an asset, and has developed several new sales techniques that we have already implemented with great success.

I can provide any additional information you might need at the meeting on Friday.

Sincerely,
Andre Brett

Dear Ms. Foucher,

This is Carl Jenkins in New Client Generation. I wanted to inform you that I will not be able to attend this week's meeting as I am currently in Dubai on business. However, I will be sending my Deputy Manager Al Green, in my stead, and he will bring all requested information.

Anne Charles and Fred Tomes are two names I would like to put forth for the Deputy Manager positions. They have been of invaluable assistance to me over the past few years, and I know they would be able to pull more than their share in any situation. Although I would hate to lose them from my department, seeing them move up in the company would let me feel that the Management Team is only growing stronger.

Sincerely,
Carl Jenkins

191. Which of the following was NOT mentioned as a good candidate for Deputy Manager?

(A) Fred Tomes
(B) Miriam Sloane
(C) Al Green
(D) Anne Charles

192. What is the reason for the Friday meeting?

(A) There has been a misuse of expenditure monies, and it needs to be discussed.
(B) The company is looking to fill two positions.
(C) The current sales totals need to be evaluated.
(D) There are some business trips that need to be delegated.

193. Who will be unable to attend the meeting?

(A) Annabelle Foucher
(B) Al Green
(C) Andre Brett
(D) Carl Jenkins

194. What position does Annabelle Foucher most likely have?

(A) Department Head
(B) Accountantd
(C) Secretary
(D) CFO

195. Why are Andre Brett and Carl Jenkins writing Annabelle Foucher?

(A) They are dissatisfied with the job she is doing.
(B) They have people they would like to recommend for jobs.
(C) They have complaints about their own departments.
(D) They want to take the business trip to Dubai.

Questions 196-200 refer to the following letters.

Dear Wilslo Machine Repairs,

We'd like to schedule a time for you to come and take a look at our production line. Two of the eight machines are currently offline, and this is slowing our production process significantly. On a normal day, we are able to produce an average of 100,000 nuts and bolts and package them as well. Currently, we are only able to produce 70,000 nuts and bolts, and half of the packaging line is not up and running so we are having to do things manually. Naturally, this is **drastically** affecting our bottom line margin, and we are getting very worried. We would appreciate your coming in at your earliest convenience.

Sincerely
Derek Looms
Barried's Floor Supervisor

Dear Mr. Looms,

You should be receiving a bill following our last visit earlier this week. As you know, with a few adjustments and the replacement of five parts, we were able to get your entire production line system back up and running. We hope everything is still going smoothly.

Our repairman contacted our service department upon his return from your company and pointed out that Barried's has missed its last three scheduled maintenance times. I'm sure as a Floor Supervisor you don't need me to tell you how important performing regular maintenance is for production line machines. In fact, just two hours of fine tuning could have prevent the breakdowns you were experiencing.

Would you like to schedule a maintenance time for later this week?

Sincerely,
Wilslo Testing and Maintenance Manager
Jeremy Hood

Dear Mr. Hood,

I thank you for your recent repair work and your follow-up letter. You may not be aware of this, but I am very new to the Barried's team, starting at the company two months ago. I have to admit, your letter caught me by surprise. I had no reason to suspect the regular maintenances were not being carried out, and I want to remedy this right away.

I would like to schedule a thorough maintenance routine this Thursday to make sure every one of our machines are compliant, tuned up, and running the latest software. Please let me know what, if anything, is needed on my part. Will you need to fully shut down the production line?
I await your confirmation.

Sincerely,
Derek Looms
Barried's Floor Supervisor

196. Which of the following words is a synonym for "**drastically**"?

(A) seriously
(B) importantly
(C) efficiently
(D) apparently

197. Why has Derek Looms chosen to write to Wilslo Machine Repairs at first?

(A) He felt it was time to get the machines maintained.
(B) He wanted to meet with the new employees from the company.
(C) He wanted to upgrade the production line.
(D) He was having problems with the production line.

198. Was Wilslo able to help Barried's?

(A) Yes, they fixed one machine.
(B) Yes, they fixed the machines and wrote a follow-up letter.
(C) No, the machine was too badly damaged.
(D) No, the machines all needed maintenance.

199. What did Wilslo write to Derek Looms for?

(A) To let him know the cost of the repairs
(B) To tell him the Barried's production line needs maintenance
(C) To introduce the new Testing and Maintenance Manager
(D) To let Mr. Looms know that there was a delay on some of the needed parts

200. Why did Mr. Looms not perform maintenance on the production line?

(A) He did; he just didn't have Wilslo do it.
(B) He wanted to wait and do it once a year.
(C) He just started with the company and didn't know maintenance had not been done.
(D) He felt that the maintenance charges were way too high.

怪物講師的
詞彙題特訓班

1. After completing the form, he has
    _____ agreed to work in
    another branch.

    (A) final
    (B) finalize
    (C) finally
    (D) finalist

2. As the economy remains _____
    sound, there will be more job
    openings.

    (A) financing
    (B) financial
    (C) financed
    (D) financially

3. It is unanimously agreed that the
    company's _____ new line
    of products will dominate foreign
    markets as well as its domestic one.

    (A) impression
    (B) impressive
    (C) impressively
    (D) impressed

4. Easier access to the public
    transportations is making the factories
    in the region more _____ to
    commuters.

    (A) attract
    (B) attraction
    (C) attractively
    (D) attractive

5. The recent survey indicates
    _____ few companies regard
    the product quality as the most
    important thing.

    (A) although
    (B) that
    (C) despite
    (D) which

6. We take great _____ in
    announcing that we are offering
    special incentives to all of you.

    (A) please
    (B) pleasing
    (C) pleasurable
    (D) pleasure

7. You are entitled to health benefits if
    _____ have lived in this country
    for more than one year.

    (A) you
    (B) your
    (C) yours
    (D) yourself

8. It _____ true that the manager
    arranged the breakfast meeting
    in order to keep an eye on her
    employees.

    (A) offered
    (B) took
    (C) provided
    (D) became

| 正確答案 | 1. (C) 2. (D) 3. (B) 4. (D) 5. (B) 6. (D) 7. (A) 8. (D)

9. The supervisor does not like to allow her assistant _____ even at lunchtime.

   (A) to rest
   (B) resting
   (C) rest
   (D) rests

10. It is the manager's responsibility to _____ his staff to be competitive all the time.

    (A) bring
    (B) assure
    (C) persuade

11. Regarding the delivery, the shipping company must _____ our customers of the arrival date and time.

    (A) notify
    (B) explain
    (C) announce
    (D) suggest

12. Although the company _____ the division, most of the employees seemed not to be nervous about their job security.

    (A) was restructuring
    (B) was restructured
    (C) restructuring
    (D) to restructure

13. The prospects of the marketing department for the next year _____ optimistic enough to invest funds amply.

    (A) have
    (B) is
    (C) are
    (D) has been

14. _____ of the machine parts is guaranteed for a full one year from the date of purchase.

    (A) Each
    (B) Some
    (C) All
    (D) Both

15. The number of the complaints we are receiving _____ so overwhelming that we have to call an emergency meeting first.

    (A) being
    (B) is
    (C) are
    (D) been

16. Frequent customers will _____ a big discount this week only, so hurry up!

    (A) be offered
    (B) offer
    (C) offering
    (D) offers

| 正確答案 | 9. (A) 10. (C) 11. (A) 12. (A) 13. (C) 14. (A) 15. (B) 16. (A)

17. Any staff who voluntarily contributes to our company considerably will be _____ a special bonus.

    (A) awarded
    (B) taken
    (C) obtained
    (D) kept

18. The oil price _____ sharply owing to the unstable market nowadays, which will have a negative effect on us.

    (A) has risen
    (B) has been risen
    (C) was risen
    (D) raised

19. Once we _____ of any dietary restrictions, we will be able to make appropriate arrangements for our planned dinner.

    (A) are informed
    (B) were informed
    (C) are informing
    (D) had been informed

20. The medical supplies company made a mistake as its records seemed to show that it _____ our MRI machine already.

    (A) had delivered
    (B) delivery
    (C) were delivering
    (D) will deliver

21. The firm has increased the amount of funds invested into research and development by 15% _____ the past 4 years to maintain its lead.

    (A) since
    (B) before
    (C) over
    (D) yet

22. She _____ for the payroll department at our head office since she joined our company 10 years ago.

    (A) works
    (B) had worked
    (C) worked
    (D) has worked

23. _____ Jonathan not left the company last year, he would have been able to take over my duties.

    (A) Were
    (B) Had
    (C) Did
    (D) If

24. If it were not for our dedicated domestic management team, we _____ not be able to handle so many local client firms at once.

    (A) will
    (B) would
    (C) were
    (D) are

| 正確答案 | 17. (A) 18. (A) 19. (A) 20. (A) 21. (C) 22. (D) 23. (B) 24. (B)

25. Had you _____ here a few years ago when the restructuring began, you would have thought of quitting.

    (A) work
    (B) working
    (C) worked
    (D) been worked

26. Did a company _____ from losses due to the lack of investment, it should prepare enough capital to be prepared for the next time.

    (A) suffer
    (B) suffering
    (C) suffers
    (D) be suffered

27. Our company earns strong customer loyalty by _____ the durability of all our products even after a warranty expires.

    (A) to guarantee
    (B) guaranteeing
    (C) guarantee
    (D) being guaranteed

28. As the manager of a large team, Teresa is quite busy _____ extensive training sessions.

    (A) conductivity
    (B) conducts
    (C) to conduct
    (D) conducting

29. Thank you for _____ the contract with our company for additional 3 years as an exclusive agency in this region.

    (A) renew
    (B) renewal
    (C) renewing
    (D) renewed

30. Most of the employees _____ to working overtime throughout the week to meet the tight deadline.

    (A) want
    (B) object
    (C) refuse
    (D) promise

31. Ms. Abramoff was forced _____ with her litigation after several threats of countersuits from her client.

    (A) to cancel
    (B) to remain
    (C) to continue
    (D) to proceed

32. To present the findings of their research, the doctors from St. Mary's Hospital have decided _____ a press conference.

    (A) holding
    (B) to hold
    (C) to be held
    (D) holds

| 正確答案 | 25. (C) 26. (A) 27. (B) 28. (D) 29. (C) 30. (B) 31. (D) 32. (B)

33. To be _____ in the job interview, you have to leave a lasting impression on the interviewers.

(A) success
(B) successive
(C) successful
(D) succession

34. All international orders _____ to arrive within 30 days of confirming the order, which is a common practice according to this contract.

(A) to expect
(B) expecting
(C) expect
(D) are expected

35. _____ to become the top food provider in the nation, Alliance Foods expanded its distribution chain by twenty percent.

(A) Striven
(B) Strive
(C) Striving
(D) Strove

36. _____ its plans to merge with its strongest competitor, Tropical Gear will counter the demand for fashionable eyewear.

(A) Announces
(B) Announcing
(C) To announce
(D) Announcement

37. Although she had little experience working with computers, Ms. Lopez is often able to assist customers _____ technical support.

(A) require
(B) requiring
(C) requirement
(D) required

38. Please find the _____ forum agenda and the itinerary and let us know at least a month in advance to cancel for any reason.

(A) enclosing
(B) enclose
(C) encloses
(D) enclosed

39. For two years, the product warranty guarantees free repairs for _____ may happen to the item.

(A) however
(B) who
(C) if
(D) whatever

40. The year-end performance bonus would be awarded to _____ had the highest total sales figure for the year.

(A) what
(B) whoever
(C) whom
(D) whether

| 正確答案 | 33. (C) 34. (D) 35. (C) 36. (B) 37. (B) 38. (D) 39. (D) 40. (B)

41. The computer tech can determine
_____ employee's computer
originated the virus that attacked the
company network.

(A) which
(B) that
(C) where
(D) whose

42. The brochure handed to theater
patrons explains _____ the
tickets were more expensive than
usual.

(A) whether
(B) what
(C) why
(D) which

43. Please be assured _____ your
application form has been received
and you will be notified of the final
result as soon as possible.

(A) that
(B) what
(C) concerning
(D) of

44. Industrial Technologies, Inc. has
released a new calculator in hopes of
attracting students _____ plan
to study advanced physics.

(A) whose
(B) who
(C) which
(D) what

45. Coach Cal Santiago, _____
gymnastics team has seen four
Olympic gold medalists, announced
his early retirement today.

(A) which
(B) who
(C) whom
(D) whose

46. The much desired position of lead
researcher was awarded to Franklin
Howard, whom everyone in the
department_____.

(A) admired
(B) admirable
(C) was admired
(D) admiration

47. The client that I talked _____
yesterday expressed his gratitude for
receiving our excellent service.

(A) to him
(B) him
(C) to
(D) for

48. Alexander Petrokov's new film
"Roses,Daisies, You" is expected to
be a hit at the box office _____
it receives negative reviews.

(A) even
(B) where
(C) even if
(D) in order that

| 正確答案 |　41. (A) 42. (C) 43. (A)　44. (B) 45. (D) 46. (A) 47. (C) 48. (C)

49. The equipment rental store has a large supply of snow shovels _____ the region rarely receives snowfall.

    (A) because
    (B) even though
    (C) otherwise
    (D) since

50. The local symphony hosts _____ many summer festivals that it can raise money for local arts schools.

    (A) so
    (B) for
    (C) such
    (D) very

51. Jonathan's favorite form of acting is theater, _____ he plans to pursue a career in television and movie acting.

    (A) so
    (B) yet
    (C) and
    (D) for

52. The governor insisted that he had not accepted bribes while in office, _____ had he made secret deals with any companies.

    (A) and
    (B) but
    (C) so
    (D) nor

53. The record company noticed consumers today prefer to purchase music electronically and _____ to focus on Internet music sales.

    (A) decide
    (B) decided
    (C) decision
    (D) decisive

54. I am looking forward to the marketing workshop and _____ the urgent matter in preparation for launching the new product.

    (A) discuss
    (B) discussion
    (C) discussing
    (D) to discuss

55. All departments _____ the layout and design team are expected to submit their final revisions by the January 15 deadline.

    (A) as
    (B) because
    (C) except
    (D) once

56. Many worry that increasing the sales tax _____ an economic recession will be met with strong reactions from voters during the next election.

    (A) during
    (B) till
    (C) between
    (D) out of

| 正確答案 | 49. (B) 50. (A) 51. (B) 52. (D) 53. (B) 54. (C) 55. (C) 56. (A)

57. _____ unusually high demand, we couldn't increase our limited production capacity largely due to the regulation.

    (A) In spite of
    (B) On account of
    (C) In case
    (D) Now that

58. Members will be notified _____ any amendments to these rules that may affect their rights or obligations.

    (A) to
    (B) at
    (C) for
    (D) of

59. Many large _____ in this country have formed an association to lobby the federal government for favorable legislation.

    (A) manufacturers
    (B) manufacture
    (C) manufacturer
    (D) manufacturing

60. The warranty will expire after one year, but _____ to a discounted repair service can be obtained at the time of purchase.

    (A) subscriber
    (B) subscribing
    (C) subscripts
    (D) subscription

61. As a family dentist, Dr. Patterson decided to design _____ waiting room in a way that is comfortable and inviting to people of all ages.

    (A) he
    (B) him
    (C) his
    (D) himself

62. _____ who brought in the most money at the box office usually wins the Film Award for best actors and actresses.

    (A) Anyone
    (B) That
    (C) Those
    (D) Whoever

63. Because the market remains _____, many leading economists are predicting a cut in interest rates by the Federal Reserve Bank.

    (A) volatile
    (B) volatileness
    (C) volatility
    (D) volatilizes

64. With the rapid growth in data networks, many telecommunications companies are offering corporate clients _____ data downloads.

    (A) unlimited
    (B) unlimiting
    (C) unlimitedly
    (D) unlimitable

| 正確答案 | 57. (A) 58. (D) 59. (A) 60. (D) 61. (C) 62. (A) 63. (A) 64. (A)

還沒準備好，
怎敢上考場！

國家圖書館出版品預行編目（CIP）資料

全新制50次多益滿分的怪物講師TOEIC多益閱讀攻
略+模擬試題+解析 / 鄭相虎、金映權 著. -- 初版. --
臺北市：不求人文化, 2018.1
　　面；　公分
ISBN 978-986-95195-2-6（平裝）

1.多益測驗

805.1895　　　　　　　　　　106018311

書名 / 全新制 50 次多益滿分的怪物講師 TOEIC 多益閱讀攻略 + 模擬試題 + 解析

作者 / 鄭相虎、金映權

審訂者 / 怪物講師教學團隊（台灣）

譯者 / 林建豪

發行人 / 蔣敬祖

出版事業群副總經理 / 廖晏婕

副總編輯 / 劉俐伶

校對 / 曾慶宇、紀珊

視覺指導 / 姜孟傑、鍾維恩

排版 / 張靜怡

法律顧問 / 北辰著作權事務所蕭雄淋律師

印製 / 金濱印刷事業有限公司

初版 / 2018 年 1 月

初版五刷 / 2018 年 6 月

出版 / 我識出版社有限公司——不求人文化

電話 / (02) 2345-7222

傳真 / (02) 2345-5758

地址 / 台北市忠孝東路五段 372 巷 27 弄 78 之 1 號 1 樓

郵政劃撥 / 19793190

戶名 / 我識出版社

網址 / www.17buy.com.tw

E-mail / iam.group@17buy.com.tw

facebook 網址 / www.facebook.com/ImPublishing

定價 / 新台幣 699 元 / 港幣 233 元

시나공 토익 Reading（전면 개정판）

總經銷 / 我識出版社有限公司業務部

地址 / 新北市汐止區新台五路一段 114 號 12 樓

電話 / (02) 2696-1357 傳真 / (02) 2696-1359

地區經銷 / 易可數位行銷股份有限公司

地址 / 新北市新店區寶橋路 235 巷 6 弄 3 號 5 樓

港澳總經銷 / 和平圖書有限公司

地址 / 香港柴灣嘉業街 12 號百樂門大廈 17 樓

電話 / (852) 2804-6687 傳真 / (852) 2804-6409

2011 不求人文化

2009 懶鬼子英日語

我識出版集團
I'm Publishing Group
www.17buy.com.tw

2006 意識文化

2005 易富文化

2004 我識地球村

2001 我識出版社

2011 不求人文化

2009 懶鬼子英日語

I'm 我識出版集團
I'm Publishing Group
www.17buy.com.tw

2006 意識文化

2005 易富文化

2004 我識地球村

2001 我識出版社